ORION'S HUNTERS
Cosmic Visions

gabriel dandrade

Copyright © 2023 Gabriel Dandrade
All rights reserved.

The characters and events portrayed in this book are fictitious. Any similarity to real persons, living or dead, is coincidental and not intended by the author.

No part of this book may be reproduced, or stored in a retrieval system, or transmitted in any form or by any means, electronic, mechanical, photocopying, recording, or otherwise, without express written permission of the publisher.

ISBN (Paperback only): 9798386255107

Cover design by: (IG) @writergdand
Cover art by: (IG) @lovechloewhite
Printed in the United States of America

Table of Contents

- Prologue..................................Pg. 5
- Chapter 1.................................Pg. 22
- Chapter 2.................................Pg. 46
- Chapter 3.................................Pg. 64
- Chapter 4.................................Pg. 75
- Chapter 5.................................Pg. 94
- Chapter 6.................................Pg. 111
- Chapter 7.................................Pg. 127
- Chapter 8.................................Pg. 137
- Chapter 9.................................Pg. 155
- Chapter 10...............................Pg. 164
- Chapter 11...............................Pg. 178
- Chapter 12...............................Pg. 190
- Chapter 13...............................Pg. 203
- Chapter 14...............................Pg. 225
- Chapter 15...............................Pg. 242
- Chapter 16...............................Pg. 255
- Chapter 17...............................Pg. 271
- Chapter 18...............................Pg. 285
- Chapter 19...............................Pg. 301
- Chapter 20...............................Pg. 321
- Chapter 21...............................Pg. 335
- Chapter 22...............................Pg. 362
- Chapter 23...............................Pg. 384
- Chapter 24...............................Pg. 390
- Chapter 25...............................Pg. 409
- Chapter 26...............................Pg. 433
- Chapter 27...............................Pg. 445
- Chapter 28...............................Pg. 468

-Chapter 29..Pg. 491
-Chapter 30..Pg. 511
-Chapter 31..Pg. 521
-Chapter 32..Pg. 544
-Chapter 33..Pg. 570
-Chapter 34..Pg. 586
-Chapter 35..Pg. 600
-Chapter 36..Pg. 626
-Chapter 37..Pg. 647
-Chapter 38..Pg. 662
-Epilogue...Pg. 674

Prologue

Somewhere in the universe

There are aliens that exist. They always have existed, they exist now, and they will exist even a hundred years from now. And they are watching you, right now, eyeing your every move, ensuring that you never discover their presence. This book is here to show you that they exist, and what happens deep in the far reaches of the Milky Way Galaxy. Because while you sleep, while you go to work, while you move from activity to activity, they are there, at all times. Aliens exist, even if you do not believe in their existence. That is the purpose of this book.

As the protector of the biggest secret this universe had ever seen, Shane Vulkan had a very busy job. He had to constantly deal with enemies who cared not for revealing the secret. Worse still, he had to do battle with a larger force who was actively trying to kill him and the society he ran, the Orion Coalition. He had good days, and he had bad days, like today. And it was only just getting worse with the news from his admiral that there was a Gorog ship in the area.

A hail of lasers streaked by the bridge window, slamming into the shields and causing his ship, the *Justice*, to roll to the side, causing him to slide. He stumbled and nearly lost his footing on the slick bridge floor, grabbing onto the center console to steady himself. Standing up hastily, he stared out into the red nebula, trying to discern what had fired at them. Nothing. Either they were hiding in the veil of hydrogen gas that composed the space cloud, or they were too far away to pick out. A classic strategy, using the gas for cover. Not only would it hide them from prying eyes, it would also scramble their scanners, as the hydrogen gas would meddle with the signal. A basic and simple strategy, but an effective one nonetheless. They were less than a parsec from their destination, the blue giant star in view, yet this unseen foe was blocking their path. And Shane, no matter how hard he stared, could not make it out.

Behind him, heavy footfalls sounded as someone approached. He turned slightly to face him, already knowing who it was. He could recognize Commander Vorlax's favorite leather boots from anywhere. His friend never left his quarters without them, even if it was just for a moment. The gray alien's face looked grim as he moved closer to stand beside the older Shane.

"Vorlax?" he asked.

"Shane," the reply said.

"Who fired at us?"

"Can't tell, sir. They're still too far out of range."

"Keep the sensors on. And have your squadron ready to be dispatched as soon as we determine where those lasers came from!"

"Yes sir, right away!" Vorlax's receding footfalls sounded behind him as Shane turned back to watch the stars in front of him. Another curtain of laser fire was thrown in front of the ship, but the shots missed by quite a bit. He still had no idea who would dare to open fire upon a Coalition warship, let alone one carrying himself, but now he could see the tiny silhouette of another ship etched in the red veil of the nebular gas. It was still too far away to see which affiliation it belonged to but judging by how close they were to the capital, and by the many evil-looking pincers extending from the bow, Shane had a guess as to who was shooting at them.

"In front of the nebula!" he called back to the group of naval officers decked in blue uniforms and bearing a crest with a spiral galaxy on it. Two were human, the others were brown-skinned aliens with impressive intellects and what Shane believed was an extra 'ear' in the back of their head, for enhanced hearing capabilities. In front of them was a large circular table with a projector in the center, which was displaying various coordinates and positions relative to their ship. It showcased the nearest objects to them, including planets, stars, or the other ship that was creeping in from the top of the image into the display. Numbers showcasing the distance to the neighboring celestial bodies were constantly changing as they changed position in space, with various X, Y, and Z vectors also rendering. And there was a new marker, red, moving way faster than anything else in the area.

"I see it!" said Vorlax. The battle-hardened pilot had a lot of spirit in him, and one of the most brilliant minds in the whole navy. Subtle cheekbones, piercing, bulbous eyes, gray skin, and a long mess of tentacles draping down from his scalp, he had a very thin body build that showed traces of his aquatic heritage, including the outlines of what had once been gills, but were now a row of parallel, dark lines that were visible on his neck. His hands displayed signs of past webbing, and, though Shane had never seen them, he swore that under Vorlax's heavy boots, there were partly webbed feet as well. He had been on the force for six years and had already won many battles and accolades. He had been so amazing at his job that Shane had promoted him to his personal squadron commander.

Shane paced to the other side of the bridge, barking more orders. "Get me a scan of that ship!" The sooner they knew who they were fighting, the quicker they could deal with their attacker. As he spoke, another stream of laser blasts streaked past the bridge windows, shaking the bridge and causing alarms to start blaring.

A few moments later, the 3-D rendering of the other ship came in. A single heavy warship, *Reaper*-class, identifiable by the huge array of prongs that Shane had seen earlier, causing the front of the ship to look like a giant spider. It was for sure not a friendly that was mistaking their ship for an enemy. Heavily-armed, with a large fleet of attack fighters stored in its central hangar. A formidable foe, but still outclassed by Shane's arsenal of weapons.

"They appear to be Gorogs, sir," Vorlax told him, watching the enemy ship's weapons extend into attack position. "Estimated crew at 1,200, with a fighter squad totaling 30 ships, max."

"Any accompanying warships?" inquired Shane, knowing that if they were dealing with Gorogs, odds are they would be traveling in packs.

"Not that I can see."

Shane relaxed a little at those words. A lone Gorog ship was no match for the *Justice*. Not only was its weaponry state-of-the-art, it also had Vorlax's huge fighter squadron. The Gorogs had no chance against such a powerful foe. He heard Vorlax come up behind him.

"Permission to launch the starfighters?" he said, a little gurgle sneaking its way into his voice.

"Get the pilots ready, Vorlax," answered Shane, "but don't launch them just yet. Let's see what tricks they reveal before we send out the squadrons."

The commander's shadow on the floor bowed in respect before his receding footfalls sounded behind him, followed by the *ding* as the doors to the bridge opened up. Shane continued to watch the space where, now barely twelve kilometers away, was the warship. While it was still very small from his perspective, he could see the dark brown color and the black spot with the crest of the Squids emblazoned in the center. Despite being smaller than the *Justice*, it was very well armed with plenty of cannons, phasers and other high-tech weaponry. It had to have been modified, given the number of them. He also took notice of the large central hangar, which ran through the ship and had entry ports on both the port and starboard sides of the hull. If it came to a battle, it would probably be tougher than expected.

A moment later, the proximity alarms started whining on the bridge, and red lights flashed on and off. Shane turned back to face the crew surrounding the projector. The ship was still there, blinking subtly, but there were now thirty other engine signatures streaming away from the hangar. The Gorog starfighter squadron.

"They've launched their fleet!" warned one of the officers, eyes squinching on the rendering as he watched the ships take up an offensive formation. "At least twenty ships are closing in fast!"

Shane ran to his command post and pulled out an intercom, switching it on. "Vorlax! The enemy just launched twenty or so fighters. You sure you can take them on?"

"Of course. I wouldn't be leading this squad if I couldn't," replied Vorlax, his voice popping up on the radio. "Just like the last Gorogs who threatened us. Permission to launch fighters?"

"Granted."

Moments after the intercom went silent, attack fighters began to stream out of the two hangers in the sides of Shane's cruiser, until there was a giant armada of at least fifty bearing down on the enemy. Sleek, heavily armed, and deadly, these fighters were built to be fast, designed to excel in dogfights and destroy enemy fighters with minimal losses. Painted dark green and yellow, the ship did look like an arrow, narrow and triangular at the front before splitting into its twin turbine engines. Those engines propelled the vessel swiftly across any space, and once it reached its target, the laser cannons and missile launchers did the rest. The old workhorses had done amazing things in battle, and he knew they wouldn't fail this time either.

Back on the bridge, Shane prepared to fight. "Status check!" he ordered.

"Shields up at max, sir," reported an elderly officer at

one of the control panels.

"Cannons fully charged and ready to fire," yelled another uniformed man.

"Shield Breachers locked and loaded," called out yet another from the other side of the room, this one a reddish-skinned alien.

"Targeting systems are a go!" came a fourth reply.

Shane nodded and turned back to face the forthcoming battle. He could hear the sounds of the weapons moving into attack position, the plasma generators preparing to discharge their energy. Way off in the distance, the two rival fleets of starfighters had almost reached each other, and Vorlax was no doubt prepping his men for the ordeal ahead. He didn't know what was going to happen, but one thing he was sure of was that both sides were going to give it their all. A hard battle was all but inevitable.

"Commence attack," he bellowed. "All batteries fire at will!"

The huge laser cannons dotting the hull groaned to life, heating up for a moment, and opening fire in a series of loud, potentially deafening roars, sending explosive shells of plasma at the opposing cruiser. The breachers also charged up, firing concentrated laser beams designed to punch through protective shields. The opposing cruiser returned fire, and streams of lasers streaked by the bridge's windows. The *Justice* rocked back and forth as hundreds of plasma bolts slammed into the shields.

At the same time, the two fighter squadrons broke formation and started to spit lasers at each other like firework streamers across the black void. The Gorog ships broke their formation and began to dogfight Shane's fighters, chasing them across space and shooting at them madly. Small explosions indicated the first deaths of the battle as two lasers found their target. Who had fallen, it was impossible to tell at this distance.

A breacher cannon slammed into the *Justice's* shield, the

laser doing concentrated damage. The entire cruiser shook violently as the beam threatened to breach the barrier and strike at the hull, but it fizzled out before it could. Shane ordered a retaliatory barrage, the batteries sending out concentrated barrages to appear as distant explosions against the other cruiser. One ship fired, then the other…it was a highly volatile game of back and forth. But it was nothing new to Shane. He watched the starfighters buzz around one another, shooting each other down, feeling the floor vibrate below him as the occasional shell hit, tuning out the alarms that seemed to never end. The same routine as always. Every battle was the same. The enemy ambushes him, the two of them start to fight, the enemy initially has the upper hand before he and Vorlax and their superior tactics give the win to the Coalition. It was a never-ending cycle. Were all wars this bland to him? He didn't know.

"We have them on the run, Shane," radioed Vorlax. Shane smiled as he heard it. Vorlax's fighter was the easiest to spot out of the dozens in the field. He always looked for the one that was shooting down the most fighters and doing tricks like he'd see at a Star Run event. "Seems like they want to get their butts kicked today. We've sustained only a few casualties so far."

"Take care, Vorlax," Shane cautioned. "This isn't their usual behavior. I've never seen them give up a win this easily before."

"Sir, the battle's out here, not in there!" responded Vorlax, his voice partly obscured by an explosion in the background. "Their cruiser's also sustaining damage! You have to press the attack and breach their shields!" There was a pause, and then he added, "I'm going to!"

But Shane knew that there usually was a calm before the storm in warfare. "No! It's too easy. Not even the Gorogs would sacrifice all of these fighters for nothing." Every sense was telling him to seize the offensive and strike, but something didn't make sense. "Do not press the offensive. Yet. Understood?"

"Yes, sir." But his voice sounded almost pained as he said it. There was another loud explosion as Vorlax shot down another enemy fighter, then the radio went dark.

Shane was now watching the cruiser, which, as Vorlax had said, had been damaged. The phaser fire from their ship had given their shields a severe beating. It was the same story with the way the ship was firing at the *Justice*. It seemed...halfhearted, effortless. Like they didn't care. Again, strange. Shane's body was screaming at him, and he understood why. Nothing about their strategy made sense. He wanted to press the attack. If he pressed it now, he could wipe them all out and they could proceed onwards with minimal casualties. Yet the reverse psychology of the moment caused him to stop, as he wondered if pressing would cause him to fall right into a potential trap. So he stayed put, watching the Gorogs intentionally sacrifice their own fleet.

It was at that point that he noticed something. Staring at the Gorog warship, way off in the distance, he saw faint movement. It was almost too subtle to notice. But there was the way that it moved that unnerved Shane. Although he may have dismissed it as a trick of his imagination, he grabbed the intercom.

"Vorlax," he radioed urgently, "Is the Gorog cruiser...moving? In an unnatural way?"

"Hang on!" the commander replied, another explosion almost drowning out his voice. "Yes! Looks like some large new weapon that they have. Don't worry, we'll take care of it!"

But as he messaged his pilots to attack the cruiser, the Gorogs sprung their trap. The surprise was total. The battle immediately turned up to eleven on the intensity scale, the Gorog fighters shooting down several fighters. The cruiser's guns also began to fire more aggressively, but instead of targeting the *Justice*, they aimed down at the dogfighting squadrons, seemingly oblivious to the Gorog fighters they themselves were destroying. Shane, shocked, watched as his ships were destroyed by laser blasts and missiles in droves.

"They just started shooting at us! They tricked us!" Vorlax yelled over the radio, while dodging laser fire and missiles launched from the enemy ships. He was being tailed by a particularly zealous enemy fighter that was attempting to jam his comm link.

"Listen to me," said Shane urgently, then paused as a laser blast rocked the bridge. "Get your men organized! They're scattering our men and picking them off one by one! Get back into formation!" he said urgently, gesturing across the field. Meanwhile, the large cannon on the Gorog cruiser continued to shift its position ever so slightly.

But the battle was so fierce around them that Vorlax was unable to get his men into formation. The Gorogs picked apart his fighters, generating terrible losses. Some of them even broke off from the main battle and started to bombard the *Justice* with their weapons, rocking Shane around even more. In the distance, the Coalition squadron was doing their best to destroy their opponents, but were getting beaten badly for it.

That's when the Gorogs revealed their biggest surprise.

The cruiser had pivoted to aim its bow right at the *Justice*, and four large cannons were now pointed straight at them. All four weapons now fired a concentrated, supercharged breacher beam at Shane. It blew through two Gorog ships that were caught in its path, then in a matter of seconds slammed into the *Justice's* shields, causing a vibration so fierce it resembled an earthquake. Red filled the bridge as damage alarms sounded, and everyone was sent stumbling. Never had Shane seen such raw power on any ship, and judging by the panicky voices behind him, neither had they.

"Shane!" radioed Vorlax urgently, still surrounded by the mayhem of the fighting around him, which managed to drown out the static that threatened to block the signal. "Those were breacher cannons on the cruiser! They just fired!"

"Yep! Noticed!" Shane was trying not to panic. His brain was swimming from the cacophony that surrounded him. He turned to his officers. "How bad was it?"

"Forward shields are gone, Shane!" came the hasty reply. "That breacher just eliminated all of our remaining protection in one shot!"

"Charge our breachers now!" ordered Shane, pointing at the gunners in the room. "Disable their shields! We need to take them out before their laser fire rakes us to shreds!"

Seconds later, the ship shook violently, as several laser blasts slammed into the hull. Explosions rang out across the cruiser, knocking everyone aboard off balance. Shane pitched forward, hitting his head on the glass window and falling hard on his stomach as the bridge shook as if an earthquake had struck. Some of the crew members tumbled right through the hologram of the battle before tripping and falling. The emergency systems went into overdrive, the damage alarms only increasing in pitch.

Shane struggled to his feet, dizzy from the vibrations. His vision was blurred from his fall, and his head swam. He tasted something metallic in his mouth and, feeling his mouth with his fingers, saw that he had bit his lip. Blood was flowing from the tooth marks. As the ringing in his ears fell away, he heard the constant shouts of men running about, assessing systems, which drowned out the never-ending blare of the emergency sirens.

"Damage report," Shane called out, over the dull roar in his ears.

He caught a few words like, "Sustained some pretty bad damage" and "munitions room was hit," and some other things that he couldn't quite distinguish. His admiral, who was standing up very shakily, looked grim.

"One of those lasers hit the munitions room, sir,"

reported one of the crew, the nervousness clear in his voice. There was a large welt already starting to sprout from his forehead as a result of his fall.

Shane cringed with momentary worry. If the munitions room was hit, that meant a raging fire was on board the ship. He peered out the bridge window, watching the inferno burn from a huge hole that the bomber punched through the metal hull. "Is the reactor core okay?"

Someone checked. "Yes, sir, they missed it."

Shane faced the room, determined to avoid another attack. "Fire the breachers! All of them!" he thundered.

They charged and fired, aimed right at the Gorog cruiser, which had all of its turbolasers pointed at the *Justice*. The beams slammed into the cruiser's bow, the blue shimmer indicating a direct impact. Shane was rocked again as another laser blast thrown from the enemy tore through the hull, causing more emergency lights to go off. Shane turned to the radio. "Vorlax," he demanded. "Vorlax do you copy?"

No answer. The commander was probably too busy saving his own skin to worry about Shane right now. Or the radio was jammed. Or even damaged. One of the three. Whichever, they would have to make do without him. At this point it was every man for himself. And he could see the cruiser's blue protection fall away after that last blast. He gave the order to fire on the central link, where the reactor core would be, but before he could, someone yelled from behind him, and he looked up to see a Gorog fighter bearing down on them, the muzzles of its laser cannons glowing with energy as they prepared to fire upon the bridge. But Shane, before he could move to escape his impending death, was lifted from behind by the arms, and thrown back from the window. He hit his head hard on the floor and, after already jarring his brain once, it was just too much for him. He had just enough time before unconsciousness to see two of his senior naval officers, silhouetted against the glass, before the bomber crashed through the window and went off with a loud *boom* as the explosives detonated, creating a giant fireball that hid their faces, and blew Shane away from the window. He sailed back away from his loyal men and the explosion, and the last thing he remembered was his gut crying out in pain.

Then everything went dark.

He awoke with a start several hours later, with a bad headache and stiff back. The pain lanced through his skull as he sat up, then fell back in his bed. He felt like he had aged another decade, and his vision was still a bit fuzzy, as was his memory. As his eyesight slowly returned, his mind thought back to the events of before. The headache made it difficult to remember, but Shane's memory slowly returned. They were on their way home, they had come under fire from Gorogs, they were bombing his ship, he was about to die, but after that…nothing. Groaning, he tried to sit up again, then immediately fell back on his pillow again as his head throbbed painfully.

He finally sat up without experiencing severe pain, glancing around at the white walls of the infirmary room he was in. Realizing where he was, he immediately assessed the rest of his body, checking for injuries he may have sustained. His left leg felt stiff, and when he touched it, he felt bandages on it, realizing that he had been burned by the explosion. His eyes cast upward, finally noticing that Vorlax was sitting in a chair across from him, watching him with dandelion-yellow eyes, still wearing the blue and gold g-force he always wore when flying his ship. He stood up when he saw that Shane was awake.

"Let me just say for the record that it's a pleasure watching you nap," he said, amusement in his smooth, quiet voice, which was as deep as the ocean planet from where he was born. "The way you were tossing, turning and crying out in pain, it seemed as if you were being burned at the stake. Oh, and you snore like a fat Fromasian pig."

"What…happened?" Shane asked groggily, pressing a hand to his aching head. Thankfully Vorlax at that moment handed the leader an ice pack, which he gratefully pressed to his scalp.

"Well, the Gorog cruiser had a prototype breacher cannon designed to punch through a ship's shields in one shot," explained Vorlax. "After they broke down the barriers, some of their fighters went to destroy the bridge. They breached one of the windows, knocking you out. Thankfully one of the senior officers took charge and continued the battle. He had the cannons destroy the Gorog's cruiser vessel since its shields were down too. I also destroyed the rest of their fighters." He paused briefly, then added, "The *Justice* sustained some heavy damage, and the bridge lost some of its amazing view, but she'll live. Munitions room was the hardest hit. Fire was contained soon after the battle."

"Shouldn't I have been sucked into space?"

"The ray shields kicked in before you were pulled out. You're lucky though. You almost became another victim of space. Lord only knows how many of those we had after this last battle."

"Well, that's good," Shane managed to say, before clutching his head again as a fresh spasm of pain launched through it. When he finished, he looked up, scanning for the other face he should have seen, sitting beside Vorlax. "How many known casualties?"

Vorlax's face fell. "Quite a few. Exact number is still unclear, but our best estimates place it around 100, most of them victims of the munitions room explosion. One of them was also our head admiral, who was sucked out of the broken window. We also lost half of our starfighters."

This was far costlier than Shane had initially projected.

17

And it still did not address the fact that there were Gorogs less than a parsec from the heart of Coalition territory. He rose from his bed. "We need to let the council know of this development. Gorogs this close to Arajor…its never been seen since the earliest days of the war." He turned to Vorlax. "Send word to the council. Have them convene in the chamber later today."

"Sir? Right now? Because it's fine if you want to rest or…"

"Yes! Right now! What part of that did I stutter?"

"How close did you say?" the head council member asked unbelievingly.

Shane was sitting down in a large, brilliantly lit chamber, located near the heart of the ship, with nine white seats surrounding a long, gray table. There, seven holograms of robed people, the council of Arajor, stood in front of the empty seats. Shane was sitting on the largest chair, a white masterpiece of artistic detail tinged with gold, located in the back of the room. Vorlax was standing next to him. It was a room where Shane or other council members could meet up, no matter where they were in the galaxy. A window overlooked the hallway outside, where crew members could be seen running about to repair the *Justice's* damage.

"Less than a light year away," Shane responded grimly. "Close enough to where the blue giant was clearly visible."

There was a long silence as everyone let this information sink in. Gorogs had never dared to go that close to Coalition territory in years. And that they were carrying prototypical weaponry as well; that was particularly worrisome. There had been no forewarning, no early sign of the impending attack. It had just…happened.

Finally, someone spoke. "It's long past time someone found a way to rid us of those lunatic terrorists!" raged the hologram of a thin, dark-skinned man with misshapen teeth.

"On that, we agree," replied Shane. "The problem is that it's becoming increasingly hard to find them in the first place. They've become better at staying out of sight lately."

"That's no excuse with your apparent lack of progress in ending this awful war. We've been expecting better results from the one in charge of this entire Coalition!" This was an alien member with rough skin and horns growing out of his head.

"It's upsetting to us that your so-called 'Great Armies' have barely done anything to actually strike at Gorog territory." put in another member, an alien with pale blue skin and covered in warts. "Perhaps that's the reason for why they can stray as close as the capital?"

"My army is not incompetent by any means," said Shane with a dangerous edge to his voice, as if daring the others to question his capability to handle a threat. "They're the best fighting men in the whole galaxy, but they're not used to dealing with terrorist fighting styles."

"Terrorists? *Terrorists*? These "terrorists" have been increasing their attacks with alarming speed and have just entered sovereign airspace around Arajor itself!" pointed out the first council member. "Shane, with all due respect, this problem is getting out of hand. This war has been going on for sixteen years now, and with no sign of slowing down. It's time that you break the deadlock before the Gorogs massacre half the galaxy!"

Murmurs of agreement came from the other council members. Shane could sense their doubt in his abilities. He bubbled with anger inside. He hated it when people doubted his ability to handle situations; he had to prove himself worthy of handling such a situation like this when he took up the title of Magnum. When the council acted this way, it made him think that they didn't realize, or care, that he was trading an eye, arm, and leg into the war efforts. He wasn't sitting on a beach somewhere sipping martinis, that's for sure.

"Do you think your father would look down on you now and be proud of what you've achieved during this war?" piped up the blue-skinned alien.

"That's enough, everyone." The head council member leaned forward, eyeing Shane narrowly. The Magnum tensed up. Serizau, the most powerful member of the seven, leaned forward to allow his wrinkled face to be clear to everyone. "I think Shane here has had enough of our verbal abuse today."

"What do you want to say, Serizau?" asked Shane harshly.

"This. We, the council, have been discussing a bit about the war lately, and we want a guarantee from you that you will beat the Gorogs in five years time, or will have them at the point where there's no way that they can achieve victory. Under threat of your position as Magnum."

Shane stood up slowly. "I must be suffering from hearing loss, because it seems as though you wish to wager my entire position on the outcome of something that's not entirely under my control. You cannot do that!"

"Actually, we can. And we will, if you do not get your army in order. Because while it may be outside our jurisdiction to outright remove you, there are…other ways that we may be able to prevent you from becoming Magnum again. I'm sure that the people would love this war to persist for even longer."

Shane glared at Serizau, but he knew of what they spoke of. His next bidding to retain his office was in five years time, and although he was officially the most powerful governor of the Orion Coalition, the council had the ears of a lot of the people. They could easily manipulate the opinions of the people if they chose. "Very well, Serizau. I'll play your game," he replied. "And if that's everything that everyone wants to say, then consider this meeting adjourned. Farewell."

Shane mashed a button on his chair and the council members' holograms dissolved into nothing. The lights came back up to full brightness. Shane slowly eased his breathing, his temper settling down somewhat. Vorlax just stood there.

"That was incredibly risky of you, ending the meeting in such an abrupt fashion," the commander spoke up.

"It's Serizau," grumbled Shane. "Ever since he was appointed to the council he's done nothing but cause trouble for me. And, worse, he seems to have the ears of the other council members."

"I know. Something about him gives me the chills. And what he did was entirely illegal."

"You know that he never once spoke to the council. They just don't intervene with his decisions because he's the head council member and he can have them all fired if need be."

"Don't worry, Shane. I have your back as long as this war persists. We'll find a way to beat the Gorogs and prove Serizau wrong."

Shane dipped his head in thanks. "Thank you, Vorlax." He was grateful that the commander had his back, even in the tough situations. "Can you keep on managing the men in the army while I deal with the council, and the Gorogs?"

"Absolutely. I'll keep looking for new recruits while you keep up with running this circus," said Vorlax. "One of them will have to be mighty and smart enough to outsmart the Gorogs, right?"

Chapter 1

Earth

The night sky was a sight to behold from a dark location. It has been the source of stories, philosophies, discoveries and inspiration for more than five thousand years. In the country, far from the interference of city lights and glare, the velvety blackness revealed countless stars shining bright above the grass fields, looking like millions of tiny stellar sugar cubes dotting a velvet black backdrop. The Milky Way was a shining river of light flowing from horizon to horizon, and, if one's eyes were well trained, some fuzzy spots that marked star clusters and nebulae, giant interstellar hydrogen clouds, could be seen. On nights where planets were present, they stood out like fireflies in a sea of pitch.

As glorious as this all was, the fields and street that this scene hovered over was barren by comparison, with grass that was browning from a hot summer, though the temperature was milder now that night had fallen. The road was small, barely two lanes wide, and surrounded by dead grass that gave the entire setting a drab appearance. The temperature was cold too, hovering around the 40s, which is why it would've been a strange sight to see a teenager drag what at first glance appeared to be an army mortar down the road, with a rolled-up camp table tucked under one arm. Upon second glance, it became clear that the 'mortar' was actually a large black telescope, attached to a set of wheels, enabling it to be moved easier. It made for an odd scene, to everyone but the teenager, who, as far as he was concerned, was just doing his daily, or nightly, routine. There was nothing about his appearance to indicate anything special; brown-colored hair, combed into a swept cut, with a rounded chin, and slightly hooked nose. His blue T-shirt, gray jacket, and jeans disguised his muscles, visible but not broad enough to disfigure his lean appearance, complete with long, spindly limbs. Perhaps the only remarkable thing about him on the outside was his eyes; big with sapphire-blue irises, that saw only good and wonder in the world around him. They were looking to the heavens above now, scanning the constellations for something, until his foot was caught on a pebble in the road and he stumbled, causing him to focus on the ground below his sneakers.

    Dragging his huge telescope behind him, with a bundle of items tucked under his arm, sweat dripping down his face, Daniel Phillips stared out at the road ahead, only faintly illuminated by streetlights that had been installed years ago. Above him, the stars twinkled slightly at him as he proceeded down the deserted road, past patches of trees and even an entire forest that bordered the road on one side. There was an abundance of wildlife out and about; crickets chirped and owls hooted as Daniel lugged the heavy telescope back up the road. Fireflies glowed in the dark cast by the pine trees. In the distance, some animal let out a loud cry that disturbed the still night. Daniel took pleasure in these walks; he loved passing through the woods at night, as there was always some wildlife around to see. From bears to deer to nesting birds and everything in between, he'd seen it passing through the trees. Despite their constant presence, he never felt the need to hurry through; he savored every last step, rarely feeling threatened.

    About a quarter mile up the road, the forest gave way to lawns and homes of the country, more street lights drowning out the faintest stars. Most of the homes were deserted, the walls having paint missing or flaking off, lawns that were overgrown with weeds and vines, and a few even had broken windows or boarded-up doors. The trees in the lawn were growing tall, both in size and from the vines that adorned them like curtains, some growing inside of the abandoned ruins. The homes not decaying were occupied by older folks, most in their late fifties and older. These homes displayed fresher paint, much-more well-tended grass, and would've felt warm and welcoming had it not been for the numerous "NO TRESPASSING" signs and wire fences that surrounded the properties. The old folks some nights would sit on their porches and yell at Daniel to hurry up and keep the noise down. He took their shouts and complaints with dismissiveness. His telescope's wheels were actually very quiet, so he guessed that their grumpiness came with old age, rather than from the noise. Such was the case tonight. Old George was sitting on his porch, smoking a cigarette, and when he saw Daniel walking down the street, his telescope in tow, he leaned forward and shouted out: "Can you hurry up, please? You're blocking my view of Jeff's pumpkin patch!"

"I'm sorry, sir!" Daniel said quickly, picking up his pace again.

"I moved away from Atlanta to get away from annoying kids like you!" continued the angry senior. "And now you come in and spoil my relaxing time on the porch! I should call the cops on you! That'll teach…"

Daniel didn't hear the last two sentences. He tuned George's rambling out and kept walking, just wanting to get home. Thankfully, it wasn't that far away, and he breathed a sigh of relief when he reached the driveway.

Daniel could always tell when he reached his house. The lawn was neat, freshly cut, and the one oak tree in the front had no parasitic plants or vines growing on it, unlike most of the other residences nearby. Plus, not a single angry sign or chain-link fence anywhere. It was two-storied, with large windows, a front porch with rocking chairs, and a one-car garage that was used for mainly lawn equipment and tools needed to repair stuff. Light came through the windows out front, spilling out onto the street, making it feel warm and welcoming. Shadows moved inside, indicating that his mom was still awake. Walking onto the driveway, past his mom's sedan, he opened the garage and hauled his telescope into the house, past two bikes, a workbench with a rack of tools on it, his set of barbells, a chest freezer, and other items scattered about. He set his telescope back in its special corner, threw the protective bag over it to keep dust out, and set about putting the other supplies back where they belonged, except for his notebook, which he opened and observed all of the sketches he had made that night. Pleased at the many entries listed in the notebook, he closed it and opened the door into his house, kicking off his shoes on the doormat.

As he set down his notebook on its special shelf, Daniel's mother stuck her head around the corner. Ms. Amy Phillips was in her early forties, but still looking young as ever, with dark hair that was streaked with the occasional gray strand tied in a bun, with the same sapphire-blue eyes as her son, big hands, and ears that had unusually pointed lobes. She was wearing a black blouse, a sign that she was probably going to be doing housework for a while. "Daniel, honey?" she called to him, in a soothing voice that rang like ocean waves. "Remember to put the plastic covering on it so that bugs don't fly into it."

"I know, Mom. Already did," replied Daniel tiredly. Despite his love for the stars, hiking a mile round-trip wasn't exactly leisure work. Double-checking his telescope, he took his sneakers off and moved into the house toward the stairs to shower.

Their house was once an old farmhouse, belonging to an old farmer who owned some of the corn fields near the residence. Once he passed away, the place had sat abandoned for ten years until his mom had come along and fixed it up. Now it was one of the nicer dwellings in Salt Plains, Kentucky, USA, though *nicer* was a relative term in the town. Entering through the front door, the main hall was simple and lit up, with the living room on the left containing a sofa and bookshelf. On the right was a dining area with a table for four, with a small candle in the middle. The stairs to the upstairs were back past the kitchen, which itself was down a short hallway, and a gaming room was set aside for Daniel next to it. Upstairs, half of the four bedrooms were empty, the other two being occupied by Ms. Phillips and Daniel. The only bathroom was to the right of Daniel's room.

    He glanced outside as he passed the window by the stairs, just in time to catch a meteor shooting across the star-filled sky. Daniel sighed in a satisfied sort of way. In addition to his astronomy exploits, he had wild dreams of space most nights, about him building a spaceship and traveling across the galaxy, exploring places never before seen by humans, discovering aliens never before cataloged by mankind, becoming an interstellar traveler in an infinitely vast universe. Alas, they were only dreams of grandeur, with very little, wait, *no* chance of becoming true in his lifetime. But he could dream, right? In actuality, he was clueless about his plan for his life after high school. Putting thoughts of setting foot on a distant planet out of his head, he moved towards bed.

    He showered quickly, and after brushing his teeth, he took his day clothes, threw them into a laundry basket, and pulled on an undershirt and cotton shorts, fresh and clean. He walked to his room, switching his fan on. Pulling back the covers on his bunk bed, he climbed in, said a quick prayer, and turned off the light. He closed his eyes, then, having second thoughts, opened them to face the window. From where he was, the constellations sparkled in the window, with the edge of the Milky Way running across its left side. To Daniel, it was beautiful. As he watched, another meteor streaked across the sky, making a beautiful trail of light as it did. Thoughts of becoming a space explorer returning to his weary brain, he shut his eyes once more, and passed out in his soft bed, dreams of stars dancing in his head.

The next morning, Daniel didn't leave his bed at his normal time. Usually, he was up by no later than 7:15 in the morning to start the day. Not today. Today, he didn't want to get up. Not only was he exhausted and a little sore from dragging his scope around, he knew what today was. Monday, which meant another week of school, which meant more homework for him to do. He heard Ms. Phillips at the door. "Daniel?" she called. "Time to get up! School is today, in case you've forgotten, and I want you to be there on time to make a good impression!"

Daniel's private high school was not exactly a top-tier education center. Far from it, actually. He hated every second that he was inside, whether it was due to the smelly, unshowered bodies to the absolute filthiness of the place. Plus, he was still relatively new there, meaning that he was still befriending new teachers, new kids, and harder homework. Homework that some evenings ate into the time he'd rather be spending stargazing out in the fields at night. In addition, bullying was a major problem there as well. Daniel rolled around in his bed and pulled the sheets tighter, trying to drown out his mom's breathing on the other side of the door.

The door rattled on its hinges as Ms. Phillips banged on it with one hand. "Daniel," she shouted, "The bus will be here in less than thirty minutes! It's get up now, or miss out on breakfast!" The smell of cooking sausage began to creep in Daniel's room through the door, and it made his mouth water. He fought the urge, but he finally jumped out of bed, his hunger for whatever was making that delicious aroma overpowering his dread at going to high school.

His mom had indeed made sausage for breakfast, along with toast, and Daniel, who had dressed into a T-shirt and jeans, devoured it aggressively. His mom was an amazing cook, and today was no exception. He hoped that she would never change in that regard.

"Your backpack and lunch are by the door sweetie," Ms.

Phillips told him as he ate.

"Thanks, Mom," Daniel said gratefully through a mouthful of food. His mother probably had packed his stuff for him while he was outside last night. Finishing his sausage, he freshened up his breath and combed his hair so it looked nice. He put on his shoes and opened the front door, stepping outside into the cool, morning air.

"Have a wonderful day of school," said his mom, pulling her son into a hug before he could get out the door.

"See you this afternoon," Daniel replied, sounding sweet despite trying to pull away from her. He broke free of her grip and closed the door behind him, leaving him alone on the porch.

The bus pulled up a minute later, and Daniel grabbed his normal seat, by the window in the middle of the aisle. The smell of diesel pricked the inside of his nose, and the seat next to his had an old wad of gum stuck to its top, its age unknown. The center walkway was covered in mud from the last time it had rained, and there were flies buzzing around. Only six other kids were on board, all looking depressed. Yep. Seemed normal. The doors closed, and the bus pulled away, leaving Daniel's house behind. Yawning, he propped his head on his arm and waited for their journey to be over.

The temptation to fall asleep came to Daniel as they drove through the countryside, but he fought the urge to do so, trying to pick out something of interest in the browning fields and trees showing signs of fall. There was a farmer plowing his field with his tractor, and way off in the distance, the Blue Ridge Mountains loomed, as distant humps, some of them showing signs of white on their summits. A minute later, they crested over a hill and the town of Salt Plains, Kentucky, appeared below them, hiding in a narrow depression between two large hills, looking more and more like a ghost town.

Salt Plains had not changed much in over fifty years. Most of the buildings in downtown, even the large corporate centers, showed rusted frames, peeling paint, and overgrown greenery, even town hall, at one end of Main Street. Only the three-story Marriott on the south side of town center, and the hybrid McDonald's—Starbucks betrayed the fact that this town was living in the 21st century, and not colonial times. But Daniel could not imagine that the hotel received that much traffic, and the McDonald's was only popular, because it was the only substantial restaurant in town, despite being indistinguishable from a landfill. Were you to eat there, you would be serenaded with condiment stains and the smell of mildew, plus almost no staff. Surrounding the town was essentially nothing but farmland, as far as the eye could see, like a giant quilt covering this part of Kentucky.

The school lay two miles beyond downtown, and no matter how many days Daniel went there, he was still appalled by the sight of the building. It was basically in ruins, tangled with creepers and leafy tendrils, and had huge cracks in the mortar in some spots. Moss grew on the walls, and there was a large hole in the roof of the building. A large notice board hanging on the wall said:

WARNING! Roof of room 13 is unstable. Do not enter. Watch for falling debris!

That sign had been there for months now, since the big tornado had swept through the area, and the roof had only gotten worse since then. Sighing, Daniel grabbed his bag from his feet and walked out of the bus. He checked his watch. It was still five minutes till the bell rang, so he sat himself down on the curb by the front doors and watched the small number of kids trickling into the building. Given the small size of the school, there were probably fewer than forty kids attending this year, as Salt Plains was not a major metropolis. Most people left as soon as they could. It was Daniel's plan, even though he had no clue what he wanted to do after high school. He, like most people, didn't think the town was going to last very much longer. Not only was the town in decay, but it was constantly wracked by harsh storms, and when there were no storm to be had, drought. Throw in nothing of any interest within fifty miles and you had a community that only existed due to the nostalgia of most of its residents. Daniel was not one of those residents, and his friends echoed his sentiment. They kept leaving in droves, anyway. Except for one.

Lost in thought, Daniel didn't hear the voice calling his name at first, drowned out by the hubbub of students chatting with one another. But he soon picked it out, and his head shot up. "Daniel! Daniel!" it called, in a girl's voice.

His eyes immediately began to search the crowd for the source of that voice, his heart thudding with anticipation just a little harder. That was the sound of the one reason he had to stay in Salt Plains. The one reason he actually, sort of, enjoyed school. And after a few more seconds of scanning the parking lot where the buses were, he found the person who had shouted his name.

While Daniel had made many acquaintances during the school years, and had also made some pretty good friends too, he had only one true best friend in this town: Caitlin Wheeler. And as an older eleventh-grader with a mess of facial hair moved aside, she came into view. Caitlin was, in height and build, normal for her age, which was about fourteen, with blond, not-quite-wavy hair that hung down to her waist. Her nose was straight, in contrast to Daniel's slightly hooked nose, and, like Daniel, she had startlingly blue eyes, only more aquamarine than sapphire. These eyes seemed to pierce right through the body straight to your soul to see the good there. She was dressed in a hoodie and jeans, wearing leather boots, and Daniel, despite all his best efforts to contain it, couldn't help but smile when he saw her face. A flood of happy memories filled his brain, and the gloominess of the day melted away instantly.

"You know, I was beginning to wonder if your neighbor

had made last-minute plans to move away and you weren't going to show up today," remarked Daniel casually as she walked up. It was a troll remark that he loved to deploy some days.

"If that was the plan, you'd be the first to know," replied Caitlin, in the same casual tone. Her voice was smooth and soft, but not without a playful edge to it. No doubt she had been up to some subtle mischief lately. Chuckling, the two friends high-fived each other, and Daniel found his disdain for Salt Plains melting away like winter snow.

"I know we saw each other last week, but it feels like it's been forever," said Daniel, smiling from ear to ear.

Caitlin nodded, returning the facial expression. "It does! Seriously, why do the weekends last so long?"

"One of life's mysteries, I guess?"

She laughed. "I guess. How's your mom?"

"She's doing fine. She just got hired at the place she wanted to work at, so she's excited about that. She starts in two days. Otherwise, about the same."

"That's good! How goes your telescope watching?"

"Stellar." And then they both laughed and cringed at the terrible pun. "Don't tell Charlie that! Mr. Freeze wishes he had puns that bad."

The bell faintly rang behind them, and they started to move into the school. "Ugh, don't remind me of that movie," shivered Caitlin. "I still cringe just thinking about it."

"Well, as I said, the puns there are nowhere near as bad as Charlie's. How's he doing anyway?"

Caitlin's smile faded, but just slightly. "He's...well, basically the same. I don't really feel like talking about it too much."

Daniel nodded. "Okay." Charlie Richards, her guardian, was a conversation killer normally, so he hastily pivoted the topic. "What do you think Ms. Rebekah's going to do today?" He pushed open the door, letting the smell of body odor waft out.

"Well, last time, she had us write a seven-page essay, so, who knows?" Caitlin shouldered her bookbag better. "Anything could be on the table."

"Yeah, anything."

They reconvened after three classes at lunch break in the school's gym, which was never used as a gym anymore, but as a cafeteria. This was the one part of the school that was actually pleasant to be in, as everywhere else had such terrible ventilation that the hallways became stuffy with terrible scents. It was the only part of the school that got cleaned semi-regularly too, and as such, you were less at risk of stepping in dropped, rotting food. Daniel and Caitlin found an empty spot at the table and pulled out their lunches. Out from Daniel's lunch bag came the deli sandwich that his mom had made for him. Caitlin had a small salad. "Cheers," they said, tucking into their food.

"Well, Ms. Rebekah really gave us one week to complete that trifold display," said Daniel in annoyance, a huge bite of his sandwich still in his mouth.

"True. At least we get to work in pairs. That should help."

"Let's hope that that doesn't cut into the time for the pumpkin festival this weekend. I still want to go with you. Charlie's okay with it, right?"

"Yeah, he's fine with it." Caitlin took another mouthful of her salad and chewed slowly. "Is Ms. Phillips fine with it?"

"Eh, I've downplayed the whole thing. Besides, it's not like we're going out on a date. It's the pumpkin festival, for crying out loud!"

"What about the pumpkin festival, Daniel?" said a snide voice behind them.

Daniel tensed up upon hearing it, but it soon transitioned into more annoyance. "Really? Greg? You couldn't pick on anybody else today?"

Two huge hands seized the collar of Daniel's shirt and lifted him up into the air, pivoting him around to stare into the eyes of Greg, the nastiest student in the entire school. His straw-like, unkempt hair and scarred face filled almost his entire vision. "You think you're clever, Astro Boy?" he replied, eyes narrowed. "Everyone knows that the pumpkin festival is for people with days left in their lives."

"It's certainly not for people like you whose sole purpose in life is to wind up in prison," retorted Daniel.

He immediately regretted his words, as Greg clobbered him hard in the head and knocked him down to the ground. The bully then proceeded to pummel him in the ribs as a small crowd of students started to gather and gawk. Fiery pain rocked Daniel's entire body as he fought the urge to yell out in pain.

"Greg, stop it!" cried Caitlin, grabbing him by his shoulder. "Leave him alone! He's had enough!"

"Get off me!" yelled Greg, calling her a bad word and slapping her across the cheek, sending her falling to the ground as well. Then, feeling he had done enough damage, he tipped over Daniel's thermos and kicked Caitlin in the side as he went past, laughing to himself.

Daniel sat up slowly, feeling the bruises forming on his side. He gritted his teeth, then saw Caitlin struggling to stand as well. "Oh, God, you okay?" he asked Caitlin worriedly.

She stood up, hand pressed against her cheek. "I'm fine, Daniel. I've had worse injuries than these." Noticing that the students were still watching them, she shooed them away, then turned and helped Daniel stand up. "You alright?"

"Ugh...my ribs feel bruised, but I'll live," he said, massaging them gently.

"Do you need to see the nurse?" asked Caitlin.

"No," he said, standing up fully, then groaning when he saw his thermos contents spilled all over the last half of his sandwich. "Great. There goes my lunch." He threw the soggy bread in the garbage. "So much for a quiet day."

Other students were pointing at them, clearly gossiping behind their backs, and Caitlin decided that perhaps the cafeteria wasn't the best place to be. "Perhaps we should go."

"But we just got here," said Daniel, then saw all of the other high schoolers watching them amusingly, and he broke out in a cold sweat. His heart began to beat faster and he felt his strength weakening. "Oh, no," he whispered, his voice shaky and shallow.

Caitlin hurried him over to a quiet bench, where he collapsed, hiding his face from view. She sat next to him. "Daniel? You alright?" She felt his skin, her hand sensing nothing but cold.

Daniel knew that an anxiety attack was imminent. He had been having them for years now, and he could feel it bubbling up like a volcano inside of him.

"It's...happening...again," he managed to say quietly.

Caitlin leaned in closer to Daniel. "It's nothing," she told him. "Everything that it's telling you...it's not true. Tell yourself that."

She spoke as gently as she could, and she heard his breathing slow down a little. She placed one arm around his shoulder. "It's okay. There's nobody around. It's just you and me."

His breathing settled down, and his skin grew warm to the touch again. He inhaled deeply. "I'm okay. I'm better," he said. He relaxed. "Caught just in time. That almost was bad."

Caitlin nodded. "Still, that was the first one in a few weeks. That's not ideal. I was hoping that your virtual meetings with the counselor would help."

"They have. Just, not fully."

They stood up from the bench. "You sure you're okay?" repeated Caitlin.

Daniel nodded. "I am now," he said, his voice back to normal. "Thanks partly to you."

"No problem. I agreed to help you out as best I could, and that's what I'll keep trying to do."

They both looked around for a while, standing in awkward silence. "So…what about the rest of lunch?" asked Daniel.

Yawning, Daniel opened the door, seeking nothing except some quiet time and some solitude. He threw his bag down, which was a pound heavier than what it had been when he'd left. Three more classes had sucked out the rest of his energy for the day. At least his anxiety had settled down. He heard the sounds of dishwashing from the kitchen. His mom was probably prepping the kitchen for dinner.

"Hi honey!" she yelled from down the hall. "How was school?"

"Fine," Daniel said. "I'm heading upstairs to do schoolwork."

"Dinner's at 5:30 tonight!"

"Okay!"

He wandered upstairs and into his room, which in the late afternoon light revealed all of the furnishings within. There was a bunk bed in one corner and a dresser and bookshelves on the other. A huge map of the night sky hung over his desk, with a poster of Darth Vader next to it with the caption "WE WANT YOU FOR THE IMPERIAL ARMY." Stacks of astronomy books lined his shelves. And his first pair of binoculars were resting inside a glass display case next to the front door. Even his bed sheets were astronomy themed, with a map of the solar system prominently embroidered on them. Sitting on his wooden desk was the notebook that he used to log all of the celestial objects he'd observed—and the ones he would most like to visit as a space explorer. Making the list were Saturn, the Pleiades, and a few other random celestial objects. Of course, these were all fantasies, not things attainable in reality. Flipping through the notebook, he turned to a specific sketch he'd drawn some time ago. It was of him, next to his brand-new telescope, Caitlin next to him, after a night of observing. He had drawn it during his first night out with the new telescope. His mom had arranged a hanging-out session with Caitlin and Charlie, and both of their families had spent the night stargazing. Even though it had been bitter cold—it had happened in January, when the weather was freezing, and snow decorated the ground—it remained his best night with the telescope ever. It was also the first, and so far only, time that Caitlin had gotten to experience the magic of the night sky with him. He smiled at the thought of Caitlin, who had shown up wearing three jackets and snow pants, and yet still somehow managed to shiver the entire time.

    Daniel yawned again. He was a little tired after the day, but he had to get his work done. Fortunately, there wasn't that much to do. Sitting down at his desk, he set his bag down, took out his papers, a pencil, and began to work, starting with the list of the world's countries and capitals for social studies. He remembered that Budapest was the capital of Hungary, and that Singapore was located on the Malayan Peninsula, but he wasn't sure if New Zealand's capital was Auckland or Wellington. Well, it was a 50-50 chance of success. His math homework was a breeze; all review, no new material. He enjoyed it while it lasted. Science was no trouble either, as was history. Grammar took the longest, almost an hour by itself. But he pushed through it, wanting to be free to do what he wanted.

    While he was working on his final assignment, his phone dinged at him. He picked it up. Caitlin had texted him. *"Hey!"* the text read. *"After that fiasco at lunch, I wanted to do something fun with you to make up for it. There's a big field a short walk from my house that your telescope would be great in.*

I've attached the directions below. Would you be interested in going? Your mom's welcome too."

Daniel smiled upon reading that text. Of course he'd want to go. He finished his final assignment and ran downstairs. "Mom!" he called. "Caitlin texted! She wants to know if we want to go stargazing with her tonight! Can I go?"

He popped into the kitchen, where Ms. Phillips was preparing the chicken for dinner. "Of course you can, sweetie," she replied, focusing on carving out the bird.

"She invited you too! Would you like to go as well?"

"I'd love to! It's just that I don't know if I can, though."

"Why not?" asked Daniel. "I don't see you all that often anymore, and we rarely get to do fun things together. You deserve a break every once in a while, you know. What's stopping you from going?"

Ms. Phillips sighed, putting the chicken in the oven. "It's just…I want to meet with my future boss just so I can get used to working with her and—"

"Mom!" said Daniel, approaching her. "Come on. You don't need to focus on your life all of the time. Just for tonight, let's go do something, the three of us."

She sighed, but she eventually relented. "Alright," she said. "I'll go. I suppose that I could use some more time out of the house." She started to boil a pot of water. "Let me just finish dinner and then we can go."

She turned back to focus on preparing their food. "Thank you, mom," said Daniel. He cast a look at the crowded kitchen counter in front of her. "Do you want some help preparing dinner?"

She turned back to smile at him. "That would be great," she told him.

They ate dinner and loaded Daniel's telescope in Ms. Phillips' car, setting off on the short drive to the field. It was mainly down side roads through forest dense enough to look pitch black even with the faint light of streetlamps. There was no moon out, leaving everything dark except for what the car's headlights swept over. After peeking outside the car window again, Daniel whipped out his phone and texted Caitlin their ETA.

"You texting Caitlin?" asked Ms. Phillips, driving the car through the woods.

"Yeah," replied Daniel, sending his message. "Just told her that we would be there shortly."

"How is she doing, by the way?" asked Ms. Phillips. "Is she still trying to start selling her watercolor portraits?"

"She is. She hasn't found any buyers yet, but she's optimistic someone will want one. I don't understand how anyone wouldn't want one; they're beautiful. Heck, I'm considering asking her to make one for my room. Still, she's been getting a little discouraged. Besides that, she's doing very good."

"Back when I was her age, I was interested in the modeling business. Clay and plastic shaping, you know? Took me a while to find people who wanted to see my work, but they were out there. Caitlin's talents for art will eventually find a use. That I'm sure of."

"I'm sure of it, too."

"Oh, look, we're here!"

Ms. Phillips braked and stopped the car in front of the huge patch of grass, and both of them got out to take a look. It was surrounded on all sides by forest, but the field itself was flat and void of trees, with short grass and some more barren spots where a telescope and supplies could easily fit. A wide view of the stars spread out overhead, and the Milky Way was once again a prominent mist band dividing the black. There wasn't a whiff of a cloud or haze in sight. It would be a perfect night for stargazing. There was no sign of Caitlin, yet, but she had texted to say that she would be a few minutes late. Putting his phone in his pocket, Daniel opened the car trunk and began to unload all of his supplies, assembling the telescope not far away.

"It's definitely a little darker out here than around our house," commented Ms. Phillips, staring up into space.

Daniel looked up, to where the faint band of the Milky Way crossed the sky. "I think you're right," he replied. He turned to look back towards the horizon, then saw Caitlin emerge from the woods on the other side of the road.

She was looking as fine as ever. Her hair was tied into a braid, and she was wearing jeans and a red shirt with a dark green jacket. A lawn chair was slung over her shoulder. Her cheek was no longer bright red, and she was smiling broadly as she approached Daniel. "Hey! Glad you could make it," she said. Then she noticed the car and its driver next to it. "Ms. Phillips! So happy you could make it tonight!"

"Caitlin!" said Ms. Phillips, crossing the field to her. "Been a little bit."

"I didn't think you would show up tonight," admitted Caitlin sheepishly. "Glad that I thought wrong."

"Neither of us wanted to miss tonight," replied Daniel satisfyingly, opening the car door and throwing his hoodie over himself. "Even if it is a bit cold."

"You feeling okay after today?" asked Caitlin, and Daniel immediately tensed up. Ms. Phillips's head turned to stare at Caitlin, then at Daniel.

"Did something happen at school today?" she asked.

Daniel shrugged. "Some anxiety problems. It was only for a second. Nothing to worry about, I assure you."

Ms. Phillips raised an eyebrow, but dropped any other questions she may have had. "Alright then, honey. If you say so."

They all gathered in the field, Caitlin setting up the lawn chair next to the telescope. Daniel, meanwhile, walked everyone through the itinerary. "So, the weather looks great for tonight," he told them. "No clouds or anything. If anyone wants to see anything specific, just tell me and I'll try to find it. Otherwise, I'll be panning between different targets. Mars and Jupiter are visible tonight, right there and there." He took the old rifle sight that his mom had almost discarded and turned it on, pointing out both planets.

Caitlin nodded and sat down. "So…where to first? Impress me! You're the one with all the astronomy experience."

"Perhaps, start with the planets and work our way into deeper space from there," suggested Ms. Phillips. "Let our eyes adjust to the fainter objects."

"Okay Miss Princess. Mom too," said Daniel laughing, pointing the giant tube towards the Milky Way high up near the zenith. He checked the smaller finderscope, slowly adjusting it to the bright red dot that indicated Mars, beaming down on them. A quick glance into the telescope revealed that he was on target, Mars' reddish-pink globe shining in the field of view. "Mars is in there. Lower half of field," Daniel told his two patrons, stepping away from the telescope.

Caitlin approached the eyepiece, bending down to look. "It's small," she commented. "Smaller than I was expecting." She peered a little closer. "I think that I can see the ice cap though." She stepped back to let Ms. Phillips look into the eyepiece.

"Interesting," she said, when she saw Mars. But after a moment of extra observing, she too stepped back. "Alright, let's keep going."

Daniel nodded and moved the telescope to point towards the next object. And that's how the next three hours went by in a blur, as the three of them let Daniel move his telescope around

40

the sky and point to various celestial bodies. Although for the most part, they let him dictate what they saw, there were a few requests.

"Can you show me a nebula?" asked Caitlin, after raising her hand.

Daniel obliged, showing her a small nebula that had come from a dying star. "Our Sun will eventually look just like this billions of years from now," he told her. "Just a shell of gas floating in space."

"It's pretty," commented Caitlin, before sitting back down. She requested a few other objects as well, including a galaxy, but for the most part trusted Daniel to lead them through space. Ms. Phillips just sat there and watched, waiting for her turn to see the next big object.

As the evening wore on, and they were on the order of being out until midnight, Ms. Phillips at last told him that it was time to start winding down, as it was another school night and he needed some sleep. He nodded, but asked for one last object to look at. His mom agreed, and he adjusted the telescope away from the star cluster that it was originally pointed at and put all of his eyepieces except for one back in his storage case. He then pointed the telescope towards the east, where a familiar figure was rising.

"Before we go, I have one last thing to show you before we wrap up the evening," explained Daniel, screwing the lens into the eyepiece socket on the telescope, and adjusting the focuser. He then tweaked the telescope's aim until it was precise. "Look to the east, over there." He pointed. "What do you see?"

Both Caitlin and Ms. Phillips followed his pointer finger. "Is that Orion?" asked Ms. Phillips after a moment.

"That is Orion," said Daniel, highlighting Orion's Belt with his rifle pointer. "And it's home to the nebula you're about to see. Take a look."

Before she peeked into the telescope, Caitlin finished

bagging up her chair and set it down next to Daniel's supplies. She walked over to the telescope, peered into the eyepiece, and took a look at the mystical Orion Nebula, flowering in the field like a beautiful cosmic rose. "My word…" she whispered, staring at the star-studded cloud shining back at her. "It's beautiful." She stepped back. "Ms. Phillips, you have to take a look at this."

Caitlin's happiness was all Daniel had wanted that entire evening. He watched as his mom bent over to look into the eyepiece. "Wow…" was all she said, but Daniel could see her face lighting up as she beheld the nebula in the eyepiece.

"The sword of Orion," said Daniel. "You're looking at the sword of Orion. In mythology, he was a mighty hunter who excelled in catching his targets. He was so excellent, in fact, that the gods of Greek mythology sent a scorpion to kill him, before he could equate himself with them. He now watches over the heavens for all eternity, keeping the stars safe from enemies."

"Amazing," said Caitlin, clapping her hands. "You always amaze me with your love of astronomy, Stellar Brain," she said, grinning from ear to ear.

Daniel snorted with laughter. "Stellar Brain?" he questioned. "Have we reached the point where we're allowed to nickname each other?"

Caitlin looked surprised. "I'm sorry, if you don't like it—"

"No, no, no!" said Daniel, hand raised in a stop gesture. "Not at all. I kinda like it. Has a nice ring to it. Besides, it's not *not* true, right? I mean, I put a lot of stars into this head of mine. Not literally of course, but…" He stopped, blushing awkwardly, realizing he'd overdone it. He hastily looked around, trying to change the conversation.

"Subtle, Daniel," said Ms. Phillips a little teasingly. "Anyways, thank you for convincing me to come out. I had a wonderful, and stress-free, time. I'll load your things in the car, while you and Caitlin talk. Sounds good?"

"Thank you, mom," said Daniel, hugging her.

"Bye, Ms. Phillips," said Caitlin, also hugging her. "Until next time."

She grabbed Daniel's case of items and moved towards the car, leaving Daniel and Caitlin alone under the starry sky. "You know, you're always welcome to stay over at our house and use our guest room," said Daniel. "I'm sure my mom would be delighted to have you over."

"I know, Daniel," she replied, sounding a little bit more dejected again. "I appreciate the offer."

"I know how you feel about Charlie, so I'm just leaving this on the table in case you, you know, ever decide to leave."

Even in the faint light cast by the few stars, he could see her face fall. "I'm sorry," he said, regretting his words. "I didn't mean to—"

"No, you're fine," she told him. "Just…I wonder some days, am I really serious about this? It's a very bold thing to do with my life, and I can't help but wonder if it's the right change to make in my life."

Daniel sighed. "I wish I could answer your question. I'm still worried about our town. Like, if the rumors about it going out of business are true…where do we go from there? Do we have to move?" He sighed. "You have the wrong guy to ask these sorts of questions. All I can offer is my support and my mom's. And hopefully that's enough."

Caitlin looked relieved. "Thanks," she told him. She awkwardly looked at him from the side before saying, "Hey, before I go, can I talk to you for a sec?"

Daniel raised an eyebrow, but he nodded and sat down on the grass. "Of course! I'm not in trouble, am I?"

She laughed and sat next to him, staring up into space. "No, not that." She sighed. "Remember how we met?"

Daniel laughed. "How could I forget? Second grade.

You lost your lunch after you dropped your tray. I lost my lunch after I tripped into you. We almost went hungry, but we both managed to have enough money left to get a single order from the cafeteria to split. It tasted horrible." He smiled thinking about it. "A day that I'll never forget for sure."

Caitlin sighed happily and pulled something out of her jacket pocket. It was a bright blue stone, about half the size of Daniel's fist. She handed it to him, gratefulness on her face. He turned it over, examining it. On one side was an engraving of Orion, the hunter constellation. On the other was a short message that read TO A VERY SPECIAL FRIEND.

"It's lazurite," explained Caitlin, pausing briefly while Ms. Phillips loaded the telescope in the car. "Charlie bought it as a souvenir, and he gave it to me a while back when it became clear he didn't want it. I had it engraved and everything. Consider it my present to you for being, well, just you. Because you are special just the way you are, regardless of what your anxiety tells you."

Daniel just stared at the rock. That's all it was. A rock. A pretty rare rock, yes, but still a rock. Yet seeing those words engraved on the back caused a flood of emotion to fill his chest cavity. "Wow," he said, having a bit of difficulty forming words. "It's…well, I don't know!"

"If you don't like it…"

"No, no, no! Seriously, don't say that! It's amazing, Caitlin. It's…" He stared into the finely polished rock, which was so smooth it seemed to shine in the faint starlight. "It's beautiful. So beautiful. I—I don't know what to say!"

Caitlin gave him an all-knowing grin, a grin that only she knew how to do the way she did it. "I do," she said. "Thank you. For being such a great friend through all of these years." And she reached over and pulled him into a hug.

Daniel thankfully recovered from the surprise of it all early, otherwise it could've gotten really awkward. "You're welcome," he said, returning her hug. "Thank you for being a sweet friend. Because with you around, I feel like I have a chance. God has truly blessed me with you."

She pulled away from him, tears in her eyes that she quickly wiped away. "Never change, Daniel," she told him. "Never change at all." She rose to her feet, brushing off her jeans, still smiling broadly. "I have to…go now," she explained, starting to walk away.

"Of course," replied Daniel, standing up. "Thank you for inviting me out here. I had a great time."

"Me too." Caitlin waved at him. "Bye, Stellar Brain! See you tomorrow!"

Daniel waved back. "Bye!"

She turned and slowly grew smaller, until Daniel was by himself, thinking that life could not get any better than it already was. He heard Ms. Phillips call his name and tell him to get in the car, and he grabbed the last bits of his astronomy gear and waltzed over to the sedan with a spring in his step and joy in his heart. School did not seem daunting anymore, and with the pumpkin festival almost here, he felt like everything was going his way.

Aliens could have invaded right then and there, and he would not have cared.

Chapter 2

Earth

Daniel yawned, stretched in his bed, and opened his eyes. Pulling back the covers, he jumped out, excited to start the day out. It was Saturday, and Salt Plains' two-day annual pumpkin festival officially kicked off today. He did not want to miss it for anything.

The pumpkin fest could be traced back to 1892, when the townsfolk of Salt Plains decided to have fun with their extra pumpkins after a particularly plentiful harvest gave them a lot of leftovers. After seeing the potential for something great after the first time, they decided to bring it back, and the next year, they did the same thing. As the town grew over the years, the festival got bigger and bigger as more pumpkin patches, larger fields, and better methods of growing were developed. This year, it would be held Saturday and Sunday, and Daniel planned on attending both days.

A week had passed since Daniel, Caitlin and Ms. Phillips had observed together. And they would all be there at the festival today. Daniel still planned on hanging out with Caitlin all day, and Ms. Phillips would be working the booths, serving out pumpkin pie slices to the public. It would be crowded for sure, but Daniel did not care. He was just happy that he was able to go.

Pulling on clothes and stuffing the lazurite stone in his pocket, he walked down the stairs to the kitchen, where a plate of steaming pancakes and bacon sat waiting for him, a jar of maple syrup and a glass of orange juice sitting next to it. A note stuck to the table read:

Daniel, I'm going to work to prepare for the festival

today. I'll see you there at 11:00. Bike there safely. Love you. Mom.

Daniel sighed. Looks like he was on his own this morning. He ate his breakfast, then gathered his bookbag and placed it in its weekend spot, out of the way of the front door. He brushed his teeth and sat to watch the TV to kill a few hours while he waited for his time to leave. He turned to his collection of movies, putting in his copy of *Star Wars* and grabbing one of the candy boxes located above the fridge for such occasions. Opening it up, he reclined on the couch and let himself forget about life for a second. He allowed his brain to forget about his indecisiveness about where he wanted to go next, or his concerns over Salt Plains' imminent demise. He let them sink to the bottom of his brain, where they would not disturb him and his time watching the movie. Because that's what he could do with the things that worried him; put them aside in favor of the now.

He had to pause the movie shortly before the end to leave for the festival, which was roughly a twenty-minute bike ride away. Thankfully, most of that was downhill, but he still wanted to leave a bit early. He switched off the television, took one last look at his appearance, then hopped on his bike and took off, leaving the house behind him.

It was a crisp, clear, cool but not cold fall morning. The leaves serenaded Daniel with their colors as he passed below them, the breeze occasionally sending some of them floating to the ground. There were no clouds in the sky, although the forecast had suggested that the weather would worsen a little before the end of the evening. The streets were mostly empty, as most locals would already be at the festival by this point. There were still a few folks out tending to their lawns, and Daniel waved at them as he passed them by.

Eventually, he reached a row of cars that was at a standstill, the line waiting to park for the festival. On his bike, he passed them all by with relative ease, weaving between vehicles like a stuntman. Eventually, he came to the edge of the hill overlooking Salt Plains and found the town looking…strangely enough, splendid. Usually it always looked like a pit, except for festival weekend, where everything was covered in the smell and image of pumpkins. There were pumpkin billboards and signs, pumpkin-shaped booths, wooden trebuchets for pumpkin throwing and the color orange in general was plastered onto every building in town. All of the downtown roads were closed to cars to allow people to use them, with the line of traffic being directed to a side road that would take them to the lot. All of the usual public facilities were vacant, except for the McDonald's, which acted as the one actual restaurant during the event, albeit serving, yep, more pumpkins. The scores of booths scattered throughout the town and nearby fields would keep most of the tourists busy over the duration of the event. There were hundreds of people in view, milling about and discussing whatever seemed to be most common these days. The booths and other festival markers extended past the buildings of downtown up a forested hill to the north of the town and beyond that to another large field where the festival booths continued. Signs were everywhere, with commercial messages like **PUMPKIN THROWING! ONLY $2.00!** and **FRESHLY BAKED, WARM PUMPKIN PIE, 50 CENTS A SLICE!** and other messages crudely written on the wooden boards that lined up in front of the booths, next to roped queues full of people and tourists. Yep. That was pretty much the entire nature of the festival. There were no clouds in the sky in the distance, the white-decked peaks of the Blue-Ridge Mountains visible clearly. Hopefully the forecast would be wrong with its prediction of sketchy weather tonight.

   He rode his bike down the rest of the way to the center of downtown, parking it next to the McDonald's, and began to walk through the streets of the town, scanning for signs of Caitlin. She had told him to meet her over in the spillover field up on the hill, by the arcade games. He began to hurry in that direction, being careful to not bump into any of the hundreds of people walking the festival. He had caused a scene before during a previous festival, and was hoping to avoid that at all costs. His anxiety would never forgive him if he did.

The road to the field was built on an incline, and Daniel, for all of his fitness training, had busted his lungs up by the time he reached the top of the incline, where it gradually leveled out to reveal a wide open field, with more booths, machines and ovens set up. Everything up here was bathed in the full force of the autumn sun's light, casting a yellowish glow over the entire field. The smell of pie persisted up here as well, exciting Daniel's brain and sending endorphins through his body. He spotted Caitlin next to the arcade games, just as she said she would be. There were only five games, all extremely old classics, most from the 1980s, including an original Pac Man, Space Invaders, Galaga, and other old games that he had never even heard of. The only thing in there that was sort of modern was the pinball machine, but even that was about as old as he was. The games only came out for the festival, spending the rest of their time at the elementary school, as evidenced by the paint splatters and marker drawings that covered the facades of all five games. That did not stop the public from loving to use them; a long line had formed for each game behind Caitlin.

As Daniel approached her, she glanced down at her watch, then gave him a disapproving look. "You're late," she told him.

Daniel pulled out his phone and checked the time. He sighed. "I'm less than a minute late!" he protested, then realized that she was kidding. "But you don't really care, do you?"

Caitlin shook her head. "Not a wink," she replied. She stood up from the bench where she was sitting. "How's your morning been?"

"Ah, fine. Not much to report. Just me waiting to head

here." He smiled at her. "Do you want to start walking around? Maybe try to find my mom in the process?"

"After you, Stellar Brain."

Daniel chuckled to himself, and turned towards the pumpkin patch, planning on starting with the one they would use for fall decorations and for Halloween. Even though he was too old to go trick-or-treating, he still loved the holiday; he had spent the last few holidays hiding in the bushes, dressing like some horror movie character, and jumping out when kids came to the door. He also loved carving pumpkins; this year he wanted a big monstrosity to place at his mom's door.

As they walked through the pumpkin patch, Daniel kept an eye out for larger pumpkins. The field was divided into two parts—the 'normal' section and the 'oddball' section. The normal section housed all of the regularly shaped pumpkins. These were mainly used for pies and for Halloween. The oddball section housed all of the weird pumpkins—those with strange shapes, colors, or a little bit of both. They passed one pumpkin that looked almost pink and was twisted like a rope knot around. Another was shaped like a flower vase, wide at the top and bottom, but thin in the middle. Unsurprisingly, Daniel noticed that while the oddball patch seemed to have hardly been touched, the normal side was teeming with people hunting for the right pumpkin. Worse, Daniel was having a hard time finding a large enough pumpkin for his standards.

"How about that one?" asked Caitlin, pointing to the center of a small group of the vegetables. In the center was a pumpkin that was at least eight inches in diameter. Daniel shook his head.

"I don't think so. It's close, but not quite the right size."

"How about that one?" She pointed to another pumpkin that was also big, but not quite as large as the first one.

"Mmm...nah."

"That one?"

"Eww, definitely not!" said Daniel, laughing. She had pointed to what could have won the prize for weirdest pumpkin ever—a red-colored, mangled blob where the pumpkin was about as thick as a jungle vine and as long as a snake. That would be catapult ammo for sure; it's what happened with all the unwanted pumpkins at the very end of the festival.

"What about that one?"

"Definitely n…wait." Daniel caught himself as he saw the pumpkin that she was indicating. It was huge, larger than the other two that she had mentioned, and it was a perfect orange color. It was tall and thick and, when Daniel picked it up, it was a lot lighter than he had expected, indicating less pulp in there than normal. "This actually might be it."

Caitlin spotted a scale and measurer not far away from them. "We can check it over there."

They weighed the pumpkin in at just twenty pounds, light for its huge size. It was one foot four inches in diameter, according to the tape measure, and just over seven inches tall. Daniel was impressed. "This'll do," he said, heaving it off of the scale and starting to carry it back.

"Do you need help?

"Nah, but thanks for offering." Daniel grunted while lifting the heavy pumpkin. "Don't you want one too?"

Caitlin nodded and ran off, coming back a few moments later with a much more modest-sized pumpkin in her arms. "Doesn't need to be big to work," she said, though judging by the way she strained when carrying it, Daniel guessed that her pumpkin was actually heavier than his. He found a small cart on wheels before she popped a blood vessel and they placed their pumpkins on it.

They walked back through the patches. At the festival, they didn't bother to charge money for the pumpkins. The townspeople knew that, while many would come just for the pumpkins, most of those would see the festival's other offerings and would normally spend money on something extra, like a slice of pie, a round of throwing pumpkins, or even just a large bottle of ice-cold water. But it was a great blessing to the locals, who could just walk in, pick a pumpkin up, and leave. Daniel and Caitlin lugged their find out of the patch to Ms. Phillips' booth, which was not far away. She was managing a pie booth, and they could smell the freshly-baked goods inside even as they approached it from the rear.

"Dear Lord, that's a big pumpkin!" she exclaimed at the sight of Daniel's monstrous vegetable, once they arrived.

Daniel set it carefully down. "For all of that size, it only weighed twenty pounds." He turned, grinning, as Caitlin heaved her heavy pumpkin over to them and set it next to Daniel's.

"I actually think that my pumpkin, which is a lot smaller than yours, is still heavier," she remarked in disbelief. Despite having to carry it, she was smiling. "Who would've thought?"

"Maybe Jack Skellington cursed yours or something," teased Daniel.

"Or maybe he just blessed yours," fired back Caitlin. Then they both laughed at the reference. It felt good to put their love of movies to good use. They had gotten to the point where one could finish the other's pop culture reference without missing a beat. Ms. Phillips tended to just let it all happen naturally, as she did here.

"Whatever he did, I'm sure that both of your pumpkins will make excellent jack o' lanterns this Halloween," interjected Ms. Phillips. She held out two slices of pumpkin pie. "Do you want some?"

"Yes, please!" chorused Daniel and Caitlin together, causing them to laugh again. They reached into their pockets and started to take some change out.

"What? No, no, no," Daniel's mom said disapprovingly. "You don't need to pay for this. You're my son and my son's best friend. This is on me."

"Well, those ingredients you used didn't pay for themselves," said Caitlin, pulling out three quarters. "Here. Just take them. The pie's worth it anyway." She set the change on the counter of the booth and took one of the plates from Ms. Phillips.

Daniel's mom glanced at her son. "You too?"

"Yes. Call it a tip." Daniel poured a mess of change out of his wallet, including a quarter, four dimes, eight nickels and a whole bunch of pennies. He counted off seventy-five cents worth and set it on the counter, taking the pie slice as he did.

"Where did all of this change come from?" asked Ms. Phillips.

Daniel shrugged. "Been scrounging it up from the ground as I've gone. I've found almost two dollars' worth already." He grabbed two forks and passed one to Caitlin, then they turned and vanished into the increasing crowds before Ms. Phillips could reply.

They ate as they walked, taking small bites and being careful not to dump the food in the grass. The pie was delicious, as always. "Yum," said Caitlin through a mouthful of warm goodness. "Best pie ever."

"As always." Daniel broke off a piece with his fork and stuffed it into his mouth, letting it stimulate his taste buds. It was sweet and absolutely heavenly, made using a top-secret recipe that no one outside of Salt Plains knew. Whatever those secret ingredients were, they had this pie a notch above any others he'd had. He almost liked the crust as much too, as it was laced with a sugary mixture of butterscotch that was lip-smacking. He wolfed down the rest of his pie, Caitlin doing the same.

The sun had reached its peak at this point, and had begun to trend towards the west. More people crammed the dirt pathways and stalls of the festival, to the point where in some areas it felt like a traffic jam in a city. "More people here than I would prefer," commented Daniel. "Is there something that we can do that's not going to be mobbed?"

"The pumpkin throwing is close by," mentioned Caitlin, pointing at the line of trebuchets set up a little higher up on the field. "Let's take a look, see how bad the wait is."

They walked on over to the catapults, which looked like props from *Lord of the Rings*. Made of authentic, springy oak, with a ratcheting mechanism to throw whatever was inside the bowl at the targets lined up at the end of the range. A rotating platform allowed the settings for where the catapult was pointed to be adjusted. A stash of smaller, oddly shaped pumpkins sat in a bucket next to the machine. A large sign stood at the front of the queue to the range, displaying the target's statistics and the rewards for hitting certain areas.

"Do you want to go first, or do you want me?" asked Daniel.

"Eh…I don't feel like throwing pumpkins today," replied Caitlin. "You can, though. It's almost more fun to watch anyways."

Daniel shrugged. "Have it your way. I'll let you pick out the prize if I win." He queued up at the back of the line. Most of the people in line were kids younger than age 11, with their parents, waiting to win a prize. He felt out of place, being one of only a small handful of teenagers waiting in line. The queue moved agonizingly slow, as despite the large number of catapults, and many kids took ten minutes just to figure out their thrower. Daniel pulled out his phone and played some mobile games while he waited for his turn.

Finally, after what felt like an entire month, he reached the front of the line. He approached the booth operator, who looked like he'd had one too many beers. He eyed Daniel as he approached with several other folks, most of them kids. One of them could've been no more than five years old. "How m'ny rounds d' y'all want fur this 'yer vegetable throwin' contest?" he asked the group in an extremely thick, almost indecipherable southern accent.

"Two, please," called out a mother with her young son.

"Six!" yelled a boy from the middle of the crowd. Then his mother scolded him for his choice and said, "Just three, please."

"One." Daniel didn't want to hold up the line. One round, or three throws, was more than enough. Besides, he had less excuse for missing his throws, being older than everyone else.

When everyone had said how many they wanted, the operator beckoned each of them to a catapult. "When this yer cow horn sounds," he said, holding up a horn originally designed to attract cows to it when blown, "y'all may start throwing these yer pumpkins. 'Free pumpkins per throw. Take as much time as y'all need." A groan went up from the people still waiting in line. "If yer score is satisfactory, y'all will win a prize. Now git out there and git into y'all's positions." Everyone gladly obeyed. Daniel climbed into the command chair of his trebuchet, which was just a kitchen chair that had been hastily bolted to the wooden deck, and he felt it shift under him. He studied the controls. This was his first time, so he wanted to be as familiar with the device he was manning as possible. He saw two levers; one to control spin, another to control pitch. Another lever that was painted red was the trigger—it would throw the pumpkins. Daniel bent down to the crate full of misshapen pumpkins and loaded three into the machine. As he loaded the vegetables in the bowl, he stared out at the crowd of moving people, spotting Caitlin standing in front of a bench. She gave him a thumbs-up, as if to say *Hey. You've got this.* And that was all he needed. He climbed back into the chair, readying the catapult to fire.

The horn sounded. And Daniel slowly adjusted the machine to where he believed the pumpkins would hit the target. Without sights, there was no way of telling, but it seemed like a good guess. He closed one eye, taking careful aim, and pulled the red lever. There was a loud *whoosh* as the arm came up and over, throwing the pumpkins at the target. They sailed through the air, on a collision course with the wall in front of them.

Splat! The three exploded as they hit the wood. Two missed the target, one by a solid foot, but one hit the fifty-point ring, leaving a giant orange stain where it impacted. Not bad for a first try. Daniel reached down, taking three others, and loading them into the machine. He sighted again and fired again. Two came within a few inches of the central circle, but the third again missed, landing behind the target. Daniel groaned. So close to a prize, but not quite close enough. He glanced over at Caitlin, who gave him another encouraging thumbs-up. Nodding, he bent down to load his third round of pumpkins, reaching for another bundle of three, only to stop, reconsider, and only grab one, a fairly round green pumpkin slightly smaller than his head. He loaded it in the catapult and sighted again, focusing exclusively on hitting that bullseye. He sighted as best he could, then adjusted the pumpkin's position in the basket, then adjusted the catapult by just a hair.

Praying that he had at least gotten the pumpkin to at least partially hit the bullseye, he pushed the trigger. The bowl came up in a graceful arc, sending the pumpkin hurtling at the target once more. Everything passed in slow motion as Daniel prayed his calculations were valid. The projectile was twenty feet from the target, ten feet, five feet...

Someone behind him gasped, then there was applause from a couple of people. Daniel, realizing he had shut his eyes, chanced a glance at the target. A mass of pumpkin skin, pulp, and seeds covered the target...centered very close to the exact center of the target, but still within the bullseye's border. He relaxed in his chair, glancing over to Caitlin, who was giving him a huge smile and clapping her hands. He got off the machine, feeling quite good at himself, and walked over to the operator, who was giving him a look of admiration. "Quite some shot thar, sonny," he said. "I'll tell you what, with yer kind of aim you could become a fine deer hunter right thir, I bit." He added up Daniel's point tally. "Three-'undred and firty-five points," the man told him. "That'll give you access to these righ' here." He pulled out a large cardboard box, and Daniel looked inside. Rather than being stuffed animals and other normal carnival prizes, there were lots of cool trinkets inside; a set of toy cars, a huge bar of chocolate, a small lava lamp, and a set of markers. Daniel picked up the chocolate. Caitlin would love it, and it would be a nice treat. He set the candy bar down on the counter. "I'll take this, if you don't mind."

    The operator shook his head. "No problem, sonny," he replied. "Take it. You certainly earned 'em." Then he turned and called out to another family who had just finished their turn.

    Daniel hurried through the exit, elated with his win. Caitlin was waiting. "That was an amazing throw!" she exclaimed, congratulating him. "You hit it right in the center! How...?"

    "Lucky throw, I guess," said Daniel, scratching the back of his head and grinning.

    Caitlin gave him a mischievous look. "Always the modest one, aren't we? What did you win?"

    Daniel handed her the giant bar. "To split," he told her.

    They found a bench and sat down, opening the chocolate bar and breaking it in half. After they finished eating, they sat in silence for a bit, watching as people walked on by towards the pumpkin patches. The crowds had only gotten worse in the meantime, and nearly every booth had some sort of wait. "I don't want to deal with these crowds," said Daniel, noticing the huge line behind him for the catapults, that was previously only half as long. "Why don't we leave for just a bit and come back later when there's less people?"

    "Well, where would we go?" asked Caitlin, curiously waiting for an answer.

Daniel thought for a bit. "I have an idea," he said. "But you're not going to like it, I don't think."

A few minutes later, they were walking towards the parking lot, Daniel holding the keys to Ms. Phillips' car, Caitlin looking positively nervous.

"Yeah, you're right. I hate everything about this," she said, looking around nervously.

"Relax, Cait," said Daniel, spotting the sedan amid the mob of parked cars. "I have my learner's permit, it's not a big deal."

"But isn't it against the law to drive by yourself when you have a permit?"

"I'm not alone. You're coming with me!"

"You know what I meant!"

"Mom gave me the keys to the car. If she doesn't have an issue with it, neither do I." Daniel unlocked the car as he approached. "Don't worry, Caitlin. I'll go slow, I promise. Won't do more than 45."

He opened the driver's side door and got in. Caitlin, hands on her hips, looked around again, but eventually walked around and got into the passenger seat. "Just don't crash," she told him, putting her seatbelt on tight.

Daniel nodded and turned the ignition on. Putting the car in reverse, he slowly began to back out of the parking spot, checking his rearview mirrors. "See? Nothing to it," he said. Then, he saw another car coming down the aisle faster than it should have been and he slammed to a stop, jolting Caitlin in her seat.

"I'll accept your apology at any time!" she said sarcastically, looking behind her now, her skin a little pale, a sign that she was nervous.

"That was his fault." Daniel resumed backing out slowly

until he was clear of the cars next to him, then he threw it into drive. The sedan inched forward down the lot, Caitlin relaxing a bit more as Daniel guided them out of the aisle and onto an exit artery out of the field, bumping over the grass as they went. Thankfully, there were no more close calls in the lot, and they soon left the grass and found themselves on asphalt instead.

"That's better," said Daniel, relaxing as he turned away from downtown Salt Plains and the festival and started up one of the country roads leading away from town. Caitlin said nothing, but continued to stare out the windscreen, still looking slightly pale.

They drove for a while down winding, narrow roads, Daniel navigating them to the best of his ability. He came close to the edge of his lane a couple of times, but for the most part managed to stay within safe boundaries. They passed through more forest and eventually reached a clearing where there was nothing but fields surrounding them. Looking behind her, Caitlin could see the depression where Salt Plains lay, looking a whole lot smaller from this vantage point. She looked ahead at the road and saw a familiar road sign ahead of her.

"Turn right at the next junction!" she told Daniel suddenly.

"Right? Why?" he replied, concentrating on the road immediately in front of him.

"Just trust me, please!"

Daniel was puzzled, but he obeyed, turning right at the next branch-off road he saw. He navigated a couple of hairpin turns as he started to climb up a hill, throwing both of them off to the side as they gained elevation, passing through scattered trees and patches of forest, occasionally coming close to the edge of a drop-off, until they finally reached their destination; a scenic overlook facing the town. They came to a stop at the edge of the road and got out, reaching the stone wall that overlooked the entire town, which was just a small marking on the Earth's surface from this view. The mountains were visible as faint humps in the distance, the sun slowly dipping closer to the western horizon in the distance, behind a large bank of thick clouds.

"One of my favorite spots to just relax," explained Caitlin. "Charlie makes a point to stop here every time we return from the mountains. There's no one else around, and it's a spot to breathe and escape the hassles of life. At least, that's what I think." She turned to Daniel. "Do you like it?"

He nodded, staring down at the peaceful valley. "I do. Reminds me of my special spot; it's in the woods behind my house. There's this serene brook and pond that no one ever visits. Really nice spot to just escape the hassles of life, and it's also a nice spot to swim during the summer."

She nodded, sitting down on the wall. "Do you really think that your mom would appreciate me living at your place?"

"I meant every single word of it." Daniel sat down next to her. "If you're ready to move into our place, away from Charlie, then do it."

She nodded slowly. "I feel as though I should, it's just…" She sighed. "Am I really ready to commit to something like this? Because once I do this, I can't just, you know, walk away from it."

Daniel put a hand on her shoulder. "It's not up to me," he told her. "But whenever you're ready, my mom and I will be ready to greet you with open arms and offer you a warm home where you feel welcome."

He felt her body relax just a little. "Thanks, Daniel," she said.

"Don't mention it. Who knows? Maybe, a year from now, maybe then I'll know exactly what to tell you in a situation like this. One can hope."

They watched the sun set for a while, occasionally catching faint whiffs of pumpkin being blown up by the wind.

"Those clouds do not look friendly," noted Caitlin, indicating the giant wall of storm clouds that seemed to be blowing their way, and were now hiding the sun entirely.

Daniel saw them. "Well, when you're right, you're right." He stood up. "We should probably get back before we're stranded out here."

They both got back in the car, turned around and started back towards the town. It was a little darker now in the forest, and Daniel switched his headlights on. They turned onto the road leading back to town and drove at a steady rate, the wooded hill on their right looking almost totally dark.

"Something's off," noted Daniel. "It shouldn't be this dark right now."

"It's probably that line of storms," pointed out Caitlin.

"No, no, even then there should be some natural light filtering in. This…" He glanced over to the side, where he could barely see down the hill through the thick conifers. "This is too dark for this time of day. Look at the clock." He pointed at the dash, which had a digital setup reading 3:55. "Sunset's not for another hour at least."

Caitlin pulled out her phone. "Then if it's not the storm clouds, what is it?"

Just then, a tree up ahead on the road groaned, and began to tumble over towards the road. Both of them gasped and Daniel slammed on the gas, sending them forward and clearing under the tree just before it impacted the road with a huge thud. He braked the car to a halt, breathing fast as he stared at the huge tree that had nearly crushed them.

"What the frick?" exclaimed Caitlin, her skin now significantly whiter than normal. "What the heck was that?"

"Must've been an old tree," said Daniel, noting the huge diameter of the trunk. "It was leaning over the road. Might've finally given way, it happens around here all the time." He slowly took his foot off of the brakes. "It was probably just a one-time thing. Not a big deal."

He began to pull forward, back down the road, only for a second tree to creak and crack ahead, falling over onto the road. This time, Daniel was not fast enough, and it slammed to a halt right in front of the car, blocking both lanes of traffic. He braked the car again, now looking a little worried, and got out to check the tree.

"Another dying tree?" It may have come out as sarcastic, but Caitlin sounded genuinely nervous.

Daniel inspected the trunk. "No," he said. "This is fresh wood. Living." He looked down the trunk. "It still has all its pine needles on, look!"

Caitlin went to look. "Yeah, it still does. All of them from the looks of it!"

Looking at the base of the tree, whatever had knocked it down had to have knocked it down, as there were no clean cuts or sawdust anywhere. "Whoever or whatever knocked it over had to have done so without chainsaws or axes, because there's no sign of any tools at use on this tree!" reported Daniel, his brain immediately wondering what sort of thing could knock a huge tree like this over.

As if on cue, a third tree behind them slowly creaked and toppled over, and they both turned around just in time for the trunk to crush their car under it, shattering the windows. Then, as the forest settled once again, they both became acutely aware of another noise in the woods beyond the wildlife and rustling of leaves.

"What's that droning sound?" asked Caitlin.

Indeed, it was a constant whirring, like a jet turbine, that filled the woods. Only this noise sounded way more powerful than any jet turbine that Daniel had ever heard before. They scanned the woods, looking for any sign of the source, which was made difficult by the ever-darkening forest. They heard another tree topple over, resulting in more cracking and another thud, but they could not pinpoint the source of the droning, even as it increased in volume and pitch.

"Where is that noise coming from?" asked Daniel, largely to himself. He glanced around, then managed to look up. He froze in his tracks, staring. "Caitlin…" he whispered. "Don't move."

"What do you mean?" she asked. "There's nothing around here but fallen trees!"

"Up."

She looked confused in the faint light, but she did look up, and immediately froze as well. "No…" she whispered. "No…this isn't real. That can't be real. That's…"

"Real," replied Daniel.

Above the two of them, like something straight out of Han Solo's nightmares, was the underside of what could only be an alien spaceship.

Chapter 3

Up until that day, the worst thing that Caitlin had had to deal with was some school bullies. Sure, she had dealt with problems ranging from family unrest to trouble at school, from an attack by a bear when she was seven to Daniel's anxiety. But those were small kinds of problems. Now she was dealing with a whole other kind of problem. The big, metal, alien kind with enough lasers, missiles and other weapons to vaporize everything from here to Chicago. And it was passing through the woods, slowly lumbering its way towards Salt Plains. She could physically feel the terror creeping into her body. A mixture of amazement and terror. She couldn't move at first. She and Daniel just stood there, frozen on the road, staring at the metal ship that had emerged from the woods.

"I thought that you said that there were no aliens," whispered Caitlin to Daniel, slightly panicked.

"And that's what I thought!" he hissed back. "Until just now, that is!"

"What do we do? Do we run?"

"No! Not just yet. I don't think they've seen us. If we run now, they might spot us and start shooting! Stay still!"

"Terrible idea!" Caitlin breathed harder and faster with each passing moment, her chest heaving and falling as waves of fear coursed through her. She was shaking in her shoes. "Do you see all of those weapons? There's enough to blow a smoldering crater in the valley in place of the town!"

"Caitlin!" Daniel whispered harshly, making her turn her head in surprise. "Be quiet! Please, for the love of God, be quiet!"

Shock came over her at how angry and fearful he sounded, but she nodded stiffly and stood still, the ship passing overhead slowly until they could see the thrusters on the stern of the vessel. "Okay, now go!" hissed Daniel, vaulting over the second fallen log and running towards the town. Caitlin, startled, chased after him. A distant rumble of thunder heralded the arrival of the storm front they had spotted earlier. The cracking of trees being pushed over filled the forest.

"It's heading for Salt Plains!" Caitlin exclaimed, already feeling out of breath. "Daniel, your mom!"

"You're right!" Daniel was also out of breath, panting hard as his lungs shrunk from the effort. "And the festival! All those people! We need to warn them! We…need to…" He slowed to a stop, clutching his chest.

"Daniel!" said Caitlin, running to his side.

"I'm okay, just out of breath." He panted. "I haven't worked this hard since my martial arts lessons ended a year ago."

There was a much closer rumbling of thunder, and they both looked into the distance. A faint orange glow had appeared up ahead, and there was another sound that had joined the others; the sound of screaming people. Instantly Daniel was back on his feet and taking off at full sprint towards the town, ignoring the burning in his chest.

"Daniel!" called out Caitlin again, sprinting after him.

They burst from the street and found Salt Plains in flames, the warship from earlier hovering over the town like a metallic demon. People were running back and forth, screams filling downtown. Above them, the sky was black with billowing clouds, and as Daniel and Caitlin took in the scene, it began to rain. Another huge clap of thunder shook the earth.

"The ship! Look at the ship!" said Daniel, pointing, as two beams of light were fired down from the hull, slamming into the street and sending people scattering for cover. "We need to get down there and find mom!"

"You want to go in there?" yelled Caitlin over the constant noise coming from in front of them. "It's a warzone!"

But Daniel was already running down the hill. Caitlin,

cursing silently, bolted after him, weaving between frightened tourists fleeing the scene as lasers and rain pelted down from above. A jagged lightning bolt slashed through the heavens, briefly illuminating the chaotic scene. She was fast drenched by the torrent pouring from above, and waves of terror filled her body as more lasers were fired from the bottom of the alien ship, nearly making her pass out. But she still ran, passing by buildings that were on fire and craters in the road, weaving between hordes of frightened locals, until they had made it through to the other side of downtown, away from the attacking ship.

Now that they were no longer out in the open, the two of them got a chance to better evaluate the other hazards at play. The winds were intense, lashing at their clothes like a hurricane, with rain pelting at them from above, causing them to shiver in their, as neither of them had jackets on them. Lightning illuminated the sky like the Fourth of July, briefly casting white light onto the flying metal demon at the other end of town, which was also bathed in the eerie orange glow from the fires.

"See?" said Daniel, although he still sounded terrified. "We made it. We just need to find my mom and we can get out of here safely."

Caitlin, though pale, nodded. "Okay. I trust your judgment."

They started up the road, only for them to reach a wall of people who were staring into the valley. "Move! Please!" said Daniel, trying to shove his way through. He and Caitlin pushed through the crowds, Caitlin latching onto Daniel's hands to prevent them from getting separated. People gasped and shouted at them as they pushed through, until they finally reached the other side and resumed running towards Ms. Phillips' pumpkin pie booth. They prayed that she was still there.

Thankfully, she still was, putting up a closed sign with the arrival of the impending storm. "Mom!" yelled Daniel, startling her as he came out of nowhere.

"Daniel?" she asked in surprise, staring at her son's heavy breathing. "What are you doing here?" She leaned outside her booth window. "And what's with all the ruckus coming from the valley? Why do I hear people screaming?"

"The town's being attacked," replied Daniel, in between gasps of air.

"He's right," added Caitlin, joining in. "The town's taking fire right now. Don't know how bad it is, but we need to move before we're in big trouble!"

"What? Who's attacking the town?"

"You wouldn't believe me if I told you!" said Daniel. "We need to get to the house."

"I just don't understand why anyone would be attacking the town," said Ms. Phillips, climbing out of her booth. "You sure you didn't hear something wrong?"

A huge explosion sounded off from the valley, a flash of orange peeking through some trees. Everyone turned and saw it, and Daniel put his hands on his hips.

"Need me to spell it out for you any longer?" he asked. He pushed Ms. Phillips forward. "Come on, Caitlin!"

They started to head towards the woods, where a back road would lead them around the perimeter of downtown and eventually take them to the road to Daniel's house. "So, what exactly is attacking the town?" asked Ms. Phillips, moving at a fast walk. "Just tell me."

"There's an alien warship that burst from the forest, crushed your sedan and is now attacking the town," said Caitlin. "And I wish that I was joking."

"Daniel, is she serious?"

"I wish she wasn't, mom. But yes, unless the Chinese have some new secret weapon, it's aliens."

They heard a faint explosion in the background, drowned out by a huge clap of thunder. "Storm's getting worse," noted Caitlin, staring up at the sky as they went.

She was right. The lightning and rain had become even more intense, so that now it felt like they were standing under a waterfall. Winds whipped at Caitlin's wet, long hair, nearing tropical storm speed. Her shoes were soaked through and she shivered. But the forest was close. Once they reached the back road they would be safe.

There was another peal of lightning that briefly lit up the sky, but the forest was less than a hundred feet away. Caitlin let out a huge held-in puff of air. "Oh, my gosh," she said as if a weight was being lifted off her chest, though she was still soaked. "We're safe. Thank God."

As if God himself was listening, there was a loud mechanical roar that drowned out the winds, causing all three of them to stop in their tracks. The forest came alive with sound as the same droning noise from earlier filled the air, joining the pitter-patter of the falling rain. "What on earth is that?" asked Ms. Phillips slowly, looking over at both Daniel and Caitlin. Both of them had nervous expressions on their faces.

"There's two…" they whispered at the same time.

The forest cracked and bent as the droning increased in volume. "Mom, you need to run in the other direction," said Daniel, backing away from the trees. "Right now."

The trees splintered apart, and a dull silver mass exploded from the woods. Streamlined, whirring, and smaller than the one before it, with the same paint scheme, *another* alien ship. "*There's two?*" Caitlin scarcely believed what she was seeing. "The lamest town on Earth, and it's worth the trouble to send *two* alien ships to invade it?"

They all started running in the opposite direction, back towards the orange glow coming down from the valley. "We can discuss what's fair when we're out of this!" yelled Daniel at her.

Behind them, they heard the second ship charge up its engines, and then a laser fired from the hull and hit the ground close to Ms. Phillips, causing her to jump and increase her speed. Caitlin screamed as streams of red light fell all around her, sometimes coming close enough for her to feel the heat. Daniel just kept running, clearly trying his best to ignore the hostile aliens that were on their tail.

They reached the mass of people watching the valley attack. "Everyone, move!" yelled Daniel as he barged through the crowd. "Move! Behind you!"

Everyone turned and saw the second ship bearing down on them, and mass panic overtook everyone as more lasers fired out, several of which found their mark. An old woman next to Caitlin was hit, and she immediately screamed and vanished into a cloud of dust. Another scream of terror escaped Caitlin's lips, until Daniel's hand seized hers and they both plowed through the crowd, which was now dispersing all into the surrounding region as people ran in terror for their lives. The three of them joined the horde running down towards the center of town, and they brushed off pine needles and dirt as the lasers hit the trees above them, sending branches raining down onto everyone. The rain was still as intense as ever.

They reached downtown and found everything on fire. In addition to people running about in terror, there were other figures wandering the burning streets, clad in black suits from head-to-toe and armed with various weapons of multiple types. Alien soldiers, they guessed from their misshapen helmets. One of them threw a small stone-sized object into a window, revealing itself as a grenade a few seconds later with a loud fireball that engulfed the second story of a residence. Amid the warzone unfolding in the street, Daniel saw an opening behind the McDonald's.

"There!" he said, pointing at a relatively empty stretch of street with no alien ships or soldiers. "That way!"

They took off down the street, but as they passed behind the McDonald's, a missile fired and slammed into the top of the restaurant. The arches creaked over as gravity threatened to topple them over. Daniel pushed Caitlin and Ms. Phillips out of the way, causing them to stumble and fall onto the sidewalk. He jumped after them, as far as he could, and he managed to evade the falling ornament, which crashed down behind him in a shower of sparks. Then the entire restaurant shuddered as more missiles slammed into the side. Peeking over through the windows, Caitlin had a clear view of the town center, where a mass of alien soldiers were advancing, shooting civilians that crossed their path. Several stragglers trailed behind the main group, carrying small devices which she guessed were explosives. That was confirmed after one of them threw one into a second-story office window and fire burst out moments later. Overhead, the ships were still circling, bombarding structures with artillery. Cars were burning, buildings were crumbling, and the rain somehow could not quench the flames.

Another huge missile slammed into the restaurant, sending a wave of heat washing over all three of them and knocking everyone backwards onto the street. Caitlin slowly sat up, winded and scraped up. The McDonald's burned in front of her, another giant torch in the middle of a town full of them. On the other side of town, the Marriott hotel fell down in a rush of dust and rubble, weakened by repeated explosions. Flames roared out of the structures, forming a fiery inferno that no amount of wind or rain could quench. Bit by bit, the aliens were destroying their town, and the people inside it. Even from where she was on the road, she could see a few dead bodies in the street, innocent people that had been victims of the assault and had been lucky enough to not get dusted. Lasers zipped across the street, as some soldiers shot at something that she couldn't see. For the first time that evening, she realized: Their town was gone. Everything was either a smoldering crater or a bonfire. The people were being massacred, and it was just chaos everywhere.

There was some good news: The storm had died down

somewhat, and, even better, Ms. Phillips and Daniel were stirring next to her. Ms. Phillips sat up, clutching her forehead, blinking her eyes. She cast one look at Daniel, Caitlin, and the devastation around them, and said, only half awake, "Is this hell? Have I died?"

"Not yet you haven't," said Daniel, sighing deeply.

"That was too close," said Caitlin. "Can we please get out of here before something else goes wrong?"

Ms. Phillips stood up groggily, then stumbled forward, clutching her leg. "Ow…" she groaned. She collapsed onto the ground, grimacing.

"Ms. Phillips!" cried Caitlin, who ran over to her and bent down to examine her leg. Blood was seeping through her pant leg from a long scratch left over from something. A large bolt that was attached to the McDonald's arches sat on the pavement next to her. "Daniel, get over here!"

He ran to her side. "Help me pick her up!" he said, putting her arm around his shoulder, Caitlin doing the same thing on the other side. They lifted her up, grunting with exertion, then continued to hobble away from the destruction. They passed the wreckage of the restaurant and emerged onto the main road leading towards Daniel's house. They only had to pass the gas station and convenience store and they would be safe in the woods.

Suddenly, all of them were blinded by a dazzling white light. Everyone raised their hand to block the glare. Caitlin blinked and squinted as she stared into the searchlight of what looked horrifyingly like the alien gunship. A surge of adrenaline shot through her, and now she saw some alien soldiers on the corner of the sidewalk across the street, pointing in their direction. She froze up.

Daniel, thankfully, did not. "Caitlin, go. Run!" When nobody else moved, he yelled, in a voice that seemed to echo through the valley, "RUUUUN!"

Caitlin snapped out of her trance and bolted along with Daniel as they supported Ms. Phillips between them, moving as fast as they could. Behind them, they heard a roar of engines as the gunship started to move in their general direction. In addition, they heard shouts from the alien soldiers and metallic footfalls as they pursued them. Caitlin didn't bother to look back and check on them, she could only keep running.

A laser whizzed by her side, causing her to gasp and increase her speed, Ms. Phillips nearly slipping from under her. A couple more shots were fired in their direction, but they all hit either road or building, leaving burn marks in the asphalt. The gunship was the bigger concern, however, as a missile fired out from it and exploded in the street about twenty feet in front of them. Caitlin felt the heat wave over her skin and evaporate the rainwater on her arms. Daniel faltered for just a second, before scrambling around the fiery mess that the shell had left in the street. They were almost to the edge of the forest, and to relative safety. There they could take shelter from the larger ships and hide from the enemy soldiers. It was a long shot, but right now, it was all that they had got. And the convenience store and gas station that sat at the very edge of the town was right in front of them. Once they had passed that, they'd be out of range of the gunship's weapons. They hoped.

Caitlin sprinted as fast as she could towards the trees. They were level with the gas pumps now, the pines only thirty feet away. They were so close. Ms. Phillips, suspended between her and Daniel, whispered under her breath, "Almost there, almost there…"

"We're gonna make it!" Daniel said, his breath shallow and sweat pouring down his face.

And that's when the missile fired.

What happened next was a blur to Caitlin. There was a blinding yellow light and a boom ten times louder than any thunder she had heard over the course of the evening. A tsunami of heat crashed over her, instantly drying her and singing the hair on her head. The blast violently threw her backwards from the force of it, and she felt her shoes slip from her feet as she went flying. She crashed through one of the store's glass windows and landed next to the cashier's deck, hitting her head on the floor and landing hard, spread-eagled.

There was pain everywhere, in her head, in her arms, in her chest. She had lost all feeling in most of her body from the impact, and her arm was twisted in such a way that she thought she had dislocated it. Her shoes were gone, probably outside, and there were several sizzling holes in her overalls. Her left side was bone-dry from the heat, while her right was still dripping wet from the rain. Her brain felt fuzzy, probably concussed.

She looked to her left, where Daniel had fallen. He had crashed through a different window, had landed hard on some of the shelves in the store, knocking them over and scattering their supplies all around his limp body. He was out cold, a small trickle of blood coming from the corner of his mouth. The sight made her sense her own blood leaking onto the floor, and when she tried to stand, she saw the droplets sprinkled onto the tiles below. There was no sign of Ms. Phillips.

Darkness closed in on her vision, and she lay there, hurting and on the verge of passing out, all she could think of was that her evening with Daniel was ruined, her house was probably destroyed, her town was rubble, and she was going to die.

There was motion outside the store window, looking like blurry shadows, and she heard a gruff voice say: "Snag the three of them and put them on the ship with the others! Kill anyone left behind!" Then a dark shadow appeared in the door, looking menacing in the firelight. One of the dark-suited aliens, this one with a green cloak around his shoulders. He noticed Daniel, picked him up with one arm, and threw him outside the store. Then he saw Caitlin, feebly moving in the corner. He advanced slowly, Caitlin too dazed to respond in fear.

"Relax," the figure said, his voice cold and grave. "No need to scream. Nobody's going to hear you from here." He reached behind him and pulled out what looked like a cattle prod, only jet black and double-pronged at the top. "Here. Let me jog your memory."

Intense pain shot through Caitlin's torso as the rod delivered an intense electric shock, but it was only for a second, as she slipped into the warm embrace of unconsciousness.

Chapter 4

Grimcor, Perseus Arm
Many light years from Earth

Five years later...

      The sounds of alarms ringing woke Daniel up. Or maybe it was the migraine he had. He couldn't tell. This was the fifth day in a row that he had had one. His head throbbed with waves of pain, blurring his vision with reflexive tears, and he felt nauseous in his stomach. He hoped he didn't throw up, like he had two days ago. As he heard the sounds of movement next to him, he refused to get up. He lay there, in his bed, hoping that, after a few seconds, the migraine would lessen somewhat. But, as the alarms kept ringing, he had to get up.

      He opened his eyes, staring up at the ragged tent ceiling that covered his head. He sat up, naked save for his undergarment, looking around at his room. Unfortunately, there was not much to say about it—there were holes in the fabric in multiple places, and there were rocks sticking up from below the tent floor. He had cleared as much as he could, but there were a few boulders that were wedged in the dirt tightly, and he could not get them out. He had positioned his bed in a way so that he missed most of the rocks, but there was always one that dug into his back at night. His clothes, the same old pants, T-shirt, and shoes that he had worn for the past five years, lay on the ground, what was left of them, anyway. His pants were more like shorts, having lost everything below the knee, and the fabric up top was filthy. His shirt was rags, with barely enough left of it to remain on his body, and his shoes were missing their laces and the soles were nearly worn through. His hand reached up, to where his ragged, unkept beard was growing from his chin, and where his hair was growing long off his head. He could not remember the last time he had had a trim.

Groaning from the headache, Daniel got dressed, and departed his tent, into a dark night illuminated only by the glare of dozens of searchlights, which lit up the rocky clearing he was in. Above him, stars—but not his stars. A totally different set of constellations lay overhead, with different objects and different patterns. Perhaps the biggest clue as to the alien nature of the heavens above were the two moons, one large and blue, the other small and brown, in the sky to the west. Neither was currently in view, blocked by the high rock wall behind him. In the distance, a faint glow signaled dawn not far ahead. And while under any circumstance he would have been thrilled to be standing on an alien planet, this was probably the one situation where he just could not bring himself to take any note of the occasion.

He approached a spot at the base of the searchlights, where hundreds of other figures were gathered. Many more were still streaming in from their tents. Most were aliens, but there were at least a dozen humans too. He took a spot next to a large, bug-eyed brick-colored alien that was missing two of his eight arms. He glanced at the crowd for any new faces. The only one he saw was a smaller, green one that had its pendulous nose completely removed, and was blind in one of its eyes. It looked completely helpless and terrified out of its skin, which Daniel could understand. He then noticed that a few of the others that were present yesterday were nowhere in sight. Daniel shuddered as he thought about what could've happened to them while they slept.

Surrounding the group were about thirty guards, all of them armed with rifles and electric batons. They were all in the same uniform, a black enforcer's tactical vest and tough pants that were trained to resist blows from others. A double-swords crest emblazoned both shoulders on each of them, one blade on fire, the other covered in scarlet stains, which Daniel took to be blood. All of them were aliens of the same species—brown-skinned, with eyes that had vertical pupils, a mouth with two pointed teeth like a vampire's, slits on their necks that he believed had used to be gills, and a chin that could feature anything from tiny bumps to full-fledged, squid-like tentacles, forming an aquatic form of a beard. On a catwalk above, several other guards cast menacing looks down at the group of huddled aliens. They wore green instead of black, indicating personal servants of a high-ranking official. And, in the middle of them all, was the big boss himself; Warden Dormak, looking very pleased with himself, his crisp, clean green cloak flowing around him.

Daniel had grown to hate Gorogs over the past few years. He had learned a great deal from his fellow prisoners during his stay on Grimcor, the planet they were on; the way they kept slaves, their warlike behavior, their death camps, and everything in between. Everything he had seen backed up their claims. He hated how cruel they were to their prisoners—he bore several faded scars and one fresh, just scabbed cut to show for it. He hated their smugness and value of themselves over everyone else, and he hated their agenda—the words, *"Purifying the population,"* said everything. And now it was time to start another day at Skorjion—which, to put it frank, if there was anything worse than hell, it was this place.

Skorjion, besides being a slave camp and a cemetery, was a mine. A large, ore-rich mine filled with deposits of iron, tungsten, and other metals. Originally owned by a small mining corporation, according to those who had been there the longest, it was seized by the Gorogs and converted into a concentration camp, and they began to send their prisoners there. Once there they were subject to cruel treatment and horrific living conditions, accompanied by back-breaking labor. It was an unmitigated hell, and to Daniel, it was quite possibly the worst place he had ever visited. Not even that one visit out to the mountains where his mom almost drowned could top this.

The warden took a megaphone from one of his escorts and bellowed out, "Everyone stand shoulder to shoulder and face me in a single file line!" he bellowed out, directing his men to punish anyone who disobeyed.

Daniel hastily followed his instructions. He did not want to start the day off on a bad note. The Gorogs took pleasure in harassing those who disobeyed roll call throughout the day. If you were judged to have defied the rules of roll call, it means a harsh beating then followed by additional punishment later in the day. Daniel, thankfully, was passed over at a glance from one of the guards. An alien farther down the row, however, was not so lucky. She was unable to find a way into the row of slaves, and the guards took notice. A nod from Dormak sealed the deal. They attacked, beating her with their electric batons, which, if they desired, could transform into whips that extended out from the stick, sometimes with barbs at the end. One of them did this, and their victim screamed with pain as they lashed across her back, leaving gashes that bled green alien blood. She collapsed, as the guards continued their onslaught. Daniel seethed with fury as, after a full minute of nonstop punishment, Dormak called them off. The guards put away their whips and moved back into position, leaving the alien on the ground, bleeding profusely from a series of several nasty-looking scratches on her back. Daniel knew that they had stopped whipping her just before they killed her. She would live, but she would pay the price for her minor infraction. He wanted to help, but the Gorogs, under the warden's direction, were ordered to shoot any slave who tried to help one of his fellow inmates. So, he stayed put, still furious for the injustice of it all, trying to not look.

"Now, does anyone else wish to join her groveling in the

dust?" challenged the warden, daring another one of his slaves to step out of line even just a hair. No one moved or said a word. Everyone was averting their eyes, shuffling their feet on the dusty soil.

"That's what I thought. Now, it's time for the daily roll call!" He pulled out a list of all of the slaves that he had registered and cleared his throat. "When I call your name, you will answer me with 'here,' and will receive instructions as to where you will be assigned for the day! If anyone has any objections—" He indicated the guard to his left, who was flicking his whip and hungrily staring at the slaves. "—feel free to raise them now."

When no one answered, Dormak began to list off the names, starting with, "VELLETIC!" His voice echoed throughout the area as the speakers amplified his voice, bouncing across the canyon walls.

"Here," grumbled a large, pale-skinned alien with long antennae sticking up from his head and small wings growing out of his back.

"IRON FACILITY!" A groan escaped the alien as those words. The iron facility was where the bulk of the mine's iron was processed and refined into bars that could be melted down and forged into steel or other useful tools. The work there was strenuous, with men having to cart the iron to the factory, load it onto the conveyor belt, work the extremely hot forge that both melted the metal and kept the inside of the building at inferno-like temperatures, and then shape the metal into bars. Burns were not uncommon—Daniel himself had received one the first year he had arrived. In addition, the combination of the hard work and heat of the facility led to frequent deaths. Thankfully Daniel had worked in there recently, so it seemed unlikely that he would be assigned there today.

Dormak cleared his throat as Velletic departed. "HEHEH!" he bellowed.

"Here." A smaller alien with webbed hands and two large front incisors answered.

"MINESHAFT D!" came the orders, and Daniel relaxed as the alien moved off towards the mine. The six mineshafts all catered to a different ore, D Mineshaft being where most rare-earth metals, like actinium and iridium, came from. The work there was not the worst, as most veins of ore were smaller and easier to mine. The mineshafts themselves were dug by another group.

The roll call continued with "ELITARO!", who was assigned to mineshaft digging, and "FOLKOF!", assigned to the tungsten refinery. After a few more names, "AMY!" was called.

The group of aliens to the left of Daniel started to shift around. Ms. Phillips stepped forward, saying, very weakly, "Here." She was a mess; she had lost a lot of weight, and was covered in both whip marks and scars from the labor she did, as her older age made mishaps more common. Thankfully, she got assigned to janitorial duty, where the slaves cleaned up the quarters of the warden, the guards, made them food, and kept it tidy. It was the least demanding job of them all, so Daniel was glad that she was going there.

Unfortunately, the same could not be said for both him and Caitlin. Daniel's name was called some time later, and he was put in Mineshaft B, the tungsten mine. There the metal was highly concentrated and put into large veins, and once you added in the metal's toughness to mine, it made for highly intensive work, which took its toll on Daniel's muscles, which had nearly doubled in size since he arrived in Skorjion. Caitlin was worse off, though; she was assigned to B Mineshaft as well, specifically to extend the shaft deeper underground. Daniel knew that she would be in for a rough time, staring at her. She was also a mess, like the rest of them. Her clothes were dirty and torn, she was covered in dust, her hair was everywhere, and there was a recently healed lash on her back where she was whipped. She also, unlike Daniel or his mom, had no shoes; they had blown completely off her feet at the gas station, and had been left behind. In an environment as rocky and demanding as Skorjion, that had meant trouble at the start. She had suffered from bloody feet for several weeks after arriving, but she had thankfully adapted to the harsh conditions, developing thick calluses that could resist the sharp rocks.

Once every prisoner had been accounted for, Dormak sounded the alarm signaling the start of the day's work. Every slave got a small bowl of gruel for breakfast before hitting the mines and factories to work. It was nothing more than a few spoonfuls, and it tasted like vomit, but it was either that or starve. So, Daniel, without complaint, took the gruel. At this point, he had gotten used to its horrible taste and composition, and just took it anyway. His friends had too, knowing it was better to eat horribly than to not eat at all. After breakfast, it was six hours of work until the midday meal, then another seven hours until the evening meal, then three more hours of work before bedtime. Then the next day, the cycle repeated; roll call, breakfast, morning shift, lunch, afternoon shift, dinner, nighttime shift, then bed.

As Daniel headed off to Mineshaft B, he once again examined his surroundings. The entire compound of Skorjion was set in a large canyon that was about a hundred feet from the base to the rim. Yellow-brown rocks lined the walls, along with dead alien plants that Daniel couldn't recognize dotting the wall here and there. In the daytime, it was always shady, except around lunch, when the sun was overhead.

Sun was the wrong term to use here. Rather than a yellow, fairly small star to orbit around, like Earth's sun, Grimcor's sun was a different star—a white giant. This brilliant monster was, so Daniel guessed, fifty times the Sun's size, three thousand times brighter, and much, much hotter. He had guessed that the distance from the star to here was about the same distance from the Sun to Jupiter, at least. But that was only because of his knowledge of how the stars behaved, like this one. And it was also emitting more radiation—if you were not under shade when it was visible above them, between the canyon walls, it would take only fifteen minutes for you to get sunburned, and only two hours to mutate enough cells to cause cancer. This happened two weeks after Daniel had arrived, when an alien was caught in the sun's beams for five hours straight with no protection. Within the week, he had developed so many tumors that he had died. After this, everyone had sought the shade a little more than before, and slaves would crowd each other under shady spots to escape the white giant's deadly rays.

Once at Mineshaft B, a gaping hole in the side of the canyon, Daniel and the other slaves assigned there picked up their supplies; a pickaxe, small canteen of water, lantern, and thin gloves that protected against absolutely nothing. Then they were herded down into the tunnel, which extended hundreds of feet belowground. Dirt walls lined the shaft on both sides, supported by steel beams that held the ceiling up. As they headed farther underground, the dirt gave way to rocks the color of graphite. The only light came from faint white lanterns that were built into the rock wall. The tunnel widened and narrowed as they moved; in some places, three abreast could walk the passage, and in others you could barely squeeze through in a single file line. The air became mustier and cooler the farther they went down. Finally, they reached the spot where metals began to peek through the walls, and where the majority of today's work would be conducted. About thirty feet farther down, the mineshaft ended, and those who would be extending the length of it, including Caitlin, continued down to the end, while Daniel and the other miners stayed at the metal veins. A guard bellowed at them to start working, and Daniel, taking the heavy pickaxe in hand, began to swing at a part of the rock with a large tungsten vein running through it.

The metal tip struck the rock wall with a loud *clang*. Some rock bits chipped off. He swung again. *Clang*. And again. *Clang*. With each succeeding strike more rocks were chipped off, and cracks appeared in the stone that encased the metal. Around him, the sounds of pickaxes striking rock and the grunts of other miners filled the shaft as the other aliens set about mining the tungsten. Farther down, the slaves digging out the mineshaft were doing the same thing. The clanging noise was pervasive, but Daniel had gotten used to it after five years. It was all he could hear at this point.

A few minutes later, a hovercart entered their area of the mine. These were basically minecarts that used propulsion instead of wheels and rails to transport goods. They would carry the tungsten metals to the refinery. It was a plus side to being a prisoner in an alien concentration camp, as they, unlike a wheeled minecart, were easy to push to the factories by comparison. They were small though, so many trips would normally have to be made before the day's end, which would tire you out quicker.

Soon after this, the section of rock that Daniel was chipping away at finally broke away from the wall, a large vein of raw tungsten embedded in it. Setting his pickaxe down briefly, he picked up the slab and dropped it into the cart. He wiped his brow. This was the process that he would be repeating all day, for roughly sixteen hours or so, with only one short break in the middle. He already was sweating hard, and his muscles were aching from the exertion. He knew that it would get even worse before the day was done.

The morning dragged on in a similar manner, as Daniel hacked away at the metals, loaded them into the cart, and repeated. Ahead of them, Caitlin's group dug the shaft farther down, exposing more valuable ore. But the hours of work were starting to take their toll on the group. Daniel's arms started to burn as he swung the pickaxe over and over again. He was relieved when the lunch alarm sounded, and they were herded out of the mineshaft back into the shade of the gorge. Even though it was hotter out there, the air was cleaner and eased Daniel's burning lungs. Lunch was a thirty-minute session before the second phase of work commenced. Usually it was a bowl of filth with bits of meat and vegetables in it, and, just like breakfast, it tasted absolutely horrible. Daniel, despite loathing it, ate it anyway. It was better than starvation for sure, and while it made him gag and his eyes water, it was still food. And on the rare cold days that occurred in Skorjion, it *did* warm his insides.

  Daniel looked off to the side. Caitlin was eating at a separate area meant for the miners who were carving out the shaft. She looked very pained right now and was rubbing her shoulders frequently. Dust caked her face, at least the parts visible behind her thick, rough curtain of hair, and she must've been whipped once, because there was some bruising on her arm. Only the officers carried electric whips with barbs; most of the time it was blunt whips that delivered electroshocks that were the weapon of choice, leaving bruising where it struck. Daniel noted that all of the aliens tasked for Mineshaft B had made it until lunch hour. He expected that that would change during this next session.

  After a half-hour of resting his sore muscles, it was back into the shaft for another seven hours of mining, sweating, and hurting. As he expected, they had barely gone twenty minutes into the second phase when one of the workers, a three-eyed alien with pointy ears, dropped onto the stone floor, clearly dehydrated. The guards shouted at him to keep working and beat him mercilessly, but he could not get up. Finally, one of the guards pulled a pistol out and shot the worker dead with a laser blast. The body was thrown into the cart, and a slave was assigned to push it up, to be sent to the crematorium. Daniel seethed as the lifeless figure disappeared up through the shaft. It just was not fair. The guards took special pleasure in shooting dead those who refused to work, whether by their own decision or not. It made Daniel so angry, watching as the guards killed the other slaves. And it made him even worse knowing that trying to help out the other slaves would accomplish nothing except getting both him and the other slaves killed. Unfortunately, the three-eyed worker would not be the last to fall that day. By the end of session two, two more workers, both from Caitlin's group, had been shot dead. The second had been the alien working right next to Caitlin, and she had gotten covered in blue alien blood when the guards shot him in the head and blew his brain out, giving her even more of a zombie-like appearance.

By the time the second session had ended, close to sunset that evening, Daniel's arms were on fire from soreness, and he was covered in dirt from head to toe. He had, however, managed to avoid being whipped. Brushing some stone bits off himself, he trudged back up the tunnel to have dinner, the third and final break in the day.

Dinner occurred late at night, around 7:00 p.m., or so he'd guess. It was his favorite meal of the three, mainly because, instead of a bowl of gruel, the slaves actually got fairly decent food, at least by prison camp standards. Instead of what looked like vomit with gallstones in it, each worker received a plate with a small portion of meat with some rice-like grain and vegetables. Daniel had no clue what kind of meat it was, but it was not like any meat he had tried on Earth. The vegetables were distinctly alien too, like broccoli, but without the florets, so it looked like miniature gnarly trees, and it tasted like pancake batter. It was actually pretty good, and Daniel happily devoured his every night. It seemed strange that the Gorog captors would serve such a hearty meal to their slaves. The rumor was, so the slaves told each other, that, given the work that they did around Skorjion every day, that if they didn't get the dinner they did, none of them would last a week in the mineshafts. He believed it. He barely made it through one day here every day, and that was with the large dinner he got. And he also, despite having it every night, kept on losing weight despite it.

After dinner came the final session, which was only two to three hours long. Usually, it involved washing and cleaning up the supplies used up in the day's mining and replacing the expendable supplies that they used in the day's work, stuff like explosives and such. Surprisingly, it could be just as hard to do as digging out tungsten in the mines. After all of that backbreaking work, Daniel's muscles would be aching like nothing else by the day's end. But instead of resting, they got to work to wash and clean up the supplies, and they would flare up with the slightest exertion. The agony was enough to reduce him to tears sometimes, which often encouraged the guards to whip him, as another thing they liked to do was pick on the weaker slaves. Such was the case tonight. While cleaning his pickaxe that he had used earlier, his shoulder muscle screamed with pain, causing him to gasp in pain and drop the wet cloth he had been using. Before he could bend over to pick it up, the whip came down. *Crack!* An electric shock flooded Daniel's nervous system, temporarily shorting out his senses.

"Keep working," growled the guard who had whipped him. He then stalked down the line of slaves, watching to see who would step out of line next. Daniel shot him a venomous glance, then checked the whip mark. A small, dark line marked the path of the whip. The danger came not from the whip itself, but from the side effects it caused. Once you were hit once, your muscles would become a little more sluggish, meaning it was harder to keep up with your pace. This, in turn, made you exponentially more likely to be whipped again, which further compounded the problem. After a certain number of whips, your body would shut down. Thankfully, there was only fifteen minutes left in the workday, and Daniel let out a gasp of relief when the alarm signaling the end of the day finally rang.

A second roll call followed. This one was much like the

first, except for two things. One, this was when new slaves were introduced to the horrors of the camp. Dormak would read off of a device resembling a large iPad the names of the new inductees into the canyon's endless misery. Two, and this really made Daniel furious, they would read off all of the slaves who had fallen that day. Usually, it was about twenty per day, but on bad days, Daniel had seen more than sixty names on the list. Sometimes, one of the dead slaves would be burned on the soil right in front of the other prisoners to cower them into doing their jobs. After everyone recited the Gorog anthem, not by choice, everyone was sent to bed.

The other slaves began to trudge back to their uncomfortable tents, hoping to find at least an hour's worth of rest before roll call the next morning. Daniel did not. He instead headed in the opposite direction from the sleeping area, towards one of the canyon's towering walls, keeping an eye out for guards, his muscles complaining the whole way. He stopped next to a large boulder that was almost perfectly spherical save for a large notch that almost looked man-made, hidden deep in shadow by the canyon wall. Taking his hands, he placed them into the notch, praying for one last bit of strength, and pushed. Despite another spasm of pain, the boulder rolled to the side, slowly, exposing the small crevice in the rock. It was barely two feet high, and just big enough to allow a man to crawl through on his hands and knees. Daniel, glancing around quickly to make sure that no one was watching, bent down and ducked headfirst into the dark hole.

The tunnel was narrow and would be a claustrophobic's worst nightmare. Daniel's head and legs were right up against the cold stone walls and ceiling as he crawled through pitch-darkness. He couldn't see his own hands, and he occasionally bumped his head as the tunnel ceiling rose and fell. The tunnel space narrowed and widened like ocean waves; in some places Daniel couldn't touch the walls to his left and right, sometimes he could barely fit through the space. But after twenty feet of squeezing and crawling through black, he reached the end of the tunnel and crawled into what lay at the other end.

It was about the size of Daniel's bedroom back on Earth, with a flat stone in the center, almost like a bench, and several cutouts in the rock wall directly opposite him like cupboards. It had a single hole in the ceiling that let in light from the surface above, which, at night, was the light of Grimcor's four moons, which made night as bright as early morning. The dim, bluish glow faintly illuminated the rock walls and the ancient remains of old artifacts that had been in the room when Caitlin had discovered it two months after they had arrived.

Massaging his sore hips and back, Daniel's hand eventually found its way to a lump that was protruding from his one remaining pocket that didn't have a massive hole in it. He reached into it and pulled out the lazurite stone that Caitlin had given him. It was the one item from home that had managed to make its way into Skorjion. He had been sure that the Gorogs would confiscate it, but, for some reason, they didn't. His finger felt along the engraved words, which were still easily visible etched into the smooth blue surface. Despite years of toil, he had ensured that the stone had not received a smidgen of damage, with not one chip or crack visible. The surface almost appeared to glow faintly in the light from the hole in the ceiling. As he stared at the words, his heart ached for his own bed.

Caitlin's head stuck through the tunnel right as Daniel put the stone back in his pocket and stood up. His head nearly touched the low, rocky ceiling as he did. Caitlin squeezed in all the way and stood up as well, groaning from the effort. She rubbed her shoulders tenderly. "Ow," she said, massaging the sore muscles. "What a day. Just when I thought I knew what really hard work was like."

Daniel sat down on the flat stone in the middle of the room. "You feeling okay?" he replied, stretching his spine.

Caitlin flicked a fragment of stone off her shoulder, then sat down next to him, grunting slightly. "We're living in a labor camp. I am most certainly not okay, and neither are you."

"Yeah. Is the tunnel still causing you problems? You keep banging your head it seems."

She shook her head. "Thankfully not this time. Let's hope it stays that way. Do you want to get the supplies?"

Daniel and Caitlin had no idea what the room's function had been before they had discovered it two months into their slavery. Caitlin had nearly died on that day, after being whipped five times and being subjected to brutal harassment by the guards and by the hostile terrain. Daniel hauntingly remembered seeing her walk out of the mineshaft, bruised, beaten, and bloody all over. Yet she had noticed the boulder, slightly ajar at the time, and had spotted the crack in the wall of the canyon. Daniel investigated, and that led to the finding of the hidden room. It had obviously been used before, as upon its rediscovery there were old artifacts that looked as though they could've been left there for hundreds of years. While they had no idea what a lot of it was, there was some useful stuff as well. Topping the list was a medical kit containing many valuable supplies like bandages, lotions, drugs and even a bottle of painkiller. In addition to that, there were bottles of water and food that looked like they could carry smallpox, some pieces of cloth, and, most peculiar of all, a partially constructed map of the Milky Way, housed on a mobile phone-like device with a screen. Only by chance had Daniel turned it on, which had in turn provided some information about the galaxy that they thought that they had known. Having realized that the galaxy was home to aliens, Daniel was keen to learn if the Gorogs were the only indigenous species out there. They couldn't be; they saw hundreds of other alien types working the mines. The map helped to answer some of their questions, but also left them with many others. There were lots of objects that Daniel could identify using his astronomy knowledge, but neither the Sun or Earth was on the map. In the event of an escape, they would need a way to find a way back home. If it was still standing. That was another question that Daniel had; had the people in Salt Plains that evening survived the attack? From what they had seen, Daniel and Caitlin were the only miners from their town working in the mine. Ms. Phillips, despite her age, was still too young to be assigned to permanent work in the guard quarters, where most of the older slaves went. There had been about a dozen of them taken from the town the night of the attack, but most of them had already died years ago. Had the Gorogs spared the ones left behind, or had they all been massacred? He had no idea. It was a haunting question that troubled him deeply.

Caitlin turned to face Daniel. "Do you want to go first, or do you want me?"

"I'll go," replied Daniel, laying down on the stone table in the middle.

Having no doctor and only a few supplies to take care of the injuries and ailments received from the life of a slave, Daniel, who had been trained in first aid, had taught Caitlin the basics of medical attention and examining a wounded patient. On days where one or the other had received serious wounds, they would crawl into the secret room and administer care to one another. It was only a temporary fix, and it wasn't the care that a real doctor could provide, but it was better than nothing. After a while, they also started daily check-ups to examine their bodies and identify problems before they started. Today, Daniel was going first. Caitlin began to ask him some questions, derived from Daniel's teachings on what to ask a patient, injured or uninjured. She pulled out a small notebook containing the list and began to read off what was written on it.

"Have you been experiencing any unusual pain today?" she asked him.

"Nothing out of the ordinary," replied Daniel, rubbing

his aching shoulders.

"Did you receive any new injuries today?"

"I was whipped once."

"What did you eat today?"

"Two bowls of gruel and some strange meat and vegetables of alien origin. So nothing foreign."

"Any vision or hearing problems lately?"

"Only when dehydrated."

The questions continued for five more minutes before Caitlin cleared Daniel off of the table and she took his place. She then answered the same questions that she had asked Daniel, while he examined her body. "Your whip mark looks a bit concerning," he said, noticing the purple bruising on her back. "Does it hurt?"

"It tingles a little, but that's it," she replied, moving her shoulder around. "Doesn't hurt too bad."

Daniel nodded. "Got it. That's the only thing of concern that I noticed. Everything else looks normal, or, at least as normal as a labor camp inmate would be physically speaking."

Caitlin hopped off of the stone surface. "Normal?" She made a face and glanced over Daniel and herself. "We're just a bunch of prisoners, on an alien planet, billions, probably trillions of miles from Earth, and we're stuck at the bottom of a canyon, with no way of getting out, and we're going to die at the hands of walking squids." She rolled her eyes. "And you say that we're normal."

Daniel smiled. He wanted to have a laugh, but he was still too nervous about their predicament to do so, and had been since they arrived. His anxiety had been astronomical ever since their arrival at Skorjion, and even now, it was difficult to not look worried. Thank goodness Caitlin and his mom had arrived with him, otherwise he would never have managed.

With no one feeling like carrying on conversation any longer, they crawled back out of the tunnel into the dark canyon, rolling the stone back into its position to hide the space. Above them, peeking out from between the canyon walls, were the stars. The constellations looked different, for sure; Daniel had no idea how far from Earth they really were. For all he knew, they could be as close as 500 light years, or as distant as 50,000. It would be an important factor if they attempted to escape.

    Yes, escape had crossed his mind many, many times now. When he had been dreaming of space exploration, enslavement in a labor camp did not fit into his vision, obviously. Unfortunately, Skorjion was extremely challenging to escape from, for several reasons. One: There was only one major way in and out of the canyon; an elevator that led up to the launch platform near the canyon rim. And it was guarded by six Gorog men at all times. Two: The star they orbited. Escape would have to be either early morning, late evening, or at night to prevent radiation poisoning, limiting their time of day to escape. Third, and most challenging, the blockade of warships that hovered overhead. The reason that they knew they were there was by way of the other inmates. Apparently, a few years back, before Daniel and Caitlin arrived, a large group of roughly twenty prisoners overpowered the guards and managed to steal a ship. Freedom seemed close for the group, until a blast from a warship shot them down, right into the middle of a large group of Gorog transports loaded with troops. Their bodies were hung for months afterward as an example to those who tried to escape the camp. The thought made chills run up and down Daniel's spine.

    Another thing that bothered him was the fact that he rarely got to see Ms. Phillips these days. The last time he had had a long conversation with her was weeks ago, as most of the time they were doing different jobs in the camp. Most exchanges were fleeting and passing, like the wind that blew through the canyon. He could only guess how she was doing, but it was a constant fear of his that he would discover one day that she had died away from him. He missed her deeply, and hoped that she was managing okay.

    Trying his best to put out the wildfire of his thoughts, he dragged himself through the dark canyon to the sleeping area, where the hundreds of tents that made the entire camp's sleeping arrangements were pitched. Caitlin said goodnight and hurried over to her dwelling, and Daniel crawled into his, exhausted, sore, and ready to endure another day of subjected torture and misery. He had lost track of how many there were. They all seemed to blend together so seamlessly. Pulling the raggedy covers over his body, he settled down on his bed of stones and sticks, prayed to live another day, then shut his eyes, wondering if the misery would ever end. And as the rocks dug into his back and prodded his sore muscles, he began to question if he would live to see freedom ever again.

Chapter 5

Throughout the night, Caitlin was tormented by nightmares. Tossing and turning in her sleep, she witnessed many terrible things; Daniel being devoured by giant Gorogs, herself up to her chest in the skulls of dead inmates, being chained over a pool of red-hot lava…

She awoke, sitting straight up in bed and yelling in fright, after she saw Ms. Phillips get crushed by a giant pickaxe. Shaking and sweating, she looked around. There were no monsters, no fire, no bones, no danger at all. All she saw was the ragged tent that she called home, and the rocky soil that she had been laying on. Her back was feeling sore from the whip, and she began to shiver as cold air swept through the holes in the awning. While daytime on the planet Grimcor was hot as any summer day, nighttime temperatures could drop into the low 40s, which, when the best thing you had for warmth was a fraying blanket, was certainly very cold. Falling back onto the ground, she tried to make herself comfortable and closed her eyes, hoping for a few more hours of sleep. Unfortunately, she could not bring herself back into the blissful ignorance of dreamland. Before long, the morning bell tolled, and Caitlin, tired and sore, gave up on sleeping and arose from bed. Crawling out of her tent, she stood up and felt the chilly early morning air on her skin, making her shiver in her torn clothes. She flexed her toes, hoping to keep her feet warm, and shook fiercely, as if she were a dog getting the water out of its fur, hoping to keep her body heat from departing. She started to walk to roll call at a fast rate in an attempt to jog herself out of drowsiness.

She was so focused on the cold that she bumped into Daniel at roll call, who was looking very sluggish indeed, complete with dark circles below his eyes. The look on his face as he glanced over Caitlin seemed to indicate the same thing about her. "Rough night of sleep?" he asked.

"Yep," Caitlin whispered in reply. "You?"

"Darn rocks kept poking me awake. Didn't stay asleep for more than ninety minutes at a pop." Then he yawned loudly, rubbing his eyes to keep them open.

Caitlin sighed in defeat. "Ready for yet another day?"

"As always," came the very sarcastic reply.

A few minutes later the roll call and assignments had been given. Caitlin watched as Daniel shuffled off to the ironworks, into what was sure to be an extremely hard day indeed. Ms. Phillips, who was positioned at the far end of the row, was off to the sorting areas in the coal mines. Caitlin, meanwhile, was put into janitorial duty, much to her relief, and once the last names had been called, she hurried towards the guardhouse.

Situated at the far end of the canyon, tucked into a small divot that had been carved into the wall, the guardhouse was a large, rather pleasant-looking structure that contrasted sharply with the crude tents that the slaves got, along with 90% of the rest of Skorjion's buildings. Silvery gray with black trim, three stories tall, with windows that were still emitting warm light in the predawn light, and a rooftop deck where soldiers gambled and ate their meals, it was a place she had longed to stay in multiple times in the past. She imagined how well soldiers slept in their warm beds, without having to worry about the night's freezing conditions or rocks that kept digging into your back. But she didn't dare enter unless she was doing cleanup, since slaves who crossed the property line were shot instantly. In fact, as she approached, she heard the unmistakable sound of a blaster rifle discharging, followed by a slave with at least a dozen whip marks on his torso being dragged out of the building limply, a sizzling hole burned into his scalp. It caused Caitlin's insides to burn with rage. If only she could escape, she would do everything in her power to destroy this place and ensure that every last slave was freed.

  After receiving her cold breakfast and swallowing it down, albeit with some difficulty, she received her washcloths and sponges that she would use to clean up with. One of her rags was still dirty from use the day before and smelled strongly of mildew, but she just inclined her head in the opposite direction and stayed silent. She and her fellow inmates, a group of eight, were led into the boundaries of the guardhouse by three Gorogs armed with blaster rifles and told their schedule for the day by a loud, curse-spewing Gorog officer. They would be cleaning up the guards' rooms during the morning shift, cleaning their armor, uniforms, and weapons in the afternoon shift, and would be wiping down all of the halls to remove stains in the evening. After receiving their instructions, they were sent into the maze of corridors to clean up the bedrooms.

  There were over two hundred rooms in the guardhouse, with a little over half being used by the guards currently stationed at Skorjion. And Caitlin was convinced that the Gorog men purposely left their rooms in total shambles, just to make more work for the janitorial crew. In the first room she encountered, the bed was totally wrecked, trash was everywhere, and everything was disorganized, including multiple books and papers scattered about everywhere. It took her twenty minutes to clean, tedious working to ensure that everything was in its place. One thing out of place could result in another beating with the electric whips, something she very much did not want to happen. To her relief though, after the last of the trash had gone into the can, the supervising guard gave it one glance and told her simply, "Next." Although it didn't sound nice, that was exactly what you wanted to hear from one of the guards. The other response would be the *krak* of the electric whip striking you, followed by, "Not good enough. Get back in there." Caitlin, nodding at the guard, moved on to the next room without a cleaner and began to work there. As she did, she winced as a guard whipped an elderly alien with red eyes and unusually long arms, the sound of the electric tendril crackling down the hallway. As the old creature stumbled, she hurriedly bent over, trying to be engrossed in her work.

After five rooms, she had managed to avoid getting whipped while cleaning, and she was getting into the routine of cleaning up the guards' rooms. Make the bed, get rid of any trash, put clothes where they went, organize shelves, clean any stains on the carpet. On average, it was about fifteen-twenty minutes to complete one room. But then she got to her sixth room, and she was greeted with numerous dirt and food stains on the carpet. She groaned. That would take a lot of time to clean out. About an hour, to be exact. Her shoulder, which had already started to ache before this, began to tense up, making the work even harder. By the time she was done with the carpet, the other slaves had moved onto the second floor.

When the bell for lunch rang, she was relieved to get out of the guardhouse and go eat. Her shoulder was killing her, as she had used it consistently, and her stomach was growling for some food. Leaving the quarters, she hurried off to the eating area, grabbed her lunch of gray stew, and sat down at one of the wooden tables. Setting her bowl down, she stretched out her arm, making the muscles in her sore shoulder groan with agony. A few reps of rotating her shoulder, and it was feeling slightly better, although it would no doubt hamper her cleaning during the last two shifts of the day.

Daniel showed up a few minutes later, looking like a survivor of hell itself. His hair was singed, there were nasty-looking burns on his right arm, and there was a long bruise on his back; he must've gotten whipped during the morning. He was moving slowly, hunched over, like a zombie, and he sat down hard at the table next to Caitlin, grunting in pain and nearly tipping his bowl clean over onto the ground, until Caitlin stopped it. They did not get second helpings, so they had to be careful to ensure that they did not lose the only lunch they had.

"Rough morning?" asked Caitlin, but there was no humor in her voice.

"That would be putting it mildly." Daniel sounded tired and pained. "They had the furnaces up at max strength. Really made it feel like working inside of an active volcano, actually. Not that I ever wanted to know what that felt like."

Caitlin sighed. "It sounds like it would be a fun idea until you actually do it." She stared out at the far canyon wall. "Then you realize how wrong your thinking was when you were young."

"You got that right." Daniel sounded far away. "I mean, at least we ate well in Salt Plains." He prodded his food with his fork. "What I would give for a steak right now."

Caitlin opened her mouth, a reply on her lips, then shut it when she saw something amid the throng of eating aliens. She squinted, looking over at a mysterious, metal gate over on the other canyon wall. Neither of them knew where the gate led. It was a restricted area of the compound; none of the slaves were allowed back there, only Gorogs. Nobody knew what was back there, but rumors constantly circled among the camp's residents, including a theory that the Gorogs were developing weapons for use outside of the camp. The gate was still shut, as it always was, but standing in front of it was something that they had never seen before. Not even after five years of imprisonment in an alien camp.

A long scaly back, with a row of dorsal spines sticking out from it.

An alien rose from his spot at another table and hurried off to someplace unknown, exposing the lizard's dragon-like face and teeth. Armor of reddish-gold scales glistened under the white sun's intense light, and his legs ended with digits that had boots around them, hiding the claws underneath. His tail had a small cap on its end, where it would taper to a barb, and he was wearing a collar around his neck. They guessed that it would shock him should he try to attack anyone. He was staring at Daniel and Caitlin with huge, bright yellow eyes, looking mysterious as he appeared to contemplate their presence.

Daniel noticed it too, although his drunken nature made his brain initially incomprehensible. "Is that...a lizard?"

"Yeah. A big one, too. I think it's watching us."

Daniel peered through the throng of aliens to get a better look. "Has it been around here before? I don't think I've seen it at any of the roll calls that I can remember."

"I don't recall seeing anyone like him, for sure. And it's a he, look." She pointed at his underside, between his back legs. Daniel took one look and immediately averted his eyes, groaning in displeasure.

"You really had to call attention to it?" he asked, annoyed. "Whatever, point made."

"What's everyone looking at?"

Ms. Phillips approached them from behind, looking sooty from working in the coal mine, her hair frizzled and covered in dirt. When Daniel and Caitlin both turned back to face the gate, the strange lizard had disappeared, melding into the mass of alien workers returning from a task.

"Nothing...mom. Just thought I saw something strange," lied Daniel. That lizard was probably new and checking out the inmates anyway. He moved over on the bench to allow Ms. Phillips to sit down. "I heard the coal mines were especially terrible today from some other workers. Was it?"

Ms. Phillips rubbed some of her soot. "It was very hot, for sure, being that close to the furnaces. At least I was just shuffling the coal around and not actually working the furnaces directly." She glanced over Daniel's body. "What happened to you? I heard Dormak send you to the ironworks at roll call."

"Trust me, I'd rather not talk about how hellish it is in

that factory. Like working *inside* a giant furnace."

They sat in silence for a little bit, slowly and difficulty eating their lukewarm sludge. Once Daniel had choked the last of his down, he sighed and cleared his throat.

"I want to escape here," he said, causing both Ms. Phillips and Caitlin to drop their utensils and stare at him.

"Escape?" asked Ms. Phillips.

"Yes, escape. It's something that's been on my mind for a while now, something that I've been trying to see was possible for over a year now. Caitlin and I have thrown the idea around a little, but I think that I've found a way out that could work."

"Well, say it then," said Ms. Phillips, as Caitlin looked back and forth between them. She had expected this to happen at some point, but she was still surprised to hear it from Daniel when he finally said it.

"Do you want everyone else to hear it, then? I don't want every slave here to hear our plan and try to escape themselves."

"Okay, fair, but why now?"

Daniel turned to look at Caitlin, who looked more curious than nervous. "Look around you," he said, in defiance of all of the Gorog guards standing at the perimeter of the lunch spot. "We're not doing anything in this canyon other than working for a group of aliens that are basically Nazis, while we slowly die to harsh labor and unending torture. Now I didn't necessarily love my old life, but it sure was a lot better than this. And I don't want my last moments to be spent in a hell like this. If I die here, I want it to be because I attempted to taste freedom one more time, and not because I resigned to my fate." He glanced around at them meaningfully, at the people he called his friends. His family. It gave Caitlin a fleeting moment of warmth as Daniel looked at her, in only the way a friend could. "That's why."

Caitlin stared at him. "Have you been rehearsing that for

a while or did you make that up off the top of your head?"

Daniel shrugged. "Bit of both, maybe." He paused, then added, "Mel Gibson helped a little."

It would have been a speech worthy of any patriot, except for the obvious question. "Is it possible?" asked Ms. Phillips.

Caitlin raised her hand, a little tensely. "Daniel," she said, trying to sound encouraging. "Not to rain on your words of hope or anything, but…she's right. How do you plan on escaping the facility that no one in memory has ever escaped? Just look around!" She indicated the forty guards ready to shoot any inmate who stepped out of line. "How do you plan to pass all of those?"

"By not taking the main exit," he said, much to the surprise of the other two. "I saw this today, while working in the factory." He leaned in closer to them to whisper. "There's a path leading out of the iron facility that goes directly to the surface. There's a ledge near the guardhouse that is fairly close to the canyon floor. That path was significantly less crowded with soldiers than the main elevator, from what I saw."

"Daniel, really, I am trying to see your point of view, but I just can't." Ms. Phillips' voice cut Daniel like a knife with how defeatist it sounded. "Even if there are fewer guards there than the elevator, that's not saying much. That's still a ton of guards to deal with. Not to mention we'd have to scale up the wall without being spotted, and then, where do we go from there? We'd still have to steal a ship and get past that blockade without being shot down. And we all know how that turned out. We'd never make it out alive."

Daniel turned to Caitlin, his face downcast. "Caitlin," he said, almost pleading with her, "I can't do this alone. I know it's risky, but we're facing certain death down here if we don't try and escape. Will you help me?"

Deep down, Caitlin knew that Daniel was right. Sooner or later, the medical supplies in the secret room would run out, and they would no longer get any aid to injuries they received while working. Skorjion, being designed to kill those not fit for intense labor, would, sooner or later, be the death of all three of them. She wanted nothing more than to escape the canyon walls, to be free. Yes, she'd still be several thousand light years from Earth, with no way of knowing how to get back, but she wouldn't have to live the life of a slave on top of that. She wanted to say yes, but…there was that smidgen of doubt. Skorjion was a maximum-security facility, built to keep people within its gates, and it was obviously working; no one had escaped in a very long time, if ever. If they tried to break out, odds were high that they would perish in the attempt. She couldn't decide between the two choices, so all that came out of her mouth was, "Daniel, I don't know."

Daniel's face fell sharply at those words, and Caitlin instantly regretted her words. "Fine," he said, shoving his plate of food aside. "I guess that we'll all die together then, trapped, hopeless, without another chance to live the lives we deserve. But, you know, this isn't too bad either." Knocking his water to the ground, he stood up violently and stormed off.

"Aren't you going to eat the rest of your food?" Ms. Phillips called after him.

"I'm not hungry," came the reply. And Daniel was soon lost in the crowd, leaving Ms. Phillips looking deeply worried, and Caitlin feeling terrible for her choice of words.

For the rest of the afternoon, Caitlin had difficulty concentrating on her work. Despite her best efforts, she could not help but think about Daniel's words, his ceaseless optimism with the prospects of escape, and his crestfallen face when everyone, including herself, said no to his idea. She was so lost in thought that she nearly ended up being whipped by a guard for accidentally knocking over a pile of books, leaving her to hastily pick them up before she got caught. Trying not to think about her friend, she concentrated on cleaning one of the guards' riot armor with a wet cloth. A single imperfection could land you without a meal, so she tried her very hardest to make the metal surface as shiny as silver. Once it was clean, she moved on to cleaning the same guard's formal uniform, ironing it down and removing any wrinkles or stains that were present. Having completed her fifth set, she moved on to the next available one in line. Her thoughts could not keep Daniel's face out of them though, and soon she was having a difficult time focusing on making her work stand out.

    Four hours later though, and the dinner bell rang, sending Caitlin on her way without a single mark on her back. Heading back to the eating place, she picked up her food and a cup of water, sat down on one of the benches, and waited for the others. Ms. Phillips showed up within minutes of her arrival, having spent the rest of her day at the tungsten refinery sorting the metal out into its various boxes for shipment. She was covered in grime from the furnaces in addition to the soot from the coal mine and was still dripping sweat from the intense heat you experienced inside. They both sat there, eating their meals in relative silence, and it was clear that they were thinking the exact same thing. But as they stared around at the slaves gathering their food, they saw the same lizard from earlier, watching them from a distance, both yellow eyes locked on them. Something about his gaze deeply unsettled Caitlin, and she shifted nervously on her seat, trying to concentrate on her food.

    "Why is that giant lizard staring right at us?" asked Ms. Phillips, finally seeing it for the first time.

    Caitlin shrugged. "I don't know. He was doing the same thing at lunch." She watched as the lizard started to walk away, out of view. "Something about him gives me the creeps though."

    "Do you think he could be a Gorog spy?"

    "A spy?"

"You know, to keep an eye on the slaves and report any suspicious activity to the Gorogs."

It was an interesting thought. "He could be," said Caitlin. "Or he could just be another slave." She shook her head. "We're probably overthinking this."

After a while, Daniel showed up, now limping slightly on his right leg. To Caitlin's utter dismay, he chose a seat by himself, at a bench away from the three of them. With his back turned to her and his mom, he began to eat in silence, but from what glances Caitlin caught of his face, he was looking very depressed. Finally, the decision that she couldn't decide on earlier became clear. She knew what the right choice would be.

"Ms. Phillips," she said to her companion, "What are we doing? Certainly nothing good! We've been doing nothing but slowly die in here for the last five years. Daniel's right. We should be trying to escape, instead of wasting away."

But Ms. Phillips shook her head. "I just don't see how it can be done with all of the security surrounding us."

"We would find a way to get around them without being seen. We wouldn't just march out there and climb up the wall."

Ms. Phillips turned to Caitlin. "Honey," she said, sounding tired, "I really do want to escape, don't get me wrong. It's just…Even if we were to get past security, I'm too old to scale up those walls. I'd never make it up the rock face, and even if I did, I'd just slow you down. If you want to escape, go for it. It's probably for the best if I stay here."

Caitlin shook her head vigorously, patting her shoulder. "No. Daniel would never let you say that. He would never permit you to stay. And neither would I."

"I've already lived a long, mostly happy life." Ms. Phillips sounded sad as she said it, looking up to the heavens. "This old body of mine has served me faithfully for many, many years. But perhaps it's time for my soul to go visit our Father and join the ranks of heaven."

"Have you?" asked Caitlin. "Didn't your husband die?"

Ms. Phillips stiffened up, her face hardening somewhat. Caitlin's stomach turned. She had no intention of striking a nerve. But before she could apologize, Ms. Phillips answered. "Yes," she said, her voice shaky. "And it hurts deep down, even after all these years. But it's in the past. I've moved on from my injuries, and they haven't affected my joy since then."

"You moved on from your loss, but can Daniel?" Caitlin refused to let Ms. Phillips accept this. She knew very well that her decision would crush Daniel. And as Daniel's best friend, it would crush her too. "With his anxiety, he would never forgive himself for your death. He's lost so much family over the years, and you're the last one—no, the *only* one he's got. You have to come with us."

Ms. Phillips looked doubtful. "Let's assume I decide to escape. How do you get these tired, old joints up that rock wall? I'm not exactly as fit as I was when I was your age."

Caitlin just smiled encouragingly and said, "We'll find a way. But I promise you, we will not leave you in this canyon. No one will get left behind. No one."

Ms. Phillips flashed a slight smile of encouragement, some joy reappearing on her face. "Thanks, Caitlin," she said finally. "The more I spend time with you the more I realize why Daniel loves spending so much time with you."

"Don't mention it," she replied. "Like I said, no one will get left behind."

They parted ways to go to their evening shifts, ignoring the lizard that was watching them from the canyon wall above them like a vulture.

Later that night, Caitlin finished up her shift. Exhausted, sore and tired from scrubbing all day, she was looking forward to finding refuge in the hidden room. She passed by a group of aliens chattering with each other and checked behind her to make sure there were no guards watching. She had not yet found an opportunity to tell Daniel about the decision she and Ms. Phillips had made, since he had not spoken to her since lunch. Hopefully she would get the chance in the room, since she knew that he would not dare skip over it.

Approaching the boulder that hid the tunnel, she was stunned to find it already ajar slightly. She approached it, watching for guards, and pushed it a little bit farther out of the way. Breaths of cool air came wafting out as the rock stopped moving, contrasting sharply with the dry, warm air of the canyon floor and cooling her skin down. Getting on her hands and knees, Caitlin bent over, ignoring the pain from that day's work, and started to crawl down the rocky passage towards the hidden room. The darkness encroached her from all sides as she descended into the abyss, her claustrophobia threatening to emerge. Thankfully, the shadow was soon lifted by the ray of light that was coming from up ahead, and she eagerly shimmied forward further, causing her to accidentally bump her head on the rocky ceiling in the process, which elicited an audible gasp of pain to escape her dry lips. Rubbing her skull gingerly, she suddenly heard voices from up ahead. Daniel and Ms. Phillips must have already arrived. She shimmied forward some more as the hole at the end of the tunnel widened.

Her head poked out of the hole into the room like a mole, looking around to see who was there. No Gorogs. Just Daniel and Ms. Phillips sitting on the stone table, looking totally unsurprised to see her. Daniel was even smiling.

"Step on a puppy in there?" he asked, clearly referring to her yelp of pain from bumping her head. His deadpan delivery surprised Caitlin greatly. It was a marked difference from the brooding figure Caitlin had seen at dinner.

"Daniel!" she said, feeling her skull for the injury, where

a small welt was already beginning to form. She clambered out of the hole and moved into a sitting position. Daniel's mood swing was something she had not been expecting. "You seem…cheerful."

"I feel cheerful. Ms. Phillips said you had something to tell me?"

Caitlin stiffened. She had not been expecting that. She glanced at Daniel's mom, who was just sitting there, next to Daniel. Upon seeing Caitlin's stare, she shrugged.

"He's trying to pull your leg, Ms. Wheeler," she told her. "I already told him what you said to me."

"Mom!" groaned Daniel in exasperation. "I was just going to tease her a little! It's nothing serious!"

"I'm your mother. I still get to tell you what to do."

"I'm almost twenty years old! If we hadn't wound up here, I'd be out of the house by now! I can make my own decisions!"

"True, but when I'm around, you'll do as I say." Ms. Phillips crossed her arms and gave Daniel a commanding stare.

"But, but…" And Caitlin burst out laughing at Daniel's incessant stuttering, the first time she had genuinely laughed in a very long time. It hurt her throat a little to use those muscles, but she didn't care. It felt good to feel this way after being in absolute misery for five years. She decided to join in the fun, while it still lasted.

"Twenty years old, you say, Daniel?" she asked, unable to hide her smile. "Not with that whining. Five seems far more appropriate for someone your age."

Now it was Ms. Phillips' turn to laugh out loud. Her loud wheezing echoed off of the stone chamber, forcing Daniel to clamp a hand over her mouth, looking nervous.

"What is this, a Saturday night party?" He sounded urgent but not harsh. "Don't forget, there are still guards out patrolling, and the last thing we need is for one of them to hear noise coming from the canyon walls! Try to keep the noise down, okay?"

Ms. Phillips nodded, and Daniel removed his hand. She coughed. "It tastes like dirt."

"Because I was playing in the mud all day." Daniel sighed, then turned to Caitlin. "You really decided that you want to escape Skorjion?"

Caitlin nodded without needing to think. "No question. I do."

Daniel stood up and approached her. "It'll be extremely dangerous."

"That's a given."

"We may not survive."

Caitlin simply smiled, despite the tinge of doubt in her stomach, and said, "Better to die reaching for freedom than living hopeless in bondage…or something like that? That *is* what you said, right?"

Daniel grinned. "Close enough." He indicated for them all to come closer and laid the groundwork for his escape plan. "So, if we're going to break out, there's a few things we need to do prior to the escape. We need to have our water bottles on hand. Assume no one comes to rescue us, or we're unable to reach the hangar to steal a ship. We'll need water to survive. I would also bring food, except that would be too much to carry if we're gonna attempt to scale that rock wall. Second, we'll need to get our bearings. We don't know where north or south is, so we'll ask around, see if any of the other slaves know."

"Okay, so we need water and a sense of direction." Caitlin ran over these things in her mind. "Then what?"

"We'll make our escape during dinnertime. That way, the white giant's radiation will be less than at most other times of the day, plus, most of the guards are summoned to the eating area to watch the slaves, leaving other areas of the camp less heavily guarded. We'll slip out and make a break for it from

108

there."

"Problem is, how will we make it look convincing, like we're not trying to escape?" asked Ms. Phillips. We don't want to arouse suspicion from any of the guards."

Daniel told them, and they all laughed out loud when he was done. "That's how you want to fool the guards?" said Caitlin in disbelief, chuckling at the thought of what he was proposing. "That's the dumbest, yet most sensible thing I've ever heard of."

Ms. Phillips was shaking her head. "Normally I would've said no way, but I think considering the circumstances, it would be better for everyone if I went along."

"Glad you see the sense in it," replied Daniel. "Okay, so once that's done, we'll scale the rock wall, reach the path, and hurry up the slope out of the gorge before any of the guards become the wiser. It's risky, as I said, but I feel like this is our best option for escape."

Everyone nodded their heads in agreement. With a high-security place like Skorjion, it seemed like the best way to pull something like this off. "When would we be doing this?" asked Ms. Phillips.

"Tomorrow at dinner."

Caitlin was taken aback at this, and she could tell that Ms. Phillips was too. Neither of them had expected to be leaving the camp at all, much less by tomorrow. But as Caitlin thought about it, the more it made sense. The longer they stayed, the more energy they would drain, and the harder the potential escape would be. She nodded slowly as she saw the wisdom in Daniel's words.

"Very well then," she said. "Tomorrow."

Ms. Phillips hesitated, then slowly dipped her head similarly. "Tomorrow."

The three companions, friends and family members stood up, put their arms around one's shoulders, and prayed. "Father," said Ms. Phillips, her head bowed. "We don't know what tomorrow will bring. But we know that whatever happens, you will provide. You have led us this far and have allowed us to keep our limbs intact. We ask, with all our hearts, that you continue to provide and watch over us. And no matter what comes, in life or death, we will trust your will. We ask it, we pray it."

"Amen," they all said together.

And they departed the room, Caitlin going in last and setting the boulder back in place, prepared that, when tomorrow did come, she would either escape hell, or join heaven's ranks. Suddenly a thought crossed her mind. "Daniel!" she whispered to him. "How are we going to get Ms. Phillips up the rock wall?"

He turned to her and smiled. "Leave that to me."

Chapter 6

Morning came with the roll call's bell tolling yet again. Daniel emerged from his tent, spotted Caitlin climbing from hers, yawning loudly and stretching. He stood up, adjusted his hair, and approached her.

"Today's the big day," he said, stretching his arm out, cracking some joints in his back.

Caitlin nodded. "I'd be lying if I said I wasn't nervous," she confessed, chuckling nervously. "This is the most dangerous thing I've done."

"The most dangerous thing we've all done, frankly," pointed out Daniel. "Better than staying here, though."

"I know, I know…it's just…we may not make it."

"Of course, we may not make it! That's part of the risk involved!"

"No, I meant *some* of us may not make it. What happens should one of us die or fail to make it out?" She suddenly sounded worried, looking at Daniel with eyes that were swimming with hints of anxiety. It gave him chills, as it was exactly how he looked before he had a panic attack.

"Caitlin, I…" He didn't know how to respond. To be honest, he *hadn't* thought of that. He had always assumed that they would all make it out together, or else all die together. But losing one while the others escaped…that jarred him from his confidence. The thought of Caitlin getting killed while the rest of them made it out alive nearly sent a tear down his face. It was terrible to the point where it nearly made him reconsider, but he shoved the thought aside before it could stay in his head permanently. "I don't know what will happen. But I swear to you, I will try my hardest to ensure that all of us get out. I swear, we will all make it out alive, or we won't make it out at all. You have nothing to be worried about."

She sniffled a bit, then threw her arms around him in a quick hug. "Please be right about this," she managed to say steadily. She then pulled from him and hurried over to the roll call, leaving Daniel alone and questioning his decision to escape this early.

Roll call went without issue, with them pledging as they departed to avoid getting whipped at all costs. Caitlin and Ms. Phillips were both doing janitorial duty again, while Daniel was off to mine out iron in the mines. Hoping that this wouldn't impact his attempts to climb up the rock later, he grabbed his breakfast and pickaxe and descended into the shaft.

It was especially brutal today, the pickaxe seeming to swing slower and weigh more today, but six hours later, he emerged, sweating profusely and aching all over his upper back, his hair covered in dirt and dust, his rags of a shirt just about ready to fall off his body, and one of his shoes missing, as the sole had finally given in during the intense digging, and he had ditched the shoe, leaving his left foot bare. That being said, he had avoided the whip, meaning that his muscles were temporarily tired, but not completely drained. Hungry, he hustled over to lunch, intent on consuming as much as possible. He would need a lot of extra fat to keep him satisfied out in Grimcor's harsh environment.

He found Caitlin and Ms. Phillips at a table by themselves, already eating their food. Ms. Phillips looked especially pleased with herself, and Daniel could only assume that she had found something out that was important.

"So, I found out where north is," she told Daniel as he sat down. "The canyon runs along an approximate north-south line, with the elevator shaft leading up to the surface on the north end. So, once we exit, we can get our bearings from there."

"Well done, Mom!" said Daniel proudly, and Ms. Phillips beamed. "Now, is everyone prepared to do their part of the plan?"

They all nodded.

"And does anyone need to run over the plan again?"

They both shook their heads. "We've gone over it like five times!" said Caitlin. "We don't need to go over it again!"

Daniel nodded, but then he saw something else. The lizard from before, standing just a couple of rows over, watching them just like yesterday, wearing no emotion on its face. "Guys," he said, pointing at the scaly figure.

"What is his deal?" asked Caitlin. "I've only seen him at meal times, and he's always watching us like we're impostors or something. I don't understand why we're so fascinating to him. We're not the only humans out here."

Daniel sighed aloud. "I don't know. Whatever he thinks of us, it won't matter once we've escaped." He turned back to the others. "Anyways, we need a contingency plan in case the main one fails. I came up with this earlier today. Assuming that we're still below the canyon walls when the Gorogs figure out that we're escaping, we try to get out as quickly as possible before they can stop us. I also, um, came up with a solution for getting past the blockade."

"Oh, really?" asked Ms. Phillips, leaning forward.

"My information here is a little sketchy, since I've been forced to ask other inmates for details, but the one we want is an attack gunship. They're supposed to be highly resistant to laser blasts and come with special clearances designed to pass blockades. And they're fast, in case we need a hasty exit."

"Do you know what they look like?" asked Caitlin, setting her empty plate of food down.

That question silenced everyone in an instant. Daniel thought for a second, but he eventually shrugged. "I have no clue, other than that they're a larger ship. We'll just have to pick the right ship when we get up to the hangar and hope for the best."

"And how do you plan on getting me up the rock face?" asked Ms. Phillips.

Daniel turned to her. "I think you can make it fine without any help. The rock face isn't vertical and there are tons of hand- and footholds available, from when I checked."

"As long as I won't ruin myself climbing it, fine. When do we escape?"

Daniel smiled. "This evening. Be ready."

Dinnertime came, and Daniel and the gang met up after their work. Daniel was a bit sore, but nothing he couldn't power through while ascending the canyon wall. Caitlin and Ms. Phillips were looking healthy and fit, with no telltale bruises on them from the whips. As the bell to collect food came, the group prayed silently as they gathered up their plates, sat down and gulped down what they hoped would be their last meal in Skorjion's hell. They ate quickly, and in silence, not wanting to waste any more time that they had. Despite the time crunch, Daniel had some difficulty eating his food. On the one hand, he was excited at the prospects of escape, but on the other hand were the battle that would have to be fought to reach that goal, plus the never-ending anxiety clinging at his chest, the anxiety that worried that some of them, or all of them, wouldn't make it out alive. That had become his biggest fear. And he was determined that it would not come true. Scarfing down the last of his meat, he left his plate on the table, and amid the fears of everyone, found the courage to speak.

"Everyone, it's time."

Caitlin, Ms. Phillips, and Max all stopped chewing their food, set down their utensils, if they were using them, and leaned in to listen to Daniel.

"Mom…you're up."

Ms. Phillips obeyed, standing up from her table, clearing

her throat, and started to fake a cough. She pretended to gag and hack, almost like she was choking on something, which had been Daniel's intention, in part. She bent over, clawing at the table in an acting performance that could've been better, and toppled onto the ground, clutching her stomach in pretend agony. It was the first part of Daniel's plan; to use Ms. Phillips's pretend choking to access the infirmary corner of the canyon and proceed from there. It all relied on Ms. Phillips' ability to properly fake choking. So far, she was doing amazingly well.

"Mom!" Daniel yelled out, pretending to sound worried, bending down to find her unresponsive. Inside, he felt proud. She had nailed the trick of sounding like something was blocking her windpipe, save for the clutching of the stomach. He turned to the others, who were trying their hardest to look horrified.

Or maybe it was genuine, since when Daniel turned back to face Ms. Phillips, she was staring at him with wide eyes, having dropped the act. "There's a rock that's digging into my ribs," she admitted, grunting in what was now real pain. "I can't lay here."

Daniel groaned in exasperation and helped his mom up. "That won't work," he told them. "It's fine. I'll do it myself." He stood up to his full height and pretended to cough, just like Ms. Phillips had done. Gagging and hacking, trying his hardest to make it sound real, he grabbed at his throat and stopped the coughing, before falling down and lying there, limp.

Caitlin stooped over him, her face coming close to his. "What are you doing?"

"Pick me up like you were going to with Ms. Phillips," he hissed angrily as loud as he dared. "And carry me to the infirmary!"

"Oh…right!" Caitlin turned to Ms. Phillips, who was already starting to bend down, not bothering with the dialogue that Daniel had come up with for the act. Ms. Phillips grabbed Daniel's arms, while Caitlin took hold of his ankles, and together, they hoisted him up, suspended between them like the cables of a bridge. Together, they started to walk, taking care not to bump him into any tables or other aliens.

"Excuse us, coming through," they apologized, as they forced their way between a large group of alien inmates, all sitting in a row. No one paid them much attention, nor to Max, who was following at a close distance, trying to look normal. Unfortunately for Daniel, he was bumped several times with all of the swinging, once with his ribs hitting the edge of a wooden bench, causing him to have to bite his lips to prevent from yelling out loud in pain. But they managed to make it almost all the way through without too many hitches.

Almost all the way through. Because when they were right at the edge of the seating area's boundaries, Daniel swung out a little too far and bumped hard into the backside of a massive alien with green skin and horns growing from his head, causing him to drop the glass of water he was holding all over himself. The three of them froze, as the huge figure rose from his seat at the bench, his chest dripping water, and turned around to look directly at them, a mask of anger draped over his face.

"You've got a problem, buddy?" he asked menacingly, towering over them and causing everyone to shrink away a little.

"No, no problem!" Daniel said hastily, dropping out of the arms of his carriers and scrambling to his feet. "Sorry, I didn't mean to bump into you."

"Well, you bumping into me just cost me the only water I get until tomorrow morning." The alien's muscles rippled hard across his chest as he spoke, and Daniel had no doubt that he was incredibly strong. "Perhaps I should cost you something in return."

"Perhaps you shouldn't!" said Caitlin, speaking on behalf of Daniel.

But the alien grabbed the empty tray of food from behind him and threw it at Daniel's head like a frisbee. He gasped and ducked, the tray spinning over his head across the dinner area until it thudded into someone with a loud clang. Everyone immediately fell deathly silent upon that sound, and Daniel felt his stomach twist.

After a few moments, the crowd started parting to make room for what they all could only presume was the one they had hit. And when the last row of inmates parted ways to reveal the same giant lizard from earlier, Daniel felt terror clutch his chest. Not only was it enormous, bigger than any dog he had ever seen, but he was walking on two legs, the thrown tray clutched between a set of enormous claws that resembled steak knives. Those piercing yellow eyes were narrowed to a pair of slits.

"Did someone lose this?" he demanded, raising the tray into the air for all to see. His voice was deep and scaly, like the rest of his body, and it commanded the space immediately.

"Give that back," growled the horned alien. "That's mine."

The lizard contemplated the tray in his hand. "Seems to me as though you didn't want it," he said, showing no fear in his voice. "It's a nice tray. I think I'll keep it."

"Slug!" The yell of the big alien echoed through the canyon. "You'll give it to me, alive or dead!"

The lizard's head whipped back around to stare at the big green guy. "First of all, my name is Maximiliez," he growled. "Secondly, I don't listen to maggot-ridden filth like you. So if I were you I'd shut up and stay out of my way. Or else."

The lizard turned away, but the big alien charged at him, seized him by the tail, fist raised to swing at him. The reptile dodged it easily, and turned around to bite down hard on the alien's forearm. He yelled as dozens of sharp teeth pierced his flesh and into his muscles. He shook his arm, but the lizard was clamped down like a vice.

His arm was released, and the alien found his assailant

on his back, ripping into his skin with his claws with unbelievable savagery. Blood sprayed out and bits of skin went flying as the lizard dug in like a dog digging in the soil. Finally, the alien collapsed onto the ground, dead, a pool of blood forming around his body from at least a dozen deep wounds in his back.

The scene went into a full-on uproar, as at least a dozen other slaves, clearly friends of the dead one, yelled out loud and rushed the lizard, who immediately turned his sharp claws to them. Other slaves joined in the chaos, and soon the entire eating area was full of brawling and infighting. Caitlin hurried over to Daniel, trying her best to avoid the hailstorm of punches that were flying around her.

"Is this part of the plan?" she yelled at him fearfully.

"It is now!" he shouted back, dropping to his knees as two inmates went tussling onto the table next to him.

The guards surrounding the area shouted out loud and rushed into the fray, rifles drawn. The angry mob turned and began to take out their anger on them, ripping rifles away from the guards and shooting them dead. In doing so, the path to the escape route was suddenly opened up. "Daniel, the path!" called out Ms. Phillips above the cacophony.

Daniel saw it, and immediately bolted for it, dodging fighting inmates and guards shooting their rifles to kill. He broke free of the fighting and took off full sprint towards the ironworks as alarms began to sound through the canyon. He glanced behind him to see Ms. Phillips and Caitlin huffing and puffing after him, the riot going on behind them. They hastily ducked behind some rocks as a stream of armored Gorogs streamed out of the guardhouse away from them. But just when they thought the coast was clear, as Daniel stood up to resume running, a straggler came out and spotted them.

Caitlin ran up behind him and gasped when she saw the one guard. The guard was clearly stunned as he froze upon seeing them. But Daniel, before he could even think, rushed the Gorog, yelling maniacally as he did. Everyone's heart stopped as he lunged at him, planting his foot in the guard's chest and kicking him down. His riot stick fell out of its holder, and Daniel grabbed it and proceeded to beat him down while he was still on the ground. He struck hard, shattering the visor of the guard's helmet, allowing him to go for the soft flesh of his face, all while Ms. Phillips and Caitlin watched in horror. Another blow later and the guard lay still, Daniel discarding the stick, which had a blue spot on it from the guard's broken face.

Caitlin and Ms. Phillips stared. Daniel saw them gawking and he gestured towards the rock wall. "Come on, let's go!" he said, picking up the guard's rifle running off towards the wall.

Caitlin turned to her companion. "Did he just..."

"Yeah. He did." Ms. Phillips watched as Daniel waved them on, feeling nervous as she ran and caught up with him.

They stared up the rock wall before them. It was only about 25-30 feet high, and riddled with handholds, so it should've been an easy ascent. The problem was Ms. Phillips, who was not used to climbing such rock walls at her age. Daniel's hope was that she would be able to climb regardless. Everything here depended on time, and how little of it they used. Checking once again to make sure that no other guards were nearby, Daniel grabbed the nearest handhold, placed his foot on a rock jutting from the wall, and began to climb.

He had only been rock climbing like this before once; *once*. He had barely made it up six feet before slipping and falling to the ground. That time he had a mat below him and a safety harness on. This time, he had neither of those. Despite the higher stakes, he managed to begin climbing at a fast speed, ascending the face quickly. He glanced down. Caitlin was just beneath him on the left, with Ms. Phillips moving a bit slower as expected. Despite the alarms blaring throughout the camp, they only heard guards shouting behind them from the prison riot. *Let's hope it stays that way*, thought Daniel as he reached up for another handhold. As he had expected, his muscles were not pleased with working more, and ached hard as he climbed, but he shrugged it off and continued to climb, ignoring Caitlin's words from that morning and concentrating on climbing to the top.

About ten feet up the wall, Daniel's foot slipped as he tried to place it on a smooth rock that jutted out from the wall, kicking up some dust as he did. Left dangling by just one hand, he resisted the pull of gravity and fought against the urge to let go, feeling around with his toes for another rock, finding one, and regaining his traction. Then he glanced down, watching as the small dust cloud slowly blew over towards Ms. Phillips, who was slowly making progress up the granite face. As Ms. Phillips reached up to grab another handhold, she inhaled deeply through her nose, taking with it an entire pound of dust.

Daniel stiffened. He waited for the inevitable sneeze. It was all but guaranteed with that kind of dust. Sure enough, Ms. Phillips's eyes screwed up, she opened her mouth, and she started to intake like she was going to blow. Her nose started to turn slightly red, and her mouth opened wide. She stopped inhaling, and Daniel braced for the inevitable explosion. But it did not come. For several agonizing seconds, there was no sound. Daniel, hearing nothing, slowly relaxed. Maybe it was not meant to be. He glanced down and next to him, at Caitlin. "Well, we certainly dodged that one." he said, relief filling him up.

Before he could celebrate, though, a laser blast slammed into the rock wall beside him, making him jump in terror. He glanced to the side, where a small group of Gorogs were charging in their direction, yelling and pointing at them, their rifles raised into the sky. Daniel's heart sank, as another laser was fired their way, coming dangerously close to Caitlin's head.

"Move! Faster!" Daniel bellowed down at his

companions, who all gladly obeyed and started moving up the wall as fast as humanly possible. Stealth was no longer needed. Speed was now most definitely needed more than anything. Reaching up, finding hand- and footholds with incredible speed, and shimmying his way farther up the wall, he soon found himself near the top of the wall, almost at the pathway out.

    He caught a glimpse from the corner of his eye of more guards streaming out of the riot zone, moving like the devil as they ran at the wall. With the ravine growing darker as evening rushed towards them, the beams of searchlights began to appear throughout the camp space. Alarmed, Daniel scampered up the rest of the wall like a monkey, finding the top of the rock face and hoisting himself up. He rolled onto the pathway, then ducked as more lasers whistled by. He then crawled to the edge, peering down to where Caitlin was climbing higher up the wall, about eight feet down. Farther below, Ms. Phillips struggled to push her way up, looking flustered as she tried to climb higher. Behind them, tons of Gorog soldiers, all filtering into their area of the canyon, taking up positions behind rocks near the shelter of the infirmary.

    Then Ms. Phillips started to lose her footing. She slipped and slid but still managed to stay attached to the rock by her two hands until finally she found purchase on a small ledge and stopped herself from falling. She hastily resumed climbing as the armada of soldiers continued to fire, sending bits of rock tumbling from the wall. Caitlin climbed the wall like a spider, trying to avoid being shot at, gasping as several bolts impacted the wall right next to her face. Daniel hastily ducked for cover, realizing that their cover had officially been blown. As streaks of light flew over his head, he also realized that the others were sitting ducks while they were climbing the wall. All it would take was a shot in the arm or leg to send them crashing to the canyon floor, into the waiting masses of angry guards. On the wall, the Gorogs would eventually find their mark and put a hole

121

in their head or chest, or scare them off the wall entirely. He couldn't let that happen. He removed the rifle he had taken from the guard earlier from his back, doing the fastest examination of an alien weapon he had ever done. He was disturbed by the lack of a safety feature, but otherwise, he could tell where everything was and how everything worked. Praying there was ammo in its magazine, he grabbed the weapon, preparing to fire.

Sticking the barrel over the edge of the cliff, and around the rock, he found the trigger and let loose a barrage of rounds. He felt the recoil as the rounds discharged in a hail of red streaks. The guards saw the beams flying their way and immediately ducked for cover, buying Caitlin enough time to get a hand on the rim of the pathway. She hoisted herself up, looking shaken, then noticed Daniel, firing the rifle he had stolen.

"Since when did you learn how to shoot a blaster rifle?" she exclaimed, panting.

"About ten seconds ago," he replied, sighting down the barrel and firing at one of the guards' hiding spots. "Now get behind me!"

With a spree of blasts missing her as one of the guards stuck out from the rock he was crouched behind and firing up at the wall, she gladly obeyed. As she ducked into a small crevice in the wall behind them, Daniel continued to deter the guards from shooting at his mother. Once they reached the top, their situation would become far less dangerous. He fired again, causing a guard to hastily duck under his cover as he stuck his head out. He aimed again, only for an explosion off in the distance to jar his concentration and cause him to miss.

Down on the wall, Ms. Phillips was approaching the top, despite shots now falling all around her. Above, she could see the red blasts coming from Daniel's stolen rifle, buying her time, but she knew that it would not last forever. She was only five feet from the top, the ledge almost in reach, but when she tried to grab it, she nearly slipped again, only stopping herself in the nick of time.

"Hurry up, mom! Please!" Daniel sounded genuinely terrified as he fired off another volley of lasers. "There's more coming!"

As they had feared, reinforcements were coming around the bend. At least a dozen additional Gorogs were pouring into their end of the canyon. As they went, they shot two slaves that had broken out of the main pack and had tried to make a break for it. Daniel watched as they killed them and funneled into the iron facility, knowing they would emerge out the gate on his right. They really needed to begin making their way out.

"Ms. Phillips!" called out Caitlin. "Please hurry! You're almost there!"

"It's harder when they're shooting at you!" she retorted, as she hoisted herself up one hand at a time. Her fingers felt like they were about to snap off, and her leg muscles felt like they were about to tear in half. But she continued to fight through the pain, until she had pulled herself all the way onto the ledge, out of view of the guards down below.

Down on the canyon floor, the guards, realizing that there was only one person shooting at them, began to return fire. Lasers began to whiz by him and Caitlin, who was still crouched behind him, trying to make herself as small as possible. Daniel returned fire, which resulted in a bunch of missed shots, save for one that hit a guard on his unprotected arm. He hastily clutched the injury and ducked out of sight, as others popped up to shoot back. One hit the rock right above Daniel, sending a cascade of dust onto his head. Another missed taking his ear out by about two inches, close enough for him to feel the heat from the laser. Despite constant fire, he refused to hide for more than a few seconds, ducking behind the rock and popping out to shoot at the hidden enemy. He shot another guard in the chest, his first direct hit, and he collapsed onto the boulder he was hiding behind, limp.

In the distance, slaves were running away from the eating area, where smoke was billowing up from. As Daniel watched, the guards pivoted to shoot at them instead, gunning them down before they could get far. As the mass of running figures fell, he saw the lizard from earlier come bounding through, jumping into the mass of guards and ruthlessly ripping them apart with his own claws. The Gorogs were caught off guard completely and had no time to prepare themselves for the fury that befell them, as one by one they died to the teeth and claws of the lizard.

Once he had killed the entire squadron, he whipped around, saw everyone at the top of the ledge, bounded across the open space, and began to scale the wall as if it were flat, reaching the top in a matter of seconds, joining Daniel behind the rock.

"Excuse me," he said gruffly. "You should be going that way." He pointed up the pathway to the surface.

"In a second!" replied Daniel harshly, as more guards came around the corner into their alley of the canyon.

Caitlin turned and saw the lizard sitting right next to her. "What is he doing here?" she asked over the noise of lasers firing.

"He made himself welcome!" explained Daniel, concentrating on shooting down upon the enemy, not even looking her way.

He had killed two more Gorogs when suddenly, the rifle clicked, but no rounds came firing out. Hastily inspecting the magazine, Daniel saw the flashing red light. Out of ammo, or at least that's what he thought it meant. And with maybe seconds before the gate opened and Gorogs poured out. Desperately, Daniel inspected the entire gun, hoping to find a spare ammo container. While he saw no such thing, he did find a small green button on the left side of the gun, by the brace. When he pushed it, a small round item dropped out of the rear of the weapon.

124

Picking it up, he saw that it had another green button on the top. It looked like an explosive, in fact.

"That's a standard-issue blast grenade!" the lizard told him. "Every rifle comes with one!"

Daniel turned to face him. "How big of a blast are we talking about?"

"Big enough to wipe a squad out, if you place it right!" came the reply over the whiz of beams impacting the rock face to their left.

Daniel, fingering the weapon, then remembered the second squadron of guards that were coming up through the ironworks. He clutched the explosive in his hands, tossing the rifle aside, and waited behind the rock for the other guards to emerge. Ignoring the dust raining down from above his head, he prepared to throw the grenade at the right time.

The gate, with a loud metal *clunk*, stuttered, then opened. A horde of Gorog agents, numbering maybe a dozen, poured out, all armed with rifles and secondary pistols. Daniel, while everyone else watched in confusion, threw the explosive as far as he could, landing it in the middle of the squad. The Gorogs saw the grenade, panicked and started to scatter for cover, but not before there was a tremendous noise, accompanied by a blinding light, and a surge of dust and rock. Daniel was temporarily blinded by the blast, and Caitlin quickly ducked behind the crevice as the detonation occurred. And when it settled, there was a black stain on the rock, with a dozen dead Gorogs surrounding it. Well, eleven, as one of them was still showing signs of breathing, but his leg had been blown off his body and was out cold, so he wouldn't be going anywhere anytime soon.

"Nice throw," said the lizard, walking over to the one guard who was still alive and finishing him off with a swift bite to the neck.

Daniel turned to face them, ready to congratulate them, when through the gate, all heavily armed, at least twenty additional guards came rushing through. "FREEZE!" they all yelled, their rifles leveled right at them.

Seeing no other way out, Daniel began to run up towards the path in a blind panic. The others followed along, hoping to escape while they still could. But they had barely gone twenty feet up the path when another huge squad came charging down the path, blocking their only exit.

"We can't get out!" yelled Caitlin, the despair now very real in her voice.

Daniel, skidding to a halt, realized that she was right. There was no way they'd survive an assault from forty-odd Gorogs armed with rifles. And they also knew that after the havoc they'd caused, they'd be good as dead on that path already. Daniel faced his group. The lizard looked angry. Ms. Phillips looked worried. Caitlin, poor Caitlin, looked like she had just lost everything, the expression of grief and hopelessness that was present on her face. He wondered if he himself had that same expression written on his face.

The guards encircled them, boxing them in from two sides, rifles leveled squarely at their chests. Daniel shut his eyes, waiting for the inevitable to happen.

And that's when things went from disorderly to chaotic.

The canyon wall opposite them exploded.

Chapter 7

The blast knocked everyone to the ground, even the Gorogs, who were bedazzled by the fiery light. Caitlin was forced to shield her eyes from the glare, and she could barely make out Daniel and Ms. Phillips doing the same thing. Max had just shut his eyes, meanwhile. As the light died, they made out huge chunks of rock falling to the canyon floor, forty feet below their position, where they shattered into smaller fragments. Dust clouds flew everywhere, creating a grayish-red fog that enveloped the canyon floor. And when the opposite wall emerged from behind the dust, there was a smoking hole in the side, roughly ten feet wide. As Caitlin and the Gorogs stared at the crater, they all became aware of a noise that was sounding from above, like a swarm of metallic bees flying.

And then the sky became a warzone as a dozen starfighters dropped in from the heavens, all of them shaped like the tip of an arrow. A barrage of torpedo blasts dropped down like a swarm of locusts, setting off violent tremors that caused the ground to shake whenever one exploded. The roar of their engines sent dust and pebbles vibrating off of the canyon walls, rattling everyone to their cores. Shouting and confusion was heard everywhere. It was a perfect storm of destruction and chaos, enough to leave the most hardcore man shaken with fear and awe.

Interestingly, the Gorogs were the most rattled of all. After witnessing the assault, in one moment, roughly half of the guards abandoned the group of escapees and ran back up the path towards the surface, yelling orders at each other that were lost in the clouds of dust. The rest were left confused, looking at each other confused, not sure what to do or where to go. The canyon walls shook as the surface was ceaselessly bombarded by enemies, making the guards grip their weapons a little tighter. Then a starfighter dropped into the canyon briefly, firing lasers and destroying the Gorog guardhouse in the process before vanishing out of the ravine.

It was then that Daniel struck. He wasn't entirely sure what had happened, or what he had done to warrant it, but in the moment, for just a moment, his fight-or-flight response kicked in, and for once, it trumped any anxiety that he had at the time. His only objective, for better or for worse, was to destroy the enemy. And he didn't care by what means it would be done.

In a move that seemed totally un-Daniel, while the guards whipped around at the sound of another explosion against the opposite rock face, he grabbed a guard's rifle, removed it from his custody while he was distracted, and shot the guard in the arm, causing him to step back and tumble off the pathway down to the canyon floor. He then turned around and lunged at two of the other guards, catching them completely by surprise. The lizard took one look at him and, almost deciding that what Daniel was doing was a good idea, followed suit, extending his claws, lunging onto one of the chest of a guard and proceeding to slash through his armor as if it was made of paper. Blue blood began to splatter out onto his scales as he savaged the figure, disfiguring the guard beyond all recognition until he collapsed to the ground, wishing he had died sooner.

Caitlin isn't sure what possessed her in that moment, but it must have been the same thing that had possessed both Daniel and the reptile, because she grabbed the electric whip of another guard, wrenching it from the holster on his back, turned it on, and proceeded to lash at the other guards. The pathway erupted with the skirmish, as the three of them engaged their enemy, leaving a bewildered Ms. Phillips to comprehend what was happening around her. Caitlin couldn't concentrate on the others, just on the guards she was striking at, swinging and flicking her stolen weapon wildly. The electric whip lashed out like a cobra, wrapping around one guard's helmet and electrocuting his skull, causing him to fall over, out cold. She then cracked the whip onto a guard so hard, she nearly fell over, but it left a foot-long gash in the Gorog's leg, causing him to fall over with both pain and numbness from the shock. She stepped back to lash at another guard, and found herself back-to-back with Daniel, who was picking off the guards with his stolen rifle. Around them, the canyon wall shook as bombs went off above them, sending dust onto everyone as they struggled on the pathway. The guards didn't go down quietly, though. Caitlin was grazed by a rival guard's whip as she attempted to disarm him, and Daniel was punched in the gut, winding him and almost resulting in his undoing until the lizard ripped the guard's back up until he was dead. Thankfully, the constant bombing was helping to distract and confuse the guards, assisting the group in taking them out.

From her peripheral vision, Caitlin saw the lizard bite a guard's foot, sending him kneeling onto the ground. The lizard then jumped on his back and fastened his jaws to his skull, biting down with enough force so that she clearly heard bone breaking. She turned back to her own opponent and struck out with her whip again, causing the Gorog to stumble back in shock, and tumble right off the edge of the wall. Another guard, a female, jumped at her, but Daniel intercepted her before she could reach Caitlin and knocked her down with one punch.

The scene fell quiet. Caitlin stood, panting, the whip still sparking in her hand, shoulder numb from being grazed. Daniel looked positively demented, in his rags and the alien rifle in his hand, like a survivor of the apocalypse, wheezing from the dust and the blow he'd sustained. The lizard's jaws were stained blue with Gorog blood. Ms. Phillips was pale in shock. Surrounding the four of them were fifteen dead Gorog agents. The rest of them had fled in terror or run off to stop the aerial invasion, which was still causing the ground to shake as munitions were dropped and detonated.

As the dust settled, Ms. Phillips, still numb with shock, finally spoke. "What...just happened?" she squeaked, coughing out some dust as she did.

"We killed them." The lizard said in a no-nonsense voice. "Or if you want a more civilized word, we dispatched them. That just happened. Now, if you don't mind, I'd love to get out of this canyon before more guards show up, how about you?"

Daniel brought his rifle into a nonthreatening pose and cracked his knuckles. "I agree," he concurred. "Let's move out of here and into the open where there's more room to move around." He turned to the lizard. "Do you have a name? It was Maxim...something, I don't remember."

"Just call me Max, for short," he replied gruffly, before sprinting up the ramp to the surface.

Daniel watched him go. "Well, anyone want to reconsider leaving Skorjion in the next five seconds?"

Caitlin shook her head. "Not a chance. Let's go."

They started running up the pathway, Ms. Phillips hesitated down there for a second, until she saw them running up towards the light of the surface. Scolding herself for not paying better attention, she ran up out of Skorjion's devouring maw and towards the light of freedom aboveground.

The white giant was slowly setting on the horizon as the group reached the top of the canyon wall. Behind them, Skorjion looked small yet foreboding, the buildings looking tiny. To their left and right, huge monoliths of rock rose up from the ground, looking foreboding and grim, casting long shadows onto the ground. A barren wasteland surrounded them on three sides, but ahead of them, a dust cloud larger than downtown Salt Plains loomed.

At first this giant cloud that had formed masked any sign

of battle. But as it slowly parted, it revealed hails of lasers firing, red ones from ground level, and green ones blasting from above. A missile fired from somewhere unseen and blew the rest of the dust aside with an enormous shockwave that rang throughout the surface, revealing the warzone stretched out before them. In the distance, the rocky, harsh environment of Grimcor stretched out before them, the orange rocks lit up in dazzling ways in the setting starlight. In the foreground, a small army of Gorogs had taken up any cover they could, firing their weapons up at their adversary; a squadron of starfighters, all of them that arrowhead shape that Caitlin had noticed down in the canyon. Painted in silver with blue accents, they looked far less menacing than the Gorog's gunships that had attacked Salt Plains years ago. Sleek and swift, they were swooping down to bombard the Gorogs with merciless laser fire and bombs, while the aliens that had held a hundred slaves captive for years with an iron grip were struggling to defend themselves against this foe. It was unclear if their pilots would be any less friendly to Daniel's group, but at least they were shooting at the trapped aliens and not at the four escapees. As the aliens on the ground attempted to fend off their foe, the starfighters performed glorious loops and twists as they dodged ground-based missiles and anti-aircraft guns.

  Daniel pointed at a large building besides a large airstrip. "That should be the hangar! We should make our way there as soon as possible!"

  "How?" asked Ms. Phillips. "Do you see all those Gorogs?"

  A huge squadron of Gorogs blocked the path to the hangar, all of them hunkered down behind cover and shooting skyward. "Go around them, of course!" he replied, starting forward, clutching his rifle and grabbing the riot stick of a fallen Gorog guard in the process. Everyone else exchanged looks and started forward as well, finding whatever comfort they could in the weapons they had won.

They made their way behind the enemy lines, frequently being startled by bombs dropping and exploding in the trench. Some of the Gorog guards noticed them and opened fire on them, but Daniel's rifle shot them dead quickly. One of them rushed the group, but Caitlin shocked him with her whip before he could reach them. Most of the guards remained oblivious to their movement, focusing instead on the swarm of ships bombarding them from above.

Shortly up ahead, they came across a group of Gorog reinforcements, running through the empty launch pad towards the center of the battle to assist their men. They pivoted to rush at the group upon seeing them, raising their rifles to shoot. Daniel's weapon took two more down, and then he tossed it aside as it ran out of ammunition, proceeding to engage a guard armed with a metal staff with his stolen riot stick. Dodging a swing for the head, he struck the guard's arm, causing him to falter, then he swept the guard's feet out from under him, before knocking him out with a well-timed, if a bit clumsy, blow to the head. He moved on to the next foe, while Max jumped onto another guard's shoulders to punish him with brutal damage. Caitlin, meanwhile, found herself facing two guards, armed with weapons. Flicking the whip at their guns, the electrically charged tip contacted both men's arms, causing them to go numb and drop their weapons. A quick and surprising strong punch from Ms. Phillips to each alien's exposed head caused them to go down.

Above them, the sky was alive with laser fire, torpedoes, engines whirring, and the sounds of explosions as a horde of brown ships was launched and engaged the silver ones. One was hit in the engine and went spiraling to earth, exploding near Caitlin in a fireball hot and loud enough to leave her skin singed and her ears ringing. Fiery pieces of it flew everywhere, with a piece of fuel cell taking out two of the guards they were fighting. A stray missile exploded into the roof of the hangar, lighting the building on fire. To their left, the power generators were hit by ceaseless fire from ships, and soon were a smoldering wreckage. Several times stray laser fire struck the ground around Daniel and his group, with some coming within inches of their tussles with the enemy. One even hit a guard in the arm, taking the entire thing out and leaving a burnt stump where it once was.

That guard's screams were silenced by Max, who had abandoned all sanity by that point. His claws swiped fast and his jaws came down hard on the limbs and head of every guard near him. To Caitlin's left, he slashed down so hard, he shredded through a guard's chest armor, gutting the alien from neck to stomach. As he toppled over, the lizard leaped to his next victim, doing a similarly violent kill there. Caitlin, meanwhile, was trying to disable the three guards she was fighting, using the whip to numb the arms, legs, or even entire body of them. With the whip flying around, she struck out at the guards, trying to look tough, but stumbled as the end came back around, instead making her look clumsy. Having never used a whip like this before, she was having difficulty using it at long range. She managed to shock one unconscious by wrapping the weapon around his upper arm, then yanking it back. Unfortunately, the two other guards began to realize that Caitlin was inexperienced in weapon training, and they started to slowly approach her, one armed with a short sword, the other with a rifle.

Realizing that her weakness had been exposed, she cracked the whip at the Gorog on the left, knocking his helmet off. Another strike and the guard was lying on the ground, paralyzed from the waist down by the strand that had wrapped around his leg. Caitlin turned to face his companion, preparing to strike, only to feel a surge of terror as the whip was torn from her hands. The fallen agent had grabbed the whip with both hands, ignoring the electricity, and with his last act before he passed out, yanked it away from Caitlin with all the strength that he had left. She turned to face the other guard, who was displaying a look of delight on his face at the thought of another kill. He discarded his rifle and drew a long, curved knife, expecting easy prey now that Caitlin was unarmed. He advanced, murder in his eyes.

Caitlin took a step back and found herself against the wall of a service building. Frantically, she found nowhere to go, nowhere to run, and nothing she could do. The guard, licking his chops with anticipation of the kill, lunged. She raised her hands, involuntarily of course. The guard's knife came down like one of the many missiles that were falling from above. Her hands met the wrist guard of the guard, in a feeble effort to stop the blade from piercing her flesh. To her surprise, she felt…strong. Then her hands glowed blue. It was only for a split second, but they did…electric blue. And then they discharged a huge blast of energy that sent the guard flying back, to come landing hard on the ground near his companion, out cold. A spark of electricity flickered across him as he lay there, unmoving.

Caitlin turned her hands over to face the palms toward her head, now more afraid than she was when she was being threatened by the Gorogs. They already looked fine, albeit paler than normal, but still. What was that? Did she just unleash a shock of electricity? And without getting electrocuted herself? As explosions sounded off around her, jarring her back to reality, she lost the thought as she hastily scanned the battlefield for her friends. Laying eyes on Daniel, she ran to him, avoiding falling debris from a collapsing watchtower as she did.

Daniel had found quite a use for his stolen stick. Despite guards coming at him from all sides, some armed with rifles, the repurposed staff in his hands twirled about, knocking down guards before they could come close to him and sweeping them onto the ground. Even their strong helmets could not resist the power behind the weapon. Any ranged weapons were dealt with by Max in brutal fashion. Despite this string of successes, Daniel was feeling the pain in his already tired muscles. Fighting the urge to rest, he fought gallantly through more guards. His arm screaming from the staff work, he pushed through, not wanting to give up, not when he was so close to success. Nearly slipping on a patch of slick rock, he barely managed to block a knife-wielding Gorog's stab and strike him on the head. Another guard, seeing his opportunity, lobbed a grenade in his direction. Daniel, watching the explosive fly his way, did the first thing that popped into his mind and swung his staff like a baseball bat at the device. The metal rod sent it flying back towards the guards, taking out three in one loud blast, like an extremely volatile baseball. But the action also caused Daniel's shoulder to pop, eliciting a groan from him as pain lanced through his shoulder. Thankfully, Max arrived to level the playing field, helping to dispatch the rest of the guards.

    A troop of Gorog reinforcements then came running up to their left. Caitlin's heart sank when she saw them. There were at least thirty of them, more than the three of them could handle in their situation. But then a barrage of laser fire was thrown down from above by some fighters, and the entire squad died instantly under the hailstorm. Another explosion came from their left, a fuel cell detonating. The Gorogs were losing, and it seemed like their defeat was coming up fast. What was left of the hangar's roof was set on fire by a flamethrower from one of the ships, and a large building that Daniel assumed was the secondary power generator control room was obliterated with one torpedo blast.

    "We're almost there!" he called out, running for the hangar.

    Then another missile flew through the hangar door and hit something explosive in there, as the entire building lit up with fire that acted like a fireworks display. Daniel skidded to a halt, his heart sinking. "No, no, no!" he said, as their method of escape went up in flames.

    A stray Gorog ran up, nearly catching Daniel offside

before Caitlin intervened with her whip, and then they were all blinded by an intensely bright light from above. As they all shielded their eyes, they watched as a silver ship descended from above like some angel, engines thrumming rhythmically like an instrument. It stopped about five feet above the ground, with a rope dangling from its underside. A door opened on the side of the hull, and a green alien with a pointy nose and warty skin poked its head out.

"Did you all escape from the camp?" it yelled down at them over the roar of the ship's engines.

Everyone nodded, sensing that this was their new opportunity to escape.

"Then I suggest you get inside if you want to live!" The alien pointed at the rope before ducking back inside and reappearing with a blaster to shoot at a large Gorog troop that was blazing their way towards them. A very large troop, with easily seventy men, all heavily armed. Heading right their way.

Ms. Phillips and Max, now covered in blue splatters, ran up, after finishing off the last of a small group of guards. "Is this how we're escaping?" the lizard inquired over the noise.

"It is now!" Daniel urged them to the rope. "Get on! Quick!"

Caitlin went first, scrambling up the rope into the gunship. Max followed, getting some help from Caitlin, who hauled him into the ship. Daniel then grabbed the rope, followed by Ms. Phillips just below him. With the Gorogs closing in fast, Daniel yelled up into the ship, "Time to go!"

They slowly began to lift off, the engines humming deeply as they charged up and propelled them away from Skorjion. The camp burned below them as they lifted off of the ground and towards the warmth of freedom.

Chapter 8

Grimcor's Atmosphere

Grimcor was getting smaller behind them, Daniel could tell, and with it, all of the hell that he, Caitlin and Ms. Phillips had been through. He sat, leaning against the wall of the gunship, tired, but feeling jubilant on the inside. They had done it. They had gotten out. They were free. And none of them had been left behind. Caitlin was injured on one arm, a nasty welt forming, and they were all covered in dust, but they were all alive, surrounded by soldiers wearing silver and blue uniforms, all standing still. They paid the four dirty escapees no attention as the ship rumbled up through the atmosphere.

They examined their surroundings briefly. Blue lights lined the sides of the ceiling, casting a ghostlike glow throughout the space. At the front of the bay was a huge weapon rack, lined with enough rifle holders to fill a gun shop. At the back was what looked like a retractable cannon, complete with a door that opened to allow someone to shoot out of the back of the vessel. There were seats for troops to sit and wait to be deployed, and handholds to allow them to remain standing without falling over in the heat of combat. But none of them could even stand up and sit down, their bodies only able to slump against the wall of the room. They all were too stunned and relieved to do so.

"We made it," whispered Caitlin, her voice sounding close to tears. "We actually made it."

"You're welcome," grumbled Max from the corner, who had curled himself up like a dog, a dog with a scaly hide and dorsal spines protruding from his backside, in the corner behind the legs of two soldiers.

They all turned to stare at him. "I'm sorry," said Caitlin,

sounding indignant. "You've got a problem? I didn't quite get your name back there."

"It's Max," he replied, looking the other way. "And leave me alone." He turned his head the other way, grunting as he did. Caitlin gave him a look, but left him alone.

Ms. Phillips came over to sit beside Daniel. "You alright?" she asked him.

He slowly turned his head to face her, almost disbelief written on his face. "We all made it," he said quietly. "We're safe. I almost forgot what it felt like." He cuddled up next to her. "What did Caitlin and I tell you? We got you out safely."

As they snuggled, Caitlin came over and joined them, until all three of them were curled up next to each other, resting. Daniel felt strange, knowing that they could go anywhere. For five years, he had known nothing except the canyon floor of Skorjion, and the horror that went on there day after agonizing day. But they were free. And as they all rested, filthy and battered, for the first time in years, the thought of home felt as though they could actually become true.

One of their rescuers, a female alien with horns extruding from the sides of her scalp, walked by them to the front of the troop bay. "We're arriving at Hangar 3, port side in just a few minutes!" she called out to the occupants, including Daniel's party. "Stand by for atmosphere departure!"

Daniel and Caitlin exchanged a glance, then they both jumped to their feet and ran to the window, peering outside the ship. The reddish haze of Grimcor wrapped around a good portion of the view, surrounding the sandy ball. Next to that, an endless sea of jet black stretched out to the edge of the window. Space. Actual space. Daniel had missed his first opportunity to see it since he had been unconscious during his flight from Earth. But this…this was the real deal. No atmosphere separating them from the eternal void that surrounded them. As Grimcor grew smaller behind them, stars began to pop into view, specks against the black. Despite Daniel bracing for gravity to lose its hold over him and Caitlin, it never came, even as they ascended higher into space. But that was only temporary as they soon caught sight of the giant battleship from whence the gunships and starfighters must have first come from. Even from here, they could tell that it was huge, potentially more than a mile from bow to stern, thickly plated with armor, and boasting two rows of giant cannons on each side of the bridge that stuck out against the elegant-looking hull design. They were flying towards a hole in the side of the cruiser, probably the hangar. "Mom," said Daniel. "You need to see this."

    She came over and took a look outside, whistling at the view. "Never did I imagine that I would be able to get to space," she said, looking out across the void, then at a neighboring starfighter that was overtaking them.

    As they drew closer to the hangar, they began to see more and more about it. There was plenty of room to store ships, some of which they could already see parked. As they passed into the shadow of the warship and into the hangar itself, the endless darkness of space gave way to a brilliantly lit chamber lined with starfighters, gunships, and filled with fueling reserves and enough people to fill all of Salt Plains. There were technicians running about, some working on the damaged starfighters, pilots in flight suits talking, and several officers strutting about. Tons of small cargo carriers and other small craft were zipping about the chamber, carrying spare parts and repair tools. It looked like a miniature town, complete with a small food area at the back. Like a futuristic version of Salt Plains, if it was located in a giant box.

    The gunship they were in slowly descended towards an empty lot on the right side of the hangar. As they slowly came to a halt, Daniel felt strange, as he was now realizing that he was experiencing artificial gravity, as well as an oxygenated atmosphere that was entirely man-made. And as the troop bay door opened, he forgot about everything else but what he was seeing. To his left, Caitlin and Ms. Phillips were experiencing the same sort of wonder. Max...well, he seemed impressed, just not blown away. They slowly set foot onto the steel hangar deck, and one thing became clear; they could never return to a place like Skorjion again. The ceiling seemed like it was miles away, and there were ships as far as the eye could see. Daniel tried to jump, and promptly came back down, just like on Earth. He took a deep breath. He didn't start asphyxiating. It was fresh oxygen. Around him were dozens upon dozens of workers, many of them with special antennae, multiple arms, a third eye, all neatly dressed in uniforms as they did their work.

 Daniel suddenly became aware of his rags and looked down at himself. Dirty, covered in dust, his T-shirt all but torn to shreds, multiple holes in his pants, one of his shoes gone, and tons of red marks from recent injuries. Glancing over at Caitlin, who was standing barefoot, with just enough of her clothing left to prevent her from being indecent, she was looking equally out of place among all the well-dressed, sharp-looking soldiers, pilots, and officers who were running about the hangar. They both looked homeless. Ms. Phillips was similarly filthy, but Max, aside from being caked with dust, looked right at home. "I could really use a shower right now," said Caitlin, brushing her arms and sending small orange clouds floating into the hangar.

 "Me too," replied Daniel, feeling ashamed of his appearance.

 The soldiers who had rescued them approached them now, sending the group back to reality. While they were not smiling, they at least had their weapons pointing up rather than across at their chests. "Are you four escaped slaves from the camp Skorjion?" one of them, a green alien wearing a blue jumpsuit and with eyes sticking out from his head asked.

 Daniel glanced around at his ragged, dirty friends and reptile hitchhiker. "Uh...yes," he replied, not sure how else to phrase it. He also did not know how to greet their saviors. He was tempted to handshake, but in alien culture for all he knew, it could mean something completely different. So, he just stayed put.

    The guard looked at his companion, a tall, blue-skinned alien covered in warts and boasting two very yellow eyes, without any pupils at all. They stepped back and conversed privately for a brief moment. Daniel hoped that they were discussing their freedom, rather than discussing whether or not they were a threat and deserved to be killed. He tried to listen in, but he couldn't make out their words. Thankfully it was ultimately the better option, as the green alien came forward and told them, "Please follow me. The Magnum would want to see you."

    Although relieved to know that they weren't dead, yet, Daniel still felt uneasy. Where were they going? And who was this "Magnum?" It sounded important, for sure. But there was no sign of hostility towards anyone in their group, not even Max, who despite his menacing looks hadn't elicited one reaction from any of the soldiers. Deciding that refusal would result in their situation going bad, he started to follow them, but was stopped when he was yanked back by Caitlin and Ms. Phillips.

    "Do you really want to follow them?" she whispered, trying to keep her voice down.

    "And refusing would only serve to make the situation better, you think?" asked Daniel, trying to sound firm. "I don't think these guys want to hurt us like the Gorogs did."

    "And you know this…how? What if they're not friendly to us? Do you really just want to trust them like this?"

    "I'd rather accept their invitation and see where this leads us, rather than refuse and risk angering the people *who pulled us out of that battle and Skorjion,* I might add. Also, it's not like we have any other choice."

    Caitlin huffed loudly, but she and Ms. Phillips nodded.

She clearly mistrusted the soldiers, and after spending so long in Skorjion's gut, he couldn't blame her. But she must've seen the wisdom in Daniel's words, so she sighed and said, "Let's hope you're right, Stellar Brain."

"Let's hope wherever we're going has water, because my throat is dryer than a desert," grumbled Max, trailing after her.

Daniel also started to walk, but initially lagged behind the others, caught off-guard by Caitlin's words. She hadn't used that nickname in years. Not since the pumpkin festival, all those long years ago. It seemed so long ago…Daniel realized that he had spent years rotting away in Skorjion, while the world moved on without him or Caitlin. He again wondered what had happened with Salt Plains in his absence. Was the town rebuilt, or did everyone leave?

Such thoughts were all but forgotten as they left the hangar behind and entered into a long corridor branching off from it, which in turn had many more corridors branching off elsewhere. It felt like a giant maze, where every path you took led somewhere new. Groups of soldiers marched in single file past them, accompanied by ship crew that were hustling off to other areas of the vessel. There were even some robots around, hobbling throughout the ship. One of them, to Daniel's total surprise, looked like Mr. Mech, a fictional droid that often accompanied him on his wild space adventures that he used to so often dream about. He smiled at the thought of what his reaction to where he was now would be if he was several years younger.

Caitlin must've caught his expression and the hint of a smile he managed, because as they went along, she leaned in closer to Daniel. "How are you not nervous right now?" she asked. "We're still not home, you know. Who knows where we are or what these people are."

"We don't," he replied. "But, Caitlin, just look around you! We're on an alien ship! And we're free from our miserable slave labor! How could that not make you happier than you've ever been?"

She looked a little hurt, so Daniel leaned in closer still. "Listen. All we have to do is find someone willing to drop us off back home on Earth. That's it. In the meantime, since nobody's pointed any guns at us, how about we take in the...view–"

They all stopped in front of an enormous central room, nearly as big as the hangar that they had just left, which Daniel guessed from its larger size and busier crowds was the main corridor from which all other hallways branched off. It was lined with lights beaming down from the ceiling, a pair of monorail tracks going in opposite directions, and crew members. So many crew members that Daniel swore it was more people than Salt Plains' entire population. A train whizzed by above them, whirring loudly as it carried more men as well as some metal crates towards some unknown destination. They continued down it for a minute, past at least a hundred different species of aliens and hundreds of robots, carrying supplies and escorting guards down the pathway. The entire time, Daniel's jaw was hanging open, and if he was able to turn to look at Caitlin or Ms. Phillips, he would have seen them doing the same thing. Another train screeched overhead, filling the space with tons of kinetic energy. There were no whips, no scorching hot suns to send sweat down their foreheads. The air was crisp and cool, and it was refreshing to experience. They stared as a robot as tall as a first-story house walked by them, stepping over aliens and humans alike.

"If only anyone back home could see this," said Caitlin, awestruck.

But as they went along, they saw some things that looked blatantly out of place. They saw several aliens wearing normal clothes, including one that had a picture of the Hulk on it, and another in a stylish pair of boots. They saw several humans munching on granola bars, just like at the local grocery store, in between the other strange snacks they saw, like the bag of fried tarantula-sized bugs stuffed with some sauce that some four-eyed, red-skinned alien was munching on. They were all confused, but kept walking down the main corridor.

After a while, they left the main corridor when they made a left, passing rooms behind closed doors and a group of pilots conversing on the aftermath of the battle that they all had just witnessed along with some other personnel, and made a few more turns through increasingly narrow hallways until they came to a halt at a door that was different from all the others they had seen; the others were dark silver with blue tinges, while this was one was a lighter color with gold tinges and trim. There was a sign on the door, but it was written in a language that they could not understand.

The guards turned around to go, but before they did, the green one spoke up again. "When this door opens, go inside. The Magnum will see you there." And they turned and left without another word, leaving Daniel, Caitlin, Ms. Phillips and Max standing in the hallway, with no one around, with just the door in front of them.

They stood there for a few minutes, waiting patiently, except for Max, who started to pace after about a minute. "This is taking too long," the lizard complained. "Can't we see this Magnum person right now?"

"Have you heard of him before?" asked Caitlin. "You seem to have heard more of space than any of us have, and given Daniel's knowledge of it, that's really saying something."

"I've only known him as "the Magnum", never by his real name. He supposedly runs this large galactic state that I've only heard brought up under the title "The Coalition.""

"Coalition? You mean like a Federation, as in *Star Trek*?" asked Ms. Phillips, confused. But Daniel barely heard her speak. That name, the Coalition, was ringing a bell in his brain. The map in the Skorjion room. It had something listed on it as "Coalition." Perhaps that was this same Coalition that Max was referencing. But before he could think about whether or not Coalition soldiers had rescued them, the door slid open horizontally, giving way to reveal a pitch-black room.

A draft of cooler air ran out, crossing the line from pleasantly cool to chilly. They all peered into the room, but they could not see what lay beyond the light that was streaming in. Daniel turned to face the others. "Well, whatever the Coalition is, I think we're about to meet its ruler."

He took a step inside, no longer feeling the warm fuzzies, but he was soon swallowed up by the darkness. Caitlin and Ms. Phillips nervously followed, while Max's shadowy figure sauntered past them. It was indeed as black as tar in there, save for the light streaming in from the open door and from a handful of glowing buttons on one wall. That is, until the door slid shut without warning and left the three of them in virtually total darkness. Daniel felt Caitlin's hand lock around his forearm like a vice, reminding him rudely about her claustrophobia.

"Ow…Cait, you're cutting off circulation to my hand!" he said, feeling her grip lessen as a result.

"Sorry!" she said, sounding embarrassed.

Off to one side, Max was seemingly looking for a light switch, but a spotlight came beaming down on three chairs while he was sniffing at the wall, a sole circle of light in a void of black, and Caitlin's grip was released. Daniel approached, cautiously, half-expecting there to be some deadly booby trap that they'd have to avoid. But they made the few feet to the chairs without issue, and, not sure what else to do, he sat down. Caitlin did too, taking the seat next to him, and Ms. Phillips took the last one. Max just sat on the floor.

For a moment, nothing happened. Then a loud voice boomed through the room. "I understand you four are escaped slaves, formerly inmates of Skorjion?" It was loud, commanding, and raised the hairs on Daniel's arms that had not already been singed off. He exchanged a quick glance with Caitlin, before turning back to answer.

"Yes. Yes, we are." That was all he said. If he was indeed speaking to the "Magnum" he decided speaking less would be the smarter move. That way, there was less chance of saying something offensive. "We are slaves that escaped from Skorjion, uh, sir."

"What are your names?" came the voice again, once more filling the room with its presence.

"I am known as Daniel Phillips, sir," he stated honestly. "On my right is…"

"Caitlin. Caitlin Wheeler," she spoke up, cutting off Daniel to his surprise.

"I am Amy, Daniel's mom," came the third answer. Then everyone turned and stared at Max, who glanced around at all of them and sighed.

"Just call me Max," the lizard spoke up on the far right, sounding annoyed. "You going to show your face to us or what?"

A brief pause, followed by, "Are you three on the left of Terra, or Earth?"

This time, Caitlin answered. "Yes. We all are." She pointed back and forth between herself, Daniel, and Ms. Phillips.

This time, there was no answer for quite some time, and Max eventually lost his patience. "I've had enough of this…" he growled, rising and resuming his search along the wall for a light switch. It did not take him long to find one and switch it on, instantly banishing the darkness.

After being in complete black for so long, it blinded the three humans and caught them off guard, forcing them to shut their eyes. Blinking to slowly get used to the light, Daniel slowly took in the room's surroundings as his full vision slowly returned. They were in an office, with posters and paintings on the walls, a clock, and a red carpet lining across the room's floor in front of them. There seemed to be a futuristic espresso machine on one wall, a fake plant leaning against the opposite wall, and a hand-carved desk in the center of the room. And sitting at that desk was the one who had been speaking.

He was definitely on the older side, in his fifties, guessed Daniel. He was wearing a bright red uniform lined with blue and silver, was adorned with a muted gold cape, and was wearing a strange head adornment above his left ear, a star facing to the side, solid gold, clearly the mark of someone very highly ranked. He was wearing black fingerless gloves and boots. His facial hair was tinged with gray, his cheeks were slightly sunken in, there were hints of wrinkles forming, but his eyes and expression were surprisingly youthful. He looked like the type of person Daniel would have expected to be his godfather, the sort of guardian who promised to look after you, but who was also no-nonsense about rules and limits. He looked surprised at Max's impatience, but he soon lost that appearance and instead relaxed in his chair.

"Interesting. Perhaps the lizard's feeling a bit impatient," he said, flashing a wry smile at Max, who immediately bristled up like a porcupine. The old man put his fingers to his chin to think briefly before continuing. "I suppose I'd better introduce myself, yes?"

Caitlin shot Daniel another glance. He turned to face her, then back towards the man at the desk. "Yes, please, sir," he said, fumbling his words a bit, causing him to turn a slightly red shade in the cheeks.

The silver-haired man stood up, revealing his full height. To Daniel's surprise, he was pretty tall; maybe not as tall as him but definitely a decent height; six feet perhaps. His cloak fell down around him as he rose from his chair, his figure. He spoke again, and that same voice from before filled the room, the voice of power and authority incarnate.

"My name is Shane. Shane Vulkan. I am known as the Magnum, a title that you probably already heard from the guards who brought you here. I am commander of this ship and of the forces that attacked Skorjion, where you were being held. You are now under my protection."

Daniel glanced over at Caitlin and Ms. Phillips again, not sure who to answer that. It sounded friendly, but he had met enough school bullies who had lured him in with false friendliness before. "Okay…so what does that mean, exactly. Specifically, the bit where we are supposedly now 'under your protection?'"

The old man leaned forward onto the desk. "It means you are now under the protection of all my guards and troops. What else would it mean?"

"Meaning, how do we know if this isn't some trick?" That was Caitlin speaking, sounding a little blustered, before she heard her own tone and added, "Forgive me, sir, but up until fifteen minutes ago we were all basically slaves of the Gorogs, so I apologize if I stumble with my speech a little bit."

"No, no, no worries at all." The Magnum moved a little closer, checking in on their appearance, eyeing their rags, their dirty features and their overall unkemptness. He shook his head. "All of you look rather dry. I understand, knowing how harsh Grimcor can be. Perhaps you three would like a glass of water each?"

This time all of them nodded enthusiastically, even Max. In response, Shane took three large, ornately blown glasses of water from his desk cabinet, moved to the dispenser on the wall, filled up all the glasses, then brought them over to Daniel, Caitlin, Ms. Phillips, and Max. They all took the glasses gratefully and gulped down the icy cold water. Since they all had lost their canteens during the skirmish, they had gone an hour or two without any fluid, and their throats were parched. Daniel let the liquid cool his burning throat, his first truly cold water in five years.

"You all look like you've been through hell and back again," commented Shane. "Which you basically have. You're lucky. Most don't get out of Skorjion alive. Which reminds me…" He pulled out a small device from under his desk, turned it on, and pointed it at the three of them. "This may sting a little." He pressed a small button, and a short shock pierced Daniel's neck.

"Ow!" said Caitlin, reflexively reaching behind her. Something clattered to the floor as she did. Something fell off of Daniel's neck as well. He turned around to take a look, and saw a tiny disk, no bigger than a penny. There was one next to Caitlin as well, and underneath Ms. Phillips' chair, yet another. She was glancing around, wondering where it had come from.

"What was that?" she demanded, rubbing behind her ear.

"I just disabled the trackers the Gorogs placed on all of you. Now they can't track you wherever you go," explained Shane, setting the device down.

"Um…thank you, sir," said Daniel, sipping up the last of his water. He set the empty glass on the ground next to Caitlin's. He exhaled, his throat feeling slightly better than before.

Shane walked around the side of the desk, moving closer to them and bending down to retrieve the glasses. "Did you say five years you were trapped in Skorjion?"

"Sir…" began Daniel, then paused and asked, "Should I call you sir? Because if it offends you…"

"Sir is just fine, thank you."

"Right. Sir, with all due respect, we're just looking to return home. We were forcibly abducted from our hometown on Earth by the Gorogs, and sentenced to work in their camp. We're not looking to intrude on anyone's property or cause any unnecessary stress. And we want to be as far away from the Gorogs as possible. We don't even know where we are or what's been going on."

"Except me. I have a semblance of where we are," boasted Max, looking smug.

"Ignore him. His brain's the size of a walnut,"

interjected Daniel, savagely looking at the lizard.

Shane chuckled slightly, which did serve to make Daniel feel slightly more at ease. "Well, in that case," he told them, striding across the office to the console on the right, where the glowing buttons had been, "hopefully I can fill in some of those gaps for you." He flicked a switch, dimming the lights in the room, then returned to his seat.

"Is the show really necessary?" asked Max, staring at Shane crossly. "Just get on with it!"

The old man sighed, then leaned forward. "As you wish," he said. "I assume that you've already become familiar with the Gorogs in the past?"

They all nodded. "More familiar than we would've liked," said Ms. Phillips. "They're a bunch of crazies for sure."

"Crazy, deranged, there's a lot of words you can use to describe them," replied Shane, his voice sounding as though it could narrate the nature documentaries Daniel used to watch. "Whatever you use to describe them, they're highly dangerous and, as I'm sure you've at least heard about, want to impose themselves as the rulers of the entire galaxy."

They again all nodded.

"As you might imagine, not everyone wants to support that idea, those people being us, the Orion Coalition. We were founded 2,000 years ago to handle threats such as this, and to maintain the peace in the galaxy. I am the Coalition Magnum, its leader, or, in your Earth terms, its president, per say."

"Yes, we gathered," grumbled Max, scratching at the floor. "What else is new?"

Shane stared at the grumpy old lizard. "Where did you come from?" he asked, a bit of an edge in his voice. Max did not reply, but instead turned his head the other way, muttering something under his breath, still clawing at the floor. Daniel cast an annoyed glance in his direction. "Apologies for his behavior, sir," he told Shane. "He sort of joined our party while we were escaping and never left."

"Yes. Anyway," continued Shane, "The Orion Coalition forged an army to defeat the Gorogs, but unfortunately, their resistance has proven quite effective. It was only recently that we were able to breach their outer defenses and penetrate a major hub of their operations; Skorjion."

Daniel nodded slowly, still processing all of the information. His brain was like an old computer, as it was taking a while to come to terms with what he was hearing. "Okay, so to recap quickly, you're the leader of a group dedicated to peace and justice. And the Gorogs want to watch the galaxy burn. You two are at war and neither of you can make much headway against the other?"

"That just about sums it up." Shane sat back down at his desk, fingering a pen as he did. "Now, I too have a question. How did you escape Skorjion?" he asked them. "It's supposed to be near impossible to breach the camp's defenses."

Caitlin gave him a tired look. "Your men had a big help in our success," she confessed. "Had your fighters not started their attack right then and there, we would all have died."

"And you're of Earth, not some other group of humans?"

Caitlin looked puzzled. "Um…no, sir. The three of us were all born, bred and raised on Earth. We didn't even know that aliens or you even existed until the Gorogs attacked us five years ago."

Mentioning Earth reminded Daniel as to what he had been trying to ask since they had sat down. "Sir, with all due respect," he spoke up, trying to sound respectful, "We wish to ask your permission to return to Earth as soon as possible." He glanced over at Caitlin and Ms. Phillips, who were both nodding enthusiastically. "We've been away for five years and long for our homes. Can you spare a ship, a pilot, anyone who may be able to drop the three of us off back where we were first kidnapped?"

Shane thought for a second. "A ship to take you back home..." he repeated, fingering his short beard. "How can I make that work?" He stood up, beginning to pace, while they all waited patiently for an answer.

"I would love to oblige your request," Shane finally replied, causing Daniel, Caitlin, and Ms. Phillips to light up. Then their faces all fell as he added, "But unfortunately, I cannot do so at the moment."

Daniel stood up. "Sir?" he asked, his voice confused and hurt. "It's just one ship, nothing serious. We won't take up too much of your time! Please, please, all we want is to go home! We all miss it so much!" He felt the desperation starting to creep back in as he spoke. Surely, they were not going to be trapped when they were this close to flying back to Earth?

But Shane was shaking his head. "We're in the middle of Gorog territory right now. To leave the ship at the moment, even with an experienced pilot flying you, would be a death sentence. Plus, I'm not sure what ships are still working properly after that last battle."

Caitlin folded her arms. "How long until we can realistically fly back to Earth?" she asked.

"Soonest would be two days from now, I guess."

Daniel groaned inwardly. They were so close, so near to their goal, and yet were still stuck in outer space. At least they were in hospitable company, he thought. And, as a silver lining, they were on board an alien ship. Something that he had never expected to do at all, but secretly had always wanted to. Their circumstances could have been worse. Max, however, did not see it that way.

"What about me?" the angry lizard demanded.

"Do you have a home to return to?" asked Shane.

That question made Max furious. "What do you think? Of course I do! I've been away from it for almost ten years now! *Ten years!* I want to return there, and I want to return there now!"

Shane immediately took a step forward. "A little short-tempered, are we?" he said, reaching for a button on the wall. "Another outburst like that and I may have to call security to come handle you. At ease, please." There was no waver as he spoke, staring down Max until the lizard finally relented and sat back down on the ground, still muttering under his breath.

The Magnum sighed, then gestured at their clothing. "Well, since you can't go anywhere for a little bit, tell you what. I'll send for some men, they'll provide you with a room, where you can shower, clean yourselves, and change into fresh clothing. I'll also have my chef prepare some food, and you may feel free to join me in my own personal dining room, since you're probably starving. It's the least I can do while you're here. Does that sound okay to all of you?"

"Oh my gosh, yes," Caitlin stood up as she spoke, clearly excited about the prospect of a shower and some fresh clothing. "That would be wonderful, thank you!"

"Yes, thank you!" said Ms. Phillips, sighing with relief.

Max yawned. "Well, beats being covered in dust all day," he said, stretching his legs.

Shane nodded. "Very well. Dinner is in…" He checked his watch. "About four hours from now. Room 402. I'd appreciate it if you attended."

"We'd love to eat dinner with you," said Daniel, suddenly feeling how hungry he was. While he hadn't eaten *that* poorly during his tenure in prison, he had lost a lot of weight over the last five years, and so had Caitlin. "We'll probably need a map, though."

Shane smiled, like a grandfather would do to his grandchildren. "I'll provide the map. Now go clean yourselves! You all deserve it."

Daniel nodded, arose from his seat, said, "Thank you, sir," then started for the door. Caitlin and, thankfully, Max both did the same. They met up in the hallway as the door closed behind them, Max still sitting like some mutated dog between them.

"Do you actually think that he's going to let us go free?" asked Daniel as they met up with the guard who would escort them to their rooms.

"He does have a point about being in Gorog territory," replied Ms. Phillips. "If getting home safely means waiting a few more days, I'm all down for it. Besides, this ship seems nice enough."

"Let's hope so," replied Caitlin.

Daniel turned to her. "Do you still think he's not friendly?"

"I definitely feel a little bit better about being here after that, yes."

"I mean, anything would be better after Skorjion. The bar's not exactly that high."

"True." Caitlin yawned. "Alright, let's go find our rooms. I desperately need a shower and some untorn clothes."

"Absolutely," said Ms. Phillips.

Max shrugged. "Sure, why not?"

And off they went, towards cleanliness and hope that their lives may finally be taking a turn for the better.

Chapter 9

Skorjion

    Warden Dormak was not pleased. Not pleased at all.

    As his ship set down, he hopped out and surveyed the destruction. The main hangar was in shambles, half of its roof now inside the building, in little chunks, or burnt off entirely. Both the primary and secondary power generators were spare parts, still smoldering from the missiles that had destroyed the systems. Fuel cells had all been vaporized, and the radar center had been severely damaged. One of the central watchtowers had fallen over completely, and there were hundreds of dead Gorogs littering the field, some of them being carted off by a handful of guards that had survived. Also scattered throughout the area were chunks of debris, pockets of flame, and the remains of no fewer than a dozen starfighters, most of them, to Dormak's fury, painted brown. Approaching one of them and examining the blackened hull and twisted thrusters, he clearly made out the arrowhead style and silvery paint job of the ship. Growing angrier by the second, he stormed off towards the secondary pathway down into Skorjion, intent on finding some guards and venting his anger on them.

    Passing a ring of at least fifteen dead guards, as well as several blackened stains on the canyon wall and some blue splatters of Gorog blood, he passed through the gates into the iron facilities, still wide open. Passing through the darkened factory, he took notice of several holes that had been blasted into the ceiling, as well as several dead guards lying on the ground. One of the forges was on fire, having gone out of control as a laser blast damaged the control that regulated the intensity of its heat. Outside, he finally found some more living guards, all of whom were busy cleaning up debris and the bodies of Gorogs with the camp slaves. The order that had been present just that morning had been abandoned, with guards struggling to keep the prisoners in line. As Dormak walked by, two slaves attempted to overpower their supervising guard, very nearly succeeding until another soldier shot them both dead. Ahead, Lieutenant Jorka, temporary manager of Skorjion, was busy speaking with other guards, going through a device that kept the records of every slave in the camp so far. The second-in-command to Dormak was also a senior officer in the army, boasting shorter but still prominent tentacles that commanded attention onto his chin, a piercing stare, and a high-necked officer uniform that displayed the insignia of lieutenant, complete with a short cape dangling off his back. He stiffened when he saw the warden approaching, but quickly regaining his composure, trying not to look afraid at the look of rage on the superior officer's face.

"Ward—Warden Dormak!" he exclaimed, putting a hand behind his head and surveying the wreckage around them. His voice was timid and stuttering like crazy. "This...this isn't what it looks like—"

He never finished the thought, as the warden seized him by the throat, hoisted him off his feet using his immense strength, and shoved him into the nearest rock face. Jorka squeaked and grabbed at Dormak's tentacles, but to no avail. Dormak was nearly a head taller than the lieutenant and far, far stronger.

"Give me one reason why I shouldn't throw you in the forges this instant." Every last word the angry Gorog spoke was loaded with the kind of hatred that one only came into having from being hugely let down by someone they trusted to do something for them.

"S—Sir!" croaked Jorka, trying to find a way to brace himself against the wall, rather than be left hanging by the warden's muscular arm. "We—we had no warning! They snuck up on us! It's...not...my...fault!" He gasped for air as he tried to force out the words.

"There are several rules of leadership, and do you know what the first one is?" came Dormak's vengeful reply. "When you're in charge, everything, yes, *everything* that happens is *your* fault, not mine! Yours!" He raised the lieutenant even higher in the air and threw him into the rock wall, sending him sprawling onto the rocky soil, clutching his throat and gasping for air. The warden whipped around to survey the damage again, his cape blowing in the wind whipping through the canyon. Here he could see down the canyon to the elevator shaft, taking note of the boulders that had fallen from above and the rubble of another service building. He finally turned back to face Jorka. "You had one job," he stormed. "ONE! And you managed to fail even that!"

"Sir…"

"We are at war, Jorka. This kind of carelessness does not help us win it! This is how we lose it! Oh, in the name of…" He stalked away, his head buried in his hands, muttering incomprehensible gibberish. This was a travesty, and the heathen god Begarr only knew how long it would take to fix all the damage.

"Sir?"

Dormak turned around, realizing that he was noticing a lack of slaves repairing the damage to the camp. "Where are all of the slaves?" he demanded.

Jorka stood up slowly, brushing the dust off of himself. "We brought them to the barracks, sir. We're keeping them there until we have enough guards to manage them. Some of them got a little excited before the attack happened. Had close to a full-scale riot in here."

"We didn't lose a lot of slaves in the attack, did we?" asked Dormak. When that elicited tenseness from Jorka, the warden's horizontal-pupiled eyes bore right into the lieutenant's forehead. "How many did we lose?"

Jorka swallowed. "We went through the records, and the number came to twenty-two, sir."

Dormak's face darkened. "Twenty-two?" he repeated, taking another step closer. He also bent down and grabbed a rock from the ground, only to stop as another thought popped into his head. "Is Subject X-17 here?"

The lieutenant looked as scared as a mouse in front of a cat as he shook his head. "No, sir...we have eyewitness reports saying that he escaped on an enemy gunship."

The officer had to duck hastily as Dormak threw the huge rock at the cliff wall. Then he found the warden's head at his, close enough to feel his breath. "WE LOST X-17?!" the warden shouted, loud enough to cause other Gorogs to turn their heads at the commotion. "AND HE'S IN THE HANDS OF THE ENEMY?!"

Jorka managed the faintest of nods, causing Dormak to storm off, a hurricane of anger and fear swirling around in his head. Skorjion attacked, the facilities on the surface heavily damaged or destroyed, and twenty-two escaped slaves, including X-17. This was sure to attract unwanted attention, and there was one person in particular who he did not want finding out about this.

Unfortunately for Dormak, he did.

Several thousand light-years from Grimcor's desert terrain and harsh white giant, a huge ship floated through the endless void of space, amid a large field of asteroids. Rocks as large as mansions swirled and hurled through the zero-gravity conditions with enough velocity to smash up smaller ships completely. Openings in the treacherous field appeared and disappeared without any rhyme or reason, in a way that would scare even the most hardcore pilots and their ships away. But not this ship, as its hard armor plating simply shrugged off the space rocks and continued to cruise undeterred. Black and brown, shaped vaguely like a dagger, and armed to the teeth with cannons and phasers, the *Deceiver* was a crown jewel in the Gorog navy. It had never failed to win a battle, and excelled in destroying enemy cruisers, given that it was several times larger than most other battleships it encountered. It carried a fearsome reputation among pilots, calling it, "The Bane of Freedom." It was a ship worthy of a conqueror.

And it so happened that its commander was none other than a conqueror. And not just any conqueror. A prince.

On the bridge overlooking the ship's bow, surrounded by his aides, Prince Orvag II of the Gorogs stared out the window, his chin resting in his tentacled fingers, wondering how he should proceed. Did he make the call, or did he let it go? The message from the Perseus Arm was still fresh in his mind. For a moment, he considered letting the affair go, but at the last minute, decided something this serious deserved to be dealt with.

With five long, tentacle-like fingers with suction disks, the prince reached over to the armrest on his throne and pushed several buttons. Adjusting his green, golden-trimmed cloak, the prince fingered his extremely long beard of tentacles, a sign of royalty in the Gorog clan. Surveying the eighteen crew on the bridge with him who were in charge of ensuring they didn't accidentally ram into a planet, he sent the signal out, sat back in his throne, and eagerly waited for a response.

After an unnecessarily long delay and the prince's impatience being stretched to its limit, Dormak finally answered. The warden appeared in front of the entire bridge as a 3-D hologram, transparent against the windows that looked out at a field of endless stars. Upon seeing the prince, he started, then hastily gave a low bow, trying to look dignified despite the smoke that could clearly be seen behind him. "My lord," he began. "This is all—"

Orvag held up a hand for silence, causing Dormak to

stiffen and stop talking. "What is this blabber I hear? Did I give my reason for calling you?" The prince's voice floated across as cool, collected, with just a hint of ominousness behind it all, despite the fact that he didn't even raise his voice to speak.

The warden looked puzzled. "Sire, I…I don't understand."

Orvag leaned forward in his chair, eyes with horizontal pupils narrowing at the hologram before him. He opened a small space in the side of his throne and pulled a small, square object. He presented the silvery, glowing device to the warden. "Do you know what this is?"

"A disk drive?"

"Not quite." Orvag's voice became just the slightest more belligerent. "This is a disk drive containing a message I received not five minutes ago from one of your own men. And do you know what it said?"

The warden looked off camera, to where Lieutenant Jorka presumably was, attempting to avoid eye contact. It was foolish of him to ignore the smoke and guards carrying dead bodies that occasionally popped into range of the transmission.

"It said that there was an attack on Skorjion. The labor camp?" The prince sounded pleased with his deducting skills and picking apart of the warden's closed-off nature. "Which last I checked, you were in charge of managing it and ensuring its operations went smoothly?"

Dormak only managed to say a weak "Yes, my lord."

"Now, on said message, there were reports of 'being caught unaware.' By over a dozen starfighters. Tell me, Dormak, what exactly seems wrong with this picture?"

"The being caught unaware by over a dozen starfighters?" the warden asked stupidly.

"No! The being caught unaware at all!" Orvag's formerly cool tone was exchanged for a more savage and furious one as he spoke, causing the warden to step back in surprise.

"And not only that, but that you lost slaves and suffered severe damage to the main hangar and that the primary *and* secondary power generators were…let me remember the word…hang on…*'Obliterated?'*"

The warden lowered his head. "No excuse, my lord."

"Do not speak to me that way, these submissive words!" he slapped back harshly. "But that's not the main reason why I'm calling."

Dormak, now visibly trying not to look terrified, gulped loudly.

"The last thing that this message said was something about how many slaves escaped during the commotion. But what caught my attention the most was that Subject X-17, the most important slave in our roster, the key to multiple scientific experiments, had *escaped*?" The prince's voice lowered to a dangerous level. "Tell me, Dormak, what exactly do they mean by, 'it escaped?' Did it truly escape? Or perhaps… is this a matter that requires my personal intervention? I'd hate to be forced to come down there and waste my time in order to ensure that Skorjion's leadership is effectively doing their job!"

"No! No! No!" Dormak replied hastily, clearly unnerved by the words. "We're handling this just fine, I assure you! We're already prepared to send out men to find them and recapture them."

"That won't be necessary," said Orvag, rising from his chair. "It's clear to me that you need some supervision on Grimcor. Allow me to come over and help straighten out things."

The response was not what the prince expected. "All due respect, Orvag," replied Dormak, sounding a little firmer, "We do not need help. Besides, you have better things to do than micromanaging me and my affairs. I promise, we have everything under control down here. Sir."

Orvag sat back in his chair, unconvinced, but agreeing that such an affair was not worth his precious time. "Very well,

Dormak. That being said, I still want you to fly out here immediately. There are some matters that I wish for you to be in attendance for. Do you understand?"

Dormak bowed his head in respect. "I understand, sire. Thank you."

"Have Jorka keep up the search for the missing slaves. At all costs. Do I make myself crystal clear?"

Gulping, the warden answered. "Yes, my lord! Crystal clear! They will find him! You have my word!"

"Very well. I look forward to your arrival in the next few hours. Dismissed."

The hologram fizzled out as the communication was terminated, leaving the prince alone in his throne. Orvag stroked his chin tentacles thoughtfully as he thought about the message, and subsequent conversation with Dormak. Things were not looking good at the moment. X-17 was one of the most valuable assets to the Gorogs. If he truly was in the company of their enemy, it would be a real struggle to get him back. That old Terran may provide some clues to his whereabouts, but it likely wouldn't reveal his exact location. And given the current leadership, retrieving them from the cruiser was unlikely to ever happen in the first place. The king would never allow it to happen.

Orvag's father, King Fero-Shak, was the ruler of all Gorogs, and had been king for an impressive twenty-five years. At one point, he was the single most powerful ruler in the entire galaxy, commanding an army of millions and an empire spanning thousands of light-years. Sadly, his rule had taken a major toll on the king, and while he may have been a stronger ruler in years past, many in the army and navy believed that he was long past his prime. He was in his fifties, old by Gorog standards, and was becoming increasingly less effective as a ruler at war. Many in the army disliked his ruling style, and his ability to win battles was slowly fading away. He may have possessed the title of king, but everyone knew that Orvag held most of the real power behind the throne. The prince knew what it took to win battles; there was a reason why he almost never lost an engagement. Plus, he possessed the *Deceiver*, which stood as the biggest ship in the entire navy, and he held a highly favorable position among many Gorogs in the army. He always thought that he would've made a far better king than Fero-Shak. But the king still had plenty of friends, and though the ambitious prince had considered an insurrection before, he had always decided to wait until he more than outmatched Fero-Shak.

That being said, he still wielded a considerable amount of power over the Gorog leadership, the military, and the people too. His father had taught him from a young age how to properly present oneself to the public in a way that would cause them to support you. In fact, he probably had taught him a little too well. From a young age, Orvag had used his father's advice to bribe and bluff his way into becoming not only the heir to the Gorog throne, but also head of the navy and Battlefield Overseer, who would move soldiers and legions around during battle. Orvag was also a master of politics and propaganda, and knew that, as soon as he had enough men and power, all he had to do was come up with a reason for overthrowing Fero-Shak that sounded good enough to the people and he could become king. But until then, he used his standing to win battles and earn even more favor in the eyes of his men. It was time to exercise that power yet again.

He stood up from his throne, his imposing form commanding the room. "Send out the probes!" he ordered. "And get me in contact with the twins! Find those missing slaves or it'll be my wrath that you maggots deal with!"

Chapter 10

The *Justice*, Coalition warship

Taking a shower had never felt so good to Caitlin before.

After taking a short hike with one of Shane's guards, she, along with Daniel and Ms. Phillips, had reached a hallway with three empty rooms right next to each other, one for each of them. Although he had been offered the opportunity to sleep in one of their rooms, Max had vehemently declined, saying, "I'm my own lizard, not a pet." After splitting up and promising to meet in the hallway when dinnertime came, the three humans entered their quarters. They had all been greeted with a white-walled, futuristic but homey room with an insanely soft, big bed, chairs to sit at, a small mini-fridge, a table with chairs that had some food on it, a bathroom with a self-cleaning toilet and shower, a tablet with a downloadable map of the entire ship, a closet that she guessed was filled with clothing, and even a window that stared right out into space, providing a view of the stars that she could only assume that Daniel would admire. After a short walk-around of her room that lasted barely fifteen seconds, she had shut the door to the bathroom and changed out of her filthy rags, letting them go right into the waste chute in the wall. She had turned on the shower to the gentlest setting on the dial and opened the water valve, letting the water get nice and hot before getting under the stream.

It was glorious. Never had she felt so amazing in her entire life. As she stood under the water, the dust and dirt slowly washed off, leaving a brown trail of water rolling into the drain. Her body became smooth and soft once more as the grime from Grimcor was washed off, exposing the many marks on her skin from Gorog whips. Applying soap, she thoroughly lathered her body with as much of it as she could fit into her hand, until she felt brand-new. And as she dried herself, staring down at her newly cleaned self, she felt the weight of prison life slowly lift from her shoulders. Skorjion was just a memory now, stuck in the past, nothing more. And where she and the others were now seemed like a far more habitable place to live. Even suspicions about Shane didn't stop her from being full of joy and with a spring in her step, as she wrapped the towel around her midsection and set out to change into clean clothes.

 Before she could, though, she found a device built into the wall of the bathroom that, upon inspection, revealed itself to be a robot hair cutter. Noticing how long her hair was, she found the manual next to it, which thankfully had a set of directions written in English. Having figured out the machine, she plugged in her settings into it, and sat down in a small seat that popped out from the wall. Several robotic appendages shot out, and after some slashing and some hair falling to the ground, she stood up, her hair now back to its neat self, looking as though she had never left Earth in the first place. Shutting off the device, she exited the bathroom.

 She approached the closet doors, not expecting to see anything familiar behind the doors. She was in space after all, thousands of light years from Earth and the nearest pair of jeans. But when she slid the door open, she found herself staring at not one, but two pairs of clean-cut jeans, as if they had been pulled right from a clothing store on Earth. Surprised, she glanced through the rest of the closet. While there were some items that she wasn't familiar with, such a uniform eerily similar to the ones she had seen on the crew walking around the ship, she estimated that 55 percent of the closet's clothing, which was quite extensive, was stuff she had owned back home and had even worn frequently. Two drawers at the bottom of the closet, upon being opened, revealed multiple kinds of shirts, both short- and long-sleeved, and plenty of underwear and socks. Hanging from the racks above were a bathrobe, multiple pairs of pants and shorts from sweatpants to cotton ones, a tank top, and several jackets of all sizes and types. It was just as extensive as her wardrobe back on Earth, but it was surprising to see just how similar many of the clothing was to the stuff she had worn herself. Planning on asking Shane about it at dinner, she set about finding something to wear.

After a few minutes of debating with herself, she set down a basic pair of underwear, one of the pairs of jeans, some long white socks, a simple red T-shirt, and a leather jacket on the bed covers. At the foot of the bed, some black leather boots were waiting, taken from the shoe rack that she had found hidden in the back of the closet. Eager to change, she removed the towel and pulled on her clothes. She had some difficulty pulling the boots onto her feet, as the rigors of camp labor had left them wide and tough, but after a minute or two of tugging and twisting, she managed to put them on. Throwing the jacket on over top of everything else and zipping it up, she found a mirror and examined herself. You would have never guessed that just a few hours ago she was working in a slave camp, getting filthy as a result. She looked great and being in clean clothes again made her feel good. It was good to finally be rid of her rags.

She raided the food items on the table, finding a small meat sandwich, which she gulped down. Even a simple sandwich tasted amazing to her taste buds, who had gone for literally years without a bite of real food. She then found a bookshelf on the wall, picked up a copy, thankfully written in English, sat down in one of the chairs, and began to read. The air conditioning felt blissful, and things, for a time, felt normal. That is, until something that had been buried amidst the craziness of the last few hours resurfaced. And it was triggered when a single spark of blue-green electricity arched between her thumb and forefinger, briefly jolting her hand.

Caitlin dropped the book, staring at the spot where the

energy had appeared. She remembered what she had done with that one guard and immediately felt a little queasy. She examined her hands, looking for unnatural marks, spots, lines, and feeling for anything that felt unnatural. There was nothing. Nothing to indicate that she had, just a few hours ago, discharged actual electricity from her two bare hands. Taking her jacket off, she checked other areas of her body, eventually stripping bare naked, going to the mirror and scanning herself from head to toe. When that came out fruitless, she threw her clothes back on and hunted for anything that might've betrayed something out of the ordinary.

After a while, she gave up and walked back to her chair, sitting down and wondering what had actually happened down there and what had triggered it. She had never seen anyone exhibit any sort of symptoms like this, obviously. Perhaps it was some unusual alien virus that she had picked up in Skorjion, she theorized. Maybe years of being on an alien planet did something to her body. She pondered for quite some time, and could come up with nothing that sounded even remotely logical. She hoped that whatever it was, it would be temporary. The thought of returning to Earth with something like this was a dreadful one. She could only imagine what Daniel or Ms. Phillips would think. They would probably laugh at her and think she was playfully joking with them initially.

Before she could worry about this further, she checked the clock and saw that it was almost time for dinner. Gathering herself and deciding not to tell anyone about what had happened, yet, Caitlin prepared to leave the room, only to stop when she stared at the time on the wall. She walked over to the display, grabbed it off of the shelf, and upon examining the clock, realized that it was set for a 24-hour day, just like on Earth. She set it back, now thoroughly confused. The same clothes, the same method of keeping track of time, and yet…they were on an alien ship in the middle of space. But all around her she saw signs of Earth. Adding another question to her lengthy list that she intended to ask Shane, she walked to the door and opened it up. Then, she stepped into the hallway, and nearly collided with Daniel as she did so.

"Ooof...Sorry!" he apologized as he hastily moved out of her way, thus avoiding conking their heads together.

"No, I'm sorry!" Caitlin replied, trying not to laugh at the near-miss. "You were walking, I was the one who almost bumped into you!"

Daniel sighed. "Here I was thinking we were out of danger now that we were off Grimcor, but *no*." He was wearing jeans, like Caitlin, but had opted for a silvery-gray long-sleeve shirt and black sneakers instead. And, to Caitlin's delight, she noticed that he was smiling. It made her happy to see him lighten up a little after all the hardships he had endured.

"Why do you look like a member of some biker gang from the 1980s?" he asked, taking note of her attire.

She playfully twirled a bit. "Just trying something new. Also, where did they get these clothes? I swear I've seen people walking around Salt Plains wearing this sort of stuff."

"Yeah. It's strange." Ms. Phillips approached them from the side, looking a little miffed. Daniel turned to face her and immediately let out a slight chuckle, causing her face to turn red. "Is something wrong?" she asked him gruffly.

Daniel gave a very slight chuckle, clearly fighting the urge to laugh some more. "Nothing's wrong. Just...wow. Those pants are something else."

Ms. Phillips stared down at her pants, which were metallic gold and extra baggy, as though they had been pulled straight from a disco party. "They were the only things that fit, okay!" she said in an exasperated tone. "And why is this important? I'm starving, and Shane said to meet us in about ten minutes!"

At that moment, Max arrived, having removed the dust

from his scales. "Well, one of you is talking sense now!" he said in his trademark snide voice. "How about we continue this conversation on the go. That way, while you're all still being annoying, we're at least getting closer to food. Sound good?"

They all nodded, although Daniel shot a harsh glare the lizard's way. "Alright then, the lizard has spoken. Let's go. Does anyone have a map?"

"I do," replied Ms. Phillips, pulling out a small device. "Was on my table." She turned it on. "Okay, I know where to go. This way!"

She started off down the hallway, and the others followed, waiting for the smell of warm food.

After a couple minutes of walking, they all arrived at a doorway that was wide open. Inside, a long table lined with chairs stood center-stage, lined with empty plates and glasses. On the far wall were three high-profile chairs, with a window behind them looking outside the ship. Shane was seated right in the middle, looking as dignified as the first time Caitlin had seen him. On either side of him were two others who Caitlin didn't recognize. On his left was a blue-skinned, female alien with long silver hair, tattoos on her face and arms, and bumps on her chin and face in a symmetrical pattern, wearing a simple brown shirt and pants. On the right was a gray alien that had tentacles growing from his forehead, almost like the reverse of the Gorogs' beards of tentacles. He was in a blue-and-silver jumpsuit, with tall black boots. Caitlin hesitated upon seeing him, but Shane noticed her, and waved her in. "Caitlin! Don't just stand there! Come, sit down! The rest of you too! Dinner will be coming soon."

They obeyed, taking a seat near the Magnum, unrolling their napkins and silverware and setting everything up properly. Daniel found the chair next to her and sat down, Ms. Phillips sitting down on the other side of her. Max paced to the other side of the table, jumping up on a chair and sitting down in his dog-like stance, licking his chops.

"Dinner will be here in just a moment," Shane announced to the three of them, spreading out his hands. "In the meantime, I want you to meet my two assistants." He indicated the aliens flanking him. "This is Pantura, one of my top engineers." He indicated the blue-skinned female, who just smiled at them. "And this is Commander Vorlax, head of my personal fighter squadron." He pointed to the gray alien with tentacle hair, who waved. "Don't mind his tentacles, he's not related to the Gorogs in any way. He's from a different aquatic planet."

Pantura's smile faded as soon as Shane was done talking. Vorlax, however, gave them all a friendly look and said, "What's up?"

Daniel blushed, embarrassed. "Hi," he managed in a very small voice, causing Caitlin to snicker. She blushed too, upset for laughing at Daniel's awkwardness.

"This is Daniel, Caitlin, Amy, and Max." Shane pointed to each of them. "They were just rescued from Skorjion earlier today. They're our guests of honor until we can return them safely to Earth."

"Quick question," asked Ms. Phillips, raising her hand. "You wouldn't happen to have anything…familiar to us, now would you?"

Shane rose from his chair to address her as though he was the president. "My apologies in advance, Ms. Phillips, that not all of tonight's dinner will be familiar to you. Unfortunately, being on an alien spaceship for months on end means that beef and pork is hard to come by." He glanced towards the wall. "I hope that what we have tonight still satisfies your itch."

Everyone followed his gaze, looking towards the group of men carrying large platters and red glass pitchers full of liquid heading their way. Lining up around the table, they set down their supplies, lining them up down the table, as well as give Shane, Pantura, and Vorlax their own platters, with what Caitlin guessed were their own food. Then they all bowed in front of the Magnum's chair and hurry off. Caitlin examined their table. She counted at least a dozen platters of food, and five pitchers containing drinks. She grabbed the nearest handle, lifting it up to reveal a large pile of meat with a sign in front of it. It looked very much like chicken, but the sign said the meat was that of a "Eelepit." When she inquired about it, Shane told her that it was considered a delicacy out here. She grabbed a small handful of the meat, curious. She opened two other platters, revealing tons of vegetables on one, and some rice-like grain on the other. Daniel, meanwhile, was also opening others, most of which were alien, save for one. "Caitlin!" he called. "There's steak over here! Actual beef steak!"

Sure enough, there was a huge cut of steak on one of the platters, with a sign designating it as beef. Daniel, who was busy putting a huge chunk of beautiful-looking meat onto his plate, looked up towards Shane's chair. "You have cows out here?"

"How about saving the questions for after we eat?" He gestured towards their food. "Eat first. You'll feel better. Then we can talk."

Nodding, they gathered up their food, Daniel passing the steak to Ms. Phillips, setting their plates at their places, then grabbing their glasses to fill them up. One of the pitchers thankfully had water in it, and they both shared a pour into each of their glasses. Once their plates were piled high with steaming food, they grabbed their forks and knives and began to eat. The food, although in some cases tasting a bit unusual, was delicious after surviving on mostly vomit-inducing gruel for years. The eelepit meat that Caitlin had taken a small sample of was great, reminding her of the rotisserie meats she used to have. Even the strange-looking vegetables tasted good. To her left, Daniel was chowing down, clearly enjoying his meal. Despite this, he was maintaining a respectful approach to his food, as was Ms. Phillips. Max, on the other hand, was behaving less like a lizard and more like some lion after hauling away the kill. He had both of his front feet on the table and had taken to eating directly from the platters, making tons of grunting and groaning noises as he ate. His dorsal spines were raised high in the air, which she guessed meant that he was happy, but the sight of him eating so messily in the company of Shane disgusted everyone, particularly Caitlin. What's more, Shane kept giving him funny looks as dinner progressed, and Pantura and Vorlax occasionally snickered at a loud sound Max would make. It was embarrassing to Caitlin, and from Daniel's expression as he caught sight of the lizard, embarrassing to him also.

    Mercifully, the same people who had brought them their food soon arrived to carry off the platters and dirty dishes, leaving Max without any food to eat. Seeing this, the lizard promptly jumped off his chair, curled up on the floor, and went to sleep, just like a dog. Ms. Phillips stared at the sleeping reptile for a moment, then rolled her eyes. "No respect at all," she told Daniel, clearly agitated.

    "Well, what would've you had me do, push him off the gunship, to his death? I don't think so."

    They finished their drinks, everyone setting down their glasses. Shane then cleared his throat. "Right. Questions. I assume you have plenty."

    For a brief moment, they all hesitated, waiting for someone else to be the first to speak. "Don't be shy!" encouraged Shane. "I want to hear your questions."

    Daniel nudged Caitlin, causing her to speak up first. "Yes…um, we have two. First off, where are we currently in relation to Earth?"

    Shane turned to Vorlax, nudging him. "You're the expert here. Tell them."

The gray alien pulled out a tablet, examined it for a few seconds, then said, "We're in the Perseus Arm currently, about…say, 13,000 light years from Earth. Going at hyperspeed from here would be about a forty-minute ride."

Caitlin nodded. "Thank you." She turned to Daniel. "You do the next one."

"Yes." He cleared his throat. "We've noticed a lot of things that we're inherently familiar with on Earth. Things like the steak you had out for dinner. Things like Caitlin's jeans. I found a pair of brand-name sneakers in my bedroom closet. Heck, on the way in, we saw multiple aliens dressed in clothes that we've worn before. Where did you get those?"

"He's right. That's been something that's confused me somewhat. I think that if there were aliens shopping on Earth, we would know about it."

Shane turned to face Ms. Phillips, then glanced over at Pantura, who stood up from her seat and walked down to their level, allowing her gray pair of athletic sneakers to appear. They all stared at the shoes for a second, puzzled, then turned back to Shane, looking confused.

The Magnum sighed. "We don't usually associate with Earth's humans," he began. "But there was a time long ago where the Orion Coalition proposed to meet with Earth's leaders and merge our technologies. We offered to reveal ourselves to the world as a whole, but by the time that came around, the gap in technological advances had become so separated between their culture and ours that revealing ourselves would've caused mass panic and would've likely resulted in us doing more harm than good. So instead, we offered to keep our presence there a secret, and meet up with leaders from the Earth every few years or so. During this period, we would share some ideas amongst ourselves. We gave the humans the technology needed to shrink down electronic components. They, in turn, gave us the wonder of jeans and potato chips."

"You meet government leaders from around the world every few years?" interrupted Daniel.

"Yes. The Magnum and some of his advisers, the heads of the various alien groups, and some of their troops meet up with the UN," came Shane's response. "We call it the Pact of the Zodiac. We try our best to meet every few years or so, although sometimes that isn't possible. The Gorog Wars have been a major disruption to our plans. Just a few years ago, we had to cancel a conference due to something that the US government called the...what was it...the corona-something? Some sort of virus that was running rampant at the time, I don't remember it that much."

"And how exactly does a ship, or multiple ships, full of delegates land on Earth, away from prying eyes or ears?" Ms. Phillips sounded genuinely curious. It seemed like a daunting task to avoid all of Earth's people, especially now.

Shane raised his hand. "The UN had the same concerns. After the Zodiac Pact was signed, they knew that the convention would not remain a secret for much longer without a designated area to keep it hidden. So, they constructed a base in the desert here to keep outsiders out and us in. A base known as..."

"...Area 51!" finished Caitlin, now realizing the extent as to how far this relationship went. "I don't believe it! All this time, there have been aliens on our soil, and no one's noticed?"

"Well...not exactly. There have been a few times throughout history where people have seen the meetings taking place. None of them have ever managed to tell anyone else; there are special forces designed to blip memories in the event that our cover is blown. It was the very first clause of the Code that we and the Earth agreed to: 'No human, or alien, shall reveal the presence of extraterrestrial lifeforms or entities to the greater population of Earth, under any circumstances.'"

Caitlin nodded, then suddenly had another thought. "Wait...we were part of the greater population of Earth until a few years ago. What does that make the Gorogs who attacked our town?"

"The Gorogs have long since been stretching or breaking the Code, even though, to the best of my knowledge, they still adhere to the sacred law."

"They revealed themselves to a crowd of thousands when they attacked the town," Ms. Phillips said. "How then would they have gotten away with adhering to the sacred law if thousands would have seen their ships?"

"They would round up all the witnesses and kill them."

They all turned to see Pantura looking down at them. That was the first time all session that she had spoken. Her voice was smooth like glass, but with an edge to it that penetrated the bones, like the schoolteacher that had made questionable decisions in the past. Her eyes, which looked uncanny with their horizontal pupils, burrowed into theirs with a sternness that was haunting.

"I'm sorry?" asked Ms. Phillips.

"The way the Gorogs attack their settlements is by first encasing their target in a special laser grid barrier, so that no one can escape. Then they approach their target from two different sides. They then round up the inhabitants, taking prisoner those they want while slaughtering the rest. I know, because I've witnessed it first hand."

"Pantura is an expert in the field of alien cultures and strategies," explained Vorlax. "She knows all about the methods that the Gorogs use during battle. Taught me some too."

"So you're saying that, the strategy that you just described, that's what happened to Salt Plains when we were kidnapped?" Daniel's voice was no longer happy, instead featuring the shake that it always got before an anxiety attack.

"I'm afraid she's right," said Vorlax. "It's a brutal and incredibly effective way to subdue an opponent. We've seen entire towns—"

"That's enough you two," interrupted Shane gravely. "Read the room. Can you not see that Daniel is a bit upset?"

Caitlin grabbed his arm, being careful not to squeeze it too hard. "Breathe," she whispered. "Relax."

Daniel's breathing slowed down somewhat, although he still looked a little hot in the face. Ms. Phillips cast a worried glance towards her son, but Caitlin shook her head, mouthing that he was fine. She nodded and turned back to Shane.

"One more question. You said that it was your most sacred law that Earth's people do not know about you or the Gorogs. What does that mean for us? We used to assume that aliens didn't exist, until the Gorogs came along. Do you brainwash us or something?"

Shane shook his head. "If we had rescued you sooner, then maybe. Unfortunately, we can only create new memories up to a certain point. You've been in captivity for five years. That's way longer than what we can fix. So, no. No messing around with any of your brains."

"Great, because I would feel pretty violated if someone were to go poking around in my head," Caitlin said with just a hint of sarcasm.

Shane checked the time. "Vorlax, don't you have a briefing with your pilots to attend soon?"

The gray alien nodded. "I'd best be going then." He stood up, brushing himself off, then walked down the stairs and out the door.

"We should all probably go too," said Ms. Phillips. "We're all still exhausted and could use a good night's rest."

"Of course, of course," concurred Shane. "Don't worry about any mess that you made. My men will clean it up. If you need anything at all, I've linked an intercom in each of your rooms that will come directly to me. Just push the blue button and tell it what you need, and I'll see to it that it's provided."

Caitlin dipped her head in respect. "Thank you, Shane.

For dinner and for everything else." She stood up and started to walk out, Daniel next to her, Ms. Phillips trailing behind. Max continued to snore on the ground next to the table.

"What about the lizard?"

"Eh, Shane will wake him up and shoo him to his room, I'd think. Besides, he comes across as a bit of a stubborn jerk. And we certainly need less of those in our life."

They reached their rooms after a certain point, and Ms. Phillips broke off from the three of them to go to bed. Before Daniel could turn into his room, though, a hand came down on his shoulder. "Hey," said Caitlin, standing in front of him. "You've barely said a word on the walk back. You alright?"

"Didn't you hear what the blue alien–Pandora or whatever–said?"

She nodded. "I did. But we both already accepted that there was little chance that anyone else had survived the attack. The town was already destroyed before we were captured." Noticing that his face was not showing signs of improvement, she put an arm around his shoulder. "I'll come sit with you for a little bit. Perhaps my company will help you out a little."

She opened the door to his room and they both walked inside, shutting it behind them.

Chapter 11

Deep in space somewhere

Orvag fingered his intercom as he stared out into space. He was used to having bad days, but unfortunately, today was particularly rough. He had received word that a key battle in the Outer Arm had gone south, costing them multiple cruisers, which fell at the hands of Coalition destroyers. In addition, Skorjion's damage had turned out to be far worse than originally thought, as a rock face that had been destabilized in the attack had collapsed after strong surface winds knocked it down, blocking off the entrances to two of the mineshafts. Finally, there was the matter of Subject X-17. If what Dormak had said was true, then he was likely aboard the same Coalition cruiser that had attacked them. That would mean it would be extremely challenging to get him back, especially with the rumor that Magnum Shane himself, the Coalition's leader, had been aboard that cruiser. If Shane had indeed emerged to handle this scenario himself, that would mean additional protection and maximum security for all involved. To make matters worse, none of the probes were yielding satisfying results. All of them had so far been transmitting nothing but blank space. Setting the radio down, he leaned back in his throne, not entirely sure how to proceed. On the one hand, he had the task of getting X-17 back. On the other, his duties as wartime leader of the Gorogs.

It was not easy being a prince. Not only did he have to look out for the rest of his people and their best interests, he also had to worry about outside threats like the Orion Coalition. And with his father watching him and judging everything he did, it made for a miserable experience most days. He thought it was funny, just how hard the life of someone who had control over hundreds of thousands of people and who basically could wish for anything he wanted and get it could be. He used to think as a young prince that leading meant your days of working were completely over. And here he was, preparing to become king, and he was the busiest he'd ever been. Not to mention that his father was a terrible teacher when it came to the process of ruling. The old king was all lecturing, with no showing his son how to properly lead. Not that Orvag cared at all; everyone knew that Orvag possessed the real power in the Gorog empire. Fero-Shak was only a shell of his former self by this point. Only the law and the fear of the people stopped him from openly rebelling and taking the throne by force.

    A Gorog soldier approached him from the rear. "Sir," he said, bowing in respect, "King Fero-Shak wishes to know what we are going to do about the missing slave. He demands to have an update soon."

    Orvag sighed. Ever since the news that Subject X-17 had escaped had reached the king's ears, he had been demanding updates on the hour, or so it felt like. "Tell the king that we are still formulating a plan to get him back from the enemy cruiser. He will have his prize. I will deliver it to him, on a silver platter if he wishes. Go, tell him that."

    The messenger bowed. "Very good, sir. Dormak also sent a message, letting you know that he'll be arriving in a few minutes." He then hurriedly departed, leaving the tired prince to think of a viable plan to get the subject back. He thought and thought and thought and came up with nothing. None of his men would be able to manage to infiltrate a heavily-armed cruiser and smuggle a slave out; it was impossible. Simply destroying the cruiser wasn't an option, as the prize was much too valuable to lose. A cruiser this scale would likely have lots of built-in safety features in order to counter enemies. And even if they could, it was Shane's personal cruiser, which was basically a flying impenetrable fortress. No Gorog agent would be able to get inside successfully, no matter the skill level. But…Orvag knew two special beings who would be able to. He grabbed the intercom.

"Send up the hunters," he radioed. "I need to speak with them."

Ten minutes later, the door slid open and two men walked in. Two very dangerous, heavily armed men. Or aliens, rather. As they walked across the bridge deck, the other Gorogs in the room started to shake a little, for even they feared this pair. They were not Gorog soldiers, but rather, were bounty hunters, trained to find and capture or kill their targets. Orvag had taken to these two as his personal hunters, since they were the best in the business at political assassinations and causing mayhem for his enemies.

Foulor and his twin brother Vraxis were two of the galaxy's most feared hunters. Both were Travashians; green-skinned, large-bodied brutes with a great deal of muscle and physicality that made them fierce on the hunt. The species as a whole all had orange eyes, long, vampire-like fangs, claws on their hands and a set of black horns that jutted out from their skulls. Vraxis, the thinner of the two, was the technological genius and brains of the duo, with Foulor serving as brawn. Vraxis was wearing a black shirt with a brown jacket over top, as well as leather pants and black boots. Foulor was in a brown sleeveless shirt and pants that stopped about an inch above his ankles, allowing for proper view of his burly muscles. Foulor was incredibly intimidating from a physical standpoint, but he probably had failed his tests in school, judging by how dim-witted he could be; he acted most of the time like he had perpetually hit his head on a ceiling. Vraxis was much smarter, but was pretty scrawny, especially considering that Travashians were a subdivision of the Phiaks that prided themselves on their brute strength. Together though, they were virtually unstoppable, compensating for each other's weaknesses. They had managed to be an elite unofficial kill duo for some of Orvag's more challenging objectives in years past. He now had a need for them again.

"Foulor. Vraxis," acknowledged the prince. "Welcome back. Enjoying your stay aboard the *Deceiver*?"

"We are grateful that you allowed us to stay," replied Vraxis, nodding his head. His voice was a little grizzly, but still had a sense of charm and mystery laden behind it. "It's a lot nicer than our old quarters back home."

"Yeah!" barged in Foulor, in a more bombastic and permanently slurred tone that made him sound like he was drunk. "The food here is delicious!"

His brother gave him a venomous look and elbowed him sharply in the ribs.

Orvag spread his arms wide. "But of course! I would give my two best hunters nothing but the best living conditions one could ask for! But that's not why we're here, is it gentlemen?" He cleared his throat and brought out a projection disk. "I have your next target."

The two hunters gave each other a hungry look. "We're listening," Vraxis said.

Orvag turned the projection disk on, which lit up to reveal a blurry image of the target, taken from one of Skorjion's security cameras. "This is Subject X-17," the prince explained, pointing at the target. "A former slave of the Gorogs. He was interned at Skorjion camp until he recently broke free less than 24 hours ago during a raid. He was last seen boarding a Coalition gunship, up to a cruiser in orbit over Grimcor. I need you to figure out a way to get him back to us, where he belongs."

"How much if we succeed?" asked Foulor, blinking.

"If you return him to us *alive*, you will receive 30,000

units to split between the two of you," explained the prince. "Enough so that you won't need another bounty for several years." Then his voice went dark. "But if you return him to us *dead*, I throw both of you out of the airlock into space. This is not a kill mission; this is a retrieval. That means…"

"No removing anyone's skulls, alright," grumbled Foulor.

"Also no removing any spines or ribcages. No blowing them up, no cutting off their heads, no eviscerating them, and, yes, absolutely no disintegrations. And yes, Foulor, every single one of those statements was aimed directly at you."

Vraxis snickered, a hand covering his face to hide his expression. Foulor huffed and turned to face the wall, muttering something about the evils of profiling and labeling. He clearly was hoping for permission to kill. And yes, Foulor had removed several people's skulls while they were still alive. His brother did not like it, as he thought it was too messy and uncivilized, but Orvag was fine with it so long as it was done on a kill mission. Orvag sighed and pulled up a diagram of the ship that had attacked Skorjion, which was likely the same ship that had their prize on board.

"This is the cruiser that was sighted leaving Grimcor's atmosphere, the *Justice*. Intelligence reports suggest that Shane Vulkan, Great Magnum of the Orion Coalition, our chief rival himself is aboard. As such, it is heavily armed and guarded. Despite this, I have faith that you'll return the target to me *alive*. Understood?"

Vraxis nodded immediately, and after he elbowed his brother in the ribs again, Foulor did the same.

"Very well then. Are we in agreement?" asked the prince, shutting off the image projection.

Vraxis nodded. "Return him to you alive, don't kill him, get paid, I got it." He fingered his bandolier, which had two extra magazines for the dual pistols that were holstered at his sides. He gave a look at the belt of grenades on Foulor's belt. "But first…what's he to you? He didn't look like much to me."

Orvag's look turned dark instantly. "I'm afraid that's something only high-ranking Gorog officials can know. Let's just say that he's being used for…a means to an end."

Vraxis sighed. "Fine. When do we leave?"

Orvag gave him a look of mock confusion. "What did I say that prevents you from going now? I don't remember saying anything like that. Just go, now!"

They nodded, collected their weapons and turned to go. Before they did, Orvag called out, "I trust you won't fail me this time?"

Foulor opened his mouth to reply, but another elbow to the ribs from his brother silenced him. "Have we ever?" replied Vraxis, the smile of a hunter crossing his face.

And then they were gone, leaving Orvag alone on the bridge. The prince stared at the door, hoping that they would succeed. Walking on back to his throne, he sat down, staring out into darkness at the ceaseless void of space.

He had complete faith in the two hunters. As Vraxis had made clear, their completion streak was flawless. Every target the prince had asked them to kill, they had. Every hostage he wanted them to obtain, they did. Every mission they had led, they had succeeded. Every heist he needed them to pull, had been a perfect success. There was a reason why they were the most feared bounty hunters in the galaxy. But there was always that "first time for everything" that hovered over him. He hated it. He knew they would succeed, but that tiny doubt of failure continued to nag him, driving him insane.

Then the prince's once good mood was blown out the bridge windows, as the messenger from earlier returned. "Sir," he said, in between gasps of breath. "I…got here as fast…as I could! The king…I tried to reason with him…he would have none of…your argument!"

"At ease, *at ease*!" ordered Orvag, pushing his hands forward and standing up. "Slow down, breathe, before you pass out! What did the king say?"

The holoprojector in front of Orvag's throne suddenly flickered on, and the king was standing in the room with them. "Orvag!" he barked, making the prince stop dead in his tracks.

Orvag stiffly and slowly turned around to face his father, who's hologram was now glaring down at him. Though the hologram stopped at his torso, his broad shoulders were visible even here, and his face extended downwards into a mess of long tentacles. His head also was taller than most other Gorogs, and it was adorned with the gold crown of the king. His face was a hard mask of anger. He was the only person Orvag truly feared, but also one of the few he truly had a personal reason to despise. "Father!" he managed to say, trying to sound as warm as he could, although inside he was both terrified and afraid. "This call is most unexpected, please forgive me…"

"Silence, Orvag!" Fero-Shak yelled at him, causing the prince to shrink a little. He always knew when his father was angry; it was when he used his actual name to address him instead of "son." And his tone did not do anything to help ease Orvag also. "I think you already know the reason for my calling; about Skorjion. I've had multiple reports arrive at my location, all of them detailing what seems to be a large-scale Coalition assault on the camp, with heavy casualties on our men! Is this true?"

"Well, father, yes, but…"

"*It was a rhetorical question*!" Orvag shrunk further at the sentence and its delivery. "Save me whatever lousy excuses, misdirections, or lies you can possibly say to me! I already know precisely what happened! Including all of the slaves that went missing!"

"Yes, but…father, the damage to the camp is repairable, and we're already out hunting down those who escaped. We should have–"

"I did not call you to hear you grovel, son! It's clear to me that your supposed ruthlessness and efficiency in battle that I hear about all the time has been greatly exaggerated, and that you're slipping. I'm here to tell you that I'll be paying a visit in the next couple of days to straighten you out. This blunder on your behalf is grounds for another lesson, perhaps then you'll be less inclined to fail as second-in-command of the entire Gorog military!"

"But–" It was too late. Fero-Shak's massive frame had already disappeared from view. Orvag was standing alone on the bridge with his one messenger, still in shock from what he heard.

"He's coming here?" he whispered to himself, trying to keep his voice from shaking.

The messenger nodded, fearful. "Yes, sir. From what I heard, he sounded really angry–"

"Get out." Orvag gestured to the door, not wanting to hear anything from anyone for a second. When the messenger just stared at him confused, he yelled at the top of his lungs, "GET OUT!" causing the messenger to hustle out of the room. The prince whipped around repeatedly, staring around at the bridge, at all the officers who had turned in confusion at the sudden outburst. It was too soon…it wasn't supposed to happen yet! He started to pace, thinking desperately of a plan to turn this to his advantage. If the king was on his way here, that meant there would be severe consequences for Orvag. The king's military prowess had faded, but his ability to dole out punishments to his son had not. He vividly remembered the last time the king had arrived to teach him a lesson. On that occasion, he had been set on by a Solevar, a clawed, cat-like beast that had slashed him until he was in the medical wing, because he had won a battle, at the cost of almost all of his ships. The king had told him, "Victory is good, but a victory where you cannot continue onward and must turn back is almost as bad as defeat."

It had accomplished nothing, only serving to fuel the prince's loathing of the king. The scars he carried around made sure of that.

After pacing back and forth for a few more minutes, Orvag decided that he had no choice but to go ahead. After tomorrow, he would know whether his men were loyal to him or not. After tomorrow, he would know whether he was meant to be king or not.

He returned to his throne. The king would have to wait for a little while. In the meantime he had other business to take care of. Sitting down, he entered a set of coordinates into the holoprojector and hit the transmit feature on the armrest. The device beeped at him for a minute while he sat patiently, waiting for his call to be answered. Finally, Warden Dormak made an appearance, in the middle of sharpening his scimitar.

"You called, sir?" he asked, putting the blade down to give his attention to Orvag. "I'm literally seconds away from arriving…"

"Yes I did, old friend," the prince said, leaning back in his chair. "I have an important announcement. My father's coming tomorrow to reprimand me for the loss of the slaves. I hope you'll join me at my coronation."

The dining room was deserted and clean of all plates and glasses, leaving just the wood-carved table left. Seated at his chair, Shane was deep in thought. Alone, he had decided to wait behind to collect his thoughts from the past day. There certainly were a lot of them. First the attack on Skorjion, then meeting Daniel, Caitlin, Amy and Max…there was a lot to process.

The three humans seemed like nice enough people. It made Shane feel better, knowing that they had escaped a place of horrific suffering and had not lost their humanity in the process.

Max, on the other hand, seemed like a strange type of alien, and the kind that was prone to causing trouble. The way he had acted while at dinner still was fresh in his mind. But after five years of enslavement, to have them stay was the least he could do. But he did have some concerns about their return to Earth, and the Gorogs who prowled this part of the galaxy. And that was not the only concern that Shane had up front in his mind.

The meeting with the council from five years ago was still fresh in his mind, where his leadership had been wagered on the outcome of the war. Since then, he had come no closer to defeating the Gorogs, and though the attack on Skorjion seemed like a step in the right direction, it was only a temporary nuisance for them. The damage to the slave camp seemed to be repairable. The thought of surrendering his title had taken up full dominion over his brain cells, and he did not know how to silence it completely. But there was something else…something else that was lurking about in his head. A thought. One thought only, that he just couldn't get rid of. It seemed far-fetched, but, on the other hand…

Vorlax entered the room again. "You're still here? Something big must've happened," the commander remarked as he strode up the stairs to his chair next to Shane. "What is it this time?"

Shane sighed. "My deadline to win the war. It's less than two weeks away, and still nothing." He sounded drained. "What am I going to do…we're no closer to victory than we were five years before!"

The commander reassuringly slapped him on the back. "You're Shane! The person that I trained under, who could solve any problem he was confronted with. You'll think of something."

The Magnum rose from his seat, stretched, and started to walk down the stairs. He beckoned Vorlax to follow him, and the two old friends started to walk down the hallway towards the high-ranking quarters. As they went, they continued their conversation.

"What do you think of those four?" Vorlax asked Shane.

"They seem like good people. Daniel, Amy and Caitlin, at least. Max, I'm not so sure about."

"What are we going to do with them? I mean, they were in bondage for five years. They deserve to return home."

Shane nodded. "I agree with you. I'm just concerned about the group's future if they stay on board too much longer. After so long in bondage, I'm not sure that war would do them any favors. Lord only knows how much of that we have to deal with."

The two men turned into another hallway, walking past maintenance robots and flight crew. "Better safe on board the *Justice* than a prisoner in Skorjion's hellhole," Vorlax pointed out.

Shane took a deep breath. "Yeah. You're probably right. Still, I'd like to at least give them some basic combat training."

"To train them in case their lives are, in fact, threatened?" Vorlax asked.

"Yes."

"I can help with that. I'll teach them everything I know—wait, why? If they're going straight back to Earth, what's the point of training them to fight?"

"Call it an extra precaution in case the flight goes wrong. You never know, the flight path to Earth from this part of the galaxy is often riddled with Gorog ships. In the event of an ambush, they'd need to defend themselves."

Vorlax thought for a moment. "I suppose that's fair," he finally said. "I'll have the combat room prepped by tomorrow." He yawned. "I'm exhausted, Shane. Why don't we talk about this more in the morning? Maybe by then we'll be closer to the boundary between Gorog and Coalition space."

"Good idea. In that case, I'll see you tomorrow. Sleep

well."

"You too, Shane." And Vorlax was walking away, off to rest in his quarters, leaving Shane alone in the hallway. He continued to walk towards his own quarters, wondering exactly how he was going to solve his dilemma. He remembered the footage that he had seen from Grimcor of the four escaped slaves battling their way through the Gorog guards. Daniel, in particular, seemed to have a lot of skill in fighting of some form. But, deciding that that was a tomorrow problem, the Magnum turned towards his chambers and put his thoughts to bed before the pressures of his leadership caught up with him.

Chapter 12

Perseus Arm, 1,000 light years from Grimcor

Daniel had difficulty falling asleep that night, which was something that he never would have predicted in his current state. He was dead tired, sore, only recently fed a decent meal and cleaned up, and in need of a lot of sleep. He had been given the softest sheets, mattress, and pillow he had ever had the privilege of sleeping on, and he compared the sensation to sleeping on a cloud. They all had made it out safely and soon would be heading back to Earth. Yet he still couldn't fall asleep. He just lay there in bed, thinking about the last eight or so hours. Maybe it was the fact that outside his window was a never-ending void that stretched for forever. Maybe it was the artificial gravity. Whatever it was, he had difficulty entering the world of dreamland.

He had yet to formulate a complete opinion of Shane and the Orion Coalition at large. The older leader had taken his entire group under his protection, which he was grateful for after the labor of slave life. He also appreciated the society they had constructed for themselves here on the cruiser, which he had found out was named the *Justice*. The food, bedrooms, it was all great, and he could think positively that knowing that pretty much a simple burger with french fries and a camping mattress would be an improvement over his old accommodations. And, finally, he was not surprised that the Coalition was at war with the Gorogs; with such an evil ideology running around. However, while many of his questions had been answered, there were a few that still needed answering. And it was the nagging doubts, like the constant barrage of negative "What-ifs" that were keeping him awake.

He rolled onto his side, trying to enjoy the comfort of his new bed while shutting out the cyclone that his brain had swirled into. He tried to think of happier thoughts, such as the fact that he was literally in space. Caitlin was safe, his mom was safe, and they were now in a position to return to their old home at last. This must have worked, because before Daniel knew it, the lights in his room had switched on, causing him to wake. At first, this annoyed him, until he realized that they were way out in space, where the only feeble light available was from stars, and that without something to wake him up, he would likely keep on sleeping.

He stretched as he stood up from his bed, cracking his joints and stimulating his muscles, which felt much better after a decent night's rest. He checked the clock on the wall. It read 7:30. But, more interestingly, next to it was a small button that, when you pushed it, switched the digital display on the clock to reveal messages and notes. The only one in the inbox at that time had "Mg. S.V." written on the title: Magnum Shane Vulkan. When Daniel selected it, a typed message came up, like an email. It read:

"Hoping that this message finds you well-rested and in better spirits. Breakfast is at 8:00, in the same place as last night. I hope to see you there. -Shane."

Not wanting to be rude, and in the mood for some more food, Daniel took a brief shower, cleaned his teeth, combed his hair, and put on his clothes. He was just about to leave when he stopped dead in his tracks. He was missing something. His eye fell on the small blue stone that was resting by the bathroom door from where he had left it yesterday. He walked to it and picked it up, fingering the engraved words. He shoved it into his pocket, not wanting to risk losing Caitlin's gift to him. Pushing the button that opened the door to the hallway, he stepped outside and walked ten feet to his left, to Caitlin's door. He knocked on the door twice.

"Yes?" came Caitlin's voice from the other side.

"It's me," replied Daniel. "Did you check your clock this morning? I figured Shane messaged you also."

"I got his message, yes. I'm changing. Be out in just a moment!"

"I suppose I'd better wake Max up."

"Good luck with that."

Sighing, Daniel walked back the way he came, and then an equal distance past his door, until he came to the next room in the hall. He knocked on that door twice as well.

"What?" Max sounded tired and grumpy.

"Shane invited us to breakfast at 8:00. It's 7:52 currently. Do you want to come?"

The response was laconic and very on the nose: "No."

Daniel rolled his eyes, and pushed his face against the steel door. "Just so we're clear, I'm not bringing you any food whatsoever when you get hungry. Not a crumb. So unless you want to be hungry for most of the day, I suggest you get your scaly little butt out of bed and come eat with us."

There was a lot of grumbling on the other side of the door, but Daniel heard movement inside. Figuring that Max would join them after all, he walked back towards Caitlin's room.

She was waiting outside, leaning against the wall next to her door. "Is he coming?" she asked.

Daniel nodded. "Hopefully he'll behave himself this time. His behavior was completely embarrassing last night, in front of Shane no less."

Ms. Phillips walked up to them. "Sleep well everyone?" she asked.

"Yeah," they both replied. "You?"

"Best sleep I've had maybe ever."

They began to walk towards the dining hall, the conversation pivoting back to Max. "Honestly, having to constantly supervise Max reminds me of what raising a child might be like when I marry and have kids," Daniel remarked. "Just a never-ending hassle?"

"If your kid was of the scaly, prideful and toothy kind," said Caitlin with dry humor.

"If you had found him in the woods behind your house, what would you have done?" Daniel asked her.

"I would have grabbed Charlie's shotgun and filled that monster full of bullets until he was dead. Especially if I had known previously what his demeanor was."

"Fair enough."

"I honestly want to know what his parents thought of him growing up," commented Ms. Phillips.

"Trust me, we all do."

They continued to chat as they went along, until they reached the dining hall, where Shane was sitting in his customary spot at the head of the table. "I see you received my message this morning. Do come in! Breakfast should be ready soon!"

They all took their seats, eager for a hot breakfast and not cold gruel. There already was a full glass at each of their seats. The liquid inside was a pale purple, and seemed to pulsate with a strange light. Taking his, Daniel swirled it around, and it instantly changed color and became a bright shade of ice blue, much to his surprise.

"I see you found your glass of Glistll juice," spoke up Shane, staring down at them.

"My what?" asked Daniel.

"Glistll juice. It's a rare delicacy, made from the dilated juices of a Nrazse's intestinal tract mixed with some horrak berries and an apple. Sometimes served with the eggs of a Walrag fish, like mine." He raised his glass of the liquid, swirling it around slightly to reveal the bulbous eggs resting on the bottom, as well as change its color to that same ice blue.

"When you swirl it, the berry juice reacts with the intestinal fluids and gives it its ice blue color. Try it! I swear it won't kill you."

Over next to Daniel, Caitlin was mixing up her own drink. Ms. Phillips had already done so, and was examining her blue-colored concoction. He stared into his own glass. No eggs, but digestive fluid from some creature? He sniffed it gingerly. It had a very prominent smell to it, almost like apple cider, only *much* stronger. It made him back away a little bit. It all sounded…different, for sure. Then again, it certainly looked and smelled better than water. But the strength of the drink's smell made him look back up towards Shane's booth. "It's not alcoholic, is it?" he asked. "Because I don't drink."

"Non-alcoholic," he replied. "There is an alcoholic version available, but it's quite potent, so I don't think I'd recommend it for your first beverage."

Daniel turned back to his glass and picked it up. Caitlin and Ms. Phillips picked theirs up as well. They all turned to each other.

"Cheers," they said, clinking their glasses together. Then they each took a sip.

It actually tasted quite good. It was cold and refreshing, and tasted like sweet apples mixed in with watermelons. It also had another flavor in it that Daniel couldn't quite pinpoint; he guessed it came from the digestive fluid. But it still was tasty, and he took another, bigger sip.

"Mm…this is quite good," Caitlin piped up. "Better than I thought it would be."

Shane nodded, and then turned to face the entrance as Max walked in, looking ten years younger. Daniel noticed this too and started to snicker uncontrollably.

"Am I late?" he asked, yawning widely, once again exposing his masses of coned teeth.

"No…you're not," said Shane, who had one eye cast

down at Daniel, who was still trying his best to not laugh.

"What is he laughing at?" The lizard pointed at Daniel, who turned and faced him, still trying to hold it in. Ms. Phillips turned to stare at the lizard and became slightly red in the face.

"Eating the pillows, were we?" Daniel managed to say.

Caitlin, still busy drinking her Glistll juice, turned at Daniel's voice, and almost snorted out her beverage at the sight of Max's jaws, completely lined with feathers and what looked like toilet paper.

Max grunted out a single "Yes" before finding a spot on the other side of them, taking a napkin between two talons, and wiping away all the loose feathers from his mouth. Shane sighed loudly. Daniel and Caitlin both chuckled to themselves. Max simply finished wiping away the remnants and yawned again, waiting for the food.

A minute later, the food came in. Unlike the row of trays and platters that had filled the table up last time, this time, it was just one plate for each of them, all covered with a silver lid. The waiter set them down in front of them, brought Shane his food separately, then hurried back behind the kitchen doors. Daniel stared at his plate, wondering what was hiding underneath the lid. He expected something alien, but when he pulled the lid off, he was greeted with a sight he had not seen in years.

Caitlin just stared at the meal in front of her, not sure if her eyes were deceiving her. "Shane," she began, "What is this?"

"I figured you would be missing the tastes of home," the Magnum replied down from his podium. "So I put in a special request to the kitchen this morning to make the three of you biscuits and sausage gravy. Just the way they make them on Earth."

"Is it real?" asked Ms. Phillips in amazement.

It was. There were no tricks, no lies here. In front of each of the four of them was a huge, warm, buttery pile of biscuits and gravy, looking exactly like their families used to

195

make them. Daniel took a bite, and immediately nearly cried from the sheer joy of it. It was perfect in every way, the biscuits, the thick coating of gravy and the bits of sausage that inhabited it. On his left, Caitlin's face wore a smile Daniel had nearly forgotten existed. "Thank you!" he told Shane. "Thank you so much! This is fabulous!"

"Happy to be of service."

Breakfast was gone in a flash, and once their plates had been cleared away, with everyone still hungry for more, Shane stood up and addressed the room. "Guards? Leave us, please."

The two bodyguards at the door both turned heel and left the room, as did Max, who requested to leave early to nap, leaving Daniel, Caitlin and Ms. Phillips by themselves. Shane sat back down, reaching below his podium and pulling out a small flash drive.

"So, some good news. We should pass out of Gorog territory and into safer quadrants by late tonight. Then we can set you all up with a ship back to Earth and let you drop there safely."

"That's good," said Ms. Phillips, swallowing down her gravy. "So why do I hear a catch in your voice, Shane?"

"An intelligence officer intercepted a message from a secure Gorog transmission line early this morning, and they managed to partially decode it. The problem is that it seems to possibly refer to the four of you. Allow me to play the transmission." He pressed a button on his screen and static started to play, with voices occasionally cutting through the foggy white noise.

"...glad that you made it safely," one of the voices sounded, a younger, authoritative voice that commanded the room with a sense of danger behind it. "Be thankful that Skorjion's damage turned out to be repairable, otherwise this meeting would be far less amicable."

"Thank you, sir. What's the word on the king's arrival?"

came the other voice.

Daniel stiffened with bitterness. "That's Dormak's voice. He's the warden in charge of all Skorjion!"

Shane perked up. "Dormak? He's one of the top Gorogs. You've run into him?"

Daniel nodded. "He was the one who raided our town and kidnapped us in the first place!"

"…one of my most fervent supporters," the first voice said. "I trust your opinion on my dear father hasn't changed at all since you last stood before me?"

"No sir, I firmly believe that you are the best choice to lead us," Dormak said. "Old Fero-Shak ran out of steam about ten years ago."

"Correct answer. And what of Subject X-17? Is there any information that you wish to give me?"

"Subject X-17?" repeated Caitlin, now listening into the conversation. "Who's that?"

"Not as of right now, sir." Dormak's voice.

"Just keep searching. I have just sent out the twins to extend the search for the escaped prisoner, and any fellow slaves he may be traveling with, since the cameras show him leaving with a group. Hopefully they will yield better results than you have. Have you uncovered any additional information thus far?"

"No sir. Everyone's a little in the dark about this."

"Really? Well they'd better figure something out soon. X-17 is the key to all our future plans. We cannot hope to proceed with him not around…"

The transmission stopped, and silence descended upon the dining room. The good feelings of the morning were gone. Daniel, Caitlin and Ms. Phillips all looked slightly alarmed. Shane, meanwhile, looked disturbed, and deep in thought.

"Did you hear that?" Daniel said, indicating the transmitter. "They were talking about us!"

Caitlin nodded, face a little pale. Then she saw Shane's

face. "Shane!" she called up to him. "Is everything alright?"

Shane didn't answer, instead walking down from his podium towards them. He clearly looked bothered by something. He walked to the other side of the room and began to pace back and forth.

"What is it?" Caitlin asked again. "Is something wrong?"

"Do any of you know who that first voice belonged to?" asked Shane, sounding a little rattled.

Daniel and Caitlin exchanged a glance, then shook their heads simultaneously. "I'm afraid not," replied Daniel.

"That was Prince Orvag," explained Shane. "The heir to the Gorog throne and the leading general in the Gorog military. He's been the biggest thorn to our efforts to pick out the Gorogs from their bases and defeat them."

"What does it mean for us, if he's looking for us?" inquired Daniel forcefully.

"It means," said Shane, "That if he's involved with this, then whatever purpose you were originally serving down in Skorjion was of the utmost importance. Orvag doesn't interfere with escaped slaves unless it's a matter of extreme concern to him."

"Perhaps it has something to do with the one they mentioned, Subject X-17?" asked Caitlin.

"Could be," said Shane. "Not sure who that would be, as we picked up dozens of escaped slaves that day. Whoever they are, they must be incredibly valuable to the Gorogs. An escaped slave doesn't usually attract attention from the Gorog's second-highest ranked official."

Daniel buried his face in his hands. "Great. We're being hunted by the Gorog prince, along with all his best men, and they're after a Subject X-17, that, for all we could know, could be anyone of us."

"Us?" Shane asked incredulously. "What do you mean,

'us?'"

"If Subject X-17 was an escaped slave, that means that anyone of the escaped slaves could be him. Well, all the male ones anyway," he added, after Caitlin shot him a suspicious glance.

Shane sighed loudly. "You're right. I'll see if my intelligence officers have picked up any other mentions of X-17 in past transmissions, and see if we can't obtain some more information. In the meantime, since you all are still waiting to depart, I have something that you can do to keep yourselves occupied."

"And what's that?" asked Ms. Phillips.

"Vorlax and I both talked last night, and we agreed that, even though it's unlikely, there is a chance that a Gorog ship could intercept your craft when it leaves for Earth. We want you to have some basic combat training. He's offered to help tutor you both in basic defense and attack, and help hone your skills with weapons. Oh, and I guess the lizard too."

"You want us, the three of us," said Daniel, pointing back and forth between him, Ms. Phillips and Caitlin, "To be trained with weapons? Like, *your* weapons?"

"If you're going to ask, yes, Vorlax proposed laser rifle training for you both."

Daniel and Caitlin both pumped their fists in excitement. Ms. Phillips only showed mild enthusiasm meanwhile. "I'm getting too old for this sort of thing," she said. "I'll be happy to watch the two of you though."

"When would we start?" Daniel inquired.

"Take a couple of hours to recharge and explore the ship. Say, about…10:00 in the morning, which is over two hours away, meet Vorlax in the combat training simulator. I'll post directions onto the tablet map that you two used to find this hall last night, so that none of you get lost."

Daniel bowed his head in respect again. "Thank you,

Shane," he said. He turned to Caitlin and his mom. "Come on. Let's find Max and take some time off our feet. We'll feel better."

She nodded, and they turned to leave, Daniel's arm around Caitlin's waist. Shane watched them go, and once they had passed through the doors, contacted Vorlax on his transmitter.

"What did they say?" the fighter pilot asked Shane, while his hologram clearly applied his special anti-drying wax to his skin.

"They agreed. 10:00 today. I gave them some time to themselves. They could all use some extra rest. I told them to explore and wander around."

"Did you tell them about the drone you sent to their town to check in on it?"

"No. They've been through enough. Telling them about the dead we found there would only make them feel worse."

"That's terrible. Losing a friend is bad, but to lose an entire town…that's truly one of the hardest things we can face. I've lost hundreds of my 1,803 siblings in my life. Many more died before I even knew what the heck was going on around me. But I never lost a whole town on my home planet."

"I'm not sure you understand with that many siblings." Shane huffed. "Well, best to not disturb you at the moment. Are you planning on coming in for breakfast?"

"In a few minutes, yes. What's on the menu?"

"Biscuits and gravy, Earth-style."

"Really? I've heard that's the best way to make it."

"It certainly is delicious. Although it's also a fast means of getting high blood pressure, from my experience eating it. The amount of salt they put in it is…something."

"Looking forward to it. See you shortly."

Shane nodded and switched the transmitter off. As he sat back in his chair, the door slid open, and Pantura walked in, looking almost cat-like with her mannerisms and movements. Her bright blue skin was eye-poppingly bright against the white and red walls and steel gray floor.

"Pantura?" Shane asked. "I thought you were eating separately and going straight into the ship repair depot to work on some of the fighters damaged in yesterday's raid."

"I was," she replied. Her voice was surprisingly gruff this morning, lacking in humor and very businesslike. "And I still intend on doing so."

"Then what are you doing here?" Shane demanded. "If you're not here to eat, that is?"

"I wanted to ask you a favor," she explained. "Those three Terrans that we picked up from Skorjion; I feel like they could use someone to help guide them through the ship; a sort of mentor-figure. Someone to help answer any questions they have, since they'll likely have lots."

Shane fingered his neck and his beard. "You're not wrong, you know. I'd be here for another five hours trying to explain every way things are done around here to them. But…why you, of all people?"

"I studied social economics, remember? I also used to be an ambassador to the Chorax before I was put in engineering. I feel like I'm qualified to help them along, unless…you disagree?"

"No, that's a great idea. They're heading to the combat simulator at 10:00. If you finish your shift in the repair bay early, you might be able to catch them before lunch. And, Pantura?"

Having started to walk away, she turned back to face Shane, a question on her face.

"Beware the lizard that often accompanies them," said Shane. "He's a shifty little bugger. Gives me the creeps."

She thought about this, then nodded briefly and left.

201

Chapter 13

The three humans spent most of their time wandering around the *Justice*, taking in the sights and using their digital map to avoid getting lost. It felt strange to be around this many people, as there were hundreds of crew members wandering the central ship atrium, from aliens to humans. There was constant chatter in the air, like a busy city block, as groups of friends discussed current events with each other, sometimes in foreign tongues that the Earthlings could not understand. Occasionally, they saw a human or alien dressed in regular clothing, not unlike what they were used to seeing on Earth, even if the shirt sometimes needed two neck holes to accommodate the alien's two necks. Still, it was a bit jarring to everyone to see alien lifeforms walking around wearing Marvel T-shirts and wearing jeans or sweatpants.

Every four minutes or so, the atrium was filled with a loud roar as a train barreled through the monorail above them, usually followed by a different train going in the opposite direction. "Anyone want to check out the monorail?" asked Daniel, watching the underside of a car go past.

"Yeah, we still have time," said Ms. Phillips. She pulled up the route that Shane had downloaded onto the map. "And it looks like we'll need to take the train to get to the training room anyways."

They found a station perched above the main walkway, with an elevator leading up to it. They took the elevator up to the platform and mingled in with the dozen or so other people and aliens waiting to board. After a minute or two, a train swiftly pulled into the station and slowed to a stop, humming loudly as the magnetic breaks kicked in. The doors slid open smoothly and a dozen or so passengers walked out, their idyllic chatter adding to the already noisy station. A crowd of crew members pressed forward, and the three humans were pushed forward, passing through the doors and onto one of the many leather couches set up in the car. They squeezed into their booth and sat down, bathed in the soft blue light of the overhead lights. Other passengers boarded and took up standing positions around them, and then the doors shut and the train launched forward at high velocity.

"So," began Daniel, as the atrium sped past them, "What's the plan for when we return to Earth tomorrow?"

It was a question that had been bothering him for most of the morning. "I don't know," replied Ms. Phillips. "I'd assume that we'd check on the house, see if it's still standing first thing. It'll probably need to be cleaned after all this time. Assuming that someone else hasn't already moved in..." Her voice trailed off, wavering slightly. "In which case we'll need to find a new house somewhere else..."

"We can worry about that later," said Caitlin gently, stopping Ms. Phillips' fretting. "All I know for sure is that I may have to move in with y'all. Otherwise, we don't know enough about the status of Salt Plains to make any final decisions. So how about we end this conversation now and think of something else to talk about?"

There was a brief silence. Daniel and his mom exchanged a look, and then both nodded. "Yeah, I guess you're right," said Daniel.

The train stopped at another station, and a bunch of passengers walked out of the car, as a new batch came in and took their place. The three remained in their seats though, trying to think of a conversation starter. Caitlin hoped that it would be something trivial, something that was unimportant in the end, something that would create some laughs.

"So...what about that transmission from the Gorogs?" asked Ms. Phillips, a little quietly.

Caitlin tensed up and remained silent, but Daniel immediately jumped into the web. "I don't know," he said, though his voice meant that he clearly did know about the seriousness of that message. "I've upset a number of people in my years, but to be on the most wanted list of an entire alien empire?"

"Yeah that's not ideal." Ms. Phillips stared out the window at the rapidly-moving scenery. "At least we're in a secure ship heading away from enemy territory. That should count for something."

"Still, I get the feeling that something's not right. That something's...off. I can't quite put my finger on it though, only that I really, really want to get off this ship sooner rather than later."

"We all do, Daniel." Caitlin once again was the only calm person in their booth. "But if leaving a little later allows us to guarantee safe passage home, I'd rather opt for that. Wouldn't you agree?" She inclined her head at him. "You alright? You're sweating a little bit."

"Fine. Just a bit hot, that's all."

The train halted to a stop again. "This should be our stop," said Ms. Phillips rising from her seat. "Now let's go see what sort of training Vorlax wishes to put us through."

They all got up from their seats and left the train, shoving through the oncoming passengers and down the elevator from the station back into the main atrium. They crossed the pathway and entered a small side corridor, which the map then directed them to follow until it branched off. As they went along, Caitlin fell behind slightly, beckoning to Daniel to join her. He nodded and slowed his pace until he was behind Ms. Phillips.

"What's up?" he asked her as they passed a group of guards on patrol.

"Can I ask you something? Hypothetical, that is?" she replied, sounding a little nervous.

"Um...sure, what's up?"

She sighed. "Let's say, that, tomorrow, for instance, they found out that I had some really rare condition that wasn't going away. There was nothing that Shane's doctors could do to fix it. What would you say to me, in that scenario?"

"Well, what do you mean?"

"I mean, what words would you have for me, when you found out about this condition?"

Daniel chuckled a little bit. "That's a really strange question, you know. Well, what sort of condition are we talking about? Strange mutation on the body? Or some weird thing that you seem to be able to do?" He then checked his words, and added, "Or is it something else that I'm not thinking of?"

"Let's just call it a physical change, how about," she clarified.

"Okay. Well, in that case, I think I would have to remind you that, even with whatever you were dealing with, you're still the same, amazing person that I know and love. Sure, there may be some changes in the way we interact, but by and large there would probably be little difference in the way I looked at you. Because even with all your physical changes, you're still the same old, wonderful friend that I've known for all these years. And no body changes would ever change that for me."

Her face lit up at his encouraging words. "Thanks. That means a lot to me," she said, quickening her pace to rejoin Ms. Phillips.

"It's still a weird question, though!" Daniel called out after her, running to catch up.

They ascended another elevator up several stories and through more twisting corridors until they finally arrived at the doors to the Enhanced Combat Training Simulator, or E.C.T.S., two giant metal doors that towered over the two friends.

"Well that's certainly a first impression," quipped Caitlin, staring up at the closed doors.

Daniel had to crane his neck slightly just to see to the top of the entrance. "I don't see a keyhole or keypad anywhere, do you?"

"Not one." Ms. Phillips scanned the door itself. "And I don't see any sort of knob or handle to open the doors either."

Just then, the doors slid open with a loud hiss, revealing Vorlax standing right behind them, arms crossed. "What are you doing standing there?" he asked. "Get in here!"

Daniel gave Caitlin a funny look, then obeyed, Ms. Phillips followed right behind them. The doors slowly closed behind them, and they were left basking in the sight of the massive chamber that surrounded them.

The E.C.T.S. was huge, a giant cubical room almost a hundred feet wide and tall that towered over everyone. Reinforced metal walls lined the sides, floor, and roof. High up on the other end of the room, a set of windows peered down from an observation deck, in view of anything that transpired within it. A set of small doors lined one wall, shut closed. And in the middle, a variety of different objects were scattered haphazardly on a raised platform jutting from the floor.

Caitlin whistled in astonishment. "It's...big, for sure."

"*Big* is the understatement of the year," replied Daniel. "Just look at it!"

"Yes, it's big," Vorlax acknowledged. "Designed to fit small tanks in here for certain simulations and training modes. Don't get your hopes up, though, you're far too inexperienced in this sort of thing to be doing a pretend battle against a bipedal walker. No, you'll be starting with the basics; firearm and sword training."

"Wait, wait, wait," exclaimed Daniel. "Did you just say *sword* training?"

"Yes. Yes I did." Vorlax sounded confused.

"This isn't the Middle Ages, Vorlax, with all due respect. I'd think that with all sorts of laser rifles, ships, and whatnot, you'd have evolved past crude melee weapons."

"Don't worry. Our swords are leagues ahead of your simple sticks. Trust me."

Daniel shrugged. "Ok. Show us what we'll be using."

Vorlax approached the platform in the middle. On it was a pistol, a rifle, what looked like a submachine gun, and a rocket launcher. In addition, a long metal rod and what resembled the hilt of some melee weapon rested, shining in the white light from above. "These are the basics. You have your D-67 pistol, your FF-7B rifle, the *Leviathan*-1 RPG, and the 7-V plasma SMG for your main firearms. You also have a metal staff and a sword."

"Sword? I don't see a sword," said Ms. Phillips.

"It's that, right there." Vorlax pointed to the hilt.

Daniel couldn't help but snicker, despite his best efforts. "Vorlax, I hate to break it to you, but there's no sword. Unless the blade is invisible, I only see a hilt."

To his surprise, the alien nodded. "You're actually not that far off, Daniel. Here, take it." He picked up the item from the table and handed it to Daniel, who tested its weight and feel.

"It's shockingly light," he remarked, swirling it around in his hand. "Feels good too."

"Now try it after you push that button on the center of the crossguard."

Daniel turned the hilt over. Sure enough, a small gray button protruded from the center of the crossguard. It was almost invisible against the steel gray of the hilt, and only about as half as wide as Daniel's ring finger. He stared at it, confused.

"This whole thing isn't a cruel joke, I hope," he said, with mock threatening in his voice.

"I swear, I'm not pranking you!" protested Vorlax, though he still had a cocky grin. "Just push the darn thing already!"

Daniel sighed and pushed the button. He then gasped, as a series of loud metallic noises grated out from the hilt, and fragments of blade shot out from the top through a narrow slit, elongating to form a two-foot long metal blade that grew in his hand. Caitlin and Ms. Phillips both were staring, wide-eyed, at the weapon. Daniel's eyes cast over the blade itself. Shiny, probably brand-new, with no traces of chips or damage. The individual segments of the blade seamlessly transitioned into each other, making the sword feel like one large piece of metal. He pushed the button again, and the blade retracted into the hilt. He pushed it yet again, and the blade reformed. He swung it around, effortlessly, as it had very little weight to it. The sharp edge hummed happily as he did. He felt the blade edge with his finger, then hastily pulled his hand away with a pained grunt as he opened a small cut in his fingertip, which started to bleed.

"It's incredibly sharp," he remarked, staring at the cut in his finger. "And well-balanced, too."

"May I see it?" asked Caitlin.

Daniel nodded and handed her the sword hilt to grasp. She took it, taking a few swings too, one of which came close to chopping Ms Phillips' head off.

"Watch it, you!" exclaimed Vorlax. "We don't want any amputations in here, do we!" Then he paused and wondered, out loud, "Unless she can grow it back."

Caitlin and Daniel burst out laughing. Ms. Phillips, oblivious to the whole affair, simply turned around and said, "What? What's so funny?"

Ignoring her, Caitlin handed the weapon back to Daniel. "It's quite an elegant weapon," she told Vorlax. "It feels great."

Daniel examined the blade again, feeling the metal surface. "What's it made of?" he asked.

Vorlax turned to face him. "What?"

"The blade, what's it made of?" His gaze passed over the shiny metal. "It doesn't feel like any substance I'm used to."

"It's made of a substance called Xaphorium," the commander said. "Same metal we put on the hulls of our ships and tanks."

"Xaphorium?" repeated Daniel. "Never heard of it."

"It's not a metal on your periodic table. There are quite a few elements like that out here. It's normally a very soft, easily malleable substance found heavily in asteroids. But when you expose it to certain types of gamma radiation, its atoms realign and become much more rigid, giving it a tensile strength greater than tungsten, while being over a third lighter in weight. We use it for weapons and for ship hulls!"

"Interesting," Daniel murmured thoughtfully, still gazing at the blade. "What supplies the gamma radiation?"

"We started out with plutonium, then polonium, before settling on another metal not found on Earth called fuarenum. Its specific gamma signature yields stronger xaphorium overall. It's fairly rare, though, so samples can be pretty hard to come by, but it has an incredibly long half-life, so it's useful for long periods of time."

"That's super cool," Caitlin said. "Will we be using these in our training?"

"If I agreed to that, Shane would have my head," explained Vorlax. "So, no, you will not be using the metal ones. Instead, you'll be using these."

He reached down to the side of the platform, opened a small hatch, and pulled two wooden practice swords instead, made to mimic the metal ones.

"Now, no one's at risk of getting their arm chopped off. Just do me a favor and try not to deliberately swing them hard. They won't chop, but they'll still break bones."

He handed one of the swords to Daniel, then gave the other one to Caitlin. He then turned to Ms. Phillips, who was looking back and forth between everyone.

"No, don't worry," she said. "I'm too old for this sort of thing."

"Normally I'd disagree, but here…yeah, you're probably

right." Vorlax then turned to his new students as Ms. Phillips took a seat. "Now, Daniel. Caitlin. Take two steps away from each other and turn to face each other."

Still holding their practice weapons, they obeyed.

"Before we begin, do either of you have any prior experience with weapons training?"

"I have maybe five minutes," confessed Caitlin. "And it was with a whip."

"I practiced some staff and stick training several years back, when I took martial arts," said Daniel. "I should have some fundamentals knocked out already."

"Very well, I'd advise you to take it easy on Caitlin there, Daniel, given that information. Now, on my command, you both will start fighting each other. Slowly, mind you. And Ms. Phillips, feel free to enjoy the entertainment. We don't need to make this any more chaotic."

"Wait, hold on!" Caitlin whipped around to face Vorlax. "Are you not going to teach us any techniques first?"

"I'm a firm believer in 'learning on the job,'" he replied, backing away from them. "Now. In three. Two. One. Go!"

Daniel looked awkward. He had never fought his best friend in this way. Especially not with an alien instructing him to his right and his mom watching from a distance. Across from him, Caitlin looked the same way. For a few seconds, neither of them proceeded or did anything. They just stood there, weapons in hand.

Finally, Daniel said something. "Well, I suppose we should at least try," he told Caitlin. "I'm going to start attacking you, okay? Block my swings."

She nodded. "Ready."

Daniel paused for a second, then raised the sword over his head and swung in a slow upper-left cut, aiming for Caitlin's head. She raised her own sword to meet his and blocked it with a wooden *thunk*. Daniel followed it up with an underhand swing, which Caitlin again parried.

"Good start," Vorlax told them. "Try increasing your attack speed slightly. See how that works."

Daniel gave Caitlin a look, then swung twice more at her, both moving with a little more speed. She managed to block both strikes, but nearly missed the second parry, causing her to stumble slightly. A third overhead blow from Daniel was brought down upon her, and she barely managed to parry. But when a fourth strike from the lower right came her way, she failed to deflect it and was hit in the hip by the wood.

"Ow!" she cried, pain lancing through her hip and down her leg. The blade had hit the cap of her hip bone, causing her to pick her leg up in a reflex.

"Oops! Are you okay?" Daniel quickly asked her, lowering his weapon.

"Yeah. Yeah I'm fine," Caitlin said, through slightly gritted teeth.

"You see why we don't use Xaphorium blades when training initially?" Vorlax asked them, sounding vindicated. "In all seriousness though, that was not a bad first attempt. I've seen way worse than that for beginner swordsmen and women. Try again, same speed as before. Caitlin, spread your feet apart so you can dodge the blade too if you must."

Caitlin readied her grip on her blade and spread her feet out a little bit. Daniel resumed his onslaught of attacks, remaining at constant speed, but varying in their position, trying overhand, backhand, and diagonal cuts in an effort to break through Caitlin's defense. Though she was bruised a couple of times, she soon started to get the hang of blocking blows.

After some time, they switched, and Caitlin went on the offense. Daniel, with his martial arts training, meant that he had some experience with melee weapons, and did a little better than Caitlin, though he was still hit by the blade a couple times, resulting in bruising and pain. He powered through anyway, swinging the oaken sword around with deft ease thanks to its lightweight design.

After about an hour had passed, their blows became faster and harder, and they started to move around the room more. Vorlax intervened several times to teach them specific moves and techniques that they could use, before stepping back to allow them to resume their duel. By this time, Daniel had mastered the feel of his training sword and was twirling it about with insane speed and accuracy. Powerful strikes came down on both his and Caitlin's weapons, sending shocks down their forearms every time it happened. Occasionally, one would be hit by the other, pausing the training for a few seconds while the injured person had a moment to rest his arm. Then the action would resume. This cycle repeated itself for an hour and a half, with Daniel and Caitlin performing their whirlwind of attacks.

Eventually, though, Vorlax called for a timeout. "I think that's enough sword training for today," he said, holding out his hands and taking the two practice swords from the pair. "You all did fabulously for your first time with one. Especially you, Daniel, which makes sense given your past history."

"I was worried that this would feel drastically different from a normal weapon, but it's not that different," he admitted. "It's at least easy to handle."

"Even staff usage can greatly improve your ability to use another handheld weapon, like a sword," Vorlax told him. "And that was fine form you were showing there. I think with a little more polish and refinement, you could be an accomplished swordsman one day."

"Thank you, Vorlax," Daniel replied.

As silence threatened to descend on the room again, Ms. Phillips spoke up. "Alright, that was fun. Now, is lunch going to be provided?"

Vorlax glanced out of the corner of his eye at her. "I messaged the kitchen to have lunch delivered here shortly," he said politely. "It can't be more than a couple more minutes. Ah! There it is now!"

Two crew members in uniform had entered the room carrying trays with food on top. "Commander Vorlax!" they called out. "Where should we put the lunch you requested, sir?"

"On the center platform would be fine!" he replied curtly. "And be snappy about it!"

The men obeyed, leaving the trays on the center platform and hastily exiting the room. On the trays were several types of food to choose from. One of which was just a plate of what appeared to be whole raw fish, their heads and tails still attached.

"This one's mine," Vorlax told everyone, gently pushing Ms. Phillips aside and picking a fish up, taking a spice shaker and coating it with a white seasoning that looked like salt, then taking a bite out of its head, its eye and cranial cavity going into his mouth.

"Ew…" Caitlin said, turning a little green around the edges. Daniel felt his stomach heave as Vorlax bit off the rest of the head and chewed slowly. Ms. Phillips weirdly looked unaffected, if a bit offended. "You eat them raw?" she inquired to Vorlax.

"Cooked seafood never did it for me," the commander replied, taking another bite. "A byproduct of my constant time out of water. Unfortunately, my body hasn't quite adapted to life outside of an ocean, so I need to hydrate several times throughout the day and take a bath daily. Raw fish contains some extra minerals that cooked fish doesn't normally have."

Ms. Phillips simply went "Huh?" and then found her own lunch and began to eat, even as Daniel went green around his cheeks for a second.

Once his stomach had settled, Daniel examined the rest of the tray's contents. There were some basic french fries on there, as well as sausages on buns. "What type of sausages are these?" he asked Vorlax.

"Gerreti sausages," he told Daniel. "Very high-class meat in the Coalition's best restaurants."

Daniel picked up his sausage bun and took a bite. The meat was rich and flavorful, coated with spices that added an extra kick to it. On his left, Caitlin was sighing happily, a big bite out of her food.

"Mmm…this is really good," she said through a big mouthful of food. "I'm consistently impressed with how great alien food tastes. I'd have laughed if you'd told me, but it's true."

After enjoying and finishing lunch, combat training continued, with Vorlax moving on to the basic plasma guns that he had laid out on the table. He started with the pistol, a firearm no longer than Daniel's hand, and fairly non threatening in appearance. The weapon had a handgrip with the trigger, a small casing in the back for rounds, and a barrel-like 'tub' that sat just behind the barrel. It didn't look like much. But when he pulled the trigger in a demonstration shot, a hot bolt of energy fired out and left a round burn mark on the opposite wall.

"Our rifles and pistols and such have been designed to breach most types of combat and riot armor. The plasma inside is swirled around in this chamber just behind the barrel until it is superheated from friction, then it escapes through the barrel at high velocity to hit its target. It is a bit heavy, though, so hold it firmly." Vorlax then handed the pistol to Daniel, who felt the gun for a second, then did a series of practice shots at a metal target that rose from the ground in front of the wall. His aim was not great, to put it kindly. Though a few shots managed to hit the actual target itself, by the time his round was over, there was a large ring of marks surrounding the target on the wall behind it.

Then it was Caitlin's turn, who performed slightly better; more of her shots hit the target, with one getting close to the bullseye, but there was still a ring of burn marks on the wall when she finished. She put the gun down and removed the pair of safety goggles she had been given, walking back to Daniel and Vorlax.

"How did I do?" she asked.

"Better than he did, that's for sure," Vorlax told her. "But still not great." He took note of their body posture and facial expressions. "Are you two tired?" he asked them.

They both nodded. "We could use a break, yes," Daniel said tiredly.

Vorlax gave them a thumbs up. "Very well. How about we call it for today? Go sit down and take a rest. You both did great for your first day. We'll pick back up tomorrow, same time."

They both nodded again and sat down on the edge of the platform. Vorlax then turned his attention to Ms. Phillips. "You sure you don't want to at least try anything?" he asked. "I've known some pretty seasoned folks who could shoot a rifle just as well as a rookie."

"I appreciate the offer, Vorlax," she replied. "But I'd prefer to watch."

"You forgetting someone?"

They all turned around to see Max standing in the doorway, looking vindictive. The lizard stalked forward, his red-brown scales glistening in the combat room's bright lights.

"Where have you been?" demanded Caitlin, placing her hands on her hips.

"Sleeping," the lizard replied. "I needed some extra after that escape mission."

"It's after 2:00!"

"I could've gone for longer," Max replied smugly. "Except that I heard that combat training was taking place here, so I came to show off my own skills."

"Well," began Vorlax, "How about you show us your combat skills? Demonstrate how you dismember your enemies. We'd love to see it."

Max raised an eyelid. "Is that…sarcasm I hear coming from your throat?"

Vorlax shook his head quickly. "No, not at all. We're all just curious, you know?"

Max sighed. "Fine. I'll show you all." He strode towards the far wall several paces, before turning and facing them, as if he was waiting for something.

"I need a practice dummy, please!" he ordered.

Daniel rolled his eyes. Vorlax sighed and pushed a button on the platform. Immediately, two robot dummies emerged from trapdoors in the floor, entering onto the field switched on, armed with rifles and equipped with wires dripping from their chins to more resemble Gorogs. After a moment where nothing happened, they realized that they were powered off.

"These things were likely going to the scrapyard anyway," Vorlax mused. "Feel free to rip into them as best you can." He pushed another button, and both robots sparked to life with jerky, artificial movements. Their photoreceptors glowed green, and when they turned around and spotted Max, they changed to red and began to fire their rifles at the lizard.

"Their plasma bolts are only blanks, so they won't kill!" yelled Vorlax. "But I'd advise not getting hit by them anyway!"

Max barely paid any attention to him, as he jumped on the first dummy and proceeded to rip the arm that was holding the rifle clean out of its socket, leaving a mess of wires behind. Tossing that aside, Max then dug his claws into the base of its neck and ripped its wiring clean out, causing the first dummy to power off. Ignoring several hits from the other bot, he then leaped off like a cat as the destroyed bot collapsed on the ground in a heap of spare parts. He then used his tail to sweep the second bot to the floor, then sprang forth in a predatory fashion before clamping his jaws hard around the fallen dummy's head. He then slowly began to apply pressure, while the pinned-down opponent fired off random shots, several of which nearly hit Daniel, Caitlin, Ms. Phillipsand Vorlax. Sparks began to fly from the robot's head, until it too shut off, leaving itself unmoving on the floor.

Max stood up onto his paws, breathing heavily. The second bot's head had two giant dents on each side where Max's jaws had applied force. Both of the old dummies were lying on the ground, the arm from the first tossed off to the side a good ten feet away. The session lasted less than a minute. Vorlax was simply staring, wide-eyed, at Max, as was Ms. Phillips. Daniel and Caitlin looked less surprised.

"Now, those two are officially scrap," said Max, walking past them without another word. Vorlax didn't even turn. He just continued to stare.

"Did he just…wow," he said dazedly.

"Yeah. You should've seen him when he escaped Skorjion," Caitlin told him. "He absolutely murdered several Gorog guards, even ones with riot armor on!"

"He was with you in Skorjion?" asked Vorlax.

"Not initially. He sort of joined us partway through. None of us know anything about him, other than that he's constantly grumpy and is really good at killing everyone." Ms. Phillips sounded serious, but Daniel could see a faint hint of a cocky grin on her face.

"Interesting. Well, perhaps we should give him a medical examination. Test his blood and his anatomy."

"Max would never consent to that," Daniel told him. "We'd have to drag him, kicking and biting and roaring." Caitlin nodded in agreement.

Vorlax gave him a mischievous smile that unnerved Daniel with how similar it was to Caitlin's own. "I think we can solve this. Just leave it to me."

"What will you do?" asked Caitlin.

"Make a couple phone calls. As for you two, go enjoy

yourselves! Maybe Shane would let you use his private swimming pool. He never uses it anyway."

Before either of them could reply, the door slid open again, and this time, it wasn't Max. Standing in the doorway, looking blank-faced, was Pantura. Her arms were folded across her chest and her eyes narrowed.

"Pantura!" called Vorlax. "This is unexpected. I thought you were in engineering."

"I'm here under direction from Shane," she replied, and Daniel heard her voice for the first time, very matter-of-fact and mostly humorless. "I'm here to help assist young Daniel and Caitlin here, and Amy, in adjusting to our culture. He asked me to give them some lessons."

"That's a great idea! I'm sure Shane is happy you volunteered to be their tour guide." Vorlax turned to the two of them. "Alright you two, Miss Pantura here is going to help guide you through our wonderful little culture aboard the ship. Don't let her intimidate you, she's harmless. And remember, dinner's at 6:30! Don't be late!"

"We won't!" Caitlin told him, as they all scampered off to walk out with Pantura.

While the three's time with Vorlax was special in its own way, Pantura proved to be a far more enigmatic presence, lacking the humor that Vorlax was full of, swapping it out for a more businesslike manner. After sending Max away to nap in his chambers, the two friends followed the blue-skinned alien through the ship's labyrinth of corridors, passing a large munitions depot and the entrance to the hangar where they had come in yesterday, and taking an elevator several levels up, until they arrived in the officer quarters, where officials like Vorlax slept, stopping at a room with "Pantura Rhodtz" written on it. A passcode interface was set on the wall, and after Pantura had typed in a few digits, the door clicked and opened up.

"In here," she told them, walking inside.

Her room was much larger than the quarters they were staying in, with a giant bed, two tables, one with a transmitter and map, and another with several chairs surrounding it, a large storage area built into the wall, and a bathroom. There was also an intercom on the wall, which she probably used to contact Shane. She indicated the table, and Daniel, Ms. Phillips and Caitlin, after hanging up their jackets, sat down opposite Pantura.

"So, Shane tells me you three are both escaped slaves from Skorjion?" she asked them. Although there was no humor in her voice, her tone was far from threatening.

"Yes," Daniel said. "We all are."

"You two should be proud. Very few ever escape a Gorog slave camp, especially one as well-fortified as Skorjion. It's not an achievement you should take for granted."

"I'll feel better when we're all home safe and sound."

"I'm sure you will, Ms. Phillips. Shane told me about everything. He also said that we may be out of Gorog territory sooner than expected, so you may be getting back earlier than anticipated."

Daniel sighed in relief. "Thank you."

"Right. So, what do you two want to know about our culture first? I studied sociology for a long time, so I have a lot of information that I can divulge."

They took a moment to think about this, as to what they really wanted to know about this new side of the galaxy that they had never seen. To Daniel's surprise, despite not being the one obsessed with astronomy at childhood, Caitlin spoke first.

"About the Zodiacal Conference," she inquired. "Who normally attends? In detail please."

"The leaders of the fifty largest countries on Earth attend, as well as the Magnum, the three Deacons of the council, and delegates from the six major subspecies of the Phiaks and seven subspecies of the Quelliks. The last few conferences had only six of the Quellik groups there, as the Gorogs did not attend."

"*Major* subgroups?" repeated Caitlin. "Just how many total subspecies are there?"

"Not counting the Primitive groups, about 1,800 between the Phiaks and Quelliks," answered Pantura. Adding in the Primitives would bring the total up to 16,700."

Daniel and Caitlin's jaws both fell open. "That's a lot of alien species," Caitlin said, rubbing her forehead.

"16,700?" Daniel sounded shell-shocked. That figure was way higher than he expected it to be.

"Only 1,400 of those are capable of speech, and only about 150 of those are represented to a high degree in the Coalition," explained Pantura, in her teacher voice. "We've been trying to improve connections elsewhere in the galaxy, but the war going on has hampered things quite a bit."

"And what kind of alien are you?" asked Ms. Phillips. "I mean no offense by that, by the way."

"No, you're fine. I'm technically half-human, you know. Shane did an analysis of my DNA when I joined the *Justice's* engineering team and was found to contain human proteins. As for my other half, well, they're not a hundred percent sure. All they know is that it's Quellik in origin, so part of my ancestry is aquatic."

"Interesting. That explains the slight webbing on your fingers." Daniel pointed out the small hints of it between Pantura's digits.

"Do you have gills?" asked Caitlin. "Odd question, I know."

Pantura pulled back her shirt collar to reveal smooth blue skin. "I'd show you the actual traces, but doing so would require me to become naked. And having studied your Earth customs, I know that you would find that…offensive?"

Daniel nodded quickly. "Yeah, probably to be honest."

They asked some more questions about the galaxy, from more questions on its wildlife to its government. Then the discussion took a darker tone. "How did you and the Gorogs start fighting in the first place?" asked Ms. Phillips.

The room turned a few shades darker at the mention of the Gorogs, as did Pantura's face. "That's not exactly a happy story," she warned them, her voice very serious and somber now.

"Please," Caitlin said, sitting back in her seat.

Pantura sighed. "No one for sure knows how the Gorog Wars began. It started a little over forty years ago, when the Gorogs gained a new king, the mighty Fero-Shak. Now the Gorogs have always been a bit of a warlike group, but they usually fought amongst themselves, and had split into several rival groups by the time he became king. Fero-Shak became the first Gorog king in six centuries to unite all of the planet Tersak, and he did so by declaring that they were the dominant alien species in the galaxy. All others were to be subjugated or killed, by force if necessary."

"So they're basically fascists?" asked Caitlin.

"In a way, yes. The difference is that Earth's fascists acted too swiftly, and thus overextended themselves, leading to their eventual downfall. The Gorogs waited for almost two decades, building up their military reserve and formulating plans that would lead to the takedown of their neighbors, and eventually, the Orion Coalition. Eventually, they declared their independence from the Coalition and began causing trouble around their system. When they seized a nearby moon and killed a fifth of its population, Shane's father, Volcazan the Great, declared war. The two sides have been at war for almost twenty years at this point. When Volcazan died, Shane then took over in his place. Fero-Shak meanwhile continues to cause trouble, especially now that his son, Orvag, the Gorog prince, has joined the war efforts."

"Has any effort been made to stop them entirely?"

"Yes. The raid on Skorjion was the first Coalition strike on Gorog-sanctioned territory since the early days of the war. Shane hopes that it will not be the last one either. At the moment, he plans to strike at the other large-scale Gorog labor camp in their lands, Rhozadar, on the planet Lhassi."

"Rhozadar?" asked Ms. Phillips.

"The largest labor camp of them all, and the location of the principal wartime factories that create the Gorog army's weapons. Destroying that would effectively cripple the supply lines and severely disrupt the advances of Fero-Shak's forces. Shane hopes to attack it in the next few days, since he uncovered a special shortcut to it during the Skorjion raid." Pantura sighed and glanced over towards her window. "Shame you'll have to miss it. Shane's been looking forward to this."

"Not really," replied Daniel, scratching the back of his head. "I've had enough Gorogs for one trip. I would love to simply go back to normal for a bit, and I think we'd all agree."

Before any of them could ask another question, the door swung open and Vorlax barged in, out of breath and with his tentacles hanging down from around his skull. "Vorlax!" exclaimed Pantura, standing up immediately. "A little knock would have sufficed!"

"Sorry to barge in like this Pantura," he replied, "But it's urgent." He took a peek around the room. "Where's the lizard??"

"Uh…last I heard he had returned to his quarters!" Pantura followed Vorlax around in confusion. "What is going on?"

"It's Shane. He sent me to tell Daniel, Caitlin, Max and Amy that they're leaving now before the Gorogs arrive."

Chapter 14

Perseus Arm, roughly 5,500 light years from Grimcor

They all burst onto the bridge, out of breath and sweating slightly from running the entire way there. Daniel, Caitlin, and especially Ms. Phillips placed their hands on their knees, gasping for air. They did not even notice the dials, switches, holograms and all the crew members wandering around the crowded area, nor did they notice the giant wraparound window overlooking the entire ship. All they saw were Vorlax and Pantura running over to Shane and bringing him over to them.

"You made it! Good," he said. "Sorry about the short notice, but that seems to be what we're operating on at the moment."

"What's the problem?" asked Caitlin, standing up straight to address Shane.

"There are two Gorog ships that our scouts reported were heading this way. We're not sure how long it is until they arrive, but we want to get you all off the ship beforehand. There's a ship being prepared in the hangar for your departure."

"How long until it's ready?" asked Daniel.

"My guess would be ten more minutes. Gather anything that you need for the trip back and be prepared to board in a moment's notice. Pantura will accompany you." Shane turned to face her. "Right?"

"I'll protect them with my life," she replied, bowing and ducking off of the bridge.

"Who's leading the Gorogs?" asked Vorlax. "Have we figured that out yet?"

Shane shook his head. "Still waiting for a visual

confirmation of the cruisers. That will tell us more about our foe. If it's just a captain out on a lead, we'll be fine. On the other hand, if Fero-Shak or Orvag appears, that'll be a bigger problem. Be prepared for anything." He turned back to the three humans. "Has anyone found Max yet?"

"No, sir," said Vorlax. "But I sent some men to check on his quarters. If he's there, he'll be coming up shortly."

"Good. You three, do you need to pack anything before you leave?"

They all shook their heads. "Just the clothes that we're wearing," said Ms. Phillips. "And maybe some money for when we get back?"

"I'll handle the finances," replied Shane. "Vorlax, go get your squadron. If there's going to be a battle they'll need to be briefed. You three, stay here for now. I'll let you know when it's time to head to the hangar."

He walked off, talking to some other crew members as they ran about, checking screens and monitoring statistics all over the room. There were no seats that the three humans could see, so they moved forward, past a giant holographic table with a three-dimensional map of space, and into a slightly more open part of the bridge that terminated in a curved window staring out into space. Daniel found himself drawn to the view, where hundreds of stars sprinkled the field in front of the *Justice's* hulking silver and blue hull, wrapping around them. Caitlin moved to stand beside him.

"Get your view in while you can, Daniel," she told him. "Because we're about to leave for Earth. This will be the last time you see alien constellations anywhere."

He did not reply, for he was lost in thought. Something about this whole thing had seemed fishy. They were almost at the edge of Gorog territory, where there were bound to be ships patrolling, but it was several thousand light years of border to inspect. The odds of two cruisers being in the right place at the right time seemed…odd. To make matters worse, how had they been found in the first place. Shane seemed way too methodical to allow the Gorogs to track them all the way from Skorjion.

"Shane?" he called across the bridge.

"Yes?" The Magnum approached him.

"How did the Gorogs find us? Could they have been tracking us since Skorjion? I'm no expert in math or anything, but when there's a border this long to check, aren't the odds of two cruisers being there and immediately knowing where we are seems a bit low to you?"

"They definitely haven't been tracking us. We scanned the entire ship for potential homing devices and switched all our radio channels to a frequency that they cannot locate. Whatever it was, it has to be something else."

"Can you check for small transmissions? Like, small transmissions, from an object smaller than a starfighter?"

"What exactly did you have in mind?" Shane sounded slightly confused.

"Have the people of Earth ever introduced you to *Star Wars,* Shane?" Daniel said, moving across the bridge, looking for a potential scanning device.

"They have. I think it's supremely entertaining, but how is that relevant to small transmissions?"

"Remember, in *Empire Strikes Back*, how the Empire used probe droids to locate the Rebel base?" Daniel sounded dead confident in his assessment, as he continued to search the bridge walls for scanners. "Have the Gorogs used such devices in the past as well?"

Shane immediately stopped, then pulled his communicator out of his pocket. "Vorlax," he asked. "You've been watching the scanners of late. Has there been any, I don't know, repeating signals coming through in the last 24 hours or so? Like, really small, smaller than a starfighter. Like, the sort of signal that probes send."

There was a brief pause on the other end. "Yes," Vorlax eventually said. "There was a repeating signal. And now that I think of it, we should've been paying closer attention to probe droid signals like that."

"Enough of that! Just get the fighters ready!" Shane hung up. "This is bad. If the probes caught us, they'll have scanned the entire ship. They'll know how many troops are on board and the proper breaching points."

At that moment, an alarm started to blare and the lights all turned red. "Sir!" called out a crew officer. "The scanner just picked up two Gorog cruisers entering the region! Five clicks out and closing in fast!"

Shane ran over to the holographic table, where two sizable dots were creeping onto the map, getting closer to the *Justice's* blue icon. A second later, another officer ran up. "Sir! We're receiving an incoming transmission from the enemy!"

Shane whipped around to face him. "Patch them in," he commanded, stepping back from the hologram.

The map retracted into the table and was replaced by a gigantic digital image of a shadowy figure, sitting on a chair. "This is Commander Vraxis, speaking on behalf of Orvag, High Prince of the Gorog Empire. I demand to speak with Magnum Shane Vulkan."

Shane cast a nervous glance behind him at Daniel and the others, before turning to face the transmission. "This is Shane, Magnum of the Orion Coalition and Commander of this ship. And I demand an explanation for this ambush. Where's the actual commander of your fleet?"

"I'm leading the squadron, with permission from Orvag himself," came the sinister reply. "I'm here to collect a large bounty on a group of individuals aboard your ship. They're of top importance to the Gorog Empire and their war efforts. I'd like them to be handed over and get paid for my wasted time here, if you don't mind."

"What options do I have?" demanded Shane sternly. "And what prompted Orvag to have you lead an entire fleet by yourself, Vraxis?"

"If there's anyone who's up to the job, it's me. Let me break it down for you how this is going to play out. Either you send over the four individuals who escaped Skorjion to us, which includes three Terrans, two of them female, and one lizard, or we board your ship and take them by force. We don't care how many of your men we have to kill to reach them, Shane. Orvag really, really wants them back, and when he wants something, he'll move the whole galaxy to get it."

Shane put his hands behind his back, and waved Daniel to stand behind him. "Take Caitlin and Amy and get to the hangar," he whispered, out of range of the transmission. "Look for the large gunship. Pantura and your driver will be waiting outside."

"But what about you?"

"I'll be fine, now go!" hissed Shane, pointing. Daniel hastily nodded and ran to his friends, who were still waiting in the middle of the chaotic bridge.

"Who were you talking to?" demanded Vraxis. Then he turned to face off-camera and shouted, "Foulor! If you enter this transmission with your shenanigans, I will put you in therapy for the rest of your goddamn life! Now get back to your place!"

"What's happening?" asked Ms. Phillips.

"Two Gorog ships are closing in fast," said Daniel. "We're heading down to the hangar. Pantura's going to meet us there with our ship home."

"What about Shane?" asked Caitlin.

"He's staying behind. Listen, we need to move before the Gorogs have a chance to attack. Does anyone have a map?"

Ms. Phillips presented the tablet. "Got it right here."

"Let's go." They all ducked out of the bridge, leaving Shane behind, still talking to Vraxis.

"I was never told that my men picked up slaves during the raid," continued Shane, stalling as best he could.

"Do you deny that they could be on board?"

"No, of course not! I just wasn't informed of their presence, I suppose."

"You play a good game, Shane, but lying through my pointed teeth is something that was par for the course when I became a hunter. Now, where are they? I will not ask again!"

"If you want them, come and take them!" shouted Shane at the hologram.

"Fine. I'll pry them from your dead body if I have to. Orvag will likely shell out a nice bonus for your death. Don't say I wasn't reasonable!"

"I don't want to hear the word "reasonable" used to describe any of you scum," Shane fired back. He waved the hologram away, then grabbed the intercom on the dash. "Attention all personnel! Two Gorog cruisers are heading this way! Everyone to their battle stations!"

The three humans bumped into Max on the way, who was looking a little groggy. "What's…happening?" the lizard asked, looking around in blind confusion. "What's with all the alarms?"

"Gorogs. Here for us, from the sound of it," replied Caitlin, looking a little helplessly at Daniel. He shrugged.

"What she said. Come on, we're running to the hangar. Going to clear the heck out of dodge before the Gorogs can start their attack."

They all took off, passing through crew members running about and pilots joining them in the mad dash to the hangar. Thankfully, the wide open atrium made it impossible for bottlenecks to form, and they soon were standing in the entrance of the hangar, which was crawling with more pilots and crew running about, refueling fighter engines and restocking their weapons. In the back, they saw a large, silver-and-blue ship parked. "That must be the one Shane mentioned," said Daniel, pointing to it. "Come on." They ducked and weaved through the hangar, nearly bumping into several personnel on the way, passing underneath the engine of a starfighter at one point, until they saw Vorlax's mess of tentacles peeking through the throng.

"There's been a slight change of plan!" he informed them as they arrived. "Max, you're leaving with them also. More seriously, the transport blew a circuit in the last fifteen minutes. We're switching gears to that orange attack gunship over there." He pointed to a bright, metallic red and orange ship with a large wingspan parked not far away. "Pantura will escort you on board and fly you out."

"How long do we have?" asked Ms. Phillips. "Before we'll be cut off?"

"From my guess, five minutes. Gorog starfighters are fast, they'll be here before you know it. You should get going?"

"What will you do?" Caitlin turned to face him.

"I have to lead the fighter squadron in defense of the *Justice*. I'll be fine, now go, before it's too late!" He waved them off, and they, along with Pantura, took off towards the waiting ship.

They ascended the boarding ramp into the ship, which at first seemed cramped and narrow. Then Daniel saw the ladder leading up into a hole in the ceiling. "This is the hyperdrive deck, you fools!" yelled Pantura in annoyance. "Use the ladder!" Her angry shouts goaded Daniel into scampering up the ladder, into the central room of the gunship, where a holographic table was surrounded by chairs. Two doors were shut in the back, hiding what was there. The others pushed up behind him, staring around at the interior. At the front, four chairs were parked in front of the viewscreen.

"You three, sit up here," said Pantura, striding over to

the cockpit and sitting down in front of a huge dash with all sorts of controls and screens. She began to flick switches and power the ship up. "And buckle up! This could get hairy."

"Where will I sit?" demanded Max angrily behind them.

"You're a lizard. You have claws! Dig them into a support beam and hang on tight."

"They're not meant to be used when traveling aboard an alien spaceship!"

"Make it work!" Pantura flipped a knob on the dash and the engines roared to life, vibrating the ship like a massage chair. She grabbed the wheel in front of her and lifted it up, the ship moving in tandem and lifting off the hangar floor. Everyone lurched forward as the ship shuddered slightly.

"Guess I can cross "alien ship" off my bucket list!" yelled Ms. Phillips over the increasingly loud engines.

"Same here!" replied Caitlin, who was gripping the seatbelt straps like her life depended on it. Behind her, Max was sitting by the hologram table, gripping the table hard with his claws. Daniel tightened his seatbelt and prepared for launch. The ship's vibrations grew more intense and Pantura made final preparations as they started to inch forwards towards the dark void ahead. On their right, they could see the first Coalition starfighters launching out of the hangar.

"All systems are a go," she told them, looking back. "Are you all ready for launch?"

Daniel nodded, as did Caitlin. Ms. Phillips hesitated before doing the same. "Just try and take it easy, please, if you can," she said. "I'm not sure how my carsickness will fare on an alien spaceship."

Pantura gave a curt nod and pushed the throttle without warning, causing everyone to be pushed back in their seat from the force of the acceleration. The hangar's edges passed by them in a flash as they were propelled into the darkness of space, the gravity briefly fluctuating for a second before their ship's own artificial gravity kicked in. The engines now smoothly hummed with energy as Pantura turned them to the right. It was a glorious sound, the kind that made your adrenaline pump out and fill you with euphoria.

"What if the Gorogs see us?" said Daniel, still gripping his seatbelt.

"The hull is made of Xaphorium! It would take a serious laser blast to cause any damage!"

"That's good to know!" said Daniel, although he was still having doubts.

"Should be lined up for the jump to hyperspace in about two minutes," she said. "Hang tight! We'll get you home!"

On the Gorog cruiser *Tyrannical*, Vraxis watched the monitor as a few dozen blips were launched from the Coalition cruiser, heading towards the ships that he had launched just moments ago. "Captain Frashur," he said. "Are our ships in attack formation?"

"Yes, sir," said an elderly Gorog with tentacles hanging down from his chin to his breastbone, and eyes that were slightly bulbous.

"Good. Have them target the cruiser's starboard side defense, and prepare the boarding craft to land inside the main hangar. Make sure that the troops are ready to go when the time comes!"

The captain nodded and ran up the stairs to the next level of the bridge. Vraxis turned to his other side, where Foulor was checking his bandolier full of grenades. "What are you doing?" he demanded. "You've been checking that thing for about twenty minutes!"

"I need to make sure that it's all full!" Foulor explained, in his usual slightly slurred voice. "I can't go into battle without a full stock of grenades!"

"If you're missing one or two grenades, it's no big deal!" growled his brother. "Now get on down to the hangar and meet with the troops. I'll join you momentarily."

Foulor grunted in anger and sauntered off. Vraxis turned back to the monitor, where there was now a small cloud of ships moving his direction. But as he looked, he saw one of the ships break off from the main formation and forge a new trajectory away from the battle. "Captain," the hunter called out. "What's with that one ship that's leaving the sector?"

"We've scanned it, sir. Appears to be an attack gunship. Not sure why they're breaking formation from the rest of the fleet."

"How many lifeforms are aboard?"

"Five, sir. Thermal imaging is reading very high temperatures on one of them, sir. We're not sure why."

Vraxis stopped. Orvag had mentioned that one of his targets, a lizard, had an unusually hot body temperature. He had also said that it had a very specific heat value, one that no other species of alien that he had seen had. Looking at the reading, that reflected with this new signature. That meant only one thing.

"That's them. They're trying to escape. Have the batteries open fire upon that ship. Shoot to disable their hyperdrive, not destroy it. And get me a proper scan of the passengers as well. We're not about to lose Orvag's prize just yet!"

Back on the gunship, Pantura was punching in some coordinates. "Almost got it," she said, steering them to the left of the two Gorog cruisers lurching into view. Both ships were massive, almost as large as the *Justice*, and bearing down rapidly on the Coalition forces. Their path would take them past both enemy vessels into a safe part of the sector. "Making the jump in thirty seconds!"

There was a brief flash of light, and then the ship was rattled about, causing everyone to look around wildly. "Did we hit something?" asked Daniel, looking outside the window.

There was another flash of light, followed by more shaking. "No, those are laser blasts," replied Pantura, her voice wavering a little as she checked the scanner, then looked outside the viewscreen. One of the Gorog ships had changed position to line up their portside turbolasers with them. And every single one of those turbolasers was now spitting plasma beams their way.

"How long until the jump to lightspeed?" said Caitlin weakly, her skin turning pale again.

"Ten seconds!" replied Pantura, charging up the engines. Everyone gripped their seats a bit tighter as they barreled through space, the ship shuddering slightly with every laser. But as she reached to pull a large lever on the dash, their ship suddenly rocked hard from side to side. This time, warning lights came on all around them, and the engines suddenly quieted. Daniel did not know a whole lot about ships, in fact, he knew nothing about them, but that seemed like it was a bad thing. And Pantura's confused, deeply worried face backed up that claim.

"Hyperdrive's been hit!" she yelled, as they were jostled by another hit from a Gorog turbolaser. She grabbed the steering wheel and pivoted them hard back towards the *Justice*. She activated the intercom. "This is Pantura, contacting Shane. The Gorogs hit our hyperdrive system and we're turning back!"

"We're going back?" repeated Ms. Phillips shrilly.

"We can't survive out here without a hyperdrive!" replied Pantura harshly, increasing their speed. "We need to get you all back to safety!"

"What's going on out there?" bellowed Max from the back of the ship.

"Nothing, everything's fine!" Pantura yelled back.

"Fighters!"

The word from Caitlin was loaded with terror as she pointed at several fast-moving blips in space moving their way. Pantura cursed under her breath and veered away from the oncoming enemy. "Hang on!" she called out. "This is going to get rough real fast!"

Daniel clutched the seatbelt securing him in as they were spun around to avoid a stream of laser fire. Strong positive g-forces pushed him down into his seat as they climbed up, the pursuing fighters following like a flock of vultures. The ship shook around them as dozens of lasers slammed into them, but no damage was recorded.

"Shields are holding steady," said Pantura, concentrating hard on twisting through the laser grid.

"Are there weapons on this thing?" shrieked Caitlin over the commotion.

"Yes, but someone needs to man the rearview gunner in order to shoot back!"

Ms. Phillips immediately unbuckled her seatbelt and stood up, wobbling over to the back. "Where are you going?!" yelled Daniel in fright.

"To help!" she replied, starting to climb a ladder into a space above the central room. "How do I control it?"

"Use the handles to aim, red buttons to fire! That should be all you need!" replied Pantura, turning around for just a second to speak the instructions.

A moment later, they saw blue bolts coming from their rear, a sign that Ms. Phillips had figured out the cannons. Daniel scanned the region outside the window and saw that the Coalition starfighters and the rest of the Gorog fighters were engaged in battle some distance away. "Pantura! Can you try to lose some of our pursuers in the battle over there?"

She followed his gaze. "I can try!" She steered them towards the mess of dogfighting ships, more vibrations rocking them around as their shields absorbed enemy fire. She performed a downwards roll, spinning them around as lasers shot their way. Behind them, there was a loud thud as something heavy impacted the floor.

"*Too much, you fools!*" yelled Max, over the roar of the engines and sounds of lasers firing.

"Just grab onto something!" retorted Caitlin in anger.

"I can't grab a hold of anything when you spin like a goddamn moron!"

"Make it work!" called back Pantura, as a muffled explosion came from behind them. One of Ms. Phillips' lasers had found its mark and left a smoldering wreckage drifting in space forever.

That would be the last good luck they had that day.

Pantura gripped the steering wheel and performed a series of acrobatic maneuvers as they tore through the battlefield, laser cannons flashing around them like they were at a rave party. They grazed a Gorog fighter as they passed through, bumping them around some more, but as they emerged on the other side, there were still a ton of fighters on their tail. Perhaps even more than before. And now they were attracting the attention of the larger cruisers as well, as a huge blast missed them by feet, having been launched from a turbolaser.

"That didn't work!" Pantura was sounding desperate as the proximity alarms whined around them. She glanced down. "Shields are down to just forty percent!"

Then there was a huge thud on the backside of the hull, and a huge arc of electricity shot out from the steering wheel and up Pantura's arms. She yelled in pain, her seatbelt coming undone as her arm fell down, and was knocked out of her chair, falling onto the ground. The ship, now pilotless, continued to drift in the same direction.

"Pantura!" cried out Caitlin, as the ship rocked around them and started to nosedive. She unbuckled her seat and pulled her onto the floor, kneeling beside her. Daniel, meanwhile, saw the empty steering wheel, and, without thinking it through, jumped into the pilot's seat and grabbed the wheel, pulling them up out of their dive and slamming them all down with more g-forces. The enemy fighters followed them, spewing out more lasers in the process.

"What are you doing?!"

"I'm saving our lives, Cait!" Daniel's voice was deadly serious as he banked them right, passing by the hull of the *Justice*.

"What's happening down there?" shouted Ms. Phillips.

"Nothing! Keep shooting at them!" called out Caitlin, before turning to Daniel. "Have you ever flown an alien spaceship before?!"

"No, but I have driven a car!"

"You never had your license! And this is way different!"

"You didn't even have your learner's permit! Who else is going to fly?" Lasers fell around them as he looked her in the eye temporarily. "Someone has to save our skin!" He turned back to the window and banked hard to the left, jolting Caitlin so hard she slammed into her seat. Hastily, she scrambled to move Pantura into Daniel's chair, strapping her in, before taking her own seat and buckling hastily, all while being barely able to stand from the earthquake-like vibrations that were rocking the gunship back and forth.

The ship's dashboard was incredibly complex, and there were too many buttons to figure out in such an intense situation. Daniel found the shield readout and the scanner of nearby ships. "Caitlin, do me a favor and watch these two screens! If either of them are looking bad, tell me!"

She found them both. "Okay! Right now, there are about eight Gorog starfighters on our tail!"

"Is Pantura alright?" said Daniel, nearly slamming into the burned hull of a destroyed ship. Which team it had been on, he could not tell.

"She's unconscious, but she should be fine. If we survive!"

"'*If?*'" yelled Max from behind.

There was another explosion from behind them, as Ms. Phillips landed another shot with the turret. Ignoring Max, Daniel swung the ship around and lined up their attackers with the *Justice's* turrets. Several of the fighters were shot down and went spiraling out of control. The ship continued to vibrate as their shields kept taking a beating. Daniel found the thruster controls and boosted them forwards, swooping down through the area, rolling to avoid more lasers. Max slammed down behind them again and let loose a string of curse words. Ms. Phillips started to miss her lasers more and more as Daniel's wildly inexperienced flying got to her.

"Whoever's flying down there, you're making me sick!" she hollered down, shooting at the pursuing Gorogs.

"How many ships on us?" Daniel asked, weaving between two huge chunks of debris.

"Four!" Caitlin replied. "Watch out, more coming up behind us!" Her hands were turning blue-green again, and she hastily put them out of sight as she felt energy start to emerge from them.

They shot down two more ships, and a Coalition starfighter destroyed a third, leaving just one Gorog on their tail. Before they could celebrate, there was a horrible noise. It sounded like a generator dying after it had run out of fuel, and when Daniel chanced a glance at the dash, the shield monitor was completely red. A second later, the entire ship shuddered much harder than before, and they started to lose control.

"They've breached the shields!" he yelled, struggling to control them. He flew over the *Justice's* bow, and a wave of huge lasers were thrown up, nearly hitting them several times. Caitlin screamed as one passed right in front of the cockpit screen. He swooped around the bridge, losing more power, the ship continually shaking and giving everyone a headache.

The hangar came screaming into view. "Hold on, Caitlin, this is about to get really bad!" he told her, sweating hard as he tried to keep them on course, the ship fighting his control every step of the way.

"Are you flying down there?!" yelled Ms. Phillips from above.

"Not the time, mom!" Daniel hastily scanned the dash and started pressing buttons, hoping that one of them would be the landing gear. After a bunch of trash was ejected from the back, Daniel found the correct button. The hangar was almost in view, smoke trailing from behind their ship. At the last second, he pulled the steering wheel back, and the entire ship decelerated insanely fast, throwing everyone forward.

Crew members on the hangar deck scampered out of the way of the gunship as the landing gear scraped the floor, leaving a trail of sparks. Barrels of fuel were knocked aside and a pilot transport was bent in two by the skidding ship. Eventually, after narrowly hitting a parked starfighter, they came to a screeching, agonizing halt.

Daniel's knuckles were white, his forehead damp with sweat. He slowly turned around behind him, tense as a wooden plank. "Everyone…alright?" he said, stuttering a little.

Caitlin's face was ghostlike. "Define alright," she replied.

"Idiot!" yelled out Max's voice from behind them. The lizard was wedged between two chairs, on his back, his paws flailing in the air as he tried to right himself.

"What were you thinking?" demanded Ms. Phillips, jumping from the ladder. "Because what you just did was not smart!"

"Excuse me, I just saved all our lives!" he protested. "'Thank you, Daniel, for saving us from turning into Gorog mush!' You're welcome! Where's the gratitude?"

"Watch your mouth, young man. You do not talk that way to your mother ever."

"I'm twenty years old!"

"Can we save this conversation for later?!" interjected Caitlin. "We have a problem!"

"Another one?" They all turned to face the window, which was pointed out towards the hangar entrance. They saw troops running across the floor in the foreground, scattering all over the hangar around pieces of debris thrown by the crashed ship. At first, it looked like they were attending to the damage, but then they started taking up defensive positions around the hangar, facing the window.

Because in the distance, hurtling towards the hangar, was over a dozen boarding craft.

Chapter 15

The Unknown Sector

Prince Orvag stared into the surface metal of his gleamingly shiny scimitar as he slowly sharpened the blade. His mess of tentacles stared back at him as he worked to remove the dents, nicks, and rough patches that had formed on his blade after several years of combat and training. The scimitar was the chosen sword that the Gorogs used, for its elegant curved blade and simple design. There were no gimmicks, no high-tech infusements into the weapon, just a plain, simple metal sword forged from Xaphorium and housed in a simple sheath. Orvag carried two of them on his person normally, strapped to his back and hidden below his massive cloak. The first of the two had already been sharpened, and was back in its usual home, but the second still needed some touch-ups.

He was using a headstone to sharpen his blade. This was a special rock that was gifted to every Gorog warrior once they turned twelve, made of a special stone that was exclusive to the Gorog homeworld of Tersak. The planet, once entirely made up of oceans, had long since dried up, save for the Great Lakes, which dotted the surface and could have circumferences of a thousand miles or more. The Gorogs and other Quelliks of the planet had adapted to living on land, growing toes instead of flippers, losing the function of their gills, and becoming more used to being out of the water for extended periods of time. Nevertheless, a Gorog could not survive forever without water contact, which is why they had devised suits that could feed water or water vapor from the outside air and moisten their skin. On ships like the *Deceiver*, Gorogs were required to take baths once every two days in order to keep their skin from drying up. It was a bit annoying, but since the alternative was death, nobody complained.

The proximity alarm sounded on the bridge, but Orvag hardly paid attention to it. It was only when Warden Dormak came up behind him and said, "He's here," that he set his headstone down and looked out into space, watching the small black shuttle approach. The king's shuttle. He could tell from the gold highlights on the wings and hull. On board that ship, that small, insignificant hunk of metal, the most powerful ruler in this side of the galaxy was sitting, preparing to disembark.

King Fero-Shak had not made contact with the *Deceiver* since his last check-in call nine hours ago. Orvag had been counting down the minutes since, laying preparations for his grand mutiny. His sword was sharpened, his tongue prepared to scorn his father's name, and Dormak and his bodyguards to back him up. Now all he could do was trust the fickleness of his own men and their willingness to support him over his father. He wanted to shoot that spacecraft down, to give the order and be done with it, but he resisted the temptation. Anything less than the approval of his crew with the king in their midst could result in his exile or death as punishment. To distract his mind from the approaching ship, he pulled his handheld communicator out and contacted the twins.

Vraxis answered right on schedule. "Your Highness," his hologram said, dipping his head in respect.

"Soon, Vraxis, soon," Orvag replied, drumming his throne's armrests with his long tentacle-like appendages. "How goes the assault on Shane's cruiser?"

"We've launched the boarding craft and are preparing to take the fight to them," he replied, fingering his belt slightly. "If we find Subject X-17 or the other slaves you mentioned, we'll deal with them. Are you sure you want the others as well?"

"Yes. The other three were traveling with him when Shane picked them up. Even if we can apprehend one of them, we'll have a direct tie to our lost experiment which will make it easier to get him back. One other thing; do not engage Shane under any circumstances. You're just there to grab the slaves and get out. Understood?"

"Very good, your Highness. Foulor!" Vraxis turned around off camera. "Did you get that?"

There was a disgruntled "Yes" that could be faintly heard.

"He'll be fine. We'll report back in a second, as soon as we've recaptured your missing slaves."

"Good hunting."

The hologram faded out right as Vraxis turned to face his brother again, leaving Orvag to stare out the window and await his father's arrival. Dormak moved to stand by him.

"The king has landed in the main hangar," he informed him. "He's coming this way now."

"How many guards accompany him?" asked Orvag, fingering his chin.

"Six, from what the men are saying. Those may be a problem, sir, should things get tense."

"Those are members of the Scizorheads, the elite bodyguards of the king. They serve whoever wields the power over Tersak and its empire. Which, in this case, is me. They'll bend to my wishes, just like everyone else." The prince turned to look up at Dormak. "Now all we have to do is pray that my hunters do their job and bring us our prizes back."

"You sure the twins are up for the job you gave them?" asked Dormak.

"They're some of the best bounty hunters in the galaxy. They've never failed an assignment, nor have they disregarded any of my instructions. So yes, I do believe that they're up for the job. It's not like Subject X-17's a major threat anyways." Orvag turned back to Dormak. "I have every confidence in their ability, even in leading a fleet of ships."

"Right. I suppose that they'll be fine."

"What about you? You sure you're up to see my father deposed?"

Dormak sighed. "At one point, Fero-Shak was the Gorog that I wanted to emulate. Everyone I knew spoke of him as this godlike figure, who could cut down entire Coalition armies with just his sword. Yet the more I learned, the more I realized that he was just another Gorog. One with a lot of power, but slowly declining with old age. If he's not advancing our plot to rid us of the Coalition, he's part of the problem."

"Very good, my friend. It brings me comfort knowing that you have my back."

Just then, Dormak's wrist-mounted device beeped. He checked it. "The king's almost here," he said to the prince. "Got maybe five minutes before he's in the room."

Orvag stood up from his throne, slung his dual sheaths over his back, and adjusted his military uniform so that it was nice and crisp. He sat back down, turning his throne around to face the double sliding doors to the lifts, where the king would be appearing. His hand was already being attracted to the hilt of his scimitar, but he continued to resist the urge to lunge at the door the moment it opened. He continued to fight it, even as the seconds ticked by, right up until the doors themselves opened and six guards walked in, all armed with long spears and pistols holstered to their waists. They all took positions on either side of the door, standing at attention. Behind them, a cloaked figure advanced.

King Fero-Shak had been nicknamed "The Hammer of the Sea" by his enemies. One look at his hulking physique and menacing aura that he cast around him wherever he went told you that he was not to be trifled with. He, like his son, had a beard of tentacles that trailed down from his face, but because he was older, his were even longer, reaching all the way down to his stomach. He was showing prominent wrinkles in his forehead and his gill slits were virtually nonexistent, both of which were signs of old age in Gorog society. Nevertheless, he had not lost his signature stalk, which could send chills down even the bravest of challengers. He was dressed in the dark red and gold military uniform that only the king wore, and a thick velvet cloak was draped over his shoulders that seemed to skirt on the floor. A small crown made of gold swords adorned his head. Upon his entry, the bridge fell deathly silent, with every officer and crew member there turned to look at His Highness himself.

Orvag was the first to break the quiet. "Father," he said, still seated on his throne. "I must say you're here sooner than anticipated. Please forgive the shoddy decorum of my men, they did not foresee you being here early."

"You may dispense with the pleasantries, son. We have some problems that demand our attention first." Even Orvag was rattled somewhat by the grave tone of Fero-Shak's voice. It was a booming, no-nonsense voice that spoke as if it meant business and seemingly warned everyone around that the king was the last person you wanted on your bad side. Plus, the way he said *son* only served to confirm his theory that another lesson was imminent.

"Problems?" repeated Orvag, choosing to wait to play his cards. "If you're referring to the incident at Skorjion, work is well underway to restore the camp to its former glory. There are hunter units tracking down the escaped slaves…"

"Enough of your rambling!" barked Fero-Shak, causing everyone to freeze in fear. The king may have been old, but he still possessed that air of foreboding that made him so feared. "I did not fly all the way here to hear you make excuses about the consequences of the attack on Skorjion. I am here to address the fact that you allowed an entire fleet of Coalition starfighters to raid the camp in the first place, destroying valuable property and crippling a large percentage of our wartime production!"

"Your Highness, with all due respect," put in Dormak

from the sidelines, "Orvag was on this ship the entire time, as remote from the camp as it gets. I was in charge of defending the camp, and I blew it. If anyone should be punished, it's me."

Fero-Shak turned to face him, then advanced slowly on the warden. Dormak, despite every instinct telling him to be as small as possible, stood his ground, until his eyes were boring straight into the king's.

"When last I checked, you, Warden Dormak, were acting as Skorjion's caretaker by my *son's* appointment," snarled Fero-Shak, spitting in Dormak's face. "So, by extension, your failure is his failure also. What was that saying that I hear is so popular with you?" He thought for a moment. "Something about how, as a leader, anything that happens under your leadership is your fault?" He thought again. "Just how many soldiers did you kill under that moniker?"

Dormak fell silent at that last bit. Word of his rampage through Skorjion must have traveled faster than he had anticipated. Although the military codes said nothing about execution of lower-ranked military officers without a trial, he had figured that some would take umbrage with his decision. He had just hoped that word would not have reached Fero-Shak's ears. And now Orvag was turning and giving him a funny look.

"Did you do something?" he prompted, confused.

"I'll tell you later," replied Dormak through gritted teeth.

The king's eyes narrowed further, then slapped Dormak in the cheek, sending him reeling back. "I'll deal with you later. Right now…" He swiveled around to stare at Orvag, still seated on his throne. "…I have to teach my son another lesson." He began to approach the prince, hand reaching for his gigantic sword that seemed to be nearly as long as a man is tall.

Now, this is where everyone on that bridge expected Orvag to cower in fear at the sight of his angry father advancing his way. After all, Fero-Shak had made his reputation known through his brutality and malevolent demeanor. What no one expected was for Orvag to stand up from his throne, take a defiant stance against his own father, and say, "Dormak was right about one thing when he killed those men. That was the fact that they were all bumbling fools who couldn't shoot straight if they wanted to."

The king stopped. The arrogance in his son's voice was so prominent it almost shocked him. "You had best watch yourself, boy," he retaliated, voice dangerously low. "I could beat you within an inch of your life at the drop of a finger. I'd advise you to not make it worse for yourself than it already is." He resumed his advance.

"Beat me within an inch of my life? And how exactly do you plan to do that when you cannot even best a small Coalition ship in space combat?"

"A single fluke!" roared Fero-Shak. "This is your last warning! One more outburst and I'll chuck you into the Ocramus pit!"

Every other soldier in the room gasped. The Ocramus pit meant certain death, even for the hardiest of warriors. But Orvag didn't yield. He stood his ground, looking defiantly into his father's eyes.

"A single fluke? Or a pattern?" The prince turned to address the masses that surrounded him and the king. "Let the military records reflect that the king, who was once unbeaten in the art of ship-to-ship combat, has recently lost in several engagements with Orion Coalition ships. In his last battle, in the atmosphere of the gas giant Drogor, he and an armada of eight ships engaged six enemy vessels. By the end, he had retreated with just two, and the enemy got off with a single lost warship!"

"Now, wait one minute–"

"And that's not all!" Orvag relished every word as he brought forth all of Fero-Shak's recent failures and faults. "Let the record also state that the king's last five years of rule have been the worst for the Gorogs since the war first began! Back on

Tersak, there is corruption roaming the city streets! Our mighty empire has shrunk by a considerable margin due to Coalition attacks! Our casualty numbers are up! Perhaps, with better training and radar systems, the attack on Grimcor from two days ago could've been prevented! Yet the king deemed it not important enough!"

Murmurs broke out among the crew members who were watching the spectacle. Some of them were nodding their heads, as if they were agreeing with what Orvag was saying. But there still seemed to be no clear consensus among them.

It was Fero-Shak's turn to speak. "My loyal soldiers!" he bellowed, as if he was giving a speech. "Who was the one who gave you purpose? Who was the one who lifted Tersak out of poverty in the first place? Who was the one who lifted the Gorog name high, and elevated our race into the ranks of the greats of history?"

"And," interjected Orvag, cutting off the king. "Who is the one who has been fulfilling your purpose recently? Who is the one who has actually been doing something about the war? Who is the one who has been keeping our name great among names? I'll tell you: not him!" He pointed his tentacle finger at the king. "My brothers, my fellow Gorogs! For the last few years you have been under the authority of a king whose rule is long past its prime! Fero-Shak is no longer the great ruler he once was! He has become weak with age, his mind feeble and no longer able to properly rule over us! And what do we do with the weak and those who cannot fend for themselves?"

"We rid the galaxy of their filth!" answered Dormak, along with a small handful of other Gorog officers. "Only the strong can survive in our society! Those with the will to do what needs to be done!"

"SILENCE!" shouted King Fero-Shak, but no one paid him any attention. The prince had every eye locked upon him.

"And, let me ask you, my brothers," Orvag said to the

crew. "Does the king meet these requirements at present?"

Although most of them stood silently, shifting their weight about, a decent number of them did shake their heads no. Orvag, sensing that he was winning, pressed forward.

"And if the old king does not meet these requirements, then do we deserve a king who possesses the will to do what needs to be done?"

All but two of the Gorogs nodded their heads.

Orvag, sensing he was near victory, played his final card. "My brothers!" he exhorted. "For too long have we lived in the shadow of the Coalition and the filthy ideals they uphold! Too long have the Gorogs been mocked and scorned by our neighbors! I promise you this day, that so long as my breath resides within me, I will not rest until our sign waves above every Coalition stronghold and fortress! The name Gorog will be feared from the Outer Arm to the Galactic Nucleus! And our empire will reign as the strongest in the galaxy's history! Do you want to see this happen?!"

"YES!" came the voices of every Gorog on the bridge. Fero-Shak's once-confident stare began to wither away, replaced by fear of knowing what was about to happen.

"Do you want to see a Gorog flag on every planet?!"

"YES! LONG LIVE THE GOROGS!"

"And who will be the one who will get us there?!" called out Orvag in a loud voice.

"YOU!" The crew members had swayed to his position, even Fero-Shak's guards, as the prince had hoped. He smiled, knowing that his future was all but secure.

"HAIL THE MIGHTY GOROGS!" he bellowed throughout the room.

"HAIL! LONG LIVE THE GOROGS! LONG LIVE ORVAG!" The chants of the soldiers echoed through the vast chamber, rising to the ceiling and making the windows shake from their fervor. And there was no one who shouted louder than

Dormak, his booming voice heard over the chants of the men.

King Fero-Shak looked around in desperation, knowing that his position was compromised. He turned to his bodyguards, still stationed by the elevator, for help, but they refused to heed his calls. Frantically, he started to slink away, hoping to reach his shuttle and escape with his head. But as he started to move, Dormak moved into his path, using his massive size to sweep the king to the floor, where he sprawled onto his stomach. Fero-Shak scrambled to get up, only for four Gorogs sympathetic to Orvag to appear from the shadows with whips. They flicked the weapons, wrapping around the king's ankles and wrists with painful cracks, then hoisted the monarch into the air, suspended by all four of his limbs. The king writhed and twisted, his beard of tentacles flopping about, but he could not get free.

"TRAITOR!" he bellowed at Orvag, who was turning around to face him, even as the crew members chanted feverishly below him.

"Now, now, father, I think that it is time that I teach *you* a lesson." Orvag advanced, hatred hinging on every word that escaped his mouth. "After all, you should have to go through what I've had to at your hands."

"You think you're going to get away with this mutiny?" Fero-Shak growled, still struggling to escape, straining against the whips. "You will be executed for this betrayal! Your head will be forfeit!"

"I think your own subjects have made it clear that no such harm will come to me," Orvag said, a wickedly evil smile on his face. He approached the restrained king. "On the other hand, I'll be surprised if any of them truly care if you die."

"Release me! NOW!" Fero-Shak was on the verge of insanity as he struggled to free himself, trying to kick his captors. Dormak, seizing his electric spear, set it to the lowest power and zapped the king in his back so that only his head could move. Fero-Shak's movements fell silent, aside from the

251

crazy glares of his eyes.

"That's better," Orvag said, kneeling down so that he was at eye level with his father. "It's okay, Your Highness. You had a good run while it lasted. But as the Gorog law that you wrote says, 'There is no room for weakness in our society.' And the law must not be contradicted."

"You…" snarled Fero-Shak, teeth bared, "…shall never be king. Nor will you ever be victorious on the field of battle."

"Wrong. I've already been victorious over you. And soon the Coalition will fall in the same way." Orvag reached forward and took the crown of swords from Fero-Shak's head. "Best not to damage something so precious," he mused, dusting it off and placing it onto his own head. It fit perfectly.

Dormak approached Orvag from the side. "So, Your Highness," he said, bowing his head in respect. "What do you plan to do with him?" He indicated the helpless former king, still being strung up by the whips of the guards.

Orvag turned to face him. "You may want to stand back a bit," he warned. "Grab that ornamental pot in the corner and bring it here." Dormak nodded, grabbed a small metal pot next to the elevator door, brought it to the new king, and took two steps back. Orvag placed the pot underneath Fero-Shak, then stood up to check its placement below his head.

Fero-Shak turned to look at his son, now lording himself over him. "I am ashamed to call you my son," he growled, malice in his voice.

Orvag turned to look down at him. He contemplated the words for a minute. "No," he eventually said. "I have been ashamed to call you my father. I am ashamed to have had you as our king. And now, as your new ruler, I hereby renounce your ties to the throne, this society, and your right to live."

Fero-Shak's eyes widened at the meaning behind those words, but before he could speak, Orvag moved. With one fluid motion, the dual scimitars slid out from the sheaths on Orvag's back, came in an arc from below, and came up in a scissor-like motion. There was a stomach-churning sound of steel cutting bone, then a loud thud as the head of Fero-Shak fell into the pot from before, then the sound of fluid also filling the pot as the headless body began to spit out blue Gorog blood.

The body dropped to the floor, no longer moving. Orvag peeked into the pot, where the decapitated head of his father stared up at him with lifeless eyes. Glaring contemptibly down at it, he turned to the guards who had held the king in place. "Get rid of the body and clean up this mess," he ordered them. Then he bent down and unclasped the red and gold cloak that Fero-Shak had been wearing, lifting it up. There was blood on the collar, but it was otherwise clean. He tossed it to one of them. "And clean this up too!"

As the guards moved to obey, Dormak came alongside the new king. "Well, that's done. Now how do you intend to break the news to the rest of the Gorogs?"

"Rig the king's shuttle to explode and send one of the prisoners in the brig to fly it," replied Orvag, pulling out a black cloth and wiping his father's blood off of his two blades. "I'll send messengers to every corner of the empire, telling the populace that the king died while departing the ship, and that I have been crowned the new king of the Gorogs. If anyone finds out about the plot, kill them. While I have no doubt that the people will prefer me, best not to go in with blood on your hands." He sheathed his two swords back into their holsters.

"And what of Subject X-17?" asked Dormak.

"The twins will handle him. In the meantime, we have another pressing matter to attend to."

"The Coalition?"

"Correct," Orvag said. "And every single one of their bases and strongholds will have our flag waving over them by the time I'm done with them."

Chapter 16

Perseus Arm

"Move!" yelled Daniel, unbuckling the unconscious Pantura from her seat and dragging her towards the escape hatch. The boarding craft were getting very close, and he did not want to be around when the hangar became a full-on warzone, as the hidden guards made abundantly clear. He strained to move Pantura's body, his muscles groaning in protest and tensing up all over again. Caitlin ran to his side and grabbed her other arm, pulling her across the ship floor and towards the hatch. Ms. Phillips tailed behind, freeing Max from being wedged between the two chairs with a strong push, releasing him onto the hangar floor.

"Thank you for that," he grumbled. "But you were supposed to do it gently."

"Just get on down there!" she snapped, fed up with his entitled behavior.

Daniel jumped down into the hyperspace deck. "Push Pantura down here!" he called up. "Hurry!"

"She's really heavy!" grunted Caitlin, pushing her over the edge and letting her down as slowly as she could via her arms. "I don't know how long I can suspend her like this!"

"Just release her! She'll be fine!"

She did, and she fell in a heap on the floor with a dull thud. The impact jolted her senses awake, and she started to a sitting position, breathing heavily and staring around wildly at her surroundings.

"Ouch!" she complained, rubbing her head gingerly.

"Sorry about that!" apologized Caitlin, descending the ladder.

"You able to stand?" Daniel asked her. "Because we're going to need to run in a second."

"What…why?"

"Hey, I don't mean to sour this anymore, but those landing craft are about to pass through the hangar window," reported Max. "We should move."

"Gorogs. They're about to board the cruiser."

Pantura shook her head in confusion. "We didn't get far?"

Daniel shook his head.

"What are we standing around for?" demanded Max. "MOVE!"

Daniel opened the ship door and helped Pantura stand up. "He's right. Come on, let's go!"

Ms. Phillips jumped down from the ladder and chased after the others as they ran down the exit ramp and into the damaged hangar, passing an overturned transport as they went. On the other end, several Gorog boarding craft passed into the hangar, coming under fire from the defending guards instantly. Their armor plating shrugged off the lasers, which went ricocheting around the hangar, some of which landed close to Daniel and the others. The main doors opened as soon as each craft landed, and out came at least twenty Gorog soldiers, all armored and carrying rifles, which opened fire on the hunkered down Coalition guards. Caitlin shrieked and jumped behind some cover as a Gorog blast whizzed over her head. Everyone else ducked down into safe spots as the Gorog troops advanced into the hangar, shooting down security left and right.

"Head for the exit!" Daniel took off running for the open door, the others leaping up to follow him. More lasers came down around them, but they all missed, sending both Caitlin and Ms. Phillips into screaming fits. Pantura whipped out her own weapon and shot over at the enemy, before throwing herself through the open door hard and into the corridor. The others followed, and the instant they were, Max slammed the door shut with the emergency lockdown button next to the entrance.

"That should hold them off for a little bit," he said. "Now what?"

"We need to get to the bridge. Shane's there, so it's likely to be the most secure spot on the ship." Pantura turned to Ms. Phillips. "Do you have the map of the ship on you?"

She felt around her pockets, her face falling as she came up empty handed. "I think I left it on the ship," she said nervously.

"No worries. I know the way to the bridge. Just stay close behind me, alright?"

They all nodded at Pantura. "Okay then, I know a shortcut. This way!"

As they started to run, Shane contacted Pantura on her intercom. "Pantura, are you there?"

"Yes, Shane, I'm here! We crash-landed in the hangar, but we're heading towards your location now!"

"Exercise extreme caution!" the Magnum warned in a serious voice. "There are three groups of boarding craft scattered throughout the ship! Watch for Gorogs! And Pantura, Vraxis and Foulor are leading the assault!"

That last bit made her skid to a halt in the middle of the hallway. "The twins are here?!" she asked shrilly.

"Correction: they're on the ship. Just be careful getting here!" There was a pause. "Listen, I have to go! Keep Daniel and the others safe!"

"Shane? Hello?" No answer; the transmission had been cut. Pantura let the intercom drop from her hand. She was looking very afraid indeed, as she turned to face the others.

"This situation just got significantly more dangerous," she told them.

"That name came up when we were up with Shane on the bridge," said Caitlin. "Vraxis."

"Yeah, it did," joined in Daniel. "Who is he? And who is the other one that Shane mentioned?"

In another part of the *Justice*, Vraxis and Foulor, carrying their best weapons, stepped from their boarding craft and onto the secondary hangar's deck. The last Coalition resistance fell before them as they advanced into the hangar, scanning the area for more hostile forces. A Gorog soldier approached the two Travashians.

"Area is secure, Commander Vraxis," he reported.

"Excellent. Have the rest of the men fan out and go hunting. Remember, you're looking for these individuals." Vraxis pulled out the images of their targets again. "Bring them back here, alive and in one piece. If anything else gets in the way, kill it. Understood?"

The soldier nodded and ran off. Vraxis pulled out his rifle and cocked it into the ready position. Foulor, behind him, groaned loudly.

"Why do you get to be commander and not me?" he complained, tossing a grenade in his hands as though it were a bouncy ball.

"Because," his brother replied, clearly aggravated, "Unlike you, I have the mental capacity required to lead a group of troops like this. You would probably mistake them for the enemy and blow them up."

"I would not!"

"What about on Kramesur, when you accidentally destroyed an entire troop transport when trying to hit that Coalition tank?"

"That was an accident! The grenade bounced off the wall and landed in the transport! It's not my fault!"

"Keep telling yourself that." Vraxis sighted down the barrel briefly and then started to advance across the hangar, shooting down a guard that came running in through the door. "Stay with me. You four!" he yelled at a group of Gorog soldiers who were walking towards the exit. "With us!"

They passed through the entrance to the hangar and entered the maze of ship corridors. They encountered little resistance along the way, sniping down the few security guards who appeared to stop them. They lost one Gorog, but that was inconsequential.

"Sir!" another Gorog, a sergeant, radioed.

"What is it?"

"They've locked the doors to our hangar! We're trying to cut through the door, but one of the troops from Squad B claims that he saw a large lizard-like animal leave through the exit. It matches the description of one of the four slaves that you told to keep an eye out for."

"If he's on board, the others should be too. Stay on high alert. If you see them, be sure to immobilize them as soon as possible." Vraxis shot another Coalition soldier in the head. "Split up, and try to cover more ground that way."

The sergeant nodded and broke up the call. Vraxis killed another guard, while Foulor burst open a closed door with one of his many grenades. Entering the hallway, they began to scout the corridors for signs of their prey. They rounded two corners, and then Vraxis raised his hand for his men to stop, causing Foulor to nearly bump into him.

"Why are we stopped?" he hissed, his hand already caressing another explosive.

"Shhh...listen!" Vraxis attuned his hunter ears for the sound he had heard. It was coming from up ahead, down a small side corridor. Conversation. He gestured for his men to move up a little bit, and they took positions all alongside the corridor.

A few moments later, four individuals emerged from the hallway. There were three humans, all matching the images that Orvag had provided, and confirming the report from the sergeant, the lizard. They turned down the hall away from the group of Gorogs, still in conversation. Vraxis motioned silently for his men to switch to stun, and then slowly advance forward, muffling their footsteps on the hard floor. The four targets paid them no heed as they slowly crept closer to within firing range.

Then, without warning, four guards emerged from another side hallway on the left and began to open fire.

Daniel became aware of the sounds of laser fire from behind him, interrupting Pantura's story about the legendary deeds of Vraxis and Foulor. They turned to see a small party of Coalition troops engaged with a much larger force of Gorog soldiers, the hallway filling up with lasers almost immediately. At the head of the Gorog force were two figures that were decidedly not Gorogs. Both were aliens with olive-green skin, horns protruding from their heads, and catlike eyes. One of them was built like a freight train and had an entire bandolier of grenades slung around his body.

Pantura saw them too and immediately drew in a breath. "Shoot, that's the twins! Run!" She took off running down the hallway and the others followed after. A few blue bolts of energy came streaking by them, but neither of them hit, sparking off the wall. They hastily rounded the corner as the sound of an exploding grenade filled the hallway, followed by some indistinct shouting.

"The two in the front...those were the twins?" gasped Caitlin, seeking clarification.

"Yes," said Max grimly. "Even I can recognize those little horned devils! They used to deliver slaves to Skorjion, before Orvag started to use them for kill missions!"

"Try and lose them in the corridors!" Pantura made several turns down random side halls, the others struggling to keep up. They heard some more shouting from behind them, but despite turning their heads to check, there was no visual sign of the pursuing Gorogs. That did not stop them from running, though, as they moved with due haste to get as far away as possible from the twins and their pack of soldiers.

They ran into a pack of soldiers on the way, who started to shoot blasts of energy at them. They all darted down a side corridor, Pantura laying out some cover fire. A shot struck Caitlin in the arm, and she yelped, feeling the flesh of her shoulder burn slightly. Immediately, she felt her hands start to spark again, like they had twice before, and she hid them from view of Daniel and Pantura.

"You alright, Caitlin?" said Pantura, noticing her injury. Thankfully, that was all she seemed to see.

"Yeah, it just grazed me! Don't worry about it right now!" Thankfully, that seemed to be enough to cause them all to look away and miss the glowing hands. As more laser blasts appeared behind them and they started to move again, she brought up the rear, hoping to God that they would not see the blue-green light behind them until it disappeared.

Eventually, they reached the atrium of the ship, which was decidedly less busy than it was yesterday. "The bridge is this way!" said Pantura, turning left and resuming her sprint. Before she got far, though, five Gorog intruders appeared and started to shoot at her and the others. Pantura pulled out her pistol and shot two rounds, hitting one of the soldiers in the chest and sending him falling back. The others shooted back, forcing them all to scatter for cover. One of the monorail supports acted as cover for Daniel and Caitlin. Ms. Phillips hid behind an abandoned cart of barrels, while Max lunged at the four enemies and fell upon them with tooth and claw. Pantura headshot another Gorog before he could fire off a shot, and before long, the entire troop was dead, Max once again standing like a feral beast in the middle of some dead bodies.

"Daniel! Caitlin! Grab their weapons!" Pantura shot another Gorog who appeared from a side corridor, while the three humans gingerly emerged from behind their cover and ran over to the dead aliens, picking up their guns. Daniel examined his. It was almost exactly like the one he had used during his escape from Skorjion, the grenade still in the butt of the rifle. Caitlin was looking a bit confused at hers, though, so he came over to provide some tips.

"Trigger's here, this reloads the chamber." He pointed out the two buttons. "This is a grenade in the back."

She took it gingerly from him, but eventually settled it onto her shoulder. "Thanks," she replied, shouldering her weapon.

"Come on, the bridge is not that far!" Pantura was some distance ahead, scouting out the area ahead.

From a side corridor directly ahead, Vraxis and Foulor emerged, along with at least ten Gorogs. Pantura screeched to a halt and quickly stepped back behind an empty barrel, as the enemies fanned out across the atrium, blocking their path. Daniel and Caitlin quickly took defensive positions, Ms. Phillips ducking right behind an abandoned pile of crates right in front of them. Max, taking one look at the enemy, decided to join them as well.

"Congratulations, you've managed to postpone your inevitable capture," called out Vraxis in a mocking voice. "But, playtime is over. Step out into the open, put your weapons down, and nobody else will need to get hurt."

"Yes! Put down your weapons, so that we don't come over there and kill you!" barked out Foulor, sounding like he was drunk. It would have been funny, except for the massive belt that was lined with grenades that Daniel and Caitlin could only get frightful glimpses of.

"That's not true!" yelled out Pantura from behind her cover. "You wouldn't infiltrate this ship just to kill a bunch of escaped slaves! You would probably just blow the whole thing up! Orvag must've told you that he wants them alive!

"Well, well, I'll give you credit for being smarter than most," complemented Vraxis, with almost sincerity in his tone. "It makes no difference. Step out from behind the crates and come with us."

"What if we refuse?" called out Ms. Phillips, much to Daniel's surprise.

"Then I personally come over there, drag you out, unconscious and bleeding out if I have to, and kill any guards who try to stop me. Orvag may have said that he wants you alive, so as long as you'll recover from your injuries, he'll be fine with it."

"That's not going to happen!" Daniel picked up his rifle and fired off several rounds, hitting one Gorog in the chest and sending him toppling over. All of the other guards dove for what little cover there was, while Vraxis fired back, causing Daniel to duck down.

"What the hell are you thinking?!" shouted Pantura in anger. "They're the two most furious bounty hunters in the galaxy!"

"They're not dragging me back to Skorjion alive!" Daniel shot another Gorog in the chest. Caitlin grabbed her own rifle and joined him, the atrium filling up with blaster bolts as both sides shot lasers at each other. Ms. Phillips yelped as a bolt struck the crate she was hiding behind, creating a loud pop and a bright flash.

"Don't kill them!" they heard Vraxis call out. "Set your weapons for stun only! Remember, Orvag wants them alive!"

They all noticed that the bolt color of the Gorog's rifles changed after this command. One grazed over Daniel's head, causing him to duck down. Another Gorog was shot in the head by one of Pantura's pistol rounds. There was an explosion nearby, as Foulor threw one of his grenades in their direction, causing their ears to ring. Several Coalition guards came sprinting out of a side hallway and joined the fray, shooting two more Gorogs dead. Vraxis sniped one of them in the head, then immediately shot and killed another with rapid precision. The others took up safer spots along the walls, but still managed to be sniped by Vraxis's fast aim.

Caitlin glanced at Daniel, who was in a shootout with two other Gorogs. She glanced to her right, and saw two exposed wires sticking out of the wall. She glanced around at her friends. Nobody was paying her any attention. Letting the adrenaline build up in her body, she grabbed one of the wires and let a surge of energy into the system, hoping to short out the lights and take away Vraxis's aim. The lights flickered momentarily, allowing Daniel to shoot down one of the Gorogs, but they did not go out. She hastily pulled her hand away before anyone saw her and resumed to shoot her rifle at the enemy.

"What's going on with the lights?" yelled Ms. Phillips in confusion.

Then Foulor reared up from behind his spot, brandishing a thick metal staff, and ran like a bear at the Coalition security, roaring loudly. The guards shot repeatedly at him, but their shots seemed to have no effect on him, as he reached them all and dispatched them with brutal efficiency, using the staff as a club and cracking their helmets from the force of the blows. The entire group fell like ragdolls, and no sooner did the last of them fall that he turned, saw Daniel and Caitlin hiding behind their crates, and ran at them as well. Caitlin screamed again as Foulor rushed them.

Then Max, who had been hiding behind Ms. Phillips, lunged out of his spot and leapt onto Foulor's back, causing him to stumble and nearly fall on the hard floor. The lizard's claws dug into the bounty hunter's tough skin, and while they did not rip it to shreds like the Gorogs, it still left faint scratches amid the green. Foulor yelled, struggling to reach behind him to shake

Max off. He found the tail and seized it, pulling with all his strength. Max roared as he was yanked off of Foulor's back and thrown across the space, digging his claws in to stop him from sliding. He batted aside another grenade that Foulor lobbed at him, and the two grappled at each other, trading blows and snarls at each other.

Caitlin fired at Vraxis, who dove out of sight for seconds before popping back up and forcing her to hide from a concentrated volley he returned. Pantura clutched her weapon, peering around the edge of her barrel. "I'm heading to the other side! Cover me!"

She rose from behind her cover and fired multiple shots at the Gorogs, killing another. Caitlin and the guards kept Vraxis at bay, keeping him from poking his head out and shooting them down. Daniel, seizing an opportunity, stuck his head around his crate and shot the final Gorog guard in the stomach, sending him falling backward out of view. As he stuck his head out again, there was a sharp pain in his right shoulder, followed by a strong burning sensation. He backed off hastily, staring at the small chunk of flesh that had been carved out by the blaster bolt. He grit his teeth as agony shot through his entire arm.

"NO!" yelled Vraxis. "We need him alive! Alive, you hear me?!" Then his words were drowned out by the sound of another grenade detonating nearby, batted away by Max as he tried to tear Foulor's bandolier off his body. The twin was howling in frustration as the lizard used his back as a jungle gym.

"Brother!" he yelled out. "Get him off of me!"

Vraxis pivoted to face the two combatants, aimed his rifle, and fired in one smooth motion. The blast hit Max in the side, causing him to yell out and fall down onto the ground, in pain. Foulor grabbed his staff from where it had been tossed aside and raised it to smash Max's head, but the lizard scampered out of the way. Foulor moved to pursue, but the

Coalition guards pummeled him with lasers, causing him to stumble and hastily dive behind some more cover.

"There's too many of them!" he called out.

"We're not leaving without our prize!" Vraxis replied angrily. "Use the grenades!"

"But you said not to use them on the targets!"

"Throw them into their cover! They'll scamper and then be stunned!"

"But–"

"DO IT!"

Foulor reached for his bandolier, grabbed a handful of explosives, and threw them across the entire width of the atrium. One landed behind Daniel and Caitlin, causing them to duck as a piece of metal barrel went flying over their heads. Pantura covered her head as the heat from the blast washed over her skin. But worst of all was Ms. Phillips, who had a grenade land at her feet, forcing her to scamper from behind her cover. As she moved to get away, she heard her knee pop and give out, causing her to sprawl onto the floor as the bomb went off behind her. As she struggled to stand, Vraxis, quickly seeing an opportunity, fired his rifle at her. The stun bolt hit her square in the ribcage, immediately knocking her out.

"MOM!" cried out Daniel, witnessing the entire thing.

"She's down, Foulor! Get her!" ordered Vraxis, pointing to her still body.

Foulor nodded and rushed for her, and despite Daniel emptying an entire rifle magazine at the hunter in desperation, it only slowed him down, and he had soon scooped her up in his arm and slung her unconscious form over his shoulder.

"Now let's get out of here before more guards arrive!" Vraxis waved Foulor over towards the exit.

"What about the other three targets?"

"They'll have to wait! There are hundreds of guards heading this way, Foulor, and we'll be trapped! Move it!"

"No, *mom!*" Daniel tried to fire at them again, but the rifle clicked pathetically at him. It was out of ammunition. Throwing it aside, he faced Caitlin in horror, who was similarly looking stunned and scared at the same time.

As Vraxis stood up to run for cover, Max reappeared from the smoke filling up the atrium and leapt at him, looking much bigger than he had originally seemed. The hunter let out a very unprofessional shriek as the massive reptile, now the size of a medium crocodile, jumped on top of him and pinned him down, his teeth flashing in his face. The rifle was knocked from his hand and went skidding across the atrium floor, to where Foulor picked it up.

"Go! Don't worry about me! Get to the ship!" yelled Vraxis, struggling to breathe. When Foulor started to approach him, he cursed and screamed. "GET OUT OF HERE!"

Foulor hesitated, but as more Coalition soldiers started pouring into the atrium, he started to run away, passing the dead bodies of all of the Gorog soldiers, as well as one survivor who took off with him. Daniel and Caitlin immediately rose from their cover and approached Pantura with haste. "They took her, my mother!" he exclaimed, panting.

"I saw." She turned to the other guards and pointed over to where Max was sitting atop Vraxis's struggling body. "You two! Detain him and send him down to the brig. The rest of you follow me!" They started to sprint after Foulor, Daniel and Caitlin following. "Max! Come on!"

The lizard looked up, saw the guards approaching him, and rose, allowing them to take Vraxis into custody, while he watched the entire thing. He struggled fiercely as the guards slapped a pair of binders on him, which shocked his nervous system into a docile state. As they began to drag him away, Max chased after the others, catching up with them shortly.

"Whatever rounds that fool was carrying, they breached my scales." The lizard said, in a slightly pained voice. "Never have I seen that before."

Caitlin glanced over, noticing the wound in his side. She also noticed, more clearly now, that he was significantly bigger than before, over twice as large. "When did you get bigger?" she gasped.

"Not now, Caitlin!" said Pantura, in full sprint mode in front of the others. "After we've saved Amy!" She pulled out her intercom. "Shane, we've detained Vraxis, but Foulor is escaping with Amy! I hope things are going well for you up there!"

"Vorlax is pursuing the enemy back to their ships, but there are still a lot of Squids roaming the ship on your level!"

Sure enough, as she put the communicator away, they came upon a small troop of Gorogs waiting, blocking their path through a side passage. The group moved to hide behind cover, but before they could, Max sprinted ahead of the group, roaring furiously, claws fully extended. The Gorogs all shot at him, but their blasts were ineffective, and Max soon had reached them. His tail came out like a club and crushed two of them between it and the wall. He then ripped right through a third's armor, then picked up the arm of a fourth in his jaws and bit it clean off. Everyone watched, wide-eyed, as Max killed the entire troop by himself. Spitting out a gloved hand, he glanced over at his spectators. "What are we standing around for?" he demanded. "Are we going to go or not?"

He waited by the side corridor for everyone else, as they all slowly started forward, still locked onto Max's hulking frame. "I think we're going to need to ask him a few questions when this is over," Pantura whispered under her breath.

Caitlin nodded. Daniel, meanwhile, was moving faster than everyone else. "Come on, people!" he said, his voice high in pitch. "They're getting away!"

They all increased their speed, making their way through the labyrinth of hallways. They shot a stray Gorog down on the way, finally emerging in one of the side hangars. Parked off to one side was a Gorog landing craft, ready and waiting to fly. But as they rushed over to it, they saw that there were at least a dozen of Shane's guards standing around it, and several dead Gorog bodies lying on the ground.

"They tricked us," said Pantura, her face falling. At that moment, her intercom buzzed again.

"Pantura? Pantura, do you read?" came in Shane's voice. "A Gorog landing craft just took off from the main hangar! Scanners indicate that Foulor is on board!"

Daniel stopped for a second, letting that news sink in. But after a moment, he ran for a parked starfighter that was sitting on the far side of the hangar. "What are you doing?" called out Pantura, confused.

He did not answer. He climbed into the cockpit, studied the controls for just a second, then pushed the ignition. The engines rumbled, and the ship started to lift off.

"Daniel!" yelled Caitlin, running up to the side of the vessel. "Don't! You don't know how to fly one of these!"

"They're not taking my mother!" he yelled. Then he shut the open viewscreen on her and quickly accelerated out of there, leaving everyone there dumbfounded and worried, most of all Caitlin.

He quickly spotted two landing craft flying towards the Gorog cruisers, one of which was on fire and clearly badly damaged. He increased speed to the max, then hunted for the laser cannon controls, which he found a moment later. He gained on Foulor, laser-focused on stopping him from reaching the cruisers.

The radio buzzed. "Daniel!" came in Shane's voice yet again. "Pantura just told me that you stole a starfighter and are chasing after Foulor! You have to turn back now!"

"I'm not letting my mom go back to that hellhole!" he retorted. He attempted to turn off the radio, but found that he could not.

"The radio is hotwired, so you can't turn it off. You're not skilled enough to fly one of these things! And what are you going to do, shoot down the landing craft?"

"They've got my mother!" cried Daniel, his voice shaking with a mixture of rage and denial.

"And risking blowing her up is the right call to make?"

Daniel sat back in his fighter, watching himself approach the landing craft. He could take the shot now, disable that ship and then go save his mom. His finger sweated as it rested on the trigger, almost itching to press it.

"Daniel! We will get her back. I promise. But you aren't going to do anything in that fighter beyond making the problem worse. Turn around now, please! It is not your purpose to save her here!"

He tried to depress the trigger, to shut out Shane's words. But it was no use. Fighting tears and rage at all once, he yelled in frustration, turned the ship around, and left his mother in the hands of the Gorogs.

Chapter 17

Everyone reconvened on the bridge shortly afterwards, tired, sore, and, most of all, angry. Gone was the optimism from earlier that day, replaced with the harsh reality that everyone was dealing with. Even Vorlax was not wearing his usually charming smile. Shane stepped forward and addressed the somber group, who were sitting around the big hologram in the center.

"So, there is a lot for all of us to take in regarding this past battle," he began. "On the one hand, casualties weren't as bad as feared, and we managed to keep the three of you safe from the Gorogs, and we captured one of the Travashian twins; something that I've been trying to do for years now. But, on the other hand…"

"We lost a good chunk of our starfighters, our ship is pretty badly damaged, and Amy Phillips is back in the hands of the Gorogs," finished Vorlax, his voice somehow even grimmer than his face.

Caitlin glanced over at Daniel, who had barely said a word since it had happened. His face was parked with a permanent scowl, his eyes darting around the room almost in a paranoid sort of way. She knew that he had to be pissed for coming back and leaving Amy behind. She shuddered to think as to what could be happening to her aboard the Gorog ship.

"Yes, all that is true," Shane was saying. "The silver lining to that, is that the Gorogs didn't get ahold of Subject X-17, since that decoded transmission clearly stated that he was male. By default, they're unlikely to kill Ms. Phillips, since they suspect that she has a link to him. Why else would they take her alive?"

"That doesn't change the fact that she's on board a Gorog ship!" raged Daniel. "And even if they don't kill her, I've lived with the Gorogs enough to know that, however they're treating her, it's almost certainly not good!"

"Relax, Daniel," said Pantura. "I know how you feel, but worrying about her now is not going to help her out, nor is it going to do you any favors. The best thing we can do for her is for the intelligence agencies to keep an eye out for her in the Gorog radio chatter and then act out on that."

Daniel gave her a broodingly nasty stare. "Don't…you dare…say that to me."

"Daniel, she's right." Caitlin walked over to him and stood before him. "Worrying about her is the last thing we need to do at the moment. I'm sure that Shane will have something figured out sooner rather than later."

"Perhaps." Shane was fingering his beard. "Foulor would be taking her back to Orvag's ship, the *Deceiver*. But they could be taking her to another place as well."

"Where?"

"It's a place deep in Gorog territory. Lhassi. The heart of the Gorog's labor camp empire, and the site of their largest production center, Rhozadar. More imprisoned slaves wind up there than any other Gorog camp, and they're mainly escaped slaves and those that the Gorog empire really hates. If there's any place where she might be, it's there."

"Why bring this up now?" asked Caitlin.

"Because that's our next target," replied Shane. "We've been planning this out for a long time, and one of our men managed to uncover a special passage that cuts right through Gorog territory to Lhassi. The Gorogs don't use it, because it runs right next to a black hole. And one of our men found the entrance to it during the raid on Skorjion."

"Now," interjected Pantura, "We have the means to cripple the Gorog Empire's wartime production severely, with Skorjion under repairs. If Amy is going to be sent anywhere, it would be there. There's no place more secure other than Terzak itself."

"What about Vraxis?" asked Max.

"Well, odds are that we'll question him for information, and if he doesn't cooperate, we'll tie him from head to foot and send him off to the asteroid prisons. And all you need to know about those is this; if you're sent there, odds are you're there for life."

"So that's it?" asked Daniel. "You said that he's a known colleague of Orvag, the Gorog prince and likely the person who holds possession of my mother! We should try everything in our power to extract information out of him!"

"And we will. But unfortunately, we cannot exercise brutal methods of torture to obtain our information. We try to exercise methods that are above the savagery of the Gorogs."

"Then try something else!" suggested Daniel forcefully. "Try something from a different angle! We've got to get that information!"

The intercom buzzed, and Shane picked it up. "Sir," came a female voice on the other end.

"Can this wait for just a few moments?" Shane replied gruffly.

"Sir? It's the council. They wish to see you in the chambers immediately."

Shane put down the intercom, looking more miffed than a child who had only gotten clothes on Christmas. "If you all would excuse me," he said. "I have a meeting to attend to. We'll finish this later." He rose from his seat and exited the bridge, leaving the others just standing there. Vorlax, arms crossed, glanced around the bridge, watching all of the officers just standing there, spectating.

"Don't you all have some jobs to attend to?" he barked at them, causing everyone to disperse. He turned back to Daniel and Caitlin. "You two should probably go down to the medical wing, since both of you have blaster burns. Get patched up and

273

head back to your rooms to rest. I'll have the intelligence officers scan for mentions of your mother, and I'll send you a message if anything comes up."

"I'll come with you," said Pantura, moving to stand beside them.

Daniel nodded. "Thank you."

They all exited the bridge, but as they got into the elevator to head down to the lower levels of the ship, Daniel cornered Max. "Alright, what was that back there?"

"Excuse me?" the lizard growled, his spines bristling up in defense.

"You've been oddly quiet for the last ten minutes. What was that back there? I swear that you were bigger than normal when we were chasing Foulor. When I land back on the ship, you're back to normal size. What was that?"

Max sighed. "I'd rather not say."

"So you *did* get bigger." Daniel approached him, looming over the lizard. "I'm curious. If it's nothing of consequence, why does it seem like you're trying hard to avoid saying anything about it?"

Max backed into the wall, his teeth flashing slightly. But Daniel was undaunted, and soon Pantura was approaching him too. "What are you not telling us, Max?"

The lizard glared between the two of them, Caitlin watching in the opposite corner of the elevator. "Fine," he finally spit out. "I'll tell you as much as I can. Because even I'm not sure about where it started, to be honest."

Daniel backed off and leaned against the wall of the elevator. "Fine with me." Pantura backed off too, arms folded.

"I was raised on an ice planet for as long as I could remember, a world full of harshly cold nights and chills that sapped all warmth from your body. Where it is today, I couldn't tell you. The Gorogs came, trying to look for a location to establish a hidden base away from Orion Coalition troops. They found my home in the process and at first kept me around as company, a source of warmth against the freezing nights. Because, although I am reptilian, I am fully warm-blooded, or as they said, hot-blooded."

"What happened?" asked Caitlin.

"They eventually tried to relocate me offworld, and I resisted. Upon doing so, I could increase my strength and grow in size to repel them off. I struggled to fling them off me, but they stunned me repeatedly and eventually managed to subdue me. They sent me to Skorjion, where they used my increased size to help dig out the rocks from the wall. I could only hold the form for short periods, and then my body would need a break. I spent my periods between in chains, a muzzle strapped around my jaws, in a dark cave where only high-ranked guards would be able to enter."

"Didn't you ever try to escape?"

"I did. Many, many times I did. But they always had at least a dozen guards watching over me at all times, and would always subdue me before I could get far. And even if I was using my larger size, stunning me enough times would bring me down."

"Can you cause yourself to grow bigger?"

"Sometimes I can, sometimes I cannot. It usually comes out during moments of high adrenaline, so they would always shock me to wake it up. I can also sometimes control when it stops, other times, I just have to wait."

"So, besides greater size and strength, are there any other traits that you have that you're aware of?" inquired Daniel, genuinely curious to know.

"So far, I'm not sure. I've never really gotten the chance to know under the watch of Dormak." Then Max paused, his face looking confused. "What does it matter to you? You're heading back to your own planet once you find your mother!"

"We…just wanted to know…" began Daniel.

"It's not important, just leave me be! Please!" The elevator doors opened, and Max stormed out, shoving past them and disappearing down the hallway. They all stared after him in confusion.

"What's his problem?" asked Pantura. "I didn't see any harm in asking."

"Maybe he's just sensitive about that," theorized Caitlin.

"No, this doesn't seem like that. I think there's something else that he's not telling us." Daniel exited the elevator shaft, nursing his injured shoulder. "Come on. Let's get to the infirmary."

They traveled for a little bit in silence, until another question popped into Daniel's mind. "Pantura, you said that the hull of that gunship was made of Xaphorium?"

"Yes," she replied. "Did Vorlax tell you about that? Yes, it's extremely resistant to blaster bolts, which is why it covers the entire hull. Did he tell you about how we use it?"

"He did."

"It's an expensive metal, so we can only use it on troop transports and gunships, regrettably. Such as the one we tried to escape in.

"Very interesting," said Daniel. "Were you ever planning on teaching us about ship building?"

Pantura let loose a single chuckle. "Trust me, that's one lecture you do not want to have."

Shane's day really had to close out in the worst way possible. He had a lot of things on his plate, serious things too, such as this latest attack, the loss of Daniel's mother back to the Gorogs, or the fact that his time to figure out his position as Magnum and win the war was fast dwindling. In fact, this meeting with the council was likely to remind him of this fact. He had been pleading for good news to come to him, and thankfully, the news that they had Vraxis in custody was huge. Having Foulor in the mix as well would have been nice, but Vraxis by himself was a major turn of events. The twins were some of Orvag's most trusted officials out there. Who else would the prince trust with leading two entire Gorog cruisers and all their men? If the Coalition could get him to talk, they could have another, secret way of ending the war. If. There were so many *ifs* making their way onto Shane's plate, so many variables that could influence the trajectory of the war, his career, and the history of the galaxy, so many directions that they could go. It was maddening to him, and it did not change the fact that there were still new problems to deal with. His father had warned him that he would be constantly busy, but he had never suspected that it would be this bad.

  He barged into the council chambers, storming over to his seat and plopping down. The meeting would not start until everyone was present in the Hub of Delegation back on Arajor. The council preferred for everyone to meet in person, but with Shane busily managing the war, more often than not, meetings would have to be held via hologram, since it was more convenient that way and they could be held from any area in the galaxy, be it on another planet thousands of light years away or in the vast darkness of space. Holographic projection had really changed the entire face of the galaxy for sure since its invention four hundred years prior, thought Shane. He had debated sharing it with the Earth, but had made no move to do so quite yet.

  The lights went down in the room, signaling that the call was about to start. Vorlax was managing the *Justice*, so Shane was all by himself. He straightened his posture and waited for everyone to appear in hologram form before him. One by one, the various council members materialized in the room and glanced around at their new surroundings, until all were present. Shane rose from his seat to address everyone as they all turned to face him.

"Good evening, gentlemen," he said, and they all bowed their heads in respect, Serizau, sitting at the head of the table, dipping his head the least of all. Even though the council wrote most of the laws that got passed, Shane still held most of the power in the government, and he was to be treated as higher than the council, so it was a courteous gesture on their part.

"Good evening, Shane," said one of the council members.

"How goes the effort to bring about peace and prosperity to the galaxy?" asked another one, an alien member with rough skin and horns.

"About that, we finally might have made some progress in that area, courtesy of recent developments," replied Shane, smiling broadly, masking the facade of his problems under it. "The Skorjion raid was a huge success. We crippled their entire main production line and liberated many of the camp's slaves. The damage was severe enough that it'll take at least two weeks to repair from here. The Gorogs never knew what hit them."

"Skorjion? The labor camp on Grimcor? I thought that was deep inside enemy territory." The head council member sounded unconvinced of this news.

"It was, until the strike on the outpost on Shaanak smashed a hole right in enemy territory. The battle that I told you about in our last meeting session? That gave us the opening we needed to sneak inside the Squids' own land and strike at one of their key bases."

The head member nodded. "So, the camp was destroyed?"

Shane sighed. "Yes, Serizau, it was destroyed. And we now have the key to opening up the other major labor camp in Gorog territory, thanks to that attack. We have uncovered the entrance to the secret shipping lane that passes directly through Gorog territory to Lhassi, the location of Rhozadar, the largest labor camp in their empire."

"What about this news I hear of a surprise Gorog attack on your ship?" asked Serizau, standing from his seat.

"It has been handled," replied Shane sternly. "Two Gorog cruisers ambushed us on the way out of their lands, but they were quickly defeated, one of their ships completely destroyed."

"Really? I heard that Vraxis and Foulor were leading those ships."

"Wait, wait a second," interrupted a fourth council member sitting to Shane's left. "Vraxis and Foulor? The twin bounty hunters who always do Orvag's dirty work? What were they doing leading an entire fleet of Gorogs?"

"We're not sure…yet," answered Shane truthfully. "But one thing that we do know is that they were hunting someone…likely one of the slaves in the party that we rescued from Skorjion. Thankfully, we can ask Vraxis ourselves, since he was apprehended during the attack."

"He was?" asked someone else.

"Yes. He's being held in the brig under heavy guard. I'm planning on heading down there momentarily to question him myself."

"Those two hunters have been among the best weapons that Orvag has used against us," said the rough-skinned alien. "So many high-ranking Coalition officers have fallen to one of their kill missions, including many that I knew personally. That even one of them is in custody is a huge win for all of us."

"Let's not celebrate just yet," interjected Serizau. "Because even with Vraxis in custody, it won't matter once the Gorogs end their mourning and return to form."

"Mourning? What in Vertaz's name are you referring to?" questioned Shane.

"Didn't you hear? King Fero-Shak is dead. His son, Orvag, is now the king. It's been all over the news, surely you had to have heard about it."

Shane shook his head. "No, I have not heard about this. This was?"

"Earlier today, I believe. The report said that Fero-Shak's ship blew up in transit due to faulty engines," said another council member with very long hair and tons of facial tattoos. "They've declared a period of mourning to honor him."

"That's what the Gorogs want you to think!" Serizau replied savagely. He produced a piece of paper from his council robes. "This report came on my desk not long ago, and it says otherwise, that Fero-Shak was killed by his own son on the *Deceiver*, Orvag's prime flagship. From what we've gathered, it seems as though a lot of Gorogs have also noticed how Fero-Shak's fallen from grace in recent years, and voted to end the king's life on the spot."

"However it happened, it doesn't change the fact that Orvag is now king," said Shane. "Which is a huge problem for us. He's among the most brilliant generals we've ever faced, and now he commands the entire Gorog army. For sure, the mistakes Fero-Shak made will be corrected, and the battles we'll be fighting will become costlier. We need to find a way to strike now and land a major blow on the Gorogs before they can regroup. My suggestion would be assaulting Lhassi next, now that we have the secret route there. Skorjion's already down for repairs because of the damage we did. If we can inflict similar damage on Rhozadar, over half of the Gorog Empire's means of production will have been knocked out. Orvag or no Orvag, there would be no coming back from a loss that big. The destruction of Lhassi would essentially mean a guaranteed end to the Gorogs and their reign of terror."

"That would be devastating, for sure," said the council member seated right next to Shane, his hologram flickering a bit as he shifted around in his seat. "Do you have a force large enough to invade? Rhozadar is one of the most secure places in the galaxy, from what intelligence says."

"I already have sent messages out to the fleet at Jurkis, they can be ready to assist us at Lhassi by tomorrow. Ladies and gentlemen, it appears that the end of the war is drawing closer to us as we speak. The key card will soon be in our hands, and with that we'll finally end this war once and for all. You can forget about me leaving my office, because it's not happening. The fall of Lhassi will mean the fall of the Gorog Empire."

"I see you haven't forgotten about our little bet," said the dark-skinned council member.

"It would be kind of hard to forget about it with you all reminding me every five minutes," said Shane, rather rudely. "Also, I never agreed to anything. You strongarmed me into taking it. So if that's why you wanted to hold this entire formal meeting here, you, and by you I mean Serizau, have just been wasting their time."

All of the council members stared at each other, looking somewhat peeved by Shane's comment. Finally, Serizau cleared his throat and stood up. "Listen, Shane, our bet notwithstanding, the council also feels as though you're making an ill-advised decision, leading these battles yourself, especially after that last ambush. There's simply too much risk posed by you leading your men into battle like you've been doing for the past few months." Serizau sounded as though he'd been waiting to say this for the entire duration of the meeting. "We've invoked our yearly vote to order you to return to Arajor and lead the war from the safety of the Kraken, and to let the actual generals in the military lead the war while you give them your orders from your seat in the government."

Shane burned with anger at this. The Kraken was the fortress-like sanctuary where the Coalition's government met to discuss business circulating throughout the galaxy. It's also where the Magnum's seat was, where Shane's power was centered on, and where he would normally delegate from. These days he rarely sat in his own seat, as he preferred to lead the war from the front lines, where he could interact with his own men and supporting generals in a more personal manner. To be robbed of this made him furious. "You can't be serious," he said, his voice shaking with a mix of disbelief and anger. "You used your Dhimma, your one vote per year that allows you to check my power, to put me back on Arajor, away from my men, my generals, and from the very war that I'm trying to win for us?!"

Serizau leaned back in his chair, his fingers tapering in his lap. "It's for your own good, Shane. We'd rather you remain alive than blown up by some Gorog missile. We all know how taking you out in battle would boost the morale of the Gorogs, low as it is right now…"

"My place is on the bridge of a warship, leading my men, not stuck in a room where I cannot direct my troops effectively! You're all making a huge mistake!"

"Starting now, you are to head towards Arajor and take your seat in the Kraken. If you do not, you know what will happen. You will be found guilty of violating the very code that your forebears set in stone years ago. And losing your title of Magnum will be the very least of your concerns if that happens."

Shane sighed. Serizau and the council had him pinned down. He knew the real reason as to why they were trying to force him back to Arajor; they were trying to delay him from winning so they could put Serizau in the Magnum's chair. He couldn't overturn the law now; he would have to head home. But there was something else that he could do, something that he never would've conceived of doing otherwise. But he had to make it work.

"Very well," he finally said, the words shaking with subtle fury. "I'll set a course for Arajor. I'll play your game and direct the assault on Lhassi from the Kraken's sanctuary. But here's what I'm adding to the table. If the Gorogs are defeated, I get my right back to direct the war from the front lines." He paused, and then added, "*And* Serizau will not be appointed

282

Magnum of the Coalition after me."

There was a soft uproar among the council members. All of the holograms were staring at each other wide-eyed, scarcely believing that Shane was defying the will of the council. There was a dull roar of whispering between the people, only silence by Serizau yelling, "SILENCE!" The room fell quiet again, and Serizau turned to Shane, no longer smiling. His face was stone cold and clearly ticked off.

"Very well, Shane. I'll consider this your acceptance of our bet." He paused, thought for a brief moment, then said, "Here's what *I* want to add to this table. Unfortunately it's beyond the scope of our judicially-appointed power to remove you from office. I can't remove you from office through silly gambles like this. *But,* if you *lose* to the Gorogs, not only will your power as Magnum be stripped away from you, but you will be forbidden from working in the government again, and the only thing you will be permitted to rule over will be your own household or business that you run. That is it. Do I make these terms clear, or do I need to repeat them a second time?"

Shane was taken aback at how angry Serizau sounded, as if he could not envision the man with more power than him defying his wishes. He gave no sign of this on the outside, though, keeping his cool and relaxing in his chair. "Serizau," he began, pretending to sound friendly. "Quick question regarding what you just said. Should I prepare an impeachment trial for you or just outright court martial you and remove you from office for speaking to the Magnum in that disrespectful manner?"

Serizau immediately backed off, knowing that another hostile word could land him in big trouble. "My apologies, Magnum Shane," he said, sounding way friendlier now.

"Good. And now that we're acting like civilized men again, I'm adjourning the meeting. The next time you hear from me, councilmen and women, will be after we've won the decisive battle of the war. You can thank me at that time."

Shane ended the call before Serizau or another council member could stall him any longer. He slumped back in his chair, worn out from having to put up with the council. Yes, they were necessary to prevent a different Magnum from going off the rails and turning dictatorial, but he still wished that the one under him was more concerned with the welfare of the galaxy and not meddling in his own political affairs. It really was only Serizau; the council would likely fall into their rightful places if he was not on the council. But Shane also lacked the authority to remove a council member from office unless they were charged with a crime. He sighed. Some things would still be difficult for him even once the Gorogs were no longer a prime threat.

The door to the room opened behind him. It was Vorlax. "Sir?" he asked, staring at the back of Shane's head. "I heard shouting. Everything alright here?"

"More of the same, Vorlax," he replied, turning to face him. "I'll tell you about it in a little bit. For now, tell the navigators to set a course for Arajor. The council has ordered us to return."

"Can they do that?"

"They used their Dhimma to force me to return, more specifically Serizau did. I don't like it, but I don't dare go against it."

The commander nodded. "I'll let the men know, and tell Daniel and the others. What are you going to do?"

Shane stood up from his chair. "I'm going to suck out every little secret that Vraxis knows about the Gorogs. Personally."

Chapter 18

Deep in Gorog territory

Many, many light years from Daniel, Ms. Phillips' life had taken a major 180.

She had spent the past hour and a half in a state of pure vertigo, unable to sense most anything beyond faint signs, and feeling as though her brain had been hit by a truck. She could not move, her body still recovering from being stunned by Vraxis's rifle. She could faintly hear the roar of ship engines, but was too dazed to process which side they belonged to. It was only after a violent jolt awoke her that she became acutely aware of her predicament.

She was no longer in the welcoming, brilliantly-lit bedchamber that she had lived in on the *Justice*. She was kneeling in a dark cell, lit dimly by ominous red lights, with no windows and a solid, metal door blocking her escape. Not that she would be able to in the first place, as her hands were cuffed behind her back, a long steel cable linking them to the wall, holding her in place. In addition, a set of binders linked her ankles together as well. She could feel the vibrations of the craft she was on below her, and she imagined that they were in motion, heading to some sinister destination that she could not see.

She genuinely had no clue where they were taking her. Skorjion was unlikely, as it had just been destroyed not two days ago, so she assumed that she was being transferred to another prison to undergo more interrogations. Where that prison was, she didn't want to know. The thought of more Gorog torture sent shivers down her spine. She almost hoped that she would die, to avoid the horrors of another five years with the Gorogs, to have it be done and then ascend to join the saints in heaven. Alas, that wish had yet to be granted. She could only assume that Daniel and the others had avoided capture, considering that she saw no one else with her in the cell.

As she considered what she would do once she reached wherever she was being taken, a door slid open to the side, and, to Ms. Phillips' horror, Foulor waltzed in, a smug look on his rough face.

"We've almost arrived at your new domicile," he told her menacingly, looking outright pissed. "I still don't understand why Orvag sought you out, but whatever, it's his problem, not mine."

"I'm thirsty," she told him defiantly.

Foulor stared at her, almost contemplating her words. She was not sure that he would oblige her request, but to her surprise, Foulor backed out of the door and came back with a small container of water.

"Small sip, please," he told her, giving her the water. She cast one eye up at Foulor, raised the bottle to her lips, and drank a small portion of the vessel. It was refreshing and cold, just how she wanted it, but before she could drink anymore, Foulor took the bottle from her hand and shut the door on her face, leaving her alone and slightly cold.

After another, short period where she was lying on the cold cell floor, freezing, there was another jolt from the floor, which jarred her awake from her half-asleep state. A few moments later, the vibrations of the ship ceased entirely. The door was flung open again, and this time, Foulor was shadowed by a Gorog guard.

"Get her up," he commanded the guard, who nodded and hurried into the cell, using a key to disable Ms. Phillips's ankle binders. He did not, however, remove the ones on her wrists. Lifting her off the floor, the guard shoved her forward, and she began to walk as Foulor turned and led the way through the ship's interior. It was a small shuttle, with two pilot seats, and a third seat elevated, likely for him to use. A small ramp led out the back, underneath where her cell was located. And through a window, she saw something very large on the other side, and as she was pushed out of the shuttle, she realized where she was.

She was not, as she had expected, in another Gorog slave camp. In fact, looking straight ahead as she exited, she wasn't even on another planet. She was in a gigantic hangar, rectangular in shape, with a ceiling that looked like it was miles away, ships of all sizes lining every last square foot of available floor space, much like the main hangar on the *Justice*. The difference was a small army of Gorogs in deep green uniforms cleaning and repairing the ships, and the hellish orange-red light that bathed the entire space, saturating every surface. As they walked, two Gorog high guards, signified by their long spears, approached her group.

"King Orvag has received word that you have arrived," they told Foulor. "He is waiting on the bridge. He requests that you bring the Terran with you to see him."

"Very well," replied Foulor. "I'm heading up there now. Which route would be fastest to get there?"

"Take the inner monorail, the yellow one, Line D, all the way to its end. The elevator there leads directly to the bridge deck."

"Good. I have some affairs that need to be resolved as soon as possible."

Ms. Phillips began to worry even more. Shane had told her enough about Orvag to know that he was not a benevolent ruler at all. Yet there was nothing she could do to delay the guards or Foulor as they roughly grabbed her by the arms and shoved her along, down a narrow passageway that branched off from the hangar with more guards, performing a patrol through the heart of the ship. The corridors were relatively broad, and they brushed past without incident. They passed dozens of other Gorog soldiers, all sculking through the hallways, serving to unsettle Ms. Phillips greatly. After two more turns, they came to a halt in front of a door, which Foulor opened, revealing the cavernous interior of the warship they were on.

Ms. Phillips had no way of knowing this, but one of the things that the ship she was on, the *Deceiver*, was known for was its giant monorail system that ran to nearly every corner of the ship, dwarfing the one housed in the *Justice's* atrium. The *Deceiver,* being nearly 8 miles long from bow to stern, had need of such a transportation system, and so Orvag had commissioned the enormous complex to be built to help ease getting around. Now Ms. Phillips found herself gazing upon the monorail system, a spaghetti weave of metal, with tracks darting in and out of the central space. Trains charged at high speeds down the track, carrying cargo, supplies, and troops to every corner of the ship.

The guards pushed her onto a platform that was stocked with some metal containers. One of the tracks had a junction with a tributary, which came to rest alongside the platform, and a train was parked there, waiting. There were five cars; three of them were open for boxes and containers, with cars two and four having additional barriers and metal roofs for actual Gorogs. Foulor, Ms. Phillips, and his two guards stepped on, grabbing hold of the handles that were mounted to the roof. When Ms. Phillips hesitated, taking note of the large drop to the bottom of the chamber, Foulor turned to her.

"I'd grab onto that handle if I were you," he said slimily. "It's a long way down, and those barriers do not afford much protection."

As much as she hated the twin, Ms. Phillips complied, reaching up with both hands and grabbing hold of one of the straps. And not a moment too soon, in fact, as a second later the train accelerated forward with a surprising amount of speed, causing everyone to be forced back by the g-forces. The train merged with one of the main tracks, joining two other trains up and to the right as they barreled through the interior of the ship. The ride was a little bumpy, but everyone kept gripping the handles, making the escort look almost like a group of people standing on a subway car. Ms. Phillips, from out the side, watched as more platforms and trains whizzed by, as they continued to ride through the center for a couple of minutes, until the train hit another junction and peeled off onto another platform, where the vehicle came to a smooth stop.

Ms. Phillips was shoved yet again onto the platform, with Foulor following. "I'll take her from here," he told his guards. "Go wait by my quarters until I say otherwise."

They nodded and stayed on the train, leaving Foulor and Ms. Phillips to walk down another dimly lit hallway, the sounds of the monorail system fading behind them. More guards walked by, armed with every form of weapon under the sun, from firearms to many different types of melee weapons. Some of them dipped their heads in respect as Foulor strode past, his presence commanding the hallway. Clearly, he was respected by the soldiers, even though he was not a Gorog himself. After a while, they reached a set of elevator doors nestled way in the back of the ship.

"In," ordered Foulor, shoving Ms. Phillips inside. He followed behind her, shutting the doors and gripping her forearm tightly to prevent her from escaping. The lift began to rise at a rapid rate up through the heart of the cruiser, and Ms. Phillips broke out in a nervous sweat. Not only was she terrified at the prospect of more torture, but she was dead tired, hungry, and thirsty, and could barely stand on her own. She felt as if she were in a constant state of dreaming, only this time her dream was actually real. And it was actually a nightmare.

In no time at all, the elevator came to a halt. How far they had gone, Ms. Phillips didn't know. Nor did she care to know, as she was being led forward onto what she could only assume was the ship command deck. Two sets of stairs branched off to either side of the walkway they were on, and there was a balcony overlooking a set of giant windows. Directly ahead, facing out towards the windows, was a large, black-and-gold throne with the same double-sword insignia on the back that Ms. Phillips had seen constantly when she was in Skorjion, and what she now knew to be the banner of the Gorogs. The throne slowly turned around, revealing its occupant; large in build, with a mess of tentacles drooping down from his chin. A golden crown adorned his forehead, and a long green cape flowed down from around his shoulders. Behind the throne, a figure that Ms. Phillips recognized stood; Warden Dormak, looking as evil as ever. He smiled an evil smile as she was forced into the chamber, to stand before the throne.

"Foulor," acknowledged who she suspected was Orvag in an evilly smooth and silky voice that would have been the envy of any movie supervillain.

"Your Highness," replied Foulor, bowing low with his arms crossed.

"Please, no need for pleasantries at this rate. Orvag will be fine for now."

"In that case, Orvag," corrected Foulor. "I have one of the targets that you requested."

The king rose from his chair, revealing his tall form and gold-inlaid military uniform. "Is this her?" he asked, pointing to Ms. Phillips, who was wide-eyed with fear by this point.

Foulor nodded.

"Where are the others? There were four targets that I listed for you, yet here I only see one!"

"Security was more stubborn than we anticipated. We had to retreat, so we unfortunately only got one."

Orvag put his face into his hand. "I told you that if there was one scumbag that you had to get, it was Subject X-17! This is not him!" He stopped, then looked behind Foulor, confused. "Say, where's Vraxis? He's usually right with you!"

Foulor's face darkened. "They got him."

"Say what again?"

"I said, *they got him*. Shane. He's probably being interrogated right now as we speak."

Orvag leaned back in his chair, concern on his face. "Will he talk?" he asked.

"He's not your pet, Orvag! He only answers to money, not from any loyalty to someone." He paused. "Say, that's actually a pretty good saying right there."

Orvag turned to Dormak. "Prepare a cell and drag her down there. I'll be there shortly to…give her some company." He smiled wickedly at Ms. Phillips as she was picked up and dragged off, causing her stomach to violently heave. It was a cold smile, with no humor behind it. It made her extremely uncomfortable.

Once she was out of the room, Foulor turned back to Dormak. "With permission, I'd like to stage a rescue of my brother."

"From the *Justice?* That's impossible. Shane's ship was too much for both of you to handle, and without your brother, you'd be good as dead walking in there."

"But…"

"You two are supposed to be the best of the best!" raged Orvag. "You two only had to get on the ship, find the four targets, apprehend them, and get out! Instead, you go ahead and make a big show out of it and walk away with one of the lesser-valued slaves, leaving your brother behind to rot in a cell!"

"You told us to raid the most secure ship in the galaxy! The one that carries the Magnum himself around! Surely you would have known that, even for us, the odds of success were slim!"

Orvag glowered at him. "And here I thought you two

were immortal figures, above the Coalition's puny soldiers. Apparently, I was wrong."

"I want to get my brother out of there! He doesn't deserve to die that way!"

"You're not exactly the brightest brain out there, Foulor! After all, I firmly believe that your brother was the main reason behind your success! Take that away, and you're nothing more than a strong, tough, but ultimately dimwitted bodyguard who sounds like he's had too much alcohol!"

"If he's that important to you, let's go get him back!" shouted Foulor in anger, making a surprisingly logical argument in the process.

"NO!" roared Orvag, raising to his full height and making even Foulor look small. "I cannot spare any men at this time to go and save him from Coalition custody! Not when we're this close to the ultimate destruction of Shane's pathetic empire!"

"He's my brother!"

"FOULOR! YOU WILL NOT LEAVE THIS SHIP UNLESS YOU HAVE MY PERMISSION TO DO SO! AND IF YOU DO, I SWEAR TO THE GODS, *YOU* WILL BE PUT IN THE CELL RIGHT NEXT TO THAT EARTH WOMAN! DO I MAKE MYSELF CLEAR?!"

Orvag's screaming carried all the way to the ceiling, causing his own men to turn around in surprise. Foulor shrank back, frustrated, but ultimately yielding the point. "Yes, Your Highness," he said, sullenly.

"Get back to your quarters," the king growled, directing him towards the exit. "I'll send you a message if I have need of your talents."

Foulor, fighting the urge to leap for his throat, dipped his head and walked out, fuming on the inside. It had been a pact he had made with his brother that they would never leave each other's side, under any circumstances. To be denied that was an insult of extreme proportions. But, instead of protest, he set the elevator to his floor and began to descend.

Back up in the bridge, Orvag watched his hunter retreat, then pulled out his radio. "Dormak!" he barked. "Get up here as soon as you take care of our guest! We have a problem to discuss!"

Some time later, Orvag and Dormak convened around a holoprojected map of the galaxy, intent on finding anything that could assist them beat Shane to victory. "These are the places Shane has been in the last week," said the king, zooming in on a certain area of the galaxy. "He started out in his own territory, near Grovidor, then attacked our outpost on Shaanak with three other ships." A red trail marking Shane's path began to cross the map, showing where the Magnum had been in the past. "He seized the outpost, thus opening up a huge hole in our outer defenses. My father tried to stop them, but alas, he was not in his element and he was forced to flee back to Tersak. The fleet then split, with the three supporting ships heading into the Centaurus arm towards the Great Nothing and Diamondhead Outpost, while Shane continued along, and then attacked Grimcor and bombed Skorjion three days ago. He cripples the camp entirely, then proceeds back out of Gorog territory, the raid party on Diamondhead proceeding towards a rendezvous point just outside of our lands." He highlighted the location of the trading outpost in purple, and marked the rendezvous point on the map. "They've been targeting our centers of production ever since the war's earliest days, but they've only received the intel to the whereabouts of our primary centers and labor camps in the last few years. Note where they've been concentrating their attacks recently."

He flipped another switch and every major battle fought with Orion Coalition forces was highlighted in blue, with a timestamp next to each showing what year they were fought and the duration of the battle itself. "Every major engagement fought in the last seven months has been near factory sites or mining camps, or have outposts or fleets that stood in the way. Of those, three of those sites were destroyed, but none of them were very large. The fact that they found Skorjion and were able to cripple it that badly…that was serious oversight from all involved. Now they possess the means to basically shut down all our means of production with one attack."

"What do we do about Lhassi?" prompted Dormak. "I mean, a battle is essentially guaranteed now that they have the means to get into the planet's sector."

"True, which means we can prepare for their arrival. But they'll also be expecting us to have prepared to meet them, since they'll likely decide that we also found out what they were after."

"So, what do we do?"

Orvag pondered this for a moment, wondering how it was best to proceed. "See the outpost right here, in the Outer Arm near the border?" He highlighted a small border outpost near the edge of the galactic disk. It was a respectable base, with maybe 3,000 Gorog soldiers guarding it. A large task force was needed in case the Coalition came knocking one day, as the outpost was the first line of defense between Shane's armies and the rest of the Gorog Empire.

"Yeah, one of our border stations," said Dormak. "Designed to help keep the Orion Coalition out of our land. What about it?"

"I want you to take a thousand of their best men and transfer them to Lhassi effective immediately to buffer the defenses there. With an attack imminent, I want every available soldier to move there to counter any assault. The remaining two thousand are to be stationed on this ship in reserve in case they are needed."

"Sir, I beg your pardon for asking this, but you want us to abandon that outpost? Just…leave it up for grabs?"

"In the grand scheme of things, Dormak, one little outpost will not have a huge influence on the outcome of the war. Now, losing our largest grouping of factories on the other hand, that could very well be the deciding factor in whether or not we lose the war. I'd rather the outpost falls in order to keep the majority of our empire intact, wouldn't you agree?"

Dormak swallowed anything he was about to say. "Yes, sir," he said, knowing it was best to stay silent before Orvag, especially when he was spitting logic out of his brain. He truly was a master at military strategizing.

"Those thousand men should help Warden Trivass beef up the security around Lhassi and Rhozadar," continued Orvag. Warden Trivass was the Gorog in charge of the camp's security, much like how Dormak ruled over Skorjion. "And to ensure that the camp has a proper general to defend it, I will be going as well."

This took Dormak aback. "You're going to Lhassi in person, my lord?" When Orvag shot him a glare, he hastily added, "Not that I doubt your intentions, sir, but isn't going in person a bit of a risk? I mean, if you fall in battle, that'll be it for our efforts to defeat the Coalition. Perhaps…it would be a bit wiser to…" He paused, trying to choose his words as carefully as possible. "…stay and direct the defense of Lhassi remotely?"

Thankfully, Orvag did not lose his temper at his suggestion. "I see where you're coming from, Dormak. I appreciate your concern for my well-being, but this is war, and some risks must be taken in order to ensure a victory. I'll be fine, I promise. After all, you'll be there as well to cover my back, as will Foulor."

"You…want me there as well, sir?"

"But of course!" Orvag sounded almost insulted at the question. "You're my most loyal soldier and advisor. What would I be able to do without your counsel and combat skills? You'll be there to help keep me out of trouble. Anyways, with Vraxis in custody, there is the danger involved that is Shane feeding him money to make him talk. If he spills out any of Rhozadar's weaknesses, which he knows, we'll need to be there to counter any of Shane's attacks."

Dormak slowly nodded. "I understand, sir."

"Good. Now send out the orders to the outpost. Tell them to abandon the outpost immediately and disperse the men in the way we discussed. In the meantime, I'll make the necessary preparations to head in that direction."

Dormak started to reach for the dash on the holoprojector to send out a prerecorded message to the outpost, but then stopped as he realized there was something they forgot. "Sir!" he spoke up. "What about Subject X-17 and the other escaped slaves?"

Orvag facepalmed his hand. "For heaven's sake, you're right!" he exclaimed in frustration. "How are we going to get them back amid all of this?"

Both Gorogs sat down, Orvag in his throne, Dormak next to the holoprojector. Neither of them really had a clue as to how they should proceed with the escaped slaves. Orvag was starting to see why his father was always grumpy as king; he had to deal with a dozen different things on his itinerary, and manage all of them successfully. Now, he was managing the defense of their primary camp, the future invasion plans for Arajor, ensuring that his transfer to power was stable among his own people, covering up the dragon that had destroyed Diamondhead, and getting the lizard and his entire group back. And those were just the big things. There was no telling how many small things would be on the list in addition to all of those.

"We can't possibly risk sending another fleet to try and invade the *Justice*," Dormak said, stroking his mess of chin tentacles. "If Vraxis and Foulor couldn't do it, then no one would be able to. And we won't know where they're going to be, either. But we need them back, especially if the forthcoming invasion is going to go off smoothly."

"You're right. At this point, we should just focus on getting our prizes back before they cause us any more grief. And I think I have an idea on how we might be able to get the entire party back into our possession." An evil smile crossed Orvag's face at the thought. He pulled up a video feed from the center of the *Justice*, taken on the camera that he had put on Foulor's chest to record everything that transpired there.

"What exactly were you thinking of?"

"Using the twins to attempt to recover our lost property was our first choice of a plan," Orvag reminded Dormak, watching the group of slaves try to defend themselves from the twins. "Now, if my memory serves me correctly, there's a certain prisoner down in the brig who just arrived in, and has ties to the rest of the escaped slaves. And who could be used as leverage to release Vraxis from prison, thereby appeasing Foulor as well."

Dormak remembered Ms. Phillips. "The old Terran woman?"

Orvag nodded. "Have her cell prepared for my arrival. Bring my finest interrogators and torturers as well, and all their tricks and trappings. If she has information to tell us, we'll extract if from her, even if we need to use an IV to do it."

He turned back to the footage from the camera feed, and caught something odd in the lower part of the screen. He rewinded, because the camera view was being blocked by Max. The girl, the friend of the woman's son, was shooting a rifle, then turned to face a pair of exposed wires in the wall. Her hand glowed faintly for a second, and then she grabbed one of the wires, causing the atrium lights to flicker. Orvag fingered his chin, wondering what this meant. There was only one certain kind of being who could wield such a power, and from what

Orvag was seeing, this girl didn't even know what she had tapped into.

"And I think I have a place to start. Get me a recording device up here. Now! And tell the guards that I'm going to pay our new friend a little visit!"

The Gorog brig was a dark, ominous corridor lined with cells that was located in the very heart of the ship. Orvag and Dormak strode down the hallway, passing by guards posted in front of every occupied cell. There were dozens of them lining the hallway, as they always had lots of prisoners on board. Dormak was carrying a long metal stick with two prongs on each side and a button built into the handle. They eventually came to a cell numbered D-47, and opened it, the guards nodding in acknowledgment. Inside, Ms. Phillips was suspended against the wall, hanging by several thick steel cables around her ankles, wrists, and waist. She was still looking a little dazed, but her face immediately perked up and hardened upon seeing the two Gorogs in her cell.

"I don't suppose you've come to give me food," she said. In response, Dormak walked over to a control panel on the wall and released all of her cables, causing her to drop to the floor, where she lay, dizzy.

"First lesson of the day. Being snide with either of us will not get you very far," growled Orvag, towering over her considerably. "Now, we have some questions for you to answer. If you cooperate, perhaps I can get you a bite to eat. If you resist our interrogation, you will be punished. Severely. Understand?"

She nodded slowly, glancing over at Dormak, who was twirling around his metal staff eagerly, as though he could not wait to use it. "Yes," she said.

Orvag lifted her up and brought her to a kneeling position. "What is your relation with these three missing slaves?"

he began, shoving an image into her face. She glanced at it, seeing the faces of Daniel and Caitlin in the security feed, as well as Max lurking behind them. She recognized the picture as a shot from their escape routine, and immediately swallowed.

"I...don't know," she lied, immediately seeing where this was going. "I've never seen them before in my life."

Orvag's face fell. He turned around and pointed at Dormak, who handed him the stick. He powered it on, the ends lighting up with violet-colored electricity, and jabbed it into Ms. Phillips' side. She immediately convulsed hard from the shock, sharp pains filling her body. It was intense pain like she had never felt, and it was several seconds before Orvag removed the prongs from her skin.

"Liar," the king told her. "We have security footage that Dormak has handily provided from Skorjion, showing extended interactions with these two humans as far back as two years ago. Second thing you should know; lying to us will result in more pain like what you just experienced. Now, what is your relation to these missing slaves? The truth, this time!"

She groaned. Her feet felt numb from the shock, her entire body tingling. Her brain struggled to process information, but she managed to say, "The boy is my son. She is his best friend. The lizard we only just met." She braced for another shock, but it never came. Instead, Orvag handed the stick back to Dormak.

"That's much better," the king said, much in the same way you'd compliment a dog who listened. "Now, what's your name? The camp records we have are sadly incomplete, and we were not able to find your name. What is it?"

"Caitlin Richards," she replied, referencing an old friend of hers. Then she immediately regretted her words, as another painful shock came lancing across her body, delivered by Orvag.

"More lies. You're not making good progress here. See, I lied as well, but unlike you, I get to because I have information to get out of you. I have your real name safely in my memory, courtesy of Dormak. So, Amy Phillips, are you going to start cooperating or are you going to make this more difficult on yourself?"

She did not answer. Her entire body was starting to feel fuzzy from the concentrated jolt. She struggled to breathe, her lungs feeling like they were being sat on. Orvag exchanged a look with Dormak, then knelt down beside her.

"Listen, if you want, I can keep zapping you all day long until you give me some real answers. This thing won't kill you, but it will make you wish you were dead, for sure. Just tell me what I want to know, and the pain stops. It's that simple." Orvag seemed to relish every word he spoke as Ms. Phillips lay suffering at his feet. "Perhaps a different method of persuasion, then?"

He jabbed the two prongs into Ms. Phillips arm, just enough to pierce the flesh, but he did not turn it on. She screamed with pain as the sharp ends came out of her arm and the puncture wounds began to bleed out.

"Who are these three slaves? Tell me!" yelled Orvag, the stick raised over his head. When he got no answer, he brought the stick down into her other arm, this time fully energized. Ms. Phillips screamed out loud as more intense pain lanced through her entire body. Every nerve was on fire, every muscle having a seizure, every cell in her body wanting to curl up and die.

And as Orvag continued his never-ending torture, you could hear her screams from the end of the brig's hallway.

Chapter 19

The *Justice*

On the *Justice,* the brig was located in a heavily isolated area, separate from all other important facilities and electronics. It was far off the main pathway through the heart of the cruiser, down several flights of stairs and through lots of tight corridors. It was meant to function as a temporary holding center for prisoners caught on the battlefield itself. Shane seemed to notice that the closer you got to the brig, the darker the ship's hallways became. There was this evil aura that hung over this entire section of the ship, and it made Shane uneasy every time he crossed into it. Their brig mainly contained straggler Gorog soldiers, maybe a few officers, but nowhere near as close as to the importance of Vraxis. The fact that one of the most dangerous beings in the entire galaxy was now stored on the same ship on him made Shane shiver slightly as he reached the thick iron door that led to the cell block. He put on a straight face as the two guards at the door dipped their heads and pushed the switch to open the door.

Vraxis was somewhere in there, he knew. And he would likely resist his advances to extract information by normal means. He had interrogators who specialized in getting out information from prisoners, but he knew that, with Vraxis, it would be way more difficult than normal. But, if there was one advantage that Shane had, it was the knowledge that he was dealing with a bounty hunter, not a Gorog general. The heavy gate slowly swung open, the only door on the entire ship that didn't slide into place. Shane passed through it and took note of the dim red lighting, the occasional guard, and row after row of cell doors, behind some of which were sworn enemies of the Coalition. Vraxis, so Shane had been told, was imprisoned in cell

GS-47, and had been placed under heavy guard to minimize his chance of escape. The cell was conveniently marked by the four guards outside, always watching him to ensure they did not escape. Shane approached one of them.

"I'm here to interrogate the prisoner," he told him. "Permission to enter Vraxis' cell?"

The guard nodded and opened the door to allow Shane to pass. He passed the threshold, gazing upon Vraxis, who was strung up in the center by four thin glowing wires, wrapped around his wrists and ankles. The hunter was panting heavily, and when he saw Shane, his eyes immediately narrowed into slits. All of his weapons, and there were a lot of them, had been removed, leaving just him, his clothes, and his anger hanging.

"Just the man I was interested in seeing," he growled, his eyes narrowing further as Shane drew closer to him. He tried to move closer to him, only for the wire attached to his left arm to send a jolt of electricity circuiting down into his arm, causing him to immediately pull back and growl at Shane like a wild animal.

"Well, if you wanted me, here I am," replied the Magnum, with no humor in his voice whatsoever. He relished knowing that one of his most annoying foes was now in his custody. And now that he actually could take a good look at him, he realized that Vraxis, the leader of the twins, and Orvag's best agent of chaos, was on the smaller side by all standards, and downright tiny by normal Travashian standards. Most of their alien brethren were giants, seven feet tall at the minimum and with muscles that made even the strongest human look tiny. Shane had never laid his eyes on either twin before the attack, only hearing reports of their deeds via message, and only now did he realize that one of his most dangerous adversaries was smaller than he had expected.

Vraxis's body relaxed and he raised his chin to look at Shane down between his nose. "So, to what reason do I owe this visit? Perhaps you want to take a look at the entity who gave you and your men hell for so very long? Or, more likely, you want information that I'm holding regarding Orvag and the Gorogs, true?"

"No, actually. What I want is to inform you as to what is going to happen to you. Because, as a sworn enemy of the Orion Coalition, and one of the Gorog's biggest allies, you, by all accounts, should be put to death." Shane gave him a stare to ensure that he was paying attention and then continued speaking. "I'm faced with a tough decision. On the one hand, I could lock you up forever, or even execute you probably, so that I never have to deal with you again. I'm sure that the guards at the asteroid prison would be delighted to take you in." He remembered what Daniel had said, about finding another way, and an idea formed in his brain. "Or, I could propose…call it a truce agreement. I understand that Orvag pays you tons of money to run his work for him?"

"What's it to you?" Vraxis demanded, eyes still narrowed. "You, Shane, of all people should know what the hunters' association would do to us if we were to break our contract with Orvag. My government does not take kindly to hunters giving away personal information."

"Luckily for you, first of all, it was the Orion Coalition who gave the Hunters' Party the planet Kotor in the first place. And secondly, that question was entirely rhetorical. I have security camera footage of you telling your own men that Orvag offered you 30,000 credits to bring in Subject X-17, whoever that is, and 5,000 for any one of his three companions. So the correct answer is…Orvag offered you a lot of money to run this job for him. Enough so that you wouldn't have to work for quite some time…I'd say, a year, maybe two if you spent it wisely. Which, I doubt. 30,000 credits is a lot, but I've heard enough about Foulor to know that he's not exactly the smartest person alive. Now, this is where things get strange. I'm here and ready to offer you 1.5 million units each if you give me the information I'm looking for, if you swear on the spirit of Skarako to never work with Orvag again, and if you aid us with the coming battle of Lhassi against the Gorogs. Let that total sink in. 1.5 million credits. That would sustain you for pretty much the rest of your life, and, unless my math is wrong, is way more than Orvag offered you. All you have to do is tell me what I'm looking for. That's it. Do what I ask and your life is nothing but relaxing and comfort until you die. And I know how long you've been in this bounty hunting business…I'm sure you would at least want a break at some point. And let it be known that by doing this I could be risking my reputation by trusting you to do anything for us and not sending you to the firing range."

Vraxis's face was stuck in place. It was clear that Shane's words had penetrated through to him. He had hoped they would; 1.5 million credits was an enormous sum. That was more than his annual salary. He knew that Foulor would immediately jump at the chance to seize the money. It was clear to Shane that the idea was attractive to them, so he decided to increase the leverage he now had. He pushed a button on the wall, and the cables fell around Vraxis's extremities, causing him to fall to the floor.

"Here's another gesture of my goodwill," he said curtly. "You can choose to accept my proposal and live happily for the rest of your life. Or, you can reject my extremely generous proposal and I can have my best interrogators siphon the information I want out of you, with an IV if I have to, and then dump your rotten body on one of our asteroid prisons. And you don't have to be a criminal to know how infamous those places are for their inescapability. There you will stay until you are rotting in your cell and the flies eat your remains. You will never run another mission for anyone, and you will be judged as though you were one of the Coalition's most wanted enemies, because you are. So," he said finally, spreading his arms out, "think about it. Discuss which one you'd rather have. Comfort for the rest of your life, or eternal pain in a tiny cell thousands of light years from the nearest inhabited planet. The choice is yours. And a word of advice from me; don't pick the wrong one."

With that, he turned and left the hunter in his cell to think about his future, hoping he had said enough to convince him to make the call that he wanted. He had staked a lot of money on the line, but if Vraxis took the bait, it would be a small price to pay in the long run.

Dinner on the *Justice* was something that had lost its amazing taste by this point. The cuts of meat that Shane had his personal chef prepare for them tasted delicious, and they featured a mix of spices and meat juices that would have caused the taste buds on Daniel's tongue to sing. He just felt worn out and stressed out all at once. He had successfully saved the lives of Max, Caitlin, Pantura, and his mom, but had lost her in the process. The tension of the battle was gone, but his anxiety was ripping at his inside like some ferocious beast, refusing to let him be at peace. He took a sip of his drink, which was carbonated to a ridiculous extent and caused bubbles to go up his nose and make him hiccup. He tensed up and cast a glance up in Shane's direction. Neither he nor Vorlax, who was sitting next to him, made any sign that they noticed. Nor did Caitlin, who happened to be sitting right next to him. She was too busy munching down on her food to notice.

"Dinner's amazing, Shane," she said, even Caitlin's voice being dragged down by the events of the day. She had also showered and changed and was now wearing a fresh bandage over her blaster wound, the same as Daniel. A doctor had seen them both in the medical wing and had checked them out, and had said they would both make a full recovery by tomorrow. They had given them some pills to take that would help speed up the clotting process and left after that. Daniel was glad that nothing was truly wrong with either of them. He had no clue as to the effects of blaster bolts that grazed a person, since he had only seen them impact directly onto their targets and instantly kill them.

"Thanks," replied Shane, who was biting into one of his vegetables. "I'm glad you're enjoying your Mizar intestines. It's one of our finest delicacies. A favorite of mine to be sure."

The look of disgust that crossed Caitlin's face at the revelation that she was eating part of some alien beast's digestive tract did nothing to help Daniel's demeanor. He was sure that Max would have enjoyed his portion, except he had been delayed in the medical wing and had to sit this meal out. This came through Shane himself, who wanted the lizard to undergo some tests after the news about his size changes were made known to him. Daniel couldn't blame him. He would've been curious too if one of the random strangers he had picked up could grow in size. Pantura was also nowhere to be found, as she had elected to stay in her room and recover from the electrical trauma she received while flying that gunship. She had promised to join them later.

They were preparing to jump to lightspeed. Daniel knew this, since he had heard the alarms signaling the jump while on his way to dinner, and had seen tons of control workers darting about. It boggled his mind that such a thing was possible, even out here in a star-studded galaxy with civilizations far more advanced than Earth. Then again, it also boggled his mind that he kept seeing aliens with four arms or heads shaped like a pistol that were wearing khaki pants and cotton shirts like there were in a business-casual meeting in a cafe somewhere on Earth. He was still wrapping his head around that, to be honest. He would have predicted a lot of things would happen should aliens exist, but for them to wear the clothes he was familiar with was not one of them. It still felt weird after living among aliens for several days now. One thing that was suspicious; Shane was continually looking over at the door to the kitchen during the meal. It was probably nothing, but it was still a little strange, Daniel thought.

Dinner was gone quickly, thanks to everyone being in a hungry mood after a long day, in spite of the worrying developments. After the plates had been carted away and everyone had settled back into their cushioned chairs, Shane rose from his seat to address Daniel and Caitlin. "I just wanted to say, in front of Vorlax, that on behalf of the entire Orion Coalition, I want to thank both of you for your bravery today. You fought hard and risked your lives; and all for an organization that you had only just met."

"You saved our lives first," said Caitlin. "It's only fair that we returned the favor."

"I still wish that I could've saved my mother," grumbled Daniel. "We helped you out, and saved ourselves, but now my mom's back in the hands of the Gorogs. We know where she is, but we're making no move towards going to save her."

"We'll get her back, Daniel. You can have my word. She won't stay a prisoner for long. Rest assured, if she's in Rhozadar, we'll find her and bring her home."

Daniel nodded. "Thank you, Shane."

"I'll be honest, you two just keep on surprising me time after time," Vorlax said, speaking for the first time that evening. Daniel was convinced that he had been chewing on his food the rest of the time before that. "Shane can vouch for me that it's hard to surprise me in just about anything."

"That I can, old friend," Shane casually replied, shooting Vorlax a slightly mischievous glance. "Daniel, Pantura told me that you took control of the gunship you were on once she was knocked out...is that true?"

Vorlax turned back to face Daniel. He blushed. "I've driven a car before, it wasn't that hard," he said defensively.

"I've driven a car before and flown many starfighters.

That wasn't luck," replied Vorlax. "You managed to hold off a lot of Gorog starfighters for a good long while. It seems as though you've got a thing for flying ships like that one. Perhaps some leadership skills, too...Pantura also told me that you apparently took charge of the whole situation and saved everyone. That took real guts there."

"Well, I wouldn't have been able to do it without Caitlin acting as my spotter," he replied, giving her an encouraging glance. She smiled back at him and gave him a small thumbs-up.

"And Max...sheesh, I was going through the security camera footage from the day, and I saw what he did to those Gorog troops. Was he that way in Skorjion too?"

Daniel nodded. "Perhaps even more destructive there, Vorlax," he said. "Even Gorog riot armor was no match for his claws."

"I had to send him down to the bloodworkers to get some samples of his DNA. I've met plenty of reptiles in my time, but one who could change their size at will...he's special for sure, that one," Shane added.

"And, Caitlin, did you want to hear about what we found in the security feed of you? Something...interesting, to say the least?"

Caitlin's face immediately fell, to the surprise of everyone. She hesitated, twitching slightly and casting a nervous glance at Daniel, who leaned in and whispered, "Just ask them. It's probably nothing of consequence."

"Umm...yes, please?" she finally said slowly.

"You did well out there, today. Holding your own against the twins and their squad. Vorlax told me that you were a pretty good shot."

She let loose a massive, albeit silent sigh, her secret still safe for the moment. "So, what happens now?" she asked..

"We're currently preparing to head towards Arajor, the official center of the Orion Coalition," Shane told her. "The council there has ordered us back. From there, we'll be turning around and embarking to Lhassi, to end this war for good."

"So Arajor's the capital, basically?"

"Yeah, you could say that. Believe me, you won't want to miss it. I've taken multiple first-timers on a tour, and they all react the same."

"As for in the meantime, the combat simulator room door will be unlocked if you need to use it at any time. Be my guest and train as much as you want. Just don't damage anything important, because if you do, I will know who did it." Vorlax held up a small tablet that was linked to a security camera feed. Daniel nodded, understanding, but he wondered if he would even need it at this point. They did not expect him to participate in the upcoming battle, did they? His mom was down there, but surely, he was not reckless enough to go down there himself, right?

That is, until the intercom beeped, and Shane answered. "This is Shane, what is it?" he asked, listening to the other end. Daniel could not hear what was being said, but from the look of utter confusion and shock on Shane's face, it did not seem good. When Shane hung up the phone, his face was no longer smiling.

"It's a message. From Orvag himself. And it's for Daniel."

The bridge was crowded with officers and crew members when Daniel, Caitlin, Shane and Vorlax emerged onto the bridge from the elevator, so much so that it was virtually impossible to see the holographic projector at all. Word must have spread like wildfire around the *Justice* that Orvag, the Gorog king himself, had demanded an audience with Shane and Daniel. This, Daniel guessed, was why the bridge was far more crowded than the first time he had visited. There was a constant chatter in the air, as Coalition personnel whispered amongst themselves at whether the rumor spreading around the ship was actually true. There was a lot of doubt and curiosity in the air, and the tension on the bridge was palpable in the air.

"I would've hoped that this would've stayed more secret," Shane said, commenting on the audience that had formed around the central holoprojector. "Alas…" He clearly had wanted to keep this under wraps as much as possible. Daniel didn't blame him in the slightest.

The machine was buzzing on and off, flashing red lights around the room, a sign that there was a message impending. Daniel and his group pushed to the front of the circle, and Vorlax moved to turn the machine on. Before he pushed the answer button, he turned to Shane, Daniel, and the rest of the room.

"Before I turn this on, I must warn you that there is likely going to be disturbing content in this message, and that this is a live feed. This has not been prerecorded at all. I ask that anything that happens in here is kept under wraps for the sake of Shane and Daniel. Is that clear?"

A lot of heads nodded. Including Daniel's. "Turn it on. Please," he said. The suspense was killing him, and he needed answers to this. Why would the king of the entire Gorog Empire request to be put on live hologram in front of Shane's entire staff to speak to someone that he had never met? It made no sense. He had to know why.

Vorlax nodded back, and, after a long, hesitant pause, pushed the button. The projector immediately whirred to life and two huge figures emerged into the room. Daniel recognized one of them immediately; Warden Dormak, the man who had run Skorjion with an iron fist, and who had been responsible for quite a few of his beatings over the years. Daniel recognized that massive frame and intimidating stare even via hologram. The other figure he could not identify by his face, as it was new to him, but by his adornment. The huge gold crown and gilded robes, combined with the very long beard of tentacles, gave Daniel enough reason to assume that the second figure was indeed Orvag himself. The king was even larger than Dormak, managing to be a couple of inches taller than his companion, and his eyes, though color-changed from the holographic projection, still had a sense of malice behind them that made the hairs on Daniel's arm stand on edge. Whatever Orvag was feeling, it most certainly was not goodwill of any kind.

"Shane." Orvag let the name slide out of his mouth as if it was the name of Satan itself upon seeing the Magnum standing before him.

"Orvag." Shane replied with equal hatred. It was clear to Daniel that the two rulers abjectly hated each other, given their long rivalry and opposing views.

"I see you got my message," the Gorog king replied, voice remaining dangerously low. His eyes scanned the room, falling squarely upon Daniel to the right of Shane. The minute they did, Daniel began to feel his stomach squirming around. The most powerful king in the galaxy, and a tyrant for that matter, was staring straight at him. It was a feeling of terror that he had never felt before, and he wanted to curl up in a closet somewhere and hide until it disappeared.

"So, this is the one who helped deny Foulor the chance to capture him and his companions. The one who helped capture Vraxis." Orvag laughed to himself softly, then burrowed those evil eyes straight into Daniel's soul. He then proceeded to utter two words. Two words that Daniel had heard a thousand times before, but somehow, in the moment, felt as though he had never heard them before.

"Hello Daniel."

Daniel nearly fainted from fear. His chest clenched up again the way it always did prior to an anxiety attack. Here he was, twenty-year old Daniel Phillips, a nobody from Earth and fugitive slave of the Gorog Empire, and one of the most powerful rulers in the entire galaxy was speaking his name to him. To his right, Caitlin looked utterly petrified from fear as well. She let out a small noise, and Orvag immediately snapped his attention in her direction.

"And this must be Caitlin," the king said. "How honored to finally meet you."

Caitlin squeaked again, a noise that meant nothing but absolute terror, too terrified to notice her hands sparking like crazy and the bridge personnel who were starting to notice. Daniel tried to speak, but to no avail. Both he and Caitlin were too terrified to say anything. Shane finally broke the tension the only way he knew how.

"Enough of the pleasantries, Orvag. You have a lot of courage demanding an audience with this boy and girl, especially after you just raided our ship and kidnapped their mother! What do you want?" There was no humor in Shane's voice. Just contempt and anger that his mortal enemy had shown up uninvited to his own ship just to meet with Daniel.

Orvag turned back to Shane, the anger back in his eyes. "At ease, Shane. I'm not here to speak with you. I want to specifically address these two." He pointed at Daniel and Caitlin. "I have something to tell them that they should pay very close attention to."

Shane immediately silenced anything he was about to say, and instead opted to turn to Daniel and Caitlin. "You don't have to speak to him if you don't want to."

"Silence!" Orvag's command made a few people gasp. The king turned back to Daniel and Caitlin, eyeing both of them at the same time, one with each eye. It was a disturbing sight, and it made Daniel's stomach turn even more. "I've heard quite a bit about both of you these last few days. How you came from one of Dormak's raiding parties, and how you managed to escape Skorjion, a near-impenetrable fortress camp, almost completely by yourself, along with a certain lizard that was also in our possession. Tell me now, where is he? Where is my little science experiment?"

"He's none of your business, Orvag. He's safe with us, and he's not going back to one of your hellholes again. You have my word on that matter. You and your slimy minions can stay away from him."

Orvag's jaw tightened in anger. "Be careful what you say to me, Shane. I am ten times the ruler you will ever be. At least I don't need to be saddled with a council who pesters me from all sides and who secretly claims the Magnum's spot for themselves." The words struck a nerve with Shane, who's face went a deep shade of red at the mention of the council.

"Now," Orvag began, turning back to Daniel and Caitlin, both of whom were still paralyzed with fear, Caitlin sweating nervously. "You've caused some huge problems for me. You've damaged my property, killed many of my servants, captured my best bounty hunter, and have presented me with a new challenge, as you have refused to come quietly back to me. You have emerged as a worthy adversary for sure. I can respect that."

"Can you though?" Daniel finally found the courage to speak. "I would think that believing that genocide is the path to galactic peace would warp your perspective on what a 'worthy opponent' is. What you believe in isn't the truth. It's insanity."

Orvag laughed. It was a booming laugh that would've made anyone's blood curdle instantly. "Dormak, look." He elbowed the Gorog next to him. "This little rat from nowhere is insulting me. ME! The most powerful ruler in the entire galaxy." Then his laugh disappeared. "He should be a little more careful when speaking to me. Otherwise, *she* might be damaged beyond repair."

Dormak, reached off the frame of the video and dragged a limp figure into view. At first, the long, unkempt hair prevented Daniel from getting a good look, but as Dormak tilted her head so he could see, Daniel's throat tightened so that he was once again rendered speechless. But Caitlin, in absolute shock as well, was not.

"Ms. Phillips..." she whispered, horrified. Daniel's mom was covered in blood and bruises, and her clothes were basically nonexistent; for all intents and purposes, she was naked from the waist up. She hung limply from Dormak's strong grip, dazed and only half awake, and Daniel was convinced that she had been beaten by Orvag until she was half dead.

"So you do know her. Glad to see that she was telling the truth." His hand lowered back to his side, and only now did Daniel see the handle of the sword sticking out from behind his back. They had been prepared to kill her right then and there. Anger began to seep through the cracks in Daniel's fear-laced wall. His fists balled slowly, but Orvag noticed.

"I know," the king said, his voice completely calm. "I can feel your anger, even from here. I want you to know that she's alive...for now. Because in exactly 24 hours, I'm going to kill her, and throw her body into space to drift forever. And I know you don't want that."

Caitlin leaned in to whisper to Daniel. "He's lying," she told him, although she wasn't sure of that herself. "He's trying to get inside your head. Don't listen to him."

"Am I the one lying, Caitlin Wheeler?" The use of her last name made her tense up like a brick. "Because I assure you, I'm telling the truth here. What about you? Have you been honest lately? Does *he* know what you can do with your hands?"

What color was left in Caitlin's cheeks instantly vanished, and Daniel noticed it. "What is it?" he asked. "Is something wrong?"

"He doesn't know..." Orvag said with mock surprise. "I can't believe this. You accuse me of lying in front of Shane and his entire entourage, while you refuse to tell your own best friend of your powers? Hypocrisy is a criminal charge in the Gorog Empire, punishable by death, you know. Do not speak to me of lying when you so graciously do it yourself!"

Caitlin's face was one of despair and defeat. Daniel, who

up to this point had been unable to put two and two together, finally started to understand her strange behavior lately. Orvag grinned as he watched Daniel put the puzzle pieces together while Caitlin hid her face in her hands. Shane wished he was there to shoot the king dead, but alas, Orvag could be anywhere, and try as they might, he could see his men trying to trace the signal and failing every time. The transmission was under an extremely intense scrambler, and none of the codebreakers could crack it. Orvag was still out of reach.

"I know you're heading towards Lhassi next, Shane," Orvag told his rival. "Your recent attack patterns have betrayed you as such. Make no mistake, I will be there, with this woman, and I will be ready to meet you on the field of battle, no matter what happens. You will not outsmart me again, and you will lose there, and then again, and again, and again until there is nothing left of your all-powerful kingdom. And you will die just like my father did, with his head separate from his body." Orvag then turned to Daniel, who was almost completely distracted by Caitlin. "And to you, Daniel, I have this to say. Leave. Take you and your friend and go back to Earth. Stay there. And don't ever interfere with my business again. Because if you, your mom, Caitlin, and yourself will be treated as enemies of the Gorog Empire, and will be dealt with as one. But I'll sweeten the deal; accompany Shane and his forces to Lhassi, and I will return your mother to you. You all can return home and live a happy, normal life again, the way it was before the attack. I will give you this, on one condition. Return my lizard to me. Hand him over, and I will trade you Ms. Phillips in exchange."

"But..." began Daniel, but Orvag would have none of it.

"No buts! My patience is wearing thin with you little rats, so here's my final warning: Either you hand over the lizard and get your old life back, or you die screaming alongside Shane and everyone you know and love!" He gestured to Dormak, who nodded and threw Ms. Phillips off to the side, out of view.

"Think about it, *Daniel!*"

The hologram died before anyone could say anything else, leaving the bridge in total silence. No one said anything, to the point where a pin could drop and it would have sounded loud. Whatever good mood people had come in with had disappeared. Daniel was in a chaotic jumble of his own feelings, emotions, and thoughts. Orvag's threat was burned into his brain, the words haunting him already. He also couldn't get his mother's beaten, battered body out of his head. And there was Caitlin! What had Orvag meant about her powers? He turned to ask, only for her to be nowhere in sight. He turned to the elevator door behind him, and saw her blond hair disappearing from view on the elevator on the left.

"Caitlin, wait!" he called out, desperately running after her for some answers. Shane watched him go, no longer feeling sure that he could keep all of them safe. Orvag had just put his own intentions out for everyone to hear them, and his display of power had worked. Shane could see worry, nervousness, even outright fear on most of the crew standing on the bridge. Not only that, but Orvag had also anticipated the assault on Lhassi. The rumor of a period of mourning for the empire was wrong. Orvag would be ready to counter the invasion immediately. It was too late, ships were moving into position, and troops and ground support were being prepared for battle. To cancel now would throw a huge chunk of the military into disarray, and with Orvag helming the Gorog military, any disruption could be exploited.

"Well, that went horribly," Vorlax said. It would've been funny, had it not been for the serious tone in his words. When even Vorlax had lost his sense of humor, that's when you knew that the situation had gotten bad.

"He knows we're coming," replied Shane. "He's expecting us at Lhassi tomorrow."

"I'll send a message to the leaders of the fleet," offered

Vorlax. "I'll tell them to prepare for a hard battle tomorrow. Hopefully our numbers will do the job instead."

"Let's hope."

"What about Daniel and Caitlin?"

Shane shook his head. "Give them some space, alright? They need it after that call."

"And their mother?"

"I'll think of something alright? For now, keep marshaling the fleet for the invasion. I'll meet up with you later."

Vorlax nodded and turned to inform the fleet, leaving Shane in a bind yet again. Orvag knew of the plans for tomorrow's invasion, which almost guaranteed a harder battle, and he had just threatened Daniel and Shane in front of all of his bridge officers. Already the Magnum could see his crew looking about and chatting with each other nervously, rattled by Orvag's proclamation. On a slightly more positive note, they at least knew to expect hard Gorog resistance.

But it was only a slightly positive note.

Daniel finally managed to catch up with Caitlin after almost a full minute of hard running. When she saw him, she turned away from him and hid her face, clearly embarrassed over something. Daniel was having none of it. His questions from before kept getting vague answers, and he was done with those. He touched her on the shoulder, without grabbing too tightly. "Hey," he said, trying to sound calm, and having difficulty after that hologram. He banished judgment from his voice, while also trying to sound somewhat firm. "What's wrong? Running out on me? Not being receptive to my questions? And that look you got on your face when Orvag mentioned the lying bit? That's not the Caitlin I remember from my childhood. Something's wrong, I can tell."

"It's nothing. It's inconsequential." Caitlin tried, and

failed to convince Daniel. To Daniel's shock, he glimpsed tears in her eyes. He shook his head, and instead of walking away, stepped in closer.

"No, it's not," he said. "You wouldn't be hiding from me if it was nothing. Hey." He grabbed her hand and held it reassuringly. "You wouldn't walk away from me if I was where you are right now. You can talk to me. I won't tell anyone if you don't want me to. What did Orvag mean by 'your powers?'"

Caitlin sniffled, a lone tear came streaking down her face, but she nodded slowly and held out her hand in front of Daniel. At first, and for a few seconds, there was nothing, but then as Daniel watched, sparks of electricity began to dance back and forth between her fingers, like a tesla coil. The sparks grew in intensity until her entire hand was lit up by lightning. Meanwhile, her face was now streaming tears, yet no sob escaped her lips. Daniel finally understood everything. Her skittishness of late, the weird question she had asked him earlier, and why she had seemed more distant than normal the last couple of days. She had been hiding this all this time. He did not want to prod, but he felt it would be best if everything came out now. Delaying the questions would only drag it out.

"How long has this been happening for?" he asked as gently as he could.

"Since…Skorjion," admitted Caitlin tearfully. "It first happened during our escape; a guard came at me, and I sent him flying…somehow. I…I thought it was a one-time thing. Then it happened again, and by the time the twins attacked us, there's been this constant buzzing in my body. I only grabbed that wire because I was trying to blind the guards who were shooting at us."

"Can you control it?"

"At first it was just when I was scared. Then it started happening more, and the buzzing came more frequently. Then I controlled it willingly for the first time back in that atrium."

"You mean...you'd never controlled it before then?"

"No." Caitlin sounded utterly defeated, as if she had just told Daniel that their friendship was over. She started to shake a little. "I wanted to tell you. Really, I did. But I was worried about what you would think and I...I didn't want our relationship to change in any way. And I was afraid of this...power I now seem to have. I don't know where it came from, it just...started happening more and more!"

"Hey, hey, calm down." Daniel grabbed both of her shoulders firmly, while not too hard. "I totally get it. You have nothing to be ashamed of. If my hands started sparking out electricity at random, I would be scared as well. I'm not mad, Cait. Not even a little bit." He paused to see her face brighten just a little bit, before dropping the other half of that statement. "But you should just tell me next time when something like this happens, that way, we can work through it together. Something this big shouldn't be kept under wraps. It could be dangerous for you. And now that I know of your...let's call it a gift, I can help you find a solution, okay? What was it that you always told me when I had a strange issue that I didn't know what to do with?"

"Ask for help from someone you trust," whispered Caitlin, almost inaudibly.

"Exactly. Let's go to Shane, ask him for help, and see what he thinks. He rules over an entire galaxy, and so far he's had a solution to almost all of our problems, so he'll have a solution for your gift as well. Does that sound good to you?"

Caitlin nodded, the electricity disappearing from her hand. She dried her eyes and took several deep breaths, the warmth in her face slowly returning. "Okay," she whispered. "Let's go to Shane. But please, don't let anyone else know about this, alright? I'm not ready to let everyone know about this."

Daniel nodded. "Of course. Only Shane."

Chapter 20

Foulor paced around his quarters, feeling unable to sit down. He should have been relieved to be back in his comfortable bedroom, with soft bed sheets and a sink, even his own set of weights to build his muscles with. Yet he kept finding himself glancing over at the empty bed in the corner, with one of Vraxis's shirts still resting on top of it, neatly folded from before they had left for their mission. Normally, he would be sitting right there, polishing his rifle and changing into clean clothes, bragging about their success with Foulor. Yet, for the first time in their many years of bounty hunting, he was not there.

He hoped that he was doing okay. Foulor knew that, for the most part, the Orion Coalition treated their prisoners well, at least the ones that were stored aboard their cruisers. There was always the threat of the asteroid prisons looming overhead, though. Every bounty hunter knew to fear that dingy, dark hell. The asteroid prisons were a group of random asteroids that existed in a far, remote area of the Orion Coalition's territory, a long way from any inhabited planets. The prison complex had been built into several asteroids kept in formation by gravitational devices, and was used for only the worst prisoners and enemies of the Coalition. Every asteroid was home to a single cell inside, and there were no windows, no actual gravity, and no bright lights. To be sentenced there was a death sentence, as if you were sent to an asteroid prison, it would be for life. There would be no returning from it. And they were known to be inescapable, even by experienced veterans of the craft. Worst of all, precious few knew where they were located, as their position changed constantly, to throw off anyone who would want to break in and rescue somebody.

Shane had every right to throw Vraxis in with the other

high-tier enemies and leave him to slowly die, from loss of body mass as the effect of zero gravity, the most freeing sensation ever, slowly killed a person. Vraxis had killed so many political figures in the Orion Coalition, including some good friends of Shane. Yet, somehow, Foulor figured that Shane would not do such a thing. Vraxis was an enemy who knew many of the Gorogs' darkest secrets. Surely, Shane would know this and try to exploit them for himself? Foulor was dimwitted, but not that dimwitted. All the Magnum would need to do would be to present his brother with a fat stack of cash and he'd talk. Probably.

The door to his quarters swung open and Dormak stuck his head inside. "Is this a good time to enter the premises?" he asked.

"In simpler terms, please," Foulor asked.

Dormak grunted in mild annoyance. "Can I come inside? Please?"

Foulor nodded and beckoned the warden inside, who came and sat on Vraxis's bed, much to the chagrin of the hunter. "Don't worry about Vraxis. Your brother, though he's smaller than most of your kind, is certainly not weak. I'd argue that he's every bit as strong as the rest of you, the amount of punishment I've seen him take over the years. He'll manage Shane's advances, I'm sure."

"That's not what I'm concerned about," Foulor replied, staring at his wall. "It's whether Shane is actually angry enough to send him off to the asteroid prisons. My brother's caused him enough grief to where he may want to do that."

"That would be a very ill-judged move on Shane's part. Vraxis holds tons of Gorog information, very private information in his memory. To send him off to rot in one of those hellholes without first exploiting him for intel would be foolish."

"True, but what about after he's gotten his information? Would he still send him away?"

"Well, we really can't say, now can we?" Dormak sounded almost unbothered by the idea of Vraxis being imprisoned. "He's at the mercy of Shane now. What happens to him is dictated by what Shane chooses to do with him next."

"Why do you sound like this isn't a big deal?" demanded Foulor angrily, noting Dormak's tone of voice. "He's my brother!"

"And he knew the risk when he started working for us. I seem to recall that you accepted that same risk as well. And here you are. You're still here, still ready to accept risks. For Vraxis, well, I guess his luck just finally ran out. It was bound to at some point."

Foulor let loose a low growl in his throat, like a dog who was getting fed up with its owner. "Don't say that about my brother," he snarled.

"Really? Growling at me? And with the Travashian special snarl? Orvag and I simply gave you the jobs and the money. It was up to you to carry them out successfully, and for almost twenty runs, you did good. Excellent, even! Yet you finally failed a mission, and one of you is now sitting in a Coalition jail cell! Vraxis is in prison for his own mistake, not mine!"

"He needs to be freed!" retorted Foulor.

"Then do it yourself!" The anger finally started to creep into Dormak's guttural voice. "You're not a Gorog yourself, you can come and go as you please! If you want to save him, be my guest. I'm sure that that mission will go off splendidly." The warden rose from Vraxis's bed, disturbing the nicely done blankets. "I have nothing more to say on this. If you need anything, message a soldier and they'll bring you whatever you need."

"But–"

Dormak was already gone, slamming the door shut behind him. Foulor glared at the empty door, then let loose a yell

323

of frustration and slammed his fists against his bed. Again denied the option of Gorog assistance. It was as if they did not care anymore. And it made Foulor angrier by the second. His brother deserved to be rescued. He had done more to help the Gorogs than almost all of the actual Gorogs themselves. And now, he was being tossed aside.

Sitting on his bed, feeling lonely for the first time in a long time, Foulor hoped and prayed that Vraxis was doing alright.

Down in his prison cell, Vraxis was actually doing alright. He had not stopped thinking about Shane's proposal. The deal he had laid down before him was a lot to handle for sure. Shane had clearly meant business by offering 1.5 million credits to him. That was near the value of one entire Coalition cruiser, among the largest starships in their fleet. If he took the money, it would mean instant retirement for himself. He would never have to work again, not for Orvag, or anyone for that matter. It would mean he could settle down in a village somewhere, like he had always wanted, and enjoy his longer-than-average lifespan in comfort. And, to sweeten the deal, Shane had implied that Foulor would get the same payday as well. That was the obvious choice. Comfort. Something that a bounty hunter like Vraxis or Foulor rarely got to experience in full. Foulor would have jumped on that opportunity faster than a blaster bolt.

And yet…there was their organization to deal with. And they rarely looked down positively on betraying one's contract with an employer. In some cases, the punishment for betraying the terms of your arrangement included expulsion from the guild; or in rare cases, assassination by other bounty hunters. The Hunters' Party held a lot of power in many parts of the galaxy, and they owned an entire planet as well, for nothing but bounty hunters, who came and went as they pleased. Now obviously, if they took the money, whether they got expelled from the party or not would be irrelevant, since they would no longer need to collect bounties. But there was also Orvag's fury to deal with, something that they had witnessed several times, and was feared by the king's entire staff. That was far more important than what the Hunters' Party could throw their way. It was a tough call for Vraxis. He knew that Foulor would be belittling him about now for not seizing the opportunity. He also knew that his alternative, the asteroid prisons, was not ideal in the slightest. Most bounty hunters knew of Ralkan, a six-armed bounty hunter who could hold a machine gun in each hand, and who was widely agreed to be the best mercenary in the Hunters' Party, at least until Vraxis and Foulor came along. Ralkan was caught by the Orion Coalition and sentenced to life in an asteroid prison for serving enemies of the Coalition before the Gorogs rose to power. According to reports, he was dead after just five years in one of those cramped cells. So that was not an option either. Yet Orvag's temper remained stuck in his brain. But the Coalition supposedly had the recipe to wipe out the entire Gorog Empire in one stroke at this point…

  He made a decision. Not the important decision, but a decision. With no restraints holding him back, he walked to the front of his cell and tapped the inside of his door. "Excuse me?" he called out to his guards. "I would like to see Shane!"

  Instantly, the door swung open and in walked the Magnum himself, looking as royally decorated as always. "Vraxis! I heard that you wanted to see me," he said, entering the cell room.

  "What…how?"

  "I was just coming to check on you. I heard you call your guards as I was approaching. About time too." He sat down on a bench on the wall of the cell bordering the hallway. "So, about my offer…do you agree? Is this what you wanted me for?"

  The hunter nodded. "It is. I want to make some things

absolutely clear before we go through with this. Because there's a lot I'm risking accepting this bid from you."

"Okay, shoot."

"First, I want your guarantee that Foulor, when he and I are reunited, gets at least another 500,000 credits in addition to the 1.5 million that you offered me. So a total of two million all told. Second, and more important, I want your guarantee that you won't keep me in here if I accept. You'll give me full sleeping quarters and allow me the freedom to explore and wander about. Finally, I want your solemn guarantee that you will protect me, both from the prying eyes of my own organization and from the wrath of Orvag that will be sure to follow as soon as he hears of this. Those are my terms for accepting your proposal, Shane. If you refuse to give me what I want, you may as well forget ever offering me the money in the first place. Have I made my point clear enough?"

Shane nodded. "So, just to clarify, you want 25% more money than previously, the ability to sleep outside of your cell, and protection from anyone who may look down on this decision with ire?"

"That just about sums it up."

Shane thought about this for a moment. "I can give you everything except the freedom of wandering the ship. I have no guarantee from you that you won't betray us and try to sabotage the ship."

"I made my point perfectly clear," replied Vraxis.

"Listen, if you want to debate this all day, be my guest. I'm not the one in a cell, with the possibility of rotting away forever hanging over my head. You can choose to accept my terms, which I believe are very generous, and take your freedom, or choose to put yourself in one of those asteroid prisons."

Vraxis did not even pause. "Fine. But I still want access to the rest of the ship, even I have to be guarded at all times. I'm not being confined to a chamber, even a nice one, again."

Shane put a finger to his chin. "Fine. If you choose to explore the ship, you will be shadowed by guards in the process and, as an addition, will be denied access to weapons while on board. That way, you still get to explore and I don't fret over you going out and causing trouble."

Vraxis considered this. "Alright, deal. Just get me out of this wretched cell."

Shane nodded and opened the door, allowing the bounty hunter to exit and stretch. "Your guards will direct you to your quarters," he told him. He turned to one of them. "Ensure that he doesn't cause any trouble on the way."

The guard nodded and escorted Vraxis down the hall, the hunter keeping his gaze locked upon Shane until he could not see him anymore. As Shane watched him go, a Coalition crew member ran up behind him.

"Sir," he said, out of breath. "I hate to disturb you at the moment, but Daniel has requested your presence. He says it's important."

Shane examined the multiple samples of Caitlin's blood with a curious eye on the screen next to his chair. After scanning through all of them with a curious eye, he flipped the screen to the next slide, where several DNA tests could be seen, all of them Caitlin's. He made no sound as he glanced at the schematics presented before him. After doing more scanning without any sound, he flipped the screen again, this time, landing on a 3-D model of one of Caitlin's cells. Caitlin was sitting to his left along with Daniel, and could see the entire screen, along with everything the Magnum was pulling up. A short visit to the medical wing had resulted in multiple scans of Caitlin's body, but strangely enough, not a single needle had been used. When she had asked, Shane had replied, "We don't need actual samples in most cases. Usually, we just use a scanner and can draw a pretty accurate depiction of someone's blood and DNA that way. We only use needles when examining something that's completely new, like your lizard friend." Daniel had seemed pretty relieved at that, as Caitlin knew that he hated needles of all kinds, and that he dreaded shots when he was younger.

They were in a room just outside of the medical center, where patients could see their test results after they had visited. Shane had specifically requested to take over this room, honoring Daniel's promise to Caitlin. Caitlin had described her issue to Shane in as much detail as she could, and Shane had promptly sent in her for some tests. Five minutes later, they were in. Yet so far, Shane had given no sign as to what he was looking for. He was obviously looking for something, as he was only doing brief glances over the test screens. It was only when they reached the 3-D model of the entire cell that he stopped and zeroed in on a certain part of the cell. He highlighted it red and turned back to face Caitlin and Daniel.

"Did you find something?" she asked, hopeful for an answer.

"I did," Shane replied, pointing to the red spot in her cell. "That."

"And? What is that?" prodded Caitlin, not satisfied with just a one-word answer.

"That is your mitochondria. Your cell's main producer of energy. Call it the cell's power plant. It takes the nutrients from the food you eat and converts it into energy for the cell. It's what gives all of your cells energy and enables your body to function in the first place. Without it, you'd be stagnant, unable to do most anything."

"So?"

Shane sighed. "I'll be completely transparent; this is not the first time I've had to deal with a case like this. About fifteen years ago, there was a fighter pilot who developed the same exact symptoms, and the issue was with his mitochondria.

Looking at this rendering, it appears you have the same problem. You see, the mitochondria is supposed to look like this in a normal human cell. Observe."

He pulled up another slide next to the diagram of Caitlin's mitochondria, comparing the two. The normal mitochondria was smaller and shaped like a prescribed pill with waves on the inside. Caitlin's was much bigger, but also manifesting what appeared to be additional projections on all sides, so that it resembled a virus's tendrils rather than a part of a cell. The cell part was also pulsating like a heart, so that it also bore a resemblance to some alien creature from a far-rung planet in the Milky Way Galaxy. Caitlin was looking at the diagram with a fair bit of confusion mixed with slight worry.

"So, that's what it should look like normally?" she asked, gesturing to the normal human mitochondria. "And that's what mine looks like…right now?"

Shane nodded. "That's not even the craziest part. Take a look at this." He inserted another overlay over the diagram of Caitlin's cell. The mitochondria suddenly turned bright electric blue, pretty much outshining the rest of her cell. But that wasn't even the biggest thing about this overlay. Caitlin's eyes widened as she saw it. Daniel's did too, and he stood up to get a closer look.

"Are those…?" he began, squinting at the screen to try and see clearly, although the screen was clear enough for him.

"Electric currents. Inside of all of her cells." Much to everyone's surprise, Shane sounded very calm, as if this whole thing was just something that happened to come into his doctor's office every day. Unsurprisingly, Caitlin took some offense.

"Alright then, Shane," she said huffily, folding her arms. "Since you seem totally cool with the fact that there's actual electricity coursing through my entire body, you must have a cure for it. Do you have like a shot, antibiotics, pills, something that can treat this and make me normal again?"

Again, to everyone's complete surprise, Shane actually shook his head no. Caitlin spread her arms out, a look of complete disbelief written on her usually happy face. It wasn't a good look for sure, Daniel thought. "*No?*" she demanded, her voice a decibel closer to shouting. "You're basically the ruler of the entire galaxy, the governor of hundreds of planets, with access to huge funds and almost unlimited resources, and you can't find a cure for me?"

"Because you're not suffering from a virus, or any disease for that matter. Nor are any of your cells cancerous in any way. There's no physical aberrations of any kind. From a purely physical standpoint, you're completely fine."

"Shane, I hate to bring this up, but her being able to shoot electricity out of her hands is not being 'completely fine,'" pointed out Daniel. "In fact, I'd argue that that's not being fine at all."

"And why do you act like you've seen this before?" prodded Caitlin. "The way you just described my condition; you acted like someone else that you know came down with the exact same problem. Now, please, answer my question; can I be fixed or not?"

"That electricity is not normal electricity. It's a special variant of energy." Shane sighed. "A few years back a pilot came to the medical wing with eerily similar conditions to yours. He too could occasionally shoot electricity from his hands. He wanted answers to his condition. None of the doctors could accurately diagnose his condition. They sent him to me, and I had to do some digging in order to find his condition. When I eventually found it, it wasn't a physical affliction of any kind. It wasn't even a problem with his own body technically. It was…" He stopped, then slapped his knee almost out of frustration. "You wouldn't believe me if I told you."

"I'm pretty sure at this rate we can accept anything if it helps Caitlin out," replied Daniel tartly.

Shane sighed. "I had to travel to another planet to find a solution. Anich. It's far, way on the other side of Coalition territory. There's been a group of wizards that have lived there for thousands of years, who are sympathetic to us. I sent the pilot there to live among them and cure his condition. Five days later, he came back and was fine. He no longer was shooting electricity, and he went back to his old job perfectly fine. They would likely be able to cure Caitlin's condition as well…"

"Okay, that's far enough!" Daniel sounded like his brain was about to break. "When you say 'wizards' are we talking about the *Wizard of Oz*-type or *Lord of the Rings* type? You're not saying that, in addition to everything else we've seen, there's magic as well?"

Shane hesitated for a moment, but he eventually nodded. "Yes. This is a group of magic-practicing wizards."

Caitlin's face turned down even farther. "So, what you're telling *me*, the patient, is that my condition, my ability to spit out electricity, the thing that I'm trying to cure…is magical?"

The look on Shane's face betrayed everything. "Yes?! So you're saying I'm basically a witch now?" Caitlin's voice was getting even shriller. "Do you think that's who I want to be?"

"I'm saying that if you want your powers gone, you're going to have to go to these wizards and ask them to help fix you. I cannot help you here. It's either that or deal with them on your own."

Caitlin hid her face again. Daniel felt his stomach twinge seeing his friend like this. Usually in these situations, he was the one struggling with something. It felt as though the natural order of things was being thrown off by Caitlin's predicament. He cleared his throat as naturally as he could and turned to Shane. "Would you mind giving us a minute, please?" he asked.

The Magnum nodded. "Take as much time as you need.

I'll be waiting in the hall outside addressing some things when you're done." He rose from his seat, turned the display screen off, and left the room, leaving Daniel alone with Caitlin. He turned and gently prodded her back with his finger, causing her to look up at Daniel.

"You should go," he told her.

"What do you mean?"

"Go get your powers fixed."

"Daniel, I…you heard Shane! They're actual wizards! Not some fraud nonsense, but actual, magic-wielding wizards. First of all, as if there wasn't enough to process, now there's actual magic out there, and I seem to have it coursing through me. Second, there's the incoming invasion of Lhassi coming up, and Orvag and finding your mom and…oh my gosh, there's so much on our plates."

"Trust me, I'm freaking out over it all. I'm freaking over it more than you are, honestly! I just found out you could shoot electricity out of your two hands. That was enough to trigger my anxiety alone. And then there's Orvag with that death threat on my head *and* my mom. But my mom's something that we can't fix right now. Your abilities; that is. And if you want them gone, you should go to the only people that we know can cure them and do so. Shane did say that the wizards were sympathetic to the Coalition, right?"

"When he visited! What if they've changed?"

"Cait, you'll be fine. I'll be fine as well; I have the entire Coalition army protecting me and helping me out. The only one who should be afraid is Orvag; that little scumbag has no idea what I'm capable of. When I get my hands on him…"

"I wouldn't advise that," interrupted Caitlin. "He's the actual Gorog king, so reaching him would probably be difficult."

"He has my mom," growled Daniel. "You saw her. She was hurt badly. He needs to pay for what he's done, both to her and the rest of the galaxy."

"And Shane will handle that beautifully I'm sure," said Caitlin, some color returning to her face. "You sure you want me to leave you? If I go, no one will be able to help you out from making a reckless decision."

Daniel laughed. "I have Max with me. He never does anything risky. He'll keep me in check." He smiled at her. "Don't stay just because of me. You want to fix your problem? That's how. You feel nervous about it? Ask if Pantura will go with you. I'm sure she'd love to get up close with a bunch of magic wielders."

Caitlin gave her friend a thankful look, then placed her head on his shoulder affectionately. "Thank you, Daniel," she said, no longer sounding concerned. "For being so loyal as a friend."

He shrugged. "Gotta pay you back somehow for all the times you've helped me out."

She laughed, sitting back up straight. "Alright, if you're sure you don't need me around for the invasion, I'll talk with Pantura and see if she can come as well, for extra company."

Daniel nodded. "I'll let Shane know you intend to seek some help, and I'll...prepare for the coming battle tomorrow."

Just then, Max stuck his head in through the door. "Hey, you two. Finally got out of my tests. That was way too many needles they used. I'm going to prepare for the battle tomorrow in my room." He started to turn away and then saw Caitlin's face and Daniel sitting next to her. "Hey, is something wrong? Did I interrupt something?"

Daniel shook his head hastily and thought up a lie quickly. "No, nothing's wrong! Just...something we were talking about. It's fine, we're both fine. Nothing that concerns you at the moment either."

Max looked puzzled, but he shrugged and backed out of the room.

Shane stuck his head back in the room a few moments

333

later. "So, have you decided on something yet? I know I sound impatient, but if you're going to make a choice, it has to be very soon."

Caitlin nodded. "I'll go. As long as Pantura goes with me. Because I refuse to travel alone to a place full of mysterious wizards. I don't exactly feel comfortable making that journey by myself. If…that's possible?"

Shane nodded. "I completely understand. I'm sure that Pantura will be able to go. Daniel, will you be staying here to prepare for the battle? Or are you going as well?"

"I told her to go without me," he explained. "She doesn't need me there to fix her powers, and plus, there's that message from Orvag to worry about. She's fine with that. Right? Caitlin?"

Caitlin looked rather unsure of herself, but she nodded nevertheless. "I'll manage, Shane. Just tell me when we can leave, I want this trip to be over as quickly as possible. The sooner I can remove this…magic, or whatever it is inside me, the better."

"I'll have Vorlax prepare a ship immediately. As for Daniel, I just told Max. We're coming out of hyperspace in the next ten minutes. You'd better be ready."

"Ready for what?" asked Daniel, now a little concerned after the way Shane phrased his words.

Shane gave him a look that was almost pitiful. "To meet the Orion Coalition Council of Justice. Because we're approaching Arajor now."

Chapter 21

Arajor System
25,000 light years from Earth

Daniel was not prepared for when they emerged from hyperspace and Arajor came into view. No matter what Shane or Pantura had said about the great capital city of the Coalition, Daniel had a certain thing pictured; either a huge city spanning thousands of miles or some space station high in orbit where the council members met up and discussed treaties and delegated amongst themselves. Although Pantura had described it as a giant space station, Daniel at first did not see anything. Arajor was a gigantic white, featureless ball on one side, but with banded clouds on the other in white and blue colors, and where huge flashes of lightning could be seen on the dark side of the planet. But as the *Justice* slowly approached, a dark mass began to peek out from below the planet's uppermost layer of clouds. It was small at first, but as they approached, it grew larger and larger. Unfortunately, it was eventually hidden from Daniel's window as the ship changed course, and soon he could only see the far cusp of Arajor. Backing up and finishing cleaning himself up, he laid down on his warm bed and stared up at the ceiling, wondering what his meeting with the council members held. It had been established that Shane was not a bad person; quite the opposite in fact. But a whole council? That to Daniel seemed…well, he was not sure. It was possible that the Coalition council would turn out well enough, but he remembered his mom talking on the phone about the former Salt Plains council, and how corrupt they were. They never put any money into the town, because they kept hemorrhaging it away, and nobody in the town liked any of the members, who were labeled as "corrupt," "slime," and a whole bunch of other nasty things.

Given how the town looked, Daniel believed everything that he heard about the old Salt Plains council, and since then, he had viewed other collaborations of politicians with suspicion. He had never liked politics to begin with, and to deal with it more was not something he was especially looking forward to.

Slowly, the blackness of space outside his window began to disappear, replaced with blue as they passed into the atmosphere of Arajor. It was his first time back inside a proper atmosphere since he had escaped Skorjion, something that at that point felt like an eternity ago. It was weird to watch the stars, his constant companions throughout all of the last few days, slowly drop out of view one by one. Soon, all of them had disappeared, and Daniel could have switched off the lights in his room and he would still be able to read a book. It was weird to have natural light coming into his room again, to start dappling onto his shoulders. From his view, he could see a small, brilliant blue dot that attempted to blind him every time he tried to look its way. A blue giant, he guessed, one of the hotter star varieties out there, and one very different from the sun. But it was still a star, and it was now shining down upon him, and not from dozens of light years away either. And as it did, his skin began to tickle oddly, almost as if it had missed the warmth of starlight from a nearby star. And it felt truly amazing. Daniel let the blue giant bathe him in light as they continued to descend downwards towards Arajor's mystery space station.

A few minutes later, the ship thudded, jolting Daniel out of his bed. He glanced outside his window, and saw nothing but steel gray. Wherever they had gone and landed in, they were now inside some building. Whatever building it was, it would have to be truly enormous to fit a ship the size of the *Justice* inside. He could even see catwalks along the walls, with tiny people the size of ants racing about on them. He could see carts of materials being pushed about by tons of workers, many of which, to Daniel's amusement, were wearing plain, ordinary T-shirts, like you would find in a store inside of a mall. There was even an alien with four arms wearing one with two extra sleeves. Daniel laughed. Apparently the trend of adopting Earth's clothing went wider than he had originally thought.

There was a knock on his door, and he arose from bed to answer it. Caitlin. "Hey. Don't know if you saw Shane's message on your screen, but he wants to see us in the main hangar."

Daniel looked back and saw that indeed, there was a flashing red light on the screen hanging on his wall. "Oh. No problem, I'm already dressed. I can go right now."

"Great!" Caitlin turned and started moving towards the hangar. Daniel started to follow, only to run straight into Max, who had been standing in the hallway behind Caitlin.

"Oops! Sorry, Max, didn't see you there!" he quickly apologized.

"Don't mention it," the lizard growled, starting to walk away.

Daniel chased after him, not wanting to end a conversation like this. "How did your tests earlier today go?"

"Well, the scientists used needles, like I specifically asked them not to, but other than that…not much else was uncovered." He thought for a moment, trying to remember what they told him. "They did mention something about my body's atomic structure reacting to high levels of certain hormones, like adrenaline. I don't know, there were a lot of science words in there, I didn't comprehend most of it. That's not exactly my area of expertise."

"No, I know," replied Daniel, trying to sound polite to avoid arousing Max's ire again. "I'm not looking for a detailed explanation here. Just…curious to see if there's a reason behind your weird transformation. It's something that's been on all of our minds lately."

"Nothing that I could understand, I'm afraid. Talk to

Shane about it, he should be getting my tests back soon." Max turned away and increased his pace, widening the gap between him and Daniel. Daniel shook his head, wondering if the lizard would ever have a proper conversation with him that was not entirely one-sided. So far, he had seen nothing to convince him otherwise.

They reached the hangar a few minutes later, where there was a large assembly gathered in the center. Daniel could see Shane, Vorlax, Pantura, and several supporting crew members all mingling together. He could see Caitlin, about twenty feet in front of him and Max, starting to interact with the group as she approached them. Behind the group was a small shuttle with large, retractable wings. The ship was only half the size of the gunship from earlier, and was painted in dull steel gray instead of the vibrant orange and reds of the other ship. The biggest difference was the hangar window was now bathed in white light from Arajor's atmosphere behind it. As they grew closer, he could see the group turn and look his way.

"Daniel. Max," acknowledged Vorlax. "You're just in time for the send-off. Pantura and Caitlin were just about to leave."

Daniel eyed the ship behind them. "You couldn't have used that gunship again? I'm sure the two of them could use a ship on that caliber to transport them."

Vorlax nodded. "I wish they could, unfortunately, it's still being repaired over there." He pointed to the massive hull of the fighter, loitering in the far corner of the hangar. Surrounding it were ladders and more crew members, all barely visible between the hulks of other ships lying in wait. "We had to substitute it for the *Serenitis*, behind us. It's...not that gunship, that much is certain, but it'll work."

"As long as we can fly that shuttle to Anich, it'll serve our purposes," Pantura spoke up. She materialized on the left side of the crowd, looking rather grim. She approached Daniel, placing her hands on his shoulders. "Daniel," she began, speaking directly to him, "Shane told me about the message from Orvag. I have to warn you; Orvag is a known liar, do not trust him, under any circumstances. There's a reason that his flagship is named the *Deceiver*. Whatever he told you is a lie."

"I appreciate the concern, Pantura," said Daniel. "But I'm fine, really. I'm more concerned about Caitlin anyways." He leaned in closer to her to where he could whisper. "You'd better keep her safe from harm," he said in a low voice. "Especially since she's going to a group of wizards on a faraway planet. Not exactly the most reassuring of scenarios."

Pantura nodded. "Don't worry about these wizards. I've heard of them; they have longstanding ties to the Coalition's past Magnums. They shouldn't cause us any trouble."

Daniel shrugged. "I'm not an expert here. If you believe they'll help her, I have faith. Just bring her home safely, will you?"

Pantura nodded. "I'll protect her with my life. You have my word on that, Daniel."

Daniel bowed his head in respect. "Thank you Pantura. I appreciate it very much." He pushed past Pantura and found Caitlin in conversation with Vorlax. When she saw Daniel, she froze. She turned back to Vorlax. "Excuse me, but can you give me just a second here?" He nodded and she slowly approached Daniel.

"You sure you're up for this?" he asked her, smiling as much as he could. He was surprised that he was able to do so at all, given how Orvag's death threat was still fresh in his mind from earlier that day.

It took a moment, but Caitlin did nod. "I mean, as long as it gets my abilities removed, I'm good with it. So long as Pantura accompanies me, of course."

Daniel nodded. "Of course, it would probably do you some good to have some company." He sighed. "What is it with bad things happening to us? We've managed to withstand invasions, slavery, two battles, and only now we're finally being separated from each other. And it's all because you have the abilities of a wizard." He laughed. "It's like all of the random ideas inside my head just were spit out all at once and that's become our new life."

Caitlin chuckled. "Well, hopefully soon I'll be free of these wizard powers and can focus on making it home with you and Ms. Phillips."

Daniel's face fell instantly. "Except now the entire Gorog army stands in our way. You saw Orvag's message to us. He has my mom. Meaning that we now have to get to him in order to reach her. Assuming he doesn't kill her before then."

Caitlin's face fell as well. "I can't even imagine what Ms. Phillips is going through right now. You saw her on that transmission; they must've beaten her until she was almost half-dead."

"I know." That image of Ms. Phillips, broken and beaten to a pulp, resurfaced into his head, making him shiver and boil with rage at the same time. "Whatever happens now, her fate is now directly linked to that of this war's outcome. Which means that Shane has to win tomorrow. Otherwise, she's gone for good. And the Gorogs will never die." He paused briefly to reflect. "I can't let that happen, Cait. I would never forgive myself if something as evil as the Gorogs emerged as the dominant rulers of the galaxy. That's why I'm going to ask Shane if I can help in the battle tomorrow. Not just because of my mother, but also because I can't allow Orvag to win. Not when he'll destroy the galaxy."

To his surprise, Caitlin nodded. "If that's what you're feeling called to do, do it. I don't want to see Orvag win either, and if you can help Shane defeat him tomorrow, then you should do so. Just don't do anything reckless, will you? I want all of us to make it home safely, alive and in one piece."

"Me too, Cait. Me too."

The two of them just stared at each other, until finally Caitlin stepped forward and gave Daniel a huge hug. "Stay safe, Stellar Brain. I'll see you soon, alright?"

"Yes, you will. Stay safe yourself." Daniel released himself from Caitlin's grip and stepped away to allow Shane to move in to talk to her. After they exchanged some more words, she and Pantura boarded their ship, with Vorlax trailing right behind them. After several long moments, Vorlax reappeared, and a second later, the shuttle engines fired up, and before Daniel knew it, the ship was out of his sight, Caitlin and Pantura on board and inbound for the wizard planet. Shane soon found himself in front of Daniel's face, still staring at the edge of the hangar window where he had last seen the ship.

"Staring at where she went won't bring her back any quicker, you know," he reminded Daniel, snapping him back into focus. "In the meantime, we both have our own matters to deal with. The council is expecting us in two hours. While we wait for that time, why don't Vorlax and I show you Arajor City? I'm sure you've been dying to see our capital all this time."

Daniel eagerly nodded, but then yawned loudly. Anything to keep Orvag, his mom, and Caitlin off his mind. "I'd love a tour, if this is what this is. As long as I can go get some sleep after the fact."

"It's better than a tour," promised Vorlax. "You're going to love this, Daniel. It sure beats any museum tour you can get. It's not every day you get to tour a futuristic city and see what it has to offer. And yes, as soon as you're done with Shane and the council, you'll be able to sleep."

"Then I guess I'll have to come along." Daniel was happy to do something other than worry about his friends. He turned behind him, to where Max was standing. "Do you want to come as well?"

Max looked up, confused. "Me? You sure?"

"Yes, I'm sure," replied Daniel curtly. "It'll be fun, trust me. When was the last time you did anything really fun?"

Max thought for a moment. "You know, I really can't remember the last time I did anything that was truly fun. Closest thing I've had to that in the last…however many years it's been was when Vorlax let me loose on some old droids yesterday in the combat room."

"That long? Sheesh, no wonder you've been a huge grouch every time I've tried to interact with you. Come on! I'll do my best to not bother you at all."

Max sighed loudly, but he still managed to nod his head. "Alright. As long as you're not an annoyance, I'll come with you."

"Great!" Daniel looked back to Shane. "What about you? You coming at all?"

Shane shook his head. "I'll let Vorlax handle taking you around the city. I have to check back in on our guest in his quarters, see how he's doing. I'll join you in the Kraken facility later on though. Vorlax, is that alright with you?"

"I'll be Daniel and Max's tour guide while you interrogate Vraxis. Don't go too easy on him, though. He's a Travashian, one of the toughest alien species. He's not going to crack easily."

"Actually, I think I've managed to avoid methods of torture with this one. I let him out of his cell late yesterday, after we made a sort of agreement."

"He's not in a cell?"

"Don't worry about it, I've taken precautions. Look, just keep Daniel occupied for the next two hours, give him something to do so that he's not worrying about all of his friends. I'll handle the bounty hunter. We'll meet in the Kraken's council chamber when time's up, are we clear?"

Vorlax nodded. "You got it boss." He turned to Daniel and Max. "This way, you two. Your transport is just over here."

He led them into the other side of the hangar, to a spot void of parked starfighters, where a small open-top transport painted in blue and white colors awaited. The craft had two engines, both dwarfed by the engines on the starfighters that Daniel had seen parked in the hangar bay, and five rows of chairs divided up the middle like a church aisle. A low wall separated the guest seating from the driver's seat, which was armed with a steering wheel and various knobs and switches to control the vehicle. Vorlax, unsurprisingly, went straight for the driver's spot and sat down. "Don't just stand there you two!" he chided Daniel and Max, who had stopped to stare at the craft. "Get in!" He switched the engines on, causing the area around them to vibrate from the noise and heat. In response, Daniel and Max hastily climbed aboard and took seating positions, Daniel on the benches, Max perched below one like he was a giant dog sitting down. Vorlax put on a pilot's headset and tapped into the microphone.

"Can everyone hear me back there?" he asked, his voice coming in through speakers built into the backs of the seats. Both Daniel and Max nodded. "That's a yes. This is Captain Vorlax speaking. Before we begin our tour of Arajor today, I must go over basic flight safety rules. Please do not lean out over the side of the vehicle while it is in the air. Remember, we're currently over a gas giant planet. If you don't fall to your death onto a floating island, you'll fall straight through the atmosphere and be crushed by the increasing pressure deeper down in the planet. And that's just as bad, so I'd recommend avoiding both fates if you can. Apart from that, sit back, enjoy the smooth ride, the sights, and we'll be touching back down on solid ground in about two hours."

Daniel fastened the seatbelt that was next to him and secured it tight. Max simply gripped the back of the seat in front of him with his talons. The taxi vibrated beneath them as it slowly began to rise into the air, Shane watching them depart from behind. They started to inch forward, the hangar opening drawing nearer to them. They passed through the shields, and Daniel was hit by the first blast of fresh air in several days. He took a deep breath, letting the air fill his lungs. It felt completely unnatural after breathing artificially-created air for almost an entire week. This was photosynthesized, pure, normal air like the kind that you would find on top of a hill on Earth. Daniel's lungs relaxed as he breathed, as if they had been waiting for this moment. But his breath soon was lost as they pulled away from the *Justice*, through a hole in the side of the building where the cruiser was parked, and he saw the city.

    The building they had just exited was enormous, as large as a decent-sized city back on Earth. Stretching out in front of them was the floating city that Pantura had described, although calling it a city was a stretch, as this was bigger than any city that Daniel had seen on Earth. It was broken up into dozens of huge artificial islands spaced closely together, linked by multi-storied bridges spanning the white void below. On top of these islands were massive, hugely complex structures linked by more bridges and catwalks. Skyscrapers towered over them like mountains. At the base of each island, a large thruster's base could be seen pumping out blue light as it kept the city from spiraling under gravity to its fiery demise. The buildings were all painted light gray with blue accents, like the Coalition ships Daniel had seen, and they almost seemed to shine like polished metals under the light from the blue giant. He noticed that several had neon lights covering a wall or two, with large windows overlooking everything.

    "Welcome to Arajor City, you two," Vorlax said, dropping his tour guide voice for a moment of seriousness. And then he turned up the engines some more and turned their craft towards the heart of the city, leaving the cruiser hangars behind. As they drew closer, they kept seeing more and more little details in the structures below them. The long platform that linked the cruiser hangars to the rest of the city was dotted with factories and what appeared to be more Coalition starfighters, all of them *Arrow*-type.

"Those are our starfighter manufacturers below us," confirmed Vorlax, noticing where Daniel and Max were looking. "Currently working overtime to deliver us more small ships for the war."

"That's where every Coalition starfighter is made?" asked Max.

"Yes. We make the parts separately and then deliver them to the assembly lines to put together. Of course, we have some other facilities in other areas of our jurisdiction, but I'd say roughly 95 percent of our starfighters are made and tested right here in the city. A safe place to do so given that the Gorogs never venture this deep into Coalition territory."

"There goes some more ships, over there on the left," pointed out Max, looking at five ships being wheeled out onto a flat stretch of the platform, away from buildings.

"Those ships just came off the assembly lines. They're entering the testing phase now. If we're lucky, we may see some test flights going on around the city."

"That's...honestly amazing," commented Daniel, noticing how efficient the process seemed. Although he couldn't see any workers, he noted the different sections of the platform, each tailored for a different job to streamline the process of building starfighters; hardware manufacturing, component assembly, and a final line to piece the individual ship parts together. Remarkable, really.

They flew past the starfighter factories and entered a more residential area of the city. The industrial complexes were replaced with housing complexes that loomed large over the three of them, with lush, multi-colored garden pathways and resort-like shopping centers spread out in between the buildings. The entire area was split between two giant islands, each nearly seven times as large as all of Salt Plains, with four huge bridges linking the two. "One of many residential areas in the city. This one is for the middle class residents in the city. Granted, there's very little difference between the lower and upper classes in Arajor; we try our hardest to ensure that everyone can lift themselves up into higher areas of society. Every residence comes equipped with a multi-biome botanical garden designed to capture the feel of multiple alien planets, so that everyone, no matter where you're originally from, can feel like you're at home again."

    Daniel marveled at one of those garden biomes below them, which was decked out in vibrant colors unlike any Earth plants he was familiar with. "Are those alien plants down there?" he asked Vorlax.

    Vorlax glanced where he was pointing. "Yes. There are hundreds of thousands of ecosystems preserved in these gardens. You'll find plant species from all across the galaxy residing right here in the city. Especially the main city gardens, which I'll show you. That biome right there is a Forrex biome."

    "Forrex biome?"

    "The alien mother planet. Has a more diverse ecosystem than any other planet in the galaxy. It's also where all alien life originated from. It's been sitting uninhabited for a while now, but we have many of its flora here, for all to enjoy."

    "Uninhabited? Why don't you just…go back to Forrex? I mean, you could rebuild, right?"

    "I wish it were that simple, Daniel. While yes, we could easily restore the planet to its former glory, there are tons of radioactive deposits leftover from a time when the many alien species fought each other, which renders large chunks of the surface uninhabitable for many alien species. And not only that, but the planet's orbit in the Milky Way has taken it into a dangerous zone of the galaxy, near several black holes. And I'm sure you can imagine why that would complicate things a bit."

    "Black holes would make it hard to live there, yes,"

agreed Daniel.

"Shame. I've heard stories of the great civilizations that used to live there. I would have loved to see where alien life began."

They passed by the residence area and flew around to another large island where there were no tall buildings or botanical gardens sprawled out around them. Instead, three huge, mall-like structures, once again linked by bridges, resided there. Vorlax flew their taxi down closer to the buildings, to where Daniel could see hundreds of figures walking on the paths below them. He could also see huge screen signs on each building, displaying products on them and alien languages that he couldn't read. One of them was, however, written in English, and it read "LOCALLY-GROWN PRODUCE, HALF-OFF NOW!" The buildings, he guessed, were some kind of shopping center.

"This is one of nine main shopping centers. If you need something important, odds are it'll be in there," explained Vorlax. "There are tons of stores for food, clothing, housing supplies, and everything you'll need to furnish a house and live here. If you're looking for something random, odds are it'll be inside one of those buildings."

"Holy cow, imagine how long shopping inside one of those would be," Max exclaimed, gawking at the huge buildings. "Just how much space is in there?"

"Between all three buildings, almost five million square feet of space is equipped for stores. So, yes, I'd imagine it takes a very long time to get everything you'd need. Of course, most people don't shop this way, they just order their things remotely and have it delivered. I hear a lot of towns on Earth are doing the same thing."

"I mean, online ordering was never a thing in my town," admitted Daniel. "Salt Plains was a backwater town in every way."

"He's understating it, honestly," put in Max. "I heard

some guards talking about it a few years ago, and their description made it sound like the most pathetic, miserable, lonely little place in the entire galaxy. Honestly, it's a miracle it even existed for the Gorogs to…"

The lizard stopped talking and turned to Daniel, who was not looking pleased with Max's comments. Vorlax didn't seem too happy either. "Was that too far, or…?"

"Perhaps next time try to know when's the proper place to stop talking," Vorlax said, turning back to focus on driving the speeder. Daniel said nothing, but instead propped his elbow up on the edge of the wall and marveled some more at Arajor.

Back on the *Justice*, Shane had finally reached Vraxis's quarters. He was a little nervous, as he was about to find out whether or not his idea worked. If it did, it meant that everyone would get off happy in the end. If it did not…Shane may have hated Vraxis for the damage they had done, but even he wished the asteroid prisons upon no one except Orvag himself. To be sentenced there was to be sentenced to death, and a painful, agonizingly slow death at that. He would have been less concerned with Foulor, since he was less cognitant than Vraxis and would likely take whatever route guaranteed him freedom. Vraxis would be challenging, however.

He knocked on the door and had it opened by one of the guards. He passed through the threshold and stared at Vraxis, who was sitting back against the far wall, on his bed. As the door slammed shut behind him, Vraxis rose to his feet, almost miffed that Shane had come back so soon.

"Back already?" the hunter asked, folding his arms. "To what do I owe the pleasure of this specific occasion? Another proposal?"

"Yes, I am," replied Shane. "So, what do you think of your new room? Better than your old cell? Oh, by the way, be sure to push that panel into the wall. You'll like what's inside." He pointed at a small protruding piece of the wall, which jutted out into the bedroom. Vraxis reached over and pressed it, and a small minifridge popped out of the wall, with several racks for storing items.

Vraxis sighed. "Alright, you made your point, Shane. This is a very nice room. Probably nicer than what I had when working for Orvag. But you didn't just walk in here to ask how the accommodations were. Just spit it out, what is it that you want?"

"Another proposition," replied Shane.

"Oh, great, more bargaining. My favorite." Sarcasm hinged on Vraxis's words. "Tell me."

"I have 50,000 units sitting in my office in Arajor City. If you answer these two questions, you'll get that early as a taste of the payment to come. The rest of the money you'll get once you've finished honoring your end of the bargain, when assisting us in the attack on Rhozadar tomorrow. Understood?"

Vraxis nodded. "Fair enough." He was smart enough to recognize that a little honor and trust was required from both parties. "What do you need me to answer?"

Shane moved in closer to him, taking a seat on the bed. "Have you been to Rhozadar before?"

"Yeah. Loads of times. Orvag had Foulor and I run some of his slaves there sometimes for money."

"Good, that's good to know. Now. Where would the slaves in the camp be taken to in the event of an attack?" Shane was hoping to get at a certain point soon.

"Where? There are multiple places there that they could go to take shelter."

Shane racked his brain for details from the few scattered reports he had heard and seen. "I mean, where would the slaves go to be kept under guard, to be safe from any attack, either from the ground or the air?"

Vraxis thought for a few moments, then his face brightened with recognition. "Oh, you mean in the event of an attack from multiple angles. Yeah, they would go to C-bunker. It's located in the center of the complex, and is basically a bomb-proof shelter. If the Gorogs were to keep them anywhere, it would be there."

"Okay." Shane turned to go, but then stopped and turned around to face Vraxis again. "One other thing. When Orvag was giving out your targets for the last raid, did he say what he was planning on doing to them?"

"Well, if my memory serves me right," said Vraxis, "Orvag was after four targets. Two female Terrans, one male, and then a strange male lizard-type creature. I wasn't sure about it when I saw it. However, he did say that only one of those targets was high priority. He referred to him strangely…I'm not 100% sure."

"Subject X-17," finished Shane. "We already know."

"The point of the raid was to get him back, alive, to the custody of the Gorogs. Orvag was using him for some experiment. Said it was going to help out the Gorog Empire's future plans. If getting him back wasn't possible, then one of the other three was, since they had been in contact with X-17, and they could be used as leverage."

"Wait, wait," interrupted Shane. "The Gorog Empire's future plans. Did Orvag tell you about them?"

Vraxis shook his head. "We both inquired about it, but he was tight-lipped. There were whispers though. Apparently it's a highly secret plan that, so the rumor goes, leads straight to an attack on Arajor."

Shane nodded slowly. "Alright, thanks," he said, his voice lacking emotion. That answer meant that Orvag hadn't sabotaged the transmission in any way, as he had sometimes done before. Ms. Phillips had really been there with them, and not just been digitally inserted. He opened the door to exit. "Just a reminder, although we've let you out of your prison cell, you will still be accompanied by security at all times until you further prove that you can be trusted, alright?"

Vraxis nodded again. "Totally understood, Shane."

"One other thing." The Magnum leaned in dangerously close to Vraxis's face. "If I find out that this whole thing was a trick, and that none of the conversation we had meant anything, it won't be the asteroid field we'll be sending you to. It'll be a death via the nearest airlock. So don't do anything that might tempt me to do so."

Vraxis's face remained unchanged, even if his body language leaned back just a bit. He slowly nodded. "You have my word, Shane. This is no trick."

Shane nodded, still not fully convinced, then turned to the guards behind him. "Have two men assigned to Vraxis whenever he leaves his room. Under no circumstances are they to leave his side."

"What if I need to take care of some business?" piped up Vraxis, raising his hand like he was a student in school.

Shane sighed, loud enough so that Vraxis could hear his exasperation. "Scratch that, under no circumstances, unless he's defecating in the restroom, are the guards to leave his side. And, before he interjects again, they're allowed to be indecent in private as long as they're within earshot of the guards." He turned back to Vraxis. "Any necessary changes to the policy that you wish me to grant?"

Vraxis shook his head.

"Very well. Lunch will be arriving in your cell in about two hours. Don't get into trouble before then."

He left and shut the door behind him, digesting this information. Orvag was potentially planning on attacking Arajor. Big surprise. He had figured as such years ago, since that was what the Gorogs would ideally want. But it still offered little comfort as to how it would transpire. And from what Vraxis had just said, Orvag was being incredibly secretive about it.

He walked off to get ready for his meeting with the council, choosing to bury these thoughts deep down inside.

After over an hour of flying around the city, Vorlax set the taxi down on one of the landing pads next to a high-class residence area. He, Daniel and Max all disembarked, letting the blue giant's solar rays hit them in the face. Ahead of them was a lush garden rich in flora. "We still have a half-hour until we need to be at the Kraken," Vorlax told them. "I thought I'd let us stretch our legs for a little bit. Besides, this is one of my personal favorite spots to visit in the entire city."

Vorlax had a point. As they passed the threshold of the garden, the gray, blue and red colors of the bridges and buildings were replaced by blue-green grass that had been planted on the surface of the island. Trees taller than Daniel's house loomed over them, their branches and yellow leaves obscuring the star above them. Bushes with flowers of all shapes, sizes and colors surrounded them, some of them in full bloom. And the wildlife; there were small lizards climbing up tree trunks, which Max took a particular fancy to, birds with three tails and iridescent blue plumage that chirped overhead, and insects of all sizes buzzed around them. Daniel noticed a few familiar ones, including two bumblebees like the ones that pollinated the flowers in his front yard. Behind them, however, a four-foot tall mantis that was standing on its hind legs was devouring some small furry animal, causing Daniel to look the other way. There were also some alien species that he had no reference to, such as a large flying beast that almost looked like a monkey, except its eyelids opened horizontally, and it had four eyes and scales. There were also small, stick-like mammals walking around on the paths, next to full-sized aliens and humans alike, and a multi-headed fish that was swimming in a manmade stream that they passed over during their walk. "There are over two hundred different species of creature within this one garden. All together, there's about 8,500 total alien species, flora or fauna, that all dwell in Arajor's gardens.

Daniel whistled. "8,500?"

"All of them are docile towards humans and aliens our size. The predators that are hostile have their own island that's only accessible by speeder. Hunting beasts for sport is one thing that certain aliens who live here, especially those where hunting is a part of their planet's culture, take part in."

"You really have thought of everything, haven't you?" Max asked, and Daniel was almost certain that he meant it this time. If he did, it was one of the only true compliments that the lizard had uttered since he and Daniel had met.

"We tried to, yes."

They found a bench to sit on overlooking part of the floating city. Now that they weren't on the speeder, Daniel could see other small craft flying around the city, traveling between destinations like flies. On their left, one of the residential complexes towered over them like a mountain. Before them, dozens of metal islands supported other areas of the city, such as another housing complex and a huge mess of buildings in the distance that looked suspiciously like some kind of amusement park. One thing that Daniel did notice was how some islands looked older than others. "So...how did y'all build this city in the first place?" he asked Vorlax.

"The Coalition has always resided in this star system, ever since it was founded two thousand years ago. But for the first seven hundred years or so, the main headquarters were located on Delvor, Arajor's largest moon." Vorlax pointed at a large sphere that was peeking out from behind one of the buildings in the distance, rising over the cloud tops. "After a while, we converted the old base into our star cruiser factories and rebuilt the main government headquarters on a floating island over the surface of Arajor Prime, designed to perpetually float over the surface. Since then, more islands have been constructed to accommodate others who've wanted to settle down in a secure place, and the city continues to grow to this day. Even now, there are more islands being built on Delvor, waiting to be placed in a designated spot in the city."

"And what if the Gorogs, or some other threat, tries to come and attack the city?" Max said, his neck twisting around to look in Vorlax's direction.

Vorlax laughed. "They'd be in for a bad day for sure. Where you're sitting down, Max, is the most secure facility in the entire Coalition. There's a permanent blockade of a dozen of our finest warships that constantly guards the planet from attack. Most armies wouldn't even make it down to the surface. Even if they did, you see those right there?" He pointed to a small island about half a mile away from them. Although the haze of Arajor's atmosphere was making distant objects foggy, the shadow of two giant cannons poked out through the fog. Daniel estimated that each barrel was a hundred feet long, at least. "That's one of fifty military batteries scattered throughout the city. Each of those guns has enough power to punch through the shields of a Gorog freighter, and each island also comes with surface-to-air missiles and phasers designed to rip holes in the hulls of enemy vessels. Oh, and let's also not forget the dedicated army that lives here at all times and is trained to stop any ground assault. The bridges help too, since they can be blown up and hinder advancing troops. It would take a colossal army to take this city, and even if they did, the losses would be enormous."

Max nodded. "That's good to know."

"The last time this city was attacked was during the Infernite Wars, one thousand years ago. Back then, it was still in its infancy, and our defenses were weaker than they are now. The attacking force was eventually beaten, and after that the city's defenses were made stronger and increased in number.

Since then, no enemy has even managed to get close to Arajor itself, not even Orvag himself."

Daniel stared out at the city, watching at the rays of the star above them slanted down further and further. "It's getting late," he noted.

"Yeah. That's one difference between Earth and this place," replied Vorlax. "We may be floating, but the gravity of the planet still causes us to rotate with it. A day here only lasts about seventeen hours."

"How do you plan your schedules then, when you have seven less hours in your day?" Daniel asked.

"Usually everyone here sleeps around seven hours of their day. Here, there is no midnight; 17:00 happens right at starrise, our version of sunrise. Breakfast usually happens at 2:00, dinner happens around 8:00, and everyone's typically asleep starting at 10:00-11:00. But because we're orbiting a gas giant, nighttime only lasts about two hours, as the planet's core passes between us and the star. Every other time, the atmosphere filters in weak solar rays, causing it to resemble dusk. It's different from most other planets, but you get used to it," Vorlax added, smiling at Daniel.

"When did you first come here?" Daniel asked him. "You seem to know a lot about this place."

"Me? Well, it was about twenty-two years ago. I was only seven at the time, but I wanted training to enlist in the Coalition's starfighter division, the Zodiac Force. Rumblings of war were in the air, and they had started to enlist for a potential conflict. I spent ten years training to become a pilot, hoping to fly with a squadron. By the time I graduated, the war was in full force, and I joined a squadron to help battle the Squids, as my fellow pilots called them."

"When did you meet Shane?"

"I've known Shane for a very long time, but I first met him when I was still training in the academy. His father,

Agammor the Mighty, was still Magnum when I met him. He was an ambitious young man, who wanted to destroy the Gorogs the first chance he got. Not long after, Agammor was killed in battle and he became Magnum. He recognized my ability to fly a ship and promoted me to be on Belt Squadron, the group of pilots who fly under Shane himself. After helping to win several major battles, he had me promoted again to Squadron Commander. I also function as an…adviser of sorts, as you saw when he called me earlier."

Max nodded. "It's nice to have a friend like that, I'd assume. Me? I've never really been that great at making friends."

"What do you mean?" asked Daniel.

"It's difficult to say. I just hate almost everyone I meet, since I either find them annoying or boring. The only friend I ever had was a fellow lizard on my old snow planet, but it's been so long that I forget his name. I doubt he's still alive."

Daniel sat back on the bench. "I'm sure you all can guess that Caitlin is my best friend. I've known her since I was very young, for almost fifteen whole years at this point. She's the kindest, most amazing person I've had the privilege of knowing. She cares for everyone, even the people she hates, and she…well, there's no one I'd rather be lost in space with than her."

"You two are only friends? Yeah, right. There's definitely a thing going on there, right?"

Daniel nearly fell off the bench at Max's comment. "No! No! Absolutely not!" He stopped, considered his words, then added slowly, "But I can see why you'd think that. But there's no…thing between us. We're just friends, that's all."

Vorlax leaned in closer to Daniel. "Between just you and me, Daniel, if a thing doesn't ever develop between the two of you at some point, I'll cut my tentacles off, deep-fry them, and serve them with butter. Because you two deserve better, I'll tell you that. Being taken hostage by the Gorogs wasn't fair."

"Glad someone sees it that way."

Vorlax leaned in. "Once this is all over, I'm sure that I'll be able to help you find a new home. A nice home. You all deserve a normal life. You'll have some amazing stories to tell, but I can imagine that you'd want to be back with your own kind." He stared out across the slowly deepening atmosphere, watching as the shadows lengthened before him. "I had a lot of siblings. Over a hundred, in fact. And, despite their never-ending numbers, I still miss them a lot, and can't wait until this war is over and I can go see them again."

Daniel managed a smile. "Thanks, Vorlax," he said gratefully. "I'm glad I got the chance to meet you."

"As did I, young Daniel."

They sat on the bench watching speeders fly past for a long time, to the point where Max even fell asleep on the ground at Vorlax's feet. Daniel was getting drowsy too, having been deprived of a decent night's sleep since before the Gorog raid. But at last, the commander made the call to resume their trip around the city. They reached the taxi and resumed their trip, leaving the garden behind and heading deeper into the city. As they did, Daniel could see nothing but densely packed islands of buildings and more buildings, stretching on forever into the distance. "So…just how large is Arajor?" he asked Vorlax, curious to know.

"If you're referring to the planet, its diameter is about 80,000 miles wide," the commander replied. "But if you're referring to the city, it's about 90 by 70 miles, or at least that's what my estimates tell me. It keeps growing every year though, so in five years it'll likely be a mile or two larger in every direction. The Kraken is right at its center, about 20 miles from where we are, so it'll be a moment before we arrive."

"Um…quick question, just because I'm curious about this," piped up Max. "Why is your government building, the center of your entire empire, called, of all things, *the Kraken*? It seems like a dumb name to me."

Vorlax chuckled slightly. "That's a funny story. So, the Kraken is actually the third different government building we've erected in that spot. I've already mentioned the original, and then we replaced it with a larger building about five hundred years ago. Then, about ten years ago, the third building was built in place of the second. It's not officially called the Kraken, per say. Its official name is the Coalition Diathon, as set forth by Shane and the council. But about four months after it was finished, at one of the Zodiac Conferences, your Earth leaders gave us a full roster of your mythical creatures list, large and small. One of them was the kraken, and a lot of people started nicknaming the building the Kraken. Even Shane got in on the joke eventually, and that's when the Kraken essentially became its unofficial name. It's even funnier because very few people are actually aware that the building's actual name is the Coalition Diathon."

"So the building looks like an actual kraken?" asked Max, sarcastic as always.

A few minutes later, he found out. They rounded around another apartment complex and saw a gigantic building not far away. From all of the infrastructure radiating out of it, and lighting, it was blatantly obvious that it was the central hub of the entire city. It sat on a giant island, much bigger than any of the other ones that they had seen. The building on it was…shaped interestingly, to say the least. Situated in the back was what appeared to be the main building, but radiating out from it were eight long extensions that wrapped around from the side to encircle a huge opening in the front of the building, and that happened to bore a striking resemblance to a set of giant tentacles. A hangar opening, since there were so many ships flying into it, acted as its gaping maw, swallowing up ships as they sought to land. The building managed to tower over most of the buildings near it, and as Daniel got closer to it, he could see that some of the projections coming out of it had to take up their own mini islands. It was imposing in every way, and in the slowly fading light, was brightly blue from all the spotlights.

Max was speechless, a rare occurrence. "Huh," he finally said. "So that's why it's called the Kraken."

He was not wrong, Daniel thought. The building's eight projections, hangar maw between all of them, and huge size did warrant it being called what it was. The chrome gray and blue glistened in the dimming light of the blue star as they approached. They eventually joined a crowded stream of vehicles all of which were queuing to enter the Kraken's hangar. Vorlax turned around as they drew closer to the building's projections, which were now looming large over them.

"I should also mention that a lot of the council members want to remove the building's 'tentacles'. You know, we're at war with the Gorogs, we can't have our building resembling the visage of our enemies, all that nonsense. I disagree, plus a lot of important things are housed in those projections. Communication for the whole city, the control center for the defenses…plus, I think those projections give it character. You don't see too many buildings like it."

Daniel nodded. "I agree. It's…strange for sure, I'll give it that."

They passed into the reach of the Kraken's tentacles. Up ahead, a shielded gate barred any further access. A female Coalition guard stood outside, checking IDs. Above the gate, one of the projections had a row of guns attached to the underside, all of them aimed at the people below. "You'd be dead before you even set foot in the compound if you tried to circle around the gate," Vorlax revealed to them. The queue grew shorter in front of them as they neared the lasers. Daniel watched nervously as they passed under the watchful eye of the resting cannons. He was sure that they were safe, but just looking down the barrels was giving him anxiety.

They reached the guard at the front. "Vorlax!" she

exclaimed upon seeing the commander's gray face.

"How's your day going, Trisha?" he asked her.

"Doing alright so far," she replied. "Are you here on business?"

"Yes, I'm escorting these two. Shane and the council have summoned them to appear before them in just a few minutes. They're not in any trouble or anything, just here to see the council."

"Very well. You have your ID ready?"

Vorlax fumbled with his uniform's pocket, finally pulling a small card out. "Right here," he said, handing it to Trisha to scan. She did, and handed it back.

"You're all clear, Vorlax," she told him. "Spot C-11, inside."

"Thank you." The gate's laser grid went down, and Vorlax pulled the speeder past the boundary of the gate, which reactivated behind them. They approached the maw of the Kraken's hangar door, passing by the outer defenses. They passed into the building's shadow, causing everything to dim save for the blue lights that lit the path to the hangar. They reached the threshold of the interior and Vorlax slowed their speeder to a crawl, passing by other parked speeders.

He found their parking spot, marked with "TAXI SPEEDER PARKING. SPOT NO. C-11." He landed their vehicle and shut the engines and other systems off. "Door's opening behind you," Vorlax called behind him. "Watch your step as you disembark!"

Daniel carefully stepped off the taxi and onto the solid ground of the building floor. Max did so a little less gracefully, stumbling and almost slamming his head onto the ground. The two of them regathered their balance after being on a swaying vehicle for a combined total of almost ninety minutes. Once he had, they could take in the size of the hangar they were in;

double that of the *Justice's* main hangar, and big enough to fit a city much larger than Salt Plains inside. But whereas the *Justice* was always crowded in its hangar, both from parked ships and their crew members, the Kraken's was less so, with ships scattered more sparsely here. There were also fewer people running about as well, although Daniel did see some workers come jogging across. Max was also watching people go by, eagerly sitting down next to the taxi like some excited dog. But before either of them could sightsee anymore, Vorlax interrupted from behind.

"The exit is this way!" Vorlax told them, grabbing Daniel from under his arm and dragging him away from the taxi. "Shane and the entire council are waiting for us! And they do not take kindly to late visitors!"

"We're still on time!" protested Max, who started to follow them. "Why can't we sightsee any longer?"

"Because if we don't hurry, we'll miss the addressing of the council from Shane. And if you miss that…well, you'd better not come back here or you'd never leave this place alive."

This ominous statement now repeating over in his head, Max stopped complaining and followed Vorlax out of the hangar.

Chapter 22

Hyperspeed

    A long way away from the safety of the Kraken and Arajor, Caitlin and Pantura were hurtling towards the planet known as Anich on their small shuttle. Caitlin was already missing the comfort that the *Phoenix* provided during her voyage on that ship, as their little ship was not very comfortable at all. The seats were hard, with almost no cushioning, and her back was sore while sitting down. In addition, there was no fridge to munch snacks from, nor were there living quarters with books to read. The interior consisted only of two rows of chairs against a wall, some empty weapon racks, and an elevated one-person cockpit that Pantura was occupying. There were also no windows outside the cockpit viewscreen, and little soundproofing, given how loud the engines of the shuttle were inside. Caitlin was growing tired of not being able to take a nap, after having little sleep the last full day. She approached Pantura, hoping to get a solution to her problem.

    "Hey! Are you able to dampen the sound of the engines? I'm trying to nap back here and can't because of the constant roar."

    Pantura didn't even turn to face her as she concentrated on keeping the ship's course stable. "Open the cabinet just above the access door. You'll see some earphones in there. Put those on and it'll cancel out the noise."

    She resumed her work before Caitlin could protest any further. Her shoulders slumped in resignation, but she backed into the ship, unzipping and taking off her jacket and tossing it onto one of the seats. She opened the cabinet that Pantura had indicated and pulled out a set of earphones. She put them on, and the engines' roar was instantly silenced. She looked towards

Pantura, who was still flying the ship. Shrugging, she stretched her body across several seats, shutting her eyes and hoping to sleep as much as she possibly could. Although it was uncomfortable to stretch across that many chairs, she was still relatively comfortable, using her jacket as a pillow, only for the ship to start vibrating below her like the rattle of a snake. This sensation forced her back awake, and she soon was forced to sit up as a particularly intense bout of shaking nearly gave her a headache. Angrily staring at the row of seats that were denying her a decent sleep, she decided to forget trying to sleep and just sat down on one of the seats. Boredom was something that she had yet to feel the entire ride to Anich, as worry about her powers, plus the fact that she was going to meet actual wizards to help cure her, silenced any bored feeling that she may have felt otherwise. She wondered if maintaining a conversation with Pantura would be the best way to help keep her engaged on something besides the obvious. She stood up and approached the cockpit again, taking off her earphones and tossing them aside.

"So...these wizards that Shane mentioned," she began, asking something that had been on her mind for a while now. "Do you, the expert on the galaxy's cultures, know anything about them?"

This time, Pantura turned her chair around to face her as she spoke. "Yes. They're known as the Ostila Madors, *Magic Wielders* in the old tongue once spoken by all alien descendants. They are friendly to the Coalition; we've even fought alongside them in the past. But not much is known of their culture or how they manifest their magic. They tend to keep a low profile on Anich, and don't socialize with us much. Shane's fine with that, honestly. He's always viewed magic with some..." She searched for a word that wouldn't spook Caitlin. "...suspicion," she finished. She gave Caitlin a reassuring look. "I wouldn't worry about your powers too much. If they are a part of the same magic they wield, they'll be able to fix you right up in no time."

Caitlin's lip corners managed to uptick slightly, and she bowed her head. "Thanks, Pantura. That means a lot."

Pantura nodded and dipped her head down as well, only to be interrupted by a rapid beeping from the ship. She checked the dash. "Navicomputer says we're here," she announced, backing the shuttle out of hyperspeed slowly. They slowed down slowly but surely, the streaks of light outside their window growing shorter, until at last they were back to stellar points of light and Anich loomed right in front of them.

The planet was perhaps the most visually stunning that Caitlin had seen so far. For one, it looked like a twin of Earth in terms of climate, with tons of green and blue patches covering the surface. Even more impressive, there were hundreds of stars within close proximity of Anich, surrounding the planet and bathing it in their glow. Beyond that were thousands more, stretching on for forever, to the point where they couldn't even see past the boundary of the star cluster. Something in Caitlin's memory jarred as she saw the thousands of stars that she and Pantura were encased in. She remembered Daniel's words to her at their last stargazing session; he had referred to what they were in as a globular star cluster, a massive, old ball of stars that orbited the center of the galaxy and contained some of the oldest stars out there.

"Welcome to one of our many Starfields. Or, as you Terrans call them, a globular cluster," Pantura said, piloting the ship towards the lush surface of Anich in front of them. Caitlin felt immeasurable pleasure with herself at remembering Daniel's astronomy lessons to her. She smiled, imagining him geeking out at being inside an actual star cluster.

They dove into the planet's atmosphere, a fireball forming around their ship as they passed into the atmosphere. The shuttle vibrated like crazy as the atmosphere around them buffered the ship. Caitlin grabbed onto an overhanging handle to steady herself, while Pantura concentrated on flying through the flames. Thankfully, the turbulent entry did not last long, and soon they were within cruising altitude, below the clouds but still unable to see the planet's surface. That was, until a huge, dark shape loomed out of a cloudbank ahead of them, and Pantura steered to avoid ramming into a mountain.

"We're entering the mountain ranges. That means we're getting close," she told Caitlin. "The navicomputer says we're about twenty miles out. Once we're within two miles of the temple, we'll land and continue the rest of the way on foot. We don't want to disturb them or have them mistake us for Gorogs or another enemy."

They cruised along for another minute or two, Pantura having to steer around two more mountains as they did, until finally the computers indicated a flat spot of ground where they could set down the shuttle, and was reasonably close to their destination. She steered the vehicle down towards the ground, setting it down on its landing gear as gently as she could. The ship powered down, and the back door slid open, letting a wide shaft of light inside. Caitlin, blinded for a brief moment by how bright it was, shielded her eyes as she walked out of the ship and into the brilliantly lit daytime. Pantura was right behind her.

They had landed in a clearing in a mountain forest. Huge, spruce-like green trees loomed over them and their ship as they made sense of their surroundings. Peeking over the top of the clearing at one end was the peak of a huge obelisk-shaped mountain that stretched forever into the heavens. There were clouds, just like on Earth, but beyond that the light of thousands of stars poked through and dappled the ground as it filtered down through the leaves. There was a brisk wind blowing, and Caitlin ducked back into the ship to grab her jacket before they left it. Pantura, meanwhile, was scanning the area with a device to mark their coordinates so they wouldn't get lost.

"Okay, I have our position," she told Caitlin as she came out of the shuttle. "Now we'll be able to find our way back here no matter what. According to the map, we're about 1.5 miles southeast of the coordinates Shane and Vorlax gave us. If we head this way, it should lead us to the temple." She pointed to her right, into a stretch of forest bare of bushes and other low-dwelling plants. "Caitlin, do you have everything you need?"

She nodded. "I do."

"Good. Give me one second." She ducked back inside their ship, and came back out with a small bag. "There's some water bottles and a protein bar each in this bag, along with some first-aid supplies. Odds are we won't need them, but you never know." She slung the bag over her shoulder, and then started off in the direction she indicated. Caitlin followed hastily, feeling the adrenaline levels rising throughout her entire body. She prayed that these wizards would be able to cure her of her powers, as she was growing paranoid that they would only keep on getting stronger from here. She didn't want to be returning home with them either. People would only ask too many questions.

They passed under the shade of the trees, past small bushes and flower patches, a smell very similar to pine needles drifting through the air, exciting Caitlin's nose. It was a very familiar scent, one that made Caitlin homesick for her old house back on Earth. Sure, Charlie hadn't been the best guardian out there, but her house always smelled fresh thanks to all the small conifer plants planted in her old backyard. Pantura continued to lead them through the woods, their route slanting downwards as they pressed on farther from the shuttle and clearing. The scanner she had brought had been calibrated to look for the same traces of magic that was on Caitlin, but as they walked for about ten minutes, they had not found any such traces anywhere. Not only that, but Caitlin was also feeling as though they were being watched. She kept looking around for signs of a predator lurking in the shade, but there were none; the high level of brightness ensured that there were very few spots where something could hide. Despite this, Caitlin still felt unsafe, and although she still had her pistol from the ambush in its place, she had no idea how much ammo it had left, or whether it would be any good against whatever it was that was stalking them.

She was just about to tell Pantura her feelings when the scanner she was holding started to flash blue. She came to a halt, looking around at the trees around them. She then lowered her head to look at the ground, noticing leaves displaced about six feet in front of them. She took another step forward, her free arm extending forward and waving around at the space in front of them. When that yielded nothing, she stepped forwards again, and this time, her hand passed straight through an invisible bubble in the woods. She retracted her arm in surprise, then stuck it through again, the membrane shimmering as she did. Caitlin just did what she had been doing most of her week so far and just stared as Pantura examined the mysterious anomaly.

"This is it," she finally said, approaching Caitlin with the scanner. The readings were the exact same as the magic traces on Caitlin, only much stronger and more precise. "The border of the Ostila Madors' lands. Once we cross that line there's no telling what will happen."

"That's cool, but, I'll be honest, Pantura," said Caitlin, hoping to get her concerns out of the way quickly. "This forest is creeping me out. I think there might be something watching us."

"You mean like a predator?" Pantura looked behind her, and then all around them. "Where would a predator hide? There are no caves in the mountain face next to us, and no suitable cover to hide behind. You're probably just experiencing some adrenaline spikes from your powers. Besides, if there *is* somehow a predator…" She pulled out a small box from her belt, which in a matter of seconds began to extend into a long rifle barrel and brace. She brandished it threateningly at a tree, the huge muzzle waving around threateningly in the air.

Caitlin shrunk away from the huge gun as it came near

her. "I see," she said, as Pantura collapsed it back down to its original size.

Pantura nodded. "Come on," she said, gesturing to Caitlin. "Let's see what lies on the other side of this bubble."

They approached the spot where it was, which now looked like a continuation of the forest as normal. But as they kept walking, they eventually were absorbed into the membranous outer wall. It felt surprisingly viscous, yet not wet or slimy in any way. As they kept walking, they eventually popped out onto the other side, and were greeted with a strange sight.

"Well, this was not what I was expecting," said Pantura, staring up at the night sky above them. Even around them, the forest had radically changed, now looking as though nighttime was upon them. Behind them, it even continued onwards, looking as though the path they had just taken in the daytime was now entirely in the dark.

Caitlin's sense of danger only heightened under the night sky. "I'm not sure this is the best idea after all, Pantura. Maybe we should go back to the ship and just fly closer to the temple."

"Relax. This is just one of their spells. This is completely normal. In fact, this will make our job even easier for us, since we'll now be able to see the temple lights." She pressed onwards, ignoring Caitlin's concern. Caitlin, looking nervously around them, followed.

They pressed on deeper into the forest, which was now much harder to navigate because of the dim light. But mercifully, just two minutes farther into the woods, they saw a light up ahead. A torch, mounted onto a stick stuck into the ground. Besides it, running approximately parallel to the direction they were going in, was a dirt path. Turning to their right, they could see another torch further down the pathway. "See? We'll be fine," said Pantura, stepping onto the path and into the light of the torch.

As Caitlin moved to do the same, some of the leaves behind them rustled, and they both stopped dead in their tracks. Pantura was especially perturbed. "Alright," she whispered as loud as she dared. "Maybe there's more to your predator story after all."

"See?" hissed Caitlin. "I told you there was something after us!"

There was another rustling, this time to their right. They whipped around to face the noise, their concern slowly being replaced by literal fear. "I heard something!" Caitlin whispered to Pantura. "It sounded like growling."

"Let's just start walking this direction. Follow the lights!" she replied, starting to walk.

But as she did, the forest next to them disgorged something out of its shadowy depths. It landed straight on the pathway, between them and their destination, and growled at the two of them. It was easily a full three heads taller than Caitlin, probably more, and although most of its body was hidden in shadow, two faintly glowing purple eyes with V-shaped pupils and two huge tusks jutting out from underneath its chin could be seen. Behind it, what little light there was exposed the trailing tendrils coming out on multiple spots on its back. It pawed the ground with huge front paws and growled at Caitlin and Pantura again.

"A Shervide!" exclaimed Pantura in terror upon properly seeing the beast. "Run!"

They both took off running, but the Shervide was already there, blocking their escape route into the woods. They then used the pathway, not bothering to watch for roots or rocks in the pathway as they tried to put as much distance between themselves and the monster's growling.

"Please tell me about what's trying to kill us!" Caitlin panted as they ran for their lives.

"A Shervide is a very dangerous predator that lives in

the mountains of several planets!" replied Pantura, trying to conserve her breath as she sprinted. "They can move extremely quickly to chase down their prey and can scale vertical surfaces to reach it!"

"Great!" yelled Caitlin, trying to keep her balance as she nearly caught her foot on a tree root jutting out of the pathway. She glanced behind her, seeing the monster sprinting after them on the mountain wall itself, somehow defying gravity as it chased after them, its huge white teeth flashing in the light from the torches.

"We have to find water! Shervides hate water! If we can find a small river we'll be fine!" Pantura looked around frantically for any signs of water, but the dark forest hid any trace of a stream. The sounds of the chase also hid any bubbling water. They chanced another glance back behind them, only for the cliff face to be vacant of the Shervide. They both skidded to a stop, out of breath, with Caitlin sweating from her forehead. "Where did it go?" Pantura asked, looking around wildly.

Suddenly, two purple eyes came flying out of the forest on their right, rapidly getting closer to them. The Shervide burst out, its jaws wide open as it prepared to bite Pantura's head off. Caitlin screamed, and Pantura's eyes grew wide as dinner plates as she stared down her death right in the eyes. The Shervide's fangs were so close, but right before they chomped down, the monster was sent flying by an invisible force, landing hard on the ground a good distance away.

Both Caitlin and Pantura swiveled around to see what had knocked such a huge creature aside, and saw a hooded figure standing on the pathway. He was hidden in shadows, his cloak hiding and facial features, and he appeared to be carrying no weapons. But as he approached, the Shervide snarled from the forest and lunged at the strange person in the pathway. As it did, however, they stuck their hand out, and a blue-green light came out, and the beast was sent back another ten feet. The hooded figure then made a couple motions with their arms, then placed his hands together and extended them apart from each other. A long sword, with handle and everything, materialized out of thin air, falling right into their hand. The figure swished it around several times and came at the Shervide, swinging it with deadly accuracy as the blade slashed at the monster's face, leaving a deep cut on its chin. The Shervide roared, and swiped at the figure with his paw, only for them to roll on the ground out of the way.

Then from the cliff, another hooded figure lunged from off of it, and landed on the Shervide's back, driving what looked like another sword into the creature's back. The monster's body convulsed, a howl of pain escaping its jaws as it tried to throw the second figure off. But they refused to budge, distracting the hunter while the first hooded man slashed at the Shervide's face with his sword. The massive creature slowly began to back away, and it finally turned tail and ran, the second figure flipping off its back as it tore off into the dark woods, out of sight. The two of them didn't lower their swords until the sounds of it tearing through the woods vanished away into the darkness.

Caitlin and Pantura, who had been watching the Shervide with tense bodies and held breaths, finally let them loose and collapsed onto the pathway. "No more surprises tonight, please," Caitlin whispered to Pantura.

Pantura glanced down at her hand. "Caitlin, your hand," she whispered back.

They both looked down, to see her hand sparking wildly with electricity. And it wasn't just the one; as she took her other hand out from behind her, it too was alive with lightning crackling across it. Caitlin stared at the two of them with horror. "It's never happened with both hands before!" she said, alarmed.

The sound of footsteps approaching caused both of them to look up. Both of their hooded saviors were approaching them, resting on the side of the path. One was broader in build than the other, while the other was lankier and less muscular in build. "You two alright?" the big one asked Pantura and Caitlin.

Pantura nodded, rising to her feet and dusting herself off. "Yes, I think so. Caitlin?"

Her hands instantly stopped sparking as she turned to look at Pantura. "Yes, I'm uninjured." She stood up as well, scratching the back of her head. "Uh…thanks for saving us from that monster."

"No problem. What are you doing all the way out here?" asked the smaller hooded figure, in a female voice. "The nearest settlement is fifty miles away."

Pantura cleared her throat. "We're looking for the Ostila Madors' temple. We're both Orion Coalition agents, and we need to speak with them."

The larger of the two hoods perked up at the mention of the Ostila Madors. "You're looking for the Ostila Madors?"

They both nodded. "Please."

The two hooded figures exchanged a glance that neither Pantura nor Caitlin could see, and then they both reached up and pulled their hoods back, revealing their faces. The bigger of the two was human and male, with a buzzcut of hair and a short mustache, along with a rare pair of green eyes, and not just any green; sea-green, piercing, like the water you'd see in the tropics. His partner was also human, but female, sporting a long braid that disappeared into the cloak she was wearing and a straight-set jaw. Caitlin and Pantura exchanged a look themselves, wondering if the gesture was good or bad for them.

"I am Baracath," the male told them. "This is Erwid. We are both members of the Ostila Madors."

"It appears we stumbled upon you just in time," said Erwid, folding her arms. "That Shervide was moments away from tearing both of you apart."

Caitlin's eyes kept darting back and forth between the two of them. Neither of them looked any different from the other humans she'd met. Yet she had just witnessed one of them pull a sword out of thin air and take down a huge predator with it. "You two are both wizards?" she asked, then cursed herself at how dumb the question sounded.

Pantura's face turned slightly red, but Baracath laughed out loud. "I suppose that's one way to address us as," he said, smiling. Then he noticed Caitlin's embarrassment. "Don't worry about it. You're not the first to have called us that."

Caitlin's cheek color faded somewhat at that, and she shook her head. "I assume that that's not technically the term that you go by when out in public, right?"

Baracath shook his head. "No, but I don't take offense at it either." He turned to Erwid. "We should bring them to the temple before another Shervide or some other predator comes for us. They're everywhere out in these woods this time of day."

"I agree," Erwid replied. "Besides, they were looking for us. And look." She pointed at Pantura's engineering uniform, which had the Coalition's patch logo on her shoulder. "They're of the Coalition alright."

"We can take their requests inside the walls of the temple." Baracath turned to Pantura and Caitlin. "We'll take you to the temple. You'll be safe there. Erwid, you know how to do a Time Spell. The Shervides won't come out if it's daytime, and it'll be safer for all of us."

She nodded, and she pulled back her cloak to allow both hands to come out. She held out four fingers with one hand and began to swivel her hand in a circle. The sky began to turn rapidly as she did, the stars above seeming to grow brighter as she did. As she moved her arm, her hand glowed blue-green, the same color that Baracath's hand did when he summoned the sword. And, now that Caitlin could see it clearly, it was the same color that her electricity became when her hands started to spark. Before long, the forest around them was brightening, the veil of the night disappeared, and their surroundings were indistinguishable from when Pantura and Caitlin first landed.

"Alright, the spell's been disabled," Erwid told Baracath. "We should head back to the temple before the Master comes after us."

"I agree," he replied. He turned to face Pantura and Caitlin. "Please follow us," he told them, before starting to walk away down the path, Erwid joining him.

Caitlin turned to face Pantura. "I guess we follow the wizards," she said.

Pantura sighed. "Yes, we follow the wizards."

They caught up to Baracath and Erwid and joined them as they walked down the path past more spruce trees and tons of bushes with gold-colored flowers that emitted a sweet smell like cane sugar. The sounds of birds calling resumed as they went along as animals once asleep awoke confused, before starting their morning activities. The breeze changed as well, whipping at the edges of the wizards' cloaks. They passed into a less dense strip of forest, allowing them to properly see the sky above them, and the countless yellow stars shining above them, casting their solar radiation down onto the group as they went along.

After a while, the two wizards came to a halt in a clearing of forest. After looking around at the vegetation and surrounding mountains in the distance, with no large trees within a hundred feet of them, Baracath turned around to their guests. "Take my hand," he told Pantura and Caitlin.

"What? Why?" demanded Pantura.

"It'll make the remaining mile we have to walk a little more bearable," he replied callously, looking slightly hurt at Pantura's offense.

Pantura immediately choked back anything else she had to say. "My apologies...what was your name again?"

"Baracath."

"Baracath, yes. My apologies for my rude tone. May I grab your wrist instead?"

"Yes, that'll work." He glanced over at Caitlin, who was also looking uncomfortable. "You too, miss."

Caitlin scooted back a little bit at his hand reaching out, but she eventually grabbed onto his wrist as well. "Grip it firmly," Baracath warned. "This will feel weird."

Pantura and Caitlin only had time to exchange one look of confusion before their senses were thrown completely askew by the ground literally dropping out below their feet. It felt as though they were falling into the void, yet they remained locked onto Baracath's wrists. All sense of direction was lost as they tumbled down for what felt like several seconds. Caitlin screamed as they dropped, while Pantura was fighting the urge to do the same. Finally, they landed on solid ground again and promptly fell down onto their backs, while Baracath remained standing. Erwid was already there.

Caitlin sat up, her brain swimming from the journey she had just had. She had had no idea what had happened, and her vision was all fuzzy, meaning that she couldn't get a bearing on her surroundings.

"Your eyesight will adjust in a few seconds," Erwid told them. "Everyone falls when they teleport for the first time."

Caitlin's vision finally cleared, and she stood up slowly, Pantura doing the same a few feet away. The mountain clearing they were in was gone. Instead, they were now standing in a large, flat field, bigger than a football stadium. Mountain peaks towered over them on the left, and on the right, a huge cliff rose up into the sky, with a giant waterfall cascading down. Straight ahead was a massive walled structure, colored in golds and dark reds, with the base of the waterfall inside. The peaks of several buildings could be seen poking out from above the wall.

"The temple," whispered Pantura as she stared at the building in the distance.

"Indeed," Baracath said. "Come, let us go inside."

They all dusted themselves off and walked down the

field to a large, medieval-esque gate in the wall. The gate doors were made of metal, but were already wide open, and above it on the wall, several more individuals stared down at the party as they approached. Caitlin saw four humans, but also three aliens, one of whom had four arms as they passed underneath the ramparts and into the temple's courtyard.

    The second they were past the wall, Caitlin's eyes started to pop out of their sockets as the sight of the temple interior. The dirt path had given way to reddish-brown pavers arranged in a geometric formation, forming a central square that was surrounded by flowers. Several buildings were arranged around the center, including one that had an open first floor and resembled a kitchen. All of the structures were, as the exterior had suggested, painted in dazzling red and golden colors that captured the light of the stars above. At the opposite end of the square was a multi-leveled building that seemed to reach the heavens above. Two giant watchtowers flanked it on either side. The courtyard had a few people walking about, but it was, for the most part, empty. As they continued to walk, Caitlin could look down the paths, to a large open area at the end of one of them, and to what appeared to be a path that went all the way up the cliff face on their right. Pipes came out of the walls of the buildings and into the ground.

    "Up here," Baracath said, exiting the courtyard and passing over a bridge that went over a stream. As the rest of them passed over it, Caitlin could see that the huge waterfall fed into the stream they were crossing over.

    They passed two more aliens, both of whom had long necks and small heads, and started up the stairway that led into the main temple. Behind them, the sound of a ship's engines firing up sounded, and as they all turned around to look, a small shuttlecraft, similar in size to the one that Pantura had flown to Anich, rose up from behind two buildings and launched into the sky.

After ascending two more flights of stairs, they found themselves facing two huge wooden doors that were all that stood between them and the temple interior. Erwid and Baracath approached them and pushed on them simultaneously, causing them to swing open and let a draft of hot air escape. "At the end of this hall will be Daimyo Shurgen, our leader. You can give your request to him. If you need anything else after you're done, come find one of us and we'll do our best to help you." After finishing his words, Baracath pushed Pantura and Caitlin into the temple, then slowly shut the doors behind them, leaving them inside the temple.

"Well, that went better than expected," remarked Caitlin, fanning herself with her hand, for the interior of the temple was much hotter than the outside.

"Aside from the monster attacking us, yeah, I'd say that went well," said Pantura. "Come, let's go meet this Daimyo and see about getting you fixed."

The temple inside was supported by large wooden columns going up to the ceiling, and there were torches sticking from the wall and lighting up the inside with an orange glow. At the very end of the hall, an elevated throne sat, and sitting on it was a middle-aged man, who didn't even seem to notice that there were people walking down his temple. He paid no heed to either Caitlin or Pantura as they drew closer to him. It made the both of them feel rather uneasy, especially as their footsteps echoed throughout the interior.

"Is he sleeping, Pantura?" Caitlin whispered to Pantura.

"I'm not sure, but he sure looks like he's out cold," Pantura replied. "Again, let's try to be discreet about this, we want this to be as short as possible, and we don't want to anger anybody while we're here."

They finally arrived at the foot of the throne, where Daimyo Shurgen was still seated, seemingly asleep. Sure enough, his eyes appeared closed, and he remained unresponsive, even as Pantura and Caitlin waved in his direction to try and grab his attention. "Uh, excuse me?" Pantura finally asked. "We've been told to seek your council by some of the other wizards here, and we could really use your help in trying to solve a problem that we're dealing with. Can you hear me?"

Daimyo Shurgen's eyes opened suddenly as if on command, and he moved from slumping in his throne to sitting up straight in a matter of moments. It happened quick enough to make Pantura instinctively take a couple of steps back. Even Caitlin was unnerved by the sudden change. His eyes were deep green, like leaves in the summer, and he sported a short beard that was braided on either side of his chin. A set of wavy hair covered his pale head, with one strand that braided down on his right. Several rings adorned his fingers.

"I can hear you just fine," Shurgen finally spoke. His voice carried through the entire chamber as if it was being spoken through a megaphone. "There's no need to assume that I was asleep, Pantura."

Caitlin turned to stare at Pantura, who was looking puzzled and concerned. "How do you know my name?"

"Your friend next to you. I heard her comment from down here," he explained, resting an elbow on his armrest.

Pantura just stared, then finally shook her head. "Great Daimyo," she said, getting down on one knee, and dragging Caitlin down to her level as well, "We are honored to be before you today. If you would please allow our requests to be heard…"

"What are you two doing?" Shurgen asked, leaning down to get a better look. "We don't really do formalities around here, you know. We all find that formality around here just doesn't work all that well, so you can stop addressing me like I'm the king and talk to me normally. I understand everyday English, you know."

Caitlin got off her knee as soon as he said it. Pantura took a little longer, but she too, shrugged and stood up. "In that case," she said. "Do you mind helping us with our problem that we want fixed?"

"That's better." Shurgen was smiling, as if he didn't really have a care at all. He leaned back in his chair. "Now, what can I help you two ladies out with today?"

Pantura opened her mouth to speak, but Caitlin elbowed her. "I'll say it, don't bother," she said, stepping forward. "Daimyo Shurgen," she said, addressing him directly. She held out her hands, just as she had done for Daniel, and the same blue-green lightning started to crackle out of her fingertips. Although it was nothing new to Caitlin by this point, in the darkened hall of the temple, it cast an eerie glow around her surroundings.

Shurgen watched her hands with great interest, even rising from his throne and walking down the steps to Caitlin in order to get a better look. He watched the electricity spark out, which by now was reaching halfway up her forearm. He observed its frequency, and even reached out and touched two of Caitlin's fingers, letting the energy transfer over into him. He finally took two steps back and made motions with his arm, which by now Caitlin took to mean that he was casting a spell. Although she couldn't see any change, she could feel her body buzz and her hairs raise on end.

"I see," Shurgen finally said, lowering his arms. "You appear to have the gift of magic in you, Miss...I never did get your name."

"Caitlin," she replied, the lightning disappearing from her hand.

"Miss Caitlin. As I was saying, that electricity is magical in origin. It's an early sign that someone possesses similar power to the rest of us in the Ostila Madors. Those were my first symptoms, way back when I was younger. Lightning coming out of my hands, a strange sensation that filled my entire body..."

"I understand that it's magical in origin," replied Caitlin.

"Shane, the Magnum of the Coalition, already confirmed that for me. The problem is, I don't want it. I don't want to deal with this for the rest of my life, if it's permanent. I don't need everyone I know looking at me like I'm a freak." That last part was true, but only for a few people; odds are most people wouldn't even recognize her at this point, and most of the people she knew were probably dead anyways, after everything they've learned about the Gorog attack on Salt Plains.

"So, just to confirm, this is the issue that you've come to me with." Shurgen said, seeking clarification. "You have magical powers and you don't want them around?"

Caitlin nodded. "If you can remove them, please do so."

To her dismay, and Pantura's as well, Shurgen shook his head. "I'm afraid that it's impossible to remove magic entirely from someone. Once the Madorax has chosen someone it can never go away."

"Madorax?" repeated Pantura.

"The name of the magic we use," replied Shurgen, turning his head to address her. "If someone is found with abilities such as these, it means the Madorax has chosen someone to wield its magic and manifest it in the real world. Once a person is chosen, they cannot change it back."

Caitlin felt utterly defeated. She hoped that she was hearing things, that what she was hearing was not true. To be stuck with her powers forever–that was not the outcome she wanted. "So, you can't help me remove these powers? Shane told me you cured a pilot who also wanted them gone!"

Shurgen thought about it briefly, and, to her surprise yet again, he nodded. "I remember him, this pilot. Good young man, with a bright future in the Coalition's fleet, if I recall." He took a few steps closer to Caitlin, letting his black cloak drift across the floor. "I didn't cure that pilot of his magic. He wanted me to cure him, but just like you, I couldn't. Once the essence of the Madorax is inside of you there's no removing it."

Caitlin's face fell. Pantura cast a nervous glance in her direction.

"You've only been able to exercise a semblance of control over your powers by this point, correct?" asked Shurgen. "And, also, while we're talking about this, when did they start to emerge?"

"They started to emerge less than a week ago, that was the first time they appeared," said Caitlin, shifting her weight around nervously. "It's only gotten stronger since then, and yes, I've only been able to make it happen a few times on command. Most of the time it just emerges whenever it feels like it."

Shurgen scratched his beard. "The way I see it, there's only one way you can make your powers disappear, and it was the same way that I helped your pilot friend out. Right now you cannot control your abilities well. My offer is; allow me and my fellow Madors to help you focus your control and enable you to precisely manipulate your power. That way, while you'll still have it within you, you'll be able to keep it bottled down inside you should you choose."

Caitlin heard the proposition. It definitely was not what she wanted. She would have much preferred a straight cure instead. But if what Shurgen was saying would help her silence her power, she decided it would be better than just allowing it to keep emerging whenever. But she decided to take it up with Pantura. "If I may, Daimyo Shurgen, please allow me to discuss this with Pantura for a minute or two."

"Of course you can!" Shurgen exclaimed. "You don't need my permission! Go ahead, talk it over. Take as much time as you need. I'm not far away if you need anything." He ascended the stairs back to his throne and sat down, while Caitlin and Pantura took a few steps away into a corner next to one of the wooden support beams.

"I want to take his offer," Caitlin confessed to Pantura. "If it helps me keep my powers down and inside, I want to do it. If it's the only way to help me out."

Pantura agreed. "Do it," she told Caitlin. "As long as it accomplishes our goal. I'll let Shane know that it might be a couple of days before we return. Besides, I've always wanted to stay among the Madors and see more of their culture. It's one of the few things not very well documented in the Coalition's records."

"Alright. You sure Shane will allow this? I mean, what with the whole invasion about to go down?"

"Yeah, I'm sure he'll be fine with it. I'm not a fighter at heart, and I'm sure he's glad that you're far away from danger. I think he's starting to take a liking to both you and Daniel."

"If you think so. Just don't have him tell Daniel, alright? He's been incredibly anxious for a large portion of our stay with the Coalition and I don't want him to suffer any more than he likely already is."

"I'll be sure to let Shane know that," Pantura told her.

Caitlin nodded, and she stepped out from behind the column and approached Shurgen's throne. The Daimyo leaned down from his chair again as she drew near. "I'll take your offer," she told him. "I'll train and learn to control my powers, but as soon as I'm able to keep them under wraps, I'm done. That's all I want. Can you do that for me?"

The Daimyo didn't even wait to nod. "I can do that easily. It'll probably take a day or two at least, but we'll have you all ready to where you can keep it under wraps. Wait!" he added, noticing Caitlin's mouth open again. "If you're going to ask about the logistics of it all, don't worry. Your sleep and food schedules will be taken care of."

Caitlin dipped her head in thanks. "Thank you, Daimyo Shurgen," she said.

"Please, call me Shurgen," he replied. "Is there anything

else that needs to be brought to my attention tonight?"

Caitlin shook her head.

"Good!" Shurgen turned to look straight behind them, to the door. "ERWID!" he shouted, his voice booming throughout the entire temple interior, causing Pantura to reflexively put her ears over her head.

A moment later, Erwid materialized beside Shurgen's throne. "You summoned me?" she asked.

"I did," the daimyo told her. He indicated Caitlin and Pantura. "You were one of the two who brought these two into the temple, correct? I want you to go find them rooms and bring them a proper meal. Oh, and for the love of all that is good, please reset the Time Spell that you manipulated. Everyone's a bit...pissed that their sleep schedule got interrupted."

"Gladly." Erwid waved her hands around, and Shurgen nodded in approval. "That should do it," she told him. She turned to Caitlin and Pantura. "You two, please follow me. I'll take both of you to some empty rooms that you can use."

They followed her out, exiting the temple to where, once again, the sky was now dark. Caitlin stared up at it for a good fifteen minutes, still in shock that it was all simulated. If that was what she was going to learn here, maybe this whole journey would be worth it after all.

As they walked down the stairs, tired and hoping for some sleep, little did they notice the giant probe watching them from above, its giant red eye fixed upon Caitlin and Pantura.

Chapter 23

The *Deceiver*

Orvag watched as the small ball of Lhassi came into view ahead, peeking through the bridge viewscreen. He could see the small blips of Gorog cruisers forming a dense blockade around the planet, the first line of defense against any impending invasion. He was convinced that it would be able to resist invasion from most forces, but against Shane's massive fleet, he was here to ensure that the defenses would hold.

Lhassi was a smaller planet, only half the size of Grimcor, and was even more depressing than the deserts of that planet too. Lhassi was a former volcanic world, and as a result, most of its terrain was covered in a thick layer of ash that made the entire planet resemble a nuclear wasteland. The volcanic activity had long since ceased, but the ash and dark, smoky atmosphere remained. It was basically uninhabited outside of the occasional stronghold and, of course, Rhozadar. The camp had been assembled in the highlands, where volcanic ash was less common, and where the atmosphere was a bit more tolerable. It was also one of the only places where water was left, which was absolutely critical for the camp and its guards to run.

Dormak approached Orvag from behind. "Excuse me, Orvag," he said, holding several pieces of paper. "This just came in. One of the probes spotted one of the three targets that Vraxis and Foulor missed in their raid." He presented him with an image. "It appears as though it's the younger of the Terran girls. The one with powers."

Orvag studied the image. She was there, alright, as was another individual who Foulor was listed in his briefing, a blue-skinned engineer who was also present during the assault on the

Justice. "Where was this taken?" he asked, not seeing any clues.

"Anich, sir," replied Dormak. "It seems as though, as we suspected, her abilities are Madorax-related."

"Perhaps." Orvag gave the picture another look, clearly looking for something. "Did the probe catch how strong the defenses were?"

"Sir, you're not possibly thinking about diverting troops now to go recapture one slave, right?"

"No, no, you moron!" Orvag stood up and faced Dormak, tossing the picture aside. "I'm talking about a preemptive strike on the sorcerer temple! That's a threat that needs to be addressed if we're going to invade Arajor in the next few days."

"You want to *attack* the temple? Preemptively?" questioned Dormak. "I would think that that would be an unwise decision. The Madors are amazing fighters, what with their magical abilities. You'd need a sizeable force to raid the temple, hundreds, if not thousands of Gorogs."

"I've already selected Captain Villus for the task. His fleet is close by and equipped with 800 men and four tanks. There's less than fifty sorcerers in that entire temple."

"Even so, why now?" Dormak was clearly unconvinced. "The Madors have been waiting out this war since the very beginning. Attacking them unprovoked now would be an unwise decision, as it could get them involved in the war and give Shane and the Orion Coalition another powerful ally."

"True. But here's the thing." Orvag turned to him, face clearly showing signs of some hidden knowledge that Dormak was unaware of. "The Coalition and the Madors signed a deal that when Arajor, the big capital city of the Coalition, was attacked next, because they foresaw it happening sometime, they made an agreement that the Madors would assist them in battle. And that agreement was signed using Madorax energy itself, so that it would be legally binding to anyone who carried the power.

Tell me, Dormak, why do you think that would be a problem for us, we who have been planning to invade Arajor for years now?"

The warden did not need to be told twice. "I understand, sir. Still, I don't see the benefit in attacking them now versus after the assault on Arajor."

"If we attack them now, they won't suspect anything, because they've been left alone in their temple for over a thousand years with no outsider interference. If we come in there and unleash a surprise attack, they won't be prepared to counter it. If we wait until after Arajor, they'll be prepared for us and be much harder to defeat."

Dormak sighed. "Still. I don't like doing this. Antagonizing one of the strongest groups of individuals in the entire galaxy…I don't like it. It's a major risk for sure."

"You will thank me later once those sorcerers are on their knees begging us for help," Orvag replied, standing up from his chair. "For now, let's focus on getting down to Rhozadar and setting up the defenses." He looked behind Dormak, puzzled. "Where's Foulor?"

"In his chambers," said Dormak. "He was none too pleased with what you had to say about his brother. I don't blame him for wanting to get him back. I would want to rescue my brother from Coalition prison if I could. Assuming that he was still alive."

"Shane almost never kills his prisoners. To assume that he'd defy expectations and kill Vraxis is foolish. If anything, he would send him off to prison with the other lunatics in the asteroid belt. It's where the worst of the worst go, the ones that the council of Arajor don't interrogate for war crimes."

"True, but still, shouldn't we at least allow him the opportunity to go out and try to negotiate with Shane to get him released? I mean, the two of them have been inseparable for years."

Orvag laughed out loud, a booming, psychotic laugh.

"You suggest that you let Foulor, that Foulor, negotiate with Shane and try to release his own brother? Do you even hear yourself?" He laughed some more, causing some crew members to turn and stare. "No offense to Foulor, he's an amazing tank and a brutal fighter, but using his brain has never really been his strong suit. He would probably negotiate and agree to his own surrender and capture if he tried."

There was a beep from the lower bridge deck, and Orvag stuck his head over the balcony. "What is it?" he called down to his men.

"It's a transmission, sir," a communications officer replied. "From Rhozadar. Warden Trivass is making contact."

"Put him through," the king commanded.

A second later, a skinny but cloaked Gorog appeared in holographic form in front of Orvag. "My king," he replied, in a deep, heavily accented voice. "We are honored by your visit. We received your message about the impending Coalition attack. We have begun to prepare the defenses for battle."

"Very good, Trivass," commended Orvag. "Tell your men that, effective immediately, they are to report to me and Warden Dormak along with you. I have several thousand extra troops on board my ship, who will be assisting us in defending the camp."

"That's good to hear. Should I move all of the slaves to the safe bunker?"

"Not yet, but we will soon. Concentrate on readying the surface-to-air weapons and preparing the troops for ground assault. We expect a very large invasion force here sometime tomorrow."

"Very well, Your Majesty." Trivass dipped his head in respect. "I will continue to make preparations. We look forward to your arrival."

The transmission died out and Dormak turned to Orvag. "Should I give the order to Captain Villus to redirect his fleet towards Anich?" he prompted.

"You may," replied Orvag, watching as Lhassi grew larger in the window, revealing the lanes of volcanic ash and rays emitting from a few large impact craters in the southern hemisphere. They were almost at the blockade, which was slowly parting to allow them to pass.

Dormak sent the message. "There. Now all we do is wait and see who wins, and whether or not the Madors become a very serious threat to us in the immediate future."

They stood at the balcony, watching Lhassi approach them slowly, the blockade disappearing behind them. After a while, Dormak glanced behind him, as if he was missing something. Abandoning his post next to Orvag, he started to stride towards the exit.

"Something wrong, Dormak?" asked Orvag.

"I'm going to check on Foulor. Just to see if he's doing any better."

He left the bridge, descended the elevator, boarded a monorail train back through the center of the ship and stayed on for a few minutes, until the train stopped at a station near the center of the ship. From there, Dormak climbed several flights of stairs and passed down several hallways, until he finally reached Foulor and Vraxis's quarters.

The door was closed, and Dormak approached it and knocked. "Foulor? Foulor are you in there? I just want to check in and see how you're doing!"

There was no answer. That raised the warden's suspicions, as Foulor would never stay silent if he was called, even if he was mad at him. "Foulor? Please answer the door! I don't want to have to come in there myself!"

When there was again no answer, Dormak moved to fiddling with the door controls, hoping to manually override the settings. After a few moments, he managed the right combination and popped open the door, it sliding open with a loud hiss. He stuck his head inside, and saw no sign of Foulor anywhere. He crossed the threshold and entered the room itself, and again saw no sign of the hunter. Neither was there any sign of his bandolier of grenades nor any of his prized accessories, which would normally hang on a shelf in the back. There was, however, a note on Vraxis's bed. Dormak walked over and picked it up and read it. The handwriting was crude, but he could still read every word:

"Dormak and Orvag, I know that you cannot provide assistance to me to help rescue my brother from prison. By the time you read this message, I will have already left. I am going to attempt to free him from prison, even if it means defying your orders. I hope you understand."

Dormak crushed the note up, realizing what this meant. No sooner had the paper fallen out of his hand did his radio beep. Orvag.

"Dormak, a ship just launched from the main hangar! The twin's ship! What's going on? Is Foulor not in his quarters??"

Dormak pushed the button to answer. "No. He's not. He's going to Shane."

There was a long pause from the other end, followed by the sounds of commotion as Orvag overturned something large, possibly a table. A scream cut through the audio, and then there was more silence. "Fine. If he wants to leave, let him," the king eventually growled, panting slightly. "We cannot distract ourselves from the immediate task at hand. Prepare the troops to hand."

"What happens if he returns?"

"We deal with him the same way we deal with all deserters. The Ocramus pit."

Chapter 24

Arajor

Shane was waiting in his office when Daniel, Max and Vorlax walked in. The Magnum was seated on a large office-style chair, painted the same blue and silver colors of the Federation, and was wearing a uniform with gold trim that Daniel guessed was meant exclusively for formal events such as this. A large window overlooked downtown Arajor City, where skyscrapers could be seen towering in the distance. Mountains of paperwork were stacked in front of Shane on his desk, and there was a peculiar sound that was floating through the office as well.

"Is that...what I think it is?" Daniel asked incredulously, listening as an all-too familiar music number came from a small speaker on Shane's wall. "That's *Star Wars* music, isn't it? Gosh, I haven't heard that in years."

"You missed when Earth gave us *Star Wars* for the first time back in 2000," Shane told him, smiling at the memories. "When it was first shown to us, back then, some of the aquatic aliens tried to have it banned. I was getting complaints from them about how the character of Jar Jar Binks seemed like a negative stereotype of their own race. Thankfully, we reached a deal on the matter, and Star Wars exploded over here. Easily one of the most popular things that Earth's given us out here. I even tried to have the opening title music become the new Coalition anthem. Unfortunately, the council rejected my offer." He sighed. "It's been way too long since the anthem was revised. The version we use now was written almost two hundred years ago."

"Yeah, John Williams always made some amazing anthem-worthy pieces of music," agreed Daniel. "If anyone deserves to have an anthem written based on one of their tracks, he does. I used to argue with my mom that he was the greatest composer of our time. She was always more of a Danny Elfman fan at heart, it was always something that was brought up any time we watched a movie."

"I see," Shane replied. "I assume Vorlax told you the meaning behind the origins of the Kraken's name?"

"I did, Shane," the commander spoke up.

"Yeah. That whole fiasco also started happening around the time Earth gave us *Pirates of the Caribbean*. I had to make a public announcement about how Davy Jones wasn't actually a Gorog, because that's all everyone ever talked about for weeks once the first copies reached households. Ugh, that whole meeting was just a big circus. I still haven't fully recovered from the paperwork."

"I hate to interrupt, Shane, but you need to be in the council chamber in about five minutes," said Vorlax, checking the wall clock.

"Right, right," the Magnum said, standing up from his chair. "Well, let's get this over with. Vorlax, stay here and monitor any calls I get. And watch the lizard as well."

"What?" demanded Max, his face darkening. "I thought I was coming as well!"

"Daniel will not be perceived as a threat by the council members, at long as they have eyes to see. Max, on the other hand, would be much more likely to get security called. Besides, if they found out that you're a walking monster in disguise who butchers Gorogs, they'd likely imprison you, experiment on you...you get the picture. It's best if only Daniel goes."

Max huffed. "I hate it when you all make statements that contain actual logic that I can't refute easily." He stormed off to the corner and sat down, resting his lower jaw on his paw like an angry dog.

Vorlax rolled his eyes. "I'll watch over him. You two

should go."

Shane nodded and put an arm around Daniel as they left the office, taking another long path through the Kraken's labyrinthine hallways and open spaces, all painted in pleasing shades of blue. As they walked along, they passed dozens of Coalition personnel, most of them members of the elite class or bureaucrats. There were no Earth-style outfits anywhere in sight; everyone was dressed in proper, well-groomed attire. The lighting was regal, a soft blue color that came from fancy-looking lights mounted on the walls. They climbed down two flights of stairs and across a bridge that went over the main hangar before they finally stopped at a set of double doors that barricaded their way. They stopped, and Shane turned to Daniel.

"Listen to me very carefully," he told Daniel. "The less the council knows about you, the better. Be very cautious about what you tell them, because once you say something before them it'll go on the record, where no one, not even me, will be able to delete it. Do not say anything about how you came from Earth, or anything about your former status as a Gorog slave." He thought for a second, then added, "And say nothing about Max either." He thought for another second. "In fact, it might be best if you don't say anything to them unless questioned."

Daniel nodded. "Very well. Don't speak unless spoken to."

"Exactly."

Shane pushed the button that opened the huge double doors, which slid back to give way to a cavernous room that took up the entire backside of the Kraken's floor plan. The path ended right in front of them, and Daniel and Shane stepped across the threshold, allowing them to look down over a balcony hundreds of feet into a sharp drop. Above them, the ceiling towered over them, and directly across the gap was a semicircle of chairs, each and every one of them occupied by a human or alien wearing elaborate robes and bearing the insignia of the council, a gold engraving of Orion's Belt, on the right side of their chest. There were seven council members in total, including one sitting in the center of the group who was glaring down at Shane as he walked in. In fact, all seven council members were giving Shane looks of resentment upon seeing him.

"Good afternoon, members of the council," said Shane, coolly keeping his voice low despite the angry faces of the council members.

"Shane," the council member in the middle of the seven, a human with frizzled gray hair, said. "Glad to see you obeyed our directive and came promptly to see us."

"Don't remind me, Serizau. I'm here to talk business only, and I want this meeting over with sooner rather than later." He opened a hatch on the barrier separating he and Daniel from the deadly fall and pulled a switch forward, causing the platform they were standing on to slide forward closer to the council, a set of stairs forming behind them. "Now, I seem to recall you not divulging the reason behind this impromptu meeting to me when you last contacted me on my ship. So, I speak on behalf of the other council members here when I ask: Why are we here today?"

Serizau's eyes narrowed at Shane's comment. "We're here to ask, completely of our own volition, to approve this document that we've put together over the last month. It stands ready to be signed into effect as soon as you and the Gorogs approve the terms here."

"You never ask me to sign anything that you write down of your own volition. Also, why do you need the Gorogs to approve…" Shane's voice trailed off as the realization sank in. "That's a peace treaty, isn't it? You want the Gorogs to sign it in order to end the war, don't you?"

"You're acting like that's a bad thing, Shane. That's not a good look for you. If the people found out…" Now Serizau's voice trailed off as he spotted Daniel's face, positioned next to

Shane. "Who is that next to you?" he demanded. "Do they have clearance to be in this room?"

"Yes, I gave him my own," retorted Shane. "This is Daniel, someone who I've been watching over this past week. He's one of the ones who defended my ship during the recent raid, and who distracted the Gorogs on Skorjion to allow my men to steal the key card to Lhassi's shields."

"Really?" Serizau exclaimed. "Him? He looks like nothing more than a simple commoner, not a military agent!"

Daniel's anger bubbled up slightly at the derogatory expression. After all that he had been through, he believed that he had moved above the title of "commoner." He opened his mouth to reply in force, but Shane, seeing the motion out of the corner of his eye, interjected hastily.

"Appearances can be deceiving, can they not, Serizau?" he asked rhetorically. "We needed a commoner to lure the Gorogs into a trap. I mean, no one would suspect him of being a capable threat. But he is, and he even saved one of my finest men during the ambush. Without him, we wouldn't have the key to the Gorog Empire's destruction." Shane turned and gave Daniel a hard pat on the shoulder. "We owe him a great deal for what he's done."

Daniel blushed slightly, but Serizau did not return the gesture. "And where exactly is he from?" he asked, leaning forward in his chair, causing the other eight council members to turn to stare at him.

Shane turned to Daniel and poked him, causing him to involuntarily stand up straight. "Um…I'm from…"

"He's from Ooban," interjected Shane again. "He's from Ooban. His family are distant relatives of mine, and they've fallen on hard times. I offered to help him out until his parents could sustain themselves again."

"Ooban?" Serizau looked unconvinced. He stared at Daniel, as if he was trying to look for something that would give him away. "And how long has he lived on Ooban?"

Daniel started to sweat nervously, but Shane again piped up. "His whole life. Nearly 21 years of it."

Serizau was prepared to ask another question, but thankfully another council member with rough, uneven skin and horns spoke up before he could; "That's enough, Serizau. Leave the poor kid alone. Can't you see he's looking a bit nervous?" He turned to Shane. "Listen, Shane, about that treaty."

"You're making a mistake," Shane said adamantly. "The Gorogs will never sign a treaty with us. Have you all forgotten that they issued an ultimatum years ago to destroy us with no treaty?"

"That was almost twenty years ago," spoke up a third council member, this one with long hair and a narrow body. "We are hoping that the Gorogs have become more receptive since then, and are more willing to make peace with us."

"Alright, let's say that we attempt to put a cease fire on the floor with Orvag. What are the terms we'll be setting forth?"

One of the council members grabbed a document from in front of his chair and handed it to Serizau to be read aloud. He cleared his throat and began to speak. "The Orion Coalition will henceforth concede the territories already in occupation by the Empire of the Gorogs. The Coalition will acknowledge these territories as part of the Gorog Empire henceforth. In addition, the Coalition will also halt the production of wartime materials and the drafting of troops, provided the Gorog Empire returns this gesture likewise. The Coalition will no longer engage in warfare with the Gorogs, unless…"

"That's enough!" barked Shane, causing Serizau to nearly drop the document. "Do any of you have ears to hear the language written in that document? That's not a peace treaty. That's us allowing the Gorogs to continue their persecution of other alien races uninhibited. If they sign that document, they'll have unlimited freedom to destroy any alien race they choose to.

That stands in direct violation of everything we've stood for over our entire history."

"Do you think we want to cow to the Gorogs' demands? No!" another council member explained in frustration. "But this war has persisted for over twenty years now! And over the last few years, we've been losing soldiers at an alarming rate. The longer it persists, the more troops will die on the battlefield."

Shane averted his eyes from looking directly at the council people. The troop losses were a major issue for him, and although he was positive most of his army would gladly lay down their lives to oppose a force as evil as the Gorogs, their families would likely not take so kindly to their sacrifice.

"Shane," began Serizau. "You have to realize that the public's opinion on the war has grown decidedly less favorable recently. The losses of troops and the fact that we've been in a deadlock, with no real headway made to hasten the Gorogs' defeat, has sparked a growing interest in ending the war sooner rather than later."

"That's not true!"

Shane whipped around to see Daniel stepping forward, and instantly his heart skipped several beats. He felt a sense of pride that Daniel was stepping up to defend him from the council's slander, but at the same time was hoping that he did not land in trouble for his words.

Serizau instantly found Daniel's gaze, and his own hardened in response. "Well, Shane, it seems your relative can speak up for itself after all! I was wondering if he was deaf or just plain dumb!"

Shane pleaded internally for Daniel to shut up, and let him do the talking, but his attempt at telekinesis failed, as he continued to speak. "At least I speak on behalf of the common people in this galaxy! You just speak on behalf of your own ego and self-indulgence, you warty old fool!"

Serizau and Shane's face went beet red, Serizau's

hardening into a rage-filled mask. "How *dare* you, young man! I should have you executed for that! Do not call me names, you little sh—"

"SERIZAU!" yelled one of the council members, causing everyone to jump. "If you do not shut your mouth this instant, we will have you court-martialed! Now sit back down and delegate as we're supposed to!"

"Seriously, what is your problem?" another council member with short tusks on his jaw asked. "I've never seen you this angry!"

Serizau looked around, his face red from rage, but he did take several deep breaths and sit back in his chair. "My sincerest apologies, everyone," he said, rather meekly. "I...don't know why I said that."

"Well, that just cost you your ability to speak for the rest of this meeting," said the council member with rough skin. "From this point out, I'll be acting as head council member in your stead. Now give me your notes."

Serizau looked horrified at this, but he did not complain and handed him his notes, then simply sank deeper into his seat, fuming.

"And as for you," that same council member said, glaring down at Daniel. "You have some real guts to speak that way to the head council member. We'll chock it up to lack of decorum this time, but Shane, please, if he's going to be before us..."

"My apologies, councilman. He's just passing through. It won't happen again." The Magnum breathed a huge sigh of relief. That could have been bad, Daniel speaking that way. "Anyways, now that we've got that out of the way," continued Shane. "Where were we in our conversation again? I don't remember after Serizau's little temper flare right there."

The rest of the council members all cleared their throats. "Well, young Daniel," the one with rough skin said, "Perhaps we

397

owe you an apology for those comments back there. Please, continue with what you were saying earlier."

"Thank you, men and women of the council," replied Daniel, and Shane almost took a step back at how formal the greeting was. "As I was saying earlier, Shane has made progress towards breaking the deadlock with the Gorog Empire, because, as I'm sure has been made clear, he led the assault on Skorjion, one of the Gorog Empire's main labor camps and a principle supplier of wartime materials. The camp is currently inoperable due to the damage inflicted on it during the attack. And now we also possess the means to do the same to the other main Gorog labor camp on Lhassi, Rhoza–something, I'm not fully sure, thanks to the key card he recovered there as well."

"And how would you know about the attack on Skorjion?" asked one of the council members.

"Because I used to be a slave there," replied Daniel honestly. "I'm not from whatever planet Shane said I was. I was kidnapped from my *real* home planet and forcibly taken there to work in the mines. They treated me, and the two other members of my party, my mother and my best friend, like we were nothing. We were dying of thirst and malnutrition, but still forced to dig in the mine shafts all day long. It was only through Shane and his successful attack that I am alive today, to tell you this. It was through Shane's own efforts that he was able to reach all of those slaves, including me, who were suffering down in that pit. Without him…" Daniel turned and gave the old man a grateful look. "I would be as good as dead right now."

Shane felt…strange. He didn't recognize the emotion inside of him at first. It was something that he hadn't felt in a very long time. And the last place he had felt it, he had realized, was at his residence, on Arajor's moon. He had felt it when his son had given a special report on him at his school and he had watched the video. It was pride. Pride for Daniel. As if he were his own son. After going for so many years without seeing his family, it felt strange to feel as though he had found another son, lost in the galaxy and the victim of an evil ideology.

The council members were exchanging looks. Finally, the rough-skinned member, the one who had substituted himself in Serizau's place, spoke up. "Shane, is all of this true?"

Shane jerked back around to face the council and nodded. "Yes. Anything that was said that I already didn't tell you in the past, it's all true. Every last word of it."

The rough-skinned alien glanced at the clock on the wall to the right of the council ring. "Give us five minutes to convene amongst ourselves," he said to Shane, who nodded and brought the platform back to its original position. Once they were far away from the council seats and the nine members were engaged in conversation, he pulled Daniel aside.

"You weren't supposed to do that," he told him scoldingly. Then he sighed, and added, "But I'm glad that you did. Thanks for sticking up for me."

"You did it first," Daniel replied. "You saved me. And Caitlin too. And you've been trying to get us all home safely, my mom included. And if the council can't recognize the good that you've been doing, then I will."

The old Magnum smiled, letting his still-white teeth show. "Let's see what they have to say."

After a while, the council reconvened, and Shane extended the pathway yet again to hear what they had to say. "We wish to hear the words of Daniel here, Shane. We want to know, as a survivor of Skorjion, what were some of the things that the Gorogs had you do? What did they subject you and the other slaves to? Your answer will determine our response to your argument over the peace treaty."

"How specific are we talking?" asked Daniel.

"Be as specific as possible. This is for the record, by the way. We've never had eyewitness testimony of the events in the Gorog slave camps."

"Well, for starters, we were given a tent to sleep in, all 160 or so of us. We had one blanket that was covered in holes and paper-thin as well. They dragged us out of bed super early in the morning, about two hours before it was even light outside. Our breakfast and lunch were poor prison food, and all vomit-inducing no matter what it was. From that point on, it was nothing but grinding in the mines and mining materials, or working in the smelters and refining the raw materials, and those furnaces reached 110 degrees commonly. I pretty much saw at least two slaves die and get cremated every day I was there, which was never a concern of the Gorogs because they had fresh slaves arriving every day on ships. Only the fittest made it longer than a month. How the three of us lasted five years is beyond any of us…"

"I think that's enough," the rough-skinned member said. "Shane, in regards to your treaty, we're not sure if we can shut it down altogether. For right now, the best I can promise is more stringent terms and some more time. Say, two days from now. That should hopefully follow after the invasion of Lhassi. At that point, we'll make a more decisive evaluation. Does this sound like a good compromise?"

Shane nodded. "More than fair. I appreciate it, you eight. Can you also do me one easy favor as well?"

"That would depend on what it was, but let us know your mind," a female council member spoke up.

"This is just for you eight. I don't want Serizau to hear any of this." It was a request Shane figured would get turned down, but they actually sent Serizau out of the room temporarily. Once Shane was sure that he was in the clear, he said: "I think something's wrong with Serizau. I'm not sure what it is, but I'm sure I'm not the only one noticing that he's been getting angrier over these last few meetings. I would like someone to take action and look into this. Just to make sure he's alright. Or if something fishier is going on. He's been grouchy before, but this…this really is something else."

"Of course we can do that," said the acting head council member again. "We'll keep an eye on him, make sure that he doesn't cause trouble. If that's all, then consider this meeting adjourned. And remember, Shane, you cannot leave to lead tomorrow's campaign from the battlefield. You'll have to do it from your office."

Shane's head dropped. "Very well," he said, no longer cheerful. "I'll be upstairs, picking out a commander to lead the siege. You all know where to find me if you need me. That is all." He turned around and retracted the platform again, it slowly hissing back into its original spot, and he then stormed out with Daniel right behind him. Once the double doors had shut behind them, Daniel spoke up.

"Are your meetings always this eventful?" he asked, as they strode through the corridor and back up towards Shane's office.

"Unfortunately yes," replied Shane. "Before Serizau took over they were actually helpful and collaborative with me. Once they elected a new head council member though…it's been rocky from that point on."

"I see why you don't really like them."

"You have no idea."

With nothing else to do, Daniel returned to the *Justice* with Vorlax and Max, leaving Shane behind in his office, as he had some things to do before he could join the three of them also. Upon reaching the warship, he headed straight for the combat room, determined to get some training done while there was still time to do so. Vorlax had warned him that there were only three hours left until they left Arajor to rendezvous with the other ships in the invasion fleet, so he hustled through the ship's hallways, all of which were crowded with crew officers and soldiers heading for Lhassi. He found the main atrium of the ship, following it down to where he needed to go, until he was finally opening the door of the E.C.T.S. and walking inside.

The room had been reset to its default appearance, but Daniel quickly used the controls on the table to open the gun rack and slide a target out from the ground. Grabbing a rifle, he got into position and started to hit the target with lasers, trying out both the semi-auto and automatic modes built into the weapon. He sprayed lasers, imagining the target was Orvag's face, causing hundreds of little dots to appear, each marking a shot that he had made.

The message to him from earlier still lived rent-free in his brain. To be honest, it would probably haunt him for the rest of his life, given his anxiety problems. But if there was a bad time to be worried about anything, now was it. With so much at stake, he refused to bow to his fears and continued to let loose lasers into the targets. With each volley, he thought of Orvag's message and the threats he had made, on him, on Caitlin, and on his mom. His anger began to boil as he opened fire, until he had run out of plasma cartridges and had to stop. Frustrated, he set the rifle down on the table. He had managed to keep his thoughts about the message within himself during the council meeting, largely thanks to Vorlax's tour, but now that he was by himself and hours away from war, it was all he could think of.

He was tempted to go back for another gun, but instead decided to try something else. Something that he had only used once before. He shut the gun rack door closed, and instead opted to push a different button. This time, the rack of melee weapons slid out of the central platform, and he reached out and grabbed the retractable sword that Vorlax had shown them when they had first trained in this room. He felt its weight, and gripped it in his hands, then pulled the switch on the handle. The blade slid out as if it were coming out of a sheath, and extended to its full length, about two feet long. Daniel gave it a few swings to refamiliarize his hands to it, and after deciding it felt good, started to practice swinging it around as he used to at his old martial arts studio back home. That had been many years ago at this point, but some of the skills he had learned with the half staff were still there in his brain, and the longer he swung the weapon, the more old memories of his dojo floated to the surface of his brain. His swings and strikes became less erratic and more precise as he practiced, and he pulled out a practice dummy, one of the few ones Max had not destroyed, and started to practice swinging at it without actually touching the dummy.

Yet as he practiced, striking and stabbing, the image of his mom, bloody and beaten, once again resurfaced in his head. His moves became more aggressive, quicker, as Orvag's face started to pop up on the dummy he was attacking. He felt the rage from before once again taking hold of him as he grew less careful, until he finally yelled out loud and swung the blade as hard as he could. The weapon sliced through the metal of the robot's neck and sent its head flying off to one side, a loose pipe spraying oil everywhere, some of which got on Daniel's sword. Breathing heavily, he stopped and let his weapon point drop to the ground, his emotions in turmoil as he watched the dummy's head stop rolling to one side. The headless body just stood there, on its little pole, still standing upright.

"Letting some steam out?" said a voice behind him. Daniel whipped around. Vorlax. The commander was standing in the doorway, hands on his hips, his head tilted as he stared at the decapitated dummy behind Daniel, the sword still positioned at the end of a diagonal stroke.

"Uh, yes, I am," Daniel replied, honestly too. "Just wanted to get some additional practice in before the battle in a few hours."

"I can see that. I was just wondering why you decided to go full executioner on that practice dummy. What did it ever do to you to deserve such a messy fate?"

Daniel stared at the oil still bleeding out from its neck, then noticed his sword had the same stuff on it. "I...well, Vorlax, the thing is..." He sighed. "It's that message from Orvag that came in."

Vorlax waited to answer as he started to walk towards Daniel, only speaking once he had closed the gap. "The one where he specifically asked for you and Caitlin?"

Daniel slowly nodded. "Yes." He shuddered. "I just...the image of my mom, so broken and helpless, and the fact that they've been torturing her all this time most likely. She means more to me than anything else in the entire galaxy, and knowing that she's being held on the same ship as the most powerful king in the entire galaxy...Vorlax, it's tearing me apart. I don't know if I can be of any use to you all tomorrow. I feel emotionally compromised. All I want at this point is to make Orvag pay for what he's done, and to get my mother back. This whole thing has just become personal for me, something that I hoped it wouldn't."

Vorlax nodded. "I totally understand. That message was calculated to frighten any who heard it. I certainly was." He noticed Daniel's sword. "Do you want to go a few rounds?"

Daniel saw where his eyes were looking. "Sure, I guess. Anything that'll help me defend myself tomorrow."

Vorlax reached to his belt and detached another similar-looking sword hilt from a clip. He activated the blade, causing it to slide out, then took a defensive stance with the weapon. "I'm ready when you are."

Daniel similarly took up a defensive position. They started to circle around each other, still in defensive positions. Each of them watched for an opening in the other, swords ready to strike. Vorlax decided to add some conversation as well.

"So, your mother and you, you were close?" he asked, making the first move and swinging a single downward cut at Daniel that he easily blocked.

"She was the only parent I grew up with. I never knew what happened to my dad but he never was there to raise me." Daniel responded in kind by adding two more swings, both of which Vorlax was there to parry. He then stepped to the side, throwing in some more strikes at Daniel, all of which met the metal of Daniel's sword.

"Would you save her under any circumstances?" asked Vorlax, the two of them exchanging blows regularly now.

Daniel rolled under a horizontal cut from Vorlax's weapon and immediately regained his defensive posture. "Any circumstances," he said in a determined voice, stabbing forward with his weapon so that Vorlax had to block it.

"Even killing Orvag?" came the reply as Vorlax blocked three consecutive strikes from Daniel.

That question only hardened Daniel's face even further. "Absolutely," he growled, his attacks becoming a little bit quicker and stronger in the process. But Vorlax was unfazed, blocking all of Daniel's advances while also throwing in a few attacks of his own.

"We may share the same opinion of Orvag, but that doesn't mean we just kill whoever we choose," said Vorlax, stepping forward and aiming a very strong blow at Daniel's head that had enough power behind it to cause his arm to buckle.

"He's killed so many people!" retorted Daniel, swinging even harder now. The sword in his hand swished over Vorlax's head, coming very close to the tentacles on his scalp.

"True, but in the Coalition, everyone gets a trial and a chance to live another day, even the worst of the worst. That includes Orvag. When our organization was founded, we made an effort to avoid being judge and executioner to whoever we chose. The earliest Magnums knew that it was a recipe to become more like the very empires that we sought to abolish and liberate."

Daniel did not respond, but instead kept increasing the ferocity of his attacks, and also showing less care about not cutting Vorlax. Still, the commander remained cool, blocking Daniel's attacks as though they were nothing. And it was only serving to heighten the tension in Daniel's body.

"Your mom will be safe, Daniel," said Vorlax, noticing his opponent's increased tension and lack of logic in his motions. "They're not going to kill her. You need to relax!"

"Orvag needs to pay!" shouted Daniel, swinging at Vorlax so hard he was sent off-balance. As he stumbled, Vorlax grabbed his weapon and tripped Daniel up, sending him sprawling onto the floor. When he finally turned around onto his back to get back up, two sharp swords were already at his throat.

"And he will. But doing so through revenge will not do you any favors, Daniel. Trust me, I know." Vorlax turned both swords off, the blades sliding back into their handles. He sat down next to Daniel, setting both weapons aside. "About five years ago Shane and I were returning from a campaign in another system. Our ship was ambushed by Gorogs, and although we defeated them in the end, they managed to kill the head admiral in the process, who was a very good friend to both Shane and I. Shane managed to make peace with the tragedy after a few days, but I was hurt. I wanted to make that ship captain pay, and he had managed to escape the battle. But about two weeks later, we found them again. This time, I didn't let him escape. We utterly destroyed his entire ship and him along with it. And the last thing he saw was the hologram I sent him of myself, letting him know that I was the agent of his destruction. I thought it would make me feel better. But instead, my decision to kill him in cold blood now is one of the few things I truly regret doing in my life."

Daniel's face slowly softened as he listened. "How did you manage to push through it?"

"I had to go through a lot of personal discovery in order

to make peace with my friend's death and my own act of revenge. Took a few months. But I managed it."

Daniel laughed a sarcastic laugh. "I still can't believe that we're here. I went from a normal kid on Earth to a slave of an evil alien empire to now being part of the group that's going to stop the evil alien empire. Even if we all do make it out, my life is forever changed by what's happened here. So many of my friends are dead from the Gorog attack, and the ones that aren't likely won't recognize me." He took a deep breath before he went into panic mode, letting the air fill his lungs. "Vorlax…I'm not sure what I'm supposed to do."

The commander's face was oddly touching, the look of pity he gave Daniel as he listened to his story. "I wish I could understand what you've been through to get here, Daniel. But don't worry, we'll put Orvag in his rightful place soon enough. And then you can go back to Earth and live the rest of your life as it should've been lived. You'll all be a family again, just as you were before. But until then, it's not my job to fulfill your purpose in life."

Daniel looked down again. "In fifteen years of normal life, I couldn't figure out what I wanted to do with my life. What makes you think that I'll be able to figure it out when everyone's working against me?"

"I don't know," the commander replied. "Perhaps, just hope. Hope that you will find out what you've really been looking for all this time."

Daniel smiled again, then he stood up. "Do you want to go another round?"

Vorlax stood up as well, nodding eagerly. "Maybe two more and then we go get some rest. We have a busy day tomorrow, after all."

He tossed Daniel the other sword and drew his own out. They readied their weapons and their stances and clashed their blades together with a loud clang of metal that rang throughout the entire combat chamber. But before they got too far into their second duel, Vorlax's transmitter rang loudly.

"Vorlax, where are you?" Shane's voice said in an urgent tone. "I need you on the bridge right now!"

"What's the matter Shane?"

"You're not going to believe this, but the blockade is being hailed. By Foulor."

Chapter 25

Anich, Temple of the Ostila Madors

Caitlin was up bright and early the next day to start her training. Although Pantura was still asleep in the room next to her, she headed out her door and into the morning light coming over the mountains in the distance, although now she knew it was only an illusion and nothing more. She skipped steps on the way down as she entered the courtyard of the temple, eager to start gaining the knowledge as to how to remove her powers the best. She was a little hungry, but feeling much better than yesterday after a good night's rest. The temperature was warm, there were barely any clouds in the sky, and it felt like a good day to be alive. But it would be even better once her powers were gone.

There was no one out and about in the courtyard, so she headed over to the kitchen and got a plate of breakfast. Strangely enough, nobody in the kitchen used any sort of magic for cooking; only for cleaning up dishes and floors. Indeed, the plate of scrambled eggs she got were made by hand, with no outside tinkering of any kind, including the magical kind. She found a spot to sit besides some bushes and started to eat her food, which was, like most of the meals she had had while out in the galaxy, delicious.

"Enjoying your eggs?" asked Erwid's voice. Caitlin looked up from her plate to see the young sorceress standing right in front of her, a similar plate of eggs in her hand as well.

"Yeah," replied Caitlin as soon as her mouth wasn't full of eggs. "Surprised you don't use any magic to cook it. I would've thought that that would speed up the process."

Erwid sat down on the bench next to her. "It usually does," she said, taking a bite of her food. "But Shurgen likes his food prepared the normal way, so that's just how the kitchen does every plate now. Plus, I think the homemade ones taste a little better."

"I can see that." Caitlin finished chowing down on the rest of her eggs, wiping her mouth with her arm.

"Where's your blue friend?" asked Erwid.

"She's still resting," Caitlin replied. "I figured I would let her be."

"No, that's fine. Anyways, do you want to get started? Shurgen said that Baracath and I would be helping you out today."

"Yes, I would love to get started," replied Caitlin, standing up and stretching her body. "Just tell me where to go."

"Over there, down that pathway," Erwid explained, pointing down a path that led from the main square into a darker portion of the temple. "I'll meet you there in just a second."

Caitlin obeyed, following that path until it reached a large open space with a couple of trees in the center. Around her, the time spell was wearing out, and the hundreds of stars overhead were starting to peek through the veil of the magic. The square slowly became brighter as Caitlin waited for Erwid to show up. And a couple of minutes later, she did.

"So, before we begin," she said as she approached Caitlin. "Tell me, what exactly have you been able to do with your powers up to this point? Tell me everything, no matter how small."

"Well," Caitlin started, "I've been able to control it in minor ways, such as it popping up on my hand." She brought the electricity back to demonstrate to Erwid. "I've also shocked a couple of guards that were trying to kill me in moments of fear, and short-circuited some wires with my hands. That's basically the extent of it."

"That's mostly the raw essence of the Madorax coming out through you," Erwid said. "When it's all sparky and electricity-looking, it's unrefined." She held out her own hand for Caitlin to see, and a blue-green light came from the palm of it. It was still sparking a little, but way less than what Caitlin had done before. "This is what it looks like when the energy output is refined."

Caitlin nodded in understanding. "Okay," she said.

Erwid closed her hand, extinguishing the light. "That's your first test. Refining your power. Once you've done that, the real fun begins."

"How do I do that?" asked Caitlin.

"Close your eyes, and reach out with your hand. Try to look for the power source that is within. Look for the Madorax. Once you find it, concentrate on it, and that should be everything you need."

Caitlin closed her eyes, reached out with her hand, and began to search her body for the sensation of the Madorax that she normally felt whenever she was pumping with adrenaline. But after she had searched for a minute and found nothing, she began to doubt whether or not it was true. She felt no essence within her.

"Take deep breaths," Erwid said after a while. "Relax. Remove all signs of stress."

Caitlin did all of those things, and still felt nothing. "I'm not feeling anything," she said, putting her hand down in frustration and opening her eyes. "I can't find it."

Erwid approached her and had her reach her hand out again. This time, she put her own hand next to Caitlin's. "Try again," she said. "Feel for the buzz within you. It'll feel like a buzz."

Caitlin closed her eyes again and tried to feel for the mysterious buzz within her. This time, she felt something weird in her abdominal area, a weird sensation unlike anything else she had felt. A buzz. She locked onto it and concentrated as hard as she could, and immediately, a glowing blue-green ball appeared on the palm of her hand.

"You did it!" exclaimed Erwid. "Now, hold it there, just for a few more seconds! Don't let it fizzle out!"

Caitlin focused on keeping her power flowing as normally as it could. "Now what?" she asked, eyes concentrating on the light coming from her hand.

"Okay, you can stop!" said Erwid, and Caitlin obeyed, the light disappearing from her hand. "That was the first step! And you did really well."

Caitlin checked the palm of her hand for any traces of discoloration or anything else that would betray that she was just spitting out energy from her hand in concentration. But there was nothing. No weird spots, no swelling, nothing. "Okay, that's done," she replied to Erwid. "Now what?"

"Now," came the reply. "The actual fun starts."

Erwid led Caitlin to another part of the temple, since another group was set to use the square they were in. "The next step in your training is to take that focused Madorax energy and put it towards something more useful. After all, a glowing light isn't going to stop anyone who's trying to kill you."

"Wait…I don't want these powers," explained Caitlin, realizing she had never told Erwid why she wanted training. "I don't want them. I don't need people I know to look at me like a freak when I start defying the very laws of physics."

"Sure, but you never know when something like this might be useful. If you're up against an enemy, what are you going to do if you have to fight? It's not like you have to parade around town brandishing your sorcery skills to everyone around. You're getting that choice now."

Caitlin sighed. "That's a fair point."

Erwid backtracked a little bit so she could be next to Caitlin. "Just between you and me, these powers, when I first started getting them, I felt the exact same way as you. I didn't want them. But I've learned over time that these powers are a gift, not a curse. They've done me so much more good than harm over the years that I've had them. And they'll likely do the same for you."

Caitlin was unconvinced, but decided to go along with it for now. "So, please continue what you were saying before I interrupted you, okay?" she asked.

"You're fine, Caitlin. As I was saying, you want the energy in your body to go to more than just a glowing sphere that does nothing. Which is where the molding process comes in. Watch." She brought back the glowing sphere on her hand, which she held there for a few seconds. She then slowly began to move her arms around in similar patterns to when she and Baracath confronted the Shervide in the woods. Slowly, glowing trails of magic began to appear in the air in front of Erwid as she concentrated, her arms waving around, until there was a longsword made entirely of blue-green, transparent outlines in the air, complete with a crossguard and grip. She grabbed it, and to Caitlin's surprise, it didn't phase through her hand, instead handing in her grip just like a real sword.

"See that stick over there?" Erwid asked, pointing with her free hand. Caitlin followed her finger and saw it resting on the temple wall. "Grab it."

Caitlin did, holding it with both hands. It was a thick stick, made of wood, designed for fighting with. It looked like one of the sticks Daniel used to train with back when he was a martial arts student.

"Now, try to strike me with it," said Erwid, not even grabbing the sword with two hands.

This request took Caitlin aback. "You sure Erwid?" she asked. "I don't think that sword is going to block this…"

"Just trust me," Erwid said, reaching over with her other hand and raising the sword into a defensive position.

Caitlin was confused, and worried that she would knock Erwid out, but she raised the stick over her head and brought it down towards Erwid's head. To her surprise, the sword came up out of nowhere and stopped the stick hard in its tracks. The sound of the blade swishing was unlike any sound Caitlin had ever heard, an almost watery swoosh.

"We can use the Madorax's energy to create almost any weapon or item that we need. From shields for defense to weapons of all kinds for offense. That includes ranged weapons, but most of the time if you want to take a target at range out, you'd just do this…" She grabbed another ball of energy from her hand and this time pulled her shoulder and other arm back as if she were a baseball pitcher winding up. Her hand glowed like a sun for a second, and then it fired out a beam of pure energy into the sky, away from the buildings. Caitlin gasped aloud as she felt the heat from the blast as it went past her.

"That attack has high explosive value, for when you want to breach something," explained Erwid. "But those are just a few examples of the crazy things you can make with the Madorax energy."

"Do you want me to try some out now?" Caitlin asked, anticipating the answer already.

"Absolutely! Go ahead, see what you can make. I'm not expecting you to make anything elaborate or fancy, but just…anything really. Just try it out!"

Caitlin nodded and attempted to bring back the blue-green sphere from earlier, which thankfully she was able to do much more easily this time. Once she was there, she stopped, not knowing where else to go from there. "What do I do now? I'm still new to this whole magic thing, you know?"

"Picture the weapon or item that you want to make in your mind, then start moving your arms like this." Erwid demonstrated for her, putting her hands together, then spreading them out and forming two giant counter-clockwise circles with them, before finally putting them back near each other again. "Do that and you should see some results."

She was hesitant to use her magic more, but Caitlin pictured the item she wanted in her mind. She didn't think of something violent; she wanted something she had not been able to touch in a long time; an artist's pen. She imagined her old pen, with all its dried paint stains and broken clip. She began to move her arms in the motion that Erwid had described for her, placing her hands together and then slowly moving them counter-clockwise. As she watched, she could see blue-green lines start to appear in front of her, forming the shape of the pen. She could see the tip being almost written into existence, along with the push button on the top. But when she completed the motion with her hands, only about two-thirds of the pen was completed. She reached out to touch it, only for it to disappear the second she did. She recoiled instinctually, not sure what she had done wrong.

"Don't worry, you'll get the hang of it!" encouraged Erwid. "It should take a few attempts to get right. I wouldn't expect you to get it right on the first try…in fact, that would be basically unheard of." She checked the watch on her arm. "I have some matters to take care of elsewhere in the compound. Can I leave you here to keep working on this? Baracath or myself will check on you periodically, okay?"

Caitlin nodded, already summoning more Madorax energy. "Okay. I'll keep practicing."

"I'll leave you a little something." Erwid quickly made a magical diagram of the motions for the item creator spell. "There, use that to help you out. I'll be back soon."

She left Caitlin in the corner, with her diagram still spitting out bolts of lightning. Caitlin continued to concentrate, following the steps listed as best she could, but she still could not manage to complete the design of the pen. She tried again and again, but the closest she could get to finishing her design were four missing lines of energy. She tried moving her arms at different speeds, making different hand gestures, concentrating harder, even attempting to picture one of her other pens, but she still could not manage to complete it to where she could grab it out of the air.

She was waving her arms around for about thirty minutes before someone else came down into her corner, that person being Pantura. "I was told you'd be over here practicing," she told Caitlin as she approached. "Still no luck?"

"Not yet," said Caitlin, making the pen for the fortieth time. "Still trying to actually finish making this pen." Her concentration slipped as she spoke, and the lines drawn in the air fizzled out. She slapped her knee in frustration. "I just can't seem to finish the darn thing in the first place!"

"I really wish I could be of some help to you now," said Pantura, noting her frustration. "But last I checked my occupation was engineering, not teacher of magic, so I'm afraid you'll have to keep trying without me. I'll be here for emotional support though, if that helps."

Caitlin shrugged. "We'll see." She glanced over Pantura and saw that she was not carrying a plate. "Didn't you want some food? The eggs this morning were really tasty."

Pantura put her hands up in a carefree gesture. "I'll get it later. I'm not hungry right now."

Caitlin kept trying for another hour, and still not making the pen all the way. She came within one line from completion twice, but never enough to where it stopped it from vanishing. Eventually she threw in the towel and sat down next to Pantura. "This is ridiculous. I'm never going to be able to do this!"

She said it right as Erwid entered the corner and came upon her, allowing her to hear every word. "That's not true," she said immediately, walking towards them and causing Pantura to start a little bit. Erwid knelt down next to Caitlin, who was sitting on the side looking dejected. "Lesson I learned from years of being taught how to wield magic. No matter how impossible it seems now, you can get through anything if you put your mind to it. It took me two years to learn that lesson. Now I'm giving it to you now."

"How can I learn how to properly wield magic when I can't even make something as basic as a pen with my mind?" Caitlin asked in frustration. "I can't even complete that! How can I be expected to make a full-on sword with my mind when I can't do that to start with?"

Erwid leaned in a little closer. "Just between the two of us, a little trade secret," she said quietly. "I personally find that concentrating on good memories and thoughts helps me focus when I'm learning something like this. Try it with yourself, see if it works."

Caitlin thought for a moment. Unfortunately, a good deal of her memories were tainted by the bad times of the past five years. She scoured her brain for something truly happy, a memory that she could depend on. After a few moments, she landed on the perfect one; an old memory, from before the Gorog invasion, but it would do nicely. With the image of the nebula from Daniel's last stargazing session firmly set in her brain, she stood up, stepped forward, reached out her hand, and began to concentrate. The memories of that night came back as the Madorax energy formed on her palm, and she began to move her arms around in the motion described. The blue-green lines of energy began to form in front of her as she shut her eyes, thinking of the blue stone she had given Daniel, and the last truly happy exchange between the two of them. The pen outline became more defined and clear, but Caitlin's memories kept her going as the final lines began to be filled in.

Erwid was staring at the sight in front of her. "Caitlin," she said. "Look."

Caitlin opened her eyes up. Her arms settled down back into the final position. In front of her was a fully-outlined pen, shining extra bright with blue-green light. She reached a hand out to grab it, and found that she was able to do so. It felt solid to the touch, just like the real thing. She twirled it around in her hand, the energy constituting it buzzing with life as she did. She gasped in astonishment, her face lighting up as she realized that she had done it. She had made a pen using only magic.

"Well I'll be…" mouthed Pantura, moving in closer to examine the item in Caitlin's hand.

"That's some fine handiwork right there," complemented Erwid, stroking a finger along the spine of the pen. "You should be proud, Caitlin. Even though it took a little longer than normal, you managed to create your item. But, if I may ask, why did you choose a pen?"

"It's a reminder of home," replied Caitlin, staring longingly at the replica of her artist's pen. "I used to draw to pass time when I was younger. Daniel would come and help out some days." She laughed. "He was terrible at art, but that didn't stop him from trying to add to my drawings."

Erwid nodded. "This Daniel, is he a friend of yours?"

Caitlin watched the pen slowly disappear from her hand. "He's my best friend in the entire world. And I wouldn't trade it for anything."

"And does he know about your powers?"

Caitlin tensed up a little, but she then relaxed somewhat as she realized that her secret was already out. "Yes," she said. "I…didn't want to tell him at first. I almost didn't. But I did. I don't want our friendship to be any different from what it was before…" She stopped, realizing that she was about to mention her home of Earth and her years inside Skorjion. She quickly thought of an alternate scenario. "Before we had to restart our lives elsewhere."

It was technically the truth, and Erwid seemed to acknowledge it, as she nodded and stretched her back. "Well, now that you've made your first weapon, you're now ready to branch out and try other items. See about making weapons and other items that you're familiar with. I'll leave two other spell diagrams with you so you can keep practicing, and I'll bring you lunch to eat in a little bit. I'll bring some for you as well," she added, speaking to Pantura.

She left them again after making two new diagrams for Caitlin. Both of them were variations of the default movements used to make the pen, but with additional movements and gestures of the hand for basic shields and weapons. Now that she had already made an item using magic, it took her much less time to make a sword for her second item. After five tries, a long, glowing blade was in front of her, which she picked up out of the air and began to swing around and test. The weapon was light as a feather, and she was able to swing it as gracefully as she could. Which, for her, meant overreaching, stumbling and nearly chopping Pantura's head off multiple times as she failed to mind her surroundings. After the third close call, Pantura hastily backed away, angry.

"Why don't you go over there?" she said in annoyance. "You're getting *very* close to my neck with that blade."

"Sorry!" apologized Caitlin, backing up away from Pantura before continuing to swing her weapon around. Although she still stumbled now, at least Pantura was out of danger of the reach of her sword. She practiced maintaining her balance and keeping her footing stable while swinging, and gradually grew accustomed to wielding a long, sharp-edged weapon that was made entirely from magical energy. By the time Erwid came back with lunch for both her and Pantura, she had ditched the sword and was working on creating the default shield.

"I see you've already moved on to the shield," she noted, setting down a plate of meat and vegetables in Pantura's lap, and another on the bench next to her.

The default shield was not big, just under two feet in diameter, but the Madors made up for it by possessing the ability to dual-wield if necessary. Plus, according to the diagram, the edges were sharp enough to act as weapons in their own right. The shield was round, with the grips and silver buckler detailed in with the rest of the energy lines, but not much else. Still, despite this, Caitlin was having some difficulty creating just one of these items, even more so than the sword, but upon seeing the plate of food with her name on it, she dropped her activity and sat down next to Pantura to eat. Lunch, like breakfast, was also quite good, and everyone ate everything on their plate. Once the last bits of vegetables were gone, Erwid took the three plates and caused all of them to disappear right in front of everyone, as they disappeared in a cloud of blue-green smoke, causing both Pantura and Caitlin's eyes to pop out of their heads in disbelief.

"How?" exclaimed Pantura, staring at where the small stack of plates used to be.

"That," said Erwid, "Was another spell. I just sent all of those dirty plates back to the kitchen. But that's not important. It's time to continue Miss Caitlin's training."

Caitlin raised an eyebrow, somewhat amused. "Causing dinner plates to disappear?"

"That, and potentially a lot more. Believe me, plates will probably be something that you rarely make disappear after this."

Caitlin raised her other eyebrow. "You're killing me with this indirect answer, Erwid. Just tell me before the anticipation makes me go insane!"

She meant it jokingly of course, but her tactic worked, and Erwid skipped straight to the point. "Alright. Grab my hand," she said, reaching hers out towards Caitlin. She turned towards Pantura. "And that goes for you too."

They obeyed, Caitlin grabbing Erwid's hand, and Pantura touching Caitlin's shoulder. The same warp effect from earlier came upon them, as they dropped out into the same dimension that they had entered back when they had first arrived. After several seconds of vertigo-inducing falling, they landed back on solid ground, Pantura comically falling over backwards as they landed. Caitlin stumbled as well, nearly losing her balance before she managed to steady herself, blinking as bright spots swam in and out of her vision.

They had moved onto the perimeter wall surrounding the temple complex, where they had a view of the surrounding mountains and grassy fields. There were snow caps on some of the highest peaks, and lush conifer forests that hid the temple from outsiders. The breeze was much stronger up on the wall, and Caitlin shivered, wishing that she had not left her jacket back in her room.

"How do you keep doing that?" demanded Pantura, putting a hand on the rampart for balance and sitting down. "Teleporting around."

"I'll get to that in a second. For now, it's time for Caitlin to learn the process of Madorax Hopping."

Pantura stood up. "So, what, do you toss a coin to choose between a normal name or some crazy gibberish that no one knows how to pronounce?"

Erwid ignored her, proceeding with the lesson. "As you may have seen last night, it's possible to fire out beams of Madorax energy, which can be used as an attack." She raised her hand up, which glowed bright blue and discharged a large pulse of brilliant light that temporarily dazzled Caitlin and Pantura. The energy sailed over the walls and impacted a distant boulder in the field.

"I see, but how do I do that?" asked Caitlin.

"You have to concentrate the energy at a single point on your palm, then mentally tell it to release." Erwid demonstrated again for her. "Once you've done that, you can direct the beams wherever you want, which allows you to do stuff like this." She took several steps back, then broke into a sprint. Before either of them could comprehend what was happening, Erwid had vaulted over the wall rampart down towards the field. Pantura recoiled from the edge of the wall, while Caitlin gasped and ran to the edge. Erwid was in freefall for what seemed like forever, but right before she shattered her legs, she fired two concentrated pulses of Madorax energy, which launched her skyward into a graceful arc over the field. She launched herself again as she came down towards the ground, and continued to repeat it until she was on the far side of the field. She then turned around, the two of them still staring at her, until she propelled herself over the wall and onto the rampart with a particularly powerful blast, landing right next to Pantura and startling her.

"Whoa!" exclaimed Caitlin, awestruck. "How do you do that for so long?"

Erwid sat down on the wall. "The trick is timing your blasts. If you do it too early and it won't do much to stop your fall, too late and you'll have already broken your leg. But first, you'll have to master actually firing out the energy from your hand."

Caitlin looked down at her hands, the calluses visible from Skorjion's mines. They seemed to feebly pulse with energy, and she wondered if they would glow in the dark once nighttime came. She rubbed them together, letting the power transfer between them and down her arms. She began to concentrate as Erwid had instructed earlier, letting her right palm light up again.

"I should warn you," Erwid added, speaking up hastily. "The feeling that you get is quite weird on the first few discharges."

Caitlin barely heard her, instead focusing inside her. As she did, she willed the energy built up on her palm to be released forward. There was a buzzing that traveled down her arm, almost like pins and needles, and then she was launched backwards by the sudden pulse that fired out from her palm. She tumbled backwards, falling onto the hard stone walkway, scraping her elbow in the process. Grunting as her arm stung from the impact, she stood up, dusting herself off, and shivering again as another cold breeze came blowing up and over the wall. Looking around, she saw Erwid watching her closely, indicating for her to try again. Pantura was also watching closely, but probably for research purposes more than anything. Frustrated, she tried again, succeeding in launching herself back again and nearly vomiting up her lunch in the process.

"You alright?" said Pantura, standing up from where she was sitting in surprise.

"What's happening?" asked Erwid, kneeling on the ground in front of Caitlin.

She managed to swallow her lunch before it escaped her entirely. "I can't resist the recoil," she said, standing up and brushing off her knees. "It keeps blowing me backwards."

"You're not discharging correctly," Erwid reasoned. "Try again, and this time try to maintain your posture. And try to keep yourself steady while you practice, and bend your knees; that helps a lot. Just watch out for that drop behind you. A student accidentally launched himself clear into the courtyard, and landed on his neck. He wound up being paralyzed entirely as a result."

Caitlin nodded, not feeling any better about her practicing. She concentrated again, trying to hold the energy in one place, without her moving as well. She raised her arm, bending her knees slightly to absorb the shock, and released the pulse. The recoil was still felt, and it knocked her back, but she managed to stay on her feet, while the energy sailed over Pantura's head and off between two distant mountains, joining the many stars in the sky as another point of light.

Erwid's head was cocked to one side as Caitlin relaxed her posture. "Well, that attempt seemed way more fruitful than the first two."

Caitlin shook her head to clear out the dizziness she was feeling, and then nodded. "Yeah. Managed not to fall over this time."

"Good shot, too. Right in between those two mountains."

"Thanks."

"Great!" said Pantura, still sitting down on the rampart. "I still have no clue exactly what is going on."

"You will, hopefully," Erwid replied. She looked overhead at the sky, where all of the stars were slowly rotating. "We should proceed on to the next part of the training. If you would please follow me..." She started off down the wall towards the nearest stairwell down.

"Wait!" Caitlin called, confused. "You're not going to let me practice at all?"

"There will be time for that later today," explained Erwid. "For now, it's time to show you the last thing that you can master as a Madorax wielder; the *Plavoris*."

She walked away, and Pantura's confused expression remained on her face even after she had disappeared from sight. "The what now?" she asked. "I hate all this riddle talk and secrecy nonsense."

Yet she still followed Erwid and Caitlin down the wall as they moved towards their next location.

She led them outside the temple, through the gate and into the big open field in front of it. There, Erwid was joined by Baracath, who had just returned from a routine patrol. There were no other sorcerers within sight, save the few on the temple's ramparts, and no trees either. It was just Caitlin, Pantura, and the two sorcerers standing in a grassy field.

"The *Plavoris* is the third and final major task you can learn as an Ostila Mador," explained Baracath. "It is a very powerful charge of Madorax energy that is much stronger than any other usage of the magic. It is also unique to each sorcerer; it's very rare for two sorcerers to have the exact same *Plavoris*. Take Erwid's, for instance." He stepped back to put the attention of both Caitlin and Pantura on her. "You've already witnessed hers. Her Time Spell is something only she can do."

Erwid raised her hands and began to swivel them in a small circular motion. The sky bubble above them, which was moving normally a second ago, stopped, then slowly began to rotate backwards, the hundreds of suns in the sky moving in the opposite direction to where they were supposed to go. The sky darkened, the air cooled, and soon the night sky was staring down at them, where the daytime sky used to be. A quick reversal of Erwid's arm movements and the dark sky was quickly overtaken by the same familiar daytime sky as before. She stopped the movement and the sky settled back into its original place, the many stars once again lighting up the field. "Shurgen's not going to be pleased with this manipulation," she said.

"I'll let Shurgen know about our reasons for tampering with the temporal dome again," said Baracath, clapping his hands together. "That's an example of a *Plavoris*. A really powerful but not sustainable usage of Madorax energy. Mine is a little different."

He reached out his hand, holding it out as if he were reaching out for something, and suddenly, he picked out a small laser pistol out of the thin air, taking it in his grasp. "I can use my *Plavoris* to access items even when they're far away from me. I don't even need to teleport there; I can grab them if I need something. Makes it really helpful when I leave the key to my room in some random spot."

Pantura chuckled. "I wish I had something like that for my paperwork. Some days it feels like it keeps on running away to where I can't find it."

"So how do you figure out what someone's Plav…their

Plav…the…ugh!" Caitlin exclaimed in frustration at stumbling over her own words. "Their special ability is?"

"The *Plavoris*," said Erwid. "And it depends on the sorcerer. Sometimes, it can take months or even years to figure out what their connection to the Madorax is. Sometimes, it can take just a week or two. And we won't know what it is until we see it. So I'm afraid you'll just have to wait if you want to see it."

"I'm really just curious, but if it's too difficult to figure out then I won't bother over asking again. Besides, I'm never going to use it anyways, so…"

"Totally fine," Baracath replied. "That's really all we have to teach you about the Madorax, so as long as you keep practicing, you should eventually reach a point where you'll be able to master control of your powers; including keeping them out of sight. If that's how you still wish to proceed?"

Caitlin nodded. "I'll be honest with you two," she said. "I'm not as concerned about my abilities going haywire anymore. What I can do…it's…well, it's kind of cool. But I don't want anyone else to witness my powers and take the wrong message from it. So yes, I'd prefer to proceed with burying them deep down."

Erwid nodded. "Of course." She extended her hand. Caitlin took it, and so did Pantura. Once again, they teleported, landing back inside the temple courtyard, which was now way more busy than this morning, with Ostila Madors dressed in cloaks walking around and chatting with each other.

"I don't suppose there's a special spell that allows you to teleport around like that too?" asked Pantura.

Erwid shook her head. "That ability is something that only the daimyo and his three advisers can use. So, while we'd love to teach you how to use that, I'm afraid it won't be today."

"Besides that, we have nothing else to teach you," explained Baracath, who appeared not far away. "You keep practicing these skills that we have shared with you today, and you'll be in a position to where you can hide your abilities. But before Erwid and I leave you to manage other affairs, we want to offer you something."

Erwid briefly vanished, then reappeared a few moments later with a large piece of cloth in her arms. "This is one of our robes that you've been seeing us wear all day. Designed to help us blend in with the shadows. If you wish, it will be yours to wear. But do not think that you have to accept it from us. It's entirely up to you."

Pantura stepped forward and took the cloak in her hands from Erwid, letting the hem fall to the ground, and rubbing her fingers over the woven fabric. "What is this made from?" she asked. "I've never felt fabric like this in my years of engineering and experience."

"I'm afraid that's one secret that we unfortunately cannot tell you," Baracath explained, smiling. "Only Ostila Madors can know how these are made. And since you are not one, and Caitlin doesn't want to be…" He shrugged. "You get the point."

Pantura admired the soft fabric some more, then handed it to Caitlin. "What do you say?" asked Baracath. "Do you want it?"

Caitlin looked down at the cloak in her hands. It was indeed very soft, and very black as well, and it seemed to almost disappear into the shadows cast by the group as they stood around. She was tempted to take it, as they were offering it to her freely, but after some contemplation, she shook her head. "I appreciate the offer, Baracath," she finally said, "But I don't have any need for it at the moment, I don't think. I'm perfectly happy with my clothing at the moment."

Baracath nodded. "No worries," he replied. He took the cloak back from her. "If there is anything that you need, don't hesitate to ask one of us. I'll be up in the temple with Shurgen."

"And I'll be managing a group of other new students," added Erwid, pointing to a back pathway that extended to the left of the temple. "Just down there."

"You sure you'll be fine on your own?" asked Baracath, folding his arms.

Caitlin nodded. "I remember everything. I'll probably be training on the wall, out of the way of everyone else."

"Good. If we're nearby, we'll keep an eye out for you." Baracath turned to face Erwid, giving her a look, then turned back to Caitlin. "In that case, stay out of trouble, and we'll see you around."

He vanished, and after Erwid nodded and smiled at her, she teleported too, leaving Caitlin and Pantura in the middle of the temple square. The two of them exchanged a look before Pantura shrugged.

"I'll get used to it eventually," she said. "So…temple wall?"

Caitlin nodded. "Yes."

On top of the temple wall, surrounded by mountains, with the glorious waterfall behind them, Caitlin continued to practice the techniques she had been taught, not only creating items and weapons but also dual-wielding two different items, such as a sword and shield. This was what she was doing now, swinging her sword while occasionally raising her shield to pretend block blows. Pantura, meanwhile, continued to watch from where she was seated, some distance away, in order to avoid Caitlin's sometimes clumsy swings. Her form had seen some marginal improvement over the past hour, but was still highly unrefined.

After she stumbled again and almost face planted into the wall, causing both of her weapons to disappear into the air, Pantura stood up, deciding to do what she thought was best.

"Allow me to help you out here," she said, pulling out the hilt of a retractable sword from her bag and extending the blade out. "You've seen one of these before?"

"Vorlax showed Daniel and I one before I left," said Caitlin, pushing herself off of the wall and back to an upright position.

Pantura advanced on Caitlin, stopping a few feet in front of her, and took a defensive stance. "Perhaps actually fighting a real opponent would aid you in your technique," she explained. "Just for a few rounds, just to see what you got."

Caitlin did not bother to hesitate, instead conjuring up another sword to use. Taking her spectral weapon in both hands, she swung it around a little, letting the blade hum, then took a rather stiff posture, the blade raised high above her head. Pantura, rolling her eyes, quickly lunged forward without warning and managed to get the point of her sword right in front of Caitlin's chest before she even had time to react.

"Dead," said Pantura, lowering her blade. "I would advise keeping the sword closer and more centered to your body, like this." She gripped the hilt with both hands, raising it so the point was at her eye level, and centered on her spine. "Try to stab me now."

Not even stopping to consider why she was listening without questioning the command, she lunged forward, the lightweight weapon humming through the air as she stabbed it forward. It met Pantura's own weapon about six inches out from its target and was sent off trajectory, causing Caitlin to stumble again. When she returned to her old position, Pantura had barely even moved.

"See? Way more effective in case your foe decides to stab at you." She lowered her sword, letting the steel gray blade fall to her side. "Now, your turn."

Caitlin copied her defense posture, and Pantura lunged again. This time, Caitlin blocked out, and the pointed tip went past her instead of into her. Pantura faltered somewhat, but still managed to keep her balance and return to her starter pose.

"That was much better." She then proceeded to lunge out again, only for Caitlin to again block the advance. Pantura stepped back, eyed Caitlin's defensive form, then unleashed several quick attacks in rapid succession. Caitlin barely had time to block the strikes before the next one came swinging at her, and by Pantura's seventh swing, her sword was too far away to block in time, resulting in the sharp edge at her throat.

"You have some ways to go before you master the art of swordplay," said Pantura. "But don't worry. It's not something you can learn in a day."

Caitlin nodded, but then thought of something. "Quick question," she asked. "Why do you still use swords in combat? On Earth they went out of style about five hundred years ago."

Pantura shrugged. "It's a simple weapon, from a simpler time. It's elegant, relatively easy to use, and deadly in melee combat. Sure, we still use long-range weaponry in the army, but every soldier gets one of these as their final item to use. Because once you can use one of these and not be killed trying, you're ready for the army. Useful when the enemy gets a little too close for comfort." She swung her weapon around a few more times. "Being an engineer, I don't get to use mine often, but I still practice with it as often as I can, just in case. It came from my family, going back to my grandfather, when he carried it around as a member of the Arajor Guard."

She handed it to Caitlin, who examined the shiny, recently-polished hilt of the weapon. It had a chrome sheen to it that glistened under the light of the stars above, and it felt nearly as light as the spectral ones she'd been creating. "It's not that heavy," she remarked, raising and lowering the hilt. On the crossguard's center was a symbol engraved into the metal; a depiction of the constellation Orion, the three belt stars prominent, all surrounded by a diamond border.

"That's the symbol of the Orion Coalition engraved into the hilt," explained Pantura. "It was brand-new when my grandfather became a soldier." She reflected for a moment. "When the Orion Coalition was new, and we started watching over Earth, we saw this pattern of stars in the sky, what was known to the humans as Orion, the Hunter. Given that Arajor from Earth lies inside the Orion constellation, the council came to an agreement to use it for our symbol, even though from Arajor we do not see this pattern in our sky."

"Earth keeps on giving," replied Caitlin, handing the weapon back to Pantura. "Has there been anything else that we've given you of any significance?" As she spoke, she created another sword and took up her defensive posture in a wordless gesture.

Pantura drew her blade, recognizing the implication. "Well," she said, as they began to spar, "You haven't exactly given us a whole lot that was truly game-changing. Obviously, Shane probably already mentioned all of your clothing fads. We had never even heard of jeans before the Zodiac Conference of 1975. And then there's smallpox, which we received at the 1946 convention, which had already been delayed a year because of some world war that was raging at the time. That caused quite a massive killing in some parts of the galaxy, but thankfully we eliminated all of the viruses within a few years."

Caitlin shuddered and almost missed blocking a crucial strike at the realization that, although she knew World War II to be the most violent and destructive war in human history, to these people living in the galaxy, it was insignificant next to the gigantic conflicts that they had fought, and were still fighting even today. She thought of the sheer number of troops that must have died just fighting the Gorog legions, to say nothing of the other wars in the past. "Oh," she simply said, continuing to maintain her defense as she spoke. "Well, at least you eliminated smallpox in a short period. It took us several centuries to do the same."

They kept exchanging blows, circling around each other, trying to find a weakness in the other's guard. Their weapons clanged as they collided with each other, each impact causing Caitlin's arm to cramp up more. "The biggest thing you all gave us was all the entertainment," continued Pantura. "Movies, amusement parks, and more. For better or for worse, there are now movie companies that make films out here. None of it beats your cinema of course, but it's a start."

Caitlin chucked as she continued to swing at Pantura. "You'll get there eventually!" she said. And then she was swept off her feet by a well-placed low kick from her opponent and went down, Pantura's sword once again at her throat.

"As will you," said Pantura, lowering her weapon, and grabbing Caitlin's hand, hoisting her up. "Now, again! And no holding back this time!"

They continued to spar as the sky darkened, heralding the oncoming night.

Chapter 26

Arajor System

The *Justice* was almost ready to go to hyperspace, Daniel could tell. All of the crew members running about, the massive amount of chatter over the intercoms, and the fact that he was about to meet up with Shane one last time before they departed for Lhassi all seemed to give it away. Once they were in hyperspace, it would not be long before they charged into battle.

Daniel was by himself, as Max was supposedly already there. It felt strange to walk the halls of the massive ship by himself, with no Caitlin next to him. He hoped she was doing okay with the wizards, and that they were helping her to fix her powers. He felt the warm blue stone that she had given him once again. He refused to leave it behind, since it was his only connection to her now that she was across the galaxy. His fingers felt the words on the stone, and immediately a pang of anxiety came bursting through his defenses. He could die in this battle. Obviously, that was a risk he was going to have to take, given everything that had happened the past couple of days, but it still bugged him. He had already cheated death three times; when the Gorogs first attacked, when he had escaped Skorjion, and when he had infiltrated Diamondhead Outpost. There was something dark about this forthcoming conflict. There was no sense of heroism in the air, no grand adventurous feel to it, it was just one battle in a brutal war that had been persisting for decades. And Daniel knew it.

He found Shane, who was talking with Vorlax, Max, and two other individuals that could not identify, as their backs were turned. "Shane!" he greeted the Magnum.

"Daniel," acknowledged Shane. "How are you feeling

today, after some training?"

"Better. What's going on? You summoned me."

Shane turned to the two strangers that he was talking to. They both turned around, revealing Vraxis's face, and, to Daniel's utter shock, Foulor's massive build. And neither of them were in handcuffs. "What are *they* doing here?" asked Daniel, a hint of anger creeping into his voice. "Especially him!" He pointed at Foulor.

"Foulor surrendered to us about an hour ago, saying that he was hoping to negotiate a deal with us for Vraxis's release. He promised that he would help us win the assault on Rhozadar in exchange for his release and Vraxis's. Of course, what we never told him was that Vraxis had already agreed to help us for a large sum of money. They're going to help us identify weak points in Rhozadar's ground defenses, and then they'll be free to spend their fortune."

Daniel did not lower his guard. "They could be tricking us, you know," he said, tensed up, hands raised slightly over their normal position. "This could be another of Orvag's plans."

"You need to remember, they're not Gorogs. They're bounty hunters. They only serve money, not any ideology in this galaxy, besides the one that pays them the most of course."

"And I regret living by that code somedays, just to be absolutely clear," grumbled Vraxis. "But you offered each of us a lifetime supply of riches. I'd have to be insane to refuse."

"You never said that we both were getting paid today!" complained Foulor. "I thought it was just going to be you!"

"Shut up, and that's not what I told you."

"I, for one, and I can't believe I'm saying this, agree with Daniel," piped up Max. "I told you, Shane, that you should put them in the airlock and eject them both into space. We don't need to deal with more colorful characters on the eve of this battle."

"And, I told you, Max, that they are going to help us win

this conflict. End of discussion."

Daniel folded his arms. "So, we're all friends now, are we?"

Vraxis gave him an evil look. "Don't think that we're now best friends just because I agreed to stop hunting you down. Your little lizard is going to cause me to go to therapy, since his teeth are all I see now in my visions, after he jumped on me."

"If you want, I can make it worse," snarled Max, looking like a spawn of the devil with his toothy grin. He unsheathed his claws, making Vraxis look even more uncomfortable.

"I'm sorry for kidnapping your mom, Daniel!" exclaimed Foulor, approaching Daniel as if to give him a hug, only to be stopped by a raised hand from him.

"I don't think we're at that stage yet, Foulor," he said as harmlessly as he could. "Maybe one day though?"

Foulor looked a little hurt, but at the mention of the possibility in the future, he started to jump up and down with excitement. "Yay!" he exclaimed, clapping his hands together. "Someday!"

Vraxis's uneasiness was replaced by yet more embarrassment at the sight of his buffoon of a brother. "Alright, that's enough, get behind me," he growled, causing his brother to slink behind him. He turned back to Shane. "The *instant* the Gorogs are in retreat, we're getting out, you're giving us our money, and we're leaving for retirement. Do I make that clear?"

Shane nodded. "Understood." He turned to Vorlax. "You sure you can manage Daniel and Max and get them prepared for battle?"

"What, do you not trust me?" asked Vorlax. "If I can be their tour guide for a couple of hours, I can get them prepared for battle! Watch me!"

Shane laughed. "I wish I could, but I have paperwork to attend to back on Arajor. Just do me a favor and don't screw this whole operation over in my absence, will you?"

Vorlax raised his arms in a mock posture of surrender. "Again, do you not trust me?"

Shane smiled. "I'm kidding, Vorlax. There's no one I'd rather have leading this military campaign than you. You'll do great, I'm sure. Just keep an eye on those two, will you?" He indicated Vraxis and Foulor.

"I'll take them off your hands, how about?" interrupted Max, poking his head between the two of them. "If they make a motion that hints that they're turning and running, I'll kill them for you. If they try to switch sides again, I'll kill them. If they do *anything suspicious*," he said, directing it at the twins, "I'll kill them faster than you ever could."

Vorlax nodded. "You have my permission to do just that," he replied. He turned back to Shane. "You'd better get going. We're making the jump to hyperspace in like five minutes."

Shane nodded. "Good luck everyone. I hope to see you all alive by tomorrow at dusk. May the Belt light your way."

"As well as yours," replied Vorlax, making the same hand gesture that Shane had made earlier. Shane returned the motion, dipped his head, then turned and left. Vorlax watched him go.

"I guess that means that I'm in charge now," he said, straightening his dark blue and silver flight suit. "Everyone, I have to prepare my squadron for the battle. I'd suggest everyone get some rest. Especially you, Daniel. And Max, again, keep an eye on the twins for me, will you? We don't want them getting themselves into any unnecessary trouble."

"Aw, seriously," protested Vraxis. "Do you seriously not trust us?"

The look on Vorlax's face provided all the answer that he needed. "No," he said. "Max, please escort them to their chambers."

"Gladly," the lizard replied, pushing Foulor forwards,

causing the much bigger hunter to stumble a little. Vraxis gave a possible hurtful look in Vraxis's direction, then slinked off after the two others, where they soon disappeared into the crowd of soldiers marching in formation towards their posts.

Vorlax sighed. "Let's hope the weight of responsibility doesn't get to me before we win this battle," he quipped. He stared at Daniel, who was still standing and looking at him. "Why are you still here?" he asked. "Go! Get some sleep while you can! You'll be needing it!"

"Why??" yelled Vraxis at Foulor as soon as Max disappeared into their room's lavatory. "Why, oh why, did you have to get delusions of grandeur and try to come out and bargain for my release??"

"You were in prison! I wasn't just going to leave you behind!" Foulor shot back.

"I had everything under control! Shane was never going to kill me! We could have flown off into retirement together, but instead, you needlessly got yourself captured!"

"Dormak and Orvag weren't going to send a rescue party, so I thought that if I came by myself, perhaps I could have negotiated with Shane…"

"No! You didn't need to do that! I had already worked out a deal with Shane, and would have come to pick you up as soon as the Lhassi campaign ended! All you had to do was be patient, which lest we forget, is one of the central trademarks of a great bounty hunter! Instead, you blindly tried to come out, and negotiate for my release!"

"How is negotiating for your freedom a bad thing??"

"Because, Foulor, you're not good at it! Your specialty is breaking people's skulls and blowing things up, not trying to bargain with the leader of the Orion Coalition!"

"Are you two going to quiet down in there, or am I

going to have to start maiming you two to get you to shut up?" yelled Max from behind the bathroom door.

Both twins turned to glare at the closed door. "Look, Foulor. I appreciate you having my best interests at heart, but you could have just stayed with Orvag." Vraxis lowered his volume and softened the tone of his voice. "You didn't need to come all the way out here on my account."

"I'm sorry, I just didn't want to sit around in our room all day while Orvag did nothing to help you get free."

"I'm sure he's preoccupied with the fact that we are all preparing to invade his largest labor camp." Vraxis sighed. "It's too late now. You're here, and I've already made the deal with Shane. We're locked into this whole thing."

Foulor sat on the bed, glancing over at his grenade bandolier sitting next to him. "How much did Shane offer to pay us should we help him?"

"A million credits, even more, each."

Foulor whistled. "Right. That's a lot of money."

"Forget 'a lot of money.' That's enough to retire and never work again. Think, after this rotten business is over, we can go settle down, like you've been asking me to do for a long time now. We can travel to Oxola and stay by the water, in that beachfront house that you found."

Foulor nodded slowly, although his movement was not committed. He glanced over at the wall, then sighed. "Listen, Vraxis," he began.

"Yes?"

Foulor sighed again, louder this time. "What if we, you know, are wrong about…"

"What? Just say it."

"The…whole retirement thing." It was not what Foulor had intended to say. He had meant to ask whether or not working for Shane would be a better idea in the long term, assuming they ever came back from retirement to continue hunting. However, he knew that, deep down, Vraxis would just shoot the idea down. Retirement was something that he had been seeking for almost a year now, saving up percentages of their collected bounties to put towards it. This latest payment from Shane was the perfect final reason to quit after tomorrow. "You sure that we're ready to just…walk away from everything?"

Vraxis turned to stare at him. "Yes," he said. "I've told you before, I've never really enjoyed working as a bounty hunter. It's been something that we've only been doing because it pandered to our skills the best. The instant we had the funds to retire, I wasn't going to refuse the opportunity."

"No, I get that," his brother replied. "It's just…normally I'm terrible at remembering things. I can barely remember what I ate yesterday. But the one thing that I can remember regardless is what you told me when we were in exile, living on that isolated moon, trying to survive another week without starving."

"And what's that?"

"We were sitting around a campfire, hungry, because our food for the evening had been eaten by wild animals. We were pretty despondent at the time, I recall. But you turned to me and said, 'We don't have to worry, Foulor. This whole business, it's only temporary. One day, we're going to get off this rock, and then, we'll do amazing things together, you and I.'"

"'Because our clan will never fall apart,'" finished Vraxis, remembering that moment.

"Do you think we've truly done amazing things since then?"

It was a question that pierced Vraxis's normally iron will and cut right to his bone, but before he could think about it, Max emerged from the bathroom, yawning and showing both hunters his many teeth. "Alright, that's enough conversation from you two. I'm going to nap by your bed, Vraxis. Don't get any ideas while I rest. There's a guard outside who will report any suspicious behavior if he sees anything. Got it?"

Vraxis could only stare at the lizard as he moved and laid down on the floor next to the bed. "Whatever," he eventually replied, yawning and taking his shirt off. "Come on, Foulor. Let's appease Mr. Grumpy over here and get some rest."

Daniel was dreaming again as he slept on his bed. This time, it was the first Gorog raid that was flashing in his mind, causing him to stir on his sheets. Although it had happened years ago, it was still vivid in his memories, and his dream had plunked him down right in the thick of the throng, right where he was all that time ago. He was running through downtown, evading blaster fire, the ground shaking around him as missiles destroyed buildings and flipped cars from the explosions. A sedan came crashing right behind him, nearly sending him flying into the wall next to him. He jumped over laser blasts, some of which nearly left sizzling holes in his legs. He hastily glanced to both sides of himself, looking for Caitlin and Ms. Phillips, but they were nowhere to be found. It was just himself, alone in a sea of destruction, surrounded by enemies, the ground furiously shaking below him.

A particularly furious bout of shaking jarred him awake, and he found that the shaking was not, in fact, part of his dream. The ship was shaking around him periodically, causing his balance to be thrown out of whack and him nearly to fall over. He reached the window as quickly as he could, just in time to see small ships dogfighting outside, spewing lasers at each other. His adrenaline kicked in as he realized that they must have arrived above Lhassi, and he changed into new clothes, not even bothering to do his hair, and ran out, to where soldiers were running around, shouting orders as they sprinted down the hall past Daniel's door. He shut it behind him and took off running, having a feeling that Vorlax was waiting in a specific part of the ship.

Sure enough, Daniel found the commander waiting in the main hangar, where he was busy barking orders at a pilot. He turned and saw Daniel sprinting towards him. "There you are!" he called. "Where have you been? The battle started ten minutes ago!"

Daniel skidded to a stop, out of breath from his run. "Sorry," he said, breathing heavily. "I was sleeping."

"Well, stop sleeping and get to the dropship down over there!" chided Vorlax, pointing down the hangar at a large dropship, the same model that had airlifted him and Caitlin out of Skorjion. "Max and the twins are already onboard, waiting! The instant that we can breach the blockade, you're taking off!"

"Vorlax, I…"

"Daniel, I can't talk for very long. But this is your last chance to reconsider going down there! Do you still want to help out today?"

"Yes!"

"Then get going! I'll communicate with you again once you're on the planet! Good luck!" He sprinted off before Daniel could finish his sentence. The ship shook some more, and Daniel, trying his hardest to keep standing, stumbled across the hangar to the parked dropship.

The engines were glowing faintly as he approached, but the side hatch was still wide open, and he could see at least twenty Coalition soldiers, plus the scaly hide of Max, standing in formation. Daniel reached the vessel just as another huge blast rocked the *Justice*, causing him to nearly face-plant into the wall. He regained his composure and took a spot next to Max, who was sitting patiently on the ground. Behind him, Foulor and Vraxis were seated, idly twiddling their thumbs while they waited to get moving, weapons in both of their hands.

"You're late," the lizard hissed. "I was thinking that we were going to leave without you."

Daniel put his mouth next to Max's ear. "Not a chance,"

he whispered back. He moved away, examining the inside of the dropship. At the front of the troop bay stood what he guessed was the detachment's commander, judging by the markings on his uniform. "Has there been any briefing or anything?"

"Not yet," replied Max. "They're probably waiting until the blockade's ready to fall to brief the soldiers."

"Got it," replied Daniel, as the ship swayed from another explosion. He turned behind him to glance down at the twins. "How have they been?"

"Surprisingly idle. Almost a little too idle, if you ask me." There was deep distrust in Max's voice. "I don't like it. It's as if they're waiting for us to become complacent before they strike."

"I can't say that I disagree," replied Daniel, casting one eye at Vraxis, who was leaning back against the wall of the troop bay. "Foulor I feel would be too dumb to cause any problem by himself, but Vraxis…" That uneasy feeling came circling back as he stared at the hunter. "He could definitely cause some trouble should he choose to betray us."

"You know, I can hear you," Vraxis spoke up, not even bothering to look in Daniel's direction.

Daniel stiffened. "I…meant no offense," he said, for those were the first words that popped up in his brain.

"None taken," replied the hunter, exhaling dejectedly. "I understand. We tried to turn you into Orvag, plus we've been enemies of Shane for years…I totally get why it would be hard to trust us."

"Well, I'm glad that your hunter ways didn't *completely* remove your ability to be honest," Max said, with scathing sarcasm scattered in his words. "You'd better not throw it away, or I'll be feasting mighty good." He licked his chops.

"Would you stop with the threatening remarks?" asked Vraxis angrily. "They're getting on my nerves."

Max smiled wickedly. "I didn't hear the magic word…"

442

Vraxis's face looked as though it had been struck by lightning, but he growled in his throat and said, "*Please*, stop with the threatening remarks."

"Better," said Max, sounding satisfied at last.

The commander at the front of the troop bay suddenly tapped a button on the wall, activating a beeping sound that jolted everyone's attention up to him. "May I have everyone's attention please?" he called, in a drill sergeant-esque voice. He was alien, sporting a grizzled brown beard and a mop of similarly-colored hair, but red-toned skin and four arms sprouting from his torso. Everyone turned at attention when he spoke, Daniel and Max included.

"Vorlax, the commander of this operation, has given us instructions on the infiltration process of Rhozadar, the primary labor camp complex of the Gorog Empire. As you might have already noticed–" He pointed into the back, to where Vraxis and Foulor were seated. "–We have special guests on board, Vraxis and Foulor. Do not worry. The twins have graciously offered to help break us into the camp, and deactivate the shield generator that protects the entire complex. I am carrying the key card that can gain us access into the generator's control panel, stolen from the Gorogs during the assault on Skorjion earlier this week, and saved during the surprise ambush two days ago."

Daniel felt a little hurt at not being mentioned. Surely, with something this important to the war effort, he would have gotten at least a quick mention? But the commander continued his briefing without so much as pausing.

"The shields are designed to withstand ships and their weaponry, but not individual soldiers. We will be landing here, just outside the generator." A map of Rhozadar materialized in front of him. The camp was huge, sprawling over many acres of land, and the shield bubble, represented in red, surrounded all of the facilities. A blue dot appeared on some flat ground just outside the generator. "Our group, along with three other dropships, will pass through the shield, to the generator plant building, near the center of the camp." A highlight came upon a small building near the exact center of the facility. "We will disable the shields there, which will allow our dive bombers to swoop in and take out the rows of factories. We will exit the battlegrounds from where we landed. In the event the dropships are taken out, an extraction team will lift us out here, just to the northwest of the landing site."

"Any sort of opposition?" asked a soldier.

"We have confirmation that King Orvag himself, along with Warden Dormak, the head of Skorjion camp, are on site and directing the battle from the main command center. Thus, expect heavy and skilled resistance from the Gorog troops. But as long as the key card makes it to the main generator, we'll be able to shut down the shield generators. Vorlax is sending a ground force to act as a diversion to clear the camp of most of its troops, but we'll still need to be quick in order to avoid unwanted attention."

"Let's hope that this goes according to plan," whispered Max to Daniel.

"Are there any other questions?" asked the commander.

Everyone shook their heads.

"Then prepare your weapons. And may the Belt keep us safe." All of the soldiers checked their ammunition, and loaded their guns. Daniel checked his pistol, and found the magazine to be full of plasma rounds. Max stretched his limbs and cracked his neck.

The dropship suddenly lurched upwards, and Daniel grabbed onto a handle dangling from the ceiling to stable himself. A hologram of Vorlax appeared up front. "We've just breached the Gorog blockade! I'm sending the army down to distract the Gorogs. You are clear to head for the landing area! Good luck everyone!"

Chapter 27

Lhassi

The dropship lurched again, this time forwards, and the side hatch swung and slammed shut, sealing off the troop bay. Air began to pump into the space from vents on the ceiling, filling up the chamber. Then the ship accelerated, sending everyone hurtling back slightly, and Daniel saw the walls of the hangar give way to the darkness of space through the troop bay's window. He also could see starfighters dog fighting each other, shooting lasers at the ship they were tailing. One Coalition starfighter vanished in a ball of flames as a Gorog ship shot it down with a well-placed missile. The view of the surrounding battlefield was limited, however, and Daniel could only see pieces of the starfighters dueling through the area. The dropship was constantly shaking, sometimes violently from a rogue laser blast, but no crazy evasive maneuvers had to be performed, meaning that no Gorog ships were tailing them. Through all of this, the Coalition soldiers kept calm, staring stoically ahead, hands gripping their assault rifles, while Daniel, Max and the twins kept trying to get a bearing of their surroundings, burst of terror filling them up every time the gunship rattled or shuddered.

The sky outside the window began to lighten as they entered Lhassi's atmosphere, fire beginning to fly past the window as they came streaking down like a missile. The ship vibrated more, and Daniel had to grab the handle again to steady himself. Then just as soon as the ship started shaking, it stopped, and they were in the clear, above the dark terrain of Lhassi, a planet famous for its thick atmosphere, dark days, and even darker nights. Daniel could only see dead plants, dark, rolling hills covered in volcanic ash, and more dropships landing on the ground, carrying the army that Vorlax had mentioned. Coalition soldiers were pouring out of the landing craft, sprinting off towards a location that Daniel could not see from the window. He guessed it was Rhozadar. Sure enough, a hail of laser fire was thrown up around the ship as they approached the drop zone, forcing their craft, along with the other three flying next to them to swerve to the side to avoid it. One of the four dropships was hit in the wing and sent into a nosedive towards the ground, but the others all managed to escape below the sightlines of the lasers behind a high ridge and touch down on the ground faster than Daniel had seen any other ship do.

  The instant the door opened, he leapt out of the dropship, feeling a little claustrophobic. Being in that tight of a space, with that many people, all while getting shot at had awoken a cold sweat on his forehead. But he barely had any time to register that before the squadron leader started barking orders from the troop bay and the rest of the troops poured out of the dropship and began to sprint up the ridge they had parked behind. Max poked his head, dragging Vraxis along with him, while Foulor lingered behind meekly. Daniel indicated the direction that everyone was running and took after them.

  At the top of the ridge, their group merged with the other three dropship squadrons, including the one that got shot down and had crash-landed. Before them was Lhassi's infamous labor camp, Rhozadar, the location of the Gorog's primary assembly lines. The huge complex was surrounded on three sides by walls, with the ridge acting as a natural barrier, since it dropped out forty feet vertically to the camp paths below. Mounted on the walls were at least a dozen mounted turrets, all equipped with barrels as long as a car. Rows of factories were belching smoke into the air off in the distance, and there were dozens of Gorogs everywhere you looked. There were no slaves in sight, and Daniel guessed that they had all been herded into one spot to be watched over by the guards. One of the gates was spitting out

Gorog troops into a field to the east of the camp, where the rest of the dropships would be waiting. The army would be coming down from there to engage with the Gorog soldiers any moment now.

"We need to get to that building," the commanding officer said, pointing at a small rectangular building near the heart of Rhodazar. "Everyone, start making your way down the ridge to that wall." He pointed at the corner where the wall met the rock face. "Then, be as silent as you can."

From his command post, Orvag surveyed the dismal gray surroundings that he was defending. Lhassi had never been a beautiful planet, but even he found the darkness to be a little much for him, given that his home planet of Tersak was utterly beautiful and blue. Nevertheless, Lhassi was ideally located right in the center of Gorog territory, and his father had deemed it a perfect place to build one of their labor camps. Later, he expanded the camp and made it the center for the empire's principal production lines. Tanks, pieces for starfighters, weapons and other wartime tools were made here, made using the raw materials shipped from other camps, such as Skorjion. Thus, it was absolutely critical that they could hold the camp and prevent it from suffering the same fate as Skorjion. They had herded all of the slaves into bunkers to prevent their escape in the chaos, but it would not matter if Rhozadar fell.

He knew that the Coalition was close. He could see his troops filtering out to the northeast, to meet an army that had supposedly landed beyond the shield generator and was approaching. He had figured that Shane would try to attack. The opportunity to completely shut down over half of their war production was too great to ignore. He hoped that he had brought in enough men to defend the camp. He had four thousand soldiers all lined up to defend the camp, after he had contributed a few extra rifles to the Anich campaign. Dormak approached him from behind.

"We just received word that Shane is not leading the campaign from the *Justice*, as we previously thought," the warden told him. "Apparently, he had to stay behind on Arajor, so his squadron leader, Vorlax, is acting in his stead."

"Who?"

Dormak pulled up Vorlax's profile on the hologram. "He's Shane's commander of his personal fighter squadron, and a very skilled tactician as well. He's incredibly deliberate with his battlefield advances and is known for causing high Gorog casualties whenever he's involved in a battle. But he's not Shane."

Orvag nodded. "That's good. But even so, Vorlax is a talented pilot, and thus he will know some strategies to outmaneuver our army."

"Yes, sir," replied the warden. "But they can't really do much damage without disabling the shields first. Their dive bombers won't be able to get through to destroy the factories with them still up."

"Yes," replied Orvag, staring at the largely empty camp. "What is their plan to destroy the shields? They wouldn't dare send a whole army to wade through Gorog forces just to flip one switch."

"Maybe they're planning on sending a small strike force to shut the shields down?" suggested Dormak.

"Possibly," replied the king, adjusting his cloak strap with his beard of tentacles. "I want every available Gorog not engaging with the enemy out on the gray fields to be extra vigilant with their patrols from this point forward. If they see any Coalition soldiers, I want to know about it!"

"Yes, sir!" Dormak ran out of the room, leaving Orvag to turn back to the window and watch the distant explosions from troops attacking each other begin to sound off in the old lava basin.

The strike team reached the wall of the camp, where it was just a ten-foot jump down from the edge of the ridge to the cobbled rampart down below. Troops began to hop down onto the wall, doing their best to stick a silent landing. They began to disperse out into the camp, rifles pointing forward, ready to shoot if a Gorog showed its tall head. Daniel scooted to the edge of the rock face, then lowered himself down onto the wall, bending his knees to absorb the impact. Vraxis and Foulor followed, Vraxis sticking the landing, while Foulor clumsily demonstrated why he was not the most agile of aliens and keeled over when he landed. Max leapt off the wall like a predator and came down on all fours, barely even breaking his stride in the process. Daniel pulled his pistol and came beside the twins.

"Where to?" he asked.

"I haven't been to this part of the camp that much," hissed Vraxis. "But if we cut through between those two buildings, we should avoid two major Gorog hotspots."

"You lead the way," replied Daniel. "

They scampered down the nearest stairwell, and proceeded through the camp floor, Daniel's nerves completely shot from fear of discovery. He had his pistol drawn at all times, scanning the surroundings for signs of enemies. Foulor looked equally paranoid. Vraxis just kept low and did little else to betray what he was feeling. Max just sprang through the camp grounds, muffling his footsteps as he did. Around them, the rest of the infiltration party, about 75 troops in total, advanced, growing closer to the shield generator plant at the heart of the complex. They passed between run-down buildings and underneath the barrels of turrets, which darkly loomed over them in the shadowy light.

They were almost a third of the way to their target and not a single Gorog had opened fire. Daniel's confidence began to come back, as he started to wonder if their task was doable.

Then a hailstorm of laser fire came from a ring around them.

At least thirty Gorogs emerged from atop the roofs of buildings, all of them drawing weapons and opening fire on the Coalition soldiers below. Four soldiers near Daniel went down in a matter of moments, while everyone else scrambled for any cover that they could find. Daniel ran out of the open and under the eave of a small hut. There he took his pistol and began to open fire on the Gorogs on the opposite roof. He shot one in the chest and sent it plummeting off the side of the building to splat on the ground. The twins took shelter behind him, while Max started to ascend the side of the nearest building, intent on getting up close with the attacking Gorogs.

"There goes your element of surprise!" Vraxis yelled, as if he was disciplining Daniel. "Every Gorog within range is going to be heading this way now!" And then he ducked as a Gorog launched an RPG, which missed his target and exploded a speeder parked next to one of the buildings.

The blast was big enough for Orvag, in his crow's nest, to witness. Dormak saw it too. "Down there!" he said, pointing at the tiny strands of laser fire that were darting between buildings. "There's your strike team!"

Orvag did not need telling twice. He ran to the nearest intercom. "As many troops as you can spare from the forward assault, send them back to the camp! There is a strike team invading, and they're going for the shield generator plant!"

Down on the ground, the Gorogs advanced, pushing on the trapped Coalition soldiers, sniping them out of their cover one by one. The soldier right next to Daniel was dropped by a well-placed laser shot to the head, causing him to duck down in terror. There was another explosion nearby that rang his eardrums. The blast dislodged a chunk of a building's wall off, which fell towards Foulor, who was paying attention to the Gorog fire coming from ahead.

"Foulor! Watch out!" yelled Daniel leaping from his cover and moving to push him aside. Remarkably, he was able to move the much bigger alien out of the way before the debris impacted the ground where he was with a loud thud.

"Thank you for saving my life!" said Foulor, staring at the massive hunk of building that was lying in pieces just a few inches from him.

"You're welcome!" Daniel barely turned to him as he immediately pivoted to shooting back at the enemy.

"Enough playing in the dirt, Foulor! We need to get to that shield generator room before the entire army arrives!" Vraxis yelled. He shoved his old rifle into Daniel's face. "Give me a weapon, a proper weapon, so that we may help you!"

"Not a chance!" Daniel yelled back. "You'd turn on us in an instant!"

"Alright then, give my *brother* a proper weapon!"

Daniel stopped firing at the rooftops. He considered the words of Vraxis. Foulor would be a safer bet than Vraxis, since he would be less likely to turn on them. He looked at his surroundings, seeing that the fallen soldier next to him had a grenade belt on, and made a decision.

"Foulor!" he called, shooting another Gorog down as he said it.

"Yes?" came a weak voice from where Foulor was cowering.

"See those grenades?" Daniel pointed to the bandolier. "Take them and start clearing us a path to the shield generator room!"

Foulor looked confused. "You serious?"

"Dead serious! Get to throwing, it's what you do best!"

Despite the battle raging around them, Foulor's face

brightened immediately, and he reached out for the bandolier, taking it from the dead soldier. He put it on himself, grabbed two grenades, one in each hand, and, to the shock of every trooper on that battlefield, ran straight out into the open pathway, yelling as if he was facing off against a foe four times his size.

"Idiot's going to get himself killed!" groaned Vraxis, sounding more annoyed than worried that his brother was about to die.

Yet despite dozens of Gorogs shooting at him, nothing fazed Foulor, who started throwing grenades up into Gorog hideouts and cover, causing the troops to scatter before the device detonated. "He's clearing a path for us!" yelled the squadron commander. "Everyone follow the crazy bounty hunter!"

The soldiers scrambled out of their cover and pushed forward at a fast pace, shooting down stray Gorogs who dared to show their face. Ahead, Foulor was charging in more or less the correct direction, clearing out camped Gorogs who were lying in wait to ambush them. They passed the bodies of dead Gorogs and Coalition soldiers, but thankfully, the squadron commander, the one carrying the key card to the shield generators, was still up and running. Sporadic bouts of fire came flying around them, but most of it missed them as they ran through narrow passageways and past large areas of cover. They were covering ground fast, thanks largely to Foulor's efforts. But when they were only twenty yards from their target, they ran straight into Foulor, who had stopped, panting.

"Out of grenades," he gasped. To Daniel's surprise, he wasn't lying; the entire bandolier, which was full when Foulor had taken it, was completely empty. Even Vraxis was in shock.

"You used an entire bandolier of grenades just blowing up Gorog cover?" he said, slightly dumbfounded.

Foulor nodded. "There may have been a few that I just threw into a building or two, just for fun," he admitted.

Before Vraxis had a chance to speak, likely to chastise his brother for wasting grenades on building demolition, Max poked his head down from a nearby roof. "Less talking and more moving!" he barked down at them. "The generator controls are inside that building there, with the domed roof! Your way is clear!"

Daniel nodded, then turned to see all of the Coalition soldiers standing around aimlessly. "You heard him! Let's get moving!" he shouted at them, frustrated with their lack of haste. He sprinted out into the open, covering the remaining distance left in no time at all. After turning to their commander, who nodded, the other soldiers joined him beside the building, pressing against the wall as close as they could. They could see no Gorogs on the roofs, and with everyone gripping their weapons tightly, they inched around the wall bit by bit until they were right next to the door. Beyond that, the shield's control panel.

One of the soldiers slowly opened the door, and the others started to filter in. The sounds of Gorogs yelling and lasers firing began to escape from the building, but within a few seconds silence returned. Daniel poked his head into the building, seeing a bunch of alien bodies on the floor dressed up in white uniforms, along with three Coalition troops.

"All clear!" one of the soldiers hissed, and the rest of the strike team cautiously entered the building, save for two who waited outside to watch for approaching Gorogs. The commander entered the building, holding the vital key card in one hand. "Find the control panel!"

The shield generator whirred with power as the soldiers spread out through the building. The structure was a maze of power banks, cabling, and pipes, and it took a moment to find the controls. Once the soldier had identified it, Vraxis and everyone else came scampering over, moving to power the shields down, for they knew that the instant they shut them down, the dive bombers would be launching from above to flatten the camp.

"Give me the key card," ordered Vraxis, bending down in front of the controls in front of everyone. The commander obeyed, handing him the slip, which was inserted into a card reader on the upper right. The scanner came on, and after a moment, the device flashed green, and the monitors all switched on, allowing Vraxis access. The hunter immediately got to work, pushing buttons and disconnecting all of the wiring from the generator, before finally pulling the plug by hitting the emergency shutoff button. The device powered down, the whirring slowly dying away as the machine's source of energy ran dry.

The commander immediately messaged Vorlax. "The shields have been disabled! You're all clear to send in the bomb squad!"

"Excellent work!" replied Vorlax. "Now get your men out of there before the whole camp is destroyed!"

Before they left, Max ripped open the control panel and tore out the wiring so the Gorogs could not switch the shields back on, sending components scattering onto the floor. Once the control panel was a mess of destroyed electronics, the group hastily ran out of the building, back the way they came. All they had to do was reach the far wall and then they'd be safe from the attack.

"The shields are down!" Dormak said urgently. "That strike team reached the generator building!"

The radar beeped from the side, and the warden went to check on it. "And it appears a squadron of bombers are heading this way right now!"

"Where are the troops I ordered?" demanded Orvag, scanning the surroundings for the army he had requested.

454

"Still bogged down with the Coalition army, sir," replied Dormak grimly.

Orvag was fuming. He would not tolerate another defeat under his watch, and especially not one this severe. "Tell the army to pull back. I don't care how many men we lose to the Coalition's forces. Man the anti-ship guns and blow those bombers out of the sky. Use the tanks if you have to!" He stormed past Dormak, approaching the elevator shaft that went down all the way to ground level.

"Where are you going?" asked Dormak.

"I'm going down there myself," replied the king, hatred written on his face. "Stay up here and direct the battle for me. You're in charge now."

"What are you going to do against that entire squadron?"

Orvag left the elevator shaft and stared down to where the Coalition strike team was fleeing through the camp. His eyes fell on one particular individual, who was not in uniform, nor was carrying any rifle. They turned around to reveal a young face, one that Orvag had seen not long ago. His throat let out a low growl.

"I won't need to deal with the entire squadron," he said, eyes narrowing on Daniel's head. "I only need to take out one."

Dormak nodded. "I've sent every Gorog in the camp to intercept the approaching forces before they can escape."

"Good. Shoot down the cliff face as well. Whatever you have to do to keep them stuck in the camp, do it."

"And the boy?"

"He's about to wish that he had never been born."

Back on the ground, Daniel and the group were sprinting towards the wall they had entered in, hoping to reach it and scale up the cliff wall away from the camp. They passed the wreckage of buildings leftover from Foulor's grenades, and were passing tons of Gorog bodies, all from the ambush from earlier. They were close, and as far as they could tell, there were no Gorogs nearby.

They were now in sight of the wall, but as the troops started climbing the stairway up to the ramparts, Daniel heard a strange noise from behind. He turned around and saw one of the mounted turrets start to turn their way. "No, wait!" he called out, dragging Foulor back before he, too, climbed the stairs. Vraxis had also noticed the guns, and scrambled away from the wall. The turrets fired, and a huge hole was blown into the stone wall, sending cobblestones and Federation soldiers flying through the air like rag dolls. Max ran to Daniel's side and knocked aside two stones that were on course to shatter Daniel's spine. The wall collapsed into a heap of dust, leaving their planned exit unusable.

The commander's body poked out from below the rubble, his eyes staring straight ahead. Daniel estimated that over half of the surviving squadron had been eliminated by that single blast. And now there were more shots being fired their way, one of which vaporized a surviving troop, who screamed as he dissolved into ash. Everyone again dove behind cover, out of sight of the turret's giant barrels.

"Now what?" Foulor asked Daniel's group, who were all crouched next to each other behind a wall.

"We find a different way out," said Daniel. "And try to take out those turrets along the way so that the bombers can do their work without being fired upon."

"How?" asked Max. "We don't exactly have anymore grenades after Foulor here used up every single one!"

Daniel scanned their surroundings, and saw that one of the dead Coalition soldiers was carrying an RPG of some sorts. "The rocket launcher!" he said.

"Daniel, don't do it!" warned Max, sensing what he was about to do, but Daniel rolled out into the open before he could say anything else. He scooped up the weapon as he stood back up, pivoted to aim right at the turret, and launched the rocket. The force launched him backwards, into a parked speeder, while the missile left a trail of smoke that dispersed into the wind. The turret was hit right beside one of the gun barrels, and the whole thing erupted in flames, creating a giant torch that was visible for miles. Everyone shielded their eyes as the light died away.

Before everyone could blink out the bright spots in their vision and resume their search for a way out, hundreds of Gorogs came charging around the bend, all soldiers from the army that Orvag had initially deployed into the field. Streams of laser fire once again began to rain down around the vastly outnumbered squadron of Coalition soldiers, who took up as much cover as they could and blasted away at as many Gorogs as they could see. Daniel ran out of the street and around to the other side of the building, intent on escaping as soon as possible. He ducked behind an empty oil barrel and fired two more rounds from his pistol, shooting an enemy soldier dead in the process. Max joined him there, watching the corner for any snooping Gorogs. All he could see though were the crouched forms of other Coalition troops as they fought for their lives.

"Where did Vraxis and Foulor go?" the lizard yelled, looking around wildly for the two Travashians.

"You lost them?" Daniel cried, shooting down two more Gorogs with well-placed shots from his weapon.

"They were right next to me a second ago!" the lizard protested.

A few Gorogs broke off from the main pack and rushed their hiding place, armed with short swords. As they came near, Max leaped out from behind the barrel and viciously dispatched all of them with ruthless efficiency, ripping into one of them with his claws. In the process, Daniel was accidentally sprayed with blue blood, causing him to miss one of his shots. "Max!" he shouted, wiping his forehead with his hand and causing his fingers to come back sticky. "Gross!"

Max finished off the second guard, and jumped back behind their cover. "It's some blood! It's not poisonous!"

They continued to hold down their position as best as they could, but after several more shots, Daniel's magazine had been completely drained of plasma. "I'm out of ammunition!" he yelled, tossing his pistol aside and grabbing the rifle of one of the killed Gorogs. He opened fire, shooting down another wave of Gorog soldiers that were rushing their spot.

From above, a low droning sound came, and when Daniel looked up, at least a dozen small, nimble-looking fighters were dropping towards the camp. "Bombers!" exclaimed Max. "We need to get out of here now before those things destroy the whole camp!"

"What about the others?" responded Daniel forcefully, glancing over to see that the one Coalition soldier in their view had been shot in the head and killed.

"Leave them! It's every man for himself at this point!" Max looked past Daniel to where the stone wall went past the ridge edge. Smack in the middle was another stairway up to the ramparts. "The stairs!" he said, pointing. "If we can get up those stairs, we can jump down to the other side and run for the landing zone!"

"Okay!" Daniel did not have time to question the decision, but if it got them out of the camp, he would take it. He fired several more rounds with the stolen rifle, then bolted across the alleyway and took shelter behind a guardhouse, killing three more Gorogs while taking heavy fire in the process. Max bounded across, managing to get shot in the hip, but continuing uninhibited to the other side. The lizard collapsed behind Daniel, grumbling in pain loudly.

"They got me!" Max yelled, clutching his hip with his left hand.

"Can you walk?" Daniel inquired, raising his voice to

speak over the ceaseless sounds of lasers firing.

Max nodded.

"Then let's make a break for the stairs on the count of five, okay?" Daniel gripped his gun and laid down some more covering fire. There were still way too many Gorogs to deal with, and there was no way that they would be able to take them all on. They had to get out before their enemy's number was too many. "One…two…three…four…"

Before he could hit *five*, a huge bomb dropped from the sky, released by one of the dive bombers, and slammed into the side of the building above the Gorogs. The wall collapsed into huge chunks of rubble, all of which fell right onto the army, sending a huge cloud of dust that spread out through the street, blinding everyone. Another bomb followed the first, and landed in almost the same spot, taking care of any soldiers that had survived the first one.

Daniel lowered his rifle. "The way's clear!" he said, standing up. "Let's go now before more Gorogs arrive!"

He scampered out from behind the guardhouse with Max limping behind him. Around them, the bombers were in the process of leveling Rhodazar. Behind them, the bombs were coming in hard and fast, leaving plumes of fire behind as markers. The mounted turrets threw up a thick veil of laser fire in retaliation, downing several ships in the process, which crashed into buildings. Daniel was within sight of the stairs, he had only a few more yards to go.

"Daniel Phillips! How exciting is this?"

He stopped dead in his tracks at the mention of his name. By that voice as well. He recognized that voice, the way it delivered his name with such contempt. Max's low growl betrayed the one who was approaching them. He turned around.

King Orvag was approaching from in front of a wall of fire, his royal robes blowing in the wind, stirred up by the Coalition ships as they flew overhead. He was even more massive in person than Daniel had ever imagined, his forehead at least a couple inches taller than his own. Those burning yellow eyes were narrowed dangerously thin, and the king's mock beard of tentacles waved in the wake of the bombers. There were two swords strapped onto his back, each of which were curved slightly and probably wickedly sharp as well. A cold lump formed in the back of Daniel's throat as he realized that this was Orvag. The King of the Gorogs and the most evil ruler in the galaxy. And he was standing just twelve feet away.

"I've heard so much about you these past few days!" the king continued, and Daniel gripped his rifle a little tighter as he leveled the barrel straight at Orvag's chest. "You've caused me quite a few headaches recently! And no doubt you are a big reason for why the Coalition is overhead, spewing out bombs to destroy my labor camps!"

Max let loose another low growl. Daniel's finger rested on the rifle trigger, but he did not depress it. "What do you want?" he demanded, keeping the weapon aimed at Orvag.

The king spread his arms out in a welcome gesture. "I would advise keeping that rifle away from my chest," he warned. "Unless…you don't want to see your mother again?"

Daniel stiffened until he was as rigid as a board. "Where is she?" he demanded, refusing to drop the weapon's muzzle.

"Oh, she's fine. Not by your standards, mind you, because if she were that way she wouldn't be half dead inside a jail cell." The tone of Orvag's voice almost seemed to hint that he enjoyed this, bragging about how horribly he treated his prisoners.

Daniel's anger burned against Orvag, and he was tempted to shoot him dead right there. Orvag could see this though. "If you shoot me now," the king warned, "I will give the order to execute your mother in her cell, and you will not be there to mourn her remains! Make your next move wisely, *boy*."

Daniel was reminded of a long-forgotten memory at the

delivery of that last word. It was the same insult that Greg used when he was the bully at his old high school. With every instinct telling him to shoot Orvag dead, he slowly, hesitantly, lowered the barrel of his rifle. Max continued to growl in his throat, baring his teeth at the Gorog king.

"That's better," said Orvag, in his silky smooth yet demonically possessed voice.

"Where is my mother?" repeated Daniel, his hands clutching the rifle so hard his knuckles turned white.

Orvag laughed a truly bone-chilling laugh and took two more steps closer to Daniel, who in turn stepped backwards, one step closer to the wall. "You haven't forgotten about my proposal yet, have you?" he asked.

Daniel remembered his ultimatum from the message. He shook his head and narrowed his eyes at the king. "First, show me my mother, alive, and then I'll consider it."

Orvag smiled. He pulled out a handheld holographic device, switched in on, and immediately a live feed came up from what appeared to be a jail cell. Inside, Ms. Phillips was strapped to the wall, with three Gorog guards surrounding her, one of which was zapping her with electricity using a long pole. "This feed is live," the king explained. "At this moment, my guards are putting your mother through her daily bout of electroshock therapy. It's never enough to kill, mind you, but it sure does leave the recipient exhausted and sore for the day."

Daniel stared, wide-eyed as his mother was zapped again by the guards. She looked just as bad, if not worse than where she appeared in the message from yesterday. She was struggling to hold her head up straight and her body hung limply from her chains. Orvag shut the transmission off.

"I'll free the both of you from my custody, officially, if you give me what I want." Orvag gestured towards Max, who was crouched with his spines bristling up. "That's all you have to do, Daniel. You can have your normal life back, with all the things that you missed during your years in captivity. Is that not what you want more than anything in the world?"

A bomb exploded nearby, sending sparks flying around the three verbal opponents and bathing them in flickering orange light. Daniel did not trust Orvag at all. But he also did not think that he was lying about Ms. Phillips. He had no reason to not believe that Orvag's men would execute her the instant Daniel shot him. He glanced downward slightly at Max. He had every reason to hand the lizard over to the Gorogs. He had not exactly presented himself as the kind of creature that you wanted to be around. Although he had been invaluable during their defense of the *Justice*, nothing else much convinced Daniel to protect him. And given the choice between his mom and some strange lizard that he barely knew, he would choose his mother in a heartbeat. But before he did the deed, there was something else that he had to do.

"I'll do it. I'll give you what you want," he finally said, causing Orvag's stern face to brighten with delight. "But before I do, there's something I have to know."

Orvag's posture loosened. "You only have but to ask," the king said, his voice sending another round of chills down Daniel's spine.

"What did you want with me?" he asked. "You said that you've been watching me ever since I escaped. What is it about me that's so appealing to you?"

Orvag's face hardened again. "Oh, I've had men keep an eye on you for way longer than the past few days," he said, each word delivered in an almost snakelike manner.

"But why?" Daniel demanded. "Why take an interest in some random kid from Earth that you happened to kidnap during a raid?"

"Because we needed test subjects for an experiment we were conducting." Orvag continued, beginning to circle around Daniel and causing him to move to keep Orvag in front at all times. "And since every type of creature under the sun lives inside of all our labor camps, like Skorjion, it made an ideal testing ground."

"And what of Subject X-17?" Daniel replied. "The one you've been hunting ever since we escaped! The one that escaped with us? You want me to hand him over to you just so I can get my mom back? What's he to you?"

Max looked up at Daniel confused, but Orvag laughed out loud again. "My dear, naive little boy," the king said, silencing his chortles. "You don't need to hand over Subject X-17 at all. Why, you've already done your part."

"But why was he so important to..." Daniel stopped, realizing that Orvag had used the second person to describe Subject X-17. "Hold on, did you just say..."

"Did you honestly believe that the lizard next to you was X-17?" exclaimed Orvag incredulously. "Well, you were mistaken. It was *you* who was assigned that moniker by Dormak. It was *you* that we were watching constantly why you were going about your days inside Skorjion's canyon walls. It was *you* who we sought after the most once you escaped. The lizard...well, that was more of a secondary objective."

The words sank into Daniel's soul like stones in a pond. "I...I..." he stuttered, unable to form words. *He* was Subject X-17? It did not make any sense. "*Me*? Why did you label me as Subject X-17?"

Orvag continued to circle, bringing Daniel closer to a patch of fire. "We needed to know how strong you native humans were. And since you were the strongest of the three that we found, Dormak chose you to watch over."

"And? What did you find?"

"Initially we thought all the rumors about the weakness of Earth's humans were true, the more we watched you. But then you escaped, we found the little hidey hole where you were illegally using materials to heal you and your little girlfriend's injuries, and all our theories were flown out the window. But don't worry. Your actions at Skorjion, on the *Justice,* and here have given us all the information that we need."

Daniel felt dizzy, realizing that the Gorogs had been watching him for over five years of his life. He wondered what else they knew about his personal life; his relationship with his mom, his friendship with Caitlin…who knows what else they knew about him?

"You have my respect, Daniel," Orvag said, sincerely even. "It's not often that an adversary like you comes along and completely blows away my expectations. But, unfortunately, I cannot allow nuisances to get in the way of my mission, even the ones I respect." He pulled out a pistol and in one motion stunned Max with it. The lizard grunted and immediately collapsed into a heap, unconscious at Daniel's side. Daniel instinctively backed away from the still body of the lizard, closer to the flaming building.

"Alright, the lizard is yours!" he said, putting his hand out instinctively. "Now please, return my mom to me!"

More bombs dropped around them, sending dust cascading from the eaves of roofs. Orvag slowly advanced, causing Daniel to back up and lower the barrel of his rifle more.

"Of course, of course," Orvag said, wickedly smiling. "You two both deserve to be together again, wherever that may be."

The way he said it made Daniel quake in his shoes, and he took another step back. He was now very close to the flaming building, which was creaking and hissing behind him, and making him sweat from the heat.

"Don't worry, Daniel. I'll give her back to you…as soon as I send you off to a better place. After all, you've experienced what hell is like. It's about time you found out what heaven's like too."

Immediately the king pulled out his pistol again and shot

Daniel's right hand, causing him to yell in pain and drop the rifle. He clutched his injury, where a huge burn mark extended through his hand and to the other side. He turned back to Orvag, grimacing, and found the king's pistol leveled squarely at his chest.

"You know, perhaps I was wrong about the intelligence of humans like you," the king mused, as Daniel raised his hands slowly. "You never learned how to mind your surroundings. Not even after everything you've been through. Take my advice." He cocked the pistol. "And learn to pay attention to which building you stand close to."

He moved the pistol to point at the burning building behind Daniel, which so happened to be an active oil refinery. And inside were hundreds of barrels of explosive gas. The barrels were designed to resist external fire; but not a plasma charge. He fired the weapon, and immediately took a few steps back. Daniel followed the laser into the burning inferno, and before he could run, the building erupted in a colossal explosion, blowing him like a ragdoll through the air and sending a wave of fire over his body that engulfed him. The hot wind blew Orvag's cape out, but when the dust settled, the entire refinery was ablaze, and there was no sign of Daniel anymore.

A buzz came from Orvag's hologram. It was Dormak. "Sir!" he yelled. "We've managed to repel the Coalition ground troops, but we're still evacuating the camp before the bombers finish it off! Where are you?"

"I'm by the second oil refinery!" replied the king over the crackle of the bonfire nearby.

"The one that just got destroyed?"

"Yes! Send me a shuttle to land at the nearest landing pad! And tell the *Deceiver* to head for our rendezvous point! It's time we begin our invasion!"

Orvag hung up the message and walked past huge bits of fiery debris, ignoring the intense heat on his skin, and stood over the unconscious body of Max, who was laying down in the street, out cold.

"You're coming with me," the king said, seizing Max by the tail and dragging him away from the burning oil refinery, leaving Daniel to die in the fiery wreckage.

Vraxis and Foulor were still inside the camp when the explosion happened. They had stayed with the other Coalition troops, but Gorogs and bombs had reduced their number to just seven survivors. They were about to reach the alternative exit when the oil refinery erupted like a volcano, pillars of fire emanating from the location. It was at that point when they realized that not all of their party was there.

"Where's Daniel?" Foulor asked, looking around wildly and failing to see the mop of brown hair anywhere.

"Who cares? We're almost out of this godforsaken place!" replied Vraxis, following the soldiers towards the exit.

"He was close to the location of that explosion last I saw him!" protested Foulor, stopping and looking back. "I think we should go back and grab him!"

"The whole camp is swarming with Gorogs, and the Coalition is dive-bombing it anyways! You'd never make it there! Besides, if he was over there, he's probably already dead!"

"No!" Foulor sounded adamant, more so than usual. "I'm going to at least check!"

"Don't!" called Vraxis, but Foulor turned and ran back into the camp, disappearing behind a production line. Groaning, Vraxis reluctantly followed his brother. "Leave us a ship so that we may escape!" he ordered the remaining soldiers, before running after Foulor.

They found the entire street on fire when they reached the oil refinery, the heat intense enough to make even the twins, whose skin was fire resistant, hesitate to go in. At first, a scan of the area revealed no sign of Daniel. But upon closer inspection, a hand could be seen amid a pile of debris thrown from the building. Without thinking, Foulor sprinted into the flames, knocking aside chunks of rubble the size of a coffee table. He reached Daniel, hoisted him onto his back, and sprinted back to Vraxis, setting down Daniel on the pathway. Burn marks marred his face, arm, and leg, and his clothes were in tatters, blown away by the heat. Although his eyes were shut, the left eyelid was sagging inward, seemingly betraying that the eye itself was completely gone. But upon checking his pulse, he was indeed still pumping blood.

"He shouldn't be alive after something like that," Vraxis said in astonishment, staring at the injured body of Daniel. He turned to Foulor. "Why did you do that? We could've been gone by now, on our way to get rich and retire!"

Foulor stood up and stared Vraxis in the eyes. "Because," he began, his voice clearer and losing its trademark drawl as he spoke, "It's the right thing to do."

"You didn't have to do that? What did he do for you?"

"You said you wanted to do amazing things? This is a start, brother." He picked Daniel up again. "We need to get to the ship before the spirits come and take him."

He sprinted off, the unresponsive Daniel draped across his shoulders. With more bombs dropping nearby, Vraxis rolled his eyes, intent on finishing this conversation, and started to run after his brother, the sound of the collapsing factories filling the entire camp.

Chapter 28

Anich

Night, or the illusion of it, had descended upon the temple of the Ostila Madors. The courtyard was deserted, the ramparts silent save for a few select watchmen patrolling the premises. There was almost no sound, save for the chirping and hoots of wildlife and the gentle whisper of the wind through the trees. And in the square from earlier, Caitlin was still awake, training to control her power.

She was wielding a long javelin with a long point, which she was using to spear one of the straw targets set up in the training square. The weapon's blue green energy casted a ghostly glow around the area, and the javelin hummed with power as she spun it around, slamming the sharp end into the straw target, which thudded loudly with every blow. Her technique was no longer as sloppy as it was, although she still stumbled every once in a while. She had essentially trained for almost twelve hours straight, since a day on Anich was only nineteen hours, versus the 24 she was used to.

After some more training, she retracted her weapon and sat down, out of breath. She was exhausted, having only stopped to eat dinner and use the facilities once. Sweat dripped down her cheeks, and a lot of her muscles were sore. She decided to call it and go to bed. She had done enough today anyways, and she would likely be training more in the morning, judging by how she could still feel the buzzing in her chest that had been lingering there ever since she had told Daniel about her powers.

She stood up, took a sip from her water bottle, then left the space to go back to her room. She was ready to hit her bed, when she ran into Erwid coming down the stairs to the main temple.

"Caitlin! My goodness, up at this hour training?" she exclaimed.

"Yeah," she replied, wiping her forehead and grabbing her jacket from where she had set it down. "I just called it for the night, and I'm heading to bed now." She sighed. "I thought I could get everything done today, but it turns out I'm just not cut out to do such a thing."

"Most people aren't," replied Erwid, folding her hands over each other. "Why do you want to go back so soon anyways? Is there someone that you have?"

Caitlin smiled. "I guess you could say that." She sat down on a nearby bench. "His name's Daniel. He's been my best friend for over ten years now at this point. He…well, I guess you could say that…"

"I know you're from Earth, Caitlin," interrupted Erwid, causing her to stop suddenly.

"Well…Erwid, it's not…" Caitlin stopped fumbling her words, breathed in deeply and finally, simply answered, "Yes."

Erwid cocked her head to one side. "How then did you two wind up out here? It's a long way from your home, that's for sure!"

Caitlin's head lowered ever so slightly. "The Gorogs. They came into our town, ravaged it all, killed most of its people, and took me, Daniel, and his mom as captives. We were imprisoned in one of their slave camps for five years, toiling away, until we finally tried to escape. The Orion Coalition found Daniel, his mom and I, and we managed to get away on board one of their ships. We thought we were able to go home, but the Gorogs came after us and attacked our ship. Daniel's mom…she wasn't so lucky."

Erwid nodded slowly. "That sounds like it was traumatic."

"I'd be lying if I said it wasn't," said Caitlin softly. "I just worry for Daniel, sometimes, you know? He's not exactly the most confident and self-assured person out there and between all of this, he has a lot on his plate. And now he finds out I have magic…I don't want to put that unnecessary strain on him. It's not fair to him."

"Then don't," replied Erwid, placing a hand on Caitlin's shoulder. "I'm sure Daniel is smart enough to know that you are the same person that he's known for so long, with or without the Madorax coursing through you. The question is, do you think that?"

Caitlin looked down at her feet. "No, I don't, honestly."

"Then that's your problem. It's not Daniel, it's you. Maybe you should learn to trust yourself a little bit more, and then perhaps you'll finally understand that he cares for you, regardless."

It cheered Caitlin's mood a bit, those words. She smiled. "I'll remember that. Thanks Erwid."

"No problem."

A bell started to clang above them, from one of the towers in the corner. Erwid stood up, staring at the tower, only to find the sorcerers running back and forth like ants, shouting at each other. "What's going on out there?" she said, staring up at the rampart and teleporting herself up to it, leaving Caitlin behind to simply stare at the soldiers running around in a panic, while doors started to slam open behind her as sleeping Madors woke up in a daze.

A missile suddenly flew out from behind the wall and slammed into the watchtower, silencing the bell and causing everyone to run away as fast as they could. Erwid suddenly materialized beside Caitlin. "What is it?" she asked.

"Gorogs," Erwid replied, brushing some dust off of her cloak. "Prepare yourself. You may be using these abilities sooner than you thought."

She sprinted off, shouting at the top of her lungs to wake everyone up, while also banishing the time bubble at the same time. Night turned to day in an instant, and Caitlin was overwhelmed as dozens of figures in cloaks poured out of buildings and towards the ramparts facing the field. Even Pantura left in a daze, bumping into Caitlin in the street.

"What's…going on?" she asked, rubbing her eyes. "Are those…Gorog missiles I hear?"

"Yes," replied Caitlin. "Better grab a weapon or something."

Pantura immediately came out of her sleep-infused daze and ran back to her room. Caitlin turned around and ran to the wall along with some other sorcerers, sprinting up some stairs and onto the top of the wall, to where she could see the approaching army. Around her, the other Madors, about thirty in all, were staring down at the Gorog force. Erwid and Baracath were standing next to each other, faces grim. Even Shurgen was there, assessing their enemy.

The Gorog force was in the couple of thousands, mostly foot soldiers, but there was a quartet of tanks and a long-range heavy cannon mixed in with the regular soldiers, all of whom were wearing armor and carrying huge assault rifles. In the lead, a Gorog officer in high-ranking attire approached the wall, six guards flanking him.

"Greetings, Ostila Madors of Anich!" the commander addressed the wall of sorcerers. "I come on behalf of the Gorog Empire, and His Majesty, King Orvag. We come in peace, seeking negotiations with you for one certain slave that escaped from our encampment years ago, and to guarantee that you will not side with the Orion Coalition in the war, choosing to remain neutral instead."

Caitlin shuddered at the allusion to herself. Erwid and Pantura both shot glances in her direction, Pantura elbowing her in the ribs. "Don't say anything," she warned.

"If you return our property to us, and guarantee that you will not ally yourselves with the Coalition, we shall depart in peace. Refusal to acquiesce to our demands will result in us having no choice but to engage all of you in battle, resulting in unnecessary bloodshed."

Shurgen stepped forward, until he was standing right at the edge of the wall. "I am Shurgen, and I speak on behalf of all the Ostila Madors standing on this wall today. You come here, to our sacred temple, threatening us with violence while you tarnish the grounds upon which we stand?" His voice was far more serious this time around, and it felt weird to hear the same person that had seemed so laid back less than 48 hours ago sound so grim.

"We only want the girl and your word!" the commander shot back. "Release her to us and we shall leave you in peace!"

"And how do you expect us to trust you and that you won't attack us anyway?" demanded Shurgen, sounding completely unconvinced.

"You cannot," the Gorog replied, craning his neck upwards to look Shurgen directly in the eye. "But I will say this; we will act on behalf of King Orvag, Lord of the Gorog Empire, and he will act in his own self-interest, which, right now, is your cooperation."

Shurgen bent over the wall to make his voice heard. "Well, you can tell your king that we will not bow to his demands, and that should he attempt to take his "property" by force, that he will be met with the full might of the Ostila Madors. If it's a battle he wants, a battle he shall receive!"

He barely had finished his sentence when several laser shots came from the ranks of the Gorogs, nearly hitting Shurgen, who backed away from the edge of the wall. "Very well!" the commander replied, and then without missing a beat he turned around and walked back through the soldiers as they rushed forward to open fire on the ramparts. Everyone ducked behind the stone as hundreds of lasers came flying over their heads, including Caitlin and Pantura, who hit the deck faster than anyone else on the wall.

"Lovely!" exclaimed Baracath sarcastically. "Now we have the whole army to deal with!"

"Yes!" replied Shurgen over the constant noise of lasers moving at rapid velocities. "Give them hell!"

Baracath nodded and conjured a large shield up using magic. "Sorcerers! Form shields! On me!" he yelled. All of the other Madors on the wall stood up, blue-green shields popping up on their forearms and weapons in their free hands. But when Caitlin tried to replicate their movements, she could not. All she got were a few faint lines being drawn in the air.

Then she forgot completely about her weapons as Shurgen's head reappeared amid the rest of the cloaked sorcerers, looking very angry. As he stuck his head over the wall, through the magic shields, the Gorog commander, bizarrely, raised his hand in a nonverbal order to stop firing. Shurgen finally reached the edge of the ramparts and stared down at the couple thousand Gorogs waiting with rifles drawn.

"I never got to finish the terms of our confrontation," Shurgen explained, without any humor in his voice. "If you would allow me, let us level our negotiations fairly."

He raised both of his hands into the air, and both started to glow with fiercely bright light as the Madorax began to spread down his arms. Then, Caitlin's eyes grew huge as the figure of Shurgen began to float in the air, without any additional support at all. He rose above the rest of the sorcerers on the wall, and raised his arms higher until they were well above his head. Down below, the Gorogs were looking around in confusion, as the wall below Caitlin started to shake. She thought it was an earthquake at first, until she saw how bright Shurgen's hands were glowing with energy, and she realized that the vibrations were being caused by *him*. And not only that, but down on the playing field, a rift was being carved into the earth, separating the Gorog army from the base of the wall, sealing the temple off in the direction of the grassy field. The soldiers hastily backed away as the chasm slowly approached them, the dark abyss seeming to stretch down straight to Anich's core.

Then Shurgen moved forward, passing above the edge of the wall until he was directly over the giant rift he had just created. His body continued to glow blue-green as he drifted closer to the enemy, like some supernatural entity. The Gorogs, perhaps wisely, opened fire on him, but none of the lasers did any damage against the shield that Shurgen conjured up. It became clear to Caitlin that Shurgen had mastered the Madorax energy within him. Not only was he flying through the air with what appeared to be not a whole lot of exertion, but his weapons were defined and clear, and nothing like the fuzzy tools that Caitlin sometimes made. Given that he was the master of the entire temple, she guessed that had something to do with it.

Eventually, Shurgen dropped the shield and, without so much as blinking, discharged a huge burst of Madorax energy from the palm of his hand, which rocketed down onto the waiting Gorog army, sending a huge group in the middle of the phalanx flying in all directions. A huge volley of return fire was sent, but the shots were once again ineffective at slowing down Shurgen as he fired off another beam of energy, taking out more Gorog troops.

While Shurgen occupied the soldiers, Baracath, Erwid, and several other sorcerers leapt off of the wall, over the rift, and down onto the field, using their powers to slow their fall before they landed. Shouting a fierce-sounding war cry, they unloaded their powers onto the hapless Gorogs, who managed to miss every single one of their shots as huge chunks of their number were tossed aside by magical weapons and shockwaves of blue-green light. Those who stayed on the wall sniped using long-range weapons conjured up using Madorax energy, including longbows, javelins, and even a couple of what appeared to be rifles made entirely of blue-green light. Caitlin peered out over the wall to see beams of energy flying back and forth between both sides, the Gorog's red-colored lasers standing out like a sore thumb amid all of the greenery surrounding the base. Then one of them found their mark, and a short, female sorcerer with dark hair keeled over backwards, a sizzling hole burned into her chest from the mark of an enemy rifle.

    Caitlin tried to summon her weapons again, and again was denied. She could hear the sounds of warfare echo all around her as she concentrated as hard as she could, trying to create anything, even a simple staff. Only a few lines of energy managed to materialize in the air before her concentration was broken and she lost all her progress. Frustrated, she tried again, and again the same result occurred. Pantura, who was shooting at the army with a pistol, looked down and saw Caitlin stumble again on her weapons.

    "You alright?" she called down, raising her voice over the ceaseless sounds of yelling sorcerers and laser fire.

    "I don't know what's happening! My weapons aren't being created!" Caitlin replied back, starting to sound stressed. She tried again, and again was foiled as another sorcerer near her was downed by a Gorog's aim. In the distance, she heard the first tank shell fire off and slam into the ground on the other side of the wall. More of the Madors were jumping over the walls to get to the Gorogs below, including the one right next to her, only serving to further distract her mind and causing her to once again break her concentration. She nearly yelled in anger, but instead, she focused her brain as much as she could, taking deep breaths and trying to picture the weapon in her mind; a simple but effective sword, since that was what she was used to. Slowly but surely, the outline of a simple sword appeared in her hand, the hilt and crossguard slipping into her hand as the blade slowly formed, the energetic lines becoming more defined as the process went on. As she felt her hand close around the warmly pulsating handle, she looked up at Pantura, who was still looking straight at her.

"Well, you have a weapon now!" she told Caitlin, shooting over the wall.

Caitlin clenched her weapon hard in her fist, peering over the side of the wall again. The Gorogs had been pushed back away from the wall by a large group of Madors, led by Shurgen, Baracath, and Erwid. But behind the ranks of enemy soldiers, they saw the four tanks slowly advancing their way, each of them the size of a small bus. One of them launched another shell, which impacted the soil just on the other side of the rift, causing sorcerers to scatter before the blinding flash.

Pantura stared hard at the dark masses, which she was having trouble making out. "What is that? Behind the Gorog ranks?" She squinted more. "Are those tanks? And a heavy cannon?"

A few moments later, she found out. The dark mass suddenly flashed bright yellow for a split second as another tank fired, and then a trail of smoke came flying out of it as the plasma missile it had discharged came straight for them. Pantura saw it coming and leapt to the side as it bore down on them, but Caitlin was not quite fast enough. The missile slammed into the wall below their position, causing the wall to vibrate, the mortar to crack and the rampart to come crashing down to the ground, taking Caitlin and another sorcerer with it. She screamed as the ground tilted and dropped four stories to the field below.

"*Caitlin!*" yelled Pantura as she watched her fall, landing just a few feet from the giant rift that Shurgen had made.

The impact of the wall on the ground jostled every bone in Caitlin's body, and her head swam as she struggled to stand back up. She felt her ribs creak as she stood up, and an intense bout of pain caused her to bend over and grit her teeth. The other sorcerer was on the ground, screaming, as the fall had broken his leg nearly double and there was a big shard of his tibia sticking out from his shin. Above them, Pantura's head stuck out from the edge of the break.

"Are you okay?" she called, before she was forced to retreat from a volley of Gorog lasers.

"Pantura?!" cried Caitlin over the sounds of the battle. Then her voice was lost as another tank shell detonated on the wall, sending another huge chunk of it falling to the ground, crushing another Mador with it. Caitlin scrambled to her feet and found her sword still in her hand, pulsing with energy. She stared out across the battlefield, to where row after row of Gorog soldiers waited. Gripping her weapon tight enough so that she developed white knuckles, she started to run towards the mayhem, only to skid to a halt as the rift Shurgen had carved earlier loomed in front of her. She backed up, scanning the canyon for an easy jump, and found no ways to cross nearby. However, the gap was not that big, and she could feel her hands pulsing with Madorax energy. Her body still felt as though it was constantly charged with electricity, and an idea came to her head. It was a crazy idea, an idea so risky that she knew that Daniel would never approve of it. But with nowhere else to go, she took a deep breath, contemplated her life's decisions, and, after saying a silent prayer, ran and leapt clear over the rift, the abyss stretching below her. She then fired off a pulse of energy that launched her forwards and brought her over to the other side of the rift, right into the middle of the battle.

There were at least seven Ostila Madors battling it out with entire Gorog platoons. One of them was Baracath, who was taking on five Gorogs at once, using just a rectangular shield made of energy, and a real, genuinely metal scythe that left deep wounds in the stomach of one unlucky Gorog. The evil-looking weapon flashed in the light of the stars above as Baracath wielded it effortlessly one-handed, backing off the other Gorogs as he did, the shield deflecting blaster bolts. Caitlin ran beside him, not even saying a word, and cut down a Gorog with her sword, before blocking another's overhead attack.

Baracath heard the noise and turned to face her after dealing with another huge Gorog soldier. "What are you doing out here?" he demanded, taking down two more enemies with a single swing of his scythe. "I thought you were going to stay inside the walls!"

"I'm not leaving you to fend off this whole army yourself!" she replied, ducking as Baracath used his shield to take out the soldier she was fighting.

"You're not fully trained! You cannot expect to survive with how inexperienced you are!" His scythe slammed into the ground, creating a tidal wave of energy that knocked down five Gorogs. "And besides! I thought you didn't want to use your powers!"

"I'll make an exception for this!" she replied, using her sword to cut the legs out from another Gorog soldier. "It's the right thing to do!" She turned to face him. "Now, what can I do?"

Baracath fired off the same beam of energy that Shurgen had used earlier. "Just stay alive!"

They both advanced up the line of Gorogs, all four tanks firing at will way ahead of them. A missile came streaking by them, throwing up a huge cloud of dirt, which showered dust on all of them. Laser fire surrounded them, yet thanks to Baracath's massive shield, all of the shots were safely deflected. "Jump!" he yelled, as the shaft of his scythe elongated until it was twice as long as it was, and he spun around the blade in a motion that would have wheat farmers jealous. Caitlin jumped as high as she could, which turned to be significantly higher than expected, as she leapt at least ten feet into the sky, aided by the raw, untamed power which was coursing through her entire body, even down to her feet. She felt sparks coming out of more than just her fingers, as she felt power arcing through every blood vessel in her body. As she floated downward, she conjured a second weapon; a small throwing knife, which slipped into her free hand. When she landed, she brought her sword down on another Gorog who was not wearing a helmet, the blade doing as much damage as you would expect.

Baracath ran beside her, taking out another Gorog with his scythe before turning to face her. "Impressive jump!" he commented, taking out another Gorog nearby.

"Thanks!" she said, before ducking and taking out another huge Gorog with a well-timed stab of the knife.

In the distance, they heard another shell fire out from one of the tanks, which sailed in a graceful, fiery arc, over their heads. As they followed the projectile, it flew over the wall and slammed into a building behind it, the only clue to its detonation being the muffled explosion that sounded from behind. And then, while they were momentarily distracted, another shell slammed down right next to them, causing Baracath to go flying back and Caitlin to lose her sword as she sailed back as well, landing hard on the grass. She hastily scrambled back up, only to lose Baracath as several more sorcerers entered the playing field, brandishing weapons.

"Baracath?" she called out. She turned around, only to find herself facing opposite what was perhaps the largest Gorog she had ever seen. He was easily two heads taller than her, covered in metal armor, and wielding no weapons besides two sets of brass, clawed knuckles, which he had fitted onto the stiff parts of his finger-tentacles. He stared her down, and Caitlin knew that this was not his first rodeo. He reminded her of Greg, back at school on Earth, and that was all she had to think about before her entire body was coursing with Madorax energy, making her skin crawl and the tips of her fingers crackle with electricity, as before. The outline of another sword appeared in her hand, which slipped into her grip, and she struck the same defensive posture that she had done with Pantura.

The Gorog did not say a word, but instead cracked his

479

neck and approached Caitlin with quite a saunter, the clawed knuckles looking razor-sharp in the starlight from above. Caitlin, meanwhile, advanced cautiously. She knew that her opponent could end the fight in a single blow, so she softened her muscles and prepared to dodge any blows that would be thrown her way. She remembered Daniel's strategy when he would fight Greg back at school; use their size against them. Big opponents could not maneuver quickly, so use that to your advantage.

    The two of them met in the middle and Caitlin hastily ducked below a swing that would have instantly killed her and jabbed her sword into the Gorog's ankle. He roared, and his fist came down fast at her face. She rolled to the side, stumbled as she stood back up, then dodged another wild swing from her opponent, taking the opportunity to stab at a chink in his armor as she did. Unfortunately, this time she missed, and she had to hastily duck down below another swing, but before she could get a safe distance away, the Gorog angrily roared and swung a backhand at her. The steel knuckles' sharp edges sliced right through her clothing and left three long cuts on her back, causing her to yell out in pain and stumble forward, dropping her sword in the process. She whipped around, immediately dodging another death-dealing swing from her opponent, her back stinging like crazy as her injuries were disturbed by her movements. She could feel the warmness of her own blood seeping out, but she barely even registered that, preoccupied as she was.

    She ran to a safer distance, the titan Gorog lumbering after her like some horror movie monster. Unlike Greg, he was in control of his own movements and was delivering precise, trained strikes, not wild, out of control swings. He was clearly trained well, and judging by the fresh, green blood on his knuckles, Caitlin assumed that she was not the first Mador he had faced that day. She conjured up another weapon as fast as she could, managing to create another throwing knife, this time attached to a glowing cord of energy, before she was once again moving out of the way of the Gorog's advances. A huge left hook came her way, and she performed a motion that Daniel had taught her several years ago after Greg caused trouble in the local middle school; the drop and roll. Dropping down, she rolled underneath the swing, came back up, and swung the knife out, her hand still firmly grasping the cord at the end. But she had had no training with this sort of weapon before, and the dull side of the knife is what hit the Gorog in the stomach, pinging off and landing in the grass without doing so much as a shred of damage.

    Caitlin tried again, awkwardly spinning around to try and aim the blade correctly, only to again miss. Now the Gorog could tell that she was far less experienced with this sort of weapon, and he advanced, not even flinching when Caitlin tried again, and again failed. But then she managed to hit the Gorog in the hand, and while that did not deter his movement towards her, it did knock one of the clawed knuckles out of his hand, leaving him with one less weapon. Caitlin tried and tried again to land a solid blow, all while her opponent closed the gap between her and him one step at a time. She was sweating heavily, her breathing fast, her heart beating ten times faster than it ever had before as her death drew closer.

    Then she managed to get lucky, and another throw of the knife managed to land blade side first, passing underneath his outstretched arm and sinking into the exposed leg of the Gorog soldier, where there was no armor to stop it. He shouted aloud in agony as Caitlin withdrew the blade back to her hand, without a single drop of Gorog blood on it for some reason. At first, she felt exuberant; she had managed to hit her target correctly. Then that sense of accomplishment was replaced by raw pain as the Gorog abandoned the slow saunter and rushed at her like a bear before she could react, his knuckle-less hand swinging and colliding with Caitlin's cheek. The softer tentacles absorbed some of the impact, but it still rang her brain around and sent her sprawling onto the grass, pain lancing through her skull. Then, while she was still dizzy, the Gorog picked her up by the throat with one hand and raised her to his level, lifting her off her feet. Caitlin clutched her throat as the life began to be squeezed from her, the tentacles wrapping around her neck like a giant, slimy set of snakes. She gasped for air, but she was already running dry of it. She managed to not drop her knife as her hands instinctively went to pull the tentacles off her throat, to no avail.

The Gorog brought her closer to him, as if to admire the girl that he was about to kill with his two bloodshot, bulbous yellow eyes. It was this that ended up being his undoing, as Caitlin, still struggling to remove the vice around her neck, took the knife that she had in her hand and, with her vision becoming fuzzy, did the one thing she could do and jammed the point of the weapon as hard as she possibly could into the Gorog's face. She was aiming for the bridge of his forehead, but her aim was off, and the knife penetrated the eye of the Gorog instead. There was a horrible squishing noise as the weapon burst through the cornea and passed through the retina into the brain. The Gorog stopped smiling, his face almost refusing to comprehend what had just happened. Then Caitlin, with her strength almost gone, pulled her arm back.

She fell to the ground, her throat no longer being choked, the knife still in her hand. She felt something spritzing her, and looked up to see the Gorog fall down backwards, a huge hole in his face dripping blue blood, which had gotten all over her. Upon glancing down at her knife, she found the collapsed left eye of the Gorog impaled on the blade, a part of the nerve still attached to it. She screamed and dropped the weapon, the knife disappearing into the air, leaving a Gorog eye staring up at her in the grass. Her stomach now violently upset, she hastily moved herself away from the disturbing image, coughing as she did so as her throat was able to breathe again. She wiped some of the blue blood off of herself as she limped off in the direction most of the combatants were.

Most of the Gorogs were in retreat by this point, thanks to mostly Shurgen, who Caitlin could still see floating over the heads of the enemy soldiers, shooting down at them with beams of energy. The biggest problem were the tanks, which were still shooting at the wall and blowing out huge chunks of stone with every shell. But as Caitlin ran in that direction, ignoring the pain in her back, she saw Erwid and Baracath leap into the air and disappear on top of one of the tanks, and a few moments later, it erupted in a huge cloud of fire, the barrel of the cannon landing about ten feet away from the wreckage. Two more successively followed, as two more tanks were destroyed. With their biggest advantage gone, the Gorogs started to run, most of the Madors not even bothering to pursue them into the woods at the other side of the field. Slowly, they disappeared from view, until the field was full of nothing but dead bodies, some smoldering tank parts, and the standing Madors.

Caitlin came to a halt, and dropped to her knees, exhausted and hurting. She was pretty confident that she had at least bruised a couple of her ribs, and her back was still cut open from the Gorog's knuckles. Her throat felt dry, and her pants were filthy from the dust thrown up by the wall. She took her ripped jacket off, tossing it aside, then slowly stood up, gritting her teeth and falling back onto all fours as she tried to approach the victorious sorcerers returning from the battle.

Erwid, whose cloak was torn and whose face was covered in dirt, saw her first. "Caitlin!" she exclaimed in surprise, running to her side. "What happened? I thought you were staying behind the wall!"

"They shot me down," she replied. "I'm hurt, but not badly." That was a lie, as she was hurt pretty badly, in fact. She winced in pain as her back stung again from the scratches there.

"You're bleeding," replied Erwid, rubbing her finger over Caitlin's back scratches, once again causing her to wince and tense up.

Baracath was next to run on over, taking note of Caitlin's pained expressions. "Is something wrong?" he asked.

"Caitlin's been injured," Erwid told him. "Get to the temple and prepare mats for the wounded. And have the healers standing by. We're going to need their help. And tell Shurgen to seal up that rift!"

Baracath nodded and teleported away. As he left, Pantura ran across the field over to where Caitlin was standing, a worried expression on her face. She was still carrying her sword in her hand.

"She's alright, just a little beat up!" said Erwid, anticipating the question. "Can you help get her back to the temple, where she can be healed?"

"Yes," replied Pantura, bending over so Caitlin could put her arm over her shoulders. She propped her up as they slowly began to hobble back towards the temple, walking past dozens of dead Gorogs as they did.

Shurgen floated down next. "Just sealed up the canyon. Gorog get you?"

Caitlin nodded. "Yeah, a little."

"I see. Well, Baracath just told me something interesting. He said that you leapt abnormally high and began to spark all over your body as if there was a thunderstorm inside of you. I don't doubt that he's telling the truth, but I also wanted to hear it from you."

Caitlin shook her head. "It's been a long day to remember details, but yes, I remember doing that."

"It seems you have been gifted with Madorax lightning. Interesting. Not many sorcerers get to use that skill." He stared at her. "Something tells me there's a lot more to you, Caitlin, than I previously thought."

"Are you about to go wise sage on her?" asked Pantura. "Because if you are, I'd like to be a solid distance away before I start hearing Confucianisms and riddles."

Shurgen laughed. "I would never!"

He floated away as Pantura led Caitlin back to the temple.

Caitlin was on her mat for almost an hour, waiting for one of the Mador healers to come pay her a visit. She wished that it was more comfortable, especially given the bed she had been sleeping in on the *Justice*. It was made of a bamboo-like substance, with several layers of itchy fabric acting as a mattress. Not only did it dig into her shoulder blades, but it also irritated her back scratches, and although they had stopped bleeding and been bandaged up, it still stung everytime she shifted her weight.

She was surrounded by at least two dozen other injured sorcerers, all of which had suffered wounds in the attack. According to Baracath the last time she had asked him as he was walking past her mat, he had said that almost thirty of the fifty sorcerers in the temple needed treatment of some variety, and that five of them had perished in the battle, including the one that had fallen from the top of the wall with her, who had been crushed by a huge chunk of debris. Unfortunately, while the Gorog tank did limited damage inside the walls, one of its victims was the storehouse where the healers kept all of their special herbs to aid in healing injuries, so they were forced to scavenge in the forests for more. Given that she could see them starting to go up and down the ranks of at rest sorcerers, she assumed that they had the necessary ingredients. She was itching, quite literally in fact, to get off her mat.

Pantura had been watching over her this entire time. Having escaped with nothing more than a small cut on her arm, she had simply bandaged herself up and had done nothing except periodically engage in conversations with Caitlin. "How are you feeling?" she asked.

"The same as the last time you asked me," replied Caitlin, sounding annoyed but smiling regardless. "Sore."

"Right, right," said Pantura, fingering the hilt of her sword absentmindedly. "Sorry. I'm just, you know, a little bored with how slow things are going."

"I am too," said Caitlin, sitting up on her mat and grunting in pain as her ribs creaked again. She suspected that at least one of them fractured in her fall. "What do you think they're doing over there?" She pointed to where the healers were bent over the forms of other sorcerers, making strange motions with their hands and whispering some spell that they could only imagine the words to.

"Whatever it is, it's probably something beyond my explanations," Pantura exhaled. "This whole trip has defied everything that I know about the straightforwardness of the galaxy. I mean, I knew the Madors were real, but seeing their work in action…it's very different from just hearing about it."

"Guess you'll be adding to your lesson on the galaxy's people and cultures?" asked Caitlin softly, smiling mischievously again.

"Probably. I think I'll be adding a section to it on the Madors, since, so far, they've managed to do nothing but stump my brain." Pantura contemplated for a second. "Yeah. That's what I'll do." She chuckled. "I've lived in the galaxy my entire life, and of course it's magic that finally does me in."

It was some levity they all needed, especially once Baracath came stalking over again, his hood down and resting against his shoulders, allowing his hair to move with the breeze flowing through the temple courtyard. "Pantura," he addressed. "Do you mind if you leave Caitlin and I for a moment?"

Pantura glanced down at Caitlin, who nodded. "Go. I'll be fine," she told her. Pantura, in return, stood up and walked off, behind a building, leaving Baracath next to Caitlin's bedside. He knelt down on the ground next to her.

"How are you feeling?" he asked her, his voice unusually soft compared to what Caitlin had heard over the duration of her visit. Gone was his usual gruff tone. It was refreshing to hear coming from Baracath.

"I've said this to Pantura many times now," the reply came, Caitlin sounding exasperated but also understanding at the repetition. "I'm doing alright. Or at least I will be as soon as your healer friends over there come patch me up."

"I'm not talking about your physical injuries," clarified Baracath, leaning in a little closer. "I'm talking about your mindset. About your connection with the Madorax."

The mention of the Madorax, for the first time that entire visit, did not cause Caitlin to stiffen up. Instead, she let her shoulders drop and sighed. "I don't know, Baracath. On the one hand, I still have some grave misgivings about walking around with this sort of ability. On the other, they did save my life today, so perhaps my initial response to them was…wrong."

"And what of Daniel?" Baracath asked, prodding deeper. "Do you think that he'd still feel the same way about you walking around with these powers? All anxious?"

That made Caitlin think for a moment. "Again, Baracath, I'm just really not sure. Maybe, I mean, he's not really been acting like himself lately and it's making me nervous. I just don't know what doing nothing about my abilities would do for his brain." She sighed. "He's the sweetest person I know, but, to be honest, he's not exactly the most clear-headed."

Baracath moved and sat on the mat next to her, folding his hands in his lap. "I'll be honest," he said, a surprising amount of gentleness again filling his voice. "I haven't exactly met a ton of people over my life. My Madorax connection was forged early, so I was sent here as a young boy, and I've never left. But," he added, turning to look at her. "This Daniel, that you've been describing to me, doesn't seem like the scatterbrained type. He survived Gorog captivity. He helped you to escape their camp. That takes a sound mind to do."

Caitlin turned to stare at Baracath. "Wait...who told you about Skorjion and our imprisonment?"

"Pantura," he replied. "While you were training earlier I...pulled her aside and had a discussion with her. She told me about how you and Daniel escaped. And how he's been trying to locate his mother ever since you two got ambushed. I would do anything to get my mother back from where I lost her. Perhaps this time, maybe, he needs someone with your abilities to help him out. Someone who can help him do things that he himself could not do."

Something about that statement touched Caitlin's heart right down to its very fibers as she began to wonder if she had been looking at everything all wrong. Maybe Baracath was right. Maybe Daniel did need a sorcerer to help him save his mom. If so, then she would have no other choice than to be that sorcerer for him. She glanced down to her hands and let just a touch of Madorax spark along her fingers.

"You have been given great power, Caitlin. Very few sorcerers in our history are chosen to bear Madorax lightning, and the ones that do are only chosen because the Madorax judges them to have pure hearts who will defend against the evils of the galaxy. And no matter what you do, you cannot hide that inside yourself. The only thing that you can do is decide what you will do with the power you have been given, be it personal or magical."

Caitlin thought about Daniel, about all the times his anxiety had gotten the better of him. She thought of all the times she was in pain, seeing her best friend broken inside. She wondered what Charlie would have done, as he had understood people. She, not so much. In the end, she slowly nodded. "Maybe you're right, Baracath. Maybe I have been looking at this all wrong." She looked back his way. "Do you really think that? That Daniel will be fine with me keeping my powers around?"

Baracath chuckled. "Perhaps you should start with having a bit more faith in your friends," he said, although Caitlin could tell that he was only half-joking.

The healers came and patched up Caitlin's scratches and ribs. When they had finished applying a strange ointment onto her injury sites, she stood up and stretched. "Alright, then. Do you have any more training for me to do?"

Baracath shook his head. "You have accomplished everything that you have needed to accomplish here for now. I cannot unlock your *Plavoris* for you. That will be up to you, and you alone. What I can tell you is this. If you wish to unlock it, look inside yourself, and decide, once and for all, what you wish to do with your powers." He made a motion with his hand. "Otherwise, Erwid and I have done everything we can for you." He tapped her chest with his finger. "Go, return to the Coalition. And go accomplish what you've set out to accomplish."

Before Caitlin could respond with a thank you, Pantura came running over. "Caitlin, I just finished talking to Vorlax. We need to get back to the shuttle right now and leave for Arajor immediately."

"Pantura, can we wait just a few more minutes?" replied Caitlin, clearly not responding to the urgency in Pantura's voice. "I need to speak with Shurgen before…"

"*Caitlin!*" yelled Pantura, causing her to jump. She turned to face the blue-skinned alien, finally noticing the panicked expression on her face.

"What is it? Is something wrong?"

Pantura's face fell further. "It's about Daniel. And it's not good."

Chapter 29

Arajor

"Ladies and gentlemen of the Council, I regret to inform you that the attack on the Gorog facilities on Lhassi, known as Rhozadar, did not go completely as planned. Despite our best efforts, heavier-than-expected resistance prevented us from totally destroying the camp, and although our bombers did manage to do serious damage, our analysis of the battle shows that the factories and camp infrastructure is repairable. In addition, we lost over a thousand men, including…"

Shane could not bring himself to say Daniel's name. Vorlax's message to him was burned into his memory. The horrified voice of his usually quite chirpy commander, combined with the descriptions of what happened, presented him with all the images he needed to recognize that things had gone badly for Daniel and for the mission. Feeling guilty, he simply shut his mouth and let the sentence dangle in the air.

"This is why you don't gamble something this important on something as unpredictable as war," came Serizau's voice from the high council chair. "Because you never know exactly how a battle is going to go, even if the odds are highly stacked in your favor. I would think that after our soldiers beat the Gorogs on Revora, in spite of being outnumbered six to one, you would have known that."

They were all back in the main council chamber inside the Kraken, where all seven council members stared down at Shane, who refused to open his mouth, instead hanging his head in silence.

"You know the deal we made, Shane. You have only a little over 24 hours before we strip away your title and ban you from government service for life." The rough-skinned council member sounded almost sad as he said. "Unless you can come up with a miracle victory in that time, you will have to abdicate."

Shane cast his eyes down. "I know," he said, voice shaking. "I accept full responsibility for what happened on Lhassi and recognize that it was my fault. However, I cannot back this peace treaty with the Gorogs. I just can't. It's against our oldest laws to allow an evil this pervasive to run free in the galaxy. And signing that treaty will allow the Gorogs to destroy whoever they choose within their own land. You'll be sentencing hundreds of thousands, if not millions, to death."

"Alright, then what would you have us do?" asked Serizau, folding his arms. "Look at your people Shane! They're on the border of rioting in the streets over the countless deaths of the soldiers. We're nowhere closer to winning the war, and at the rate we're going, we never will, not with Orvag now king. Something has to give way, and we'd rather yield a small percentage of the galaxy's territory than risk civil war among our own people, thus allowing the Gorogs to conquer the entire galaxy."

"That doesn't change the fact that you're still condemning all those people to death. We have a duty, *I* have a duty, ever since the last great war, to ensure that no one is unfairly killed by the wiles of tyranny again. This treaty breaks our most sacred principle. Never in our two thousand year history has it been broken once before. Not even under extreme circumstances."

"The circumstances, Shane, have changed," said Serizau softly, and Shane knew that he had made his mind up. And if he had, then the other council members had as well. Arguing further would get him nowhere, and he had to check in with Vorlax soon anyway.

"Fine," he said, gathering his notes that he had brought with him. "If that's what you think, then fine. Sign that treaty and have all of those people's blood on your hands. I'm wiping myself of all this. But before I leave, Serizau, let me ask you this. Do you think the Gorogs will be content with the land they get from this treaty? Or will they just wipe all of you out regardless, as their code decrees? *You* can be the judge of that yourself!"

He gathered his belongings and stormed out of the council chambers, not even bothering to give the customary adjournment farewell before doing so.

His speeder docked in the *Justice* a few moments later, and he was already aghast at the state of his flagship. The hull was covered in holes punctured into it by suicide bombers, including a huge one nestled in the neck of the bridge, exposing the elevator shafts to space. In the hangar, the damaged remains of Coalition starfighters were being worked on by hundreds of crew members, some hulls bent and twisted beyond all recognition by anti-spacecraft missiles. Then there was Vorlax, whose face was grim as expected, but it was the look of sadness there as well that really made Shane nervous. He disembarked from his taxi, and the two friends shook hands, feeling that anything else would not be appropriate.

"How bad is it?" asked Shane, as they walked through the ship to the medical wing.

"It's really bad," he replied, which made Shane even more nervous. "We judged that it would be better to treat him on the ship, since we have the same medical expertise and tools on board, and moving him could result in his death." They passed injured crew members, some of whom were being rushed to the medical wing on stretchers pushed by nurses.

"Which areas were affected?" Shane prompted, wanting to know the extent of the damage.

They rounded a corner, passing into the medical bay. They entered the first waiting room on the left, and Vorlax, his eyes somber, pointed into the operating room. There, looking like the remnant of a nuclear blast, bathed in the blue light of the medical wing, was Daniel. His hair was singed, and his shirt was gone entirely, allowing easy viewing of his many burns. His right arm was deformed beyond all recognition, marred by burns, with bone and tendon visible. His left leg was similarly charred, the pant leg burned off his body by the heat of the refinery blast. His face was turned away from them, but Shane could see the hint of burns on the left side of his face as well.

"Most of his burns are thankfully within our technology's healing capabilities," explained Vorlax. "However, his right arm, left leg, and left eye remain to be seen. Half of the flesh is gone from those areas and his eye seems to have been scorched shut by the fire. The doctors are still evaluating what can be done about those areas."

"Where's Max?" asked Shane, suddenly noticing the lack of the lizard's obvious presence. Then he realized that he was not the only one missing from the room. "And where are the twins?"

Just then, Foulor walked in, followed by Vraxis. "We're right here, Shane," said Foulor, sitting down on one of the benches. "We were just cleaning up after the battle."

"Regarding Max, though, we cannot help you," added Vraxis, sitting down next to his brother. "We've been reviewing the footage from the battle, and we've discovered that Orvag stunned him and dragged him away after destroying the oil refinery. It's almost guaranteed that he's back in Gorog custody."

Shane turned to Vorlax, trying his best to maintain composure. Even with Max, who had done nothing except be rude and selfish the whole time, he did not want anyone to suffer the fury of the Gorogs, and especially Orvag in particular. Not even Max.

"How long until Caitlin and Pantura return from Anich?"

he questioned, hoping for some better news than what he'd been getting.

"Little over an hour, assuming they left right after I sent them the message," replied Vorlax.

"Well let's pray that she gets here soon," said Shane, pressing his face to the window to stare at Daniel's body. He knew that the Coalition's medical staff were among the best in the galaxy, trained to fix almost any injury that came their way, but with Daniel...he just wasn't sure.

"Vraxis," said Shane, turning to face the hunter, who was still seated on the bench. "How many Gorogs were there? Inside Rhozadar?"

"More than we were expecting," replied the hunter, looking up at Shane. "Orvag foresaw our distraction and had a huge army on standby, ready to funnel into the camp to destroy any infiltration strike. Thankfully my brother here had his explosive expertise on standby as well."

"Yeah," said Foulor, who did not look up at Shane like his brother. "It still wasn't enough to save him though." He pointed through the window, where the doctors were hooking an IV up to the body on the mat. Shane was surprised to detect a hint of what resembled guilt on the face of the hunter.

Vraxis turned to Shane. "We've done our part. Now, we expect you to hold your end of the bargain up as well."

Shane turned to face him. "Pardon?"

"You offered us a lot of money to do the things we did, Shane. We fully expect the amount you promised us, and, just so we have a means of transportation, a ship as well. We're not in this for your little war. And we'd prefer to be as far away from Orvag as possible when he finds out about our involvement in the Rhozadar attack. If you don't mind." Vraxis folded his arms, as if he were a bratty child waiting on his reward for good behavior.

Shane sighed. "Not a big deal. If it's money you want,

it's money you shall receive." He approached Vraxis. "Enough for you to live in comfort until you die. Maybe you'll even find some real friends while you're at it."

Shane stormed out, leaving Foulor looking confused, Vraxis even more so. Vorlax stared at them and shook his head in disappointment.

"And here I thought that deep down, underneath all that tough skin, after all the atrocities you've committed, there was a chance that you had changed." Still shaking his head, the commander followed Shane out of the wing.

"What's all this about?" asked Foulor, tapping his brother on the shoulder.

"Let's get out of this wretched place," said Vraxis, dodging the question. Then he stood up and left before Foulor could repeat the question, leaving him alone in the room to watch the doctors operate on Daniel.

The shuttle came flying through the hangar at breakneck speed, whipping around to park in a vacant spot that Vorlax had reserved for them. The second the engines had died down and the exit ramp had lowered, Caitlin was sprinting off the ship into the hangar, nearly bumping into barrels of fuel and maintenance workers as she did. Pantura called out from behind her, but Caitlin paid her voice no attention as she ran across the hangar and into the many hallways of the *Justice*. She did not slow her pace one bit, constantly saying "Sorry!" as she bumped into crew members and robots walking around with heavy boxes in their arms, yet still running as she passed into the ship's main atrium, dodging more people as she did.

She almost had a head-on collision with Vorlax as she ran, as he emerged behind a group of crew members running in formation. She did her best to screech to a stop, only for her shoes to lose their grip and her to tumble over, coming to a stop right in front of the pilot. She scrambled to her feet, about to keep running when Vorlax stopped her with a stop gesture of his hand.

"Easy, Caitlin!" he warned. There was no sternness present, but there was a lot of mixed emotions present in those words, which made Caitlin even more nervous. She managed to stop herself from running and turn to face Vorlax.

"Where's Daniel?" she said, as calmly as she could, which amounted to her voice breaking as she said it.

Vorlax's face went dark, and, gesturing for her to follow him, he started to walk away, towards a side opening in the atrium that led to another corridor. Caitlin tailed him, growing nervous, her stomach feeling ill as they slowly passed through the ship, past diminishing numbers of Coalition soldiers and dimmer lighting. It was the same path she had taken when she had gone to get her powers evaluated, and soon they were turning into the same medical wing as before. Shane was waiting outside.

"You made it," the Magnum said, sounding incredibly relieved, yet sad at the same time. "I've been waiting for you."

"Where's Daniel?" she asked a second time, looking past Shane to see if she could see him.

Shane's eyes darted downward, making Caitlin even more uneasy. "Shane, you're killing me! Where is he?" Her voice became shriller and she considered forcing her way past the Magnum in order to get into the medical center.

Shane pointed at the room on the left. "In there, but I must warn you…" he began, as he never got the chance to finish his sentence as Caitlin ran into the room and stopped herself in front of the window, where she had a full view of the dozen or so doctors going over Daniel's burned body.

Vorlax had told her that the damage was severe when he had messaged her, but what she saw was even worse than anything she could have imagined. The burns, the twisted remains of his arm…it made her want to throw up again at first, but the more she stared at the body, the more she realized…that really *was* Daniel on that table, burned and charred almost beyond recognition. And he was dying.

Shane caught up to her, and Caitlin turned to face him, tears already forming in the corner of her eyes. She blinked quickly, trying to dry them, but only succeeded in sending one of them down her left cheek. "How…is he?" she managed to say, her voice shaking from her rapidly chaotic emotions.

"Bad." The single word from Vorlax hit her like a freight train. "The doctors are still running tests on him, to see if they can fully repair his body. But the outlook's not looking good. Those are some of the most severe burns I've ever seen in my life, and they're not exactly small."

Caitlin hid a sob from the ears of both Shane and Vorlax, using her hand to mask it. "Is he…he…going to…to…" She tried to finish the sentence, but she could not bring herself to say the cursed word, the word she feared more than anything else in that moment, because she knew if she did, she would collapse to the ground and cry.

"To die?" finished Shane, and Caitlin nodded slowly. The Magnum sighed. "That remains…to be determined. However, I would think it to be extremely likely that he would survive. Our medical technology and practices are hundreds of years ahead of Earth's, and those are all my best physicians and surgeons going over his body. If anyone will save his life, it's them." He paused, then slowly, somberly, added: "The bigger question is, will he fully recover from his injuries? Even with our technology he may suffer permanent damage from those burns. And we've already established that he's lost an eye to the fire."

"You mean, he's half-blind for life?" asked a horrified Caitlin.

Vorlax's face was twisting her heart from the inside. "We're…not sure that he'll be able to walk again, actually."

Caitlin collapsed onto the bench, the news and images already slamming her emotions into a bloody mess. More tears came out from her eyes, and she buried her face in her hands to hide it.

Shane approached her. "Listen, Caitlin, I know you want to stay by Daniel's side, but you're not going to do anything useful to help him by sitting here. Go, get some rest. From what Pantura told me, you've also had a rough couple of days. The doctors should have some less ambiguous news to report in less than an hour. Once that report comes in, I'll let you know."

Caitlin wanted to stay. Her feelings demanded it. She wanted to run into that emergency room and sit right next to Daniel, but her common sense was agreeing with Shane. Her eyes still watering, she nodded slowly and rose from her seat. Shane made a subtle gesture to Vorlax, who walked to Caitlin, put his arm around her shoulders and led her out of the room, trying his best to comfort someone who was unlikely in that moment to be comforted.

She was not surprised that she couldn't sit still around her room while she waited for an update regarding Daniel. She just couldn't wait. Her worst fears had been realized. They had split up, and one of them had gotten hurt in the process. She was praying that he'd emerge from this alive. She had no doubt that Shane was telling the truth about the skill of his doctors, but, then again, Shane had clearly expressed doubt himself on the process. She paced around, the minutes dragging on for an eternity as she waited for her door to open. She tried to take a nap, but found herself too restless. She tried to read a book, but none of the words jumped out at her. She was simply too preoccupied to do anything else but fret.

Finally, after Caitlin had finally cleaned herself up and changed into a fresh set of clothes, she heard the door hiss open.

She hastily pulled the hoodie she had found in her closet over her head and opened the bathroom door. She expected to see Shane standing there, but instead, Commander Vorlax stared back at her, his face almost expressionless as he stood there, framed by the arch of the door. He was out of uniform, instead wearing a black set of pants and a black shirt, his tentacles forming a tangled mess behind his head.

Caitlin approached him, incredibly nervous as to the response. "Well?" she managed to whisper, her dry throat preventing her from talking any louder. "Did the results come back in?"

"Yes," came the reply. There was a pause, then, after sighing loudly, Vorlax continued. "Do you want the good news first, or the bad?"

A sort of relief filled Caitlin at that, as at least there was some good news involved. "Uh…let's go with the good news first."

"Okay." Vorlax loudly cleared his throat. "After thorough examination of the body, as well as a patching up of the majority of his burns, the doctors have determined that Daniel will not die of his injuries."

A huge weight was lifted off of Caitlin's chest in that moment. Death was out of the picture for Daniel. "Okay," she said slowly, sounding a little more hopeful.

"The bad news is…" He stopped and put his hand to his forehead, as if he was trying to find the words to say. "Although we've managed to heal most of the minor burns on his body, the doctors have already discovered a dangerous virus infecting the left leg and right arm, where the burns are the worst. The infection is spreading rapidly and already covers most of those two areas."

Caitlin's optimism disappeared as Vorlax's words did. "Go on…"

"The physicians tried using drugs to kill the viruses, but

there's simply too many of them to kill. And the virus is threatening to enter Daniel's wider bloodstream. If it gets in there it would mean certain death for him, in his weakened state." Vorlax's voice was incredibly bittersweet. "They've decided there's only one option that will involve Daniel's survival." There was another long pause, as pain appeared on Vorlax's face as he prepared to deliver the news. "They would have to remove the infected parts entirely in order to prevent them from entering the bloodstream."

It took a minute for the news to sink in, but once Caitlin realized what the doctors were proposing, she was shocked. "No. No!" she exclaimed, placing her hands on her head in disbelief. "No! You want to amputate on him? Remove his limbs?!"

"We don't have a choice," replied Vorlax. "This is literally the only option the doctors gave us. I'm sure they would've presented us with a better solution if it existed."

"No! You can't operate on him!" Caitlin's voice was becoming shriller. "You can't!"

"As opposed to what, him dying?" shouted Vorlax, the grief and rage sounding almost foreign to his voice. "Caitlin, the surgeon said that if we don't remove those affected areas soon, our one option will be gone and Daniel will be dead. For good!"

"What if there's another way?!"

"There isn't!" The two words cut like a razor through the tension of the room, both causing Vorlax's eyes to water and Caitlin's heart to be broken clear in two. The commander just stared at her, then slowly repeated, as clearly as he could say it: "There isn't. There's nothing else we can do. Believe me, I wish there was, I desperately wish there was something that we could do besides this option. Shane wishes there was, Pantura wishes there was, I suspect even Foulor wishes there was. But there's not."

Caitlin sank to the floor, both mentally and emotionally, even as she stood there. "Well…what do you need me for?" she

501

choked, her tongue having difficulty spelling out the sentence. "Do you need my consent?"

Vorlax slowly shook his head. "The doctors have already begun preparing for the cryogenic freezing and separation of the infected areas. I'm just letting you know what's about to happen to him." He moved closer to Caitlin. "Do not make the mistake that you're the only one on this ship who cares about what happens to Daniel. This decision broke all of our hearts. Why do you think Shane couldn't bear to come visit you instead? But it's the only decision we've got."

Caitlin turned her face away, hiding the fact that her eyes were once again welling up. Vorlax, seeing the damage his words had done, turned to leave, but then turned back at the last second. "One more thing," he said. "One of the nurses found this in Daniel's pocket. It was the only item they found on his person." He approached Caitlin, who looked up at him, and dumped a small object into her hand. "Does this look familiar to you?"

Caitlin glanced down and opened her hand. In it were two small, blue fragments with some words carved into them. Upon a closer glance, she could make out the words that she had carved into the stone, all those years ago. The lazurite was broken clean in two, and the break was so jagged that it looked unlikely that the two halves could be joined. The realization that Daniel had been carrying it around this whole time reduced Caitlin to tears yet again. She slowly, painfully, gave a single nod. "Yes," she whispered, her voice shaking. "I recognize it."

Vorlax took one look at Caitlin and decided that he had done enough damage. "I'll give you a while," he said, turning to leave. But right before he shut the door behind him, he cast one last look at Caitlin, who was still standing there, looking devastated. The words came out, something he had not had to speak since Shane's first admiral died in that Gorog attack, all those years ago. "I'm so sorry, Caitlin. For everything."

He shut the door behind him, but Caitlin barely noticed, her eyes locked on the lazurite fragments in her hand. She thought of all the memories that had led her to make the rock, all the highs and lows of being friends with Daniel, including his wit, his knowledge of space, and his anxieties. Now he was but a shell of his old self, burned and crippled, and they were even further away from finding Ms. Phillips. And, unlike all of the other bad situations they had been in, this one there was no avoiding. Daniel would never walk again.

She had managed to survive one devastating event after another while maintaining her composure, for the most part, but this time, she was powerless against her grief, and as her tears began to fall onto the carpet, she finally caved in. She dropped to her knees, the lazurite fragments falling from her hands and clattering to the floor. She found a pillow from her bed, buried her face in it, and started to cry.

You could hear her sobbing from outside her room.

Shane paced furiously around his chambers, trying to think of a solution to the problem at hand. He was struggling, racking his brain for any ideas that could stop the Gorogs before they overwhelmed their armies. But every time he thought he was getting somewhere, Daniel floated to the front of his mind, horribly injured, beyond repair. He balled his fist, his pace quickening, his breathing growing more and more frustrated. His anger began to bubble to the surface, his anger at the Gorogs, his anger at his own mistakes, his anger that the Coalition was about to cede the war to a group of extremists, and, most of all, his anger that he had listened to his instinctual gut and encouraged Daniel to participate in a war that was not his. He felt his temper building, a feeling he was not used to, and he eventually snapped, shoving the chair in front of his desk aside and grabbing a book on his room's desk and throwing it at the wall as hard as he could. He then grabbed a mug from the same spot and lobbed it as well, throwing it and shattering it into a hundred tiny pieces. He fell to his knees, screaming in rage loud enough to penetrate the soundproof walls, and enough to cause Vorlax, who had just slid the door open, to back off a few steps. Shane, locked onto his emotions, only noticed him after the commander had, rather hesitantly, cleared his throat.

"Vorlax," the Magnum said in surprise, hastily standing up and trying to make himself look distinguished, despite his messy hair and red face. "I didn't think you were going to be back until later." He paused, then asked quietly, "Did you give her the bad news?"

The commander nodded slowly, looking as depressed as he ever had. "She reacted about as expected," he said sadly. "I still don't appreciate you making me responsible for telling her that. That was one of the worst things I've ever done to anyone. I still feel guilty over it!"

"I told you, Vorlax, I couldn't bring myself to tell Caitlin the news. The poor girl has already had enough trauma happen to her. I can't imagine how she's feeling right now."

"Bad enough to where I could hear her sobbing in her room even as I was walking down the hallway!" yelled Vorlax, his anger now on the surface. "And yet, because you couldn't bear to deliver this terrible news yourself, you left me to do it?!"

Shane was taken aback by the anger in Vorlax's voice, but soon found himself standing over his friend. "Yes!" he said, now yelling as well. "And you know why? Because I wouldn't have been able to do it in the first place! No matter how hard I would have tried, my tongue would've become twisted upon itself! You can't even imagine how hard this is for me!"

"For *you*?" demanded Vorlax, his tentacles curling at the ends, a sign that he was crossing from angry to pissed really quickly. "How about for Caitlin?! For the girl who loves Daniel more than anyone else on this ship, who is, at this very moment, alone in her room crying, and *you're* the one who thinks deserves sympathy?!" Vorlax began to approach Shane, his fists clenched tightly as he rose to his full height. "What the devil gives you that right to say that?!"

"You wouldn't understand!" Shane fired back, becoming defensive.

"WHY?" Vorlax shouted, making Shane jump a little.

"*You wouldn't!*"

"TELL ME?"

"BECAUSE IT'S MY FAULT!" shouted Shane at the top of his old lungs, causing him to be out of breath and panting, while Vorlax stared at him, no longer yelling. He raised one eyebrow in Shane's direction.

"*Your* fault?" he repeated, sounding bewildered and out of breath as well. "How is this situation, in any capacity, your fault?"

Shane sat down in his chair, his eyes casting downwards. "It's my fault that he's like this," he said softly. "I encouraged him to go to battle. I encouraged his deeds this past week." The Magnum glanced in Vorlax's direction, looking winded. "It's by my fault that he was next to that oil refinery."

Vorlax processed that for a second, but then he shook his head. "He made that choice, Shane. He chose to go to Lhassi of his own accord. Orvag is who left him in that state, not you. If that's why you're feeling guilty, stop. That's not your fault."

"There's something else, Vorlax." Shane's voice was even more guilty than before. "Something that I haven't been telling you these past few days. Something that I've been doing in secret, without your knowledge, or anyone else's for that matter."

Vorlax folded his arms, his tentacles uncurling. "Okay," he said. "What?"

Shane took a deep breath. "Remember that conversation we had, all those years ago? About finding the right people to be the downfall of the Gorog Empire?"

Vorlax nodded. "I remember discussing that with you."

"Well, I've never stopped looking for the right people to be a member of a group like that. But so far, I've been unsuccessful. None of the possibilities in the military that I've looked at have matched the requirements that I've been looking for. They've all been strong, tactical, or sneaky, but never all three, which were the things that made the first group so effective." He paused. "So imagine my surprise when, after reviewing the footage from the Skorjion offensive, one of the Terran slaves that we picked up from the camp, a young one too, had exhibited reasonable strength in combat, had executed a tactically sound plan, and had managed to nearly reach the surface above the canyon through stealth alone. Then imagine my surprise when one of his companions, a talking lizard from the prehistoric era, comes out with a form that looks like a smaller version of the legendary Drakons of old, and his other companion, another Terran, female this time, is found to have Madorax energy coursing through her veins."

Vorlax nodded, an idea of where this was going starting to form in his head. "Go on," he said.

Shane averted his eyes like a child caught doing something wrong. "I immediately saw, in Daniel, the perfect candidate for the program. But…he was still young, and wanting nothing more than to save his mother from the Gorogs once she was taken. I couldn't in good conscience order him into battle, not like this. But with the war only growing more violent and my time to end it growing thin, I resorted to a measure that, in hindsight, I regret doing. At my request, my chefs inserted samples of *Muttosa* into his food."

Vorlax knew what *Muttosa* was, in fact, there was hardly a soul in the galaxy that did not know what it was. *Muttosa* was a flower whose pollen contained an incredibly powerful drug that, when ingested, caused whoever consumed it to become reckless, to make rash decisions, in the name of the thing they wanted most. The Gorogs had used it as a weapon to thin the number of soldiers from the military, seeing as how many of them would desert the army or die trying to defend it as a result of the pollen's manipulative toxin. And hearing Shane admit to giving it to Daniel sent his rage back up to surface once again.

"I immediately regretted giving him the pollen, and told my chefs after that first breakfast to stop inserting it into the food. But all it took was less than a gram to start the effects. So, with that unable to be corrected…"

"I've heard enough, thank you very much." Vorlax's tentacles were curling yet again, warning Shane that he was growing furious again. The commander's face was masked so hard with the emotion that he looked as though he would burst a blood vessel.

"After Vraxis and Foulor attacked us, I had time to stop him, and I tried to discourage him from participating in the battle of Lhassi. My efforts failed. The drug was still in effect, and he went charging off to battle, the capture of his mother only enhancing the pollen's effects. And before I knew it, he was being flown back with fourth-degree burns, the victim of my own hubris and the idea that someone as young as him could lead a stealth group of elite warriors." Shane averted his eyes away from Vorlax. "There. That's the whole story. I have nothing else left to hide."

From how his tentacles were bent almost double in rage, Shane expected Vorlax to start chewing him out in the least discreet way possible. Yet instead, the gray-skinned commander, whose face certainly gave the impression he was going to yell, walked over to Shane, knelt down in front of him, and spoke softly. "I have a lot of reasons to be mad, Shane. I have every right to start yelling in your face right now. But I'm not going to. Because what I'm about to say will mean more if it is spoken with a whisper." The room's walls seemed to shrink down onto them as Vorlax inched closer to Shane.

"I know what you're going to say," replied the Magnum. "It was my fault, I messed up badly, and now the galaxy is doomed because of my own pride."

"You're still thinking about yourself," said Vorlax. "And no, that's only the tip of the iceberg that I want to say about your actions these past few days."

"Please enlighten me," Shane mused dejectedly, sounding as though he barely even cared.

"You swore an oath when you agreed to become Magnum, the instant you agreed to take the oath of office and lead the galaxy as its main keeper of the peace and guardian. You swore," continued Vorlax, his voice growing more and more angry as he spoke, "to be above the barbarians that threaten the Orion Coalition, to pledge yourself to integrity, to put the needs and concerns of others over yourself, and to be, above all else, discerning in your judgment. Do you remember giving such an oath when you took office?"

"Yes."

"Well, with this one action, you stooped to Orvag's level to use *Muttosa* pollen, a drug that you yourself banned, you lied to me, to Daniel, and to everyone on this ship, you placed your own needs to retain your position of authority over the lives of a bunch of innocent Terrans, and, most grievous of all, you exercised the same twisted logic that our enemies use, where the ends justify the means." The ire in the words made Shane's skin crawl. "And for what? We're still right in the same spot that we were before we found Daniel's group! Meaning that all your efforts were in vain!"

"What would you have me do?" asked Shane, still sounding as though he did not even really care all that much.

"'What would you have me do!' Shane, anything but what you actually did! Do you not realize that, what–do you even hear yourself?!" Vorlax's voice raised itself by a handful of octaves as his anger started to boil over. "You literally deceived everyone on this ship just to have some kid from Earth, who came from a place that's essentially no different than hell, *lead your attack group?*"

"I–" began Shane.

"No! No excuses!" Vorlax sounded like an angry father as he continued to rage. "You were the one who did that, not anyone else!" He took several deep breaths, his tentacles uncurling somewhat. "You know, before today, I would have agreed with you about Serizau being a bit of a jerk, but after what I just heard, I'm not so sure anymore."

"Don't say that!" growled Shane, standing up again and staring Vorlax directly in the eye. "You know that he's a terrible fit to be Magnum!"

"What makes you think I give a damn about your position, after all you've told me?" Vorlax said, and Shane could swear he saw actual venom coming from his pilot's mouth. He began to push the Magnum back towards the wall. "You broke the oath of office. You lied to me, the one person who you actually trust enough to tell your darkest secrets with, and you sentenced Daniel to a wheelchair for the rest of his life! And, speaking of which, you *also* signed his mom's death wish, seeing as how she's still not safe with us!"

The more Vorlax yelled, the more Shane shrunk in size, his ego and his pride being smashed down by his friend's words. By now, he had backed up against the wall entirely, and had nowhere else to hide. Glancing around in a panic, he looked for something that he could say, but before he could, Vorlax was once again in his face.

"I hope you're happy, Shane," he spat out. "Because your father would be so disappointed in you right now." He paused, then added, as savagely as he could, "Just like I am."

He turned his back on Shane, leaving the Magnum emotionally drained. "Vorlax, wait!" he called out after him, but the commander slammed the door shut behind him, and left Shane without his most trusted friend, feeling no different than a criminal in prison.

Chapter 30

The *Deceiver*, 18,000 light years from Arajor.

  Ms. Phillips was pretty sure that she had been forgotten about by the Gorogs. She had been chained to the wall of her cell for what felt like forever at this point, and it had been quite some time before a guard or worse: Dormak or Orvag had stopped by to pay her a visit. The only signs that her existence was still known to the Gorogs was the plate of food that slid through a slit in the wall just an hour ago and the occasional bottle of water that was spit out by a machine in the wall every so often. Besides that, her door had not budged once in almost seven hours. She was paranoid that her guard was going to be let down, and then Warden Dormak would come barging through for another round of torture. And that was something that kept her awake constantly, although her conception of day and night was completely thrown out of wack by the dim red light filtering through from the foggy light overhead, and the lack of a timepiece in her cell. Not that it would have mattered anyway; her cell smelled like a sewer and there were no comfortable spots to sleep.
  The majority of her wounds had begun to scab over, although a few cuts on her arm occasionally would start to bleed again every once in a while from movement. Her muscles were cramped and stiff, and her right eye was partially swollen shut from beatings. Her entire body was in severe pain from the electroshock therapy she had undergone, supervised by an all-too happy Dormak. She suspected that the Warden enjoyed subjecting his prisoners to barbaric pain, seeing as how every once in a while she'd hear earsplitting screams from other cells coming through the ventilation ducts, signaling that the Gorogs were in another torture session. She had not known whether or

not they had actually killed anybody using those methods, but she could imagine that that was their one wish as they were beaten, bruised, cut open and shocked with ruthlessness. That had been her wish at one point. Just for it all to end. She knew that escape was extremely unlikely from a place like this, especially for someone like her, so at this rate she was simply living in her cell and praying to God to grant her passage to heaven sooner rather than later. She could only hope that Daniel and Caitlin made it back to Earth safely. They were adults now; they could take care of themselves. At least she hoped they could.

As she was twiddling her thumbs, waiting to see if Gorogs would walk in that door, she heard the sounds of scuffling come from outside her door. She stood up, walking and trying to get close to the window so that she could see outside into the hallway. The chain attached to her wrist prevented her from getting all the way up to the wall, but she was still close enough to see a small picture. She heard the sounds get closer, the grunting and cursing of Gorog guards, then saw two pairs of black boots drag the scaly body of some creature through the hallway and into the prison cell next to hers. There were a few more profane comments from the guards, a sound like a rattlesnake hissing, then the door slamming shut with a loud metallic thud.

Ms. Phillips watched as the silhouettes of the guards vanished back the way they came, then walked to the window that divided their two cells. Her chain had just enough length on it to permit her to stare into the other room, and she grabbed the ledge of the window with the tips of her fingers and tried to peer into the other cell. Her weak strength made her slip and fall a few times, but eventually, she managed to get enough of a good grip to where she could take a long peer into the dark room next door.

As she had guessed, it was not humanoid, not even

slightly. It was definitely reptilian, with a huge row of dorsal spines on its back that jutted out like porcupine quills. She could see its massive claws peeking out from its hand, looking like knives in the faint light. But it was only after it turned its head to face the door and she could see its glowing yellow eyes and vertical pupils that she recognized it.

"Max?" she said, shocked to see the lizard again.

"Ughhh…you?!" Max likewise said in a surprised voice. "I thought you were dead!"

"I thought you were safe!" Ms. Phillips retorted, looking behind the lizard for any sign of Daniel or Caitlin. Given how she had last seen them with the lizard, during the raid, she could only assume that they were somewhere nearby. "Where's Daniel and Caitlin? Are they alright?"

"They should be fine…or at least I hope they are." Max seemed more interested in figuring out the locking mechanism to his cell door than to the plight of his friends.

"Did they not go straight back to Earth?"

"No. They did not."

Ms. Phillips sighed. So her one wish for them did not come true. Great. "Well, where are they now?"

"Relax, Ms. Phillips," the lizard said, clearly hearing the worry in her voice. "They're both fine. Just fine. They're still with Shane, at least that's where I think they are."

All the lizard got was a blank stare. "That's not very helpful, Max," she told him.

The lizard groaned in annoyance. "Well, that's the best I can do. Still, if anyone's going to keep them safe, it's him."

That eased Ms. Phillips just a bit, but there was still something that she felt was not right. "So, why are you here and not they?" she asked Max. "I thought you all were together."

"We were," Max replied dryly. "That was, until Orvag sent the Coalition a message, and he must've mentioned that you were still alive, because Daniel decided to lead an entire group of soldiers by himself back into Gorog territory to find and rescue you, and I got stunned in the process and captured. Oh, and did I mention that Caitlin's basically a witch at this point? It's true, we found out that she has magical powers that only a few possess. Did I mention that?"

Ms. Phillips could not even register what she had just heard. At any other point, she would have laughed and treated it all as a big joke. But given that she had done that when some of her old friends said that they believed in aliens, and she was now in a prison cell aboard an alien starship, she decided to assume that it was true. Which was not exactly comforting to say the least. "Caitlin has what now?" was all she managed to get out of herself.

Max shook his head and laid down on the floor of his cell. "What does it matter, anyway?" he said, looking like a dog that was just yelled at by its owner. "We're stuck here. And this isn't some random Gorog cruiser that we're on either. This is the *Deceiver*, the flagship of their entire navy." He picked his head up to look at the window. "Speaking of which, how did you end up in the belly of the most high-profile ship in this corner of the galaxy?"

Ms. Phillips shrugged, and gritted her teeth with discomfort from the pain that resulted. "You're asking the wrong person," she admitted. "I just complied with what they told me to do, be it awake or unconscious. I didn't really bother to ask where they were taking me."

Max stood up, and approached the window to look Ms. Phillips in the eye. "Have you been to speak with a large Gorog, bigger than Warden Dormak even, who has really long tentacles growing off his chin, a crown that always adorns his head, and an ego the size of a planet?"

Ms. Phillips nodded. "Yes, I have. Twice actually." She thought for a second. "The first time it was for a round of torture, but the second's...my memory's really foggy on the matter.

Dormak had just done me in with a brutal round of electroshock therapy, so I wasn't really thinking straight, but I seem to recall hearing something about delivering a message to someone, I couldn't tell you who though."

"That was the Gorog king that you were meeting. Orvag," explained Max, a primal growl building in his throat. "He's the most vile, inhumane creature ever to walk this galaxy. He was the one who created the labor camp programs that you and Daniel became a part of. He, more than his fellow Gorogs, is a force that will end you in a second if you do not play it safe around him. He has a reputation for a nasty temper that will emerge every once in a while, and when it does, someone always, *always* dies. But Shane already told you that, didn't he?" The lizard's voice was low and cautionary. "Has he been to see you since that message was recorded?"

Ms. Phillips shook her head. "No. Dormak came by once for another round of torture, but Orvag hasn't been to see me since that second visit."

"Well let's hope that stays that way," said Max, lowering himself down from the window. "Orvag is not the kind of person who takes prisoners and leaves them in a cell. Even if he does, it's only a matter of time before he comes down here and empties out the cell. And I don't mean in the kicking-you-out sense."

Ms. Phillips swallowed nervously. "Okay…"

"Let's pray that the Coalition finds us before then. But I'm not confident in their ability. Even I have no idea where we are, since I only woke up after they were dragging me down the hallway. Hence, why you probably heard our little skirmish outside."

"You resisted them?"

"Eh, one of them's permanently scarred on his arm, courtesy of these things that they forgot to lock." He flashed his claws at her, and Ms. Phillips could see the drying blue Gorog

515

blood faintly visible in the cell light, looking black against the pale tips. She chuckled. She normally would have never reacted in such a way to someone getting badly injured, but she made an exception for her captors.

Max sheathed his claws. "Anyways...how are these cells? They're at least roomy."

"I suppose that's one positive to them. Maybe the only one."

Max looked Ms. Phillips in the eye. "Don't worry. I'm sure that Daniel is still desperately trying to find you. And from what I heard Shane tell him, he's going to assist him in any way that he can. And if anyone can locate one ship in a galaxy of over a hundred billion stars, it's him. The question is, where exactly are we?"

On the *Deceiver's* bridge, Orvag admired the swirling pink clouds as he silently drifted among them, along with another, smaller battleship off his starboard side. Dormak was standing next to him, looking out as well.

"Isn't it beautiful, Dormak?" asked the king, admiring as they passed a protostar that was still being born. "You really picked the best rendezvous point for our ships. Not only can the Coalition's scanners not penetrate the hydrogen gas, but it also provides quite the view while we wait."

"Thank you, Orvag," the warden replied, humbly dipping his head in acknowledgment.

Orvag sat on his throne and reclined, propping his ankle up. "It's a glorious day, Dormak. Not have we taken care of those annoying little slaves, but we have our little science experiment back in our custody as well. Now, all we have to do is amass the rest of our fleet, and not even the entire Coalition army will be able to stop us from ruling the rest of this galaxy. Then, we can finally fulfill my father's wish for a perfect galaxy, without the rot that's poisoning it from the inside."

Dormak nodded. "Let's hope that our plans aren't discovered before then."

"Yes, let's." Orvag grabbed his sharpening stone and began to go along the blade of one of his scimitars. He peered over the edge of the balcony to where his communication team was sitting. "Have the commanders of the *Injustice* and *Warlord* reported in yet?"

"No, sir!" a Gorog officer yelled up. "They have not!"

"Get them on the transmitter and verify that they're close by!" replied Orvag. "I've been waiting fifteen years for this invasion, and I'm not going to let any of my commanders screw with my vision for it!"

"Yes, Your Majesty!" the officer replied, sitting down at his post and preparing to transmit to the two ships. Orvag groaned as he leaned back in his throne again, taking a sip from the cup on the armrest.

"When this whole war is over, and my army has lost its use, I think I'm going to feed the incompetent members of the army to some monsters," he confided to Dormak. "I'm sick and tired of my genius being thwarted by incapable soldiers and officers."

"I've heard Volkanu is rife with monsters of all kinds," replied Dormak. "We can just dump them all there, and let them see who survives the longest. It would be some quality entertainment for the both of us, especially after the brutality of this conflict."

Orvag nodded. "I agree. We both need some respite after leading this war for so long." He stared out the window. "I finally understand why my father lost the ability to rule effectively after a certain point. The pressures of the king's life got to him."

"You're worried about the same thing happening to you?"

"Not worried...just duly noting for now. It won't be as important once the Coalition has been destroyed." Orvag watched as a smaller warship crept into view from the side. "Our people have suffered long enough. It'll be a great day when this war ends and we're finally at peace again. The only thing we have left to do is kill Shane."

As they continued their long talk, a messenger ran up behind them and bowed in front of Orvag. "Your Majesty," he said, with a sense of urgency. "This just came in. There's something you have to see."

"You can just tell him here, you know," Dormak scolded the servant indignantly. "You don't have to make him get up from his throne."

"No, Dormak, it's fine," responded Orvag, rising up and cracking his back. "I could use a walk every now and then anyway." He threw his cape behind him and started after the skittish messenger, who darted down the stairs into the main control housing for the *Deceiver's* systems. They passed by two rows of Gorogs working on the ship's damage logistics, through a group of weapons tacticians, before reaching the three intelligence officers who relayed information from the main hub deep in the heart of the ship to Orvag. They were gathered around a pair of large monitors that had some security camera footage playing in repeat. Security camera footage that happened to come from Rhozadar, noted Orvag, seeing the dark outlines of the factories in the background.

"This was sent to us by some of the cleanup crew. They were sifting through the cameras when they found this clip here." The messenger indicated the screen, where the figures of several Coalition soldiers were shooting their way through the camp. Orvag also caught a glimpse of Daniel, brandishing a huge rifle, but then, next to him, noticed another figure. One that looked strangely familiar.

"That's Vraxis!" Dormak ejaculated, disgusted.

Sure enough, the green skin and horned head came into view at the mention of his name. And as the footage started to repeat itself, he caught Foulor in the act of helping the Coalition as well, throwing round objects onto the roofs of buildings, before a bright flash on the camera lens exposed them as grenades. Orvag had figured that they would have consented to be sidelined from the war at the very least. Even sent off into retirement. But to go from serving him faithfully to betraying him in a matter of days? No matter how much money Shane had offered the two of them, he could not see it happening. Yet those were definitely both twins throwing and shooting weapons with the Coalition, at the subjects of the king who they had pledged to serve less than three days ago.

Suddenly Orvag went from calm to rage-filled in a second. "*Traitors!*" he yelled, slamming his fist into the wall of the bridge, startling Dormak and causing all of the Gorogs within ten feet to turn around and stare nervously. "Who do they think they are?! I offer them a free place to live, all the comfort they could ever want, protection against their Hunter's Party, and now they turn on me?! *Traitors!*" he repeated, causing everyone to take a step back, sensing another legendary Orvag outburst coming.

Dormak turned to the intelligence agents. "Are there any other clips from Rhozadar showing the twins? Any at all?"

"This is the only one that they've sent us so far. I can request additional footage if you so please," one of the agents replied.

"Do it." Orvag's voice gave his agents no leeway. "Every last bit of footage from that battle."

"We'll see what we can do, Your Majesty."

Dormak and Orvag nodded and returned to the throne balcony, where they continued to stare out the window at the pink clouds swirling like interstellar cotton candy outside their window. The king turned to his friend. "This situation just got a whole lot more personal for me, Dormak," he confided.

"What? About the twins?" the warden replied.

Orvag nodded. "Shane thinks that he can take away my two best agents and assassins from me. Somehow, he found a way to seduce my own men into turning against me. And not just a couple of random guards; the twins. The most feared bounty hunters in the galaxy! And he thinks that he can have them betray me and get away with it?!"

Dormak glanced around, completely lost for words. He opened his mouth to respond with "Yes" before he decided that saying that would result in Orvag losing his temper and another Gorog guard being caught at the receiving end of his wrath. Instead, he cleared his throat, took a sip of water, and said, "No. Of course not."

"See? You get it." Orvag slumped on his throne, looking angry but also weary at the same time. His eyes followed as another ship emerged from hyperspace a short distance off the port side and moved to join formation with the other ships in the cloud. That was the fourth one. There were still five more en route.

"Is the army being prepared down in the hangar?" the king asked Dormak.

"They should be," replied Dormak.

"Good. Have Captain Hoch inform the soldiers that they are free to use whatever violent means they want once we eventually get to Arajor. But tell them that they are forbidden to harm Shane. I want that slimy bastard to be skewered like the rotten fish that he is on the point of my sword, if it's the last thing I do!"

Chapter 31

Arajor, on board the *Justice*

Mirrors had become the one thing that Daniel hated more than anything else.

He had woken from his coma, still groggy and still sore, his skin tingling. He had been confused when he had opened his eyes, on a great many things even, including what time it was, where he was, and, strangest of all, why he could only see the right side of his surroundings. And why only his left arm was there to push him into a sitting position. Then he had seen Shane and Caitlin sitting on the chairs in the medical room, their presence telling him that he was safe back on board the *Justice*, but their faces telling him something else entirely. And once Daniel had asked about his status, it took just one gesture from Shane towards the mirror next to his bed to reveal the horrific scarring around his left eye, or, more accurately, left eye socket. A steel patch covered it up, but Daniel did not need confirmation to know that there was no eye underneath that plate. He then discovered the truncated stumps of his right arm and left leg, his arm amputated off a few inches below the shoulder joint, and his leg removed about halfway down the thigh. The procedure had gone well, Shane had said, but it did not change the fact that he was missing half of his limbs, and an eye. He had said that they had saved as much skin as they could have, which was why certain patches felt as though they were tingling, but that a dangerous virus that was infecting the most severe burn areas necessitated the amputations. It was of little comfort to Daniel, who found himself feeling more defeated than he ever had in his life.

Shane gave him a special hoverchair that he could control with just his one arm, and it took some effort to climb into it off of his bed. While it did make getting around actually possible, it was unwieldy and was a challenge to get the hang of. It had been a hassle to reach his bedroom, where he was now, even with the supervision of Shane and Vorlax, who helped to steer his chair in the right direction and avoid bumping into the walls and other people walking through the hallways. And it was even harder to get it through the door into his bedroom, given how sensitive the chair was to his commands.

He floated into the bathroom, narrowly squeezing through the door, and paused in front of the mirror, bracing himself for the horrible sight again. His face, marred by burned tissue, hauntingly stared back at him. There was a clear line where the burns began, as the skin became darker-colored and more uneven. The line cut down from the edge of his hairline, where a small patch of his brown hair had been singed off, down adjacent to his nose, before tapering out on the right side of the point of his chin. That was ignoring his eye patch. He turned his face away, the sight of his own self proving too much to bear. He instead floated over to his bed, parked his chair, and sat down on the edge of his bed, which proved to be a difficult task, as he nearly fell in the process. As he reflected on the horrific turn that he and Caitlin had taken in their travels, he felt his one good eye watering, the other too burned to even produce tears by that point.

A short time later, Shane walked into the room, looking equally as depressed. Daniel only paid him the slightest of glances as he walked in, not making a sound as he found his way to one of the chairs, pulling it across to sit directly across from him. Shane sat down in it, folding his hands across his lap and taking a deep breath as he did.

"How are you doing?" the Magnum asked him, leaning forward to allow his soft words to be heard better.

Daniel shook his head slowly. "Not good," he said. There was no sugarcoating, no optimistic follow-up. Two words, delivered raw and with a sort of burden to them. They told Shane a lot more than just the two words themselves.

"I wish…no, I'm sorry you feel that way. Truly, I am." And for the first time since that first dinner, Shane truly meant it. He knew that he was going to tell him as well about his plot, and he knew that he was going to face the heat again, but he did not care. He had hidden his activities in the dark for too long.

"I owe you an apology, Daniel," he said, thinking about his choice of words. "For not being more supportive of your efforts to return to Earth. While I could not possibly place your mom over the stake of the entire galaxy, I wish I had done more to help you out."

Daniel cast his gaze upwards at Shane, and the Magnum's stomach twisted at how badly messed up the boy's face was from his burns, now that he was bathed in brighter light. "What do you mean, Shane?" he asked, sounding only partially invested in it.

"I mean, I wish I had been the supportive figure that you had needed when you came to me the first time, about your plight. When you asked me to help you return to Earth. And especially once Ms. Phillips was captured." He leaned closer. "When I was sworn into this office, I pledged myself to a code. A code that states to put the needs of others over my own wishes. And I broke that code with you."

"Shane, you only ever were supportive of me and my mission. I get that you are at war," Daniel replied, still not taking the hints. "In what way did you break the code with me?"

And Shane, bracing himself for the storm, inhaled deeply and revealed everything to Daniel, about his old mission, his wager with the council, how he had seen the makings of a great leader in Daniel, how he had tried to use his own confusion to manipulate him into making a rash decision, and how he had drugged his food to enhance those desires. He mentioned how he had immediately regretted his decision, but how his own fear stopped him from stopping Daniel, and how his own inaction led to Daniel's injuries. At the end of his story, he said, "I have no excuses for my behavior. I acted rashly and in my own self-interest, and you were hurt as a result. And I could never make that up to you."

Daniel thought that he needed a repeat, since he was having trouble processing the words that he was hearing. But as he thought about them, he realized that he did not. Shane had lied to him, to Caitlin, and to everyone around him. He had been the reason for his injuries, or a big factor in that. He was angry, oh yes, and he considered chewing out the old man in front of him. Yet, he was simply too worn out to scream, or yell, or even talk louder than a whisper. He had just been through too much at once. Getting his anger in check, he simply said, his fury only barely in check; "Why?"

"The High Council wanted to sign a treaty that would allow the Gorogs to roam free on the planets that they already have dominion over. Such a treaty would allow them to kill whoever they wanted in their lands without any outside trouble. I refused to let that happen, but I also let my own pride get in the way."

Daniel found his eyes averting from Shane once again. "You promised me that you would help me find my mom and safely return us to Earth!"

"A promise that I have every intent to keep, Daniel."

Daniel's head snapped back up to look him directly in the eyes, his face a hard mask of rage, something that Shane had never seen before. "And where's the assurance that you offer me, after you just admitted that you left me in this shape? Horribly burned and crippled?!"

Shane sat back in his chair, almost seeming to sink deeper into the cushioning. "I have none," he admitted, standing up from his chair. "All I can offer is my apologies, and a guarantee that you'll be well treated by my own caretakers as long as you're on board this ship." He started to leave, then turned back around. "I'm so sorry."

He left the room without saying another word, leaving Daniel even more bitter than before. He swung his leg onto his bed, wrapped himself in his sheets as best he could, and tried to find some comfort in his sleep, where he could be blissfully unaware of his own circumstances.

It was some time later that he was jolted awake by the sound of his door sliding open again. Frustrated at being awoken from his peaceful rest, and expecting it to be Shane again, he sat up in bed and prepared to shout some choice words at the person in the door. But when he saw Caitlin's face staring back at him, he shut his mouth and bit his tongue, his anger almost melting away in the process.

"Caitlin!" he said, genuinely surprised. "What are you doing here?"

"I came to check in on you, but if you're busy resting, I can come back later," she replied, starting to back out of the room.

"No, no!" exclaimed Daniel, beckoning her back with his arm, and nearly tipping backwards in the process. "Come in, please!"

She nodded and sat down in the same chair that Shane sat in earlier. "Do they hurt, at all?" she asked him, her face expressing deep concern for her friend.

He shook his head. "They stopped hurting a while ago," said Daniel, staring at the stump of his right arm. "But, sometimes, I can still feel the tips of my fingers, where they used to be. I can, sometimes, get these phantom sensations, where I can feel the sheets below me, even though my hand is gone. I…don't honestly know how to explain it."

"I can understand that."

Daniel eyed Caitlin's hands, which were folded in a strange way. "I've been meaning to ask you, did you get your powers fixed?"

Caitlin leaned forward, not smiling. "There was a slight change of plans once we reached the wizard temple," she said. "But that's not important right now." She inched closer to Daniel. "Right now, I'm here to spend some time with my friend who's going through a rough period." She glanced over her shoulder at the clock. "That being an understatement of course."

Daniel did not smile, but instead averted his eyes away from Caitlin. "You were right the first time, Caitlin. I shouldn't have trusted Shane as much as I had. I was wrong."

"Why?" asked Caitlin, surprised to hear that coming from Daniel.

"Shane's the reason for my being like this," said Daniel bitterly. "He had my food drugged in order for me to go out and accomplish missions that would help him win the war with the Gorogs. All of my strange behavior the last few days; it's been because of the drugs he gave me."

"Shane?!" exclaimed Caitlin, horrified. "*Shane* did that?"

Daniel nodded. "Look where he's put me. Now, not only are we no closer to rescuing my mom, or returning to Earth, but I'm also now permanently disabled for the rest of my life. And all because I had the decency to trust someone that I had never met!"

His voice started to shake again, the same way it always did before an anxiety attack. Normally Caitlin would have some words to say to help ease Daniel into a calmer state, but this time, she kept her mouth shut. She had nothing to say, and that hurt her to realize.

"I'm going to ask that we leave, and head back to Earth," continued Daniel, his voice breaking. "There's clearly nothing else left for us here. Of course, I'll have to explain to everyone as to why I look like this, and where I've been…oh, that's right, everyone we knew is dead, because a horde of aliens blew our town to bits!" He almost seemed to grow larger from his anger, his rage giving him strength, Caitlin tearing up to see him so bitter and emotional. "Who knows how long we'll last, given that the Gorogs will probably come for us next, and just kill the both of us anyway!"

He was now shouting as loud as he could, his voice carrying through the door and down the hallway. "Why did *we* deserve such a terrible fate? *Why?* All I wanted was to live a normal life! I didn't ask for this! I just wanted to be like everyone else, living out their own lives without any trouble! *It's not fair! IT'S NOT FAIR!!*"

At that instant, his rage dissipated, replaced by nothing more than tearful sobbing, as he collapsed into Caitlin's waiting arms, who held him gently as he cried out all of the pain he'd been through the last week. With no words of encouragement to tell him, all she did was place his head on her shoulder and let him release all the hurt he was feeling. She had figured that this was going to happen, but it still cut her deeply to see. She squeezed his body, feeling like crying herself.

"You're right, Daniel," she finally said, whispering it in his ear. "It *is* not fair. None of this is." She let her words sink in. "You deserve so much better than what you've gotten. You deserve the whole world, the whole galaxy, for how sweet you are, how funny your sense of humor is, and how unbelieving caring you are, even about people that you've never met. And all you've gotten in return is me. The world's lamest self-taught artist, who bears magical powers."

She felt his breathing slow down, his body relaxing, so she released him from her grip. "There's something that I've been meaning to tell you for years, but until recently I never knew how to best say it to you."

Daniel wiped his eye with his free arm and slowly

nodded.

Caitlin took a deep breath, mentally preparing herself. "If there's one thing that always stuck out to me about you, Daniel, it's always been your relentless optimism and hope, even when in the midst of your anxiety spells. Even when things were looking bad, you almost always managed to find something positive to think about. It didn't always come immediately, but eventually it did. After all these years, it's been the thing that I always loved the most about you."

"That was before all of this happened," replied Daniel sullenly, gesturing to his broken form.

Caitlin leaned forward, her face full of the same hope and encouragement that Daniel had displayed when discussing the escape plan for Skorjion. "Even with your injuries, with all of your scars, although your body has been broken by circumstance, inside of you is the same optimism that I remember from the Daniel I met when I was just a little girl. And the only thing that can take that away from you is yourself."

She saw Daniel's face sort of twitch, as if he was still unconvinced. So Caitlin continued. "What happened was indeed terrible, both because of Shane's deceit, and how you got hurt badly as a result. But the Daniel I met would've found a way to improve his circumstances, no matter how dire they were. He would've seen that we're in an alien society with technology beyond anything we have on Earth, and that somewhere in this vast galaxy was a solution to his problem. But most importantly, he would have seen that others were at risk, and would have found a way to help them, even if it was from the restrictiveness of a hoverchair."

"I'm not the old Daniel," he replied sullenly. "I'm half of what he was. I'm just a nobody, Cait. Who doesn't know what to do right now."

"Wrong. That's not true."

"How do you know that?" he asked harshly, giving her a

bit of a nasty glare. But Caitlin was unfazed, and she gave his hand an encouraging squeeze. "How do you know what I am now? What makes you think that I can bounce back from this?"

"Because you're not the old Daniel. You're better than him. You have survived so much, and done so many amazing things. And if you could fly an alien spaceship like you could, you can do anything. You've been searching for your purpose all throughout this adventure. And if it's not you looking for an answer, I'll do it for you."

"Even if you could," replied Daniel, "How can we be sure that my mom hasn't already been killed by Orvag and his minions?"

"Perhaps we can answer that for you," came a deep voice. Daniel turned to see Vraxis standing in the doorway, a rifle slung over his back. "May I come in?"

Daniel nodded, and the bounty hunter moved to stand next to Caitlin. "I thought you and Foulor were collecting your reward from Shane and then moving on?" asked Daniel, confused.

"Well, seeing as how you helped save the lives of both myself and my brother, and that we were not quite as successful in saving your life, I figured that you could use some…emotional support? Although Miss Caitlin already seems to have that covered at the moment…"

"No, please!" protested Daniel. "Stay! This is a pleasant surprise!"

"I'm here too!" came Foulor's slurred accent as the larger twin barged through the door like a rhinoceros.

"I thought I told you to load our ship with our newfound riches!" his brother exclaimed, as if he was surprised to see Foulor standing there next to him.

"I asked some of Shane's crew members to do it instead, and they said yes. So I'm here now!" explained Foulor with the energy of an eight-year-old. Vraxis simply rolled his eyes and stayed silent.

"I'm here too," said Pantura as she walked in, still wearing her dirty clothes from the Anich skirmish. Vorlax was trailing behind her. "You've been through a hell of a lot of trouble these past few days, Daniel. Caitlin's right. I only met you recently, but from what I've been hearing about you, you definitely deserved better than what you got."

Daniel gave an accusing stare to Caitlin. "Have they heard our entire conversation?"

Caitlin blushed sheepishly. "I asked them to come here to help you out. I told them you were feeling down and needed some help. They all said yes, even the twins. Foulor didn't even need to coax Vraxis down."

"I do have a heart, thank you very much," grunted Vraxis.

"But…why?" asked Daniel. "Why would you all come here just for me? Some random kid who barged into your lives from a slave pit? You all barely even know me."

"That's not true." Pantura knelt down beside him, placing her hand on top of Caitlin's. "In just a short time, I've learned more about you than I have of just about anyone on this ship beyond Shane. I've learned about how you were stripped from your home, how you've never known your father, and how you desperately want your mother back. I've been a witness to some extraordinary bravery and chivalry, and it's come from a source that I would have never predicted, even with all my years of studying alien cultures. It came from the random kid who barged into my life from a slave pit."

"We're all here Daniel, because we've been in similar circumstances ourselves," explained Vorlax, as he joined Caitlin and Pantura down at Daniel's level. "I already told you about my friend. He was a talented young man with a bright future in the navy, cut short by a Gorog kamikaze fighter. I still remember when the crew spacewalked to recover his body, and the sight of his burned, frozen self as he was brought on board. I still sometimes don't forgive myself for what happened to him, as it was my fault those bombers made it to the bridge in the first place."

"For me, I lost my mother when I was very young," said Pantura softly, her voice already starting to shake from the memory, like she was unlocking some forbidden doorway inside her mind. "She and I were living in a village, peacefully, many years ago. She was out collecting crops when the raid burst in through the gates and started to burn down the homes. By the time the hunters had finished looting every building, half of the villagers, including my mom, were dead. She never stood a chance, and I was too young to do anything about it. I don't want you to go through the same process."

Then, to the shock of everyone, Vraxis, the quiet, always serious, no-nonsense twin, spoke up. "I was a strange case, on my home planet," he began, his tone flat. "The Travashians, my people, prided themselves on their physical bulk and their brute strength. I was born with neither, even though Foulor received both traits. I was the subject of constant ridiculing and mockery, until I was finally exiled from my own kingdom, just because I relied more on my brain than my muscles. Foulor had himself exiled as well, refusing to leave my side. We lived as nomads, barely surviving on the scraps we could gather, until we finally got a gig working with the Hunters' Party collecting bounties. But even more than forty years after we were exiled, I still have yet to return to my home planet. I barely remember the mountains where our cities were built, or the flying shriekers that lived in the atmosphere, feeding on the xenon in the clouds."

"What we're trying to say, Daniel," said Vorlax, "Is that we feel your pain. We know what it's like to lose a family member, to feel out of place in a group. You've shown all of the best qualities of a great person; leadership, bravery, humility, but most of all, heart. And so help me, I will not let that be wasted."

He stood up. "We want to help you. All of us."

Caitlin stood up as well, and she stood next to the others, the five of them facing Daniel as one. "We're going to help you get your mom back. And give Orvag the karma that he deserves."

Daniel felt something creep back into his core. It was an older feeling, it was almost foreign to him, but it was there, and it was not what he was expecting. It filled his entire body, and he felt himself relax, his frustration, grief, and anger vanishing into dust. Because the sensation he was feeling was peace. Not just any peace, either. The peace that came from knowing that you were loved, the peace that came from knowing that you were safe, that you had support backing you.

He had not felt it since before the attack on Salt Plains.

At that moment, Shane walked in. He looked ready to speak up, and was probably there to offer up some solution to Daniel, but he stopped himself upon seeing the gathering, standing as a group. The five of them all turned to stare at him, their faces falling upon seeing him stand there. Shane froze, then immediately turned a shade of beet red that Daniel had only ever seen Caitlin reach. The Magnum stood there, awkwardly, while Vraxis folded his arms and said, "Yes?"

Shane swallowed. "I'm terribly sorry, am I interrupting something?"

"Uh, yes," Foulor said matter-of-factly.

Shane's face transitioned into a shade of magenta, but he then sighed. "Well, I suppose it's just as well that you're all here." He sighed. "I need to apologize to all of you, not just to Daniel. I lied to all of you, and put you all in danger for something that was never going to work."

Daniel heard Vraxis audibly mouth "Darn right you did," and he managed a smile.

"As leader of the Orion Coalition, I had no right to do what I did." Shane glanced over at Daniel. "Because of me,

Daniel got hurt. I promised him that I would help him and his entire family make it home safely. So that's what I'm going to do."

"You're going to help him find his mother?" Vorlax asked.

Shane nodded. "Starting now. I don't even care about my bet with the council anymore. If I'm exiting the office, then I'll be doing it while doing the right thing at least." He paused, then glanced around the room, at the faces there, some familiar, some fresh. "I cannot expect you to trust me like you have, because I threw it all away with my actions. And there's no way that my words will make you forgive me. I can only ask for your support. And if you choose to reject it, then I understand. It's no more than I deserve now."

For a moment, the room was silent, and Daniel could see the enthusiasm on the old leader's face disappearing with each passing second of quiet. He had every reason to not trust Shane. He was partially in his hoverchair because of him, after all. But he had been given a second chance at life after narrowly escaping death. So, he shifted his weight forward, causing everyone's heads to snap in his direction, managed to get his behind in the cup of his hoverchair, and swung his leg over forward, grunting as he struggled to do so. He got into the proper position, activating the motion controls and started to float towards Shane.

"You have mine," said Daniel. "You may have messed up, Shane, but my mom always talked about second chances. This is one from me."

Shane's face brightened slightly. "You…sure, Daniel?" he asked. "After what I did, I don't think…"

"Don't think?" Daniel moved a step forward. "You're talking about my mother here. I am going to be there when she's freed from the Gorogs. And since I am on your ship, I am going with you, and if you don't like it, then, I don't know…deal with it."

"I'm going too," said Caitlin, stepping forward.

"So am I," answered Vorlax.

"And I!" Pantura declared.

"Me too!" yelled Foulor enthusiastically.

They all turned around to stare at Vraxis, who was still standing against the wall. The twin sighed. "In for a penny, in for a pound," he muttered, stepping forward. "But I want my money ready to go as soon as we get back! Is that clear?"

Shane nodded. "Clear." He faced the rest of them. "Alright. We just need to figure out where the Gorogs are currently hiding."

"Orvag told me something, when we were having our little exchange on Lhassi," said Daniel, fingering his chin. "He said that he had been watching me in Skorjion ever since we had gotten there, and that he had been taking that information and saving it for later."

"Why would he be watching you?" asked Vorlax, leaning in. "I thought you were just one of his raiding party captives!"

"No." Daniel turned to Shane. "I'm Subject X-17."

"Pardon?"

"*I* am Subject X-17! The missing slave they were after! It's me!"

Gasps came from at least two people. "*You're* the one they wanted? Not Max?" Caitlin was in complete disbelief.

"But if you're the one they wanted so badly, then why did Orvag try to kill you?" said Vraxis.

"Weren't you sent out to try and capture him?" asked Shane.

"We were," the twin explained through gritted teeth. "The only reference image he gave us was a still from a security camera in Skorjion, and Orvag never explicitly divulged which one of you was X-17. He told us to bring in all four of you, just in case, since any one of you could be him or be related to him. And that still doesn't answer the question. Why did Orvag try to blow you up if you were his most wanted target?"

"He said that he had all of the information he needed from me," said Daniel, that feeling of dread creeping back into his body. "And that he was testing to see if the rumors that Terrans were weak was true."

Vorlax exchanged a nervous glance with Shane, and Daniel caught it out of the corner of his one eye. "What is it?" he said, noting the expressions on their faces.

Shane turned to Daniel. "There have been whispers, rumors from within the Gorog Empire, from our sources, that the King's planning an invasion of Arajor, and has been for some time. But since Tersak, the Gorog homeworld, is on the other side of the galaxy, the rumor goes that he's planning on setting up a staging area inside Coalition borders."

"He did mention something like that to us," Foulor jumped in. "To act as an intermediate staging area for his army before the actual invasion of Arajor. From the way Orvag talked about it, he had been planning this for months, maybe even years."

Finally, the puzzle pieces clicked in Daniel's brain, and he finally realized why Shane and Vorlax were suddenly so nervous. "He's not just planning on using any planet for his staging area," he said, his blood pulse quickening.

"No," said Vorlax. "He's planning on invading Earth."

In no time at all, Shane had assembled everyone into the briefing room to discuss the problem at hand. The twins were there, Vorlax was there, along with his finest pilots, and even Daniel had made it after some bumps on his hoverchair. The holoprojector was on, displaying a large Gorog warship of a model that Daniel had never seen before.

535

"Listen up!" barked Shane, although everyone was already paying attention to him. "Here's what we know. The Gorogs are planning to invade Arajor, and, according to Daniel and multiple reports, will be using Earth as a rendezvous point for their troops. Since we are bound by the Zodiac Code, it's up to us to stop the enemy before they can invade the Earth and expose extraterrestrials to the world. The operation is being led by Orvag, the King, as I'm sure you all have already guessed."

Several heads nodded in agreement.

"Orvag was last sighted leaving the battle of Rhozadar, going to his flagship, *Deceiver*. It's the alpha ship in the Gorog fleet and a symbol of their might, but it's a very elusive vessel, with sightings rare, even in Gorog territory itself. We can only assume that wherever that ship is currently parked, several other warships are moving to meet up with it and amass their forces."

"The current issue is," added Vorlax, stepping forward, "Is that we have no idea where the Gorogs are currently grouping up. They could be anywhere inside the galaxy and we'd never know. Now, Orvag's not foolish enough to group up his ships in the open, since our spies would catch wind of their logs and movements. Given that, he'll have chosen a spot that's both isolated from high-traffic areas in the Gorog Empire and someplace where it would be hard for scanners to detect a large grouping of ships. But it would still need to be fairly close to the border in order to conserve fuel, within about five hundred light years of it, in order for it to work. That still leaves over a hundred potential sites near the border closer to Earth."

The sites popped onto the map of the galaxy as Vorlax spoke, all of them highlighted in red dots. "Orvag could be at any one of these locations," said Shane, pointing at the rows of dots. "And, as you could imagine, in the time it would take us to check out each of them, Orvag could easily invade Arajor, perhaps twice over if he really tried. What we need is a way to track the ships moving into the rendezvous point, so that we can pinpoint the precise spot. The bad news is that Orvag just beefed up the firewall on their navigation servers, so our intelligence agents cannot hack into them and get the information that we need."

"Have you tried seeing if any Gorog ships have abandoned their posts at the border?" asked Daniel. "I mean, there should be some stationed there, right? If any of the cruisers have seemingly disappeared from the line, see if you can find the time when they did and track where they went from there."

"We also tried that too," explained Vorlax in frustration. "And for a moment it worked fine. But then the signal from the ships went silent and we were unable to track them. And it's not like it would have been much use either, since they traveled in random patterns to throw us off, so we couldn't figure out their trajectory and where their destination could be."

"I think this is enough stalling for now," said Vraxis, who pushed himself off of the wall he was leaning against and walked up to the holoprojector. He shoved past Shane and began to randomly push buttons on the control panels.

"What are you doing?" asked Shane, more confused than angry.

"I lived with the Gorogs for years, collecting bounties for them. Now Orvag was pretty tight-lipped with me about his empire's secrets, but one thing he had to teach us in order for us to successfully deal with his defecting troops earlier on in the war was to track the signatures of Gorog ships through less conventional means."

"'Less conventional means,'" repeated Pantura, folding her arms. "Like what?"

"All Gorog ships run on a unique radium iodide-based alloy that emits a distinct pattern of radiation. All you have to do is calibrate your device to scan for wavelengths between 340 and 360 nanometers, and you should…"

Vraxis pushed a few more buttons and the red dots

disappeared. Then, with the pull of a lever, the map turned green and hundreds of tiny signatures registered on the map. "Only Gorog battleships give off a signature strong enough to register on the scanner, otherwise there would've been a million more," said the hunter. "But, as you can see…" His finger pointed at a large clustering of dots about a hundred and forty light years from the border. "Right there. That's your meeting point. No other area in that sector has a clustering of capital ships that dense."

Shane had a look of constant surprise on his face. "Well, consider me impressed, Vraxis," he said, nodding his head in admiration. "Your intellect is truly impressive. You sure you won't reconsider your desire to leave?"

"As soon as I help Daniel over there, I'm out," he replied. "But I still appreciate the chance." Vraxis moved back, restoring the original map on top of the radiation filter that he had implemented. Vorlax took a closer look at where the dots were gathered, which was on top of a large pink blotch on the map, far from any inhabited systems nearby.

"The Veil of Carathal, the Great Nebula," he said, whistling under his breath. "A perfect place as any to amass a large group of battleships before an invasion. Our scanners wouldn't get half a light year into hydrogen gas that dense."

Daniel floated his chair over to examine the blotch. "Looks like a combination of emission and dark nebulae." He pointed at two large dark patches that almost appeared superimposed on the pink. "Those areas are perfect for a ship to hide in. Or several. With no stars nearby, it would be hard to spot them even if you were already inside the nebula."

Shane looked even more stunned than when Vraxis used the radiation filter. "How do you know all that?" he asked.

"All I used to do as a kid was stargaze," he replied, using a knob on the control panel to zoom in on the nebula. "I know a lot about these sorts of objects."

"That's right, he does," vouched Caitlin. When Vorlax shot her a questioning look, she shrugged and said, "What? We used to look through his telescope all the time."

"Alright then," said Shane. "At least now we know where to go, but we'll need to act quickly before they can deploy and travel to Earth. There's no telling how close Orvag is to having the soldiers he needs. Thankfully, two ship captains just finished their battles, and can be here in about seven hours from now." The Magnum turned to Vraxis. "Is there anything that we need to know about the Gorog's forces?"

"Most of their capital ships should be *Reaper*-class," he replied. "Which I'm sure you've had to deal with before. The *Deceiver* is another story. It's an *Avenger*-type heavy cruiser, and is much bigger than the standard Gorog warship. Even if you destroy the support ships, it'll take some impressive firepower to bring down Orvag's ship."

"Noted," Shane said laconically. He turned to everyone. "Very well. That's where we stand at the moment. I would suggest everyone get some rest. Because as soon as those other captains arrive, we leave immediately for the nebula. Does anyone have any questions?"

No one raised their hand, except for Foulor. "Where's the restroom?" he asked, way more discreetly than he should have.

Vraxis turned red again, and stormed to his brother, somehow making himself look bigger than Foulor's burly muscles. "How about I show you where it is, while also teaching you how to be more discreet around people of authority?" He placed a hand on Foulor's shoulder and led him out of the briefing room, engaging in conversation that Daniel could not understand.

An awkward silence fell upon the room. "Uh...okay," resumed Shane, hesitantly. "Alright, where was I? Okay, any other questions that are actually relevant to the briefing?"

No one else raised their hand.

"Okay, then the meeting is adjourned. Dismissed." He waved his hand and the pilots and ordinary crew members began to filter out. Pantura trailed behind them after switching the projector off. Daniel and Caitlin turned to go as well, but before they could, Shane stopped them.

"Before you go," he told them, "There's something that I wish to show you. If, Daniel, you want a solution to your…" He searched for the right word. "*Problem.*"

Daniel exchanged a look with Caitlin. He figured that Shane meant his disability, in which case it was an absolute yes. She nodded. "Let's at least see what he wants to say," she said quietly.

"Okay." He turned back to the Magnum. "Yes, I would. Lead on. If it can actually help fix up my body."

It turns out that the place Shane wanted to take them was outside of the *Justice*, since after they reached the hangar they boarded a taxi very similar to the one that Vorlax had driven when Daniel had first toured the city. They had left the hangar and had begun to fly between towering buildings separated by dozens of bridges. Arajor was just as beautiful as before, with the blue giant high in the sky giving the silvery colors a slight tint. Hundreds of small hovercraft zipped through the skies, forming orderly chains of vehicles that looked like freeway traffic on Earth. And down below, encircling many of the structures, were the same expansive gardens dressed in exotic colors that provided a stark contrast to the buildings above them. It was still amazing to witness, even though Daniel had already seen it.

Caitlin, who was sitting next to Daniel in the speeder, had never seen the city before though, and Daniel thought, amusingly, that she would pass out from the sheer scale of the buildings they passed as they drove through the center. Her eyes popped out of their sockets, her jaw almost on the floor with every sight they witnessed. She barely made a sound.

"Welcome to Arajor City, Miss Wheeler," Shane said from the front. The Magnum had decided to drive the speeder himself, even rejecting Vorlax's offer to fly it for them. Shane had promptly told him to go to the bridge and prepare for the battle immediately.

"It's beautiful, isn't it?" asked Daniel, looking down at some wildlife walking around clearing below them.

"Yeah," replied Caitlin. "I'm jealous you got to experience this before I did."

"You were visiting a group of wizards!"

They eventually reached a large building not far from the Kraken's hulking structure, which was built into a tall island that stretched down a long ways towards the cloud cover below, and was surrounded by several satellite islands equipped with heavy turrets. They passed through a security checkpoint where Shane flashed his ID and they parked in an exterior hangar, disembarking onto the platform. The building was not that big, with an ellipsoid roof that was painted golden, providing a stunning light show in the starlight from the blue giant. Shane opened the door to the inside and after passing through several long, dark corridors, and descending an elevator, they reached a gigantic open space that was row after towering row of shelves, piled high with components, metal parts, and discarded trinkets.

"These are the science archives," Shane explained, as he switched the lights on and bathed the entire room in blue light. "Anything that can't be stored on digital records, we keep here. You'll find just about anything in here, from discontinued weapons to failed inventions, and everything in between. It's really easy to get lost in here, because there are six floors of random parts going down. Stay close." He directed them a few rows down, passing the remnants of an ancient ship in the process, its hull still mostly intact outside of several massive claw marks gouged into the metal. Daniel shivered to imagine what hulking beast did that. He could also see several large-scale guns and what looked like a prototype tank sitting in one of the corners. They eventually reached a row with a sign overhead that read "Medical Instruments" in big, bold letters. They walked down the row, which seemed to go on forever, until Shane finally stopped in front of a large steel box, bigger than Daniel, with a keypad in the front. Shane waved his card in front of it, and the box beeped and slid open, revealing what was inside.

It was a set of what appeared to be robotic arms, unused and fresh off the manufacturing line, the silvery paint still retaining its new sheen. As Daniel peered into the box, he also saw a set of legs, and another, smaller box with its lid closed. Shane reached in and picked up one of the arms.

"This was part of a special program that our engineers developed in order to help out soldiers who lost limbs in battle. The mechanical arm would attach to the severed end of a limb and would feature all of the functionality of a normal human arm, while also being more durable than the old arm. The arms were made from cured Xaphorium, so they're stronger than steel, but also no heavier than the arm they would replace."

Daniel took the arm from Shane. It was shockingly light, lighter than its appearance would suggest. His burned face stared back at him, reflected off of the shiny surface. "It's very light," he said.

Shane nodded. "The wiring in the arm was designed to mimic the behavior of the human body's nervous system, meaning that the body's real nerves would not be able to distinguish them from other nerves. Thus, your brain would be able to control it just like your normal arm."

Daniel handed the arm to Caitlin, who whistled as she felt its lack of weight. "How come these are locked in a vault down here and not in mass production?" he asked.

"That arm alone is worth over 8,000 credits," replied Shane. "The military decided that a soldier's arm wasn't worth that much money. Once they canned the program, the mechanical parts were shipped to the archives, where they've been in storage ever since."

Daniel nodded. "I see." He took the arm back from Caitlin, and handed it back to Shane. "So, you could use those to restore the functionality of my missing body parts?"

"Yes. All of them," replied Shane. "There are ocular prosthetics in there as well, so we'll be able to restore your vision and your ability to walk. There's several copies of each arm, so one of them should be able to fit on your body."

"Wait," interjected Caitlin, a thought occurring to her. "Doesn't it take months, or even years for a severed nerve to properly heal and reconnect? We don't have that kind of time."

Shane laughed. "On Earth, maybe it would take that long. Out here, we do things a little differently. We'll administer a catalyst that will speed up the process greatly. Should reduce the healing time to just a few hours instead of a few months." He turned to Daniel. "Would this be something that you would be interested in doing? You'd be able to move freely again."

Daniel did not hesitate. "Yes. I'll do it," he said firmly, staring at the robotics in the vault. "But before we do the procedure, there's just one thing that I want."

Chapter 32

The anesthesia finally began to wear off, and Daniel slowly stirred back into the present day. He opened his eye and yawned, feeling incredibly drowsy. He was also rather miffed, as he had been in the middle of an incredible dream, of him exploring space and battling monsters the size of tanks in some random forest where the trees seemed to have arms and clawed fingers. It had been a happy dream, only for it to give way to the hard truth of reality. He missed the days where his younger self was naive enough to believe that his dreams of space travel were as happy as they would be, and not, in actuality, a nightmare.

He slowly sat up, blinked twice, then stopped, squinted at the far wall, and blinked again. His vision seemed…different. Previously, the left half of his vision was black, and he could not see anything there. Now he could see Caitlin, sitting on a chair on his bedside, perking up as he stirred awake.

"Rise and shine, Stellar Brain," she said, standing up and moving closer to him. "You feeling alright?"

"Well…yeah, actually," replied Daniel, surprised he felt this good. "I…can see you."

Caitlin's face brightened even further. "You can?"

"Looks like the nerve and wiring have established their connection," said Shane, sauntering in, but looking a year older than before. "Try raising your right hand."

Daniel, his spirit feeling rejuvenated, did. To his amazement, the bedsheets slowly lifted up, until the handiwork of the surgeon was revealed. Attached onto his arm, almost looking like an extension of it, was the robotic arm that Shane had revealed to him. Only, from a distance, you would not have been able to tell the difference between it and a real arm, for Daniel had requested to have the robotic parts painted to match his skin color, to allow it to blend in better. The only clues were the visible line separating flesh from metal, and the joints that stuck out of the metal. He tried making a fist. The robotic fingers responded in kind. He waved his hand. The arm did just that. He released a nervous laugh, as he bent his new arm as if the old one had never been removed.

He then removed his bedsheets and revealed the leg below. Like his arm, it had been painted to better hide its robotic origins, with only a few telltale clues to reveal as such. He swung his legs around to allow them to hang off the bed. Not only did it feel as natural as his old leg, but there were even five toes on the foot that he could flex. He made an effort to stand, almost expecting to fall over, but instead he stood up straight, feeling slightly off-balance, but only just. He reached his full height, not using anything else as support, and took two steps forward. All of his movements felt completely natural, almost unsettlingly so even, but he did not care. He was just elated to have full motion of his body back.

He found the mirror and stared into it. His hairline was still a little singed off where the burns spread, and there were hints of scar tissue, but the big thing he noticed was that his left eye was now covered by the same skin-colored metal of the other two replacement parts. Here, the line was even more subtle between flesh and metal. Even the photoreceptor that acted as a substitute eye was colored blue, and was really the only true clue to Daniel's old injuries. He closed just his left eye, and saw the blue light disappear for a second before popping back up again.

"They're not made of flesh and bone," admitted Shane, still sounding a little guilty, "but they're the next best thing."

Daniel rotated his arm about the shoulder joint. "But it sure beats the hoverchair," he said, testing the full range of motion in all of his cybernetics. He turned to Shane. "Thank you for this."

Shane smiled. "Don't thank me yet," he said, holding up his hands. "I've got another surprise for you. Caitlin too."

Caitlin whipped around to stare at him. "A surprise for who now?" she asked.

Shane ended up leaving the medical wing, Daniel and Caitlin following. As they traversed the same old corridors, Daniel marveled at the fluidity of the motion of his new additions. In fact, as he kept a normal pace after Shane, he started to get the impression that they were even more fluid than his human arms. There was no jankiness, no grinding, no stiffness at all. He had been worried leading up to the procedure that the cybernetics would be subpar compared to what they were replacing, but so far, that had not been the case. Even with his new eye, the camera feed going into his brain was indistinguishable from the retina in his right eye. It was simply remarkable.

Caitlin moved back a bit to walk alongside him. "You doing good?" she asked him. "I wouldn't know what it's like to have robot body parts, so, I'm just curious."

Daniel smiled, having known her long enough to know when she was joking. "I'll say, it's not as bad as I imagined," he said, holding out his right arm for her to see the motion. "These things are pretty capable, just from what I've seen."

"Yeah. And having them be painted over with skin tones was a great idea."

"Thanks. I mean, if you don't have to show everyone around you that you're part machine, you might as well not. To a point, of course." He tapped next to his photoreceptor.

"True," she replied. "I guess we both walk away with permanent souvenirs from this little trip." She held out her hand to reveal the subtle blue-green light of the Madorax energy.

"You'll need to show me how that works once we have a minute," Daniel said, staring at her glowing palm.

"I'll give you a full course on it," replied Caitlin, closing her fist and shutting off the light. "It basically needs one in order to fully explain it."

Shane led them down into a part of the ship where they had never been, past large boxes scattered throughout the hallway, and past quite a few pilots in flight suit gear, until they finally stopped in front of a door with a keypad on the lock. Shane once again scanned his card, and the door slid open with a hiss. Inside was a room that looked like a high school gym locker room, if that locker room was built in the year 2100. Aside from the silvery paint scheme and bright blue lights shining from above, the benches in the middle of the space, and the row of lockers lining the edge of the wall, with doors about as tall as Daniel, were essentially no different from a gym's on Earth. Shane approached a pair sitting right next to each other and opened the one on the left. Caitlin shoved past Shane first and got in front of the locker to see the contents inside, blocking Daniel from seeing what was inside.

"Caitlin, I…I can't see!" he exclaimed, trying to peer over her shoulder.

"Wow." Caitlin turned around, something dark blue and gold in her hands. It was some form of clothing, seeing as how Daniel could make out a sleeve dangling from her arms. But there was something about the design of the fabric and the fact that there was a connector at the cuff of the sleeve that made Daniel suspicious, and soon he recognized what it was.

"That's a spacesuit," he said, pointing. He peered behind her into the locker and saw a pair of black gloves, a pair of black boots, and a gray helmet with gold accents inside, along with the metal rack where the suit was hanging originally. "Yeah, look. That's an airtight helmet right there."

Shane opened the second locker. Inside it was another spacesuit, this one slightly larger than the first one. Besides that, it looked identical to the first one, dark blue with gold highlights, a gray helmet with a visor, and black gloves and boots. Daniel could also see a pale gray belt sitting nearby with several item pouches attached. He reached inside and took it out. The aluminized fabric felt surprisingly lightweight, especially for a spacesuit.

"I had these laid out for you two while Daniel had your procedure," explained Shane. "They've both been tailored to measure your dimensions, and are ready to be worn by their new owners. That is, if you still want to participate in the coming battle."

Daniel turned to Shane. "Like it or not, Earth has been dragged into this whole affair," he said. "Someone has to defend it from invasion, and since we're already here…" He turned to Caitlin. "Unless you disagree?"

She set her suit down and shook her head, losing the visage of uncertainty that had been written all over her face for most of their outer space excursion. "Let's get this nimrod," she said.

They each went back to their rooms with their suits clutched in their arms, and set about changing into them. Each suit had a inner shell of breathable fabric that would keep their temperature at the proper level, and built-in plant-based solar pads that would photosynthesize oxygen for them, without the extra weight of a oxygen tank on their back. There were special clamps on the sleeves for the gloves, with similar ones on the legs for the boots. The body and legs were one piece, with a single airtight zipper up the front, and finally, the helmet module clamped down onto the shoulders using vacuum seals, where it would not budge, even if it received a violent knock against a hard surface. It was a fairly simple process for both of them to slip into their suits, and even after they were on, complete with the gloves and boots, another remarkable thing about the suits came into focus.

Daniel found his movement unimpeded, even as he stretched as far as he could. There was no limiting range of motion, no bulky feeling. It was as if he was wearing a specially-designed wetsuit, except built for outer space. The fabric was comfortable against his body, and felt nonrestrictive. He placed his helmet on a dedicated clip on his back where it would stay until he needed to put it on. Now dressed for the harsh vacuum of space, he left his room and, like he had a few days before, nearly collided with Caitlin in the hallway.

"Oh! We really need to stop doing this!" exclaimed Caitlin, despite having a dumb grin on her face. Daniel smiled, although he could not tell if she was smiling at their poor ability to avoid collisions or the fact that she looked amazing in her spacesuit, the blue and gold popping in the light of the hallway. Her hair was tied back into a braid, out of the way. "You look...great!" she said, admiring Daniel's suit. Apparently, he looked amazing too.

"Thanks, you too," he said. He rubbed his forehead, his fingers brushing between his skin and the metal attachment of his photoreceptor covering. "You ready?"

She nodded. "As I'll ever be. Besides, I can at least defend myself this time." She flexed on him by flashing her Madorax energy at him, casting an eerie glow that reflected off their suits' gold highlights.

"You've gotten over that?" asked Daniel, as they started to walk down the hallway.

"Still haven't," came the reply. "But I can at least keep it under wraps when I need it to be, and, you never know, it could be useful. It saved my life when I was at the temple."

"Right. We all know about that," said Daniel, adding just the faintest hint of sarcasm to his voice. "You never did tell me about how your wizard experience went. We were a bit...preoccupied beforehand."

"It's not that important," replied Caitlin, looking a little awkward.

"No, please." Daniel bumped her on the shoulder. "I

want to know what visiting a group of actual wizards is like. Tell me."

Caitlin laughed a little bit, warming both of them up on the inside. "Well…it's about what you would expect. A lot of magic, some of it crazy, but everyone was super friendly, surprisingly, and it all went smoothly until the Gorog raid arrived. Though, they never really stood a chance."

"I heard Pantura whispering about how some all-powerful sorcerer created a literal gorge using his bare hands, then proceeded to destroy half of an army by himself. I think his name was…Shorgur? Something like that."

"Shurgen," corrected Caitlin. "And, yes, everything part of that is true, believe it or not."

"Well, at this rate, I think we've both come to expect that literally anything can be possible," pointed out Daniel.

Caitlin laughed again. "You're not exactly wrong there."

They passed through the hallways, still carrying on their conversation, until they reached the hangar, which was absolutely swarming with activity, with crew members and pilots darting back and forth, warming up starfighter engines and ensuring that all systems were good to go. Vorlax and Shane were interacting with another pilot who had clearly come forth with some questions. Judging by Vorlax's stern look, it was a pretty tense argument.

"I would love to give you permission to sit this one out," the commander was saying. "Unfortunately, this is one battle that I cannot let you walk away from. Even after what happened above Lhassi. And I hope I don't have to remind you as to what the cost of desertion is. Being court-martialed is something that no one wants to go through, and I'm sure you don't want to either. So, just calm your nerves and go get ready to fly that ship and shoot down some Gorog fighters."

The pilot hastily backed away before running off into the maze of ships. Vorlax shook his head as he left, then he saw

Daniel and Caitlin approaching off to the side. He nudged Shane, who was still watching after the pilot, and he turned and saw them as well.

"There you are!" he said, sounding delighted to see them.

"What was that about?" asked Daniel, looking confused. "You both seemed rather…well, peeved, with that pilot. Did he do something?"

"He tried to get himself off of the strike force for this battle," explained Shane. "Said that he lost his wingman during the Rhozadar campaign, and didn't want to suffer the same fate. He threatened to desert too, which led to some amazing lecturing from Vorlax here."

"We heard," replied Caitlin, folding her arms. "We're not used to seeing him angry like that."

"Really? You should've seen me when I found out about the drugs he put in Daniel's food," the commander said, throwing shade in Shane's direction. "I just about burst a blood vessel in my brain."

"Listen, I'd be happy to hear this story later, but for now, are there any updates regarding the Gorog positions, or when we're leaving for the nebula?" Daniel was tired of standing around and talking, and wanted to take action instead.

"As of about 45 minutes ago, the Gorogs have not moved from their position," said Shane. "The other captains are still about an hour out, though. We should be able to leave around then."

"By that point there could be more warships waiting in the nebula," said Daniel. "We should strike now, so that we can eliminate the ships that are there, and take Orvag out of the picture. Once he's gone, the rest of the fleet will scatter."

"There's only two ships ready to depart at the moment, Daniel." Shane's voice was understanding, but also grim. "As much as I agree with your argument, leaving now would not do any good for any of us. It's best if we wait and amass a greater force before we go to attack the enemy fleet."

He stopped for a second. "Though, it would be a major concern if more Gorog warships arrived before we did. Or, heaven forbid, the rest of the fleet, so that they depart for Earth." He turned to Vorlax. "Any ideas?"

The commander shook his head. "I'm drawing a blank here. But you two are both right. We can't leave now, we don't have the necessary firepower. But we also take a serious risk by waiting around, as that gives Orvag more time to grow his fleet."

"Wait a second," Caitlin spoke up, coming forward. "What if we go first, to the nebula, and distract the Gorogs while you get the ships that you need? That should buy you enough time until you can arrive in force."

"That's a terrible idea," Vorlax said automatically. "You're one ship, a very good ship, but still only one of them, against God knows how many Gorog warships with enough firepower to wipe out an entire city, plus however many starfighters they have in waiting."

"Not so fast, Vorlax," said Shane, putting his arm out. "She may have a point here."

"Point? What point? The kind of point that leads to death?"

"You forget, the nebula's gas and magnetic fields hamper the scanners of our ships. The Gorogs used similar tracking on their warships as well. Their turbolasers would have terrible aim in the nebula."

"Okay, but even so, what of all those starfighters? Those run on a different tracking system and will swarm them."

"Not if we hide in the denser parts of the gas," interjected Daniel. "If we can hide inside of a protostar that's still forming up, we can lose any ships that are tailing us."

Vorlax looked from him, to Caitlin, and back to Daniel. "You're talking about flying a ship into what will eventually turn into a star, something that is insanely hot, and could crush you from the insane pressure inside. That's perhaps a greater death wish than trying to engage an entire Gorog fleet by yourself. What kind of ship will be able to withstand such intense forces?"

"The gunship we meant to take to Earth, before Vraxis attacked us," replied Caitlin, who by now had clearly thought all of this through. "Pantura told us that its hull is made of Xaphorium, a metal stronger than any on Earth. And in case you've forgotten, there's a heat shield that can resist intense heat. And finally, it's our idea, and we feel as though it's a good idea, and if you have an issue with it, then you can discuss it with Shane, because there's nothing that you can do that will stop us from carrying out this idea. Right, Daniel?"

He nodded. "Absolutely."

"But, that gunship…I don't want it to be damaged at all. I'd hate to see that paint scheme get wrecked in any way."

"Vorlax, that paint scheme is terrible," said Shane. "Way too bright in my opinion."

"Don't worry, we'll return it in good condition, no scratches at all. Does it actually have a name?"

Vorlax shook his head. "Never could think of a good one, if you ask me. Not that that's important right now." He sighed. "Very well." He turned to Shane. "Please tell them that this is a terrible idea, please?"

Shane, to Vorlax's dismay, shook his head. "If that's their choice, then it's their choice. I cannot influence their decision in any way, and even if I could, I refuse to do so." He smiled at them. "Go, and may both of you be safe out there."

"Wait!"

They all turned and saw Pantura running after them, dressed in another spacesuit, this one colored dark red instead of blue. "I'm going too!" she said, having clearly sprinted to reach them on time.

Shane raised his hands. "Alright, may the three of you be

safe out there, and don't get any ideas about…"

"Hold on!"

"Oh, for the love of all that is holy…" grumbled Shane as both Vraxis and Foulor came around the bend. Neither of them were in a suit, instead keeping their more traditional uniforms, allowing Foulor's muscles to bulge through. Foulor's bandolier was slung over his shoulder, and Vraxis was carrying a sniper rifle.

"Do you have room for two more?" Vraxis asked, lowering the barrel of his sniper to point at the floor.

"I didn't think you two would actually show up," Caitlin said.

"Well, we were considering ditching in, and then Foulor decided that he really, really wanted to blow some more stuff up. Besides, we're clearly not going to get paid until Shane returns, so, might as well go along with everyone."

"Thanks for the help. And I promise that you will get your money," said Shane, forcing a smile out, causing it to look like the Joker's grin. "Now that we're all here, how about the five of you take off and execute Caitlin's idea?" He raised his finger before Foulor could open his mouth. "They'll explain it on the way."

He looked around, and saw everyone still standing there. "What are you waiting for? Me to forgive all of your sins? Go, go! Now!" He shooed them away. "We'll be right behind you!"

They all hustled out of there and climbed into the same orange gunship, the ramp retracting behind them. They climbed the ladder to the main deck single file, taking up positions around the atrium. Vraxis and Foulor glanced around at all of the fancy tech. "Never thought I'd be back on this ship," said Vraxis, setting his sniper rifle down in the corner.

"Be grateful that you're not a prisoner this time," his brother told him, sitting down next to the large holoprojector in the center.

Pantura took the pilot's seat and started the ship, lifting them off the hangar deck and flying them out into space. Daniel and Caitlin sat next to her, staring as the bright, artificial lighting of the *Justice* was replaced with the fainter, but natural light of the stars. "Next stop, the Great Nebula," announced Pantura, punching in the coordinates and pointing the ship towards a spot of sky that looked blank from their angle.

Daniel turned to Caitlin, who looked up at him. They didn't say anything, but instead nodded as Pantura pulled the lever that sent them into hyperspace, the stars transforming into comets as they entered warp speed.

It was about an hour to their destination, and time seemed to slow down as they hurtled through interstellar space. Daniel's thoughts would not stop dwelling on his mother. He finally had her location, and was on his way to save her. And he was prepared, with an entire army that had his back and was ready to die, not necessarily to save her directly, but to end the evil that was imprisoning her. And that was good enough for him. But, as with anything he had done so far, there were nagging doubts tugging on his gut. What-if statements clouded his mind, about failure, and all of the possible negative outcomes of the battle, just as they had done before. He must have betrayed the fact that his mind was wandering, since Caitlin elbowed him sharply out of nowhere.

"You alright?" she asked him. "You look nervous."

Daniel sighed. "It's a bit hard not to be," he said. "I mean, this is it. We're actually close to saving my mother from the Gorogs, this close to being done and ready to go home, but…"

"Let me guess. Your anxiety is giving you second thoughts?" finished Caitlin, one eyebrow raised.

Daniel nodded. "We've come so far, through so much

pain and loss, and what if everything we've done has been for nothing?"

Caitlin leaned in to him. "Then we'll face that change as it comes, too. Like we have with everything else. Because that's all we can do. Adapt. And I have faith in Shane and the Orion Coalition. Faith that our mission will not be in vain. Faith that everything will turn out okay."

Daniel nodded slowly. "I've never really been a person of faith, Caitlin. I've always been about the results, and the likely outcomes of events like this." He stared at the stars whizzing by. "But maybe it's time that I start showing a little more of it in what I do."

Caitlin smiled broadly. "There's the Daniel I met," she said, slapping him on the shoulder.

"We're coming up on the nebula," said Pantura over the intercom. In the back of the ship, Foulor was jarred awake by the announcement.

"Did you have to interrupt my dream about that buffet?!" he said, his voice sounding as though he had had one too many cocktails.

"Not when we could be heading straight into a warzone!" replied Pantura, beating Vraxis before he could answer. Except, Vraxis was also asleep, even after the intercom announcement. Foulor pointed to his body, propped up against the holoprojector table.

"What about him?" he shot back. "He's still asleep!"

"You know what he'd say to you if he was awake," interjected Caitlin, adding to the argument. "He'd drag you out and lecture you away from the three of us. It's just a dream, Foulor. You can always have another one."

Foulor grumbled and sat down, looking sullen, but he did not argue further.

"We're here," announced Pantura, bringing the unnamed ship out of hyperspace. It slowed back to normal speed, the stars becoming points of light again. And when they emerged, they were no longer surrounded by black velvet; instead, they were surrounded by cotton candy.

The nebula surrounded them on all sides, the hydrogen gas swirling like clouds, glowing in dazzling shades of red and pink. Scattered nearby were tons of globules of dark gas, which Daniel knew were protostars; the first stage of stellar evolution. They were slowly being heated up and compressed into a future sun, the solar winds and gravitational forces working to further condense the protostar. And there were dozens in view, with hundreds of even thousands likely scattered throughout the entire nebula.

Caitlin's eyes reflected the nebula's soft glow. "It sure beats all those Hubble pictures back home," she said, looking around.

"I'd love to share the view too, but we need to calibrate our scanners to work around the presence of this hydrogen gas. Otherwise, we're as blind as a bat in this nebula." Of course Pantura was the one who was immediately getting down to business.

"You have bats out here too?" asked Daniel.

"Yes, although they're nothing like your Earth bats. Ours are actually blind," explained Pantura. "Yours can at least use their sonar."

"Okay…so, how do we calibrate the scanners?" asked Daniel.

"We need to account for the extra hydrogen gas in the field. Could you please push that green button for me?" She indicated a large green button on the copilot's side of the dashboard. Daniel reached over and pressed it.

"Now please hold down that switch until I tell you to," said Pantura, pointing to a small black knob next to the green button.

Daniel moved to do so, but Caitlin got to it first. "Now

what?" she asked.

"Wait…wait…" Pantura stared at the scanner screen for a few seconds, which flickered slightly as Caitlin held the button. Eventually, a pop-up flashed, reading "REBOOT ENGAGED" and the screen went blank. "There. You can release it."

Caitlin lifted her finger. "Anything else that you need?"

"That should be it for now," she replied. "Just give me a few seconds to account for the foreign elements and we should be good to go."

He nodded and leaned back in his chair, joining Caitlin in admiring the gorgeous view outside their window. The nebula almost seemed to pulsate with light, the pink gas fluctuating slightly, like a beating heart. Between the globules of protostars, brilliantly blue stars glowed like diamonds against the backdrop, including a large cluster of them some distance away that cast this soft glow throughout the entire region.

"I didn't even realize how stunning they were up close," Daniel remarked, his breath taken away from him by the incredible vistas.

Caitlin nodded next to him. "Still not as impressive as that conjunction with Saturn, remember?"

"I do," replied Daniel sadly. "But only barely by this point."

Caitlin gave him another encouraging look. "Don't worry, Daniel. We'll be back home sooner than you think. And once we are, we'll have another starwatch session. Does that sound good to you?"

His face brightened a little, even though he did not look her way. "Yes. I think I'd like that very much."

"Look, I appreciate the sentiment between you two, really, but instead of reflecting on the past here, how about we look for the hidden Gorog fleet? And then we can worry about what comes next afterwards." Vraxis sounded half-asleep, but he still managed to sound grumpy, per usual.

Caitlin snickered a little bit, but then began to sweep through their surroundings. "Do you see any Gorog ships?" she asked Daniel.

Daniel stared out the window. "Not at the moment, no." He turned to Pantura. "Any luck with the scanner?"

"Should be just another minute or so," she replied, focused on the screen. "Just have to enter in the correct elemental spectra or we'll be no better off than before."

"Whatever that means," called out Vraxis from the back of the ship.

She rolled her eyes. "Why did we have to take them along?" she lamented. "All they do is argue with us over every little detail."

"Because," began Daniel, "We could use more than just the three of us on this mission. Plus, they have insider knowledge of the *Deceiver* and its leader, and have established that they are incredibly savage fighters. If we're going to infiltrate the capital ship of the entire Gorog fleet, we need some insider information to help us out."

"Still don't understand why they have to be so difficult about it," Pantura said, turning back to her work. She fingered the screen just a bit more and entered in some numbers. The scanner jumped back to life. "Alright, it's working again. Now let's find some Gorog ships."

But after traveling through the nebula some more, there had been no sign of any Gorog ships. "Maybe we're looking in the wrong spot?" suggested Caitlin after about five minutes. "This is a huge nebula anyways."

"You're not wrong in that regard," replied Pantura. "But we're getting signals from a large area of the nebula. And we're right near the heart of the nebula, where it would be most logical for Orvag to have hidden his fleet. We should be seeing signatures popping up soon, if that's the case. If we don't, that means that he's closer to the outskirts, or…"

"Or what?" asked Daniel.

"Or the fleet already amassed and they've been sent to Earth already," finished Pantura grimly.

Caitlin shuddered. "Let's hope that they're still here."

"I'll turn us a little bit. Maybe that will help somewhat." Pantura angled the ship more into the nebula's core. "Keep your eyes locked on that scanner. The minute it starts beeping at you, that means we're getting close."

They proceeded onward for a few more minutes, and the fear that they were too late and the Gorogs had already left grew. They passed through the central star cluster into a new section of the nebula, still hoping to see a signature pop up.

"Still nothing," reported Daniel for probably the fourth time. "Pantura, I don't think they're in this section of the nebula. Should we contact Shane to see if there's any word on whether the Gorogs have been spotted near Earth?"

As a backup, Shane had sent two nearby cruisers to watch for Orvag's fleet behind the Earth's moon. Their only mission was to watch for the enemy fleet and let Shane know if they arrived. If the Gorogs had indeed left the nebula, the two cruisers would have seen them arrive at Earth. "Good idea," said Pantura. She immediately reached out to Shane, who thankfully answered quickly, materializing out of the dashboard in front of them.

"Pantura, I didn't expect you to reach out this soon," he said, acting as though he had just been interrupted. "Have you found the Gorog fleet?"

"Not yet," she said. "We were wondering if your two cruisers had anything to report on the matter since they were deployed there."

"If Orvag had indeed sent his entire fleet to Earth, they would've told me," the Magnum replied. "I have yet to hear anything except radio silence from them."

"Well, if they do reach out to you, let us know," replied

Pantura.

"Alright. We are en route at the moment, and should be arriving there in less than an hour. Keep us updated."

"Yes, sir." The hologram disappeared, leaving Pantura to steer the ship into a new direction.

It was at that point that a shadow fell across the cockpit.

The gunship screeched to a halt, everyone suddenly very tense. Daniel and Caitlin exchanged a nervous glance. Even Pantura was looking a touch uncomfortable. In the back, neither Vraxis nor Foulor could see what was going on.

"What's happening out there?" they said, sounding nonchalant, oblivious to the tension that everyone else was feeling.

"My God," whispered Daniel, just barely loud enough for Caitlin and Pantura to hear.

Above them, a dark mass floated, blocking the light from the stars there and purring with the same, Transformer-esque noise that had first graced Daniel's ears the night the Gorogs attacked. The cruiser outline, dark as it was, was evil-looking, with multiple sharp edges sticking from its bow, and rows of laser cannons jutting out from the hull.

"An assault warship," whispered Pantura. "*Reaper*-class."

"Is that bad?" asked Daniel.

"Bad, but not as bad as it could be." Even though they were sure that the enemy ship could not hear them, they were taking no chances.

"Can they see us?" asked Caitlin, also hushing herself.

"I can't tell," replied Pantura, staring up at the ship. "They don't seem to be changing course or anything."

"Should we move?"

"No! If we fire up the engines now their heat scanners will for sure pick it up and expose us. Let's wait this out and see if they miss us."

They sat there for several agonizing seconds while the much larger ship passed over them like the angel of death. The light returned to their faces as the star the ship was blotting out was uncovered. The ship continued its original course, without hesitating or turning around once.

"I think it missed us," said Pantura, relieved.

Daniel sat back in his chair, feeling relieved for a brief moment, before making the mistake of looking right and seeing another Gorog ship emerging from the gas, this one straight on a collision course with them. "Pantura…" he said, the fear coming back into his voice.

She turned and saw it too. She cursed, violently. "That's a problem," she said, watching as its massive hull drew closer to them. She stared at it for one second, then sat back in her chair and put her seat belt on.

"Maybe it won't hit us…" said Caitlin nervously.

"No, that's totally going to hit us. Everyone, strap yourselves in!" Pantura called out behind her, alerting Vraxis and Foulor. "Things are about to get a whole lot faster!"

"Did you find the fleet?" asked Foulor.

"Yep! Put your seatbelt on!"

Everyone strapped themselves into their chairs, Daniel and Caitlin hardest of all. Gripping the handles built into the belt's waist strap, they watched in anticipation as the warship drew uncomfortably close to ramming distance. Daniel's blood rushed through his body, and he began to sweat nervously.

"This is where the fun really begins!" Pantura alerted them. "Brace yourselves!"

She suddenly opened up the throttle, which launched them forwards like a catapult on an aircraft carrier. Daniel and Caitlin were pushed back into their seats by the intense g-forces, causing Daniel's vision to blur slightly. The Gorog ship vanished from their window as Pantura piloted the ship faster than Daniel had seen any ship go thus far. She reached over to the holographic projector and managed to call Shane.

"Shane, I don't know if you can hear me!" she yelled, sounding panicky. "We found the Gorogs, but we've been exposed! We could use that extra help really soon!"

"You were spotted? By how many?" the Magnum asked.

Daniel checked the rearview camera to see both ships altering their course to move into attack position. And he could also see several other ships emerging from the nebula as well. "How about the entire fleet?" he answered over the roar of the gunship's engines.

"We're still at least—but hold on!" replied Shane, the transmission beginning to cut in and out. "We'll be there in about—and then—"

The hologram fizzled out. "Shane? Shane, are you there?" cried Pantura, sounding more worried than she had ever sounded. She swore again. "They're jamming the signal!"

A laser blast came streaking down from one of the enemy ships, coming very close to their port side wing. Pantura immediately engaged evasive maneuvers, but was met with a deadly hailstorm of fire that came raining down around them. She tried her best to navigate the maze, but still managed to get clipped in the stern hard. The shields made an unpleasant noise as the blast rippled across the ship, knocking everyone around.

"Try not to get us killed here!" yelled Vraxis, holding on for dear life as his body, only anchored down by a waist belt, was thrown about by the ship's dynamic movements.

"I'm doing my best here!" retorted Pantura, swooping around a phaser blast, the concentrated beam threatening to inflict severe damage on their shields.

The scanner finally began to beep, and Daniel at first took the several signatures present on the map to be the warships that were firing at them. Then at least a hundred others came into view, and Daniel immediately saw what was coming. "We've got starfighters coming!"

Pantura saw the screen. "Vraxis!" she yelled. "Do either you or Foulor have experience manning turrets on starfighters?!"

"Say no more!" He turned to his brother. "Foulor!" he yelled. "Get up that ladder and shoot down the Gorog ships that are about to be chasing us!"

Foulor did not need to be told twice. He unbuckled his seatbelt and climbed the ladder up to the reverse turret, all while Pantura threw the ship about in order to dodge laser fire from the Gorog warships. "Okay, I'm here!" he yelled down to the others. "How does it work?"

"Use the handles to aim and the red buttons on them to fire!" called Pantura. "That should be all you need!"

"Let's hope he doesn't kill us all!" said Daniel, holding onto his handles with all his might.

They soared through the nebula, a swarm of deadly starfighters approaching and blocking the way back to the other Gorog ships. Pantura, white-knuckled, gripped the steering wheel. "Daniel, I need you to control the forward guns. Caitlin, monitor the shields and damage. And keep holding on! This is going to be rough!"

She pressed a button and a set of handles popped out of the dashboard to land in front of Daniel, who grabbed them and saw that they were set up identically to Pantura's description of the turret's controls. The ship was turned hard to the left, to point straight at the approaching mass of enemy ships. "Diverting power to the forward shields!" called out Pantura as they charged at the mass of starfighters.

There was a storm of laser fire thrown their way as the Gorog starfighters came at them head-on like a cloud of locusts. The ship shuddered and vibrated as the shields took a heavy beating. Daniel found the triggers for the forward cannons and fired a concentrated volley into the swarm, destroying a small handful of ships as the lasers raked through the starfighters. Then the fleet parted as the ship charged right through the center of it,

Pantura concentrating as hard as she could as she threaded the needle like a daredevil.

"Shields down by eight percent!" informed Caitlin, staring at the screen like a hawk.

"As long as none of them read zero, we'll be fine!" replied Pantura, rolling the ship 360 degrees in order to avoid more laser fire from the pursuing starfighters, which were circling back and starting to chase them in earnest. More warbling came as the shields repelled the laser blasts, jostling everyone on board around more.

"Foulor!" yelled Vraxis, still clinging to his chair in the back. "Get those blasted fighters off our tail before I get sick!"

"Working on it!" he yelled down in protest, firing up the rear-facing turret and swiveling it to point at the Gorogs. A deadly stream of constant laser fire came shooting out from the twin barrels, destroying several more Gorog ships. "I got some of them!"

"Has he ever used a turret like this before?" Daniel called back to Vraxis over the roar of the engines and the sounds of cannon fire.

"No!" came the reply. "He specializes more in ground-based weapons! He's never had to shoot a turret on a ship like this!"

"Great!" said Daniel. "Just great!"

But Foulor was, for all of their doubts about him, doing a pretty great job keeping the fighters off their tail. But their shields were still taking a huge beating, and were becoming less and less effective at absorbing the constant barrage of lasers. There were simply too many starfighters to deal with.

Pantura swung the ship hard to the right, almost giving Caitlin whiplash as she was caught off guard by the violent motion. "Shields are down to sixty percent!" she warned, her vision seeing tinges of gray from all of the maneuvers.

"Where's Shane?" asked Daniel. "We need him to get

here soon!"

The scanner beeped again, showing more signatures moving at high velocity towards their position. "More starfighters incoming!"

Pantura glanced at the scanner. "Those are *Venom* fighters!" she exclaimed in horror.

"Are they worse than the ones chasing us now?" yelled Caitlin, her skin showing signs of paleness.

"Much worse!" replied Pantura, turning the ship to face the Gorog warships, where a second cloud of objects was heading their way. She dived deeper into the nebula, swooping around dense patches of gas, the two groups of ships merging to form one massive armada that chased them like a bunch of angry metal hornets. Pantura yanked the ship to the side, hoping to find shelter in a nearby protostar, but before she could, disaster struck.

"Pantura!" called Vraxis from the back. "Be careful around those *Venom* fighters! Orvag's been testing a new weapon with them over the past few months and, well, you might want to watch your arms!"

"What sort of weapon?"

"It's a special missile that will stun the pilot unconscious when it hits! I know, because I used one on this ship when Foulor and I attacked the *Justice!*"

On cue, the scanner began to flash wildly, and the previous beeping was replaced by an alarm that rang through the ship. The swarm of ships was still chasing them, but now a new signature, different from all the others, was moving significantly faster than their pursuers and gaining on them rapidly. Pantura saw it and immediately diverted power to the engines, the sudden acceleration catching everyone off guard. She turned the ship around in a wide arc, heading back towards the Gorog warships, but the new signature was already right on top of them. She and Daniel saw it closing in fast and braced for impact.

But it never came. The signature flew right past the ship, and as it did, the missile came into focus. Everyone watched as it blew right past them, almost seeming to miss them entirely. For a moment, everyone felt relief. Then the missile exploded in front of the ship, and several small nodes were ejected from the casing, latching onto their hull as it passed through the missile's fireball. For a second, nothing happened, then Pantura shrieked as a painful jolt of electricity arced from the steering wheel and traveled up her arms. She let go of the steering wheel, and with no boost from the gas, the ship began to slow down.

"Pantura!" yelled Daniel, unbuckling his seatbelt in a haste and hurrying to her side.

"I'm fine," she said through gritted teeth. "Just tingling a little bit. I…" She tried to lift her arm, but only her right one responded. Her left arm remained unmoving, limp on her lap. "My arm's not moving!"

"Those nodes were designed to stun a pilot unconscious," said Vraxis, also unbuckling his seatbelt and stumbling as another powerful blast rocked the ship. "You're lucky you're still awake."

"Who's…flying the ship then?" asked Pantura in a daze.

"What's happening down there?" called down Foulor from the turret. "Why are we slowing down?"

Aghast, Daniel saw their speed slowing down, the swarm of starfighters gaining on them. "Vraxis, take Pantura and get her off of the chair," he said, bending over to push her off.

"What? Why? You're not going to fly the ship are you?" the hunter asked.

"Watch me! I did it before!" said Daniel, pushing Pantura out of the pilot's chair and sitting down in her place. "Caitlin, take over my seat. You shoot now."

Caitlin hesitated for a second, but then came forward and strapped into the copilot's chair. "Now what?" she asked, watching the monitor show the approaching swarm of Gorog ships.

Another laser blast rocked the ship. "We survive," said Daniel, grabbing the steering wheel and pushing it forwards. The ship roared back to life and accelerated, causing Vraxis to nearly face plant onto the deck. He banked the ship left, not too harshly though, and all of the Gorog fighters, seemingly caught off-guard, increased their speed to catch up. The engines howled as Daniel guided it through the nebula, slowly getting closer to the Gorog warships. Behind him, Foulor continued to shoot at the enemy fighters, slowly whittling down their numbers little by little.

Then another squadron was launched from the warships above.

The scanner showed another fifty signatures heading their way, and Daniel dove down, putting as much distance between them and the reinforcements. He looked around in haste, looking for a safer place to go, then saw a protostar close by. Remembering his idea to Shane, he directed their path to fly straight into the surface of the globule.

"What are you doing?" asked Caitlin, going white again as they approached the ominous form of the protostar.

"Buying us some time!" he replied, diving right into the gas.

As Daniel had hoped, most of the Gorog starfighters followed them into the protostar, still shooting at them. He concentrated as he struggled to keep their ship flying straight. Alarms sounded as the heat and pressure readings began to climb to unsafe levels. The ship creaked, but he did not turn back. He kept the throttle open and their trajectory straight.

"I hope you know what you're doing!" called Vraxis from the back, who could still see out of the cockpit glass.

"Me too!"

Behind them, Gorog fighters began to explode as the intense heat and pressure got to them, even though the scanner by this point had been rendered useless by the forces. Others turned around, but there was still at least two dozen zealous pilots on their tail. Daniel banked slightly left, hoping to lose some of them in the dense, almost opaque gas. The pressure readings climbed higher, and the ship's metal groaned as it tried to resist the gravitational weight of the protostar. He prayed that the cockpit and turret glass would hold up, because if they broke, it would all be over.

The ship was violently rocked by the forces, the metal creaking still, and the heat from outside slowly seeping into the atrium. Sweat poured down Daniel's forehead as he began to roast inside his spacesuit. And yet, the warning lights on the sensors began to disappear. The heat readings and pressure readings began to decrease. The ship cooled down. And behind them, there were no Gorog ships in sight.

"We made it!" exhaled Caitlin, breathing a huge sigh of relief. Daniel echoed her; it seemed as though they had successfully gotten away. And ahead of them, their view was slowly growing brighter as they pushed out of the protostar's gravity and back into the main nebula.

They burst from the dark globule and into the glorious pink of their surroundings. But before they could celebrate their success, their hope turned to despair as a hundred Gorog starfighters blocked their path.

Behind the swarm, like the very agent of Satan itself, came the *Deceiver*.

Chapter 33
The Great Nebula

Orvag had had trouble believing what he was seeing.
Initially, upon receiving a transmission from one of his captains that a lone Coalition gunship had found their hiding place, he had dismissed it as nothing more than a faulty reading of the scanners and had proceeded to do nothing. But after another warship reported the same thing, he had turned his own scanners on and found out that the report was accurate. Ahead of half of a Gorog squadron of starfighters was a small, yellow signature, buzzing around a nearby quadrant of the nebula. Surprised, Orvag had ordered his men to determine the kind of ship they were dealing with. A quick scan later revealed that it was a specially-modified gunship, painted bright orange and red, with a unique wing style that he had rarely seen before. In fact, there had been only one other ship he had seen in his life with the same wing style, and it had been sent to him by one of his probe droids. Curiously, that ship also was painted orange, and that ship had been carrying Subject X-17, or, as he had found out, Daniel. But he had destroyed him on Lhassi. The odds of anyone surviving that oil refinery were slim, and even if they did, they would barely be clinging to life. And any pretense about it being flown by someone else came to a screeching halt when a scan of the ship revealed two of the exact same signatures that the probe droid caught earlier than week.

"Impossible," the king muttered.

"Excuse me?" asked Dormak, who was watching over the bridge's crew like a vulture, waiting to pounce on anyone not doing their job.

"A single Coalition ship." Orvag thought about telling

him about Daniel, but he instead turned to his intercom and grabbed it. "We have a Coalition ship trespassing in this nebula. Blade Squadron, report to your ships immediately. Find the ship and destroy it!"

The proximity sirens began to flash and screech throughout the *Deceiver*. "One ship?" repeated Dormak, sauntering over to Orvag's throne.

"One. And it matches the signature of another ship that was around when Vraxis attacked Shane. The same ship that attempted to flee with Subject X-17."

"You mean Daniel?" asked the warden. "I thought you killed him."

"Apparently not even the fires of the refinery were enough to get rid of him," snarled Orvag. He turned to Dormak. "Any word from the other captains?"

"Not yet. They haven't checked in in about a half hour."

"Watch the transmission log like your life depends on it," Orvag ordered him. "Because it may if a Coalition armada materializes here."

He stormed off to his throne, but refused to sit down, watching as the dozens of Gorog starfighters buzzed around the nebula, chasing the one small, gold signature that refused to disappear despite being outnumbered. His anger bubbled as he watched his ships slowly blip out of existence, victims of his enemy's lasers. He ordered another batch of starfighters into battle, hoping to either corner them or blow them apart, but before they could reach their target, the enemy signature vanished. They had flown into one of the globules housing a potential star, and multiple ships followed them in. Thinking quickly, Orvag sent his ships and had them wrap around the star, forming a barrier through which no ship could get through. Sure enough, the signature reappeared on the near side of the globule, and was soon cornered by sixty Gorog starfighters. They had nowhere to go without getting shot.

Orvag turned back to Dormak. "Prepare the transmitter for a message. Open frequency. I want them to hear the words from my mouth."

"That's a big warship," whispered Pantura in fear as the *Deceiver* approached them like a predator on the hunt.

"We're trapped!" exclaimed Caitlin, horror giving way to defeat as she saw the masses of Gorog fighters outside the window.

Inside the gunship, Daniel sank into his chair with the realization that there was nothing else that he could do. They had been boxed in and could not possibly move without getting shot down. Behind him, Vraxis's face was full of worry. Even Foulor jumped down from the mounted turret. Then, confusingly, the transmitter began to beep.

"Is that Shane?" asked Caitlin.

"I don't know," replied Daniel, hoping to God that it was indeed Shane announcing that the cavalry had arrived. Instead, Orvag shot out of the projector, his holographic form seeming to fill the entire ship with menace as he emerged.

"Daniel Phillips. Caitlin Wheeler." The delivery of their names made them both cower in their seats. There was nowhere for them to hide from the presence of the king, nor was there Shane to provide retorts and threats. "I have given you every opportunity to mind your own business in a conflict that you have no part in. I have graciously offered to leave you be, assuming that you echoed my opinion. Yet, at every turn, you have threatened my empire, caused trouble for me, and refused to heed my warnings. Even when you, Daniel, were subject to my wrath and refused to die. So, this time, there won't be any trace of either of you two left for my traitorous hunters to find."

"We were never *your* hunters!" Foulor raged, storming up to the cockpit and getting up in Orvag's business. "We made our own decisions, for *our* own benefit! You were just two shortsighted to see that!"

The thundercloud that came upon Orvag's face at the sight of Foulor was dark. "You…" the king said, voice shaking with fury. He tried to peer into the back of the ship, searching for Vraxis. "Where is your brother?"

Vraxis was shaking his head *no*, and, funnily enough, so was Pantura. Yet Foulor once again spoke before his brain could stop him. "He's not tolerating your nonsense and crap any more either!" he yelled, surprisingly managing to lose his slurred voice in the process. "He wants nothing to do with your kingship *or* your poor payment rates! He's his own person as well and he wishes to be done with your evil regime! You didn't even pay us that good!" And, as if the situation was not volatile enough, he flashed an extremely rude gesture at the king for good measure.

For a second, the silence, save for the slow burn of their engines, filled the ship. But only for a second. "*Traitor!*" roared Orvag, causing Foulor to recoil in shock. "*How DARE you speak to me that way! I was the one who made you what you two are today! I was the one who gave you the reputation as the most fearsome bounty hunters in the entire galaxy! And now, you have the audacity to come before me and tell me off, simply because you only work for money?!*"

Orvag's wrath filled the entire ship, and Vraxis face palmed himself. So much for subtle negotiation. Foulor had just thrown away their best shot at staying alive. Now, any chance of them being simply captured was gone.

"Since it's clear to me that the Coalition warped both of your brains, and possibly filled them with Munlok dung," continued the king, malice hinging on every syllable, "You can die alongside the filth on that ship. Not that you, Foulor, had a brain to begin with anyways, seeing as how you really pissed me off every single time you uttered a single word! But don't worry. You'll get the ultimate, permanent retirement that you both deserve now." The king turned back to Daniel and Caitlin. "As for you two, may the gods have mercy on your souls. Because you'll be lucky if they grant you safe passage at this point."

The hologram disappeared, and everyone turned their gaze to the horde of parked Gorog ships. They could see their weapons powering up, swiveling to aim straight at the gunship. Everyone saw the barrels of their weapons lighting up, preparing to discharge their plasma rounds, and they all braced for the flash of heat followed by the cold embrace of death.

But before they could be blown out of the sky, the ships peeled back. They abandoned their positions and flew off to another part of the nebula. Soon, they were almost completely alone save for a few stragglers. Everyone looked around, totally confused. Where did they all go? And why?

"I heard you needed some assistance," came the voice of Shane faintly on the radio.

From out of the nebula's gaseous swirls emerged a small armada of Coalition ships, with the *Justice* proudly in the lead, turbolasers already in position to fire upon the enemy fleet. Behind it, four warships flew in formation, looking like a flock of giant, slow-moving geese flying in formation. Daniel sighed in amazement, staring at their salvation. They had been saved just in the nick of time.

"Managed to scoop together a few friends to help you all out," the Magnum said, his physical form appearing on the holoprojector. "It's not an entire army, but it'll do."

Pantura had a huge grin on her face. "Shane, you amazing, amazing person," she complimented, standing up from her position on the floor.

"I hope I'm not late."

"You're right on time," said Caitlin, her skin looking less pale as she heard his voice come through.

"Glad I'm not late to the party. I'm sure neither are they."

Daniel turned to look across the nebula, and saw a mass of starfighters emerging from the hulls of the Coalition warships, taking formation opposite the Gorogs. "Don't mind us," came Vorlax's voice from the gunship's radio. "We're here to help!"

"I would get over here before the Gorogs see you," Shane pointed out kindly.

"Right." Daniel grabbed the steering wheel and fired up the engines, flying them past the Gorog ships and across the nebula. All of the warships barely paid them any attention, focused as they were on the bigger threat at hand. They gracefully swooped through the pink mist and parked itself beside Vorlax's squadron. Bombers and attack fighters kept entering the group, and Vorlax himself parked his own specially-marked ship next to Daniel, the special markings adjacent to the cockpit giving the commander away.

"Have you ever been in a real space battle before?" asked Vorlax over the radio, sounding ready to shoot down some Gorog ships.

Daniel would have laughed if the Gorogs were not amassing their own armada across the way. "Can't say that I have," he replied, gripping his steering wheel tightly.

"Well, you're about to get a hands-on introduction right now," said Vorlax. Daniel could only assume that he was smiling cockily inside his starfighter.

Daniel nodded to himself. "Foulor!" he said, turning around to face him. "Can you please get back in the gunner's chair? You have my full permission to blow up as many Gorog ships as you'd like."

Foulor gave a wicked smile. "With pleasure," he said, climbing back up the ladder to the cannons.

"I'll keep an eye on Pantura in the back," Vraxis offered. "Make sure she doesn't get stunned again."

Pantura gave him an irritated look, but eventually nodded. "I appreciate the gesture," she said, walking slowly back

575

to the living quarters.

Daniel watched her go, then turned the radio on. "Shane, can you do us a favor and attempt to clear us a path to the *Deceiver*?"

"You got it, Daniel," said Shane, surveying the battlefield from the bridge. "Vorlax, you caught that?"

"Roger," he replied, hands on the controls for his starfighter. He opened the intercom between all of the starfighters waiting to attack. "Attention all pilots!" he called out. "We're going to attempt to breach the Gorog defenses and clear a path so Daniel and his team can reach the *Deceiver* without too much trouble. Your only goal is to eliminate the Gorog starfighters and keep them at bay. Understood?"

All of the pilots acknowledged with "Roger that, sir."

"Commence attack!" came Shane's voice over the radio. "And may the Belt give you the strength to survive this battle!"

Every single Coalition starfighter fired up their engines and started forward, Vorlax leading the charge. Daniel upped the power to their ship's thrusters and joined the charging armada, Caitlin holding onto her seatbelt. The Gorogs delayed their reaction at first, until some of their own pilots activated their own ships and launched forward as well. The two fleets found themselves on a collision course with each other, and neither one of them slowed down as they barreled at each other.

Shane had left the radio on to keep on giving directions, and everyone could hear him belt out "Fire at will!" from where he was on the bridge. A second later, streams of plasma flew overhead and impacted into the Gorog's warships, sending shockwaves of energy rippling across their shields. A return volley came from them in retaliation, and soon the cruisers were engaged in a heavy firefight, sending lasers darting between the two fleets as they rushed towards each other.

"Ready weapons!" called out Vorlax over the intercom, extending his laser cannons from his ship. The other pilots around him did the same, Caitlin grabbing the forward cannon controls and leaning forward, as the giant squadron of Coalition ships met with the Gorogs.

Instantly, chaos exploded in the peaceful and serene nebula, as the ships buzzed around like flies, trading weapons and swarming around isolated members of each squadron. Vorlax vanished from Daniel's sight as he banked to the left and swooped around a trio of Gorog fighters, who peeled out of view with their lasers firing. A Coalition ship briefly popped into view in front of them before it was shot to pieces by multiple Gorog fighters, who were then destroyed by a ship they could not see. Daniel dove downwards and righted their ship, then put two Gorog ships right in the path of the forward cannons. Caitlin spotted them, took the bait, and destroyed both after a brief yet furious volley.

"Nice shot!" said Daniel, concentrating on weaving through a dense cluster of dogfighting ships.

"Thanks!" replied Caitlin, also concentrating on her own task.

They passed through a narrow opening in the swarm and rose up through the spherical mass of ships, blasting another one apart as they went.

"Watch out for those two ships up there!" warned Caitlin, keeping half an eye on the scanner.

Daniel rolled around them as Foulor shot one of them down, fully concentrating on keeping them in one piece.

From his command post, Orvag could only watch as a huge Coalition squadron came charging at his own ships. Ever since he had seen those cruisers emerge from the pink gas, he had been unable to move, just fixated on those ships. He had expected Shane to intervene with his plans, but with four backup cruisers? That had barely factored into his plan, as he had figured that they would not be able to get the necessary forces in time. The large starfighter squadron heading his way begged to differ. Dormak had to intervene in order to give the command to attack, but as he was finishing it, Orvag was snapped out of his trance.

"That's a huge force," he commented slowly, as if he was barely comprehending the magnitude of the setback he was now facing.

"You're not helping by sitting here as though Gorzak has hypnotized you," chided Dormak, referencing one of their gods. "Are you here or not?"

"I'm here," he growled at Dormak. He turned to his men. "Charge up all weapons and divert as much power as you can spare to the shield generators! All batteries have my permission to fire at will! Target the command ship!" He stared out the window as he watched his ships begin to surge forward. He smiled wickedly at the sight. "It's hunting season, after all," he added sinisterly.

His men, also seemingly frozen at the arrival of Shane, sprung into action and obeyed their orders, targeting the *Justice* with ruthless accuracy and precision, the turbolasers whirring to life and spitting out massive plasma bolts with the destructive power of a ballistic missile. Orvag watched them go to work, then turned around and sat back in his throne.

"I knew that Shane would want to stop them before we encroached on Arajor's sector," the king mused in a low voice.

"What do you think the Coalition wants?" asked Dormak, staring at the fleet outside.

"Victory," replied Orvag, staring as the various starfighters darted around the nebula like the strider insects that danced on the surface of the water back on Tersak. "He'd know I'd be here. If he can take our invasion fleet out, and more specifically, me, it would mean defeat for sure. Losing the labor camps is one thing, but losing me…"

"I assume the boy—Daniel—wants to save his home

planet as well," theorized Dormak.

"That, and something else as well."

Dormak looked confused for a second, until he saw the king marking the orange ship on the battlefield, swooping around like a bird in flight. Then he remembered who they had down in their holding cells. "The boy's mother?" he asked.

"Tell some of your men to go watch over her cell. And prepare the others for potential boarding parties."

"Boarding parties?"

"Oh, yes," said Orvag slowly, staring into Dormak's eyes. "I'm counting on them to show up. And I want any maggots who step foot on this ship to be greeted with a hole in their chest and a smoking rifle in front of them."

Back on the battlefield, the space was becoming congested with smoldering remains of starfighters as each side whittled down each of their rival's number with increasing proficiency. Daniel's ship was being tailed by two Gorog starfighters, and although he had stronger shields than the standard starfighters that were dancing all around them, they were definitely taking a further beating from the constant laser fire.

"I need those ships gone, Foulor!" called Daniel into the back of the ship. "Like, right now!"

"Your fancy flying isn't helping!" yelled the twin, despite shooting down one of the fighters as he spoke.

In the back, Pantura had managed to wedge herself into the corner of one of the rooms, and was managing to stay still even as they cartwheeled through space. Vraxis was attending to her stunned hands, applying small stimulations to rekindle her nerves.

"Are they still numb?" he asked her, applying pressure onto her palm.

"I'm getting some feeling back..." she answered, curling her fingers, then instinctively grabbing onto the bolted-down lamppost as the ship swerved hard to the right and nearly sent her sliding onto the floor.

"I swear, they're going to make me sick!" complained Vraxis, trying his best to keep the device steady as he applied pressure onto other points on Pantura's hands. "Does he seriously not know how to fly properly?"

"About that..." said Pantura, trying to brace her feet against the walls so she would not move. She reconsidered her next words briefly. "You know what, it's not really important. Best saved for some other time."

Vraxis was too concerned to care. "Fine." He pressed down hard on the very center of her palm, and her fingers all reflexively curled. "There," he said, setting the device down. "You should be good."

She nodded and attempted to stand up, only for another intense maneuver to send her sprawling onto the ground. She tried again, succeeding, and stumbled out of the door and into the atrium. The ship shuddered and vibrated, but she managed to reach one of the seats without falling over and strapped herself in. Vraxis came up as well.

"Pantura!" exclaimed Caitlin, managing to glimpse her from the corner of her eye. She turned to look at her, but was rudely jarred when the ship abruptly pulled up, a jarring movement that rattled everyone's brains.

"That was your time to shoot!" said Daniel, a bit ruder than he meant to, for sure, but he was too busy trying to keep them alive to bother.

"Sorry!" Caitlin turned back and resumed her task, blowing up another Gorog starfighter who crossed into the path of the twin laser cannons. Daniel pivoted their ship and swooped around a pair of dogfighting ships, while Foulor knocked another enemy ship out of the battle.

"I'm being swarmed!" came a voice from the radio, the signal briefly popping back in in between the constant white noise from the lasers. "I'm–aghhhh!" There was a loud sound on the other end for a second, only to be replaced with another Coalition pilot frantically screaming on their end of the radio, before they were inevitably replaced by the sounds of a destroyed ship. Then, Vorlax's voice came over the radio, sounding, to the worry of Daniel, incredibly scared.

"I have six Gorog ships on me! Someone help me!" came his distress call. "They're all over me!"

"I see him!" said Caitlin, pointing across the battle. Sure enough, Vorlax's starfighter was visible, smoking from one engine, with multiple hostiles on his tail. Daniel boosted the engines and flew through a haze of ships and lasers, the shields depleting significantly as they took the brunt of the force. But, even as the ship groaned in protest, it stayed on course, and brought the pursuing Gorogs into Caitlin's crosshairs. She fired upon them, destroying two easily, and managing to send a third into a chaotic spiral before the others broke off from Vorlax and ran.

"Thank you Daniel!" exclaimed Vorlax over the radio, sounding relieved.

"No problem!" radioed Caitlin.

They heard Shane's voice break through the radio once more. "Alright Daniel, we're charging up the main phaser to punch through the *Deceiver's* shields. Once that happens, you'll have a thirty-second window to get through before it gets patched. So you'll need to be quick!"

"Understood, Shane!" replied Daniel, steering around a hunk of smoldering wreckage leftover from a Gorog ship. "Just get those shields down and we'll handle the rest!"

"Good luck!" Shane put the intercom down, then turned around to survey the rest of his ship. "Get those shield phasers charged and ready to fire! We'll only get one shot at this!"

"Sir!" called out one of the crew members from the side of the bridge. "We've got trouble!"

The Gorogs had already charged up their shield busters and had fired several concentrated beams of energy at the Coalition's cruisers. Everyone braced as the phasers raked across the shields, causing sparks to fly from the monitors and the ship to shake uncontrollably. The damage alarms went off, but the ship managed to hold together.

"Shields are down by–" began one of the tech crew.

"No damage reports!" barked Shane. "Get those busters online now!" He ran to the intercom. "Vorlax, I hope you're doing better out there than we are in here!"

"I doubt it!" replied the commander, concentrating on blasting another Gorog starfighter that was swerving around his shots. "There's a lot of these buggers! We're taking some heavy losses."

"Just shoot as many as you can! The moment we get Daniel inside the *Deceiver* we can concentrate on eliminating the supporting ships! Keep those fighters away from the main cruisers while we prepare to breach those shields!"

"Roger," replied Vorlax, shutting off his radio and destroying another starfighter, his ship passing through the fireball. He scanned the field for Daniel and the others and found them being chased by a Gorog starfighter that was dodging all of their lasers.

"I can't get this guy off our tail!" said Foulor, still draining ammunition like it was going out of style. "He's too…too…quick!"

Another laser blast rocked them, and Daniel grunted hard from the jostling. "Just keep trying! He'll have to make a mistake eventually!"

"Daniel, the stern deflector shields are down to ten percent!" warned Caitlin, briefly pausing her targeting to check on the monitor.

"Just keep shooting! We've got to give Shane more time!" Daniel dove straight down and caused everyone to experience hard negative g-forces as they plunged through the throng. Their pursuer followed them, still trading lasers with Foulor as they went. He shot them again, getting dangerously close to hitting one of the engines, and Daniel performed extreme maneuvers in the hopes of getting the Gorog off their tail, but to no avail.

"Shields are at 5%!" Pantura yelled. "Another direct hit and we'll be exposed in the back third of the ship!"

"*Foulor!*" yelled Vraxis. "Get that blasted fighter off our tail now or you'll never hear the end of this from me! Even if we're dead, you'll never hear the end of this from me! I swear it on my grave! You hear me?!"

Vraxis's yelling must have worked, since Foulor became so spooked that he unloaded the rest of the plasma magazine and hit the Gorog starfighter, causing it to lose control. "I hit it!" he said triumphantly, sounding like an excited child on Christmas.

"Great!" said Vraxis mockingly. "Now keep up your good luck and shoot some more!"

"Um...the turret's not firing," Foulor said.

"What?"

"There's also this word on the screen that I'm only now noticing that says, '*Out.*' Do you think that's part of the reason?"

"Imbecile!" shrieked Vraxis. "You used the whole bloody magazine?!"

"Calm down, Vraxis!" Caitlin blasted at him. She picked up the intercom. "Shane, how close are we to the shield breaching?"

"Ten more seconds!" he replied.

"Make it quick, please!" she said. "We're extremely vulnerable in the back quadrant, so we could use some help!"

"You want some help? Here—" He was briefly interrupted by some loud noise in the background, and by Daniel dodging some more burning wreckage. "Look outside your window!"

"You look! I'm driving here!" said Daniel.

Caitlin peered outside her window, and watched as a concentrated beam of energy flew across the nebula and slammed into the side of the Gorog flagship, delivering a deadly blast of plasma for several seconds until it finally subsided, leaving a large patch of the *Deceiver* without its shimmery blue look, and punching a circular hole in its hull.

"You've got about thirty seconds to get inside before the generator comes back online!" warned Shane. "Make it fast!"

Daniel juiced up the engines and spun them around in a circle, allowing more enemy ships to come under fire, and then sped up and charged headlong at the opening. "I'm giving it all to the engines!" he said, the ship accelerating under his supervision.

"You're draining it away from the shields!" said Pantura.

But they were rapidly gaining speed, the opening in the ship's hull growing larger by the second. The engines droned like giant insects as they barreled through space. Daniel's palms sweat underneath his gloves as he concentrated on aiming correctly. He could see enemy ships closing in around them, rocking their ship with laser blasts as they tried to stop them from reaching safety.

"Shields are gone!" reported Caitlin. They began to hear the metal creak as dozens of concentrated lasers slammed into them.

"Everybody hang on!" called out Daniel, pushing down on the accelerator as far as it would go.

"Don't miss, don't miss, don't miss..." Caitlin repeated over and over as the opening, impossibly small, drew closer to swallow them up. They shook like crazy, buffeted on all sides by laser fire, the alarms flashing red and blaring into everyone's ears. It looked as though they were going to slam into the side of the hull.

Everyone held their breath as Daniel course corrected ever so slightly. The opening was small, it was getting bigger, it was large enough to fit their wingspan, it was right on top of them...

Daniel slammed on the decelerator as the opening's true scale loomed over them, the hole in the hull getting closer. There was a bump as the edges of the wings clipped the sides of the opening, then a bigger bump as they ship collided with the fragile interior of the *Deceiver*, smashing through corridors and walls as the engines sent them through the ship, knocking everyone around and causing sparks to fly from just about everywhere. The viewscreen cracked as they rammed through solid metal. Despite all this, Daniel managed to keep the ship stable until they exploded from the claustrophobic interior and into one of the main hangars, where they bumped into parked starfighters and maintenance equipment, the engines igniting a fuel cell that erupted in a blinding flash of orange. Finally, the ship scraped against the bottom of the hangar and came to rest in a pile of debris left by its own destruction.

Chapter 34

Orvag felt the shields sputter out from the force of Shane's breachers. He felt something thud faintly into the side of the hull, and he heard the proximity alarms switch to the higher pitch of the breach alarms, that only sounded when major exterior damage had been sustained. But it was only when Dormak came running up when the full extent of what had happened became clear.

"The starboard hull has been breached!" he said, his voice more panicky now. "We've been boarded!" In his hands, one of the hangar's security cameras was pointed at the still body of Daniel's gunship. "They came through the gap Shane burned through our shields and busted through the hull into the central hangar!"

"Who boarded us? How many?" Orvag rose from his throne to get a better look, watching as the small shadowy figures of Gorog soldiers ran up to the downed ship, weapons in their hands. "That's Daniel's ship!" he said. "Were there any other ships?"

"None, Orvag. Just them. Scanners are detecting lifeforms aboard. Five of them, to be exact. We're not sure what they think they can accomplish with a force that small…"

"I do." Orvag turned to face Dormak. "I want you to take as many guards as you can spare. Go to the main reactor and defend it. They'll try to destroy it for sure, thus bringing down the ship." He turned to face the rest of his men. "Evacuate the bridge! All of you! Get to the secondary bridge and resume piloting the ship from there! All of you! Yes, even you!" he barked at his intelligence officers, who were giving him questioning looks. He then pulled out his intercom. "All batteries, concentrate your fire on Shane's warship! If you bring it down, the rest of the supporting cruisers will have no one to take orders from!"

"What do you plan on doing?" asked Dormak, once he had set the radio back down.

"Ensure that Daniel, the boy, finds his way here." Orvag's voice had lost its wit. "Because this time, I want to ensure that he's properly dead by the time I'm done with him."

They turned to face the tablet screen, watching as five distinct entities left the safety of the crashed gunship's armored hull, lasers beginning to fly across the hangar as they engaged with the pack of Gorog guards.

"You really think that he's that big of a threat?" asked Dormak. "He never seemed that way, from what I saw of him."

"He may be from Earth, but, believe me, there was something about him, when I confronted him on Lhassi. He's not like the other humans we've captured. He clearly has leadership skills, and there's no telling what else Shane's put into his brain. Besides, the rest of his people will be either dead or dying, as soon as the invasion fleet gets out of this godforsaken nebula. He would want to protect them, for sure." He pulled out one of his swords, letting the sharp blade rest on his forearm menacingly.

"So you'll take care of him, I'm sure. What of the other four?"

"Eject them from the airlock. It'll be more amusing for us when we don't have to clean up after them."

Deep in the belly of the ship, Ms. Phillips and Max had no way of knowing that rescue was a lot closer than it seemed. In fact, at first, they did not even realize that they were under attack. Without windows in their cells, they could not look outside and see the ships buzzing around. All they felt was occasional vibrations and the pitter-patter of Gorogs running outside their cell block. "Is something happening out there?" asked Ms. Phillips, rising from her bench and trying to look outside.

"Don't know. Don't care. It's probably nothing anyways," replied Max in his usual indifferent voice from the next cell over. "They haven't come to check on us in a very long time. It's not the time to assume that they would now."

"It doesn't sound like nothing. Look." Ms. Phillips moved to the window facing the corridor outside and peered out, seeing nothing out of the ordinary at first. But then she heard the sounds of alarms faintly blaring in the distance, and the flashing red lights. "There's warning lights on in the hallway down there. Looks like there might be some emergency out there."

"Probably just a drill." Max had appeared in the window, and was looking at Ms. Phillips quite condescendingly. "They happened all the time in Skorjion."

"This doesn't look like one," said Ms. Phillips, noticing a large group of about a dozen Gorog troops running up the prison block past their cell. "A big group of guards just ran past."

As she continued to stare out through the glass, a message came piping through onto her intercom. "Attention, all personnel!" came the voice of Dormak. "We have Orion Coalition intruders on this ship. They've landed in the main hangar and could be roaming the ship at any time from this point onward. Everyone is to be on high alert and keep a look out for them at all times. They are all heavily armed and extremely dangerous. If you see them, shoot to kill. We're not here to take prisoners this time around! Repeat, Orion Coalition intruders in the main hangar! That is all."

The ship shuddered again as Ms. Phillips processed that announcement. "Intruders?" she repeated.

"Intruders? What do you mean 'intruders?'"

Ms. Phillips came away from the window to look at Max. "They just said that there are intruders on board. Intruders from the Orion Coalition."

Max raised an eyelid. "You sure that's what it said?"

"I know what I heard, Max," she replied, feeling really excited on the inside, but afraid to move too much for fear of disturbing some of her injuries.

Max's face brightened a little at the news. "Well, let's hope that whoever they are comes and rescues us, and doesn't just leave us trapped down here." He turned away from the window. "Those must be laser blasts, what's rocking the ship. It can't be anything else, if there are Coalition agents on board. No way a boarding party would've been able to get on board without assistance from a fleet."

Ms. Phillips immediately lost some of her jubilation. "Laser blasts? Are we safe in here?"

"There's shields protecting the ship," explained the lizard. "No lasers are going to breach the shields. At least, so long as they hold. Hopefully, they will."

"How long do they last?" asked Ms. Phillips.

"Who knows?" replied Max. "They can last forever it seems, but they have a point where they'll give up eventually. When they do, you'd better hope that you're off the ship."

"Great." Ms. Phillips sat down against the wall. "So, who do you think is leading the fleet? Shane? Vorlax? Or perhaps someone else?"

"Well, Shane was in some hot water with the Coalition High Council, last I heard. Said that he was not allowed to leave Arajor under any circumstances. So it's probably someone else."

"Arajor? That's the capital city, correct?"

"Yes. Shame you were captured when you were. It's easily one of the most beautiful cities in the galaxy. You would've loved to see it in person. Shame that we're just going to be left down here."

"Don't say that. I have faith in whoever's leading the charge."

At that moment, another announcement came in over the loudspeakers. "Attention, all guards!" came Dormak's voice again. "The hunters Foulor and Vraxis have teamed with two Terrans! If you see either of them, shoot on sight! They are officially traitors and are to be dealt with as such!"

Ms. Phillips's head was swimming. "Vraxis and Foulor, working against the Gorogs?" she said incredulously. "I thought they were Orvag's best hunters!"

Max nodded. "They were. We caught Vraxis just after you were taken, and Foulor, being too dumb to make a logical decision, surrendered himself to us a day later. Turns out, when it comes to bounty hunters like them, money does all the talking."

That made sense to Ms. Phillips, unlike the announcement that two Terrans were in the ship as well. That had made her worried, because the only ones she could think of were Daniel and Caitlin. Why they would lead the boarding party was beyond her, after all they'd been through.

At that moment, a huge blast rocked the ship, and power briefly cut out in the cell block. The cells went dark, leaving Ms. Phillips about as blind as a bat. She heard rustling from the cell next to her, and the sound of metal creaking. "Max?" she called out.

"One second!" he replied.

"What are you doing?"

There was no answer, and when the power was restored after a few seconds, and Ms. Phillips went to check on the window between their cells, Max was gone, the cell door pulled open by several sets of sharp claws.

"Shane!" radioed Vorlax over the radio. "Daniel made it inside! Now we need help taking out these heavy cannons! They're destroying our ships!"

Shane steadied himself as the bridge of the *Justice* was rocked by more shield breacher fire. "On it!" He turned to his men. "All batteries, target those supporting cruisers! Maximum firepower!"

The *Justice's* cannons unleashed a heavy attack on the Gorog fleet, bruising their enemy's shields and destroying the occasional starfighter. As the assault continued, the cruiser on the far left suddenly flickered, the blue sheen fading from its hull. Its weapons stopped firing and it appeared dead in space.

"The power's out on that cruiser on the left!" Shane yelled. "Focus your fire there! Send those foul Gorogs back to the abyss they climbed out of!"

A hailstorm of lasers were thrown up at his command, directed towards the disabled ship. Numerous little fireballs appeared to dance across its hull, the ship listing to one side as severe damage was inflicted upon it. After a concentrated blast with a shield buster, the rear half of the cruiser exploded, sending chunks flying across space, the front half floating of its own volition without any stabilization or engines.

"Good work, Shane!" Vorlax radioed. "That's one cruiser down!"

"Four more to go!" Shane replied, the ship faltering a bit as a Gorog phaser slammed into the *Justice's* shields, the communication briefly turning to static.

"Sir!" called out a bridge officer. "The shields are down to forty percent!"

"There's no turning back now! We've committed!" Shane turned around to fixate his gaze on him, stoically resolved. "Press the attack! Take out the rest of their support ships! But hold off on the *Deceiver*! We need to allow Daniel and his team time to accomplish their task!"

The *Justice* vibrated again as another heavy dosage of blasts rippled across the shields, Shane almost losing his balance in the process.

"How long should it take for them to bring down the main reactor?" yelled Vorlax over the radio again.

"Hopefully not long! Just give him as much time as possible!"

Daniel ducked behind his cargo container as more laser fire came streaking by him. Taking his pistol in hand, he shot twice back at the small squadron of Gorog personnel who had positioned themselves between the five of them and the exit. To his left, Vraxis was shooting through a narrow gap in a pile of debris that was the perfect setup for his sniper rifle to shoot from. Foulor, meanwhile, had grabbed a minigun from the crate of weapons that Pantura had brought on board, and was spraying it like crazy, the plasma cartridges flying out of the side of it in huge numbers, filling up one guard with dozens of burning holes. Pantura and Caitlin were crouched together, Pantura using her rifle to shoot down Gorogs who showed their face, and Caitlin, who was mainly watching everything.

"You didn't grab a weapon?" Daniel asked, taking a second to shoot another round before looking back.

Caitlin raised her hand and it lit up blue-green, the same blue-green color that it had the first time he had seen it. "Don't need one," she said, slowly waving her hand around, and causing a series of lines to appear in the air, forming the outline of a long javelin with a long tip. The weapon almost looked fake, but it found its way into Caitlin's grip, upon which she stood up for a brief second and lobbed it at the Gorogs, impaling one of them clean through the chest before it disappeared, as though it had never existed.

Daniel just stared, lowering his pistol briefly. "Okay, then. Never mind." He looked past her to Pantura. "Did that just happen?"

"Yes," she replied, shooting another Gorog down. "Yes it did."

There was a loud explosion as Foulor threw a grenade

into the few remaining enemies, taking out two more and sending the rest scattering for their lives. "The path's clear!" Vraxis hissed, lowering his rifle and standing up from his cover, slinging it across his back.

Everyone stood up, putting away their weapons and gathering around each other in a circle amidst the smoking hangar. "Now what?" asked Caitlin, looking around for any signs of incoming Gorogs.

"Someone needs to wait in the hangar and ensure that we have a way out." Daniel pointed at the large hatch on one wall. "And we'll need a working ship if our ship doesn't start."

"I'll stay behind and ensure that we can escape as soon as we're done here," volunteered Pantura.

"Good." Daniel turned to Foulor. "Do you want to cause some real destruction today?"

Foulor's face perked up like a dog being offered a treat. "Excuse me?"

"All of those explosives attached to your bandolier," said Daniel. "Vraxis, can you two find your way to the main reactor and rig it to blow?"

Vraxis shouldered his rifle. "You don't need to ask. I'll make sure he gets there. *Without* attracting unwanted attention, right?"

"I guess," said Foulor, although he still sounded excited to go with them.

"I'll go too," said Caitlin, stepping forward, but Daniel reached out an arm to stop her.

"What are you doing?" he hissed. "I thought you were going to stay with Pantura."

"She'll be fine. Besides, the reactor core will likely be crawling with Gorogs. The twins, with all their skill sets, could use some extra firepower."

"Caitlin, as much as I would love you to help out, I'm not sure that I can manage properly if your life is in danger. I

593

don't think I can."

"Then don't. Daniel, I'll be fine. I promise."

He laughed. "That's exactly what we all said before we escaped Skorjion."

She put her hand on his shoulder. "I mean it, this time."

"Don't worry, Daniel," interrupted Vraxis, walking forward. "We'll make sure she returns safely. Under oath of our gods."

Daniel felt the warmth slowly returning to his face. He nodded. "Okay, then. But be careful."

"And what are you going to do?" asked Foulor.

"I'm going to have a look around. See if I can't find the brig in the process. Or I'd settle for Orvag as well."

Vraxis tossed him a small projector. "Here. This is the device we got to navigate around this ship. Follow the blue pathway to the monorail in the center of the ship and take the yellow train to Station Five. That will let you off at the main bridge."

Daniel flipped the device on, and a detailed map of the warship, complete with a marking where he was, popped out. "Thanks," he said, turning it back off. "Anything else that needs to be said?"

No one spoke a word.

"Then let's split up," he said. "We'll meet back here as soon as everything's done. Good luck everyone." He turned to Pantura. "Did I hear Shane say something about the Belt or something?"

She nodded. "'May the Belt guide you to safety.' It's a famous saying of good luck before a daunting task."

Daniel jerked his head at her. "What she said."

They all nodded and went their separate ways, Vraxis leading his brother and Caitlin towards the front of the hangar, while Pantura ducked back inside their ship. Daniel watched as they all slowly grew smaller, until they finally passed through a small door some distance away and disappeared. Once he could no longer see them, he pulled up his map and started to walk through the hangar, through a doorway and into the ship's dark, red-lit interior.

    The hallways on the *Deceiver* were much smaller than the *Justice's*, and it would have been difficult for three Gorogs to walk abreast down one of them. The faint light made it difficult for Daniel to see his targets, even with his new photoreceptor being way more sensitive to light than his eye. He ran into three Gorog guards on the way, all of whom he easily dispatched, the first using his pistol, after a brief shootout, and the second and third using the retractable sword he had grabbed from the crate, slicing the guard's neck and dropping him silently before he could raise the alarm. Moving cautiously, he worked his way through the claustrophobic and dark hallways, until he heard the sound of wind whooshing up ahead.

    He rounded another corner and saw the source of the noise; a gigantic atrium that seemed large enough to house the entire *Justice* inside of it. Running across the space, going from one end to the other were two pairs of maglev rails that ran parallel to each other. And as he glanced from one side of the cavernous room to the other, he saw a train come streaking around the corner and fly past where he was. He glanced down at the nearest rail and saw that he was standing on the edge of a station platform. Daniel turned to face the wall behind him and saw a yellow line painted onto the steel. There was also a map placed onto the wall below that, but it was written in a language he did not understand. However, the image on the map told him everything he needed to know, as there was a clearly-laid out diagram of the *Deceiver's* interior. He could see the bridge marked clearly on the map, and could tell exactly where he needed to go.

    As he was studying his surroundings and the map, a bell chimed nearby, and he turned around to see another train pulling in, slowing to a hard stop at the station platform. There was a single Gorog on board, but he was dead before he knew what had happened, a hole shot in his chest from Daniel's rifle. Aside from him and some cargo containers, there was nothing else on board, and since Vraxis had mentioned the yellow line, and this seemed to be it he shrugged and went aboard, finding a handrail to grab onto.

Then the train lurched forward and shot into the atrium, the station, and the hangar, fast getting smaller behind him.

The train zipped through the atrium at high speeds, whizzing past openings in the wall with large catwalks crossing overhead, other stations, and trains going in the opposite direction, most carrying large numbers of Gorogs towards the bow of the ship. The wind was fierce, and Daniel had to use both hands to stay securely upright. Thankfully, his robotic arm made it easy to grab hold of the handrail, the servomotors tightening his grip on it and locking him in place. He made sure that he had grabbed his suit helmet from where he had set it, next to the weapons crate inside their gunship. Sure enough, it was attached to his back, ready for use whenever it was needed.

After just a few minutes worth of travel, and an intermittent stop midway through the journey, the train began to decelerate to a halt at another station, and Daniel, after verifying his location, hopped off. Taking his weapons in hand, he walked onto the platform, the train pulling off to its next destination. He entered another dimly-lit corridor that branched off from the station, traveling down it cautiously. He ran into no guards, but it wasn't until he came to a pair of elevator shafts that traveled upwards that he lowered his defenses. Pressing the button, the twin doors on the left opened, and, after another brief hesitation, he passed through them and took a position inside the lift. The doors slammed shut behind him, and he began to quickly ascend vertically through the *Deceiver*. At first there was nothing to see, but after a brief moment, a window in the shaft allowed him to look out across the massive hull, facing towards Shane's fleet, which was still engaged in battle with the Gorogs. Lasers darted around him, and he could start to feel the cruiser vibrating with each impact. Then, as soon as it had appeared, the sight of the battlefield disappeared, and the doors behind him were opening.

He slowly stepped onto what he could only assume was the bridge, his rifle raised and ready to shoot. The massive window overlooking the carnage outside, the hundreds of crew officer seats, and, of course, the giant gilded throne sitting on a balcony gave it away. The throne had its back turned to Daniel, and he cautiously circled around it, expecting to see Orvag in there. Daniel knew that the Gorog king would have set a trap for him, and he fully expected to encounter him. Yet, as he got within view of the front, the throne was empty. Confused, he peered over the balcony, where more controls were visible below. He descended the flight of stairs, taking his rifle closer to him, and pointing it around corners. He took note of the stark lack of Gorogs, not even the main navigators. Every seat was empty, and from the looks of it, they had been abandoned in a hurry, as a few had drink cups sitting next to them with liquid still inside. Still, Daniel refused to lower his rifle, keeping it raised, and waiting for someone to show their face.

"Back from the dead already, Daniel?" came the all-too familiar, unsettling-as-always voice.

"I never left," replied Daniel, now more alert than ever. "Surprised?"

"Speechless. I would've never expected anyone, not even Foulor, to walk away from that explosion. I still can't wrap my head around it." There was a brief pause from the disembodied voice. "Still, I'm pleased that you didn't get off unfazed by it."

"You may regret that. You've pissed me off. And you don't have an oil refinery to act as your plot armor this time, Orvag. Why don't you come out of hiding? Show me some of your Gorog hospitality that you guys are famous for!"

"Oh, I will." Orvag sounded excited, like he had been waiting for this day for a long time. "I'll give you a party that you won't be able to forget. Or walk away from."

"Where's the brig, Orvag?" Daniel demanded, glancing around him and checking every crevice he could find. After a second, he saw something suspicious that caught his eye.

"What does it matter? As soon as I'm done with you, she's next. I should've killed her when I had the chance."

Daniel smiled, then pointed his rifle at a dark corner that was shrouded in shadow. He fired it, letting the plasma round impact the wall just to the right of Orvag's head, marked by the faint sheen of his crown. The king immediately emerged hastily, face a hard mask of anger, his bulbous eyes narrowed into slits. The flashing lasers from outside flickered across his features, which were just as menacing as last time.

"This time, you're the one who won't be walking away. You're not going near my home planet. Shane is outside, nibbling away at your invasion fleet, and your precious flagship is about to turn into a giant bomb, courtesy of your old hunters."

"By which time I'll already be gone," snarled Orvag. "As soon as I deal with you."

Daniel advanced, letting the faint light flash across his robotic appendages. "I'm not asking you again. Where's the brig?"

Orvag did not answer. Instead, he took two steps forward, expecting Daniel to retreat. To his surprise, the boy was unfazed this time. In fact, Daniel took a step forward himself, determination crossing his face.

There was another muffled explosion, followed by more vibration. "I'm not afraid of you anymore," said Daniel. He tossed his rifle aside and grabbed the hilt of his sword, letting the blade shoot out. "And I don't need a rifle to stop you."

Orvag growled in his throat. "I think it's time that I teach you one last lesson," he said. He reached behind him and pulled out his two scimitars, letting the blades fall to the steel floor, scraping against it and making an eardrum-assaulting noise. He then struck a defensive pose, both weapons leveled at Daniel's chest. In response, he grabbed his hilt with both hands, refusing to break eye contact with the king.

    Then Orvag broke into a sprint, Daniel doing the same. The two of them charged at each other, meeting with a shower of sparks as their blades collided with a loud clang.

Chapter 35

The twins shot down numerous Gorog guards in their path as they charged through the heart of the *Deceiver*, Caitlin bringing up the rear as she struggled to keep up. She had been running for nearly five straight minutes now and was out of breath, while Foulor and Vraxis barely broke their concentration as they swept aside any enemies that crossed their path.

"Are you sure that this is the right way to the reactor?" she called out, letting her magic sword drop to her side.

"We lived on this ship for over a year, Caitlin!" Vraxis replied, sniping a Gorog head that appeared out a side hallway. "I know where we're headed!"

Foulor took out a small wave with his minigun. "He's right, you know!" he added. "We don't agree on much, but he knows where he's going more than I do!"

They had left the monorail behind them, and were moving quickly through the heart of the warship, hoping to reach the main reactor before their position could be locked onto by security. Staying in any one place in time, Vraxis had said, would be very dangerous, as hundreds of Gorog guards would swoop down at any time and trap them. Thus, stealth while moving quickly was the motto of the hour, as the three of them battled their way through the red-lit hallways. This was surprisingly difficult, not least to Foulor yelling loudly while he unloaded large quantities of ammunition from his minigun.

A short while later, they came to a roadblock, as over a dozen guards were camped down a long corridor, preventing anyone from going past them. At the end was a bright light that seemed to pulsate like a living organism. "That's the reactor core, just behind those guards!" pointed out Vraxis, taking cover as more lasers were shot over his head.

"Can't we find another way in?" asked Caitlin, ducking

behind the corner. "There's gotta be another entrance!"

"They'll have posted guards there, too! We need to break through here!"

They returned fire on the guards, who refused to yield and blasted their cover with multiple lasers. "I can't get a clear shot!" complained Foulor, who's minigun was given no time to charge up in between Gorog volleys.

"Use one of your explosives!"

"I'm saving them for the reactor!"

Vraxis groaned and turned to Caitlin. "Don't you have magic now? Why don't you use your wizardry to help us clear a path?!"

"I've struggled with ranged attacks! I can't do it consistently!"

"Well, right now, we're in a terrible spot, so unless we break through soon, we'll be swamped by guards! You have to break us inside!" He shot a guard dead briefly in between sentences. "Just do it!"

Caitlin, still hesitating, threw aside her sword and concentrated, trying to drown out the sounds of rifles firing and the twins yelling at each other. She let the Madorax energy build up inside of her, then let loose the charge, just as Erwid had taught her to do. Her arm flew back, but the blast sailed around the corner and landed next to a group of guards, who were knocked back through the open door by the force of it. The stunned Gorogs shot back, but Caitlin, crouched safely behind the corner, charged up another shot, releasing it and taking out two more guards. Foulor, seeing the guards confused by the dazzling beams of energy, broke out of his cover and unloaded the rest of his magazine in the corridor, all of the remaining guards falling before his wrath. When the dust settled, the corridor was lined with Gorog bodies, and two large burn marks leftover from Caitlin's energy blasts. Vraxis and Foulor just stared at her for a second, her hand still faintly glowing.

"That was awesome!" exclaimed Foulor.

"Wow," Vraxis said, actually sounding impressed for once. He then pointed his rifle down the hall they had just come from and shot two more guards without even looking. "Now, can we go ahead and finish our mission now?"

She nodded and they passed through the hallway, stepping over the guards as they went, Foulor shooting one that was still showing signs of life. They entered the reactor chamber and were greeted with a massive room, lined with a multi-story series of catwalks, stretching up a hundred feet or so. They surrounded the huge reactor column, which descended from the ceiling, tapering to a point that was glowing like a star, linked to a large, round base with hundreds of dials and monitors on it.

And coming from behind the column were at least several dozen Gorogs, all armed with armor and heavy-duty rifles. And tailing them all was Warden Dormak, carrying a gigantic warhammer with a huge spike on one end, wearing thick metal protection on his chest and an evil glare on his face. The guards took up defensive positions around the reactor, weapons leveled at the three trespassers, Dormak striding through the defensive line, gaze locked on the twins.

"*Traitors!*" he yelled, slamming his hammer down with a loud thud. "Helping out the Orion Coalition! I thought you two were better than this!"

"So did I!" barked Foulor, his minigun already raised to point at the warden's head. "We were never your property, Dormak! It's time you get that idea in that thick skull of yours!"

The warden eyed them coldly. "Kill them," he ordered his men, backing behind the line. The Gorogs opened fire, and Caitlin hastily dove behind cover once again.

"Any bright ideas?" she yelled at the twins, who were hiding safely behind a large support pillar.

"Survive!" yelled Vraxis, shooting one of the guards with his sniper.

Caitlin whipped out another sword, the weapon dropping into her left hand as the magic lines connected. She then fired out another beam into her right hand, missing the entire line of Gorogs and slamming into the wall behind them.

"You want some of me?!" she heard Foulor yell off to the side. "*Here!*" A stream of blaster bolts launched from the barrel of his minigun, cutting down a large chunk of the enemy line. Then a grenade thrown by a guard forced him to duck behind the pillar as it detonated. He reemerged and fired off a few more shots, until the barrel stopped rotating and refused to fire more.

"I'm out of ammo!" he yelled, ducking again as a Gorog came forward with a rocket launcher and deployed it. The projectile slammed into the ground near Caitlin's hiding spot, and she felt a wave of heat wash over her, singing her hair slightly. The line of Gorogs pressed forward, starting to box them in. Caitlin could see that, in just a few moment, they would be surrounded and would have nowhere safe to hide. Remembering one of the tricks deployed by the Madors during the Gorog raid, she discarded her sword and swapped it for a large shield, then, praying for her idea to work, rose from her hiding spot quickly. As she expected, every Gorog in the line stopped, swiveled to point at her, and unloaded a ton of laser fire at her.

"Get down!" Vraxis barked at her. But Caitlin refused, the shield taking the brunt of the lasers as they repeatedly slammed into it, the impacts rippling across the blue-green surface. With her free hand, she charged up another blast and lobbed it around the shield's perimeter. She expected it to knock back the Gorogs she was aiming at, but instead, the blast vaporized two of them into dust, their helmets falling to the floor. She immediately covered her mouth, shocked.

"Nice shot!" called out Foulor, who now had a window to emerge from his cover. Now carrying a huge stick with a thicker end, almost like a club, he bear-rushed the line of guards, who scattered as he came at them, the reduced number of lasers ineffective at stunning him. Vraxis followed him out of his cover, shooting a guard who was coming at them from behind, while Caitlin pocketed her shield and traded it for a long spear, running past the crates she was hiding behind and knocking out another guard with a blow to the head. She turned to find Vraxis and Foulor in the chaotic scene, and instead saw Warden Dormak, his huge build stepping closer to her, his hammer scraping against the metal floor.

"Caitlin," he said, raising his hammer and gripping it with both hands.

"Dormak," she replied, a sword sliding into her other hand, so she was now dual-wielding weapons. Remembering her fight with Pantura, she struck a defensive posture, bending her knees and preparing to dart as soon as Dormak came at her.

And came at her he did, as the warden roared like some wild beast and charged her, the hammer raising surprisingly quickly over his head. She jumped aside, the hammer slamming into the floor with a huge *CLANG*, leaving a sizable dent in the metal. Dormak whipped around and swung the hammer at her head, only barely missing her as he ducked under it. She then stabbed forward with her spear, expecting it to pierce the exposed armpit of the warden, but instead, it bounced off his armor chestplate, knocking her briefly off-balance. She dodged another skull-crushing blow, missed a swing from her sword, and then tried to fire off another beam of Madorax energy. Dormak's hammer deflected it, sending it exploding onto the ceiling of the reactor chamber. She ducked underneath another hammer swing, but before she could fully recover, a surprise backhand came out of nowhere and sent her flying back, both of her weapons flying out of her hands. She landed hard, her cheek stinging and her chest winded. She scrambled to her feet, replacement weapons materializing into her grip, as Dormak charged her once again. She once again dodged the first strike, but then the hammer came swinging around like a baseball bat. Her shield took the brunt of the impact, absorbing most of the power behind it, but it was still strong enough to knock her into a support pillar. The impact caused her to bite her lip, and she began to bleed slightly. Dormak seemed unfazed, approaching once again.

Grunting with pain, she stood back up and prepared herself to meet the rapidly approaching warden, who was looking more and more confident in victory.

On the bridge, Daniel and Orvag were locked in a colossal duel of blades, and, much to Orvag's fury, his opponent was not yet dead.

Orvag, the king of all the Gorogs, was naturally a very skilled fighter. He had been trained to use dual swords for years, and was considered to be a deadly duelist in battle. The problem was that such a skill was rarely demanded of him, and he had not had a chance to hone his abilities in the last few days, resulting in his skills being a bit rusty around the edges. Daniel, on the other hand, had less overall training than Orvag, but still had Vorlax's lessons stuck in his mind, plus his old martial arts training, which included some melee weapons. On top of that, although Orvag was dual wielding, Daniel's single blade, combined with the added strength from his time in Skorjion, almost put them on equal footing. Almost.

Orvag lunged at him with an overhead strike, which Daniel raised to counter. The two blades collided repeatedly, generating loud clangs and sparks as Orvag pushed Daniel down the steps and into the lower deck of the bridge. Daniel's sword was a whir as he parried each of Orvag's blows. Often, there were a lot of close calls, with him only barely able to block in time. What was really deciding the victor, though, was the raw power behind Orvag's strikes. Even when dual wielding, the king had some serious force behind each swing, and it was starting to wear out Daniel's left arm. Nevertheless, as he dodged a savage diagonal cut, he continued to hold his own, even sneaking in a few offensive strikes at certain points.

Then Orvag got crafty, and faked a blow with his left sword, instead coming inside Daniel's defensive box and elbowing him in the face, jarring his senses. The king used this opportunity to disarm his opponent, Daniel's sword clattering across the bridge floor. Suddenly defenseless, Daniel avoided two more strikes, then saw Orvag swinging across at his neck with both swords. In an act of fear, he instinctively raised his right hand. It should have been a pointless gesture, as there would have been little Daniel could have done to stop those two razor-sharp weapons from decapitating him, just like Fero-Shak. But, instead of the weapons going through his arm, there was a metallic *clang*, and Orvag went stumbling back, completely stunned and in disbelief.

Daniel glanced briefly at his right arm, remembering that it was, in fact, no longer made of flesh. He realized, right there, that he had a huge advantage over Orvag. And not a second too soon, either, as the king recovered from his initial surprise quickly, and attacked Daniel again. Each of his sword strikes was met with Daniel's robot arm, which acted like a special defensive wall protecting his vital chest and head. Orvag tried overhead, underhand, sideways cuts, but all were blocked by Daniel's arm. Then, as Orvag unleashed a flurry of attacks, Daniel's left leg, his robot leg, came up and kicked the king in the chest, sending him stumbling back. Daniel used this opportunity to roll behind him and scoop up his sword off the floor, rising back up into the same defensive position as before.

"You know, for a king who's killed more people than probably any dictator from Earth, I expected him to be a little bit better at swordplay." It was probably Daniel's anger that brought out the taunting. There were no pleasantries, no negotiating, no civilized talk happening here. It was war, and one of them would not be leaving this ship alive.

Orvag's face burned with malice as he considered his foe once more. "Shane has certainly taught you well," he said coldly, twirling his right-hand scimitar about. "And imparted to you his arrogance and pride, as well."

"You'll find that there's a lot more about me that you'll hate," Daniel fired back, lunging at Orvag and swinging down a hard overhead blow.

They continued to duel across the bridge, Orvag backing Daniel up the stairs to the top deck with a furious offense. Daniel blocked blows from every side, using his new limbs as additional defense against those twin scimitars. Orvag was clearly vexed that he had been unable to breach Daniel's defenses successfully, and his swings were becoming a bit more wild. Daniel continued to play defense, occasionally striking out at the king, never making contact but still proceeding to force Orvag onto the defense temporarily.

As he was coming in for another strike, Orvag feinted a blow from his sword and instead kicked Daniel in the chest, sending him stumbling back in front of Orvag's throne. Yelling loudly, the king lunged, both of his weapons coming down hard for a vicious blow. Daniel raised his sword just in time, locking blades with Orvag. The two of them stared each other down, neither of them giving in to the other's push. Daniel felt his arm begin to tense up as Orvag's stronger body pressed down on him. Gritting his teeth, he saw the elevator door close by. But there was no way he'd be able to make it there safely without getting cut down. He felt his sword lowering as he fought to keep it up, and Orvag's face twitched with delight as he pushed down all the harder.

Outside the bridge, Vorlax was shooting down straggling Gorog fighters as they clashed with the now-larger Coalition force. One of them was shot in the engine and went spiraling towards the *Deceiver's* bridge, unable to veer off of its course. Daniel saw it coming in hot out of the corner of his eye, and with a terrific shove, broke off from Orvag's push and leapt away from the bridge's window. The starfighter slammed into the bridge, shattering part of the window and creating a massive vacuum as the air began to rush out into space. Daniel sank his sword into the floor, gripping the hilt as his feet were pulled towards the hole in the bridge. Nearby, Orvag was holding onto the railing of the balcony, slowly crawling his way towards the emergency panel on the wall, still holding onto his weapons. Daniel felt his anchor give a little, sending fear crawling down his body. He frantically looked for something solid to grab onto, but there was nothing.

Eventually, Orvag reached the emergency panel and mashed a button on it. A large, red shield expanded to cover the hole, stopping the air from rushing out. Daniel's body landed back on the ground, still somewhat shocked, but not enough to notice Orvag glaring in his direction. Pulling his sword out from the floor, he stood up and rushed for the elevator doors, opening them hastily as Orvag chased after him. He leapt inside and pushed the first button he saw, then watched as the king threw one of his blades at him. He gasped, raised both his arms to protect himself, and then heard the sound of the blade clanging off of the closed doors of the elevator.

Sighing loudly, he sank to the floor, panting. He whipped out his communicator. "Pantura, status report. How are things going at your end?"

There was a brief pause of static before her voice came through. "Daniel! I'm glad you're still okay! Things are getting a bit hectic down here!" She temporarily paused to interrupt with the sounds of laser fire. "They sent a ton of Gorogs to the hangar. I'm doing my best to hold them off, but I'm not sure I'll be able to get our ship ready to go before you all get back!"

"Just do the best you can! I'll keep you informed on our progress!"

"Got it!"

He hung up, and Pantura, crouched behind a barrel in the hangar, shot back at the roughly two dozen guards that were all bombarding her with their weapons. Two of them fell, but the others drew in closer, pinning her down under her cover. Sparks rained down on her, and when she tried to get in a clear line of fire from her cover, her hand was shot clean through, causing her to yell out and drop her rifle. As she stared at the hole in her palm, she heard the Gorogs shouting at each other and advancing in her direction. Knowing that she had seconds before she was completely overrun and executed, she grabbed her rifle off the floor, ignoring the pain in her hand, and prepared to take down as many guards as she could.

She heard the guards calling to each other, and then heard more shouting, followed by the sounds and flashes of laser fire. There was a sound like nails scraping on metal and the screaming of several Gorogs, as well as strange grunting and heavy breathing. Seeing no lasers flying over her head, she stuck her head out from behind her cover to see Max, in his massive twelve-foot long glory, biting at the head of a fallen guard, all while the others shot at him, their lasers doing nothing against his scaly hide. With their attention momentarily off her, Pantura pulled out her rifle and shot down three Gorogs in rapid succession, and as they turned around to shoot back at her, Max leapt up from behind, roaring furiously, and ended two guards' lives with one savage swipe of his long claws. A second later, and silence descended upon the hangar, Max's face and body splattered with blue blood, looking more animalistic than ever.

"M–Max!" exclaimed Pantura, a little unsettled by his appearance. "How did you escape the brig?"

"Power went down for a moment," he replied, tongue sliding in and out like a snake's. "One thing I learned from my time in Skorjion: Gorog cells use hydraulics to keep the doors closed. Without power, you just need something to slide into the door cracks and you'll be free." He flashed his claws in her direction. He stared around. "Where are the others? I know you didn't come alone."

"Reactor core," she replied. "They're going to blow the reactor core."

"Half of the ship will be guarding that room." Max turned to stare at her. "Do you know which way they went?"

She pointed to the other side of the hangar. "There! They went that way. And take this, it'll help you pinpoint their location." She tossed him a small tracker, and he caught it.

"You sure you don't need my help?" Max asked.

"I'll be fine! Just go! They likely need your help more than me!"

Nodding, Max ran towards the open hallway on all fours, while Pantura turned to eye another approaching troop of Gorog soldiers. Grabbing her rifle, she popped out from behind her cover and opened fire at them, the hangar returning to a warzone.

Dormak slowly advanced on Caitlin, who had her back to a support pillar and was slowly going pale with fright. The warden's hammer scraped against the ground behind him, making the same unholy noise as before. She looked around, seeing the twins grappling with three Gorog brutes, of no help to her. She turned back to face Dormak, whose face was alight with malicious delight as he prepared to bring down his hammer on Caitlin. Thinking quickly, she charged up a beam of Madorax energy and lobbed it at the warden's chest. The move caught him off guard, and he was sent backwards, grunting as he landed hard on the floor, the hammer thudding next to him. Caitlin sprang to her feet, conjuring up new weapons.

Dormak dusted himself off, no longer smiling. "That's the last mistake you'll ever make, Miss Caitlin," he growled, using her real name again. He picked up his hammer and charged like a bear, Caitlin rolling to the side of his charge. The warden pivoted mid-run, striking out with the handle of his hammer at her head, but she was already out of range. She tried to blast Dormak with two more energy blasts, but the warden spun his hammer and deflected both of them. Her shield then absorbed a heavy swing, and although she was sent skidding backwards, it felt less jarring than the first time. But no sooner had she recovered did Dormak use his hammer to send a barrel of supplies her direction, swinging it like a club and sending it flying across the room. And as she recoiled from the near-miss, the warden was charging at her again. She swung her javelin at him, striking him in the head and sending him stumbling, dropping his hammer in the process. He went headfirst into a pile of crates, winded and a little dazed. A small cut popped out on his forehead, left there by the tip of Caitlin's weapon. She took a couple of steps back, still on the defensive.

On the other side of the reactor core, Foulor was grappling with his two opposing Gorog brutes. Each of them was a head taller than he was, but his raw strength held him in place as he wrestled both of them, growling like an animal. To his left, Vraxis was playing cat-and-mouse with another one, a long sword in his hand, darting around heavy blows from the brute's steel knuckles. He landed a cut on an exposed part of his thigh, causing him to stumble and yell out in pain, before swinging wildly at Vraxis's head. It missed, but the following uppercut sent Vraxis flying back, onto the floor.

"Stop playing with those brutes and help me out!" he yelled at Foulor, moving out of the way of his angry opponent.

Foulor, letting loose a terrifying loud warcry, gave a huge effort and heaved both Gorogs backwards, sending them both crashing to the ground. Seizing a metal pole from the ground, he knocked one out with a hard strike to the head, before the second swept out Foulor's legs and dropped him. The hunter rolled onto his opponent and proceeded to beat the pulp out of the other brute, refusing to hold back his punches. The brute tried to cover his face, but Foulor shattered one of his arms with nothing but raw force and proceeded to whale on him until both of his fists had Gorog blood splattered on them and the brute was lying still. Rising to see another dozen Gorogs charging into the reactor core, he turned to Vraxis, who was clutching his rifle.

"More incoming!" he said, grabbing the metal pole off of the floor.

Vraxis turned around, saw them being rushed, and dove for cover as more laser shots filled the room.

Back over on the other side, Caitlin was blasting Dormak with energy, trying to hold him at bay. The warden had retrieved his hammer and was advancing on her again. Having realized that charging at her was a foolish option, Dormak had opted for a slower approach, closing in the distance between them slowly, allowing him to use his hammer to block any attacks. Caitlin, fear creeping its way back inside her, knew that Dormak had figured her out and tried to hold him back, to no avail. Then, when Dormak was a stone's throw away, the worst thing that could have happened happened; she failed to discharge energy from her hand.

She stared down at her hands, still glowing blue-green, but no longer pulsating the way they had before. Dormak, sensing his opportunity, charged at her once more. Caitlin felt a sword slipping into her hand, and moved to dodge the charge. But Dormak had anticipated the movement, and instead of raising his hammer, extended his arm to grab her. Caitlin felt all of Dormak's muscle lift her up and throw her across the room, her weapon falling from her grip and her body impacting the ground hard. She attempted to rise, but Dormak was already on her, kicking her down and leaving bruising on her ribs. Pain shot through her body as the warden delivered another ruthless kick to her. She attempted to claw away from his attacks, breathing shallowly, but Dormak easily trailed behind her.

"You would have been better off staying in Skorjion," the warden taunted her, following behind her slowly. "I would have graciously extended more of Orvag's hospitality to you and your friends."

She turned herself over so that she was now facing up at Dormak's face, almost hidden by his tentacles. "The only thing that you would have extended to me was death," she snapped back. "Because that's all that you dish out to others!"

Dormak stopped briefly. "Mmm. You're probably right about that. Still, your efforts were all in vain regardless. You may have gotten lucky and escaped, but I'm still going to kill you now, so it makes no difference!"

He lifted her into an upright position, and proceeded to punch her hard twice, knocking her down the second time. Coughing a little, she spat blood out of her mouth, her jaw in intense pain. Before she knew what was going on, she was lifted back up again, and punched again, this time sending her brain into a daze. Her vision went fuzzy, and she could feel fluid coming out of the corner of her mouth. She was kicked again in the ribs, and she cried out, everything turning slightly gray. She tried to rise, but collapsed, her body too injured to do so. She saw Dormak's outline walk away from her, bend over, and retrieve his hammer. He started to walk towards her and all she could do was wait for the warden to deliver that last, killing blow and end her suffering.

Yet Dormak did not immediately kill her. Instead, he grabbed her by the throat and lifted her off the ground, her feet dangling in midair. She choked, trying to break free of his grip, but it was in vain, for the warden had an iron grip and would not let go. She then tried the same tactic she had used to kill that Gorog brute; she conjured a small knife and, using all of her strength, tried to jab it into his eye. But before she could stab him, he dropped his hammer and used his free hand to grab her wrist, twisting it painfully and causing her to drop the knife.

"You've conjured your last trick, Caitlin," snarled Dormak. "I may have underestimated you initially, but you now die!" He picked up his hammer and aimed the spike on the end at Caitlin's torso. Before he could drive it into her, though, something huge slammed into Dormak from the side, sending him out of Caitlin's field of view. She fell, gritting her teeth in agony, rubbing her throat gingerly. Somehow, she managed to get into a sitting position, groaning in pain as her ribs ignited like fire. She turned to follow the warden, who was standing up, looking enraged. Between him and Caitlin, over two hundred pounds of lizard stood, spines bristled and nostrils flared, inch-long claws visible on the tips of his digits.

"Max?" she said, her brain only barely able to process what was going on.

"You!" growled Dormak, eyes narrowing. "You're supposed to be rotting in your cell!"

"I was," retorted Max, voice dangerously low, perhaps due to his massive size. He was easily three times larger than his normal dog-sized frame, now looking less like a lizard and more like a full-blown dragon.

"Has life outside of Skorjion made you soft?" Dormak's voice was more snide than anything, although there was maybe still a hint of questioning in there.

"Maybe." Max craned his neck to look behind him, and, for perhaps the first time Caitlin had remembered, there was no sort of condescending stare, no arrogance, not even a hint of ego in those yellow irises. He then turned back to Dormak, flexing his claws. "But that won't stop me from ripping the flesh clean off your bones."

Dormak charged him again, the hammer swinging around for a blow that was sure to kill should it land. Max moved aside, then swung at Dormak with his claws, missing him. In this form, the lizard was far larger than the warden, although Dormak was no slouch either, rising up to meet his opponent with a ferocious yell.

Vraxis ran up from behind Caitlin, taking notice of Max. "What's *he* doing here?" he asked. "He's supposed to be in a cell!"

She didn't reply, and instead stood up, her body wobbling as more pain lanced through her. She hoped that her ribs were not broken, although the sensations coming from her chest did not give her confidence. "Where's Foulor?"

Vraxis pointed to where his brother was punching some Gorog security guards. "He'll be fine! Let's go kill this son of a grozlak!" He ran towards Max, leaving Caitlin to steady herself and to start walking slowly after him, gritting her teeth.

Dormak and Max were locked on the other, each of them trying to break through the other's defenses. Max was bigger, but Dormak was an elite fighter and dangerously fast for his size. Max tried to swipe at him, but he barely made contact most of the time, only managing to leave shallow scratches in Dormak's arm one time. The warden, meanwhile, was dancing around his opponent, his hammer coming very close to Max's body. Then Max made a tactical error and left his entire flank exposed, allowing the warden to leave a huge bruise in his side. Max roared and swung at hims with his claws, this time managing to score flesh and leave three parallel, bleeding cuts on the warden's leg. Dormak gritted his teeth, refusing to yell out in pain, and unleashed a furious offensive, leaving massive bruises in Max's side whenever he found an opening. The lizard yelled out in pain constantly, retreating backwards, trying to stall those terrible blows from injuring him further. He attempted to bite at Dormak, but the hammer met his open jaw instead and sent him collapsing onto the ground, three teeth breaking off from his mouth, where he lay, in pain and barely able to move.

"You're an old relic, Max," the warden growled, standing over his opponent and putting his foot on Max's stomach, the lizard groaning from the bruises there. "Soon, the Gorog Empire will have no need for beings like yourself." He gripped his hammer tightly. "You really thought that you could kill me by yourself? You couldn't even properly kill Vraxis when he attacked!"

Dormak then stopped as a strange sound filled the air. He wondered what it was. He felt a strange sensation in the center of his back. He then felt it slip further through his body. Then he saw the glowing blue-green outline of a sword poke through his stomach, blood seeping out around it in the process.

Caitlin rose up from behind him, the handle of her sword almost fully inside of Dormak. "He didn't kill you by himself," she told him, no ounce of joy left in her voice. She had rarely wanted to do harm to someone in the past, but for Dormak, the Gorog who had captured her and tortured her for five years, she wanted nothing more than to end his life right then and there.

Dormak was in shock initially, but he then started to laugh. "Really? You really think that you will be any different than him? You don't have the spine to finish the job."

In response, Caitlin narrowed her eyes and yanked her blade out of his stomach. The warden made a tiny noise, then started to foam at the mouth. His breathing became more shallow, but his eyes still displayed every bit of hatred as they always had.

Then Max, standing up from where he was laying down, flashed his claws at Dormak once more. Eyes narrowed down to slits, he roared, dug his claws into Dormak's face, and pulled in opposite directions with one, violent motion. Caitlin hastily averted her eyes at the last second, although her stomach still heaved slightly from the sounds of liquid splattering all over the room. When she uncovered her face, she saw Max, standing there, panting, with something that looked like gray cloth hanging from his claws. The warden's body remained upright for a few more seconds, and then it keeled over, his face, with half its flesh missing, staring lifeless up at the ceiling.

The three of them stared at the body for several seconds, until Foulor came up from behind. "Took care of the last of them," he said nonchalantly. "What did I miss?"

Vraxis glared at him, then pointed at Dormak's body. Foulor followed his finger, and immediately his smile disappeared.

"Oh," he said, noticing the mauled face, then noticing Max, almost eight feet tall, with Gorog flesh between his claws. "Oh, shoot. Sorry, Vraxis, I didn't know."

"Next time read the room better," his brother replied, shouldering his rifle and walking off. "Come on, let's get this place rigged to blow."

They walked off, taking the explosives from Foulor's belt and attaching them to support pillars. Caitlin, no longer feeling nauseous, but still wincing slightly, approached Max, whose face had finally relaxed into a normal pose.

"You're big again," she noted, looking up at his face.

He shrugged. "What more do you want me to say? I already told you, I don't know how it happens."

"I wasn't going to ask about that," she replied, holding her side tenderly. "I was going to thank you. For saving me."

"It's nothing. You came after me first. It was the least I could do." He glanced off to one side, looking a little…sheepish? It was an odd expression for the lizard to wear on his face. He grumbled a little, then added, "I suppose I should also say thank you, for saving my bacon too."

She nodded. "Don't worry about it. It's what friends exist for. Now come on. Let's go help the twins rig this ship to explode."

Max looked surprised at her words, but he soon nodded enthusiastically and bounded off towards the twins, who began

617

yelling at him to drag over some fuel cells from the corner. Caitlin lagged behind, reaching for her communicator.

"Daniel? Daniel, do you copy? A progress report would be amazing right about now!"

The elevator doors opened, and Daniel ran out, knowing that Orvag could be right on his tail. Sweating from his forehead and scared for his mom, he ran through the corridors, pistol in his hand and ready to shoot any Gorogs in his way. He found a train parked in the station and jumped on board just seconds before it took off. Then, exhausted and sore, he collapsed against a pile of cargo, feeling sick to his stomach. That fight had drained him physically and mentally, and it took his communicator buzzing to jar him awake.

"Caitlin?" he asked, hearing her voice slice through the garbled static. "Are you okay?"

"I'm fine," she replied. "The twins and I are preparing the reactor core to explode. Did you find your mother?"

"Not yet, but I did find Orvag." Daniel peeked over his shoulder briefly. "Listen, Cait, I need some help over here. I held my own, but I can't beat him by myself. If you could get to my coordinates, we should be able to overpower him. Meet me by the *Deceiver's* hyperdrive as soon as you can!"

"I'll be right there!"

They hung up, and Daniel shut his eyes, exhaling loudly. He figured that Orvag would chase after him, but he was hoping that he had a decent headstart on the king. He stood up to watch as trains whistled past him, the *Deceiver's* central atrium passing by in a blur. The hyperdrive for the warship was located towards the front of the vessel, and given how important a place it was, it would be an ideal place to meet up with Caitlin and the others. Then, they could trap Orvag and deal with him once and for all.

"You know, when I first proposed to Dormak to invade

Earth, I bragged to him and said that I could take over the entire planet with just one warship's worth of troops and resources. After seeing how difficult you are to kill, perhaps I was correct in assembling an entire fleet to attempt to take your rotten world down."

Daniel turned around to see Orvag standing two train cars back, looking as angry as ever. "How did you catch up to me so quickly, Orvag? You can't teleport around, can you?"

"Do you really think that, as captain of this ship and the king of the empire who made it, that I wouldn't know every conceivable shortcut and secret passageway within this hull?" Orvag took several steps forward as he said it, crossing onto the car behind Daniel's.

"Good point," he replied, pulling out his sword hilt. "And you may need a new fleet after this. Because I don't imagine any of your ships leaving this nebula alive."

"You might have thwarted me here, thus denying me the opportunity to invade Earth and Arajor," said Orvag, drawing both of his scimitars, "But at the very least, I'll be able to exact my vengeance on you."

Daniel's blade slid out from his hilt. "You want vengeance?" He pointed his sword at the king's chest, defiantly showing no fear. "Come and take it!"

Orvag wasted no time in leaping across the gap between their cars and swinging down at Daniel, who blocked both blades with his own. The two of them resumed their duel, whizzing past guards on catwalks and support beams as Orvag put Daniel on the defensive with a furious attack. And, as Daniel blocked strikes with his weapon and his robotic arm, he began to realize that Orvag had adjusted his strategy to better counter his own. Feeling a cold hand begin to clench around his heart, he dodged a vicious downward cut and came with a backhand blow, which the king easily dodged. Daniel lost ground as he came perilously close to the exposed edge of the train car, while Orvag pressed his advantage. Daniel barely had time to parry each of the king's blows, and eventually, the king broke through his defense entirely and kicked him off the edge of the train. His sword went into the corner of the car, and he was left dangling a hundred feet off the ground moving at fifty miles per hour, with nothing but his fingertips keeping him on. Orvag approached the edge, glaring down at his helpless opponent.

"You've been a boil on my neck long enough, Daniel!" he shouted down at him, using his boot to push Daniel's left hand off the ledge, leaving him holding on by one hand. "You could have gone home and rested in peace, away from a conflict that was never yours to begin with! Instead, you elected the way that led you here, right to your death!" He kicked at Daniel's right hand, his robot one, which barely held on as it slid back slightly. Terror filling his body, Daniel felt his body tighten up, like it always did before an anxiety attack. *No!* he thought, fighting the urge. *Not like this! Not like this! Fight him!* His body wanted to let it all end, as Orvag tried again to kick him off the train car. Daniel's leg nearly hit a support beam as it went flying past. Orvag tried once again to push him off, leaving Daniel holding on by just a finger.

Fighting the urge to drop, he reached up with his other hand, found the ledge, and, with an almighty effort and assist from his robotic limb, pulled himself so hard he grabbed the roof ledge above him and kicked Orvag in the chest. The king went stumbling back, and Daniel used the opportunity to pick up his sword and swing it hard at Orvag's chest. He barely brought his two weapons into position, the metal clanging together loudly, the shock of the impact traveling down Daniel's left arm. They exchanged several more rapid blows, Daniel's sudden attacks throwing Orvag off his game, and allowing Daniel to score the king's left hand with the edge of his weapon, causing him to drop one of his scimitars into the cavernous drop below them.

The king yelled out, staring down at his suddenly empty

hand for a second, while Daniel regathered himself. Now enraged beyond all reason, Orvag unleashed a flurry of rapid-fire attacks, striking at metal and flesh as he tried to break Daniel's guard. Their swords were blurs, with the sounds of metal clashing regularly filling the space, but they had finally reached even terms. Then Orvag made another crucial mistake, as Daniel got inside his box and elbowed him in the chin. Then, he swung his weapon and found the king's beard of tentacles, severing three of them and sending them below them.

Orvag roared in pain, blue blood dripping from the stumps on his chin. Daniel felt a sense of pride at landing an actual hit on the king, but that quickly turned to regret as the king unleashed another savage series of attacks, putting Daniel back on the defensive. Even with his robotic arm, Daniel found himself unable to block all of the king's attacks, and he was cut on the cheek thanks to a mistimed parry. Once more, he found himself backing towards the edge of the train car. Then Orvag came in, swung at Daniel with an intense strike, knocked his weapon aside, and sent it spiraling away from him, dropping to the atrium floor.

Orvag lunged at him, thinking that Daniel was helpless without his sword. Instead, he was punched in the face and sent reeling backwards. And not a moment too soon, either, as their train slowed to a stop at their destination, and Daniel jumped off of the vehicle and ran for the nearest corridor, fumbling his communicator in the process.

"Caitlin? Where are you?" he yelled into the device as loud as he could. "I'm in a bit of a situation right now and could use some backup!"

"We've set the charges and are heading towards the hyperdrive!" replied Caitlin, sprinting down a hallway, the twins and Max right behind her.

"Caitlin, you're going to have to cross the atrium to get to my location!" Daniel glanced behind him briefly to see Orvag entering the corridor also, chasing after him. "And please hurry! Orvag is after me and he's pretty pissed, I'd say!"

He hung up the message. "Come on!" Caitlin shouted at the others. "Daniel's in trouble!"

"Yes, we know!" Vraxis retorted. "You've only told us like five times!"

Unfortunately, as they reached the atrium with all the trains, they found the catwalk to the other side blown in half, with some guards finishing off the last extension on the other side. "Great, now how are we going to get over there?" asked Max, panting. "Fly across?"

Caitlin glanced around, growing more worried as the nearest catwalk she saw was a decent ways away. But something about Max's words gave her an idea. A reckless idea, sure. But it was the only way she could think of to get across. "You three will have to find another way across the gap. Try to aim for that catwalk and meet us at the hyperdrive. If you can't get there in time, head back to the hangar and help Pantura get us a ship out of here."

"What about you?" demanded Max.

"I'll be fine, just go!" she ordered them. They all gave each other confusing looks, but eventually backed away from the broken platform, leaving Caitlin thinking about Erwid's lesson on flying.

"Okay," she told herself, concentrating hard on her power. "Wait until you're close to the ground and then let it loose. It's as simple as that. Of course, if I mistime it, I'll be dead, but let's not think about that, okay?" She backed up, letting the Madorax fill her entire body. She felt electricity course along every vein, and she then, after a deep breath, took a running start and leapt over the edge.

The freefall was terrifying. She wanted to scream as she fell, but she resisted the urge, instead, letting her power travel down her arms and into her fingers, where it collected, waiting to be discharged. She dropped past a monorail track and fast hurled towards the ground. It rose up to meet her, but she held in her energy, waiting until she was mere seconds away from impact. She then, with all her mental fortitude, directed her arms downwards and slightly behind her and discharged all of the energy stored up in them.

    She actually closed her eyes right before she fired off the blast, so she missed the initial launch, but when she opened her eyes, she found herself soaring like a bird across the huge gap in the ship, getting huge air and weightlessness as she sailed in a tall arc overhead. She started to laugh as she started to drop back towards the ground, and she prepared another blast and released it, sending herself skyward once more. She whooped out loud, not even caring that two Gorog guards heard her excited shouts and started shooting at her. The lasers all missed her by a mile, as she sailed across the atrium towards the monorail station that Daniel had marked. She narrowly missed a passing train as she descended towards the platform at rapid speeds. Right before she impacted, she let loose one final, smaller burst of Madorax power, cushioning her fall and bringing her to a manageable speed. She still stumbled and fell, but she barely cared. She felt exhilarated, until she remembered Daniel. She whipped out her radio. "Daniel? You still there?"

    Down in the hyperdrive room, Daniel finally burst in. "Yes! I'm here! Hurry!" He charged onto the catwalk that extended over another huge pit in the room, which led to four giant pillars cracking with electricity. In the center of the room, just below the level of the catwalk, a bright, glowing dot was visible, pulsating energy with every second. He hastily tried to find cover, but there was none. He began to grow worried, looking for anything that would help hide him from Orvag. "Caitlin? How long until the bombs in the reactor room go off?"

    "We set them for eight minutes, so about four more minutes!" she replied. "Vraxis has a manual detonator though!"

"Listen, he may need to set off those bombs early. If Orvag gets in here, then—"

He stopped as the sound of a laser rifle firing cut through the room, echoing off the walls. It rang in his ears, loud as ever, but he barely even noticed the sound. What he did notice was the strong burning sensation in his stomach, and, as he looked down, the hole that had been punched right through his spacesuit and through himself, still sizzling with heat. And behind him, standing in the entrance to the hyperdrive room, holding a smoking rifle, was Orvag.

Daniel sank to the floor, body already going numb with shock and pain as he comprehended the fact that he had been shot. He could not stand up, forced to watch as Orvag discarded his rifle aside and drew his one remaining scimitar. The front of his robes were stained blue from his severed tentacles, and his crown was hanging from his head at an odd angle. There was malicious delight written all over his face, for he knew that Daniel was powerless to stop him. He drew closer, and Daniel did not even try to move. He knew there would be no point.

"So ends the story of Daniel, once and for all," the king said, moving closer, bringing his sword up higher and preparing to raise it over his head.

Daniel's hand reached out feebly and managed to pick up his communicator. "Vraxis," he said, a little weakly, "Vraxis. Blow the reactor core. Now. You—you have to."

"Requesting confirmation, Daniel. Did you say *blow* the reactor core?" the hunter requested.

"You heard me. Do it. And get everyone ready to leave as soon as possible. I'll—be right with you." He hung up, and watched as Orvag approached him, raising his weapon over his head, ready to bring it down on him.

"Just who did you think you were to stand in my way? In the way of the most powerful ruler in the entire galaxy? Who are you?!" Orvag shrieked at him, and he started to bring the weapon down, and Daniel braced for the cold sting of death.

Then the entire ship vibrated like an earthquake, and everything went haywire.

The reactor room was completely vaporized in the resulting explosion, as the entire ship's power system failed and triggered the chain reaction that they wanted. The blast filled the corridors, the sound heard all the way towards the stern of the ship. And it knocked Orvag off-balance and caused him to stumble forwards and drop his weapon; right into Daniel's waiting hand. Grunting with effort, he stood up, and pointed the tip of the weapon right at Orvag's chest. The king looked shocked as he stood, at swordpoint, with his back now to the edge of the catwalk balcony, overlooking the center of the hyperdrive room.

"Who am I?" repeated Daniel, gritting his teeth with pain from speaking. "My name is Daniel Phillips. Son of Amy Phillips and child of God. Citizen of both Earth and the galaxy." He took a step forward, letting every word count. "And the one who rids the galaxy of your filth!"

He kicked Orvag over the balcony with his mechanical foot, the king almost seeming to fall in slow-motion as his royal cloak fell from around his shoulders, his crown slipping from his head. He landed on the central power source, where he lay for a second, looking surprised.

And then there was a violent flash of bright light that nearly blinded Daniel, filling the entire room from corner to corner. And when it subsided and he could see again, Orvag was gone, his crown lying on the floor nearby, without a head to sit atop.

Chapter 36

On the bridge of the *Justice,* Shane was routing the last of the Gorog ships. It had been an incredibly difficult battle, and one of his warships had ended up retreating after sustaining critical damage from a run of suicide bombers. But he had more than equated their losses. Two of the Gorog cruisers were entirely destroyed, their hulls still smoking in some spots, being left to drift across the nebula for eternity. A third was being ripped apart by a constant barrage of laser fire. And, to make things even better, the Gorog starfighter squadron had been completely defeated, with just a few survivors retreating back to the relative safety of the cruisers.

"We're returning now, Shane. We've mopped up the last remnants of Gorog resistance out here," radioed Vorlax, sounding jubilant. "The boys and I are returning to the hangar now."

"Great work out there today, Vorlax!" Shane complimented him. "Get up to the bridge as soon as you can. You'll miss out on the fireworks otherwise!" He switched off the radio. "All batteries, target that damaged support cruiser on the right! Finish it off!"

As the cannons sounded off once again, one of the officers approached him from behind. "Sir, we're reading a strange energy surge from the core of the *Deceiver.*"

"What kind of surge?" Shane examined the tablet with the readings on it, showing a clear spike in the energy output from the ship's reactor. As he studied the readings, his communicator beeped, and he answered it. "Hello?"

"You may want to get the fleet ready to jump to hyperspace!" came in the voice of Vraxis.

"What did you do?" Shane demanded.

"We rigged the main reactor to blow, and, as of about

twenty seconds ago, activated the explosives."

"Where's Daniel and Caitlin?"

"They're right behind us, Shane!" Now Max's gruff voice came in through the radio. "The reactor wasn't completely destroyed, but the damage was severe enough so that it will self-destruct in about ten minutes! We're heading back to the hangar now!"

"Don't leave until Daniel and Caitlin get back!" ordered Shane, sounding overly concerned. "Do you hear me? Do not abandon ship without them! That is an order!"

"Understood! Vraxis, out!"

The transmission cut back to static, and Shane was left staring out the window of the bridge, watching as the lasers flew towards the Gorog cruisers, hoping that they would all make it out alive.

He would not be able to face himself in the mirror if they did not.

In the hyperdrive room, Daniel finally found the strength to stand up, his stomach wound stinging like crazy. He started to move towards the exit, knowing that he still had to rescue his mom. Since she was not on the bridge, he figured that she would be held in the brig, which, according to his map of the ship, was not far from the hyperdrive. As he continued to walk slowly forwards, groaning in pain, he ran into Caitlin, who charged in and increased her pace at the sight of the injured Daniel.

"Are you alright?" she exclaimed, stopping in front of him and noticing the blaster wound in his stomach.

"I'm…" He could not bring himself to say that he was alright, because it was blatantly a lie. Instead, he sucked in air and said, painfully, "Not fine. Not fine at all."

"Where's Orvag?"

"Dead, at least that's what I hope happened. We

need…to go…rescue my mother!" He almost collapsed onto the ground, but Caitlin ducked under his arm and supported him. She reached into one of her belt's pockets and pulled out a small bottle that resembled a bug spray canister.

"Pantura told me about this. It can alleviate the pain for a time and heal injuries faster. Hold still, this might hurt." She bent down, Daniel exposing his stomach for her to get to. She gently depressed the bottle cap and sent a small spray of liquid onto the affected area. It burned like acid, and Daniel bit his lip to prevent himself from screaming in agony. She sprayed a bit more, and it hurt again, this time a bit less than before. She pocketed the bottle, and allowed Daniel to get used to the sensation.

"Ouch," he said finally, but he could already feel the area hurting less from the bottle spray. His strength began to return to his body and he stood up to his full height.

"You should go," warned Caitlin. "I heard Vraxis on the radio talking to Shane. Sounds like we have less than ten minutes until the ship explodes."

Daniel nodded. "Get back to the ship with everyone else. I'll join you as soon as I pick up my mother."

"Be careful!"

He nodded and ran past her, off into the dark corridors. He could feel the ship vibrating more and more frequently from explosions, and he hoped that Vraxis's estimate was correct. The brig would be a very short trip, but getting back to the hangar; this would be close. He increased his speed, moving now at a full sprint, his boots echoing down the hallway as he did.

He ran into no guards between the hyperdrive and brig, and when he finally reached the cell block, he ran straight into it, taking quick glances through the windows to see if he could spot his mom. For about two hundred feet, he saw nothing that resembled his mom. Then he came to a junction and saw, down on the left, two guards going from cell to cell with rifles. He ran down to them, and before either of them knew what had happened, they were both lying on the floor, out cold. Daniel then checked the cells they were hitting, marked conveniently by open doors. And inside one of them, stunned and lying on the ground, was Ms. Phillips.

"Mom!" yelled Daniel, running up to her and assessing her condition. She was still covered in cuts and bruises, and her clothes were all tattered again, but he could feel a weak pulse on her wrist. He sighed in relief, wanting to hug her tightly, but was interrupted by reality. Feeling more blasts rocking the *Deceiver*, and remembering that his time was very limited, Daniel lifted her onto his shoulders and started off on a sprint back to the hangar. He had no idea how bad her condition was, but the sooner he got her to Shane's medical wing, the better. He did not slow down once, not even around corners. He grunted with exertion from carrying her, but his robotic limbs helped the burden greatly.

His communicator buzzed as he was leaving the cell block. "Daniel, if you can hear me, you'll want to aim for the Gorog shuttle on the right side of the hangar," came in Pantura's voice. "I was unable to get our ship ready for flight in time, so we're stealing a ship from the hangar. Meet us there ASAP!"

"I've got my mom safely with me, and I'm on my way! Don't leave without me!"

About halfway to the hangar, there was a huge explosion that rocked the entire ship and sent Daniel sprawling on the floor. The ground shaking like an earthquake below him, and the lights going out in some sections of the corridor, he increased his speed greatly and ran full speed the rest of the way back to the hangar. The hallways were deserted, as all of the Gorogs had either died or were fleeing via escape pods or by ships. He nearly slipped several times on the smooth metal floor, but he had no time left to be cautious. He had to get to safety now.

He burst back into the hangar, which was already suffering damage, as a series of explosions burst through a far wall, ripping through the metal and sending beams and debris hurtling onto the deck. At the other end, near the opening into space, was the shuttle that Pantura had described. As he emerged into the hangar, he saw its engines switch on and start to lift off the ground.

He resumed his sprint, the ship falling apart around him. Great holes were torn in the floor as fire tore through it, leaving large chasms in the deck. A huge beam fell from the wall and landed hard just in front of Daniel, forcing him to jump over it, nearly dropping Ms. Phillips's unconscious body in the process. He could now see Pantura and Caitlin standing on the access ramp to the shuttle, waving him on frantically.

"Hurry!" Caitlin shouted anxiously across the hangar.

Daniel narrowly stumbled clear into an open chasm in the hangar deck, recovering at the last moment, then dodged a falling support beam from the ceiling. Their escape was less than a hundred feet away, and he dodged and weaved through more falling pieces of debris as explosions tore through the hangar structure, carving out holes in the floor. A parked Gorog starfighter went tumbling into a massive sinkhole, vanishing from sight. Daniel stumbled, the entire hangar shaking below him, Ms. Phillips threatening to slide off his shoulders as he ran. He grabbed her arm and leg to hold her in place, keeping his eyes locked on Pantura waving him onto the ship.

Then the ray shield covering the open door, the one thing keeping air inside the hangar, rippled and vanished as the mechanism exploded as the self-destruct sequence reached it. Suddenly, Daniel and everyone else was being pulled towards the gigantic hole in the side, winds whipping at his face and lifting him off the floor. Ms. Phillips slipped from his shoulders and started flying towards it, her body going limp as she drifted away from Daniel.

"NO!" he yelled, grabbing her arm and then grabbing an exposed pipe sticking out from a hole in the floor. He felt the wind trying to drag him to his death, and he gritted his teeth as his arm muscles tensed up, sending pain rocketing down his body. Yelling with exertion, he was relieved when the emergency ray shields came back up and he dropped onto the floor, Ms. Phillips almost falling into the hole in the process. Daniel watched her drift closer to the hole and lunged after her, grabbing her arms yet again. She dangled over the edge, Daniel's muscles screaming to stop, even as she started to pull him into the opening. He tried to stop moving, but his head came over the hole, allowing him to stare into the darkness, with no sign of a bottom. He felt his stomach approach the edge, felt his body tip over...

Then he was suspended in midair over the hole, Ms. Phillips now feeling light as a feather. He floated for a second, feeling completely weightless and confused out of his mind. Then he started to float *up*, his body seemingly defying the artificial gravity.

"Whoa, whoa!" he exclaimed, as Ms. Phillips passed the edge of the hole and back over the hangar floor. He lost his grip on her, but by then it did not matter. He felt the strange sensation release him and drop him and his mom onto the floor. He grunted in pain, sitting up, turning to look behind him, and saw Caitlin standing there, palm outstretched and glowing blue, looking both worried and relieved at the same time.

"What are you doing?" he yelled over the cacophony engulfing the hangar. "You need to get out of here!"

"Not without you!" she fired back. "No one's getting left behind! Not this time!"

Daniel wanted to complain, but he shook his head, planning on dealing with this later. Standing up, thoroughly pained, Daniel lifted Ms. Phillips's body back onto his shoulders, his muscles complaining yet again. They both turned to run to the ship, and found that the ray shield had appeared to block the hole in the hangar; between him and the others. About ten feet of open, airless space lay between them and safety. The access ramp had been shuttered, most likely as a result of the sudden loss of air pressure. Despair started to manifest inside Daniel, as he saw no possible way to get to safety. At his side, Caitlin looked the same way. They had left their spacesuit's helmets on their gunship, and they had nothing else to protect Ms. Phillips. They could possibly survive space for a second or two, but Daniel's mom was already in weak condition. Any exposure to space could potentially kill her.

"Daniel? Caitlin?" came in Pantura, sitting at the controls of the shuttle. "What's wrong?"

"The ray shield's blocked us from reaching the shuttle!" she reported. "We could make it without a helmet, but Ms. Phillips could be a different story! Any exposure to open space could kill her in this state!"

"Did you check your spacesuit belt for emergency pressure wraps?"

"For *what?*" asked Daniel.

"It's a small disc with a sticky side and a button in its center. There should be one on each of your belts!"

They both hastily reached into their belt pouches, the sounds of explosions drawing closer. Daniel found one in his belt and lifted it out. "Got one!" he radioed.

"Good! Now slap it on Ms. Phillips' chest and push the button!"

"You've got less than a minute until the ship's reactor completely fails!" came in Max's gruff voice. "You'd better hurry!"

Daniel set his mom down on the floor, took the disc and adhered it to Ms. Phillips's chest, pressing the button. A glowing, plastic-like sheen started to envelop her body, encasing her from head to toe, like a transparent coroner's bag. She looked like a dead body, but Daniel could see her chest faintly rising and falling, so she was getting air.

"Now send her to the shuttle! I'll go open the access ramp!"

Daniel went to pick her up once more, but Caitlin raised her hand again and started to lift Ms. Phillips up, sending her towards the edge of the ray shield. The shuttle's ramp came down again, and Pantura floated down to the ramp's edge, her spacesuit helmet clamped down on her shoulders. Beckoning to them to send Ms. Phillips over, Caitlin pushed forwards, sending her through the ray shield and into the zero-gravity conditions, where she floated on over to Pantura, who safely retrieved her.

"The rest of you need to jump over now!" she told them over the radio, as she sent Ms. Phillips's body up into the ship.

Daniel turned to Caitlin, who was looking a little nervous. "Have you ever been into space without protection before?"

She shook her head nervously. "Never."

"Yeah, me neither. On my mark, okay? One, two…"

"*Look out!*"

A huge chunk of the hangar ceiling had dislodged over them and was falling towards them. They both ran out of its path seconds before they got crushed. The edge of the roof clipped one of the shuttle's engines, jostling it and nearly knocking Pantura off it before landing on the edge of the hangar floor, taking a huge bite out of the surface and sending it through the ray shield. When the dust settled, there was now a fifty-foot gap between them and the access ramp.

"Daniel?" exclaimed Pantura, staring at the two of them in horror.

"Pantura, we need to go now!" radioed Vraxis urgently. "The ship's gonna blow any second and our engine is leaking fluid!"

"Daniel, you have to get on the shuttle now!" barked Max through the radio.

Yet, as he and Caitlin stared across the gap between

them and safety, they knew that jumping now would be a death sentence. A ten-foot gap was one thing, but a fifty-foot one was too wide. They would be dead before they reached the access ramp.

Maybe it was the fact that Ms. Phillips was out of harm's way. Or maybe it was the fact that he could not see another option. But Daniel, instead of trying to leap across the void, turned to Caitlin. "Do you have any more emergency suits in your belt?"

She shook her head slowly, even as flames encroached around them. "No," she said weakly, sensing the doom approaching them.

Daniel turned back to Pantura, looking at them expectantly. Waiting for them to leap to safety. Instead, however, he picked up his radio, and spoke two sentences that everyone on the shuttle was hoping they would not.

"We can't get across. Go without us."

There was a momentary pause. "You're not serious, are you?" Vraxis radioed back.

"I am," he replied. "Go, save yourselves! Don't worry about us!"

"How?" Now Foulor was on the other end of the radio. "You're both going to die!"

"Thirty seconds to reactor failure!" warned Vraxis, voice shaking.

"Daniel..." He heard Max's voice, no longer gruff or scratchy, no longer deep, but instead, shaking and emotional, something that he had never heard from the lizard before. "You've got to come back."

Daniel, for a moment, hesitated. Max had finally dropped his tough-guy facade, and it was almost upsetting to hear him in despair, after not caring about much of anything the past few days. But he finally spoke into the communicator. "Just go, we'll be right behind you! Go, please!"

634

The shuttle hesitated, and then, after a few moments, it started to pull away from the hangar, Pantura continuing to stare at them through her helmet as she stood on the access ramp, getting smaller and smaller. Finally, she turned away and climbed into the ship, passing through the ray shield and closing the ramp behind her. She slowly took off her helmet, letting the oxygen in the shuttle fill her lungs, yet feeling devoid of air at the same time. She saw Foulor and Max approach her from the cockpit, looking equally shocked and saddened.

A few moments later, the *Deceiver's* main reactor failed.

To illustrate the size of the blast, imagine a nuclear warhead being dropped on a city, detonating, wiping out everything within ten miles of the initial explosion, destroying everything in the process. Now take that imagined thought, quadruple the size of the blast, give it a shockwave that ripples the very fabric of space-time, and the brightness level of a supernova. That is what happened when the *Deceiver's* reactor failed. Being a large ship that ran on a lot of volatile fuel sources, the result was a ship that, should it be primed for destruction, would go out with a huge bang.

Shane was bedazzled by the initial explosion, still insanely bright all the way across the gap in space. Same with Vorlax, who also could not see a thing. Eventually, the brightness was toned down, and Shane could see the massive shockwave rippling across the nebula, blowing away gas and the destroyed husks of starfighters left to drift in the void. There was no sign of the rescue party.

"Any word from Daniel or the others?" he asked one of his communication officers.

"No sir, but we're keeping the scanners running constantly. If they try to reach us, we'll know," she replied, turning back to her screen.

Vorlax came up beside Shane. "That shockwave is getting really close. Now I don't think that we'll be completely destroyed should it hit us, but I would prefer not to be around here when it reaches this spot."

"I'm not leaving until we have the rest of our people on board," the Magnum replied, staring out the window at the ballooning ripple in space, a beautiful, if deadly sight to witness. "The second we see them, we'll get ourselves ready for hyperspace."

"Sir!" called out one of the bridge's crew members. "We're tracking a Gorog shuttle approaching us. Its origin appears to be from the *Deceiver*."

"That's them! Prepare for the jump to lightspeed and open the port side hangar doors!" Shane darted over to the window, where he could see the tiny blip emerging from the white blast behind it. "Try to contact them! See if we can patch them through!"

The communication officer nodded and started fiddling with the controls, attempting to get a signal through. The shuttle was now on the holographic map of the region, approaching fast. "Hangar doors are open, sir!" called out a crew member.

At that moment, static came over Shane's intercom. "Shane, are you there? Do you read me?"

"Vraxis! We're relieved that you're all still alive!"

"You'd better be ready to jump to lightspeed fast! That shockwave is chasing us, and I don't want to be stranded out here!"

"We're preparing to jump now! You may proceed to the port side hangar!"

"On it! Coming in now!"

The small shuttle roared over the front of the *Justice* and dove below the line of the bow, out of sight for the bridge, the ring from the blast close behind. "Captains of the *Constitution, Nobility,* and *Odyssey,* you may make the jump to lightspeed!

Rendezvous at coordinates 0-34-3542!"

The support ships powered up their hyperdrives and started to warp away. Shane waited until the security cameras showed the Gorog shuttle parked in the hangar, and for confirmation from his bridge officers, before giving the same order to the *Justice*. With the shockwave almost upon them, Shane felt the engines power up to full strength and propel them into lightspeed, the explosion rippling over their old spot harmlessly.

For a brief moment, his adrenaline was shooting through his body, barring him from thinking clearly. Then, as he slowly relaxed, he realized something. They had done it. They had beaten the Gorogs, and beaten them badly. He did not know how the incursion mission had gone, if Orvag had died or was still alive, but either way, this was a huge victory for the Orion Coalition. "We won," he said softly.

Vorlax slapped him hard on the back, causing Shane to lurch forward and exclaim. "That's the Shane I remember!" he said, laughing heartily. "Man, we beat those suckers so badly that I don't know if they'll ever recover. That's what they get for threatening to invade Arajor!"

Shane nodded, smiling. "Let's go check on the others. See how they're doing."

They both left their admiral in charge of the bridge and descended down the elevator and into the rest of the ship. They passed through the corridors and reached the hangar, where they could see the shuttle parked near the center. As they walked past pilots and maintenance workers attending to damaged ships, Shane eagerly anticipated seeing Daniel and the others returning in triumphant victory. But when the view of the shuttle's access ramp came into view, he saw five individuals talking with the hangar's general manager. And one of them was unconscious and slung over Foulor's shoulder. Shane increased his pace, hoping that he was just seeing things.

"Shane...wait up!" called out Vorlax, increasing his speed as well.

Sure enough, the Magnum could not see a sign of Daniel or Caitlin. He bumped into two workers on the way to the shuttle, navigating a tight shortcut between two starfighters. Max caught notice, and started to walk towards him.

"Where's Daniel and Caitlin?" Shane asked, as the lizard walked right up to him.

"Turn us around, now," Max ordered, rising to his full height, on just his back legs.

"What? What do you mean?"

"Daniel and Caitlin didn't make it onto the shuttle in time," explained Pantura, running up to the Magnum. "The emergency ray shield in the hangar malfunctioned during the self-destruct sequence and trapped both of them inside."

Shane was in shock. "*What?*"

"Shane," Pantura told him, approaching him, her helmet tucked under her arm. "There was nothing any of us could have done. We only had one emergency breathing wrap to spare. They chose to use it on her." She pointed at Ms. Phillips, whose head was lolling over. "We couldn't have gotten her to safety otherwise."

"You need to turn this ship around," said Max, his voice rising in volume. "We can't just leave them there to potentially die!"

"We can't," said Vorlax, walking up behind Shane.

Max whipped around to look at him. "*Why not?*"

"The hyperdrive was damaged in the fight. We're working to repair it, but we cannot risk changing coordinates," explained Vorlax, a bit coldly. "If we try to change our position while in lightspeed, the generator could overload, explode, and scatter our pieces throughout the Centaurus Arm!"

"We can't leave them!"

"Why do you care?" Vorlax's tone was a bit harsher than

usual.

"Calm down, Vorlax," ordered Shane.

"No, I'm curious." The commander stared Max in his burning yellow eyes, refusing to look away for even a second. "Why do you care now? All of a sudden? Every impression I've had of you on this ship has made me believe that you're a selfish, sloppy, sleazy little reptile who only gives a damn about himself, and who never cared for anyone in the world, past or present!" Vorlax let his words hang in the air for a second. "So why do you now, completely out of nowhere, want to save someone you've abjectly hated these past few days?"

The lizard returned Vorlax's steely gaze. "He came for me. Normally I would have doubted it myself, but Pantura told me everything, how he had pledged to come save both his mother and I from the brig, and how he had refused to condemn me to Gorog slavery. And you know what? Out of every friend I've ever had, he was the only one who refused to abandon me, even after our differences! And if it's not noble to return the favor by saving his life, I don't know what is!"

The silence that came upon Vorlax at those words shut his mouth. Shane, on the other hand, stepped forward. "I will try to have the hyperdrive fixed before we reach the rendezvous point. We'll try to return to the nebula as soon as possible." The Magnum looked past Max. "Foulor!" he yelled. "Bring Ms. Phillips to the medical wing! The rest of you, go get cleaned up. There's nothing more you can do at the moment."

They all nodded and walked past them, vanishing in a crowd of technical workers. Shane turned to Vorlax, arms folded and a stern expression on his face. "That was uncalled for, my friend," he told the commander.

"I was just curious. You know what he's been like these past few days."

"That doesn't give you the excuse to harp on him in a threatening way. Believe me, I've gotten in trouble plenty of times for that. And Max should be the least of our concerns."

Vorlax sighed. "You're right. Do you think Daniel and Caitlin are alright?"

"Well, Daniel survived an oil refinery, and Caitlin's an Ostila Mador now, so, if I have to guess, they probably found a way to survive that explosion."

"You sure? That reactor meltdown was massive. You saw what that shockwave did to starfighters near the *Deceiver*, it warped their hulls!"

"Then we'd better repair the hyperdrive fast. And hope that if they survived that we're not too late. Go, get up to the bridge. I'm going to talk to Pantura about the mission specifics."

The commander nodded and walked away. Shane watched him go, then turned to stare out the hangar window, where the stars were whizzing on by. Daniel was back there, back where they had just come from. He was pretty confident that he had survived the initial blast, and that he was alive, wherever he was now.

He could only hope that he was still that way when they returned.

Daniel slowly shuddered and opened his eyes, jarred awake by something slamming near him. He sat up, blinded by the dark chamber he was in, and blinked several times, just like he did when he stargazed, to adjust his eyes to dimmer light. He stood up slowly, his boots making soft noises as he stepped forward, trying to get his bearings. He took a deep breath, then saw his spacesuit helmet sitting nearby. He walked over and grabbed it, inspecting it, then slinging it onto his back.

He shivered. The gunship's heating system must have been fried in the explosion. Even in his spacesuit, designed to keep him warm, it felt a little cold. He could see chunks of metal drifting on by in the cockpit window, which had cracked over from fast-moving pieces of *Deceiver* repeatedly hitting it. He stumbled on past the holographic projector, stumbling on the slanted floor in the process, and bent down to where Caitlin was lying, looking unconscious.

"Psss! Cait!" He shook her, and she stirred, groaning. She blinked, sitting up, and glanced around her, looking thoroughly confused.

"Uhhh…are we still alive?" she said, shaking her head.

"For now," Daniel replied, helping her to stand up. "Your idea worked."

The idea was to use the gunship they had flown in as a bunker, since Pantura had revealed that its hull was made of Xaphorium, the super tough metal. With seconds left until reactor meltdown, the two friends had decided on a whim to use it to safely weather out the explosion. They had sealed themselves inside, but the blast was so powerful that it sent them spinning out of control. They both were knocked unconscious in the process, slamming their heads into the walls as they lost all sense of direction. The hull had taken a beating, but it had remained intact. "I honestly can't believe that actually worked," Caitlin confessed, chuckling slightly.

"Be glad it did." Daniel looked around, trying to see if there was anything of value in sight. "Now all we have to go is figure out how we're going to get back to the fleet."

"Did they leave?"

Daniel walked to the cockpit window. "I don't see Shane's ships. They must've bailed during the explosion." He turned back to face her, noticing that she was looking a little pale again. "Hey. We'll be okay. We can survive for however long is needed."

"I'm cold," she complained, hugging herself and shivering, her breath visible escaping her lips.

She was right, Daniel knew. He could feel the temperature slowly dropping around them. Without a heating system, the gunship would slowly revert to the frigid temperatures of space, and even with oxygen, the cold would be certain to kill them both. He glanced around, and spotted the monitors of the ship, switched off without any power. "Can you try to use your sorcerer abilities to power those monitors?" he asked Caitlin. "Without any readings, we're essentially at the mercy of the elements around us."

She nodded, stood up, and crossed the atrium to the cockpit and released a slight burst of energy into the dash. About half of the dials turned on, and as Daniel sat down in the command chair and examined the readings he was getting, he felt his stomach drop. In fact, he felt his stomach sink all the way to the floor as he noticed the various warnings he was getting.

Caitlin noticed his face. "What is it? What's wrong?"

Daniel turned to face her. "The schematics show that both engines are leaking coolant. Right now, all of the fuel in the engines are heating up, and unless we can patch the holes, the entire ship will explode."

Caitlin's face lost more of its color. "Can we fix it?"

He shook his head. "No. We can't stay here. We have to exit the ship."

"To where? There's no planet to exit on!"

"To nowhere. But if we stay here we both die." He stood up from the chair and crossed over to a door marked AIRLOCK in big, bold letters. "Out there. We'll have to spacewalk."

"But your suit is compromised," pointed out Caitlin. "And both of ours are not doing great at keeping us warm. You can't go out with that hole in your stomach."

He noticed the hole burned into his suit when he was shot by Orvag, and groaned. "Hey. Can you see if there's anything that would resemble sealant? We need to patch this hole."

She nodded and started rummaging through the crates bolted to the floor. Daniel did the same, hoping to warm up through his own movements. "Do you have any holes in your spacesuit?" he asked Caitlin.

She shook her head. "No. I'm all fine."

They searched for a little bit, and thankfully, they did not have to look long, as Caitlin pulled out a small roll of what resembled tape at first. Upon second glance, Daniel could see that it was much shinier than tape, and had a similar metallic sheen to their spacesuits. He still was not fully convinced though. "You sure that's it?" he questioned.

"I mean, it's all shiny, like our suits, and it appears to have an adherent surface. It's the best I can see in those crates." She showed him the shiny roll. "That looks right to me."

Daniel felt the roll. It felt like his suit fabric, which eased him just a bit. Still, he requested that several layers be added to the hole, just to be safe. While Caitlin patched up the opening, Daniel felt his skin freezing over from the cold. They were running out of time.

"There. That should do it." Caitlin stepped away from the now-patched hole in Daniel's suit. "We should probably make sure that it's sealed up."

He nodded and, still shivering, stood up, picking up his helmet from off the floor and attaching the clamps onto his shoulders. The helmet came down over his head and rested against the top of his head comfortably. He had Caitlin put her hand in front of the patched opening while he shut the helmet visor, letting the plant-based fibers built into his suit generate oxygen. He took a deep breath, feeling crisp air fill his lungs. Caitlin kept her hand in position for a bit, then stepped back, giving him a thumbs-up. "I felt nothing leaking," she said. "You should be fine."

Daniel nodded, letting his brain adjust to his limited range of vision. "Go. Put your helmet on too."

She grabbed hers from where she had set it down and put it on, letting it clamp onto her shoulders and seal off her entire body from the outside elements. "I can breathe," she said shakily, her voice now appearing over Daniel's onboard radio.

"It's strange, isn't it?" He started to walk towards the airlock, peering through the window in the door, his cold breath fogging up in his helmet. "The second door's gone. Once we open this door here, we're getting pulled out into space. We'll need your powers to steady us, since they appear to operate independently of the elements."

Caitlin approached from behind, her face staring at Daniel behind her closed helmet visor. "Understood. Be ready to steady us once we launch."

An alarm started to blare from the cockpit, and Daniel knew that they were almost out of time. "Ready?"

"No," she replied honestly and nervously.

"Good. Ready, and…now."

He reached out and pressed the button to open the door. Instantly, they felt the wind whip at their bodies and suck them off of the ship and into space. Their view went from dark to light as they were dazzled by the surrounding nebula. Daniel spun around like crazy, losing all sense of direction as he tumbled through space past debris for several seconds. He saw a bright flash from some distance away amid the chaos, their ship detonating from the inside out. He went flying towards a huge piece of ship, but was stopped by Caitlin, who grabbed his foot and used her power to send them into a controlled stop, where they floated, in shock and a little bit dizzy.

"I've got you!" She pulled up to his height and grabbed his hand, squeezing it. "Stick together," she told him over the radio. "There's nothing to stop us from moving forever out here."

"You still remember Newton's laws after all these years?" Daniel replied, calming down slightly.

"You helped me get through physical science that year, you know," she told him.

He nodded slowly as they settled into position, letting in the view through his helmet. The pink clouds of gas floated around him, littered with debris from both the Gorog cruisers and the Coalition starfighters. As he took in the view, he became of something else, something that almost felt unnatural.

"We're zero-g," he said slowly, realizing that he felt lighter than air. There was no planet, no moon, no artificial gravity generator out here to give him mass. He was an object without mass, floating in space, a sensation more freeing than any he had ever felt.

"Yeah," whispered Caitlin. "It feels amazing."

"When I was a kid, this was my life goal. To experience the freedom of no gravity just once." Daniel felt a jumble of emotions fighting for dominance inside him, yet as he stared across space, he felt, weirdly enough, joy start to emerge triumphant. Not joy in the sense of an amazing accomplishment, but a somber joy, the kind that recognized that he, possibly minutes from death, had finally achieved his goal. He felt his eyes watering slightly, but he could not get his hand into his helmet to wipe them. "This…this is…"

He felt Caitlin come up alongside him, her hand resting on his shoulder. "Everything you wanted it to be," she finished softly. "And I'm here, able to experience the magic of it with you too."

"It's a pity," whispered Daniel, staring at the star cluster in the distance. "I would love to spend my entire life out here." He turned to Caitlin. "How long do you think we have?"

"Not long, given how I'm still feeling cold." She gazed into Daniel's eyes, their blue irises locking on each other. "You know that, we may not get out of this. Shane may not get back in time. This…may be it for us."

Daniel nodded. "I know." He felt no anxiety, no fear, not even anger at their predicament. "But, for the first time, in my life, in spite of that, I…well…I feel peaceful. We saved my mom. And if her life means my death, then that's something I'm willing to do."

He saw Caitlin blink out tears. "You ready for this?"

He shook his head, gazing at the view one last time. "No one ever is." He turned to her and gave her a look of encouragement. "But at least I'll die beside my best friend, knowing that we won."

She gave him a look that was equal parts mixed joy and sadness, and then, without warning, she threw herself onto him in a huge hug, squeezing him around the chest. He held her head on his shoulder, feeling her body shake slightly.

"Goodbye, Stellar Brain," she whispered, her voice laden with sadness, tears falling into her helmet.

The words hit Daniel like a freight train, and he felt his eye squeeze out a couple of his own tears. Closing his eyes, he comforted her. "Goodbye, Cait," he replied, hugging her tightly.

And as their consciousness started to fade, even as debris swirled around them, they kept their tearful embrace locked until the very end.

Chapter 37

The Coalition search party was in full swing in the nebula. Pantura, back in her spacesuit, floated among the husks of a Gorog cruiser's hull, a small jetpack on her back propelling her forward and a flashlight guiding her way. Behind her, over a dozen Coalition soldiers also in protective clothing shined their flashlights on every broken ship piece or piece of debris they found. A safe distance away, outside the new debris field, the *Justice* was parked, a huge searchlight sweeping the area.

"Any sign of them yet?" Pantura said over the comms.

"Not yet, miss," replied a soldier. "We'll keep searching though!"

Her flashlight shined into a dark, sheltered area below the wing of a giant piece of the *Deceiver's* hull. Again, there was nothing. She began to grow worried. She had expected for Daniel and Caitlin to survive the initial explosion, but as her radio remained silent and no traces of them were found, doubt started to creep in. She scanned the immediate field of debris and again found nothing.

"Pantura! We found them!" came an excited voice in her helmet. "About three hundred feet to your right!"

She turned around and boosted her jetpack thrusters, boosting her through space at high speeds. She could see the small group of soldiers surrounding a small object, their flashlights pointed at it. She slowed herself to a halt next to them, pushing past one of them. Sure enough, she recognized their blue spacesuits, their arms wrapped around each other. They made no sound or movement as Pantura slowly floated towards them, and her heart briefly sank. Were they dead?

She brought up her vital scanner and waved it near them. It beeped at her several times, indicating a pulse. She sighed in relief. "They're alive." She waved to the soldiers. "Get them on board the *Justice*. Quickly! No telling how long they've been out here for."

"Yes, ma'am!" The search party came forward and grabbed the two friends, separating them from each other. They started to fly back, Daniel and Caitlin each held by the arms between two soldiers. Pantura excitedly switched her radio on.

"Shane?" she messaged. "We found them."

"You did?" he replied, sounding as relieved as she was. "Are they alive?"

"Yes. The search party's bringing them back now. Start charging up the hyperdrive. We can go home. I'm coming back now."

She turned and started flying towards the cruiser, leaving the debris field behind, and with it, the remnants of the once-mighty Gorog fleet.

Daniel felt something hot and bright shining down upon his face. It reminded him a lot of Earth's Sun, the warmth it gave him in the summer. Alas, he knew that it could not be so, as he was dead, and the light surely was the approaching gates of heaven waiting to greet him.

"You awake yet, sleepyhead?"

He slowly opened his eyes, realizing that he was not dead, but just in the medical wing of the *Justice,* right back where he was just a day ago. He sat up, noticing Shane sitting across from him, looking very pleased. He noticed that there were oxygen pipes going up his nostrils, and he felt very dazed, until Shane pressed a button and released them from his nose, allowing himself to breathe once more.

"How long was I out?" he groaned, placing a hand on his forehead.

"About a day and a half," said Shane.

"How did you find us in all that debris?" he asked, blinking and adjusting to the medical light shining overhead.

The Magnum nodded. "Pantura led a search party and swept the whole field until we found you. And Caitlin too." He indicated the bed next to Daniel's, where Caitlin's long blond hair could be seen poking out of her bedsheets. "You were both suffering from hypothermia. Caitlin's suit was missing thermal shielding on the arm and yours was compromised when Orvag shot you."

Daniel remembered that incident and slowly lifted up the bedsheets to reveal the bandages over his stomach. "How bad is it?" he asked.

"Not bad. We were able to repair just about all of the damage to your intestines. Your digestive tract should be all fine." Shane stood up from his chair, approaching Daniel's bedside. "You should be very proud of yourself, Daniel. You and your friends managed to not only rescue your mother, but also defeat the two highest-ranked officials in the Gorog Empire. With Orvag and Dormak dead, the rest of the soldiers will have no leader to follow. And you saved both your world and my own."

Daniel shook his head in confusion, details slowly returning to his memory. "How's my mom?" he asked. "She didn't look so good when I found her."

Shane nodded. "She'll live for sure. And she'll likely make a full recovery. She was badly beat up, but it was nothing that my doctors couldn't handle. She's unfortunately still in a coma, but hopefully not for much longer."

Daniel laid back onto his pillow, warm joy filling his body up. They had done it. They had actually done it. They were all safe once more. And this time there was no Gorog Empire to threaten them. He let a smile cross his tired face, and inhaled deeply. And to take his smile even bigger, he heard motion in the bed next to him, and he turned to see Caitlin staring straight at him, looking elated.

"We won!" she cried happily, leaping from her bed and throwing herself onto Daniel before he could fully sit up. He fell backward, only to be picked up by Caitlin and hugged again, hard, her arms crushing his torso.

"Cait…yes, I'm really glad we won, and that you're happy, but…ow…you're crushing my ribs!" He gasped for air as she released him and scooted back, looking a little red in the cheeks.

"Sorry," she said sheepishly, rubbing the back of her head. "Just got a little excited."

"And you have every reason to be, and more," Shane added in, spreading out his arms in a very father–like posture. "The others are waiting for you outside. I don't think they've left the bench for fifteen hours. They're looking forward to seeing you again."

The two of them glanced at each other, then back to Shane, until a thought struck Daniel. "Wait…aren't you no longer Magnum? I thought you were going to lose your position if you failed to defeat the Gorogs in time."

Shane laughed. "Funny you should mention that. I get a call from the council asking for my resignation papers while I'm going back to come rescue you two. Serizau was all up in my face, until I calmly told him that I had won, and that Orvag was dead. The look on his face…such disappointment has never before been seen."

"I assume he's enraged at your surprise success?"

"Oh, he is, but he can't touch me anymore. While you were still in your coma, I paid Vraxis some extra money to go ahead and do some…investigating on Serizau. Turns out, through a second party, Dormak was bribing him to try and force a peace treaty that would let the Gorog Empire live in peace. Vraxis may or may not have found all of his secret transmissions and linked them to the Gorog Empire. From there, it was no trouble at all to kick him off of the council. The other council members thought that the treaty would be better long-term, but after that battle, they all changed their minds."

"So, an all-around win for us?" asked Daniel.

"I'd say so. Now go, into the hallway. I'm sure all of the others would be thrilled to see you."

They both got off of Daniel's bed, pulled a shirt on, and, expecting a mob, walked out of the medical wing. They turned to see Vorlax, Pantura, Max, Vraxis, and Foulor, all seated on a bench outside the door. The minute they did, though, Foulor's eyes widened and he sprang from the bench. "THEY'RE ALIVE!" he yelled in delight, causing the others to jump in fright, then turn and see Daniel and Caitlin standing there, waving awkwardly. Everyone rose to greet them excitedly, complimenting them and shaking their hands.

"That was insanely brave, what you did," Pantura told them. "Braver than anything I could do, for sure."

"You have my respect for your deeds today," put in Vraxis, shaking Caitlin's hand vigorously.

"I've witnessed many displays of courage in my years of service, but that, what you did, was above anything I expected." Vorlax, the commander of Shane's entire squadron, sounded genuinely impressed. "You helped to bring down the Gorog Empire."

"Man, it…it was nothing!" stuttered Daniel, blushing fiercely. Caitlin was also flushed, but trying to hide it behind her warm smile. Eventually, they came to Max, who was looking relieved to see them.

"Happy to see us?" asked Caitlin, anticipating a snooty remark.

"Actually, I am." Max approached them, his yellow eyes big and lacking any rage. "You came back for me. You were the first people I met who came back to try and save me from my enemies. And try to deny it all you want, but Pantura told me everything you said. So…thank you. For saving my life when no one else wanted to."

There was genuine sincerity in Max's words, and it touched Daniel deep inside. "We may have our differences, Max," he told him. "In fact, I suspect that we'd agree on very little. But that's okay. Because, at the end of the day, you saved our lives first. And it's only fitting that we returned the favor in the end. Regardless of our differences."

Max absorbed those words, and then recoiled slightly as Daniel held out his hand to shake. The lizard paused, then, slowly, retracted in his claws on his front foot and returned the gesture. "You, Daniel Phillips, are full of surprises," he praised him.

"Same about you," Caitlin said. "You were easily four times larger than normal when you killed Dormak."

"Still think I know how I can do that?"

"I'm not saying that, but, you know. It's a unique trait. I don't know anyone else who can do that, do you, Daniel?"

He shook his head. "None. Not even one."

Max sort of puffed out his chest. "Perhaps you all were right. Maybe we should look into that more."

"I'm sure my researchers would love to run some more tests," said Shane.

They all laughed at the look of horror that crossed Max's face at those words. "You know, there's some other things we think you ought to see," said Vorlax. "While you were waiting to be pulled out of your coma. Come on, follow me."

They followed Vorlax out of the medical wing and to the hangar, where, at one end, the orange-and-red gunship was parked, a flurry of maintenance workers surrounding it. "We recovered the wreckage while Pantura searched for you two in the debris field. We salvaged all we could and fabricated new parts where necessary. And fixed the paint scheme too. It's a bit duller now. I understand you got a bit attached?"

"It was a lot of fun to fly," admitted Daniel.

"I completely understand. Though, to fly the ship, you had to steal the controls away from Pantura...twice!"

"I was stunned!" she protested, and they all laughed again.

"Only thing is, we still haven't named it," pointed out Vorlax. "I've been trying to think of a name for a while, but nothing's really appealed to me. I thought that you would be a good fit to name it, since you seem to like it."

"Me?" Daniel was a bit surprised, but he stared at the regally curved hull and the broad wings and massive engines. He admired the vivid paint scheme and giant laser cannons. "Well, it was destroyed in the battle, and has been largely rebuilt from its wreckage. And it has the color scheme of fire. Maybe something like the *Phoenix*?"

Vorlax nodded slowly. "You know, that never occurred to me, but I really like it. I mean, she's all yours, so you could name her whatever you wanted, but, whatever, that doesn't matter."

Daniel whipped to face him. "Say what again?"

"The *Phoenix*. She's all yours. You need a way to get home, so that's it."

He turned to face Caitlin, who looked just as stunned as he did. "Vorlax, I—this is an amazing gift!" she stuttered out. "I just wish that there was something we could do for you!"

"You did," he replied. "You defeated Orvag and Dormak. I think that that's a fair exchange."

The two of them, in shock, slowly walked towards their new spaceship, admiring its size from a short distance away, so that they could see the still-unpainted sections of hull, some of them with burn marks from Gorog lasers. The cockpit windscreen had been replaced, as had the failed engines, indicated by the bright and shiny metal components.

"We also repaired the pressure suits we gave you,

they're on board too," added Shane. "You shouldn't freeze in them anymore. They're yours to use however you want."

Daniel's facial muscles were actually hurting from how broadly he was smiling. "Thank you, both of you!" he said. "This is amazing! I don't know how to respond, this is—"

Shane raised a hand for silence, then spoke into his communicator. "Yes, hello? Really? Alright, I'll send them right over!" He hung up. "That was one of my nurses. It's Ms. Phillips. She's about to wake up."

Daniel nervously stood outside the entrance to Ms. Phillips' room, wringing his hands and shuffling from one foot to the other. He glanced behind him briefly to see the others standing there, encouraging him on. He knew that, on the other side of the door, his mom could be waiting for him. Yet, he couldn't bring himself to quite push the button and open the door. He reached for it, then stopped himself, turning back around.

"Something wrong, Daniel?" asked Vorlax.

"She's right in there. You're supposed to push the button to open the door," added Vraxis, with just a hint of pride.

"No, it's all right. Caitlin, you should be coming in here with me."

"She's your mom, Daniel!" she replied. "If anyone should be going in there it's you. You rescued her."

But he shook his head and waved her over. "We entered this wild adventure as a group. It's only fitting that you're there too at its end."

She looked hesitant to join him, but she relented and walked over. Daniel nodded at her and pressed the button, and the door hissed open, allowing them both to walk in.

Ms. Phillips was on her bed, still passed out, but with her monitors in the corner beeping rapidly, indicating that she was about to wake. Her injuries had faded and the dried blood cleared off her face. She was hooked up to an oxygen generator and an IV pipe, which was transferring some clear liquid into her. They both approached her bedside, and Daniel, clearing his throat slightly, sighed and whispered in her ear.

"Mom? Mom, are you awake?"

For a second, she made no movement. Then, she stirred, her brain scanner lighting up with activity. She lifted her arm up and slowly opened her eyes, glancing over Daniel and Caitlin before they snapped back to stare right at them, looking confused.

"Daniel?" she said groggily, shielding her face from the lights. "Caitlin? What...what are you doing here?"

"We saved your life, mom. It's okay." Daniel was shaking with emotion as he struggled to keep his composure, fighting the urge to cry. "It's okay. You're safe."

"Is this not...the Gorog ship?" she asked him.

"No, Ms. Phillips," reassured Caitlin. "You won't be going back there ever again. You're back with the Coalition. Safe and sound."

Something clicked in Ms. Phillips' face, and she sat up slowly, letting the bedsheets fall down into her lap. She glanced around the room, still showing signs of confusion. "What...happened?"

"We infiltrated Orvag's ship and rescued you from your cell," said Daniel, taking deep breaths to calm himself. "He and Dormak are dead now. They won't be troubling us ever again."

She turned around to look at him, who was smiling at her, eyes watering slightly. Caitlin looked equally joyful behind him. She stared at Daniel's face, noticing that something looked off.

"Daniel?" she asked slowly. "Why does your face look like that?"

He stiffened and turned to Caitlin, whose smile had also

655

disappeared. She gave him a look that said, "*I don't know. Say something!*" He turned back to her, then chuckled aloud, much to Caitlin's surprise.

"That's...a really long story," he replied. "I'll tell you all about it later. For now, why don't you rest? You've had a long few days I'm sure."

"You should be very proud of your son," said Shane, striding into the room with all of his usual gravitas. "He not only saved you from your cell on the *Deceiver*, but he also killed Orvag, destroyed the Gorog armada that was threatening to invade Earth, and sacrificed himself to save your life, all in the span of less than an hour." He turned to Daniel, gratitude warmly emanating from him. "He did a great service, not only to us, but to his entire planet."

Ms. Phillips turned back to face them, looking astonished.

"Oh, and Caitlin killed Warden Dormak too," Shane added. "Can't forget about that little detail."

"Oh my," Ms. Phillips exclaimed, placing both of her hands on her head. "You really did all that in about an hour?"

"Closer to thirty minutes, but yes, we did do all that." Daniel blushed slightly, causing Caitlin to laugh out loud.

"Some things never change," she told him, punching him in the shoulder, only to retract her hand sharply as her knuckles met Daniel's robotic arm, causing them both to laugh together.

They all convened on the bridge, including Ms. Phillips, who found herself able to walk soon after she awoke. Daniel, Caitlin, and all the others were lined up in front of the window, with Shane and Vorlax facing them both.

"On behalf of the Orion Coalition, we thank you for your service," the Magnum told them. "You all helped us to defeat our enemy, something that we were unable to do in almost twenty years. Although there will still be Gorog resistance to weed out, the majority of the threat is gone now that Orvag and Dormak are both dead."

"You seven have endured a lot of crap over the past however many years," Vorlax said. "Which is why, as a reward for your efforts, we're going to give all of you something. It's also his way of apologizing for deceiving all of you." He jerked a thumb at Shane. "Do with that what you will."

"Vraxis and Foulor," announced Shane, and the twins stepped forward, both of them, Foulor shouldering a massive boomstick. They both dipped their heads before Shane and Vorlax.

"To you, in addition to your massive reward of credits, you will both receive a brand-new prototype starfighter stolen from a Gorog hangar. It's large enough to fit both of you with room to spare and to hold any items that you may collect over your travels. May you use it to enjoy your long retirement smoothly."

"Thank you Shane," replied Vraxis, dipping his head.

"Thanks!" added Foulor, nearly dropping his boomstick on the floor. "Does it come with snacks?"

"Yes, it comes with all the snacks you can ever want," replied Vorlax.

"Yippee!" Foulor bounded back to the others, while Vraxis shook his head and sauntered back, slapping Foulor in the face when he reached him.

"Pantura!" called out Vorlax. She stepped forward, looking a bit nervous. "To you, we have a promotion for you. You will receive a promotion to director of engineering of the *Justice*, supervising all of the different fields."

She was taken aback. "You're serious?" For she knew that director of engineering was an extremely high-profile job, and that she had just been put in charge of the hundreds of engineers aboard Shane's cruiser.

"I don't think he was joking…" quipped Shane, giving her a look of praise.

Pantura's normally blue skin turned pink. "I—thank you, Shane! Thank you! This means so much to me!"

He nodded and indicated to her to step forward, which she did. He took something out of his pocket and pinned it to Pantura's uniform, a small insignia with the Orion Coalition logo on it, painted bronze with a gold trim. "Congratulations," he told her.

She admired her shiny new badge, glistening in the bridge lights. Smiling broadly with delight, she stepped back and joined the others in the row.

"Max?" called out Vorlax.

The lizard came forward. "Present."

"Do you still wish to receive what we discussed in private?"

He nodded. "I do."

"Very well." Vorlax turned to the others. "Max, Shane and I had a private talk, since we had no clue how to reward him. He told us that being granted a safe haven with Daniel and Caitlin would be a substantial enough gift. In return, he promised to stop being disruptive at dinner."

"You're welcome," the lizard said, sauntering back to the line. Daniel was bewildered. Max wanted a safe haven with *him?* After all their differences? He could not understand why.

"Amy!" Shane called out, and Ms. Phillips came forward slowly, looking nervous, as she now had the entire bridge of officers looking straight at her. Daniel felt his stomach twist. He would have to do that soon. His mom stopped in front of Shane and bowed in respect.

"No need to do that here, we're not kings," the Magnum corrected her, though he was chuckling slightly. "To you, we have a very special prize. As you may recall, your old hometown was destroyed when the Gorogs raided it all those years ago.

Sadly, as our drone footage showed, it has not been repaired since. That being said, we have a solution. There's a fairly large house about fifteen miles from your old dwelling. It has enough room for you, Daniel and Caitlin, and it's located close to a much more modern town that will hopefully serve you better than Salt Plains did. It was just bought by an anonymous benefactor, and now it's yours."

"By 'anonymous benefactor,' he means that he went in and bought it for you," clarified Vorlax.

The look of utter shock that crossed Ms. Phillips's face, followed by the look of elation as she realized that Shane was serious, warmed Daniel's insides. It was the first true joy he had seen in her in years. She came forward to Shane, and, with tears in her eyes, shook his hand vigorously. "Thank you," she whispered. "Thank you so much."

"You all deserve a win," replied Vorlax. "It's nothing."

"We'll give you the address and key when you leave," added Shane.

She stepped back, still in total shock. So was both Daniel and Caitlin. With one fell swoop, Shane had just solved the last variable in the equation of returning to Earth. Daniel had been unsure how they were going to find a place to live after being gone for five years, but now, they had the means.

"Caitlin!" bellowed Vorlax, and she came forward, slowly at first, then finally took a spot in front of the two of them, shifting around nervously and wringing her hands.

"Yes?" she asked meekly.

"We have two things for you," Shane replied. "First of all, I had a lovely conversation with Shurgen over the hologram, and he's sent you this." He took the small book from the podium, which revealed that it was decorated with gold trim and a special symbol on the cover. "It contains a list of additional spells that you can learn and use, plus some other tips that he wrote down for you." He handed it to her, and she examined it slowly. "As for the second thing..." She drew close to Shane, and he passed her something small. Daniel could not tell what it was, but the way she cupped it to her body made it seem important. She nodded to Shane before stepping back, and before Daniel could ask her, he heard Shane yell out, "Finally, would Daniel Phillips please step forward?"

The way he announced his name made Daniel stiffen a bit, and he slowly walked forward, glancing back at the others, who all waved him on. He took his position in front of Shane. "Sir," he said.

Shane rose to his full height. "To you, Daniel, Vorlax and I decided not to give you a gift ourselves. We instead chose to have you pick whatever reward it is that your heart desires. Be it money, a position of power, whatever it may be. Just name it and it will be yours."

It was a proposition that had a lot of opportunities for temptation. Daniel knew that it would be easy to pick something obvious; to walk away with a truckload of credits or a high-ranking position in the Orion Coalition. Heck, he could have probably requested to be a member of the Arajor Council and would have gotten away with it. But Daniel, despite strong temptations placed in front of him, simply shrugged and said, "I don't know."

Shane raised an eyebrow. "'You don't know?' Daniel, I'm offering you essentially anything that you could ask me. Anything at all. It doesn't need to be big, you know. It could be something small, and I wouldn't take offense."

"No, I get that, it's just...I get anything I want. Anything. I want this to count." He cast his eyes downward as he tried, and failed, to come up with something meaningful. He glanced back up at Shane. "Would you mind giving me a day to make up my mind?"

"Of course, of course. You deserve a chance to think over this, maybe settle your brain down a bit after all the excitement of the past week. And when you're ready, you'll have Pantura to reach out to me and make your decision."

Daniel dipped his head. "Thank you, Shane." He joined the others in the row.

"I believe that's everything, then," said Vorlax. "Congratulations to all of you on your achievements over the past few days. Daniel, the *Phoenix* is waiting in the hangar to take you, Caitlin, and Ms. Phillips home. Thank you all again for your service, and may the Belt give you strength as you go forth into your lives!"

They all dipped their heads and dispersed, clearly satisfied with the outcome, all except Daniel, who remained conflicted and unsure about his decision as he started the long walk to the hangar. But as he joined the others, finally on the road to Earth, he let those doubts slip from his mind.

Chapter 38

Earth

Daniel slowly approached the crest of the hillside, his robotic leg thudding against the pavement below. He knew that, on the other side, was the little valley where Salt Plains originally was located. He was prepared to see the worst, to see a gaping hole in the ground where the town had originally stood. Behind him, Caitlin followed, also bracing for the inevitable sight. It had been five long years since that fateful invasion that stormy fall night, and now, finally, they were getting to see how their town had moved on without them.

Summer was in full swing in the foothills of Kentucky. The trees were in full bloom, their leaves casting ripples over the ground as the sun beamed down on them from above. After spending so long in space, feeling the warmth on his skin felt odd, almost unnatural even. He could hear birds chirping in the branches overhead and the sounds of the slight breeze blowing through the hills. Daniel inhaled deeply, letting the smells of nature in. It felt great to be back among Earth's natural wildlife, but he was still unprepared for the sight that would appear on the other side of the hill.

They both reached the hill's summit, the road now traveling down towards the valley. At the bottom, partially hidden by a resurgence of nature, was the blackened, burnt-out husk of Salt Plains's downtown core. They both stopped, letting the view sink in. They could see small trees starting to grow from main street. They saw the fallen arches of the old McDonald's, which had lost their bright yellow colors and were now heavily faded and obscured by a fallen tree. There was a huge pile of overgrown ruins where the hotel used to be. And, at the edge of downtown, the crater in the pavement next to the old convenience store and gas station, where that missile had impacted and started their five years of limbo in space. As Daniel gazed upon the ruins, he felt a sense of somber closure, knowing that this was all that was left of their town.

"It's what we expected to see," Caitlin reminded him, perhaps seeing through to his sadness on the inside. "There was no way they were going to rebuild this after the fact."

"The question is," replied Daniel, "What exactly do the others think caused this incident?"

They found their answer close by, in a field not far from where the old pumpkin fest was held. There, a large parking lot, with cracked pavement and faded parking lines, empty of cars, overlooked the old town. Lined up to one side was a row of black stones, each about six feet tall. Approaching these, Daniel could make out names engraved into the rocks, and in front of the monoliths were two words in big letters: "THE FIRE." Below that, the subtitle read: *"The disaster that burned Salt Plains to the ground."*

"They think that a fire did this?" asked Caitlin, in a bit of disbelief. "I would think a fire would cause fewer casualties than this."

"No, look," Daniel pointed out, indicating a message on the central monolith. Reading it, he said: *"On November 16, 2018, the small country town of Salt Plains was overrun by flames. The fire spread rapidly from building to building thanks to shoddy construction and a dry summer and fall. The entire town was engulfed, yet few bodies were actually found. Despite an intensive investigation, many of the people visiting the town for the annual pumpkin celebration that day were never found, and their names were also included on these stones. The cause of the fire remains a mystery to this day."* He turned to Caitlin. "So the whole 'alien invasion' part of it was never discovered by the humans. At least Shane can rest easy now, knowing that the Zodiac Code wasn't broken in any way."

But Caitlin was drifting towards a particular stone, one

two spots down from the central monolith, and she barely heard the second part of Daniel's comment. Her eyes slowly scoured the names, looking for one in particular. She passed through the R's, through Remissa, Renault, Riborka, until at last, she found the name. *Richards*.

Daniel came beside her and immediately saw what she was looking at. His heart sank, as he knew what this meant. "Cait..." he began.

"No...no. It's fine. We knew that it would be miraculous if he survived, but...I guess not." She sniffled a little. "Funny, how it works. You don't fully understand what someone means to you until they're gone, even if you hated them when they were alive."

He put a hand on her shoulder, and she squeezed it. "Charlie may not have been the guardian you wanted, Cait," said Daniel, "But he was the one you needed to endure the harsh conditions of the last five years. And though he may have been tough on you, I'm sure that if he was still around, he would be very proud of what you've done."

She slowly nodded, and wiped her eyes with her shirt sleeve. "Thanks," she said softly.

"We should probably go back and join the others," Daniel said. "Let's go to the car."

He put his arm around Caitlin and they slowly left the monoliths behind, together.

They pulled into the driveway of the house that Shane had bought for Ms. Phillips. It was a beautiful two-story building located in a large clearing surrounded by dense trees. The house was set back a ways from the main road, and the nearest neighbor was almost a quarter of a mile away. As Shane had promised, there was a decent-sized town several miles away that would provide Ms. Phillips with all of her necessary needs.

Overall, it was a perfect little country house. The one difference this time was that the massive wings of the *Phoenix* could be seen peeking out from the backyard clearing. In front of the house, Vraxis and Foulor were dragging furniture up through the front door, taking a bunch of items from a large U-Haul truck in the driveway.

"Did Shane pay for the truck as well?" asked Caitlin.

"I guess he did."

They parked their car next to the truck and got out, just as Pantura came around the corner, wiping her forehead. "It's so hot here!" she complained. "How do you manage staying upright in this heat?"

"You'll get used to it," Daniel chuckled. "You should visit in the winter. It's much cooler then. You going somewhere?"

"Yep! The twins just emptied out the last bits of furniture from the U-Haul. We're heading back to Ms. Phillips' old house to grab some more furniture."

"It's still standing?"

"Turns out no one wants to buy land around Salt Plains, not even the government of Kentucky. I wonder why that is…" She started to climb into the vehicle. "I'll be back shortly!" She stuck her head out the window. "Vraxis! Foulor! Get in, we're going for another run!"

The twins exited the house, Foulor completely shirtless and acting with swagger, making Vraxis elbow him sharply. "You really need to curb your impulses," he lectured Foulor, as they climbed into the back of the truck and pulled away.

Caitlin stared after them. "Shane really is full of surprises," she commented.

"Yeah. Almost too many of them," Daniel replied.

They entered the house, finding Max helping Ms. Phillips arrange the furniture brought in by the twins. They were both grabbing onto a large chair. "No, this should go over here,"

665

she said, directing the lizard over to one side.

"How far?" Max grunted, dragging the chair.

"To about…stop." They stopped moving. "This should do just fine for now. Although, we may have to move this again once the television gets here."

Max groaned. "Great. I can't wait."

They noticed Daniel standing there. "Oh, Daniel! Back from Salt Plains already?"

He nodded. "I feel better now." He waved at Max, who waved back slowly. "Mom, can I talk to you for a second?"

She nodded. "Of course. Max, can you please move that dining room table into the middle of that room over there?" She pointed into a currently empty room.

"Oh, of course. Anything for you!" But they could both hear some grumbling under his breath as he started to drag the table to its location. Daniel brought Ms. Phillips over into her master bedroom, which was partially furnished with tables, but just missing a bed.

"What's up, Daniel?" Ms. Phillips asked him.

He leaned against the wall, collecting his thoughts before answering. "Mom," he began. "For my whole life, I dreamt of a day where I could go into space. Where I would be able to travel to the stars, because, whenever I brought out my telescope late at night, I felt like I belonged up there. Yet I knew that I would never be able to travel up there—until the Gorogs came."

She nodded. "Okay."

"I got my wish, mom. I got to live in outer space for five years. Granted, only about one day of that was actually pleasant, but, for that one day, despite all the terrible things that were happening around us, in spite of the war, in spite of everything, I…" He searched for the words to say. "I felt like I was somewhere that I belonged."

"You're not suggesting that you're leaving, right?" Ms. Phillips asked. "Because, to me, it sounds like you're thinking about leaving and going back."

Daniel sighed. "That's not why I'm going back." He stared out the window overlooking the front lawn. "When you were taken by the Gorogs, Shane brought us to the Orion Coalition's capital, Arajor. I was able to see how things worked out here; how they functioned. It was amazing. But, amid all of this, I realized that, as technologically advanced and wondrous as the galaxy is, it, at its core, has a lot of the same problems as Earth. War's still an issue out there. So is prejudice, injustice, and corruption. And if this whole wild trip has taught me anything, it's that these people need someone to prevent evils like the Gorogs from happening again." He paused for a second, watching the leaves on the trees wave in the breeze. "I can help them, mom. I can help keep them safe."

"Does Caitlin know about your plans?"

"We already discussed it, and she agrees with me. We've witnessed people kicking down the weak enough in our lives. Besides, I'm twenty now. It's not like I can stick around here forever you know."

Ms. Phillips sat down in the chair and thought for a moment. "I suppose you're not wrong," she told him. "Anyone else know of your plans?"

"Just Caitlin, for now. I was going to speak with the others as soon as we finished getting your house in order." He leaned in to her, sensing her worries. "It's alright, mom. This is what I want."

She let her gaze wander around the bedroom, thinking about all that Daniel had lost in the last five years. But then, she remembered everything that he had gained in that timeframe, and she relaxed herself and turned back to face him. "Your father would have been so incredibly proud of you," she told him. "He wanted to help others too. And if you want to help people, even those outside our solar system, then I know better than to stop you."

He nodded and smiled at her. "Thanks, mom."

"So you're going back?" asked Pantura, as they gathered outside the *Phoenix's* access ramp, Ms. Phillips' house now in working order.

Daniel nodded. "Caitlin and I talked it out, and that's what we agreed on. We're going to work with Shane and Vorlax to help weed out the remnants of Gorogs scattered after Orvag's death. They won't quit, even with the king dead. If anyone else here is willing to assist us in this task, I extend the offer to you all now."

To no one's surprise, Pantura stepped forward immediately. "If you're going to be living with us for longer," she said, "you'll need a guide." She took a spot next to the two of them.

"Anyone else?" asked Daniel.

Then, to everyone's surprise, Max stepped forward. "Really, Max?" asked Caitlin, the instant she saw the movement. "You really want to help us?"

"If you're going after the Gorogs, then it's my fight too. They imprisoned me first, remember? Plus, you're going to need all the help you can get."

"Relax, Caitlin," Daniel told her. "He's clearly interested in helping. Who are we to stop him from doing so?"

"Thank you." Max took his spot next to Pantura.

That left just the twins. Vraxis and Foulor stood there, arms crossed. "You sure you won't come with us?" asked Daniel. "We could use your skills for sure."

Vraxis sighed. "We appreciate the offer, we really do. But the two of us have been fighting our entire lives, both for money and for others. And while we're no longer employed by

Orvag, we now have all the funds we need to never work again. We would prefer to retire and relax for a little bit, if my brother agrees."

Everyone thought that Foulor was going to run up to Daniel and beg him to join, but instead, he slowly nodded. "I hate to say this, but he's right. We could use a break."

"See?" Vraxis said, spreading his arms out. "You're learning!"

"I understand, Vraxis," replied Daniel. "If you feel like you could use a break, then go for it. If anyone's earned it, then it's you two."

The hunter shouldered his sniper rifle and slowly approached Daniel and Caitlin, examining each of them. "You two, you're not like other people and aliens I've met. I've been hunting for almost ten years, and yet, even after I tried to capture you and bring you to Orvag, you still gave Foulor and I second chances. And for that, I am grateful."

"We all make mistakes, Vraxis," replied Caitlin. "I'm glad you got to fix yours."

Foulor ran forward and attempted to hug Daniel, but his brother stopped him. "Not this time, you big doofus," he told him. He turned around and shook Daniel's hand firmly. "I wish all of you luck with your endeavors, and who knows? Maybe our paths will cross again in the future."

He turned around and started walking off into the distance. Foulor watched him go. "Wait…do we have a ship?" he yelled after him.

"Just called it in! Now get over here before someone else sees us!"

Foulor turned back to the others, and Daniel waved him on. "You two belong together," he said. "You're brothers."

Foulor considered this, then nodded and waved his hand. "Until next time, everyone!" He then ran after Vraxis, turning the corner of the driveway and disappearing behind the trees.

The minute he was gone, Max let loose a loud sigh.

"He was one word away from me killing him," he growled. "Thank God he's gone."

"Easy, Max," warned Pantura. "If you're going to live with us, you can't just kill people on a whim."

"Yeah, yeah. Don't remind me."

Daniel glanced around. "Alright, I believe that's everything. Can you two get the ship ready to go? We'll be right behind."

Pantura and Max nodded and climbed the stairs into the ship, leaving Daniel and Caitlin to turn around and walk over to Ms. Phillips, who was standing with her arms folded a short distance away.

"Will I see you two again?" she asked as they came to stop before her.

"Of course you will, Ms. Phillips," Caitlin told her. "We'll be back. Some day."

"We'll visit often, how does that sound?" added Daniel. "We'll try to make stops frequently just to check in."

"And we'll bring some of Shane's meat too, since you liked it so much."

"And we'll try to keep Max entertained whenever—"

"Alright, alright!" protested Ms. Phillips, laughing. "I get it. And I was partially kidding, too. You two are both adults now and can make your own decisions."

They stopped. "She's right," whispered Caitlin under her breath. "We are."

"I keep forgetting that," Daniel hissed back. "I'm still not used to it."

"Will you two get going already?" Ms. Phillips spoke up, clearly amused by all of this. "You're not helping this by stalling!"

"Alright, we're going. But first, come here." They both embraced Ms. Phillips in a huge double hug, as the engines started up behind them. Daniel felt the warmth of her skin below him, and let loose a single tear, knowing that she was finally home.

"Love you, mom," he whispered, letting his emotions take control for just a second.

"I love you too, son. Thank you for saving me."

"Anything for you, Ms. Phillips."

They both released her, and, after a final wave goodbye, climbed the ramp into the *Phoenix*. The ship roared below them as the engines charged up and they started to lift off of the ground, Ms. Phillips growing smaller and smaller below them. Then Pantura engaged the engines to their full strength and she was gone, her house no more than a speck surrounded by green, until it too was out of sight.

Daniel watched as Earth once again grew smaller in the rearview window of his cabin, feeling a little twisted up inside, but only slightly. Ms. Phillips was there, down on planet Earth, and he was finally leaving her. He watched as the globe came into view, the blue haze surrounding the planet filling the cabin up with light. He heard Caitlin come up behind him and sit down next to him.

"She'll be alright," she told him. "We'll be alright too."

"I just hope that nothing bad happens to her," he replied.

"Like what? Daniel, you're worrying again. There's no more Gorog Empire to threaten her. And if anything happens, Shane gave her that secure transmitter to call him with."

He nodded slowly, knowing that she was right. He turned and slowly turned the radio on next to his bed. He heard Shane's voice creep through. "Today, we celebrate the end of the Gorog Wars!" he said, clearly speaking to a crowd. "With Orvag dead, a new era of prosperity and peace that has been long overdue can finally begin! No more will we allow injustices to be committed within our own borders! We will fight to improve the galaxy, to morph it into the society that you all deserve!"

"So...wizard powers, eh?" he said after a long silence.

"I guess you could say that," she replied.

"You can make, like, anything with them? Anything at all?"

She smiled, and used them to create a pair of binoculars, which she extended out towards Daniel. He felt the hand-drawn, glowing pair, which almost seemed to shimmer as he touched it. "Wow," he said, as it started to disappear from his hand. "You really need to teach me how to do that."

She nodded and turned back to face the radio. Sounds of applause filled it as the two of them listened. "Hey," Caitlin said softly. "I have something for you."

He turned around. "What?"

She held out her hand and uncurled her fingers. Resting on her palm was the blue stone that she had given Daniel all those years ago, a faint black line carving through it. "The twins found this next to your body and brought it with them. It was cracked in two, but Shane fixed it for me."

Daniel took the stone from her and examined it, his breath suddenly shaky, his expression surprised. "I thought I had lost it!" he exclaimed, staring down at the faded words on the back. "I was so worried when I realized that I didn't have it!"

At that moment, something happened that Daniel did not anticipate. Something that surprised him more than any war or Gorog ambush in the past week, or five years for that matter. Something happened that shook him to his very core, something more unexpected than anything he had ever seen in his life. There was no warning to it, no foreshadowing. It just...happened.

Caitlin leaned close to him and kissed him on the cheek.

All at once, Daniel's brain lost all sense of reasoning, his body seemingly turning to jelly below him. Thankfully, he managed to recoup his senses before falling to the floor in a trance. "What was that for?" he asked, rubbing the spot on his cheek where Caitlin had planted her lips.

She clasped her hands innocently. "Just…for being you, I guess," she said. "And that's more than enough for me."

Daniel felt another smile cross his face. He placed an arm around her as they watched the moon pass them by. "You ready for more space adventures?" he asked her.

"Never," she said. "But hey, I've got you, Stellar Brain. And if all goes wrong, at least we'll still have each other."

They continued to embrace one another as Pantura yelled out behind them, "Express to Arajor launching in three, two, one!" Then the *Phoenix* warped into hyperspace and sent them hurtling towards their new life, a life that few humans would ever get to experience, a life among real aliens, real aliens that existed and watched over not just Earth, but the entire galaxy.

But for the first time in Daniel's life, he felt at peace with what he was doing.

Epilogue

Arajor

In his office in the Kraken, Shane stared out the window at the speeder traffic flying by. Nighttime had fallen in the city of Arajor, and the dazzling lights that decorated the skyscrapers were in full bloom, shining their glare into the circular room. He had been informed that Daniel, Caitlin, Pantura and Max were on their way back from Earth, and would be arriving in the next couple of hours. Feeling extremely pleased with how the day had turned out, he backed away, folding up his desk papers and preparing to turn his light off, until Vorlax walked in.

"You burning the midnight oil, Shane?" he asked.

"Actually, Vorlax, I was just about to leave. The others are on their way back and will be in need of a base of operations."

"Oh. So Daniel chose to come back?"

"He said that he wants to help the people out here, in any way that he can," replied Shane. "And to hunt down the rest of the Gorog survivors that escaped the battle."

"So you didn't have a hand in this?"

Shane turned to face him. "Of course not. Although, I do understand your concerns, after what I just pulled." He grabbed his folder, turned off his desk light, and started to leave. "Come to rag on me some more?"

"Actually, I came here to compliment you, old friend," replied Vorlax, causing Shane to turn and face him in the doorway.

"Really? You sure this isn't you asking me to resign? Because, I understand, you have every right to say…"

"Shut it. Just stop, right now." Vorlax had his hand up in front of Shane's chest. "You've done enough, Shane. Nobody's perfect. You messed up, in a big way, no one can deny that. But so did your father. He made terrible mistakes, as did his father, and all their fathers before that. Some things that he sorely regretted and had horrible consequences. But nobody's perfect, Shane. None of us are. It happens to the best of us. And you turned it around, you helped to reunite Daniel and his mother, and you helped break the Gorog Empire's power. You corrected your mistake. And that's all that any of us can do."

"I didn't do that much," Shane clarified. "All I did was direct my cruisers to shoot at the Gorog warships while Daniel and Caitlin's team did all the heavy lifting."

"You still helped. And it was the damage you did outside the battle in the *Deceiver*, by taking out the supporting warships, that really was the death knell for the Gorogs. Orvag's death was a serious enough blow, but those support ships…without those, there will be very little Gorog opposition left to deal with in the coming weeks."

Shane smiled at him, as they started to walk down the hallway again. "It'll take a long time to rebuild the areas ravaged by the Gorogs during their reign. I was thinking of setting up a special base for Daniel's team within those boundaries, a base of operations from which they can conduct their searches for hidden strongholds. You know more about the specific details of planets than I do, would you have any recommendations?"

"Well," replied Vorlax, "There's Bakollt, which is probably the best option. Located near the heart of Gorog territory, and has a large, sustainable atmosphere and climate, not unlike Earth, ideal for a base to live in. That would just be my choice though."

"I'll look into it." Shane rounded a corner, Vorlax right behind him. "Did the twins' ship arrive to pick them up?"

"It did. Them and all their belongings are currently heading towards the best beaches in the galaxy. They'll get to enjoy their retirement for as long as they want."

Shane smiled. "Good. I'd hate for them to waste the money we gave them."

They kept walking in silence for a bit longer, until Vorlax finally caved in. "You know, Shane, you may not be your father. But you're just as effective as him at leading the Orion Coalition. He'd be very proud of you for finishing his mission and leading us to victory."

Shane nodded and smiled slightly. "You really think so?"

"He may have been ruthless to his enemies, but, if you remember, he loved you very much, and wanted you to do great things. I was around, back when he was grooming you to be his successor. After what you've done this past week, that one incident notwithstanding, I believe that you've evolved into the worthy successor he knew you could become."

Shane stopped in his tracks to look his commander better in the eyes. "Vorlax, not a day goes by that I don't thank God for meeting you. What would I ever do without you?"

"Not much, I reckon."

They both laughed. "You know, planning that base can wait for another time," Shane said. "Do you want to get something to eat?"

"I would love to. Just don't drug my food, okay?"

"Ha, ha, that's not that funny."

They both went walking down the hallway towards the hangar, feeling hopeful and optimistic about the future, knowing that, at long last, they were finally free of the war.

About the Author:

Gabriel Dandrade was born on November 16, 2003 in Bradenton, Florida. From a young age, he loved reading books, especially ones set in the vastness of space. He wrote several short stories, which became the basis for his debut novel, *Orion's Hunters: Cosmic Visions*. He lives in Hampton Roads, Virginia, with his family and favorite dog.

Printed in Great Britain
by Amazon